THE BEST
COWBOY
STORIES
EVER TOLD

THE BEST
COWBOY
STORIES
EVER TOLD

EDITED AND INTRODUCED BY
STEPHEN BRENNAN

Skyhorse Publishing

Skyhorse Publishing books may be purchased in bulk at special discounts for sales promotion, corporate gifts, fund-raising, or educational purposes. Special editions can also be created to specifications. For details, contact the Special Sales Department, Skyhorse Publishing, 307 West 36th Street, 11th Floor, New York, NY 10018 or info@skyhorsepublishing.com.

Skyhorse® and Skyhorse Publishing® are registered trademarks of Skyhorse Publishing, Inc.®, a Delaware corporation.

www.skyhorsepublishing.com

10 9 8 7 6 5 4

Library of Congress Cataloging-in-Publication Data

The best cowboy stories ever told / edited and introduced by Stephen Vincent Brennan.
    p. cm.
ISBN 978-1-61608-216-1 (alk. paper)
1. Western stories. 2. Cowboys—Fiction. I. Brennan, Stephen Vincent.
PS648.W4B44 2011
813'.087408   dc22

                                2011014088

Ebook ISBN: 978-1-62873-155-2

Printed in the United States of America

For Andy
Only a pretty good shot, knows Cowboy Lit tho

CONTENTS

THE BEST
COWBOY
STORIES
EVER TOLD

INTRODUCTION

"Kings and cowboys I have known, and the cowboys stand above the rest.
I am six thousand miles from them at this moment and fifty-six years in
time, but they seem nearer to me than this morning's newspaper."
                                                              —*Frank Harris*

And so they seem to us all—near, I mean. We do feel this to be true, but how can it be so? The world of cowboying is not much like what it was, and the Kingdom of Cattle is past—long gone now. Despite all this, why is it that the cowboy has still such a grip on our imaginations?

Native peoples the whole world over tell stories of a time, early on in their histories, when they first settled their homelands. They call it the "dream-time." It is said to have been a time of great change, when whole peoples moved from place to place, and every new thing was named. For Americans the settling of the West was our dream-time. In those times—that seem to us not so long past but are in reality a whole world ago—America grew to become largely what she is now. This vast migration westward, with all its attendant bloodshed and suffering and hope, did indeed fix new borders and name new places. But it settled a good deal more, because in this epic struggle we also settled on an idea about ourselves—who we are as a people and what it means to be an individual American.

This idealization of ourselves finds expression in the stories we tell of that time, those places. It is a huge part of our national mythology, and like any other mythology, it is peopled with heroes. They were the discoverers, the pioneer settlers, the doomed native peoples, the miners, gamblers, lawmen and horse-soldiers, and they were the cowboys.

Especially the cowboy. Of them all, he is the one we seem most to admire, and in his image we fancy we best see ourselves. This might well be considered strange because a cowboy is only an ordinary man, doing dangerous, mostly ill-paid work, far from home and hearth. His horse, saddle, and side arms are all he owns. He lives a rough, mostly roof-less existence, on a diet of beans and beef and coffee and tobacco (when he can get the makings). He's a man without many prospects or he'd be doing something else. His best friend is often his horse. So, just what is there to admire? Yet, wildly, he is the one with whom we most identify. And in that sense at least, he is us. Why is this?

Clearly, any attempt to decode the cowboy mystique is bound to be ham-handedly simplistic, but we just might understand a little of our fascination, our attraction, by comparing our idea of the cowboy with our own view of ourselves. He's a strong man, just look at the life he leads—out in all weathers. Don't matter he's got no family, we take this as a sign of his independence. He's a free man, and so do we all count ourselves to be. He lives a life of adventure, and so would we all, even the most chair-bound of us. He's a brave man, willing and able to stand up for himself—the equalizer on his hip is badge of that. He's peaceable enough, but best don't mess with him, don't cross the line. There's always been something a little shaded, a little dark-sided about a cowboy—something he's hiding. Does he have a secret? Don't we all? On balance, he's a good man. And so we all reckon ourselves to be.

From the beginning advertisers and all sorts of promoters have understood our attraction to this common man who is also the mythic hero of our dream-time. The cowboy has been used to sell everything from cigarettes to aftershave, cars, clothes, whatever you like—so long as they can project a little of that rugged-American-individual mojo. Even politicians are quick to employ his image in their cause. Now, real cowboys, on the whole, are unlikely to run for office. But pols have always tried to glom a little of the cowboy luster. Even Presidents have been known to ape his choice in headgear, and a few, even his rolling walk.

Authors too, fast cottoned on to the idea of the cowboy story as our story. The first of these shinning literary efforts were of the penny-dreadful variety, written by hacks, pulp romances of the lives of noted Western heroes and villains. These largely invented tales, dressed up as "true biographies," flooded the big cities of the East, running as serials in newspapers and in cheap newsprint editions. They were also widely available out West. Often a ranch-hand would get one as a promotion in his tin of Bull Durham, and this might inspire his own literary effort. After a time, there were any number of real cowboys writing cowboy stories—Charley Siringo, Andy Adams, and Eugene Rhodes come to mind. At the very same time there was an explosion of magazine and newspaper articles by writers like Mark Twain and William Macleod Raine, all feeding a national hunger for participation, albeit at a remove, in our great national adventure. Crossbreed all this with the strain of (newly matured) outdoor adventure novels by the likes of Robert Louis Stevenson, Joseph Conrad, and Stephen Crane, and by the turn of the century Andy Adams, Owen Wister, Emerson Hough, and Zane Grey had invented what we now call the classic Western. And that was only the beginning. What followed was the popularization in novels, movies, radio, and television of much more than a new cultural and literary genre; it also created a new American icon, and a distinctly American type. When we look in his eyes we see ourselves.

The Golden Age of the Cowboy, or what has been called the "Kingdom of Cattle," lasted, more or less, from the close of the Civil War to the turn of the century. The four-year national conflict had devastated much of the Southland. In Texas, the cattle business had been so badly dislocated that hundreds of thousands of beeves roamed loose in the brush, ownerless, free for the rounding-up. In those heady days, there were fortunes to be made if you could gather a herd and get it to an outlet, a railhead, an army fort, or some other market. This was the time of the great cattle drives, but it only lasted thirty years or so. Before long, barbed wire and the iron-horse put paid to the free range and the long trail drive, just as the coming of the law obviated the need for the rough chivalry of the Code of the West. Except in our imaginations, where we may be said to be most truly ourselves.

Stephen Brennan
West Cornwall, 2011

AFORESAID BATES

EUGENE MANLOVE RHODES

I

"I wouldn't mind going broke so much," said Dick Mason, "but I sure hate to see the cattle die, and me not able to do the first thing to save them." He dipped a finger in spilled beer and traced circles on the table. In shirt sleeves for the heat, they sat in the cool dimness of Jake's Place—Mason, Bull Pepper, Blinker Murphy and Big Jake himself.

"Tough luck," said Murphy. "Losin' 'em fast?"

"Not so many, not yet. But the bulk of 'em are dying by inches. Dyin' on their feet. The strongest can just get out to grass and back. The others eat brush, wood and all. Hardly any rain last year and no snow last winter. Stock in no shape to stand a spring round up, so the yearlin' steers are all on the range yet. If we'd had rain about the Fourth of July, as we most always do, we might maybe 'a' pulled through, losin' the calf crop. But here it's most August, no rain, no grass—not a steer in shape to sell—and me with a mortgage comin' due right off. Feenish. And I've got a wife and kids now. Other times, when I went broke, it really didn't make no difference. Tham!"

"No, this one's on me," said Jake hastily. "Four beers, Tham."

"We're none of us cattlemen," said Bull Pepper. "And you know us Tripoli fellows never get along too well with your bunch anyway. All the same, we're sorry to see you boys up against it this way."

Lithpin Tham came with the beer. "I gueth all of you won't go under," he said as he slipped the mugs from tray to table. "They thay Charlie Thee ith fixed tho he won't looth many."

"Not him," said Mason sourly. "Charlie See, he had a leased township under fence to fall back on. Good grass, cured on the stem." The door opened and Aforesaid Bates came in, unseen by Mason. "Charlie won't lose much," said Mason. "Why should he? His stuff runs on the open range when every mouthful of grass they took was a mouthful less for ours. Now he turns 'em into his pasture. Grama high as ever it was, cured on the stem. Just like so much good hay. Been nothing to eat it for three years but a few saddle horses. Him and Aforesaid Bates, they're wise birds, they are!"

"What's all this about Aforesaid Bates?" said Bates. "What's the old man been doin' now?" His voice was acid. They turned startled faces toward him.

"You know well enough," said Mason sullenly. "You ran a drift fence across Silver Spring canyon, kept your cattle out on the flat so long as there was a spear of grass, and now you're hogging that saved-up pasture for yourself."

"Well, what are you goin' to do about it?' demanded Bates. He pushed back his hat; his grizzled beard thrust forth in a truculent spike. "Fine specimen you are—backcappin' your own neighbors to town trash!"

"Exception!" cried Bull Pepper sharply, rising to his feet. But Bates ignored him and continued his tirade, with eyes for none but Mason. "Hopper and See and me, we sold out our old stuff last fall. Cut our brands in half, bein' skeery of a drought. And if the rest of you had as much brains as a road lizard, you could have done the same, and not one of you need have lost a cow. But no, you must build up a big brand, you and Hall—hold on to everything. Now the drought hits us and you can't take your medicine. You belly-achin' around because me and Charlie had gumption enough to protect ourselves."

"Say, cool down a little, Andy," said Dick Mason. "You're an old man, and you've been drinking, and I can take a lot from you—but I do wish you'd be reasonable."

"A fat lot I care about what you wish," snarled Bates. "Reasonable! Oh, shucks! Here, three years ago, you was fixed up to the queen's taste—nice likely bunch of cows, good ranch, lots of room, sold your steers for a big price, money in the bank, and what did you do?"

Conjointly with these remarks, Mason tried to rise and Bull Pepper pulled him down. "Don't mind him, Dick—he's half-shot," said Pepper. Simultaneously, different advice reached Mason's other ear. "Beat his fool head off, Mason!" said Murphy. "You lettin' Bates run your business now?" asked Jake.

Meanwhile, Bates answered his own question. "You bought the Rafter N brand, with your steer money as first payment, givin' a mortgage on both brands."

"Now, Andy –"

"Shet up!" said Andy, "I'm talkin'! Brought in six hundred more cattle to eat yourself out—and to eat the rest of us out. Wasn't satisfied with plenty. Couldn't see that dry years was sure to come. To keep reserve grass was half the game. And as if that wasn't enough, next year Harry Hall must follow your lead—and he's mortgaged up to the hilt, too. Both of you got twice as much stock on the range as you got any right to have. Both goin' broke, and serves you right. But instead of blamin' yourselves, as you would if you was halfway decent, you go whimperin' around, blamin' us that cut our stock in two whilst you was a-doublin' yours!"

"You goin' to stand for this?" whispered Murphy. Concurrently, Andrew Jackson Aforesaid Bates raised his voice to a bellow. "Ever since you got married, you been narratin' around that you wasn't no gun man." He unbuckled his pistol belt and sent his gun sliding along the floor. "Old man, says you! Stand up, you skunk, and take it!"

Mason sprung up. They met with a thud of heavy blows, give-and-take. Pepper tried to shove between, expostulating. Murphy and Jake dragged him away. "Let 'em fight it out!" snarled Jake.

There was no science. Neither man tried to guard, duck, sidestep or avoid a blow in any way. They grunted and puffed, surging this way or that, as one or the other reeled back from a lucky hit. Severe punishment; Mason's nose was spurting blood, and Aforesaid's left eye was closed. Just as Mason felt a chair at his legs, a short arm jab clipped his chin; he toppled backward with a crash of splintered chair. He scrambled up and came back with a rush, head down, both arms swinging. A blow caught Bates squarely on the ear; he went down, rolled over, got to his feet undismayed; they stood toe to toe and slugged savagely. The front door opened, someone shouted, a dozen men rushed into the saloon and bore the combatants apart. Words, questions, answers, defiances—Kendricks and Lispenard dragged Mason through the door, protesting. After some persuasion, Mr. Bates also was led away for repairs by Evans and Early, visiting cowmen from Saragossa; and behind them, delighted Tripoli made animated comment; a pleasing tumult which subsided only at a thoughtful suggestion from the House.

"I been expectin' something like this," said Spinal Maginnis, as they lined up to the bar. "Beer for mine, Tham. Them Little World waddies is sure waspy. I'm s'posed to be representing there for the Diamond A, you know. But they wouldn't let me lift a finger. Said their cattle couldn't stand it to be moved one extra foot, and the Diamond A stuff would have to take their chances with the rest. Reckon they're right, at that. Well, it was funny. See and Johnny Hopper and old Aforesaid was walking stifflegged around Hall and Mason. Red Murray, he was swelled up at Hopper, 'cause Turn-about Spring was dryin' up on him, and he'd bought that from Hopper. And all hands sore at Bud Faulkner, on account of his bunch of mares, them broomtails wearing out the range worse than three times the same amount of cattle. They was sure due for a bust-up. This little fuss was only the beginning, I reckon. Well, here's how!"

"I hope they do get to fightin' amongst themselves," growled Murphy, putting down his glass. "Mighty uppity, overbearin' bunch. They've been runnin' it over Tripoli something fierce. Hope they all go broke. Old man Bates, in particular. He's one all-round thoroughbred this-and-that!"

As Murphy brought out the last crushing word, Bull Pepper, standing next to him, hooked his toe behind Murphy's heel and snapped his left arm smartly so that the edge of his open hand struck fair on Murphy's Adam's apple. Murphy went down, gasping. First he clutched at his throat and then he reached for his gun. Pepper pounced down, caught a foot by heel and toe and wrenched violently. Murphy flopped on his face with a yell, his gun exploded harmlessly. Pepper bent the captive leg up at right angles for greater purchase and rolled his victim this way and that. Murphy yelled with pain, dropping his gun. Pepper kicked the gun aside and pounced again. Stooping, he grabbed a twisting handful, right and left, from bulging fullness of flannel shirt at Murphy's hips; and so stooping and straddling over the fallen, lurched onward and upward with one smooth and lusty heave. The shirt peeled over Murphy's head, pinioning his arms. Pepper twisted the tails together beyond the clawing arms, dragged his victim to the discarded gun, and spoke his mind.

"I don't agree with you," he said. He lifted up his eyes from that noisy bundle then for a slow survey of his audience. No one seemed contrary minded. He looked down again at his squirming bundle, shook it vigorously, and stepped upon it with a heavy foot. "Be quiet now, or I'll sqush you!" The bundle became quiet, and Pepper spoke to it in a sedate voice, kindly and explanatory. "Now, brother, it's like this. Bates has never been overly pleasant with me. Barely civil. But I think he's a good man for all that, and not what you said. Be that as it may, it is not a nice thing to be glad because any kind of a man is losing his cattle in a drought. No. Anybody got a string?"

Curses and threats came muffled from the bundle. "Did you hear me?" said Pepper sharply. He swooped down and took up Murphy's guns from the floor. "String is what I want. That silk handkerchief of Tham's will do nicely. Give it to Jake, Tham. You, Jake! You come here! You and Murphy both laid hands on me when I wanted to stop this fight. I'm declarin' myself right now. I don't like to be manhandled by any two men on earth. Step careful, Jake—you're walkin' on eggs! Now, you take two half-hitches around Mr. Murphy's shirt-tails with that handkerchief. Pull 'em tight! Pull 'em tight, I said! Do you maybe want me to bend this gun over your head? That's better. Now, Murphy, get outside and let Tripoli have a look. You and Joe Gandy, you been struttin' around right smart, lately, admirin' yourselves as the local heroes. I don't like it. Peace is what I want—peace and quiet. What's that, Murphy? Shoot me? Not with this gun you won't. This gun is mine."

He laid a large hand to Murphy's back and propelled him through the door.

"You surely aren't tryin' to bust them collar buttons loose, are you? No, no—you wouldn't do that, and me askin' you not to. You go on home, now."

As Pepper turn to cross the plaza, Spinal Maginnis fell in step beside him. "Goin' my way, Mr. Pepper?"

The pacifist stopped short. "I am not," he said with decision. "And I don't know which way you're going, either."

Spinal rubbed his chin, with a meditative eye on the retreating Murphy.

"I don't know that I ever saw a man sacked up before," he said slowly. "Is them tactics your own get-up, or just a habit?"

Mr. Murphy's progress was beginning to excite comment. Men appeared in the deserted plaza, with hard unfeeling laughter. A head peered tentatively from Jake's door. Mr. Pepper frowned. The head disappeared.

The hostility faded from Mr. Pepper's eyes, to be succeeded by an expression of slow puzzlement. He turned to Maginnis and his tones were friendly. "Overlooking any ill-considered peevishness of mine, dear sir and mister—you put your little hand in mine and come along with me."

He led the way to a shaded and solitary bench; he lit a cigarette and surveyed the suddenly populous plaza with a discontented eye; he clasped his knees and contemplated his foot without enthusiasm.

"Well?" said Maginnis at last.

"Not at all," said Pepper. "No, sir. This Dick Mason he's supposed to have brains, ain't he? And the Aforesaid Bates Andy Jackson, he has the name of being an experienced person? Wise old birds, both of 'em?"

"I've heard rumors to that effect," admitted Maginnis.

"Well, they don't act like it," said Pepper. "Tripoli and the cowmen, they've been all crosswise since Heck was a pup. But Mason, he opens up and lays it all before us. Lookin' for sympathy? I don't guess. Then old man Bates gets on the peck like that, exposin' his most secret thoughts to a cold and callous world. It don't make sense. And that fight they pulled off! I've seen school kids do more damage."

"I didn't see the fight," said Maginnis.

"No, you didn't. You and all these here visiting waddies just happened in opportunely—just in time to stop it." Pepper regarded his companion with cold suspicion. "Eddy Early, Lafe and Cole and you, and this man Evans—that's some several old-timers turnin' up in Tripoli—and not one of you been here before in ten years. I tell you, Mr. Spinal Maginnis, Esquire, horsethief and liar—I've been thinkin'!"

"You mustn't do that, feller," said Spinal anxiously. "You'll strain yourself. You plumb alarm me. You don't act nowise like any town man, anyhow. Not to me."

"I was out of town once," admitted Pepper. "Some years ago, that was."

"Curious," said Spinal. "Once a man has put in some few years tryin' to outguess pinto ponies and longhorned steers, he ain't fooled much by the cunnin' devices of his fellow humans. But I'm no sheriff or anything like that—so don't you get uneasy in your mind. On the other hand, if you really insist thinking—Has it got to be a habit with you?"

"Yes. Can't break myself of it. But I won't say a word. Go on with your pranks, whatever they are. But I'm sure sorry for somebody."

"Well, then," said Spinal, "as a favor to me—if them thoughts of yours begin to bother your head, why, when you feel real talkative, just save it up and say it to me, won't you?

"I'll do that," said Pepper. "You rest easy."

II

Because the thrusting mesa was high and bare, with no overlooking hills or shelter of trees for attacking Apaches, men built a walled town there, shouldering above the green valley; a station and a resting place on the long road to Chihuahua. England fought France in Spain that year, and so these founders gave to their desert stronghold the name of Talavera.

When England and France fought Russia in the Crimea, Talavera dreaded the Apaches no more, and young trees grew on the high mesa, cherished by far-brought water of a brave new ditch. A generation later the mesa was a riot of far-seen greenery; not Talavera now, but Tripoli, for its threefold citizenship: the farmers, the miner folk from the hills, who built homes there as a protest against the glaring desert, and the prosperous gentry from sweltering San Lucas, the county-seat. These last built spaciously; a summer suburb, highest, farthest from the river, latest and up-to-date. Detraction knew this suburb as Lawville.

Where the highest *acequia* curved and clung to enfold the last possible inch of winnings, the wide windows of Yellowhouse peered through the dark luxurious shade of Yellowhouse Yards. The winding *acequia* made here a frontier; one pace beyond, the golden desert held undisputed sway. Generous and gracious, Yellowhouse Yards; but Pickett Boone had not designed them. They had been made his by due process of law. Pickett Boone was the "slickest" lawyer of San Lucas.

"Wildest game ever pulled off in Tripoli," said Joe Gandy. It was the morning after the sacking up of Blinker Murphy. A warmish morning; Gandy was glad for the cool shadows of Yellowhouse Yards.

"Big money?"

"O man! And the way they played it! Dog-everlasting-gone it, Mr. Boone, I watched 'em raise and tilt one pot till I was dizzy—and when it comes to a showdown, Eddie Early had Big and Little Casino, Cole Ralston had Fifteen-Six, Yancey had Pinochle, and old Aforesaid had High, Low, Jack and the game. Yessir; three of 'em stood pat, and bet their fool heads off; and that old mule of a Spinal Maginnis saw it through and raked the pot with just two spindlin' little pair, tens up. I never did see the beat."

Pickett Boone considered leisurely. A film came over his pale eyes. "And they put the boots to Bates?"

"Stuck him from start to finish. They was all winners except him and Spinal. About the first peep o' day, Bates pushes back his chair. 'Thankin' you for your kind attention,' he says, 'This number concludes the evenin's entertainment.' Then he calls for the tab and gives Jake a check for twenty-eight hundred."

"You seem to be bearing up under the loss pretty well," said Boone. He eyed his informant reflectively. "You're chief deputy and willing to be sheriff. But someway you've never made much of a hit with Bates and the Mundo Chico crowd."

Gandy scowled. "After what Bull Pepper's tender heart made him do to Murphy, I dasn't say I'm glad old Bates shot his wad. Bull Pepper here or Bull Pepper there, I'm now declaring myself that I wish I might ha' grabbed a piece of that. I can't see where it helps Tripoli any to have all that good dough carried off to Magdalena and Salamanca and Deming. Jake set in with 'em at first—and set right out again. Lost more than the kitty totted up to all night. They sure was hittin' 'em high."

"Well, what's the matter with Lithpin Tham? I've heard Tham was lucky at cards."

"Some of them visiting brothers must have heard that same thing," said Joe moodily. "Tham sort of hinted he might try a whirl, and them three Salamanca guys just dropped their cards and craned their necks and stared at Tham till it was plumb painful. Tham blushed. Yes, he did. No, sir, them waddies was all set to skin Bates, I reckon, and they wasn't wishful for any help a-tall. They looked real hostile. 'Twasn't any place for a gentleman."

"It is the custom of all banks," said Lawyer Boone reflectively, "to give out no information concerning their clients. But—" His voice trailed to silence.

"I got you," said the deputy. "But a lame man can always get enough wood for a crutch? So you know just about how much Aforesaid had left—is that it?"

"How little," Boone made the correction with tranquility.

"I'm thinking the whole Little World bunch is about due to bust up," said Joe jubilantly.

"He always wanted that Little World country, Pickett Boone did," said Pickett Boone. "Mason's only chance to pay Pickett was to get the Bates to tide him over. Pickett was afraid of that. That's off, after him and Bates beating each other up. To make it sure and safe, Bates blows his roll at poker. Good enough. The banks have loaned money to the cowmen up to the limit, what with the drought and the bottom fallen out of prices. So Mason can't get any more money from any bank. And he can't sell any steers, the shape they're in now. Pickett's got him," said Pickett, with a fine relish. "He'll get Hall too. More than that, he'll get old Bates, himself, if the dry weather holds out."

"But if the drought lasts long enough, don't you stand to lose?" Gandy eyed the money-lender curiously. "As you say yourself, the banks don't think a mortgage on cattle covers the risk when it doesn't rain."

Pickett Boone smiled silkily. "My mortgages cover all risks." Then his lips tightened, his pale eyes were hot with hate, his voice snarled in his throat. "Even if I lose it—I'll break that insolent bunch. Mighty high-headed, they are—but I'll see the lot of 'em cringe yet!"

"They've stuck together, hand-in-glove, till now," said Joe eagerly. "And Mr. Charlie See, with that bunch to back him, he's been cuttin' quite a swath. But they're all crossways and quarrelin' right now—and if the drought keeps up they'll be worse. Once they split," said Joe Gandy, "you and me can get some of our own back."

"Hark!" said Pickett Boone. "Who's coming?"

A clatter of feet, faint and far, then closer, near and clear; a horse's feet, pacing merrily; on the curving driveway Mr. Aforesaid Bates rode under an archway of pecan trees. An ear was swollen, an eye was green and yellow, but Mr. Bates rode jauntily and the uninjured eye was unabashed and benign.

"A fine morning, sir. Get off," said lawyer Boone. "This is an unexpected pleasure."

"The morning is all you claim for it," said Aforesaid Bates, dismounting. "But the pleasure is—all yours. For Andy Bates, it is business that brings him here."

"Say, I'll go," said Gandy.

"Keep your seat, Joe. Stay where you are. Whenever I've got any business that needs hiding I want the neighbors to know all about it. 'It's like this, Mr. Boone, I gave a little party last night and so I thought I might as well come over and sign on the dotted line.'"

"You thought—what?"

"I want to borrow some money of you. I gotta buy hay and corn and what not, hire a mess of hands and try to pull my cattle through."

"Money," said Pickett Boone austerely, "is tight."

"Oh, don't be professional," said Bates. "And you needn't frown. I get you. Why, I never heard of money that wasn't tight."

"Why don't you go to the bank?"

"The bank wouldn't loan me one measly dollar," said Bates, "and well you know it. If it would only rain, now, it would be different. Too risky. That's just like me. Kindhearted. Sparing you the trouble of saying all this, just to save time. Because I've got to get a wiggle."

"If it is too risky for the banks it is too risky for me."

"Whither," said Bates dreamily, "whither are we drifting? Of course it's risky for you. You know it and I know it. What a lot of fool talk! Think I've been vaccinated with a phonograph needle? You've been yearnin' for my ranch since Heck was a pup. That's another thing we both know. I'm betting you don't get it. Halfway House and the brand, I'll bet, against four thousand with interest three years 12 per cent. Call it a mortgage, of course, but it's a bet and you know it. I'm gambling with you."

"The security is hardly sufficient," said Boone icily. "I might consider three thousand for, say, two years. Your cattle may all die."

"Right. Move up one girl. If it doesn't rain," said Aforesaid Bates, with high serenity, "those cattle are not worth one thin dime. And if the cattle go I can't pay. Surest thing you know. But the ranch will be right there—and you'll lend me four thousand on that ranch and your chance on any cattle toughing through, and you'll loan it to me for three years, or not at all. No—and I don't make out any note for five thousand and take four thousand, either. You just save your breath, mister. You'll gamble on my terms, or not at all."

"You assume a most unusual attitude for a would-be borrower," observed the lawyer acidly. His eyes were smoldering.

"Yes, and you are a most mighty unusual will-be lender, too. What do you want me to do? Soft-soap you? Tell you a hard luck story? You've been wanting my scalp, Mister Man. Here's your chance to take it—and you dassent let it pass. I see it in your hard old ugly eye. You want me to borrow this money, you think I can't pay it back, and you think Halfway House is as good as yours, right now. You wouldn't miss the chance for a thousand round hard dollars laid right in your grimy clutch. So all you have to do is offer one more objection—or cough, or raise your eyebrow—and I'm off to sell the ranch to Jastrow. I dare you to wait another minute," said this remarkable borrower, rising. "For I am going—going—"

"Sit down," snapped the lawyer. "I'll make out the mortgage. You are an insolent, bullying, overbearing old man. You'll get your money and I'll get your ranch. Of course, under the circumstances, if you do not keep your day you will hardly expect an extension!"

"Listen to the gypsy's warning," said Mr. Bates earnestly. "You'll never own one square foot of my ranch! Now don't say I didn't tell you. You do all your gloatin' now while the gloatin' is good."

The three rode together to the nearest notary public; the papers were made out and signed; the Aforesaid Bates took his check and departed, whistling. Gandy and Boone paced soberly back to Yellowhouse Yards.

"Mr. Andrew Jackson Aforesaid Bates—the old smart Aleck!" sneered Pickett Boone. "Yah! He's crossed me for ten years and now, by the Lord Harry, I've got him in the bag with Hall and Mason! Patience does it."

Gandy lowered his voice. "We can ease the strain on your patience a little. More ways than one. You know Bates has strung a drift fence across the canyon above Silver Spring? Yes? That's illegal. He's got a right smart of grass in the roughs up there, fenced off so nobody's cattle but his can get to it. If somebody would swear out a complaint, it would be my duty as deputy sheriff to see that fence come down. Then everybody's cattle could get at that fenced grass—"

The lawyer's malicious joy broke out in a startling sound of creaking rusty laughter.

"That would start more trouble, sure! We'll have to make you the next sheriff, Joe. Count on me."

Joe's eyes narrowed. He tapped the lawyer's knee with a strong forefinger: he turned his hand upside down and beckoned with that same finger. "Count *to* me! Cash money, right in my horny hand. Sheriff sounds fine—but you don't have all the say. I've got more ideas, and I need money. Do I get it?"

"If they're good ones."

"They're good and they're cheap. Not too cheap. I name the price. How do I know you'll pay me? Easy. If you don't, I'll tip your game. Sure. That fence now. Uncle Sam's Land Office lets out a roar, old Aforesaid knows it's my duty to take it down. Lovely. D'ye suppose I could make that complaint myself and get away with it? Not much. That old geezer is one salty citizen. And if it comes to his ears that it was you that set up the Land Office—do you see? Oh, you'll pay me a fair price for my brains, Mr. Boone. I'm not losing any sleep about that. We understand each other."

The lawyer peered under drooping lids. "We may safely assume as much," he said gently. "Now those other ideas of yours?"

"What do you think Bates is going to do with that money you lent him? Buy alfalfa with it—cottonseed meal, maybe—that's what. So will the other guys, so far as their money goes—all except Charlie See, with his thirty-six square miles of fenced pasture to fall back on—and Echo Mountain behind that. He doesn't need any hay. Well, you've got plenty money. You go buy up all the alfalfa stacks in the upper end of the valley. You can get it for ten—twelve dollars a ton, if you go about it quietly. Then you soak 'em good. They've got to have it. Farther down the valley, the price will go up to match, once they hear of your antics. Nowhere else to get it, except baled hay shipped in. You know what that costs, and you squeeze 'em accordin'. Same way with work. They'll need teams and teamsters. You run up the price. Them ideas good, hey? Worth good money?"

"They are. You'll get it."

The deputy surveyed his fellow crook with some perplexity. "I swear, I don't see how you do it," he grumbled. "Fifty men here-abouts with more brains in their old boots than you ever had—and they're hustlin' hard to keep alive, while you've got it stacked up in bales."

"I keep money on hand," said the lawyer softly. "Cash money. And when these brainy men need cash money—"

"You needn't finish," said Joe gloomily. "You take advantage of their necessity and pay a thief's price. Funny thing, too. You're on the grab, all right. Money is your god, they say. But you're risking a big loss in your attempt to grab off the Little World range—big risks. And, mister, you're taking long chances when you go up against that Little World bunch—quite aside from money. Get 'em exasperated or annoyed, there isn't one of the lot but is liable to pat you on the head with a post-maul."

The lawyer raised his sullen eyes. "I can pay for my fancies," he said in a small quiet voice. "If it suits my whim to lose money in order to break these birds, I know how to make more. These high-minded gentlemen have been mighty scornful to a certain sly old fox we know of. They owe me for years of insult, spoken and unspoken." He had never looked so much the man as in this sincerity of anger. "Their pride, their brains, their guns!" he cried. "Well, I can buy brains, and I can buy guns, and I'll bring their pride to the dust!"

Gandy threw back his hat and ran his hand through his sandy hair in troubled thought; he eyed his patron with frank and sudden distaste. "My brains, now—they ain't so much. Bates or Charlie See—to go no further—can give me cards and spades. Mason, maybe—I dunno. But I've got just brains enough that you can't hire my gun to go up against that bunch—not even when they're splitting up amongst themselves. You listen to me. Here's a few words that's worth money to hear, and I don't charge you one cent. Listen! *Those . . . birds . . . don't . . . care . . . whether . . . school . . . keeps . . . or . . . not!*—Yessir, my red head is only fair to middlin', but I know that much. Moreover, and in addition thereunto, my dear sir and esteemed employer, those same poor brains enable me to read your mind like coarse print. Yessir. I can and will tell you exactly the very identical thought you now think you think. Bet you money, and leave it to you. You're thinkin' maybe I'll never be sheriff, after all . . . . H'm? . . . No answer. Well, that's goin' to cost you money. That ain't all, either. Just for that, I'm goin' to tell you something I didn't know myself till just now. Oh, you're not the only one who can afford himself luxuries. Listen what I learned." He held his head up and laughed. "That Little World outfit have done me dirt and rubbed it in; and as for me, I am considerable of a rascal." He checked himself and wrinkled his brow in some puzzlement. "A scoundrel, maybe; a sorry rascal at best. But never so sorry as when I help a poisonous old spider like you to rig a snare for them hardshells. So the price of ideas has gone up. Doubled."

"Another idea? You'll get your price—if I use it," said the lawyer in the same small, passionless voice.

"What part of your steer crop do you expect to be in shape to sell?" demanded the vendor of ideas.

"Twenty-five per cent. More, if it should rain soon."

"One in four. Your range is better than theirs and your stock in better shape. And you expect to get, for a yearling steer strong enough to stand shipping?"

"Ten dollars. Maybe twelve."

"Here's what you do. There won't be many buyers. You go off somewhere and subsidize you a buyer. Fix him; sell him your bunch, best shape of any around here, for eight dollars or ten. Sell 'em publicly. That will knock the bottom out and put the finishing touches on the Little World people."

"Well, that's splendid," said Boone jubilantly. "That's fine! In reality, I will get my eleven or twelve a head, minus what it costs to fix the buyer."

"Well—not quite," said Gandy. "You really want to figure on paying me enough to keep me contented and happy! What do you care? You can afford to pay for your fancies."

III

No smoke came from the chimney. Dryford yard was packed and hard, no fresh tracks showed there or in the road from the gate, no answer came to his call. Hens clucked and scratched beneath the apple trees and their broods were plump and vigorous. The door was unlocked. The stove was cold; a thin film of dust spread evenly on shelf and table, chairs and stove.

"Up on the flats, tryin' to save his cows," said Hob. "Thought so. Up against it plenty, cowmen are." Unsaddling, he saw a man on foot coming through the fenced fields to Dryford. Hobby met him at the bars. The newcomer was an ancient Mexican, small and withered and wrinkled, who now doffed a shapeless sombrero with a flourish. *"Buenos dias, caballero!"* he said.

"Buenos dias, senor. My name is Hobby Lull, and I'm a friend of Johnny's."

"Oh, *si, si!* I haf hear El Señor Juan spik of you—oh, manee time. Of Garfiel'—no?"

"That's the place. And where's Johnny? Up on the flat?'

"Oh, *si!* Three months ago. You are to come to my little house, plizz, and I weel tell you, while I mek supper. I am to take care here of for El Señor Johnny, while the young man are gone to help this pipple of Mundo Chico. *Ah, que malo suerte!* Ver' bad luck! for thoss, and they are good pipple—*muy simpatico.* Put the saddle, plizz, and come. Een my house ees milk, eggs, fire, alfalfa for your horse—all theengs. Her is ver' sad—lonlee."

"So Johnny has quit the valley three months ago?" said Hobby on the way.

"Oh, yes! Before that we are to help him cut out the top from all these cottonwoods on the reevir, up beyond the farms. Hees cows they eat the leaf, the little small branch, the mistletoe, the bark. Eet ees not enough. So we are to breeng slow thoss cows with the small calf—oh, veree slow!—and put heem een our pastures, a few here, a few there—and we old ones, we feed them the alfalfa hay from the stack. The pasture, he ees not enough. But eet ees best that they eat not much of these green alfalfa, onlee when eet ees ver' es-short."

"Yes, I know. So as not to bloat them. I noticed a mess of cows and calves in the pastures, as I came in. And up on the flat, are their cattle dying much?"

"Pero no, hombre. Myself, I am old. I do not go—but Zenobio he say no. Some—the old cows, is die—but not so manee. Veree theen, he say, veree poor, but not to die—onlee some."

"I don't understand it," said Hobby. "Drought is a heap worse here than anywhere else. Fifty miles each way, last fall, we had quite some little rain—but not here. Tomorrow, I'll go look see how come."

Tomorrow found Hobby breaking his fast by firelight and well on his way by the first flush of day. He toiled up the deep of the draw and came to the level plain with the sun. Early as he was, another was before him. Far to the south a horseman rode along the rim, heading towards him. Hobby dismounted to wait. This might be Johnny Hopper. But as he drew near Hobby knew the burly chest and bull neck, Pepper of Tripoli, "Bull" Pepper. Garfield was far from Tripoli, but in New Mexico, generally speaking, everyone knew everybody. Hobby sat cross-legged in the sand and looked up; Pepper leaned on the saddlehorn and looked down. "Picnic?"

"Hunting for Hopper, Bates—any of the bunch."

"So'm I. Let's ride. It's going to be a scorcher."

The sun rode high and hot as they came to Halfway House. The plain shimmered white and bare, the grass was gnawed to a stubble of bare roots, the bushes stripped bare; a glare of gray dust was thick about them and billowed heavily under shuffling feet. They rode through a dead and soundless world, the far-off ranges were dwindled and dim, the heat rose quivering in the windless air, and white bones beside the trail told the bitter story of drought.

"Ain't this simply hell?" croaked Pepper. "And where's the cattle? Must be a little grass further out, for I haven't seen one cow yet today. Come to think of it, I didn't see but most might few dead ones either—considerin'."

"That's it, I guess. They've hazed 'em all away from here. Hey, by Jove! Not all of 'em! Look there!" Hobby reined in his horse and pointed. Halfway House lay before them, a splotch of greenery at the south horn of Selden Hill; far beyond and high above, up and up again, a blur of red and white moved on the granite ribs of the mountain. Far and high; but they saw a twinkling of sun on steel, and a thin tapping came steadily to their ears, echoborne from crowning cliffs; tap—tap—tap, steady and small.

"Axes!" said Pepper. "They're chopping something. I know—*sotol!* Heard about it in Arizona. Chopping *sotol* to feed the cattle. C'me on, cowboy—we're goin' to learn something."

There were no cattle in the water pens. They watered their horses, they rode up the Silver Spring trail, steep and hard. Where once the *sotol* bush had made an army here, their lances shining in the sun, a thousand and ten thousand, the bouldered slope was matted and strewn with the thorn-edged saber-shaped outer leaves of the *sotol*, covering and half-covering those fallen lances.

"Think of that, now! They cleaned off every *sotol* on this hill, like a mowing machine in grass. Fed the fleshy heart to the cows—and chopped off sixteen hundred million outside leaves to get at the hearts." Pepper groaned in sympathy. "Gosh, what a lot of work! They're almost to the top of the mountain, too. If it don't rain pretty quick, they're going to run out of fodder. Here, let's tie our horses and climb up."

"Where I stayed last night," said Hobby, "the old Mexican said the young men were working up here. I see now what they were doing. Reckon there's an axe going in every draw and hill-slope." Turning, twisting, they clambered painfully up the rocky steep and came breathless to the scene of action. The cattle, that once would run on sight, were all too tame now, crowding close upon their sometime enemies in their eagerness for their iron rations; struggling greedily for the last fleshy and succulent leaves. Poor and thin, they were, rough coated, and pot-bellied, but far from feeble; they now regarded the intruders with some impatience, as delaying the proceedings. The axemen were two: Mr. Aforesaid Bates, Mr. Richard Mason. Mr. Bates' ear was still far from normal and the bruise beneath his misused eye was now a sickly green; while Mr. Mason wore a new knob on his jaw, a cut on his chin and a purple bruise across his cheek. Both were in undershirts, and the undershirts were soaked with sweat; both beamed a simple and unaffected welcome to the newcomers.

"Here you are!" said Dick, gaily and extended his axe.

Pepper glowered, his face dark with suspicion. He shook a slow forefinger at them. "Bates, I never was plum crazy about you. There's times when you act just like you was somebody—and I don't like it. All the same, there's something goin' on that ain't noways fittin' and proper. Friend or no friend, I rode out here to wise you up. And now I've got half a mind to ride back without tellin' you. What do you think you're doin', anyhow?"

"Drawing checks," answered Bates. "Checks on the First Bank of Selden Hill." He waved his hand largely. "Mighty good thing we had a deposit here too."

"You know damn well what I mean. What was the idea of pulling that fake fight, huh?"

"Why, Mr. Pepper!" said Mason in a small, shocked voice. "I do hope you didn't think Andy and me was fightin'? Why, that was just our daily dozen. We been tryin' to bring the cattle up by hand since early in May . . . like this. So we felt like we needed exercise—not to get soft, there in town. Must be you've never seen us when we was really fighting."

"Here, I want to say some talk," said Bull firmly. "That's the trouble with you old men, you want the center of the stage all the time. Information is what I want. Where's your cows and calves? There's none here. Where's your mares? We didn't see a track. How's Charlie See making it? Where's Johnny Hopper? Who, why, when, where? The Bates eye, the Mason face—how come? Tell it to me."

"I stepped on my face," said Dick Mason. "The rest is a long story."

"We serve two meals a day," said Bates. "Early as we can and late as we can—dodgin' the sun as much as possible. Cows never get enough, but when their ribs begin to crack we stop chopping. Then they go down to drink in the middle of the day, and come back up for supper. Don't have to drive 'em. Just as far as they can hear an axe they totter to it."

"After this," said Mason, "we're never goin' to work cattle that old-fashioned way again—roundups and all that. When we want to take 'em somewhere, we'll call 'em. Maybe we can just tell 'em where to go. That is," he added, "if it ever rains any more."

"And you're feeding little bunches like this all around the mountain?" said Pepper.

"Correct. We brought up two-three wagonloads of axes and Mexicans and grindstones," said Bates. "We tried to give the cattle to the Mexicans and have them pay us wages, but they wouldn't stand for it. Yessir, all along Selden Hill and Checkerboard, for thirty-five miles, you can behold little pastoral scenes like this, anywhere there's a hillside of *sotol*. They burn the thorns off prickly pears, too, and feed them, as they come to 'em. Them old days of rope and spur is done departed. See and Hopper and Red—them nice young fellows with blistered hands and achin' backs—it was right comical. Tell you while we stir up dinner— and that's after we get those doggies fed. No beef. Not a thing fit to kill. Even the deer are tough and stringy. But you first, Mr. Pepper—you was sayin' you was uneasy in your mind, if any. Spill it."

"You and Hopper bought up a lot of alfalfa down in the valley, didn't you?"

"Yes. That was for all of us. Several stacks."

"Well, Pickett Boone he went snoopin' around and found that out. From Serafino how much you paid. Ten dollars. Cash? No. Written contract or word of mouth? Just a promise. Boone says he'll pay more and pay cash. Twelve dollars! No. Thirteen? Fourteen? No, says Serafino, mighty sorrowful—word of a *caballero*. A trade is a trade. Same way at Zenobio's. But old José Maria fell for it, and Boone bought his hay, over your head, at fourteen. Mateo's too. Isn't that a regular greaser trick?"

"I'd call it a regular Pickett Boone trick, myself. Pickett Boone ought to have his adenoids removed," said Mason, with a trace of acrimony. "He reminds me of a rainy day in a goat shed."

"Well, Boone he's fixin' to bleed you proper. He sends out his strikers right and left, and he's contracted for just about all the hay in this end of the valley—cut and uncut. I'll tell a man! All down in black and white. Pickett Boone, he don't trust no Mexican."

Bates sighed. "That's all right, then. Myself, I think them Mexicans are pretty good *gente*. They sure followed instructions. Kept mum as mice, too."

"What!" said Bull Pepper.

"Yes," said Bates. "To feed what cows and calves we got under fence at Dryford, we really wanted some of that hay. What Boone didn't buy, and a couple of loads we hauled up here to my place. But for all the other ranches except mine, it's a heap easier to haul baled hay from Deming on a level road, than to drag uphill through sand from the valley. So we told the Mexicans what not to say, and how. Made a pool. Mexicans furnished the hay and we furnished Boone. The difference between ten a ton and what Boone pays—close on to four hundred tons, be the same more or less—why, we split it even, half to the Mexicans, half to us."

"Give me that axe," said Pepper.

IV

"The time to take care of cattle durin' a drought," said Aforesaid Bates sagely, "is to begin while it is raining hard."

A curving cliff made shelter of deep shade over Silver Spring. Hobby and Mason washed dishes by the dying fire; Bull Pepper sat petulant on a boulder, and lanced delicately under fresh blisters on his hands; Bates sprawled happily against a bed roll, and smoked a cob pipe; luxurious, tranquil and benign.

"We wasn't quite as forehanded as that," said Bates, "but we done pretty well. First off, Charlie See had his big pasture, knee-high in untouched grass, and everybody cussing him. Cuss words is just little noises in the air. They didn't hurt Charlie none—and the grass was there when needed. Then I built a drift fence across the box and kept everything out of what grass there is in the rough country above here. So I had me a pasture of my own. Plenty rocks and cliffs, some grass and right smart of browse. So far, so good. Then last year it didn't rain much, so See and Hopper and me, we shipped off all our old stuff for what we could get. We even went so far as to name it to the other boys that they might do the same." He paused to knock out his pipe.

"Do you know, boys," said Mason, "that old coot has to bring that up, no matter what he's talking about? Every time. Name it to us? I'll say he did. 'Sell off the old cows and low-grade—keep the young vigorous stuff.'—Lord, how many times I've heard that!"

"And did you sell?" asked Hobby.

"No, I didn't. But Bates, he told us so. He admits it."

"Order having been restored," said Bates, "I will proceed. No snow last winter, no grass this spring. It never rains here from March to July, of course; and along about the middle of April we began to get dubious would it rain in July. So we made a pool. Likewise, we took steps, plenty copious. High time, too. Lots of the old ones was dyin' on us even then."

"Just like he told us they would," said Mason, and winked.

Bates ignored the interruption. "First of all, we rounded up all the broom-tailed mares—about four hundred all told. Most of 'em was Bud Faulkner's, but none of us was plumb innocent. We chartered Headlight, sobered him up, give him some certified checks and a couple of Mex boys and headed him for Old Mexico with the mares.

"By then the cow stuff was weak and pitiful. We couldn't have even a shadow of a roundup—but we did what was never seen before in open country. We set up a chuck wagon, a water wagon, one hay wagon and two when needful and a wagon to haul calves in—and by gravy, we worked the whole range with wagons. We had two horses apiece, we fed 'em corn, and we fed hay when we had to; and we moved the cows with calves—takin' along any others that was about to lay 'em down. When we came to a bunch, they'd string out. The strongest would walk off, and then we'd ease what was left to the nearest hospital. We made a pool, you understand. Not mine, yours or his. We took care of the stock that needed it most, strays and all. Why, there was some of Picket Boone's stuff out here, and they got exactly the same lay that ours did—no more, no less.

"We tailed 'em up. I'm leavin' out the pitiful part—the starving, staggering and bawling of 'em, and the question their eyes asked of us. Heartbreakin', them eyes of theirs. I reckon they caught on mighty early that we was doin' our damnedest for 'em, and that we was their one and only chance. A lot of 'em died. It was bad.

"We shoved about two hundred of the strongest cows and calves in the roughs above here, in that pasture I fenced off. They've stripped this end bare as a bone now, and moved up to Hospital Springs. We took the very weakest down to the river. Scattered them out with Johnny's Mexican neighbors. And we had to haul baled hay to feed that bunch to keep 'em alive while we moved 'em. But the great heft of 'em, starving stuff, we threw into Charlie See's pasture. Everybody's, anybody's. Charlie didn't have a head of his own in there, except according to their need."

"That was white of Charlie See—it sure was," said Pepper, staring thoughtfully across the sunburned plain below them. "And he was the most obstreperous of the whole objectionable bunch, too. Hmn! I begin to think you fellows make a strong outfit."

"One for all and all for one—that sort of blitherin' junk," said Mason cheerfully. "Men and brothers, fellow citizens, gentlemen and boys—you ought to have seen that work. In two months we didn't rope a cow or trot a horse. We never moved a cow out of a walk, a creeping walk. We never moved a cow one foot in the wrong direction. We moved 'em late in the evenin', on into the night, early in the morning; we spoke to 'em politely and we held sunshades over 'em all day. We never slept, and we ate beans, flies, dust, patent food and salt pork. I ate through four miles of sidemeat and never struck a shoulder or a ham. And concernin' Charlie See's pasture-that you was makin' eyes about, Mr. Pepper—I've heard some loose talk that *if* it rained, and *if* we pulled through, and *if* we was lousy with money three or four years from now, and if we felt good-natured and Charlie had been keepin' in his place in the meantime, and we hadn't changed our minds or got religion, we might do this and that to make it up to Charlie. But," said Mr. Mason loftily, "I don't take no stock in such, myself. Talk's cheap."

"And who was the master mind?" asked Hobby. "Who got this up? You, Uncle Andy?"

"Why, no," said Bates, "I didn't. Charlie See took the lead, naturally, when he threw open his pasture to all hands. We made a pool, I tell you. Combined all our resources. Them that had brains, they put in brains, and those that didn't, they put in what they had. Mason had a mess of old wagons. They come in handy, too. Hopper, he thought of working his Mexican friends for pasture. Hall, he studied up our little speculation in hay; Red thought it would be a bright idea to have Bud Faulkner's mares hie them hence, and Bud, he showed us what an axe would do to *sotol* bush. I'm comin' to that."

"I had some extra harness, too," said Mason meekly. "Coming down to facts, the auditor was my idea, too. That's what I said—auditor. Remember Sam Girdlestone, that was searchin' for oil last year? Well, he come back visiting, and found us in a fix. We put him to work. He keeps track of all costs, and credits us with whatever we put in, cash, credit, work, wagons, or wisdom. We give him a percentage on our losses. He does other little chores—tails up cows, runs the pump and hunts water, chops up a few hundred *sotols* between times. But his main job is posting up the account books—at night while we relax. Likely lad, Sam. Aside from that," said Mr. Mason, "Andy is a pernicious old liar, and well he know it. Charlie See has got a little sense in his own name—I'll admit that. The rest of us have just enough brains to keep a stiff upper lip, and that lets us out. Andy Bates is the man. We may some of us dig up a bolt or two in a pinch— but old Andy Bates is the man that makes the machine and keeps it oiled. F'rinstance, Henry Hall broke out into prophecy that Boone wouldn't miss nary chance to do us dirt on the alfalfa—but it was Aforesaid that rigged the dead-fall accordin'. Bud Faulkner was feeding *sotol*, a head and a half to a cow and a half, in a day and a half. So Bates gets him a pencil and a tally book, ciphers two-three days till his pencil wore to a stub and announces that if so many *sotol* hearts a day—running in size from a big cabbage head up to a big stove—would keep so many cows alive so many days, then several more *sotol* heads would keep several thousand head till it rained, if any. We saw this, after he explained it to us, and we hired all the Mexicans north of a given point. That's the way it went. You tell 'em, Andy. It's a sad story."

"Cows, calves and stretcher cases attended to," said Bates, "we taken a long look. Way out on the desert west of Turnabout, there's tall grass yet. Tall hay— cured on the stem. It's clear away from all water holes but ours, and too far from ours for any but the ablest. We left them huskies be, right where they was. I'll say they was determined characters. Surreptitious and unbeknownst to them, while they'd gone back to grass, we edged the other cattle easy into the hills and began givin' 'em first aid with *sotol*. June, July and now August most gone—and the sun shinin' in the daytime. Tedious. Only when it would cloud up, it would be a heap worse. Look like it was goin' to rain pitchforks—but nary a drop ever dropped. Gentlemen, it has been plum ree-diculous! We haven't lost many cattle, considerin'. We've kept our stock, we've kept our lips in the position indi-cated by friend Mason, of Deep Well; and we've kept our sorrows to ourselves."

"Except when desirable to air them?" hinted Pepper. "In Jakes's place, for example? With a purpose, perhaps?"

"Except when desirable. But we've lost most of our calf crop, most of next year's calf crop, our credit is all shot, and what cash we have can't be squandered paying old bills—because we need it to buy what we can't get charged. See?

And no one knows how long it will take the *sotol* to make a stand again for 'next time'."

"There ain't going to be no next time," said Mason. "Me and Hall is goin' to keep our cattle sold off, like you said. Or was it you that advised against overstocking? I think you did. We got men chopping *sotol* on every hill and men cooking for 'em in every canyon, and another man sharpening axes on a grindstone, men hauling water to the cooks, men hauling hay to the men who haul water to the cooks, and a man hauling axle grease to the men who haul the hay to the men who haul water to the cooks. Three thousand head we're feedin' *sotol* to. Oh, my back, my back!"

"It seems to me," said Bates, "That I did mention somethin' of the kind. That brings the story to date. That's why I wrote to you, Hobby. You haven't been at Garfield long, your credit's good. We want to ease out all the steers that can put one foot in front of another, and get you to wheedle 'em along to Garfield, gradual, place 'em around amongst the Mexican's pastures, where they'll get a little alfalfa, watch 'em that they don't bloat, buy hay for 'em as needed—on jawbone—and get 'em shaped up for late sales, if any. If the drought breaks, we need all the money we can get. If it stays dry, we need all the money there is. That's the lay. If there should happen to be any steer from a brand that isn't mortgaged, you'll have a claim on him to make you safe. Are you game?"

"You know it," said Hob.

"A very fine scheme," said Bull Pepper approvingly. "But like all best-laid plans, it has a weak point. And I don't see why it shouldn't go agley as you, Billy bedam please on that one point."

"Yes?" said Aforesaid encouragingly. "Tell it to us."

"I'm the weak point," said Pepper. "I've thought seriously of shooting Red Murray in the back—some dark night, when I'd be perfectly safe, of course. Charlie See, too—worse'n Red. Most obnoxious young squirt I ever see, Charlie is. Hall and Hopper give me the pip, Faulkner sets my teeth on edge. And as for you two, yourselves—if you will excuse me for being personal?"

"Yes, yes—go on!"

"Even for you old geezers, my knees are not calloused from offering up petitions in your behalf."

"Oh, we know all that," said Aforesaid reassuringly. "But how does the application come in?"

"Tripoli, now," urged Pepper. "You have ill-wishers in Tripoli. But no one comes up here even in good seasons. Tripoli thinks you are chousing each other's cattle, cat-and-dogging all over the shop. Tripoli doesn't know of any of these very interesting steps you have taken—not even that you have driven your mares away. Tripoli doesn't dream that you are in a fair way to pull through if unmolested, or you'd sure be molested a-plenty. Just for sample, if Tripoli store-keepers, or San Lucas storekeepers, where you owed big bills—if they owed big money to one of your ill-wishers, and if they received instructions to demand immediate payment—see? Just begin with that, and then let your fancy lead you where you will. Now that you gentlemen have opened up your souls and showed me the works, what's to hinder me from hiking down and giving the show away?"

"You don't understand," said Bates patiently. "If you had been that kind of a man, we wouldn't have said a word. See?"

"I see," said Pepper. "And you haven't made any mistake, either. If my sad-dle could talk, I'd burn it. I'll be one to help Lull with your steers—and by the Lord Harry, I'll lend you what money I've got to tide you over."

"Why, that's fine, Bull, and we thank you. Glad to have you plod along with the drive, but we won't need any money. Because," said Bates, "I have already—uh—effected a loan. The best is, I've got three years to pay it in. Boone was very kind."

"You old gray wolf. I sensed it, sort of—and yet I could hardly believe it. I sensed it. You gymnasticked around and made Pickett Boone think you and Mason were on the prod; you went through the motions of goin' broke at poker, so you could trick him into lending you money—virtually extendin' Mason's mortgage. For, of course, that's what you got it for. Dear, oh dear! Ho-ho-ho! I hope to be among those present when they hang you!"

"Had to have that," said Aforesaid modestly. "Mason's mortgage is due directly. We aim to pay Hall's mortgage with our steer money, and when mine falls due, maybe someone will pay that. Lots can happen in three years."

"Give me that axe," said Pepper. "I'm working with the Little World now."

Red-faced and sweating, Andy Bates became aware that someone hailed him from the trail below. He shouldered his axe and zigzagged down the hill.

"That's Joe Gandy," said Bates to Bates. "Gee whiz, I wonder if someone is sueing me already? They have to sue. Can't spare any money now." To the deputy he said, when they met, "Hullo, Joe! What's your will?"

"Sorry Mr. Bates—but it has been reported to the Land Office that you're fencing in government land, and they wrote up for me to investigate. Made me deputy U.S. marshal pro tem. Sorry—but I have to do my duty."

"Yes I know," said Bates, without enthusiasm. "That fence, now? I did build a fence, seems like. Let me see now—what did I do with that fence? Oh yes—I know!" His face brightened, he radiated cheerfulness. "I took it down again. You ride up and see. You'll find a quarter of a mile still standing across the canyon at Silver Spring. That's on my patented land—so be you be damn sure you shut the gate when you go through. Beyond my land, you'll find the fence down, quite a ways anyhow. Wire rolled up and everything. If you find any trees tangled together or rocks piled up, you have my permission to untangle and unpile, if the whim strikes you. Away to your duty with you! I'll wait here till you come back."

With a black look for the old man, Gandy spurred up the trail. It was an hour later when he came back.

"Well?" said Bates, from beneath a stunted cedar.

"The fence is down, as you said—some of it."

"I knew that. What I want to know is, did you shut that gate?"

Gandy's face flamed to the hair-edge. He shook a hand at his tormentor, a threatening index finger extended. "You saved up that grass, turned your cattle in to eat it up, and then took the fence down."

"If such were the case," inquired Bates mildly, "exactly what in the hot hereafter do you propose to do about it? Don't shake your finger at me. I won't have it. Careful, fellow, you'll have a fit if you don't cool off. But you're wrong. Somebody told me that fence was illegal, I remember. So I hot-footed up there and yanked her down. You see," said Bates meekly, "I figured some meddlesome skunk would come snoopin' and pryin' around, and I judged it would be best if I beat him to it. That's one of the best things I do—beating 'em to it."

"You insolent old fool!" bawled Gandy. "Have you got a gun?"

Bates stared. "Why, son," he said beamingly, "I wear my gun only when I go in swimming. No need to stand on ceremony with me—not at any time. Be sure I'm awake, and then go ahead."

Gandy pulled himself together with an effort, breathing hard. "You stubborn fool," he said thickly, "if it wasn't for your old gray beard I'd stomp you right into the ground."

Bates smiled benevolently. "Give up the gun idea, have you? That's good. As to the other proposition, it's like this. I got chores on hand, as you see." He waved his hand at the hillside, where fifty cows awaited his return to resume breakfast. "Feedin' my cows. It would hinder me terrible to be stomped into the ground right now. But I'll tell you what I'll do. Either it will rain or it won't. If it don't rain, my poor corpse will be found somewhere beside a *sotol*, still grasping an axe handle in my—in his—I mean, in its cold dead hands. In that case, all bets is off. But if it ever rains, I'm goin' to heave a long sigh, and a strong sigh altogether. Then I'm goin' to sleep maybe a month. And then I'm goin' down to Tripoli and shave my old gray beard off. When you meet up with me, and I'm wearin' a slick face, you begin stomping that face, right off. Bear it in mind. Be off on your duties, now. I've got no more time to waste on you. Hump yourself, you redheaded son of Satan, or I'll heave this axe at you."

V

Strained, haggard and grim, August burned to a close in a dumb terror of silence. September, with days unchanging, flaming, intolerable desperate: last and irretrievable ruin hovered visible over the forlorn and glaring levels. Twice and again clouds banked black against the hills with lightning flash and thunder, only to melt away and leave the parched land to despair. The equinox was near at hand. With no warning, night came down on misery and morning rose in mist. The mist thickened, stirred to slow vague wheelings, vase and doubtful, at the breath of imperceptible winds; halted, hesitated, drifted; trembled at last to a warm thin rain, silent and still and needle-fine. The mist lifted to low clouds, that fine rain grew to a brisk shower, the shower swelled to a steady downpour; earth and beast and man rejoiced together. Black and low and level, clouds banked from hill to hill, the night fell black and vast, and morning broke in bitter storm. All day it held in windy shrieking uproar, failed through the night to a low driving rain, with gusty splashes and lulls between. Then followed two sunless days and starless night, checkered with shower and slack. The sun-cracked levels soaked and swelled. Runoff started in the hills, dry cañons changed in turn to rivulets, to torrents, to roaring floods, where boulders ground together in a might diapason; and all the air was vibrant with the sound of many waters. The springs were filled and choked, trails were gullied and hillside roads were torn. The fifth day saw blue patches of the sky. But the drought was broken; the brave earth put forth blade and shoot and shaft again.

Dim in the central desert lies a rain-made "lake"—so-called. Its life is but brief weeks or months at best; five years in ten it is not filled at all. Because of that, because it is far from living water, because the deepest well, as yet, has found no water here, the grama grasses are still unruined, untouched save in time of heavy rains. Shallow and small, muddy, insignificant, lonely, unbeautiful; in all the world there is no "lake" so poor—and none more loved. You may guess the reason by the name. It was called *Providencia*—three hundred years ago. Smile if you will. But if the cattle have a name for it, surely their meaning is not different from ours.

The starved life of the Little World still held the old tradition of this lonely lake. Everywhere, in long, slow, plodding strings, converging, they toiled heavily through the famished ranges to their poor land of promise and the lake of their hope.

Pickett Boone's steers were in Tripoli pens. Other small herds were held near by on the mesa, where a swift riot of wild pea-vine had grown since the rains begun. Riders from these herds were in to hear of prices. Steers were in sorry shape buyers were scarce and shy.

John Copeland, steer-buyer, rode out slowly from the pens with Pickett Boone. They halted at a group of conversational cowmen.

"Well, boys, I've sold," said Pickett Boone. He held out his hands palm up, in deprecation. "Ten dollars. Not enough. But what can I do? I can't hold them over—nearly a thousand head."

A murmur of protest ran around the circle of riders. Some were eloquently resentful.

"Sorry, boys," said the buyer. "But we would make more if your stuff shaped so we could pay you fifteen. Your steers are a poor buy at any price. Wait a minute while I settle with Boone." He produced a large flat billbook. "Here's your check, Mr. Boone. Nine thousand, eight hundred dollars. Nine hundred and eighty steers. Correct?"

Boone fingered the check doubtfully. "Why, this is your personal check," he said.

Copeland flipped it over and indicated an endorsement with his thumb. "John Jastrow's signature. You know that—and there's Jastrow, sitting on the fence. 'S all right?"

"Oh, I guess so," said Boone.

"And here's the bill of sale, all made out," said the buyer briskly. "Here's my fountain pen. Sign up and I'll be trading with the others."

A troubled look came to Boone's eyes, but he signed after a moment's hesitation.

"Witnesses," said Copeland. "The line forms on the right. Two of you. Then we'll go over to the other fellows and talk it up together. Thanks. Let's ride."

Boone motioned Copeland to the rear. "Come down as soon as you can," he said in an undertone, "and we'll finish up."

"Huh?" said Copeland blankly.

"Pay me the balance—two dollars a head—and I'll give you my check for five hundred, as we agreed."

"My memory is shockingly poor," said Copeland, and sighed.

Boone turned pale. "Are you going to be a dirty thief and a double-crosser?"

"I wouldn't put it past me," confessed Copeland. "Mine is a low and despicable character. You'd be surprised. But I'm never crooked in the line of my profession. Among gentlemen, I believe, that is called 'the point of honor.' You may have heard of it. If I made any agreement with you—depend upon it, I took the proposition straight to John Jastrow. I never hold out on a client."

"This is a conspiracy!" said Boone. He trembled with rage and fear.

"Prove it," advised the buyer. "Lope up and tell the boys what you framed up. I've got your bill of sale, witnessed. Go tell 'em!"

"They'd shoot me," said Boone, choking on a sob.

"That is what I think," said Copeland unfeelingly, and rode on.

A shout went up as the buyer overtook the cavalcade. "Here come the West Side boys." The newcomers were Mason and Murray, of the Little World, with young Sam Girdlestone attached.

"Hullo, Dick—Where's your herd? And where's the rest of you?"

"Howdy, boys!" said Mason. "Bates and See, they've gone on downtown. We didn't bring any steers. Prices too low.—So we hear."

"Boone sold at ten dollars," said Bill McCall. "I'll starve before I'll take that."

Mason smiled. "We won't sell, either. Not now. We aim to get more than twelve, by holding on a spell."

Boone turned savagely and reined his horse against Mason's. He dared not let these men guess that he had tried to tamper with the price. Stung for a heavy loss, but afraid to seek redress—here was one in his power, on whom he could safely vent his fury. "Your gang may not sell, but you'll sell, right now. Your time's up in a few days, and I'm going to have my money!"

"Well, you needn't shriek about it." Mason's brow was puckered in thought; he held his lower lip doubled between thumb and finger, and remembered, visibly. "That's so, I do owe you something, don't I? A mortgage? Yes, yes. To be sure. Due about October twentieth? . . . Let me see, maybe I can pay you now. Can't afford to sell at such prices."

"I get twelve dollars," declared McCall stoutly, "Or my dogies trudge back home."

"Oh, I'll give you twelve," said the buyer. "Prices have gone up. I just sold that bunch again—them in the pen, for twelve dollars. To Jastrow."

"O-h-h!" A wolf's wail came from Boone's throat.

"How's that?" demanded McCall. "Thought Jastrow bought 'em in the first place?"

"Oh, no. I bought 'em in behalf of a pool."

Mason unrolled a fat wallet. "Here, Mr. Boone, let's see if I've got enough to pay you." He thumbed over checks, counting them. "Here's a lot of assorted checks—Eddy Early, Yancy, Evans—all that poker-playing' bunch. They tot up to twenty-eight hundred all told." He glanced casually at Pickett Boone. That gentleman clung shaking to the saddlehorn, narrowly observed by mystified East Siders. Mason prattled on unheeding, "And old Aforesaid, he gave me a bigish check this morning. Glad you reminded me of it, Mr. Boone."

"You know, Mr. Mason," said Copeland, "You're forgetting your steer money. Here it is. Two dollars a head. Nineteen hundred and sixty dollars. Nice profit. You might better have held out for twelve, Mr. Boone. These Little World people made a pool and brought your steers—and then sold them to Jastrow in ten minutes."

"You come on downtown after a while, Mr. Boone," said Mason. "Bring your little old mortgage and I'll fix you up. Take your time. You're looking poorly."

Sam Girdlestone and Henry Hall were riding down the pleasant street toward supper, when Sam took note of an approaching pedestrian. He had a familiar look, but Sam could not quite place him.

"Who's that, Henry?" said Sam.

Hall reined in, and shouted. "Heavens above! It's Squire Bates, and him shaved slick and clean! Hi, Aforesaid, what's the idea? You gettin' married, or something?" He leaned on the saddlehorn as Bates drew near. "Heavens above, Andy—what in the world has happened to your nose?"

"My nose?" said Bates, puzzled. He glanced down the nose in question, finding it undeniably swollen. He fingered it gingerly. "It does look funny, doesn't it?"

"Look there! What's happened?" cried Sam, in a startled voice. "That man's hurt!"

Bates turned to look. Two men came from the door of Jake's Place, supporting the staggering steps of a third man between them. The third man's arms sprawled and clutched on the escorting shoulders, his knees buckled, his feet dragged, his head drooped down upon his chest, his whole body sagged. Bates held a hand to shield his eyes and peered again. "Why, I do believe it's Joe Gandy!" he declared.

"But what's happened to him, Uncle Andy?" demanded Sam eagerly.

Bates raised clear untroubled eyes to Sam's. "I remember, now," he said. "It was Joe Gandy that hit me on this nose . . . . How it all comes back to me! . . . The Bible says when a man smites you on one cheek to turn the other, so I done that. Then I didn't have any further instructions, so I used my own judgment!"

MY FIRST LESSON
IN COW PUNCHING

CHARLES SIRINGO

The next day after arriving in town, Mr. Faldien sent me out to his ranch, twenty miles, on Big Boggy. I rode out on the "grub" wagon with the colored cook. That night, after arriving at the ranch, there being several men already there, we went out wild boar hunting. We got back about midnight very tired and almost used up. Such a hunt was very different from the coon hunts Billy and I used to have at the "Settlement." Our dogs were badly gashed up by the boars, and it was a wonder some of us hadn't been served the same way.

In a few days Mr. Faldien came out to the ranch, bringing with him several men. After spending a few days gathering up the cow-ponies, which hadn't been used since the fall before, we started for Lake Austin—a place noted for wild cattle.

During the summer I was taken sick and had to go home. I was laid up for two months with typhoid fever. Every one thought I would die.

That fall, about October, mother married a man by the name of Carrier, who hailed from Yankeedom. He claimed that he owned a farm in Michigan, besides lots of other property.

He was very anxious to get back to his farm, so persuaded mother to sell out lock, stock and barrel and go with him.

She had hard work to find a buyer as money was very scarce, but finally she got Mr. George Burkheart, a merchant in Matagorda, to set his own price on things and take them.

The house and one hundred and seventy-five acres of land only brought one hundred and seventy-five dollars. The sixty head of cattle that we had succeeded in getting back from the mainland went at one dollar a head and all others that still remained on the mainland—thrown in for good measure.

At last everything for sale was disposed of and we got "Chris" Zipprian to take us to Indianola in his schooner. We bade farewell to the old homestead with tears in our eyes. I hated more than anything else to leave old "Browny" behind for she had been a friend in need as well as a friend indeed. Often when I would be hungry and afraid to go home for fear of mother and the mush stick, she would let me go up to her on the prairie calf fashion and get my milk. She was nearly as old as myself.

At Indianola we took the Steamship "Crescent City" for New Orleans. The first night out we ran into a large Brig and came very near going under. The folks on the Brig were nearly starved to death, having been drifting about for thirty days without a rudder. We took them in tow, after getting our ship in trim again, and landed them safely in Galveston.

There was a bar-room on our ship, and our new lord and master, Mr. Carrier, put in his spare time drinking whisky and gambling; I do not think he drew a sober breath from the time we left Indianola until we landed in New Orleans, by that time he had squandered every cent received for the homestead and cattle, so mother had to go down into her stocking and bring out the little pile of gold which she had saved up before the war for "hard times," as she used to say. With this money she now bought our tickets to Saint Louis. We took passage, I think, on the "Grand Republic." There was also a bar-room on this boat, and after wheedling mother out of the remainder of her funds, he drank whisky and gambled as before, so we landed in Saint Louis without a cent.

Mother had to pawn her feather mattress and pillows for a month's rent in an old delapidated frame building on one of the back streets. It contained only four rooms, two up stairs and two down; the lower rooms were occupied by the stingy old landlord and family; we lived in one of the upper rooms, while a Mr. Socks, whose wife was an invalid, occupied the other.

The next day after getting established in our new quarters, the "old man," as I called him, struck out to find a job; he found one at a dollar a day shoveling coal.

At first he brought home a dollar every night, then a half and finally a quarter. At last he got to coming home drunk without a nickel in his pocket. He finally came up missing; we didn't know what had become of him. Mother was sick in bed at the time from worrying. I went out several times hunting work but no one would even give me a word of encouragement, with the exception of an old Jew who said he was sorry for me.

A little circumstance happened, shortly after the "old man" pulled his trifling carcass for parts unknown, which made me a better boy and no doubt a better man than I should have been had it never happened.

Everything was white without, for it had been snowing for the past two days. It was about five o'clock in the evening and the cold piercing north wind was whistling through the unceiled walls of our room. Mother was sound asleep, while sister and I sat shivering over an old, broken stove, which was almost cold, there being no fuel in the house.

Sister began crying and wondered why the Lord let us suffer so? I answered that may be it was because we quit saying our prayers. Up to the time we left Texas mother used to make us kneel down by the bed-side and repeat the Lord's prayer every night before retiring. Since then she had, from worrying, lost all interest in Heavenly affairs.

"Let us say our prayers now, then, brother!" said sister drying the tears from her eyes.

We both knelt down against the old, rusty stove and commenced. About the time we had finished the door opened and in stepped Mr. Socks with a bundle under his arm. "Here children, is a loaf of bread and some butter and I will bring you up a bucket of coal in a few moments, for I suppose from the looks of the stove you are cold," said the good man, who had just returned from his day's work.

Was ever a prayer so quickly heard? We enjoyed the bread and butter, for we hadn't tasted food since the morning before.

The next day was a nice sunny one, and I struck out up town to try and get a job shoveling snow from the sidewalks.

The first place I tackled was a large stone front on Pine street. The kind lady of the establishment said she would give me twenty-five cents if I would do a good job cleaning the sidewalk in front of the house.

After an hour's hard work I finished, and, after paying me, the lady told me to call next day and she would give me a job shoveling coal down in the cellar, as I had done an extra good job on the sidewalk. This was encouraging and I put in the whole day shoveling snow, but never found any more twenty-five cent jobs; most I received for one whole hour's work was ten cents, and then the old fat fellow kicked like a bay steer, about the d—d snow being such an expense, etc.

From that time on I made a few dimes each day sawing wood or shoveling coal and therefore got along splendid.

I forgot to mention my first evening in Saint Louis. I was going home from the bakery when I noticed a large crowd gathered in front of a corner grocery; I went up to see what they were doing. Two of the boys had just gotten through fighting when I got there; the store-keeper and four or five other men were standing in the door looking on at the crowd of boys who were trying to cap another fight.

As I walked up, hands shoved clear to the bottom of my pockets, the store-keeper called out, pointing at me, "there's a country Jake that I'll bet can lick any two boys of his size in the crowd."

Of course all eyes were then turned onto me, which, no doubt, made me look sheepish. One of the men asked me where I was from; when I told him, the store-keeper exclaimed, "by gum, if he is from Texas I'll bet two to one that he can clean out any two boys of his size in the crowd."

One of the other men took him up and they made a sham bet of ten dollars, just to get me to fight. The two boys were then picked out; one was just about my size and the other considerably smaller. They never asked me if I would take a hand in the fight until everything was ready. Of course I hated to crawl out, for fear they might think I was a coward.

Everything being ready the store-keeper called out, "dive in boys!"

We had it up and down for quite a while, finally I got the largest one down, and was putting it to him in good shape, when the other one picked up a piece of brick-bat and began pounding me on the back of the head with it. I looked up to see what he was doing and he struck me over one eye with the bat. I jumped up and the little fellow took to his heels, but I soon overtook him and blackened both of his eyes up in good shape, before the other boy, who was coming at full tilt could get there to help him. I then chased the other boy back to the crowd. That ended the fight and I received two ginger-snaps, from the big hearted store-keeper, for my trouble. I wore the nick-name of "Tex" from that time on, during my stay in that neighborhood; and also wore a black eye, where the little fellow struck me with the bat, for several days afterwards.

About the middle of January mother received a letter from the "old man," with ten dollars enclosed, and begging her to come right on without delay as he had a good job and was doing well, etc. He was at Lebanon, Ill., twenty-five miles from the city. The sight of ten dollars and the inducements he held out made us hope that we would meet with better luck there, so we packed up our few traps and started on the Ohio and Mississippi railroad.

On arriving in Lebanon about nine o'clock at night we found the "old man" there waiting for us.

The next morning we all struck out on foot, through the deep snow, for Moore's ranch where the "old man" had a job chopping cord wood. A tramp of seven miles brought us to the little old log cabin which was to be our future home. A few rods from our cabin stood a white frame house in which lived Mr. Moore and family.

Everything went on lovely for the first week, notwithstanding that the cold winds whistled through the cracks in our little cabin, and we had nothing to eat but corn bread, black coffee and old salt pork that Moore could not find a market for.

The first Saturday after getting established in our new home the "old man" went to town and got on a glorious drunk, squandered every nickel he could rake and scrape; from that time on his visits to town were more frequent than his trips to the woods, to work. At last I was compelled to go to work for Moore at eight dollars a month, to help keep the wolf from our door, and don't you forget it, I earned eight dollars a month, working out in the cold without gloves and only half clothed.

Towards spring the "old man" got so mean and good-for-nothing that the neighbors had to run him out of the country. A crowd of them surrounded the house one night, took the old fellow out and preached him a sermon; then they gave him until morning to either skip or be hung. You bet he didn't wait until morning.

A short while afterwards mother took sister and went to town to hunt work. She left her household goods with one of the near neighbors, a Mr. Muck, where they still remain I suppose, if not worn out. But there was nothing worth hauling off except the dishes. I must say the table ware was good; we had gotten them from a Spanish vessel wrecked on the Gulf beach during the war.

Mother found work in a private boarding house, and sister with a Mrs. Bell, a miller's wife, while I still remained with Moore at the same old wages.

Along in June sometime I quit Moore on account of having the ague. I thought I should have money enough to take a rest until I got well, but bless you I only had ninety cents to my credit, Moore had deducted thirty-five dollars the "old man" owed him out of my earnings. I pulled for town as mad as an old setting hen. But I soon found work again, with an old fellow by the name of John Sargent, who was to give me eight dollars a month, board and clothes and pay my doctor bills.

About the first of September mother and sister went to Saint Louis where they thought wages would be higher. They bade me good bye, promising to find me a place in the city, so I could be with them; also promised to write.

Shortly afterwards I quit Mr. Sargent with only one dollar to my credit; and that I haven't got yet. He charged me up with everything I got in the shape of clothes, doctor bills, medicine, etc.

I then went to work for a carpenter, to learn the trade, for my board, clothes, etc. I was to remain with him three years. My first day's work was turning a big heavy stone for him to grind a lot of old, rusty tools on. That night after supper I broke my contract, as I concluded that I knew just as much about the carpenter's trade as I wished to know, and skipped for the country, by moonlight.

I landed up at a Mr. Jacobs' farm twelve miles from town and got a job of work at twelve dollars a month. I didn't remain there long though, as I had a chill every other day regular, and therefore couldn't work much.

I made up my mind then to pull for Saint Louis and hunt mother and sister. I had never heard a word from them since they left. After buying a small satchel to put my clothes in and paying for a ticket to the city, I had only twenty-five cents left and part of that I spent for dinner that day.

I arrived in East Saint Louis about midnight with only ten cents left. I wanted to buy a ginger-cake or something as I was very hungry, but hated to as I needed the dime to pay my way across the river next morning. I wasn't very well posted then, in regard to the ways of getting on in the world, or I would have spent the dime for something to eat, and then beat my way across the river.

A MOONLIGHT DRIVE

ANDY ADAMS

The two herds were held together a second night, but after they had grazed a few hours the next morning, the cattle were thrown together, and the work of cutting out ours commenced. With a double outfit of men available, about twenty men were turned into the herd to do the cutting, the remainder holding the main herd and looking after the cut. The morning was cool, every one worked with a vim, and in about two hours the herds were again separated and ready for the final trimming. Campbell did not expect to move out until he could communicate with the head office of the company, and would go up to Fort Laramie for that purpose during the day, hoping to be able to get a message over the military wire. When his outfit had finished retrimming our herd, and we had looked over his cattle for the last time, the two outfits bade each other farewell, and our herd started on its journey.

The unfortunate accident at the ford had depressed our feelings to such an extent that there was an entire absence of hilarity by the way. This morning the farewell songs generally used in parting with a river which had defied us were omitted. The herd trailed out like an immense serpent, and was guided and controlled by our men as if by mutes. Long before the noon hour, we passed out of sight of Forty Islands, and in the next few days, with the change of scene, the gloom gradually lifted. We were bearing almost due north, and passing through a delightful country. To our left ran a range of mountains, while on the other hand sloped off the apparently limitless plain. The scarcity of water was beginning to be felt, for the streams which had not a source in the mountains on our left had dried up weeks before our arrival. There was a gradual change of air noticeable too, for we were rapidly gaining altitude, the heat of summer being now confined to a few hours at noonday, while the nights were almost too cool for our comfort.

When about three days out from the North Platte, the mountains disappeared on our left, while on the other hand appeared a rugged-looking country, which we knew must be the approaches of the Black Hills. Another day's drive brought us into the main stage road connecting the railroad on the south with the mining camps which nestled somewhere in those rocky hills to our right. The stage road followed the trail some ten or fifteen miles before we parted company with it on a dry fork of the Big Cheyenne River. There was a road house and stage stand where these two thoroughfares separated, the one to the mining camp of Deadwood, while ours of the Montana cattle trail bore off for the Powder River to the northwest. At this stage stand we learned that some twenty herds had already passed by to the northern ranges, and that after passing the next fork of the Big Cheyenne we should find no water until we struck the Powder River,—a stretch of eighty miles. The keeper of the road house, a genial host, informed us that this drouthy stretch in our front was something unusual, this being one of the dryest summers that he had experienced since the discovery of gold in the Black Hills.

Here was a new situation to be met, an eighty-mile dry drive; and with our experience of a few months before at Indian Lakes fresh in our memories, we set our house in order for the undertaking before us. It was yet fifteen miles to the next and last water from the stage stand. There were several dry forks of the Cheyenne beyond, but as they had their source in the tablelands of Wyoming, we could not hope for water in their dry bottoms. The situation was serious, with only this encouragement: other herds had crossed this arid belt since the streams had dried up, and our Circle Dots could walk with any herd that ever left Texas. The wisdom of mounting us well for just such an emergency reflected the good cow sense of our employer; and we felt easy in regard to our mounts, though there was not a horse or a man too many. In summing up the situation, Flood said, "We've got this advantage over the Indian Lake drive: there is a good moon, and the days are cool. We'll make twenty-five miles a day covering this stretch, as this herd has never been put to a test yet to see how far they could walk in a day. They'll have to do their sleeping at noon; at least cut it into two shifts, and if we get any sleep we'll have to do the same. Let her come as she will; every day's drive is a day nearer the Blackfoot agency."

We made a dry camp that night on the divide between the road house and the last water, and the next forenoon reached the South Fork of the Big Cheyenne. The water was not even running in it, but there were several long pools, and we held the cattle around them for over an hour, until every hoof had been thoroughly watered. McCann had filled every keg and canteen in advance of the arrival of the herd, and Flood had exercised sufficient caution, in view of what lay before us, to buy an extra keg and a bull's-eye lantern at the road house. After watering, we trailed out some four or five miles and camped for noon, but the herd were allowed to graze forward until they lay down for their noonday rest. As the herd passed opposite the wagon, we cut a fat two-year-old stray heifer and killed her for beef, for the inner man must be fortified for the journey before us. After a two hours' siesta, we threw the herd on the trail and started on our way. The wagon and saddle horses were held in our immediate rear, for there was no telling when or where we would make our next halt of any consequence. We trailed and grazed the herd alternately until near evening, when the wagon was sent on ahead about three miles to get supper, while half the outfit went along to change mounts and catch up horses for those remaining behind with the herd. A half hour before the usual bedding time, the relieved men returned and took the grazing herd, and the others rode in to the wagon for supper and a change of mounts. While we shifted our saddles, we smelled the savory odor of fresh beef frying.

"Listen to that good old beef talking, will you?" said Joe Stallings, as he was bridling his horse. "McCann, I'll take my *carne fresco* a trifle rare to-night, garnished with a sprig of parsley and a wee bit of lemon."

Before we had finished supper, Honeyman had rehooked the mules to the wagon, while the *remuda* was at hand to follow. Before we left the wagon, a full moon was rising on the eastern horizon, and as we were starting out Flood gave us these general directions: "I'm going to take the lead with the cook's lantern, and one of you rear men take the new bull's-eye. We'll throw the herd on the trail; and between the lead and rear light, you swing men want to ride well outside, and you point men want to hold the lead cattle so the rear will never be more than a half a mile behind. I'll admit that this is somewhat of an experiment with me, but I don't see any good reason why she won't work. After the moon gets another hour high we can see a quarter of a mile, and the cattle are so well trail broke they'll never try to scatter. If it works all right, we'll never bed them short of midnight, and that will put us ten miles farther. Let's ride, lads."

By the time the herd was eased back on the trail, our evening camp-fire had been passed, while the cattle led out as if walking on a wager. After the first mile on the trail, the men on the point were compelled to ride in the lead if we were to hold them within the desired half mile. The men on the other side, or the swing, were gradually widening, until the herd must have reached fully a mile in length; yet we swing riders were never out of sight of each other, and it would have been impossible for any cattle to leave the herd unnoticed. In that moonlight the trail was as plain as day, and after an hour, Flood turned his lantern over to one of the point men, and rode back around the herd to the rear. From my position that first night near the middle of the swing, the lanterns both rear and forward being always in sight, I was as much at sea as any one as to the length of the herd, knowing the deceitfulness of distance of campfires and other lights by night. The foreman appealed to me as he rode down the column, to know the length of the herd, but I could give him no more than a simple guess. I could assure him, however, that the cattle had made no effort to drop out and leave the trail. But a short time after he passed me I noticed a horseman galloping up the column on the opposite side of the herd, and knew it must be the foreman. Within a short time, some one in the lead wig-wagged his lantern; it was answered by the light in the rear, and the next minute the old rear song,—

"Ip-e-la-ago, go 'long little doggie,
You 'll make a beef-steer by-and-by,"—

reached us riders in the swing, and we knew the rear guard of cattle was being pushed forward. The distance between the swing men gradually narrowed in our lead, from which we could tell the leaders were being held in, until several times cattle grazed out from the herd, due to the checking in front. At this juncture Flood galloped around the herd a second time, and as he passed us riding along our side, I appealed to him to let them go in front, as it now required constant riding to keep the cattle from leaving the trail to graze. When he passed up the opposite side, I could distinctly hear the men on that flank making a similar appeal, and shortly afterwards the herd loosened out and we struck our old gait for several hours.

Trailing by moonlight was a novelty to all of us, and in the stillness of those splendid July nights we could hear the point men chatting across the lead in front, while well in the rear, the rattling of our heavily loaded wagon and the whistling of the horse wrangler to his charges reached our ears. The swing men were scattered so far apart there was no chance for conversation amongst us, but every once in a while a song would be started, and as it surged up and down the line, every voice, good, bad, and indifferent, joined in. Singing is supposed to have a soothing effect on cattle, though I will vouch for the fact that none of our Circle Dots stopped that night to listen to our vocal efforts. The herd was traveling so nicely that our foreman hardly noticed the passing hours, but along about midnight the singing ceased, and we were nodding in our saddles and wondering if they in the lead were never going to throw off the trail, when a great wig-wagging occurred in front, and presently we overtook The Rebel, holding the lantern and turning the herd out of the trail. It was then after midnight, and within another half hour we had the cattle bedded down within a few hundred yards of the trail. One-hour guards was the order of the night, and as soon as our wagon and saddle horses came up, we stretched ropes and caught out our night horses. These we either tied to the wagon wheels or picketed near at hand, and then we sought our blankets for a few hours' sleep. It was half past three in the morning when our guard was called, and before the hour passed, the first signs of day were visible in the east. But even before our watch had ended, Flood and the last guard came to our relief, and we pushed the sleeping cattle off the bed ground and started them grazing forward.

Cattle will not graze freely in a heavy dew or too early in the morning, and before the sun was high enough to dry the grass, we had put several miles behind us. When the sun was about an hour high, the remainder of the outfit overtook us, and shortly afterward the wagon and saddle horses passed on up the trail, from which it was evident that "breakfast would be served in the dining car ahead," as the traveled Priest aptly put it. After the sun was well up, the cattle grazed freely for several hours; but when we sighted the *remuda* and our commissary some two miles in our lead, Flood ordered the herd lined up for a count. The Rebel was always a reliable counter, and he and the foreman now rode forward and selected the crossing of a dry wash for the counting. On receiving their signal to come on, we allowed the herd to graze slowly forward, but gradually pointed them into an immense "V," and as the point of the herd crossed the dry arroyo, we compelled them to pass in a narrow file between the two counters, when they again spread out fan-like and continued their feeding.

The count confirmed the success of our driving by night, and on its completion all but two men rode to the wagon for breakfast. By the time the morning meal was disposed of, the herd had come up parallel with the wagon but a mile to the westward, and as fast as fresh mounts could be saddled, we rode away in small squads to relieve the herders and to turn the cattle into the trail. It was but a little after eight o'clock in the morning when the herd was again trailing out on the Powder River trail, and we had already put over thirty miles of the dry drive behind us, while so far neither horses nor cattle had been put to any extra exertion. The wagon followed as usual, and for over three hours we held the trail without a break, when sighting a divide in our front, the foreman went back and sent the wagon around the herd with instructions to make the noon camp well up on the divide. We threw the herd off the trail, within a mile of this stopping place, and allowed them to graze, while two thirds of the outfit galloped away to the wagon.

We allowed the cattle to lie down and rest to their complete satisfaction until the middle of the afternoon; meanwhile all hands, with the exception of two men on herd, also lay down and slept in the shade of the wagon. When the cattle had had several hours' sleep, the want of water made them restless, and they began to rise and graze away. Then all hands were aroused and we threw them upon the trail. The heat of the day was already over, and until the twilight of the evening, we trailed a three-mile clip, and again threw the herd off to graze. By our traveling and grazing gaits, we could form an approximate idea as to the distance we had covered, and the consensus of opinion of all was that we had already killed over half the distance. The herd was beginning to show the want of water by evening, but amongst our saddle horses the lack of water was more noticeable, as a horse subsisting on grass alone weakens easily; and riding them made them all the more gaunt. When we caught up our mounts that evening, we had used eight horses to the man since we had left the South Fork, and another one would be required at midnight, or whenever we halted.

We made our drive the second night with more confidence than the one before, but there were times when the train of cattle must have been nearly two miles in length, yet there was never a halt as long as the man with the lead light could see the one in the rear. We bedded the herd about midnight; and at the first break of day, the fourth guard with the foreman joined us on our watch and we started the cattle again. There was a light dew the second night, and the cattle, hungered by their night walk, went to grazing at once on the damp grass, which would allay their thirst slightly. We allowed them to scatter over several thousand acres, for we were anxious to graze them well before the sun absorbed the moisture, but at the same time every step they took was one less to the coveted Powder River.

When we had grazed the herd forward several miles, and the sun was nearly an hour high, the wagon failed to come up, which caused our foreman some slight uneasiness. Nearly another hour passed, and still the wagon did not come up nor did the outfit put in an appearance. Soon afterwards, however, Moss Strayhorn overtook us, and reported that over forty of our saddle horses were missing, while the work mules had been overtaken nearly five miles back on the trail. On account of my ability as a trailer, Flood at once dispatched me to assist Honeyman in recovering the missing horses, instructing some one else to take the *remuda*, and the wagon and horses to follow up the herd. By the time I arrived, most of the boys at camp had secured a change of horses, and I caught up my *grulla*, that I was saving for the last hard ride, for the horse hunt which confronted us. McCann, having no fire built, gave Honeyman and myself an impromptu breakfast and two canteens of water; but before we let the wagon get away, we rustled a couple of cans of tomatoes and buried them in a cache near the camp-ground, where we would have no trouble in finding them on our return. As the wagon pulled out, we mounted our horses and rode back down the trail.

Billy Honeyman understood horses, and at once volunteered the belief that we would have a long ride overtaking the missing saddle stock. The absent horses, he said, were principally the ones which had been under saddle the day before, and as we both knew, a tired, thirsty horse will go miles for water. He recalled, also, that while we were asleep at noon the day before, twenty miles back on the trail, the horses had found quite a patch of wild sorrel plant, and were foolish over leaving it. Both of us being satisfied that this would hold them for several hours at least, we struck a free gait for it. After we passed the point where the mules had been overtaken, the trail of the horses was distinct enough for us to follow in an easy canter. We saw frequent signs that they left the trail, no doubt to graze, but only for short distances, when they would enter it again, and keep it for miles. Shortly before noon, as we gained the divide above our noon camp of the day before, there about two miles distant we saw our missing horses, feeding over an alkali flat on which grew wild sorrel and other species of sour plants. We rounded them up, and finding none missing, we first secured a change of mounts. The only two horses of my mount in this portion of the *remuda* had both been under saddle the afternoon and night before, and were as gaunt as rails, and Honeyman had one unused horse of his mount in the band. So when, taking down our ropes, we halted the horses and began riding slowly around them, forcing them into a compact body, I had my eye on a brown horse of Flood's that had not had a saddle on in a week, and told Billy to fasten to him if he got a chance. This was in violation of all custom, but if the foreman kicked, I had a good excuse to offer.

Honeyman was left-handed and threw a rope splendidly; and as we circled around the horses on opposite sides, on a signal from him we whirled our lariats and made casts simultaneously. The wrangler fastened to the brown I wanted, and my loop settled around the neck of his unridden horse. As the band broke away from our swinging ropes, a number of them ran afoul of my rope; but I gave the rowel to my *grulla*, and we shook them off. When I returned to Honeyman, and we had exchanged horses and were shifting our saddles, I complimented him on the long throw he had made in catching the brown, and incidentally mentioned that I had read of vaqueros in California who used a sixty-five foot lariat. "Hell," said Billy, in ridicule of the idea, "there wasn't a man ever born who could throw a sixty-five foot rope its full length—without he threw it down a well."

The sun was straight overhead when we started back to overtake the herd. We struck into a little better than a five-mile gait on the return trip, and about two o'clock sighted a band of saddle horses and a wagon camped perhaps a mile forward and to the side of the trail. On coming near enough, we saw at a glance it was a cow outfit, and after driving our loose horses a good push beyond their camp, turned and rode back to their wagon.

"We'll give them a chance to ask us to eat," said Billy to me, "and if they don't, why, they'll miss a hell of a good chance to entertain hungry men."

But the foreman with the stranger wagon proved to be a Bee County Texan, and our doubts did him an injustice, for, although dinner was over, he invited us to dismount and ordered his cook to set out something to eat. They had met our wagon, and McCann had insisted on their taking a quarter of our beef, so we fared well. The outfit was from a ranch near Miles City, Montana, and were going down to receive a herd of cattle at Cheyenne, Wyoming. The cattle had been bought at Ogalalla for delivery at the former point, and this wagon was going down with their ranch outfit to take the herd on its arrival. They had brought along about seventy-five saddle horses from the ranch, though in buying the herd they had taken its *remuda* of over a hundred saddle horses. The foreman informed us that they had met our cattle about the middle of the forenoon, nearly twenty-five miles out from Powder River. After we had satisfied the inner man, we lost no time getting off, as we could see a long ride ahead of us; but we had occasion as we rode away to go through their *remuda* to cut out a few of our horses which had mixed, and I found I knew over a dozen of their horses by the ranch brands, while Honeyman also recognized quite a few. Though we felt a pride in our mounts, we had to admit that theirs were better; for the effect of climate had transformed horses that we had once ridden on ranches in southern Texas. It does seem incredible, but it is a fact nevertheless, that a horse, having reached the years of maturity in a southern climate, will grow half a hand taller and carry two hundred pounds more flesh, when he has undergone the rigors of several northern winters.

We halted at our night camp to change horses and to unearth our cached tomatoes, and again set out. By then it was so late in the day that the sun had lost its force, and on this last leg in overtaking the herd we increased our gait steadily until the sun was scarcely an hour high, and yet we never sighted a dust-cloud in our front. About sundown we called a few minutes' halt, and after eating our tomatoes and drinking the last of our water, again pushed on. Twilight had faded into dusk before we reached a divide which we had had in sight for several hours, and which we had hoped to gain in time to sight the timber on Powder River before dark. But as we put mile after mile behind us, that divide seemed to move away like a mirage, and the evening star had been shining for an hour before we finally reached it, and sighted, instead of Powder's timber, the campfire of our outfit about five miles ahead. We fired several shots on seeing the light, in the hope that they might hear us in camp and wait; otherwise we knew they would start the herd with the rising of the moon.

When we finally reached camp, about nine o'clock at night, everything was in readiness to start, the moon having risen sufficiently. Our shooting, however, had been heard, and horses for a change were tied to the wagon wheels, while the remainder of the *remuda* was under herd in charge of Rod Wheat. The runaways were thrown into the horse herd while we bolted our suppers. Meantime McCann informed us that Flood had ridden that afternoon to the Powder River, in order to get the lay of the land. He had found it to be ten or twelve miles distant from the present camp, and the water in the river barely knee deep to a saddle horse. Beyond it was a fine valley. Before we started, Flood rode in from the herd, and said to Honeyman, "I'm going to send the horses and wagon ahead to-night, and you and McCann want to camp on this side of the river, under the hill and just a few hundred yards below the ford. Throw your saddle horses across the river, and build a fire before you go to sleep, so we will have a beacon light to pilot us in, in case the cattle break into a run on scenting the water. The herd will get in a little after midnight, and after crossing, we'll turn her loose just for luck."

It did me good to hear the foreman say the herd was to be turned loose, for I had been in the saddle since three that morning, had ridden over eighty miles, and had now ten more in sight, while Honeyman would complete the day with over a hundred to his credit. We let the *remuda* take the lead in pulling out, so that the wagon mules could be spurred to their utmost in keeping up with the loose horses. Once they were clear of the herd, we let the cattle into the trail. They had refused to bed down, for they were uneasy with thirst, but the cool weather had saved them any serious suffering. We all felt gala as the herd strung out on the trail. Before we halted again there would be water for our dumb brutes and rest for ourselves. There was lots of singing that night. "There's One more River to cross," and "Roll, Powder, roll," were wafted out on the night air to the coyotes that howled on our flanks, or to the prairie dogs as they peeped from their burrows at this weird caravan of the night, and the lights which flickered in our front and rear must have been real Jack-o'-lanterns or Will-o'-the-wisps to these occupants of the plain. Before we had covered half the distance, the herd was strung out over two miles, and as Flood rode back to the rear every half hour or so, he showed no inclination to check the lead and give the sore-footed rear guard a chance to close up the column; but about an hour before midnight we saw a light low down in our front, which gradually increased until the treetops were distinctly visible, and we knew that our wagon had reached the river. On sighting this beacon, the long yell went up and down the column, and the herd walked as only long-legged, thirsty Texas cattle can walk when they scent water. Flood called all the swing men to the rear, and we threw out a half-circle skirmish line covering a mile in width, so far back that only an occasional glimmer of the lead light could be seen. The trail struck the Powder on an angle, and when within a mile of the river, the swing cattle left the deep-trodden paths and started for the nearest water.

The left flank of our skirmish line encountered the cattle as they reached the river, and prevented them from drifting up the stream. The point men abandoned the leaders when within a few hundred yards of the river. Then the rear guard of cripples and sore-footed cattle came up, and the two flanks of horsemen pushed them all across the river until they met, when we turned and galloped into camp, making the night hideous with our yelling. The longest dry drive of the trip had been successfully made, and we all felt jubilant. We stripped bridles and saddles from our tired horses, and unrolling our beds, were soon lost in well-earned sleep.

The stars may have twinkled overhead, and sundry voices of the night may have whispered to us as we lay down to sleep, but we were too tired for poetry or sentiment that night.

THE TRUE COWBOY

H. H. HALSELL

DISCIPLINE AMONG COWHANDS AND TRAIL DRIVERS

A cowboy was not educated, but he received lessons from contact with Nature and the hardships of life which qualified him to think for himself and know how to measure men by correct standards. He was laconic in speech, using few words to express himself, but his meanings were forceful and easily understood by his comrades. He wore serviceable Stetson hats, shop-made boots, costly overshirts, and usually a silk handkerchief around his neck. The real old-time cowboy of my time never went gaudily dressed as they now do in the picture shows. His bed consisted of a ducking tarpaulin, two real good wool blankets, and in his bed a clean sack with a change of clean clothes. When a new man came into camp he was often careless in his appearance and often went dirty, but the real veteran cowboy was clean and had pride because he knew this life he was leading was all he had, and he made the most of it. That real true rider of the Wild West, with his courage, endurance, and his devotion to duty, is gone, faded out of the picture, and will never return. And now I am to sing his dying swan song:

"Fear no more the heat of the sun, nor the winter's furious rages;

Thou, thy worldly task hast done; home art gone and taken thy wages.

I am living the old trail drives over again, and in my dreams

I again see and work with some of the gay old boys.

I wish that we could live the old days over, just once more.

I wish we could hit the trail together, just once more.

Say, Pal, the years are slipping by with many a dream and many a sigh—

Let's chum together, you and I, just once more."

It is fitting someone must chronicle his deeds as they were enacted, past and gone, never to return; and no one having in a realistic manner done so heretofore—that is, in a manner to suit my view of their ways—I am, as a matter of fairness to the cowboy and the old-time cowman and as a duty to posterity, attempting to transmit to a new age the customs, habits, and deeds of men who lived on the frontier forty to sixty years ago.

I have wandered off the trail again and lost the thread of my story of the three thousand steers. At the period I am writing about, the fall of 1880, roving bands of Indians, passing through the country on their fall hunts, often burnt off a large portion of the country in order to drive the deer, turkey, and antelope on more restricted spots, so that the Indians could the more easily find and kill them. This made it hard on trail drivers and caused more trouble to hold the herds. Old grass that had been burned off in August caused new and short grass to come up, and this caused our big herd to scatter very much, and men and horses were on this account worn out at times. Old and tried cowhands won't complain, but new ones will. When we arrived near the South Canadian, the men were almost worn out and some were cross. Among the fifteen men with our outfit were two Negro cowhands—old cowhands off the Three Circle and the Three D's Ranches in Clay County. One was named Jack, and the other was Lewis. Lewis was a bad man from Bitter Creek, but a real, sure-enough cowhand.

One morning while I was out hunting some lost horses this Negro Lewis cursed out good and strong a sorry green white man for cutting his lariat rope, and the greener had to take it. On my arrival in camp the cook told me of the affair. The boss passed the buck to me, and, as I had promised my Uncle Glenn Halsell before leaving Texas I would stay with him (meaning, protect his interests) on the trail, and, furthermore, knowing this act, if not remedied, would disorganize the outfit, I struck out for the herd where the Negro was. As I went around the east and north sides, he went on down the west side toward the camp. Passing the Negro Jack on the way, I jerked his pistol out of his belt and took it along with me. Poor Jack. I can in my mind see him this day, as he looked at me and said, "Mr. Harry, please don't hurt Lewis." I was running my horse all the way, and Lewis knew there was trouble. Riding up to him, I said, "You coward—you can cuss a poor green hand, but you have not the nerve to face the real thing. I'll give you an even break. Pull your gun." He said, "Mr. Harry, I don't want trouble with you." I said, "You will either fight or get down, pull your saddle off, and turn your horse loose. If you do not do one or the other, I will kill you now." Lewis got down, unsaddled and turned the horse loose. That meant that he was to leave the outfit, but the boss or someone else persuaded me later to let him remain. I then told him he could do so by promising to behave. From that day on he did as much work as two ordinary men, and that saved the herd.

One thing that made it hard on the men was that the cook was no good. We had nothing to eat except fat bacon, sorry bread, and black coffee. Why the boss would never kill the heifers we carried along for beef, I never took pains to ask. I took it for granted that he was the boss, and I could stand what the rest put up with. But it turned out later I could not do so. Two days after this trouble, we were guarding the cattle on short grass. They were hard to hold, and all the men were up most of the night. This was a very dark foggy night, and when the night was over the fog was so dense it was impossible to see fifty yards ahead. We had in the outfit two men Earhart had met on the trail and hired. No one knew anything about them. As I rode into camp I heard one of these men tell the cook to get out that keg of molasses and open it up. The cook told them the boss had given him orders not to open the keg until he told him to. Now it really seemed to me that the molasses ought to be put to use, but there was something involved more important than a keg of molasses. The man said, "If you do not open the keg, I'll burst it open with the ax." I said, "If you do, that will be your last act." The boss came into camp, told me there had been two horses missing since the night before, and asked me to go back down the trail and find them. Starting immediately toward the trail (as I thought), which was about a hundred yards east of the wagon, I was really turned around, and instead of going east to the trail I rode due south, and that mistake saved my life. It finally dawned on me I was lost in a dense fog. I then rode down into a small creek bed that was dry, tied Sam, built a fire, and, becoming warm, went to sleep. When I woke up the sun was shining, and I rode on south, keeping west of the trail just far enough to see from there to the trail if horses should show up. Late in the evening I crossed North Canadian about one mile west of the trail. Riding up on a high hill, I saw to the south, about a mile away, a large herd of cattle being drifted onto the bed ground. I went on toward the herd, and the first man I saw was a friend of mine from Texas by the name of Stewart. He said, "Harry, we have two of your horses in our horse herd." He then told me two men came to their herd about noon, hunting for me, swearing they would kill me on sight. These men had been fired by Earhart. They wondered why they did not see my horse tracks on the trail. The reason was that I was never on the trail.

I spent the night with that outfit and next night was in our camp. Our herd moved on to within a few miles of Hunnewell, then turned east, and one cold evening swam the Arkansas River. On the opposite bank the cattle were bedded, and we built up a big log fire. It was a cold, misty night, the cattle were hard to hold, and the men were up all night. Next morning I lay down by the big log fire, sick with the flux and fever. The boss came and talked to me, asking what could be done. I said, "Nothing you can do, but tie my roan horse to a tree near me, and you go on with the herd." He offered to leave a man with me. I said, "No; you have not men enough to handle the cattle now." So the herd moved on east.

A man raised amidst the hardships and privations of a rough frontier life knows how to look to Nature for relief. Sometimes hot water is best; sometimes cold water serves the purpose. Early in life I found out nothing will beat a big warm log fire on a cold damp day to take the cold and sore feeling out. We cowboys knew what hot salt would do for cramping. We also kept slippery elm and quinine. I baked myself by that good fire until toward 11 AM Some relief came; so I said to Sam, "Can we make it to the Kansas line?" He seemed to think we could. Crawling onto old Faithful, we moseyed north and crossed the Kansas state line about 2 PM I came to a farmhouse and stayed there for ten days until I recovered. In three days one of the men came back to the camp where they had left me, commissioned to bury me, I suppose; not finding a corpse, he came north and found me. I said, "Allen, hurry on back and help save that herd." He did so. In ten days I was well, and Sam and I pushed on between a hundred and a hundred and twenty-five miles east, and caught up with the herd at the mouth of Bird Creek just where it empties into Verdigras River. I had charge of this herd from November, 1880, until the summer of 1881.

In the spring of 1881 a herd of 1,300 more steers came from Clay County to this ranch and swam the Arkansas River at the spot where Tulsa is now located. But this herd came a northeast course from Clay County and cut off about one hundred and fifty miles. Why that herd of three thousand steers went north three hundred miles, from Clay County to Hunnewell, then southeast one hundred and forty miles, was a mystery to me, but it was none of my business.

During the winter of 1880 and 1881 an incident happened that proved to me that a horse sometimes has more sense than a man. I had a favorite horse called Prince, and one cold, foggy evening I got lost in Verdigras River bottom, kept on riding, but could not find my way out. After a while I came to some fresh horse tracks and decided to hurry and catch up with the rider. Hurrying on for about thirty minutes, I came upon the tracks of two horses. I then got down and upon measuring the tracks found them to be Prince's. I had been riding in a circle. I then said, "Prince, if you can do the job better than me, you can have free rein." Old Prince turned in the opposite direction in a fast trot, and in a half hour was out of the timber bottom and on his way to the ranch.

One day W. E. Halsell and wife came out from Vinita to the ranch to camp and hunt. They came in a two-seated hack, and had a Negro boy with them. It was a beautiful May day. He selected a nice camping place on the bank of a small creek. His colored boy set up the tent, and they were preparing dinner. I rode off a short distance to drag up some wood. It had been raining hard the night before and very stormy. During the storm a smallpox patient, under delirium, had run away from a detention camp and had not been found. I found him dead about two hundred yards from W. E. Halsell's camp. He had run into a swollen stream and drowned. I came back with the wood and told Uncle Billy I wanted the spade to bury a boy who had died with the smallpox. Uncle Billy, with his wife and Negro, was gone in ten minutes. I buried the boy on the bank of that branch, and no one ever knew his grave. There was a small store at the mouth of Bird Creek. The room was about ten by fourteen feet. One day I was in this store. An Indian came in and began shooting all around my head. He was crazed with drink, and I felt it was a crisis. I looked him straight in the eye and said, "Dennis, don't do that." His name was Dennis Wolf. After emptying his gun he went off. The storekeeper said: "That Indian is jealous of his squaw." I didn't even know her, but I did know his hut was about one mile east of my camp, and I often rode by the hut on my line.

It is recorded in Genesis' act of creation that man was given dominion over all animal life. In circuses this record seems to be verified. Sometimes, however, it pays to let a good horse have his way, and sometimes it pays to follow a dog's trail if you are hungry and want a rabbit or squirrel. It has been proved that dogs' trails have led to the North Pole. Also, I have known occasions when good common horse sense was sadly lacking in irresponsible man. A good, faithful, well-trained horse will not forsake his owner, and wherever the footsteps of man have trod the dog has been his faithful companion. There is an incident I desire to mention to show that men raised from childhood in a rough frontier life must and generally do become very resourceful. A very fine Negro had been working for the Three Circle outfit a long time. He came with the herds from the Texas ranch on the Wichitas and, at this time, was working with me. Our camp was fifteen miles from where the Verdigras and the Arkansas River form a junction, and there were wide bottoms of timber on each. One cold winter evening Jack and I got lost in these gloomy bottoms on the Verdigras and wandered until dark. At the place where we then were the water in this bottom was two to eight inches deep. There were very many dead saplings handy, so Jack and I put ropes around them as high up as possible; then with the other end of the ropes tied to the horn of the saddle, we pulled down a great many. We built a big long fire with part of them; made a bed with some of them high enough to be out of the water. We then spread our blankets on the logs and slept. A tenderfoot or a jelly bean would have stood up all night in the water. If one is accustomed to a feather bed, he will need one; but a cowboy was used to the hard beds.

ABILENE IN 1868

JOSEPH G. McCOY

No sooner had it become a conceded fact that Abilene, as a cattle depot, was a success, than tradespeople from all points came to the village and, after putting up temporary houses, went into business. Of course the saloon, the billiard table, the ten-pin alley, the gambling table—in short, every possible device for obtaining money in both an honest and dishonest manner, were abundant.

Fully seventy-five thousand cattle arrived at Abilene during the summer of 1868, and at the opening of the market in the spring fine prices were realized and snug fortunes were made by such drovers as were able to effect a sale of their herds. It was the custom to locate herds as near the village as good water and plenty of grass could be found. As soon as the herd is located upon its summer grounds a part of the help is discharged, as it requires less labor to hold than to travel. The camp was usually located near some living water or spring where sufficient wood for camp purposes could be easily obtained. After selecting the spot for the camp, the wagon would be drawn up. Then a hole dug in the ground in which to build a fire of limbs of trees or drift wood gathered to the spot, and a permanent camp instituted by unloading the contents of the wagon upon the ground. And such a motley lot of assets as come out of one of those camp carts would astonish one, and beggar minute description: a lot of saddles and horse-blankets, a camp-kettle, coffee-pot, bread pan, battered tin cups, a greasy mess chest, dirty soiled blankets, an ox yoke, a log chain, spurs and quirts, a coffee-mill, a broken-helved ax, bridles, picket-ropes, and last, but not least, a side or two of fat mast-fed bacon; to which add divers pieces of raw-hide in various stages of dryness. A score of other articles not to be thought of will come out of that exhaustless camp cart. But one naturally inquires what use would a drover have for a raw-hide, dry or fresh? Uses infinite; nothing breaks about a drover's outfit that he cannot mend with strips or thongs of raw-hide. He mends his bridle or saddle or picket-rope, or sews his ripping pants or shirt, or lashes a broken wagon tongue, or binds on a loose tire, with raw-hide. In short, a raw-hide is a concentrated and combined carpenter and blacksmith shop, not to say saddler's and tailor's shop, to the drover. Indeed, it is said that what a Texan cannot make or mend with a rawhide is not worth having, or is irretrievably broken into undistinguishable fragments. It is asserted that the agricultural classes of that State fasten their plow points on with raw-hide, but we do not claim to be authorities on Texan agriculture, and therefore cannot vouch for this statement.

The herd is brought upon its herd ground and carefully watched during the day, but allowed to scatter out over sufficient territory to feed. At nightfall it is gathered to a spot selected near the tent, and there rounded up and held during the night. One or more cow-boys are on duty all the while, being relieved at regular hours by relays fresh aroused from slumber, and mounted on rested ponies, and for a given number of hours they ride slowly and quietly around the herd, which, soon as it is dusk, lies down to rest and ruminate. About mid-night every animal will arise, turn about for a few moments, and then lie down again near where it arose, only changing sides so as to rest. But if no one should be watching to prevent straggling, it would be but a short time before the entire herd would be up and following off the leader, or some uneasy one that would rather travel than sleep or rest. All this is easily checked by the cow-boy on duty. But when storm is imminent, every man is required to have his horse saddled ready for an emergency. The ponies desired for use are picketed out, which is done by tying one end of a half inch rope, sixty or seventy feet long, around the neck of the pony and fastening the other end to a pointed iron or wooden stake, twelve or more inches long, which is driven in the firm ground. As all the strain is laterally and none upward, the picket pin will hold the strongest horse. The length of the rope is such as to permit the animal to graze over considerable space, and when he has all the grass eat off within his reach, it is only necessary to move the picket pin to give him fresh and abundant pasture. Such surplus ponies as are not in immediate use, are permitted to run with the cattle or herded to themselves, and when one becomes jaded by hard usage, he is turned loose and a rested one caught with the lasso and put to service. Nearly all cow-boys can throw the lasso well enough to capture a pony or a beef when they desire so to do. Day after day the cattle are held under herd and cared for by the cow-boys, whilst the drover is looking out for a purchaser for his herd, or a part thereof, especially if it be a mixed herd—which is a drove composed of beeves, three, two and one year old steers, heifers and cows. To those desiring any one or more classes of such stock as he may have, the drover seeks to sell, and if successful, has the herd rounded up and cuts out the class sold; and after counting carefully until all parties are satisfied, straightway delivers them to the purchaser. The counting of the cattle, like the separating or cutting out, is invariably done on horse-back. Those who do the counting, take positions a score of paces apart, whilst the cow-boys cut off small detachments of cattle and force them between those counting, and when the bunch or cut is counted satisfactorily, the operation is repeated until all are counted. Another method is to start the herd off, and when it is well drawn out, to begin at the head and count back until the last are numbered. As a rule, stock cattle are sold by the herd, and often beeves are sold in the same manner, but in many instances sale is made by the pound, gross weight. The latter manner is much the safest for the inexperienced, for he then pays only for what he gets; but the Texan prefers to sell just as he buys at home, always by the head. However, in late years, it is becoming nearly the universal custom to weigh all beeves sold in Northern markets.

Whilst the herd is being held upon the same grazing grounds, often one or more of the cow-boys, not on duty, will mount their ponies and go to the village nearest camp and spend a few hours; learn all the items of news or gossip concerning other herds and the cow-boys belonging thereto. Besides seeing the sights, he gets such little articles as may be wanted by himself and comrades at camp; of these a supply of tobacco, both chewing and smoking, forms one of the principal, and often recurring wants. The cow-boy almost invariably smokes or chews tobacco—generally both, for the time drags dull at camp or herd ground. There is nothing new or exciting occurring to break the monotony of daily routine events. Sometimes the cow boys off duty will go to town late in the evening and there join with some party of cow-boys—whose herd is sold and they preparing to start home—in having a jolly time. Often one or more of them will imbibe too much poison whisky and straightaway go on the "war path." Then mounting his pony he is ready to shoot anybody or anything; or rather than not shoot at all, would fire up into the air, all the while yelling as only a semi-civilized being can. At such times it is not safe to be on the streets, or for that matter within a house, for the drunk cow boy would as soon shoot into a house as at anything else.

The life of the cow-boy in camp is routine and dull. His food is largely of the "regulation" order, but a feast of vegetables he wants and must have, or scurvy would ensue. Onions and potatoes are his favorites, but any kind of vegetables will disappear in haste when put within his reach. In camp, on the trail, on the ranch in Texas, with their countless thousands of cattle, milk and butter are almost unknown, not even milk or cream for the coffee is had. Pure shiftlessness and the lack of energy are the only reasons for this privation, and to the same reasons can be assigned much of the privations and hardships incident to ranching.

It would cost but little effort or expense to add a hundred comforts, not to say luxuries, to the life of a drover and his cow-boys. They sleep on the ground, with a pair of blankets for bed and cover. No tent is used, scarcely any cooking utensils, and such a thing as a camp cook-stove is unknown. The warm water of the branch or the standing pool is drank; often it is yellow with alkali and other poisons. No wonder the cow-boy gets sallow and unhealthy, and deteriorates in manhood until often he becomes capable of any contemptible thing; no wonder he should become half-civilized only, and take to whisky with a love excelled scarcely by the barbarous Indian.

When the herd is sold and delivered to the purchaser, a day of rejoicing to the cow-boy has come, for then he can go free and have a jolly time; and it is a jolly time they have. Straightway after settling with their employers the barber shop is visited, and three to six months' growth of hair is shorn off, their long-grown, sunburnt beard "set" in due shape, and properly blacked; next a clothing store of the Israelitish style is "gone through," and the cow-boy emerges a new man, in outward appearance, everything being new, not excepting the hat and boots, with star decorations about the tops, also a new———, well, in short everything new. Then for fun and frolic. The bar-room, the theatre, the gambling-room, the bawdy house, the dance house, each and all come in for their full share of attention. In any of these places an affront, or a slight, real or imaginary, is cause sufficient for him to unlimber one or more "mountain howitzers," invariably found strapped to his person, and proceed to deal out death in unbroken doses to such as may be in range of his pistols, whether real friends or enemies, no matter, his anger and bad whisky urge him on to deeds of blood and death.

At frontier towns where are centered many cattle and, as a natural result, considerable business is transacted, and many strangers congregate, there are always to be found a number of bad characters, both male and female; of the very worst class in the universe, such as have fallen below the level of the lowest type of the brute creation. Men who live a soulless, aimless life, dependent upon the turn of a card for the means of living. They wear out a purposeless life, ever looking bleareyed and dissipated; to whom life, from various causes, has long since become worse than a total blank; beings in the form of man whose outward appearance would betoken gentlemen, but whose heart-strings are but a wisp of base sounding chords, upon which the touch of the higher and purer life have long since ceased to be felt. Beings without whom the world would be better, richer and more desirable. And with them are always found their counterparts in the opposite sex; those who have fallen low, alas! how low! They, too, are found in the frontier cattle town; and that institution known in the West as a dance house, is there found also. When the darkness of the night is come to shroud their orgies from public gaze, these miserable beings gather into the halls of the dance house, and "trip the fantastic toe" to wretched music, ground out of dilapidated instruments, by beings fully as degraded as the most vile. In this vortex of dissipation the average cow-boy plunges with great delight. Few more wild, reckless scenes of abandoned debauchery can be seen on the civilized earth, than a dance house in full blast in one of the many frontier towns. To say they dance wildly or in an abandoned manner is putting it mild. Their manner of practising the terpsichorean art would put the French "Can-Can" to shame.

The cow-boy enters the dance with a peculiar zest, not stopping to divest himself of his sombrero, spurs or pistols, but just as he dismounts off of his cow-pony, so he goes into the dance. A more odd, not to say comical sight, is not often seen than the dancing cow-boy; with the front of his sombrero lifted at an angle of fully forty-five degrees; his huge spurs jingling at every step or motion; his revolvers flapping up and down like a retreating sheep's tail; his eyes lit up with excitement, liquor and lust; he plunges in and "hoes it down" at a terrible rate, in the most approved yet awkward country style; often swinging "his partner" clear off of the floor for an entire circle, then "balance all" with an occasional demoniacal yell, near akin to the war whoop of the savage Indian. All this he does, entirely oblivious to the whole world "and the balance of mankind." After dancing furiously, the entire "set" is called to "waltz to the bar," where the boy is required to treat his partner, and, of course, himself also, which he does not hesitate to do time and again, although it costs him fifty cents each time. Yet if it cost ten times that amount he would not hesitate, but the more he dances and drinks, the less common sense he will have, and the more completely his animal passions will control him. Such is the manner in which the cow-boy spends his hard earned dollars. And such is the entertainment that many young men—from the North and the South, of superior parentage and youthful advantages in life—give themselves up to, and often more, their lives are made to pay the forfeit of their sinful foolishness.

After a few days of frolic and debauchery, the cow-boy is ready, in company with his comrades, to start back to Texas, often not having one dollar left of his summer's wages. To this rather hard drawn picture of the cow-boy, there are many creditable exceptions—young men who respect themselves and save their money, and are worthy young gentlemen—but it is idle to deny the fact that the wild, reckless conduct of the cow-boys while drunk, in connection with that of the worthless Northern renegades, have brought the *personnel* of the Texan cattle trade into great disrepute, and filled many graves with victims, bad men and good men, at Abilene, Newton, Wichita, and Ellsworth. But by far the larger portion of those killed are of that class that can be spared without detriment to the good morals and respectability of humanity.

It often occurs when the cow-boys fail to get up a melee and kill each other by the half dozen, that the keepers of those "hell's half acres" find some pretext arising from "business jealousies" or other causes, to suddenly become belligerent, and stop not to declare war, but begin hostilities at once. It is generally effective work they do with their revolvers and shot guns, for they are the most desperate men on earth. Either some of the principals or their subordinates are generally "done for" in a thorough manner, or wounded so as to be miserable cripples for life. On such occasions there are few tears shed, or even inquiries made, by the respectable people, but an expression of sorrow is common that, active hostilities did not continue until every rough was stone dead.

In concluding we offer a few reflections on the general character of Southwestern cattle men. In doing so we are not animated by other motives than a desire to convey a correct impression of that numerous class as a whole; reflections and impressions based upon close observation and a varied experience of seven or eight years spent in business contact and relation with them.

They are, as a class, not public spirited in matters pertaining to the general good, but may justly be called selfish, or at least indifferent to the public welfare. They are prodigal to a fault with their money, when opportunity offers to gratify their appetites or passions, but it is extremely difficult to induce them to expend even a small sum in forwarding a project or enterprise that has other than a purely selfish end in view. In general they entertain strong suspicions of Northern men, and do not have the profoundest confidence in each other. They are disposed to measure every man's action and prompting motives by the rule of selfishness, and they are slow indeed to believe that other than purely selfish motives could or ever do prompt a man to do an act or develop an enterprise. If anything happens to a man, especially a Northern man, so that he cannot do or perform all that they expect or require of him, no explanation or reasons are sufficient to dispel the deep and instant conviction formed in their breasts, that he is deliberately trying to swindle them, and they can suddenly see a thousand evidences of his villainy, in short, instantly vote such a one a double dyed villain.

Their reputation is wide spread for honorably abiding their verbal contracts. For the very nature of their business, and the circumstances under which it is conducted, renders an honorable course imperative; and, as a rule, where agreements or contracts are put into writing, they will stand to them unflinchingly, no matter how great the sacrifice; but when the contract or understanding is verbal only, and not of the most definite nature, their consciences are full as pliant as are those of any other section. A promise made as to some future transaction is kept or broken, as their future interests may dictate.

DODGE

WILLIAM MACLEOD RAINE

It was in the days when the new railroad was pushing through the country of the plains Indians that a drunken cowboy got on the train at a way station in Kansas. John Bender, the conductor, asked him for his ticket. He had none, but he pulled out a handful of gold pieces.

"I wantta—g-go to—h-hell," he hiccoughed.

Bender did not hesitate an instant. "Get off at Dodge. One dollar, please."

Dodge City did not get its name because so many of its citizens were or had been, in the Texas phrase, on the dodge. It came quite respectably by way of its cognomen. The town was laid out by A. A. Robinson, chief engineer of the Atchison, Topeka & Santa Fe, and it was called for Colonel Richard I. Dodge, commander of the post at Fort Dodge and one of the founders of the place. It is worth noting this, because it is one of the few respectable facts in the early history of the cowboy capital. Dodge was a wild and uncurried prairie wolf, and it howled every night and all night long. It was gay and young and lawless.

Its sense of humor was exaggerated and worked overtime. The crack of the six-shooter punctuated its hilarity ominously. Those who dwelt there were the valiant vanguard of civilization. For good or bad they were strong and forceful, many of them generous and big-hearted in spite of their lurid lives. The town was a hive of energy. One might justly use many adjectives about it, but the word respectable is not among them.

There were three reasons why Dodge won the reputation of being the wildest town the country had ever seen. In 1872 it was the end of the track, the last jumping-off spot into the wilderness, and in the days when transcontinental railroads were building across the desert the temporary terminus was always a gathering place of roughs and scalawags. The payroll was large, and gamblers, gunmen, and thugs gathered for the pickings. This was true of Hays, Abilene, Ogalala, and Kit Carson. It was true of Las Vegas and Albuquerque.

A second reason was that Dodge was the end of the long trail drive from Texas. Every year hundreds of thousands of longhorns were driven up from Texas by cowboys scarcely less wild than the hill steers they herded. The great plains country was being opened, and cattle were needed to stock a thousand ranches as well as to supply the government at Indian reservations. Scores of these trail herds were brought to Dodge for shipment, and after the long, dangerous, drive the punchers were keen to spend their money on such diversions as the town could offer. Out of sheer high spirits they liked to shoot up the town, to buck the tiger, to swagger from saloon to gambling hall, their persons garnished with revolvers, the spurs on their high-heeled boots jingling. In no spirit of malice they wanted it distinctly understood that they owned the town. As one of them once put it, he was born high up on the Guadaloupe, raised on prickly pear, had palled with alligators and quarreled with grizzlies.

Also, Dodge was the heart of the buffalo country. Here the hunters were outfitted for the chase. From here great quantities of hides were shipped back on the new railroad. R. M. Wright, one of the founders of the town and always one of its leading citizens, says that his firm alone shipped two hundred thousand hides in one season. He estimates the number of buffaloes in the country at more than twenty-five million, admitting that many as well informed as he put the figure at four times as many. Many times he and others travelled through the vast herds for days at a time without ever losing sight of them. The killing of buffaloes was easy, because the animals were so stupid. When one was shot they would mill round and round. Tom Nicholson killed 120 in forty minutes; in a little more than a month he slaughtered 2,173 of them. With good luck a man could earn a hundred dollars a day. If he had bad luck he lost his scalp.

The buffalo was to the plains Indian food, fuel, and shelter. As long as there were plenty of buffaloes he was in Paradise. But he saw at once that this slaughter would soon exterminate the supply. He hated the hunter and battled against his encroachments. The buffalo hunter was an intrepid plainsman. He fought Kiowas, Comanches, and the Staked Plain Apaches, as well as the Sioux and the Arapahoe. Famous among these hunters were Kirk Jordan, Charles Rath, Emanuel Dubbs, Jack Bridges, and Curly Walker. Others even better known were the two Buffalo Bills (William Cody and William Mathewson) and Wild Bill.

These three factors then made Dodge: it was the end of the railroad, the terminus of the cattle trail from Texas, and the center of the buffalo trade. Together they made "the beautiful bibulous Babylon of the frontier," in the words of the editor of the *Kingsley Graphic*. There was to come a time later when the bibulous Babylon fell on evil days and its main source of income was old bones. They were buffalo-bones, gathered in wagons, and piled beside the track for shipment, hundreds and hundreds of carloads of them, to be used for fertilizer. (I have seen great quantities of such bones as far north as the Canadian Pacific line, corded for shipment to a factory.) It used to be said by way of derision that buffalo bones were legal tender in Dodge.

But that was in the far future. In its early years Dodge rode the wave of prosperity. Hays and Abilene and Ogalala had their day, but Dodge had its day and its night, too. For years it did a tremendous business. The streets were so blocked that one could hardly get through. Hundreds of wagons were parked in them, outfits belonging to freighters, hunters, cattlemen, and the government. Scores of camps surrounded the town in every direction. The yell of the cowboy and the weird oath of the bull-whacker and mule skinner were heard in the land. And for a time there was no law nearer than Hays City, itself a burg not given to undue quiet and peace.

Dodge was no sleepy village that could drowse along without peace officers. Bob Wright has set it down that in the first year of its history twenty-five men were killed and twice as many wounded. The elements that made up the town were too diverse for perfect harmony. The freighters did not like the railroad graders. The soldiers at the fort fancied themselves as scrappers. The cowboys and the buffalo hunters did not fraternize a little bit. The result was that Boot Hill began to fill up. Its inhabitants were buried with their boots on and without coffins.

There was another cemetery, for those who died in their beds. The climate was so healthy that it would have been very sparsely occupied those first years if it had not been for the skunks. During the early months Dodge was the city of camps. Every night the fires flamed up from the vicinity of hundreds of wagons. Skunks were numerous. They crawled at night into the warm blankets of the sleepers and bit the rightful owners when they protested. A dozen men died from these bites. It was thought at first that the animals were a special variety, known as the hydrophobia skunk. In later years I have sat around Arizona camp fires and heard this subject discussed heatedly. The Smithsonian Institute, appealed to as referee, decided that there was no such species and that deaths from the bites of skunks were probably due to blood poisoning caused by the foul teeth of the animal.

In any case, the skunks were only one half as venomous as the gunmen, judging by comparative staff statistics. Dodge decided it had to have law in the community. Jack Bridges was appointed first marshal.

Jack was a noted scout and buffalo hunter, the sort of man who would have peace if he had to fight for it. He did his sleeping in the afternoon, since this was a quiet time of the day. Someone shook him out of slumber one day to tell him that cowboys were riding up and down Front Street shooting the windows out of buildings. Jack sallied out, old buffalo gun in hand. The cowboys went whooping down the street across the bridge toward their camp. The old hunter took a long shot at one of them and dropped him. The cowboys buried the young fellow next day.

There was a good deal of excitement in the cow camps. If the boys could not have a little fun without some old donker, an old vinegaroon who couldn't take a joke, filling them full of lead it was a pretty howdy-do. But Dodge stood pat. The coroner's jury voted it justifiable homicide. In future the young Texans were more discreet. In the early days whatever law there was did not interfere with casualties due to personal differences of opinion provided the figure had no unusually sinister aspect.

The first wholesale killing was at Tom Sherman's dance hall. The affair was between soldiers and gamblers. It was started by trooper named Hennessey, who had a reputation as a bad guy and a bully. He was killed, as were several others. The officers at the fort glossed over the matter, perhaps because they felt the soldiers had been to blame.

One of the lawless characters who drifted into Dodge the first year was Billy Brooks. He quickly established a reputation as a killer. My old friend

Emanuel Dubbs, a buffalo hunter who "took the hides off'n" many a bison, is authority for the statement that Brooks killed or wounded fifteen men in less than a month after his arrival. Now Emanuel is a preacher (if he is still in the land of the living; I saw him last at Clarendon, Texas, ten years or so ago), but I cannot quite swallow that "fifteen." Still, he had a man for breakfast now and then and on one occasion four.

Brooks, by the way, was assistant marshal. It was the policy of the officials of these wild frontier towns to elect as marshal some conspicuous killer, on the theory that desperadoes would respect his prowess or if they did not would get the worst of the encounter.

Abilene, for instance, chose "Wild Bill" Hickok. Austin had its Ben Thompson. According to Bat Masterson, Thompson was the most dangerous man with a gun among all the bad men he knew—and Bat knew them all. Ben was an Englishman who struck Texas while still young. He fought as a Confederate under Kirby Smith during the Civil War and under Shelby for Maximilian. Later he was city marshal at Austin. Thompson was the man of the most cool effrontery. On one occasion, during a cattlemen's convention, a banquet was held at the leading hotel. The local congressman, a friend of Thompson, was not invited. Ben took exception to this and attended in person. By way of pleasantry he shot the plates in front of the diners. Later one of those present made humorous comment. "I always thought Ben was a game man. But what did he do? Did he hold up the whole convention of a thousand cattlemen? No, sir. He waited till he got forty or fifty of us poor fellows alone before he turned loose his wolf."

Of all the bad men and desperadoes produced by Texas, not one of them, not even John Wesley Hardin himself, was more feared than Ben Thompson. Sheriffs avoided serving warrants of arrest on him. It is recorded that once, when the county court was in session with a charge against him on the docket, Thompson rode into the room on a mustang. He bowed pleasantly to the judge and the court officials.

"Here I am, gents, and I'll lay all I'm worth that there's no charge against me. Am I right? Speak up, gents. I'm a little deaf."

There was a dead silence until at last the clerk of the court murmured, "No charge."

A story is told that on one occasion Ben Thompson met his match in the person of the young English remittance man playing cards with him. The remittance man thought he caught Thompson cheating and discreetly said so.

Instantly Thompson's .44 covered him. For some unknown reason the gambler gave the lad a chance to retract.

"Take it back—and quick," he said grimly.

Every game in the house was suspended while all eyes turned on the daredevil boy and the hard-faced desperado. The remittance man went white, half rose from his seat, and shoved his head across the table toward the revolver.

"Shoot and be damned. I say you cheat," he cried hoarsely.

Thompson hesitated, laughed, shoved the revolver back into its holster, and ordered the youngster out of the house.

Perhaps the most amazing escape on record is that when Thompson, fired at by Mark Wilson at a distance of ten feet from a double-barreled shotgun loaded with buckshot, whirled instantly, killed him, and an instant later shot through the forehead Wilson's friend Mathews, though the latter had ducked behind the bar to get away. The second shot was guesswork plus quick thinking and accurate aim. Ben was killed a little later, in company with his friend King Fisher, another bad man, at the Palace Theatre. A score of shots were poured into them by a dozen men waiting in ambush. Both men had become so dangerous that their enemies could not afford to let them live.

King Fisher was the humorous gentleman who put up a signboard at the fork of a public road bearing the legend:

THIS IS KING FISHER'S ROAD. TAKE THE OTHER

It is said that those traveling that way followed his advice. The other road might be a mile or two farther, but they were in no hurry. Another amusing little episode in King Fisher's career is told. He had had some slight difficulty with a certain bald-headed man. Fisher shot him and carelessly gave the reason that he wanted to see whether a bullet would glance from a shiny pate.

El Paso in its wild days chose Dallas Stoudenmire for marshal, and after he had been killed, John Selman. Both of them were noted killers. During Selman's régime John Wesley Hardin came to town. Hardin had twenty-seven notches on his gun and was the worst man killer Texas had ever produced. He was at the bar of a saloon shaking dice when Selman shot him from behind. One year later Deputy United States Marshal George Scarborough killed Selman in a duel. Shortly after this Scarborough was slain in a gunfight by "Kid" Curry, an Arizona bandit.

What was true of these towns was true, too, of Albuquerque and Las Vegas and Tombstone. Each of them chose for peace officers men who were "sudden death" with a gun. Dodge did exactly the same thing. Even a partial list of its successive marshals reads like a fighting roster. In addition to Bridges and Brooks may be named Ed and Bat Masterson, Wyatt Earp, Billy Tilghman, Ben Daniels, Mysterious Dave Mathers, T. C. Nixon, Luke Short, Charlie Bassett, W. H. Harris, and Sughrue brothers, all of them famous as fighters in a day when courage and proficiency with weapons were a matter of course. On one occasion the superintendent of the Santa Fe suggested to the city dads of Dodge that it might be a good thing to employ marshals less notorious. Dodge begged leave to differ. It felt that the best way to "settle the hash" of desperadoes was to pit against them fighting machines more efficient, bad men more deadly than themselves.

The word "bad" does not necessarily imply evil. One who held the epithet was known as one dangerous to oppose. He was unafraid, deadly with a gun, and hard as nails. He might be evil, callous, treacherous, revengeful as an Apache. Dave Mathers fitted this description. He might be a good man, kindly, gentle, never taking more than his fighting chance. This was Billy Tillman to a T.

We are keeping Billy Brooks waiting. But let that go. Let us look first at "Mysterious Dave." Bob Wright has set it down that Mathers had more dead man to his credit than any other man in the West. He slew seven by actual count in one night, in one house, according to Wright. Mathers had a very bad reputation. But his courage could blaze up magnificently. While he was deputy marshal word came that the Henry gang of desperadoes were terrorizing a dance hall. Into that hall walked Dave, beside his chief Tom Carson. Five minutes later out reeled Carson, both arms broken, his body shot through and through, a man with only five minutes to live. When the smoke in the hall cleared away Mathers might have been seen beside two handcuffed prisoners, one of them wounded. In a circle around him were four dead cowpunchers of the Henry outfit.

"Uncle" Billy Tilghman died the other day at Cromwell, Oklahoma, a victim of his own fearlessness. He was shot to death while taking a revolver from a drunken prohibition agent. If he had been like many other bad men he would have shot the fellow down at the first sign of danger. But that was never Tilghman's way. It was his habit to make arrests without drawing a gun. He cleaned up Dodge during the three years while he was marshal. He broke up the Doolin gang, killing Bill Raidler and "Little" Dick in personal duels and capturing Bill Doolin the leader. Bat Masterson said that during Tilghman's term as sheriff of Lincoln County, Oklahoma, he killed, captured, or drove from the country more criminals than any other official that section had ever had. Yet "Uncle" Billy never used a gun except reluctantly. Time and again he gave the criminal the first shot, hoping the man would surrender rather than fight. Of all the old frontier sheriffs none holds a higher place than Billy Tilghman.

After which diversion we return to Billy Brooks, a "gent" of an impatient temperament, not used to waiting, and notably quick on the trigger. Mr. Dubbs records that late one evening in the winter '72–'73 he returned to Dodge with two loads of buffalo meat. He finished his business, ate supper, and started to smoke a postprandial pipe. The sound of a fusillade in an adjoining dance hall interested him since he had been deprived of the pleasures of metropolitan life for some time and had had to depend upon Indians for excitement. (Incidentally, it may be mentioned that they furnished him with a reasonable amount. Not long after this three of his men were caught, spread-eagled, and tortured by Indians. Dubbs escaped after a hair-raising ride and arrived at Adobe Walls in time to take part in the historic defense of that post by a handful of buffalo hunters against many hundred tribesmen.) From the building burst four men. They started across the railroad track to another dance hall, one frequented by Brooks. Dubbs heard the men mention the name of Brooks, coupling it with an oath. Another buffalo hunter named Fred Singer joined Dubbs. They followed the strangers, and just before the four reached the dance hall Singer shouted a warning to the marshal. This annoyed the unknown four, and they promptly exchanged shots with the buffalo hunters. What then took place was startling in the sudden drama of it.

Billy Brooks stood in bold relief in the doorway, a revolver in each hand. He fired so fast that Dubbs says the sounds were like a company discharging weapons. When the smoke cleared Brooks still stood in the same place. Two of the strangers were dead and two mortally wounded. They were brothers. They had come from Hays City to avenge the death of a fifth brother shot down by Brooks some time before.

Mr. Brooks had a fondness for the fair sex. He and Browney, the yardmaster, took a fancy to the same girl. Captain Drew, she was called, and she preferred Browney. Whereupon Brooks naturally shot him in the head. Perversely, to the surprise of everybody, Browney recovered and was soon back at his old job.

Brooks seems to have held no grudge at him from making light of his marksmanship in this manner. At any rate, his next affair was with Kirk Jordan, the buffalo hunter. This was a very different business. Jordan had been in a hundred tight holes. He had fought Indians time and again. Professional killers had no terror for him. He threw down his big buffalo gun on Brooks, and the latter took cover. Barrels of water had been placed along the principal streets for fire protection. These had saved several lives during shooting scrapes. Brooks ducked behind one, and the ball from Jordan's gun plunged into it. The marshal dodged into a store, out of the rear door, and into a livery stable. He was hidden under a bed. Alas! for a large reputation gone glimmering. Mr. Brooks fled to the fort, took the train from the siding, and shook forever the dust of Dodge from his feet. Whither he departed a deponent sayeth not.

How do I explain this? I don't. I record a fact. Many gunmen were at one time or another subject to these panics during which the yellow streak showed. Not all of them by any means, but a very considerable percentage. They swaggered boldly, killed recklessly. Then one day some quiet little man with a cold gray eye called the turn on them, after which they oozed out of the surrounding scenery.

Owen P. White gives it on the authority of Charlie Siringo that Bat Masterson sang small when Clay Allison of the Panhandle, he of the well-notched gun, drifted into Dodge and inquired for the city marshal. But the old-timers at Dodge do not bear this out. Bat was at the Adobe Walls fight, one of fourteen men who stood off five hundred bucks of the Cheyenne, Comanche, and Kiowa tribes. He scouted for miles. He was elected sheriff of Ford County, with headquarters at Dodge when only twenty-two years of age. It was a tough assignment, and Bat executed it to the satisfaction of all concerned except the element he cowed.

Personally, I never met Bat until his killing days were past. He was dealing faro at a gambling house in Denver when I, a young reporter, first had the pleasure of looking into his cold blue eyes. It was a notable fact that all the frontier bad men had eyes either gray or blue, often a faded blue, expressionless, hard as jade.

It is only fair to Bat that the old-timers of Dodge do not accept the Siringo point of view about him. Wright said of him that he was absolutely fearless and no trouble hunter. "Bat is a gentleman by instinct, of pleasant matters, good address, and mild until aroused, and then, for God's sake, look out. He is a leader of men, has much natural ability, and good hard common sense. There is nothing low about him. He is high-toned and broad-minded, cool and brave." I give this opinion for what it is worth.

In any case, he was a most efficient sheriff. Dave Rudabaugh, later associated with Billy the Kid in New Mexico, staged a train robbery at Kingsley, Kansas, a territory not in Bat's jurisdiction. However, Bat set out in pursuit with a posse. A near-blizzard was sweeping the country. Bat made for Lovell's cattle camp, on the chance that the bandits would be forced to take shelter there. It was a good guess. Rudabaugh's outfit rode in, stiff and half frozen, and Bat captured the robbers without firing a shot. This was one of many captures Bat made.

He had a deep sense of loyalty to his friends. On two separate occasions he returned to Dodge, after having left the town, to straighten out difficulties for his friends or to avenge them. The first time was when Luke Short, who ran a gambling house in Dodge, had a difficulty with Mayor Webster and his official family. Luke appears to have held the opinion that the cards were stacked against him and that this was a trouble out of which he could not shoot himself. He wired Bat Masterson and Wyatt Earp to come to Dodge. They did, accompanied by another friend or two. The mayor made peace on terms dictated by Short.

Bat's second return to Dodge was caused by a wire from his brother James, who ran a dance hall in partnership with a man named Peacock. Masterson wanted to discharge the bartender, Al Updegraph, a brother-in-law of the other partner. A serious difficulty loomed in the offing. Wherefore James called for help. Bat arrived at eleven one sunny morning, another gunman at heel. At three o'clock he entrained for Tombstone, Arizona, James beside him. The interval had been busy one. On the way up from the station (always known then as the depot), the two men met Peacock and Updegraph. No amenities were exchanged. It was strictly business. Bullets began to sing at once. The men stood across the street from each other and emptied their weapons. Oddly enough, Updegraph was the only one wounded. This little matter attended to, Bat surrendered himself, was fined three dollars for carrying concealed weapons, and released. He ate dinner, disposed of his brother's interest in the saloon, and returned to the station.

Bat Masterson was a friend of Theodore Roosevelt, who was given to admiring men with "guts," such men as Pat Garrett, Ben Daniels, and Billy Tilghman. Mr. Roosevelt offered Masterson a place as United States Marshal of Arizona. The ex-sheriff declined it. "If I took it," he explained, "I'd have to kill some fool boy who wanted to get a reputation by killing me." The President then offered Bat a place as Deputy United States Marshal of New York, and this was accepted. From that time Masterson became a citizen of the Empire State. For seventeen years he worked on a newspaper there and died a few years since with a pen in his hand. He was respected by the entire newspaper fraternity.

Owing to the pleasant habit of the cowboys of shooting up the town they were required, when entering the city limits, to hand over their weapons to the marshal. The guns were deposited at Wright & Beverly's Store, in a rack built for the purpose, and receipts given for them. Sometimes a hundred six-shooters would be there at once. These were never returned to their owners unless the cowboys were sober.

To be a marshal of one of these fighting frontier towns was no post to be sought for by a supple politician. The place called for a chilled iron nerve and an uncanny skill with the Colt. Tom Smith, one of the gamest men and best officers who ever wore a star on the frontier, was killed in the performance of his duty. Colonel Breackenridge says that Smith, marshal of Abilene before "Wild Bill," was the gamest man he ever knew. He was a powerful, athletic man who would arrest, himself unarmed, the most desperate characters. He once told Breackenridge that anyone could bring in a dead man but it took a good officer to take lawbreakers while they were alive. In this he differed from Hickok who did not take chances. He brought his men in dead. Nixon, assistant marshal at Dodge, was murdered by "Mysterious Dave" Mathers, who himself once held the same post. Ed Masterson after displaying conspicuous courage many times, was mortally wounded April 9, 1878, by two desperate men, Jack Wagner and Alf Walker, who were terrorizing Front Street. Bat reached the scene a few minutes later and heard the story. As soon as his brother had died Bat went after the desperadoes, met them, and killed them both.

The death of Ed Masterson shocked the town. Civil organizations passed resolutions of respect. During the funeral, which was the largest ever held in Dodge, all business houses were closed. It is not on record that anybody regretted the demise of the marshal's assassins.

Among those who came to Dodge each season to meet the Texas cattle drive were Ben and Bill Thompson, gamblers who ran a faro bank. Previously they had been accustomed to go to Ellsworth, while that point was the terminus of the drive. Here they had ruled with a high hand, killed the sheriff, and made their getaway safely. Bill got into a shooting affray at Ogalala. He was badly wounded and was carried to the hotel. It was announced openly that he would never leave town alive. Ben did not dare go to Ogalala, for his record there outlawed him. He came to Bat Masterson.

Bat knew Bill's nurse and arranged a plan for campaign. A sham battle was staged at the big dance hall, during the excitement of which Bat and the nurse carried the wounded man to the train, got him to a sleeper, and into a bed. Buffalo Bill met them the next day at North Platte. He had relays of teams stationed on the road, and he and Bat guarded the sick man during the long ride bringing him safely to Dodge.

Emanuel Dubbs ran a roadhouse not far from Dodge about this time. He was practising with his six-shooter one day when a splendidly built young six-footer rode up to his place. The stranger watched him as he fired at the tin cans he had put on fence posts. Presently the young fellow suggested he throw a couple of the cans up in the air. Dubbs did so. Out flashed the stranger's revolvers. There was a roar of exploding shots. Dubbs picked up the cans. Four shots had been fired. Two bullets had drilled through each can.

"Better not carry a six-shooter till you learn to shoot," Bill Cody suggested, as he put his guns back into their holsters. "You'll be a living temptation to some bad man." Buffalo Bill was on his way back to the North Platte.

Life at Dodge was not all tragic. The six-shooter roared in the land a good deal, but there were very many citizens who went quietly about their business and took no part in the nightlife of the town. It was entirely optional with the individual. The little city had its legitimate theatres as well as its hurdy-gurdy houses and gambling dens. There was the Lady Gay, for instance, a popular vaudeville resort. There were well-attended churches. But Dodge boiled so with exuberant young life, often inflamed by bad liquor, that both theatre and church were likely to be the scenes of unexpected explosions.

A drunken cowboy became annoyed at Eddie Foy. While the comedian was reciting "Kalamazoo in Michigan" the puncher began bombarding the frail walls from the outside with a .45 Colt's revolver. Eddie made a swift strategic retreat. A deputy marshal was standing near the cow-puncher, who was astride a plunging horse. The deputy fired twice. The first shot missed. The second brought the rider down. He was dead before he hit the ground. The deputy apologized later for his marksmanship, but he added by way of explanation, "the bronc sure was sunfishin' plenty."

The killing of Miss Dora Hand, a young actress of much promise, was regretted by everybody in Dodge. A young fellow named Kennedy, the son of a rich cattleman, shot her unintentionally while he was trying to murder James Kelly. He fled. A posse composed of Sheriff Masterson, William Tilghman, Wyatt Earp, and Charles Bassett took the trail. They captured the man after wounding him desperately. He was brought back to Dodge, recovered, and escaped. His pistol arm was useless, but he used the other well enough to slay several other victims before someone made an end of him.

The gay good spirits of Dodge found continual expression in practical jokes. The wilder these were the better pleased was the town. "Mysterious Dave" was the central figure in one. An evangelist was conducting a series of meetings. He made a powerful magnetic appeal, and many were the hard characters who walked the sawdust trail. The preacher set his heart on converting Dave Mathers, the worst of bad men and a notorious scoffer. The meetings prospered. The church grew too small for the crowds and adjourned to a dance hall. Dave became interested. He went to hear Brother Johnson preach. He went a second time and a third. "He certainly preaches like the Watsons and goes for sin all spraddled out," Dave conceded. Brother Johnson grew hopeful. It seemed possible that this brand could be snatched from the burning. He preached directly at Dave, and Dave buried his head in his hands and sobbed. The preacher said he was willing to die if he could convert this one vile sinner. Others of the deacons agreed that they too, would not object to going straight to heaven with the knowledge that Dave had been saved.

"They were right excited an' didn't know straight up," an old-timer explained. "Dave, he looked so whipped his ears flopped. Finally he rose, an' said, 'I've got yore company, friends. Now, while we're all saved I reckon we better start straight for heaven. First off, the preacher; then the deacons; me last.' Then Dave whips out a whoppin' big gun and starts to shootin'. The preacher went right through a window an' took it with him. He was sure in some hurry. The deacons hunted cover. Seemed like they was willin' to postpone taking that through ticket to heaven. After that they never did worry anymore about Dave's soul."

Many rustlers gathered around Dodge in those days. The most notorious of these was a gang of more than thirty under the leadership of Dutch Henry and Tom Owens, two of the most desperate outlaws ever known in Kansas. A posse was organized to run down this gang under the leadership of Dubbs, who had lost some of his stock. Before starting, the posse telephoned Hays City to organize a company to head off the rustlers. Twenty miles west of Hays the posse overtook the rustlers. A bloody battle ensued, during which Owens and several other outlaws were killed and Dutch Henry wounded six times. Several of the posse were also shot. The story has a curious sequel. Many years later, when Emanuel Dubbs was county judge of Wheeler County, Texas, Dutch

Henry came to his house and stayed there several days. He was a thoroughly reformed man. Not many years ago Dutch Henry died in Colorado. He was a man with many good qualities. Even in his outlaw days he had many friends among the law-abiding citizens.

After the battle with Henry Owens gang rustlers operated much more quietly, but they did not cease stealing. One night three men were hanged on a cottonwood on Saw Log Creek, ten or twelve miles from Dodge. One of these was a young man of a good family who had drifted into rustling and had been carried away by the excitement of it. Another of the three was the son of Tom Owens. To this day the place is known as Horse Thief Cañon. During its years of prosperity many eminent men visited Dodge, including Generals Sherman and Sheridan, President Hayes and General Miles. Its reputation had extended far and wide. It was the wild and woolly cowboy capital of the Southwest, a place to quicken the blood of any man. Nearly all that gay, hard-riding company of cowpunchers, buffalo hunters, bad men, and pioneers have vanished into yesterday's seven thousand years. But certainly Dodge once had its day and its night of glory. No more rip-roaring town ever bucked the tiger.

THE COWBOY

EMERSON HOUGH

The great west, vast and rude, brought forth men also vast and rude. We pass today over parts of that matchless region, and we see the red hills and ragged mountain-fronts cut and crushed into huge indefinite shapes, to which even a small imagination may give a human or more than human form. It would almost seem that the same great hand which chiseled out these monumental forms had also laid its fingers upon the people of this region and fashioned them rude and ironlike, in harmony with the stern faces set about them.

Of all the babes of that primeval mother, the West, the cowboy was perhaps her dearest because he was her last. Some of her children lived for centuries; this one for not a triple decade before he began to be old. What was really the life of this child of the wild region of America, and what were the conditions of the experience that bore him, can never be fully known by those who have not seen the West with wide eyes—for the cowboy was simply a part of the West. He who does not understand the one can never understand the other.

If we care truly to see the cowboy as he was and seek to give our wish the dignity of a real purpose, we should study him in connection with his surroundings and in relation to his work. Then we shall see him not as a curiosity but as a product—not as an eccentric driver of horned cattle but as a man suited to his times.

Large tracts of that domain where once the cowboy reigned supreme have been turned into farms by the irrigator's ditch or by the dry-farmer's plan. The farmer in overalls is in many instances his own stockman today. On the ranges of Arizona, Wyoming, and Texas and parts of Nevada we may find the cowboy, it is true, even today: but he is no longer the Homeric figure that once dominated the plains. In what we say as to his trade, therefore, or his fashion in the practice of it, we speak in terms of thirty or forty years ago, when wire was unknown, when the round-up still was necessary, and the cowboy's life was indeed that of the open.

By the costume we may often know the man. The cowboy's costume was harmonious with its surroundings. It was planned upon lines of such stern utility as to leave no possible thing which we may call dispensable. The typical cowboy costume could hardly be said to contain a coat and waistcoat. The heavy woolen shirt, loose and open at the neck, was the common wear at all seasons of the year excepting winter, and one has often seen cowboys in the winter-time engaged in work about the yard or corral of the ranch wearing no other cover for the upper part of the body but one or more of these heavy shirts. If the cowboy wore a coat he would wear it open and loose as much as possible. If he wore a "vest" he would wear it slouchily, hanging open or partly unbuttoned most of the time. There was a reason for this slouchy habit. The cowboy would say that the vest closely buttoned about the body would cause perspiration, so that the wearer would quickly chill upon ceasing exercise. If the wind were blowing keenly when the cowboy dismounted to sit upon the ground for dinner, he would button up his waistcoat and be warm. If it were very cold he would button up his coat also.

The cowboy's boots were of fine leather and fitted tightly, with light narrow soles, extremely small and high heels. Surely a more irrational foot-covering never was invented; yet these tight, peaked cowboy boots had a great significance and may indeed be called the insignia of a calling. There was no prouder soul on earth than the cowboy. He was proud of being a horseman and had a contempt for all human beings who walked. On foot in his tight-toed boots he was lost; but he wished it to be understood that he never was on foot. If we rode beside him and watched his seat in the big cow saddle we found that his high and narrow heels prevented the slipping forward of the foot in the stirrup, into which he jammed his feet nearly full length. If there was a fall, the cowboy's foot never hung in the stirrup. In the corral roping, afoot, his heels anchored him. So he found his little boots not so unserviceable and retained them as a matter of pride. Boots made for the cowboy trade sometimes had fancy tops of bright-colored leather. The Lone Star of Texas was not infrequent in their ornamentation.

The curious pride of the horseman extended also to his gloves. The cowboy was very careful in the selection of his gloves. They were made of the finest buckskin, which could not be injured by wetting. Generally they were tanned white and cut with a deep cuff or gauntlet from which hung a little fringe to flutter in the wind when he rode at full speed on horseback.

The cowboy's hat was one of the typical and striking features of his costumes. It was a heavy, wide, white felt hat with a heavy leather band buckled about it. There has been no other head covering devised so suitable as the Stetson for the uses of the Plains, although high and heavy black hats have in part supplanted it today among stockmen. The boardlike felt was practically indestructible. The brim flapped a little and, in time, was turned up and perhaps held fast to the crown by a thong. The wearer might sometimes stiffen the brim by passing a thong through a series of holes pierced through the outer edge. He could depend upon his hat in all weathers. In the rain it was an umbrella; in the sun a shield; in the winter he could tie it down about his ears with his handkerchief.

Loosely thrown about the cowboy's shirt collar was a silk kerchief. It was tied in a hard knot in front, and though it could scarcely be said to be devoted to the uses of a neck scarf, yet it was a great comfort to the back of the neck when one was riding in a hot wind. It was sure to be of some bright color, usually red. Modern would-be cow-punchers do not willingly let this old kerchief die, and right often they overplay it. For the cowboy of the "movies," however, let us register an unqualified contempt. The real range would never have been safe for him.

A peculiar and distinctive feature of the cowboy's costume was his "chaps" (chaparéjos). The chaps were two very wide and full-length trouser-legs made of heavy calfskin and connected by a narrow belt or strap. They were cut away entirely at front and back so that they covered only the thigh and lower legs and did not heat the body as a complete leather garment would. They were intended solely as a protection against branches, thorns, briers, and the like, but they were prized in cold or wet weather. Sometimes there was seen, more often on the southern range, a cowboy wearing chaps made of skins tanned with the hair on; for the cowboy of the Southwest early learned that goatskin left with the hair on would turn the cactus thorns better than any other material. Later, the chaps became a sort of affectation on the part of new men on the range; but the old-time cowboy wore them for use, not as a uniform. In hot weather he laid them off.

In the times when some men needed guns and all men carried them, no pistol of less than 44-caliber was tolerated on the range, the solid framed 45-caliber being the one almost universally used. The barrel was eight inches long, and it shot a rifle cartridge of forty grains of powder and a blunt-ended bullet that made a terrible missile. This weapon depended from a belt worn loose resting upon the left hip and hanging low down on the right hip so that none of the weight came upon the abdomen. This was typical, for the cowboy was neither fancy gunman nor army officer. The latter carries the revolver on the left, the butt pointing forward.

An essential part of the cow-puncher's outfit was his "rope." This was carried in a close coil at the side of the saddle-horn, fastened by one of the many thongs scattered over the saddle. In the Spanish country it was called *reata* and even today is sometimes seen in the Southwest made of rawhide. In the South it was called a *lariat*. The modern rope is a well-made three-quarter-inch hemp rope about thirty feet in length, with a leather or raw-hide eye. The cowboy's quirt was a short heavy whip, the stock being of wood or iron covered with braided leather and carrying a lash made of two or three heavy loose thongs. The spur in the old days had a very large rowel with blunt teeth an inch long. It was often ornamented with little bells or oblongs of metal, the tinkling of which appealed to the childlike nature of the Plains rider. Their use was to lock the rowel.

His bridle—for, since the cowboy and his mount are inseparable, we may as well speak of his horse's dress also—was noticeable for its tremendously heavy and cruel curbed bit, known as the "Spanish bit." But in the ordinary riding and even in the exciting work of the old round-up and in "cutting out," the cowboy used the bit very little, nor exerted any pressure on the reins. He laid the reins against the neck of the pony opposite to the direction in which he wished it to go, merely turning his hand in the direction and inclining his body in the same way. He rode with the pressure of the knee and the inclination of the body and the light side-shifting of both reins. The saddle was the most important part of the outfit. It was a curious thing, this saddle developed by the cattle trade, and the world has no other like it. Its great weight—from thirty to forty pounds—was readily excusable when one remembers that it was not only seat but work-bench for the cowman. A light saddle would be torn to pieces at the first rush of a maddened steer, but the sturdy frame of a cow-saddle would throw the heaviest bull on the range. The high cantle would give a firmness to the cowboy's seat when he snubbed a steer with a sternness sufficient to send it rolling heels over head. The high pommel, or "horn," steel-forged and covered with cross braids of leather, served as anchor post for this same steer, a turn of the rope about it accomplishing that purpose at once. The saddle-tree forked low down over the pony's back so that the saddle sat firmly and could not readily be pulled off. The great broad cinches bound the saddle fast till horse and saddle were practically one fabric. The strong wooden house of the old heavy stirrup protected the foot from being crushed by the impact of the herd. The form of the cow-saddle has changed but little, although today one sees a shorter seat and smaller horn, a "swell front" or roll, and a stirrup of open "ox-bow" pattern.

The round-up was the harvest of the range. The time of the calf round-up was in the spring after the grass had become good and after the calves had grown large enough for the branding. The State Cattle Association divided the entire State range into a number of round-up districts. Under an elected round-up captain were all the bosses in charge of the different ranch outfits sent by men having cattle in the round-up. Let us briefly draw a picture of this scene as it was.

Each cowboy would have eight or ten horses for his own use, for he had now before him the hardest riding of the year. When the cow-puncher went into the herd to cut out calves he mounted a fresh horse, and every few hours he again changed horses, for there was no horse which could long endure the fatigue of the rapid and intense work of cutting. Before the rider stretched a sea of interwoven horns, waving and whirling as the densely packed ranks of cattle closed in or swayed apart. It was no prospect for a weakling, but into it went the cow-puncher on his determined little horse, heeding not the plunging, crushing, and thrusting of the excited cattle. Down under the bulks of the herd, half hid in the whirl of dust, he would spy a little curly calf running, dodging, and twisting, always at the heels of its mother; and he would dart in after, following the two through the thick of surging and plunging beasts. The sharp-eyed pony would see almost as soon as his rider which cow was wanted and he needed small guidance from that time on. He would follow hard at her heels, edging her constantly toward the flank of the herd, at times nipping her hide as a reminder of his own superiority. In spite of herself the cow would gradually turn out toward the edge, and at last would be swept clear of the crush, the calf following close behind her. There was a whirl of the rope and the calf was laid by the heels and dragged to the fire where the branding irons were heated and ready.

Meanwhile other cow-punchers are rushing calves to the branding. The hubbub and turmoil increase. Taut ropes cross the ground in many directions. The cutting ponies pant and sweat, rear and plunge. The garb of the cowboy is now one of white alkali which hangs gray in his eyebrows and moustache. Steers bellow as they surge to and fro. Cows charge on their persecutors. Fleet yearlings break and run for the open, pursued by men who care not how or where they ride.

We have spoken in terms of the past. There is no calf round-up of the open range today. The last of the round-ups was held in Routt County, Colorado, several years ago, so far as the writer knows, and it had only to do with shifting cattle from the summer to the winter range.

After the calf round-up came the beef round-up, the cowman's final harvest. This began in July or August. Only the mature or fatted animals were cut out from the herd. This "beef cut" was held apart and driven on ahead from place to place as the round-up progressed. It was then driven in by easy stages to the shipping point on the railroad, whence the long trainloads of cattle went to the great markets.

In the heyday of the cowboy it was natural that his chief amusements should be those of the outdoor air and those more or less in line with his employment. He was accustomed to the sight of big game, and so had the edge of his appetite for its pursuit worn off. Yet he was a hunter, just as every Western man was a hunter in the times of the Western game. His weapons were the rifle, revolver, and rope; the latter two were always with him. With the rope at times he captured the coyote, and under special conditions he has taken deer and even antelope in this way, though this was of course most unusual and only possible under chance conditions of ground and cover. Elk have been roped by cowboys many times, and it is known that even the mountain sheep has been so taken, almost incredible as that may seem. The young buffalo were easy prey for the cowboy and these he often roped and made captive. In fact the beginnings of all the herds of buffalo now in captivity in this country were the calves roped and secured by cowboys; and these few scattered individuals of a grand race of animals remain as melancholy reminders alike of a national shiftlessness and an individual skill and daring.

The grizzly was at times seen by the cowboys on the range, and if it chanced that several cowboys were together it was not unusual to give him chase. They did not always rope him, for it was rarely that the nature of the country made this possible. Sometimes they roped him and wished they could let him go, for a grizzly bear is uncommonly active and straightforward in his habits at close quarters. The extreme difficulty of such a combat, however, gave it its chief fascination for the cowboy. Of course, no one horse could hold the bear after it was roped, but, as one after another came up, the bear was caught by neck and foot and body, until at last he was tangled and tripped and haled about till he was helpless, strangled, and nearly dead. It is said that cowboys have so brought into camp a grizzly bear, forcing him to half walk and half slide at the end of the ropes. No feat better than this could show the courage of the plainsman and of the horse which he so perfectly controlled.

Of such wild and dangerous exploits were the cowboy's amusements on the range. It may be imagined what were his amusements when he visited the "settlements." The cow-punchers, reared in the free life of the open air, under circumstances of the utmost freedom of individual action, perhaps came off the drive or round-up after weeks or months of unusual restraint or hardship, and felt that the time had arrived for them to "celebrate." Merely great rude children, as wild and untamed and untaught as the herds they led, they regarded their first look at the "settlements" of the railroads as a glimpse of a wider world. They pursued to the uttermost such avenues of new experience as lay before them, almost without exception avenues of vice. It is strange that the records of those days should be chosen by the public to be held as the measure of the American cowboy. Those days were brief, and they are long since gone. The American cowboy atoned for them by a quarter of a century of faithful labor.

The amusements of the cowboy were like the features of his daily surroundings and occupation—they were intense, large, Homeric. Yet, judged at his work, no higher type of employee ever existed, nor one more dependable. He was the soul of honor in all the ways of his calling. The very blue of the sky, bending evenly over all men alike, seemed to symbolize his instinct for justice. Faithfulness and manliness were his chief traits; his standard—to be a "square man."

Not all the open range will ever be farmed, but very much that was long thought to be irreclaimable has gone under irrigation or is being more or less successfully "dry-farmed." The man who brought water upon the arid lands of the West changed the entire complexion of a vast country and with it the industries of that country. Acres redeemed from the desert and added to the realm of the American farmer were taken from the realm of the American cowboy.

The West has changed. The curtain has dropped between us and its wild and stirring scenes. The old days are gone. The house dog sits on the hill where yesterday the coyote sang. There are fenced fields and in them stand sleek round beasts, deep in crops such as their ancestors never saw. In a little town nearby is the hurry and bustle of modern life. This town is far out upon what was called the frontier, long after the frontier has really gone. Guarding its ghost here stood a little army post, once one of the pillars, now one of the monuments of the West.

Out from the tiny settlement in the dusk of evening, always facing toward where the sun is sinking, might be seen riding, not so long ago, a figure we should know. He would thread the little lane among the fences, following the guidance of hands other than his own, a thing he would once have scorned to do. He would ride as lightly and as easily as ever, sitting erect and jaunty in the saddle, his reins held high and loose in the hand whose fingers turn up gracefully, his whole body free yet firm in the saddle with the seat of the perfect horseman. At the boom of the cannon, when the flag dropped fluttering down to sleep, he would rise in his stirrups and wave his hat to the flag. Then, toward the edge, out into the evening, he would ride on. The dust of his riding would mingle with the dusk of night. We could not see which was the one or the other. We could only hear the hoof-beats passing, boldly and steadily still, but growing fainter, fainter, and more faint.

THE STORY OF THE COWPUNCHER

CHARLES M. RUSSELL

S peakin' of cowpunchers," says Rawhide Rawlins, "I'm glad to see in the last few years that them that know the business have been writin' about 'em. It begin to look like they'd be wiped out without a history. Up to a few years ago there's mighty little known about cows and cow people. It was sure amusin' to read some of them old stories about cowpunchin'. You'd think a puncher growed horns an' was haired over.

"It put me in mind of the eastern girl that asks her mother: 'Ma,' says she, 'do cowboys eat grass?' 'No, dear,' says the old lady, 'they're part human,' an' I don't know but the old gal had 'em sized up right. If they are human, they're a separate species. I'm talkin' about the old-time ones, before the country's strung with wire an' nesters had grabbed all the water, an' a cowpuncher's home was big. It wasn't where he took his hat off, but where he spread his blankets. He ranged from

Mexico to the Big Bow River of the north, an' from where the trees get scarce in the east to the old Pacific. He don't need no iron hoss, but covers his country on one that eats grass an' wears hair. All the tools he needed was saddle, bridle, quirt, hackamore, an' rawhide riatta or seagrass rope; that covered his hoss.

"The puncher himself was rigged, startin' at the top, with a good hat— not one of the floppy kind you see in pictures, with the rim turned up in front. The top-cover he wears holds its shape an' was made to protect his face from the weather; maybe to hold it on, he wore a buckskin string under the chin or back of the head. Round his neck a big silk handkerchief, tied loose, an' in the drag of a trail herd it was drawn over the face to the eyes, hold-up fashion, to protect the nose an' throat from dust. In old times, a leather blab or mask was used the same. Coat, vest, an' shirt suits his own taste. Maybe he'd wear California pants, light buckskin in color, with large brown plaid, sometimes foxed, or what you'd call reinforced with buck or antelope skin. Over these came his chaparejos or leggin's. His feet were covered with good high-heeled boots, finished off with steel spurs of Spanish pattern. His weapon's usually a forty-five Colt's six-gun, which is packed in a belt, swingin' a little below his right hip. Sometimes a Winchester in a scabbard, slung to his saddle under his stirrup-leather, either right or left side, but generally left, stock forward, lock down, as his rope hangs at his saddle-fork on the right.

"By all I can find out from old, gray-headed punchers, the cow business started in California, an' the Spaniards were the first to burn marks on their cattle an' hosses, an' use the rope. Then men from the States drifted west to Texas, pickin' up the brandin' iron an' lass-rope, an' the business spread north, east, an' west, till the spotted long-horns walked in every trail marked out by their brown cousins, the buffalo.

"Texas an' California, bein' the startin' places, made two species of cow-punchers; those west of the Rockies rangin' north, usin' centerfire or single-cinch saddles, with high fork an' cantle; packed a sixty or sixty-five foot rawhide rope, an' swung a big loop. These cow people were generally strong on pretty, usin' plenty of hoss jewelry, silver-mounted spurs, bits, an' conchas; instead of a quirt, used a romal, or quirt braided to the end of the reins. Their saddles were full stamped, with from twenty-four to twenty-eight-inch eagle-bill tapaderos. Their chaparejos were made of fur or hair, either bear, angora goat, or hair sealskin. These fellows were sure fancy, an' called themselves buccaroos, coming from the Spanish word, *vaquero*.

"The cowpuncher east of the Rockies originated in Texas and ranged north to the Big Bow. He wasn't so much for pretty; his saddle was low horn, rimfire, or double-cinch; sometimes 'macheer.' Their rope was seldom over forty feet, for being a good deal in a brush country, they were forced to swing a small loop. These men generally tied, instead of taking their dallie-welts, or wrapping their rope around the saddle horn. Their chaparejos were made of heavy bullhide, to protect the leg from brush an' thorns, with hog-snout tapaderos.

"Cowpunchers were mighty particular about their rig, an' in all the camps you'd find a fashion leader. From a cowpuncher's idea, these fellers was sure good to look at, an' I tell you right now, there ain't no prettier sight for my eyes than one of those good-lookin', long-backed cowpunchers, sittin' up on a high-forked, full-stamped California saddle with a live hoss between his legs.

"Of course a good many of these fancy men were more ornamental than useful, but one of the best cow-hands I ever knew belonged to this class. Down on the Gray Bull, he went under the name of Mason, but most punchers called him Pretty Shadow. This sounds like an Injun name, but it ain't. It comes from a habit some punchers has of ridin' along, lookin' at their shadows. Lookin' glasses are scarce in cow outfits, so the only chance for these pretty boys to admire themselves is on bright, sunshiny days. Mason's one of these kind that doesn't get much pleasure out of life in cloudy weather. His hat was the best; his boots was made to order, with extra long heels. He rode a center-fire, full-stamped saddle, with twenty-eight-inch tapaderos; bearskin ancaroes, or saddle pockets; his chaparejos were of the same skin. He packed a sixty-five-foot rawhide. His spurs an' bit were silver inlaid, the last bein' a Spanish spade. But the gaudiest part of his regalia was his gun. It's a forty-five Colt's, silverplated an' chased with gold. Her handle is pearl, with a bull's head carved on.

"When the sun hits Mason with all this silver on, he blazes up like some big piece of jewelry. You could see him for miles when he's ridin' high country. Barrin' Mexicans, he's the fanciest cow dog I ever see, an' don't think he don't savvy the cow. He knows what she says to her calf. Of course there wasn't many of his stripe. All punchers liked good rigs, but plainer; an' as most punchers 're fond of gamblin' an' spend their spare time at stud poker or monte, they can't tell what kind of a rig they'll be ridin' the next day. I've seen many a good rig lost over a blanket. It depends how lucky the cards fall what kind of a rig a man's ridin'.

"I'm talkin' about old times, when cowmen were in their glory. They lived different, talked different, an' had different ways. No matter where you met him, or how he's rigged, if you'd watch him close he'd do something that would tip his hand. I had a little experience back in '83 that'll show what I'm gettin' at.

"I was winterin' in Cheyenne. One night a stranger stakes me to buck the bank. I got off lucky an' cash in fifteen hundred dollars. Of course I cut the money in two with my friend, but it leaves me with the biggest roll I ever packed. All this wealth makes Cheyenne look small, an' I begin longin' for bigger camps, so I drift for Chicago. The minute I hit the burg, I shed my cow garments an' get into white man's harness. A hard hat, boiled shirt, laced shoes—all the gearin' known to civilized man. When I put on all this rig, I sure look human; that is, I think so. But them shorthorns know me, an' by the way they trim that roll, it looks like somebody's pinned a card on my back with the word 'EASY' in big letters. I ain't been there a week till my roll don't need no string around it, an' I start thinkin' about home. One evenin' I throw in with the friendliest feller I ever met. It was at the bar of the hotel where I'm camped. I don't just remember how we got acquainted, but after about fifteen drinks we start holdin' hands an' seein' who could buy the most and fastest. I remember him tellin' the barslave not to take my money, 'cause I'm his friend. Afterwards, I find out the reason for this goodheartedness; he wants it all an' hates to see me waste it. Finally, he starts to show me the town an' says it won't cost me a cent. Maybe he did, but I was unconscious, an' wasn't in shape to remember. Next day, when I come to, my hair's sore an' I didn't know the days of the week, month, or what year it was.

"The first thing I do when I open my eyes is to look at the winders. There's no bars on 'em, an' I feel easier. I'm in a small room with two bunks. The one opposite me holds a feller that's smokin' a cigarette an' sizin' me up between whiffs while I'm dress-in'. I go through myself but I'm too late. Somebody beat me to it. I'm lacin' my shoes an' thinkin' hard, when the stranger speaks:

"'Neighbor, you're a long way from your range.'

"'You call the turn,' says I, 'but how did you read my iron?'

"'I didn't see a burn on you,' says he, 'an' from looks, you'll go as a slick-ear. It's your ways, while I'm layin' here, watchin' you get into your garments. Now, humans dress up an' punchers dress down. When you raised, the first thing you put on is your hat. Another thing that shows you up is you don't shed your shirt when you bed down. So next comes your vest an' coat, keepin' your hindquarters covered till you slide into your pants, an' now you're lacin' your shoes. I notice you done all of it without quittin' the blankets, like the ground's cold. I don't know what state or territory you hail from, but you've smelt sagebrush an' drank alkali. I heap savvy you. You've slept a whole lot with nothin' but sky over your head, an' there's times when that old roof leaks, but judgin' from appearances, you wouldn't mind a little open air right now.'

"This feller's my kind, an' he stakes me with enough to get back to the cow country."

LOTS of cowpunchers like to play with a rope, but ropes, like guns, are dangerous. All the difference is, guns go off and ropes go on. So you'll savvy my meanin', I'll tell you a story.

One time Bill Bullard's jogging along towards camp when he bumps into a couple of wolves that's been agin a bait. They've got enough strychnine so they're stiff and staggerin'. Bill drops his loop on one easy. Then he thinks, "What's the matter with taking both?" So he puts a couple of half hitches in the middle of his string, drops 'em over the horn, builds a loop at the other end of his rope, and dabs it on the second wolf. He's snaking 'em along all right till one of these calf-killers bumps on a sagebrush and bounces too near his hoss.

Right then's when the ball opens. The old hoss will stand anything but he don't like the smell of these meat eaters, so when this one starts crowdin' him, snappin' his teeth, he goes hog-wild; and wherever he's goin' Bill don't know, but the gait he takes it's a cinch they won't be late. 'Tain't so bad till they hit the sagebrush country. Then, first one and then another bounces by Bill's head and lands ahead of him. This old cayuse starts trying to out-dodge this couple. Mr. Bullard manages to keep his cayuse headed for the camp, but he's mighty busy staying in the middle of this living lightning he's riding.

When the boys in camp see him coming down the bottom, they all wonder what's his hurry, but they heap savvy when they see what's following him. He don't slow up none when he reaches camp, so the boys hand him some remarks like: "What's your hurry, Bill, won't you stay to eat?" "Don't hurry, Bill, you got lots of time." "If you're going to Medicine Hat, a little more to the left!"

Bullard's red-eyed by this time, and of course these remarks cheer him up a whole lot. A little more and Bill would bite himself. If he had a gun, there'd be a massacre. Finally the hoss wrangler, who's afraid Bill will mix with the saddle band, rides out and herds the whole muss into the rope corral.

When Bullard dismounts he don't say nothing an' it don't look safe to ask questions.

Bill's mighty quiet for days. About a week later somebody says something about killin' two birds with one stone. "Yes," says Bill, "maybe you'll kill two birds with one stone but don't ever bet you can get two anythings with one rope."

COWBOY DAVE

FRANK V. WEBSTER

"Hi! yi! yip!

"Woo-o-o-o! Wah! Zut!"

"Here we come!"

What was coming seemed to be a thunderous cloud of dust, from the midst of which came strange, shrill sounds, punctuated with sharp cries, that did not appear to be altogether human.

The dust-cloud grew thicker, the thunder sounded louder, and the yells were shriller.

From one of a group of dull, red buildings a sun-bronzed man stepped forth.

He shaded his eyes with a brown, powerful hand, gazed for an instant toward the approaching cloud of animated and vociferous dust and, turning to a smiling Chinese who stood near, with a pot in his hand, remarked in a slow, musical drawl:

"Well Hop Loy, here they are, rip-roarin' an' snortin' from th' round-up!"

"Alle samee hungly, too," observed the Celestial with unctious blandness.

"You can sure make a point of that Hop Loy," went on the other. "Hungry is their middle name just now, and you'd better begin t' rustle th' grub, or I wouldn't give an empty forty-five for your pig-tail."

"Oi la!" fairly screamed the Chinese, as, with a quick gesture toward his long queue, he scuttled toward the cook house, which stood in the midst of the other low ranch buildings. "Glub leady alle samee light now!" Hop Loy cried over his shoulder.

"It better be!" ominously observed Pocus Pete, foreman of the Bar U ranch, one of the best-outfitted in the Rolling River section. "It better be! Those boys mean business, or I miss my guess," the foreman went on. "Hard work a-plenty, I reckon. Wonder how they made out?" he went on musingly as he started back toward the bunk house, whence he had come with a saddle strap to which he was attaching a new buckle. "If things don't take a turn for th' better soon, there won't any of us make out," and, with a gloomy shake of his head, Pocus Pete, to give him the name he commonly went by, tossed the strap inside the bunk house, and went on toward the main building, where, by virtue of his position as head of the cowboys, he had his own cot.

Meanwhile the crowd of yelling, hard-riding, sand dust-stirring punchers, came on faster than ever.

"Hi! Yi! Yip!"

"Here we come!"

"Keep th' pot a-bilin'! We've got our appetites with us!"

"That's what!"

Some one fired his big revolver in the air, and in another moment there was an echo of many shots, the sharp crack of the forty-fives mingling with the thunder of hoofs, the yells, and the clatter of stirrup leathers.

"The boys coming back, Pete?" asked an elderly man, who came to the door of the main living room of the principal ranch house.

"Yes, Mr. Carson, they're comin' back, an' it don't need a movin' picture operator an' telegraphic despatch t' tell it, either."

"No, Pete. They seem to be in good spirits, too."

"Yes, they generally are when they get back from round-up. I want to hear how they made out, though, an' what th' prospects are."

"So do I, Pete," and there was an anxious note in the voice of Mr. Randolph Carson, owner of the Bar U ranch. Matters had not been going well with him, of late.

With final yells, and an increase in the quantity of dust tossed up as the cowboys pulled their horses back on their haunches, the range-riding outfit of the ranch came to rest, not far away from the stable. The horses, with heaving sides and distended nostrils that showed a deep red, hung their heads from weariness. They had been ridden hard, but not unmercifully, and they would soon recover. The cowboys themselves tipped back their big hats from their foreheads, which showed curiously white in contrast to their bronzed faces, and beat the dust from their trousers. A few of them wore sheepskin chaps.

One after another the punchers slung their legs across the saddle horns, tossed the reins over the heads of their steeds, as an intimation that the horses were not to stray, and then slid to the ground, walking with that peculiarly awkward gait that always marks one who has spent much of his life in the saddle.

"Grub ready, Hop Loy?" demanded one lanky specimen, as he used his blue neck kerchief to remove some of the dust and sweat from his brown face.

"It better be!" added another, significantly; while still another said, quietly:

"My gal has been askin' me for a long, long time to get her a Chinaman's pig-tail, an' I'm shore goin' t'get one now if I don't have my grub right plenty, an'soon!"

"Now you're talkin'!" cried a fourth, with emphasis.

There was no need of saying anything further. The Celestial had stuck his head out of the cook house to hear these ominous words of warning, and now, with a howl of anguish, he drew it inside again, wrapping his queue around his neck. Then followed a frantic rattling of pots and pans.

"You shore did get him goin', Tubby!" exclaimed a tall, lanky cowboy, to a short and squatty member of the tribe.

"Well, I aimed to Skinny," was the calm reply."I am some hungry."

The last of the cowboys to alight was a manly youth, who might have been in the neighborhood of eighteen or nineteen years of age. He was tall and slight, with a frank and pleasing countenance, and his blue eyes looked at you fearlessly from under dark brows, setting off in contrast his sunburned face. Had any one observed him as he rode up with the other cowboys, it would have been noticed that, though he was the youngest, he was one of the best riders.

He advanced from among the others, pausing to pet his horse which stuck out a wet muzzle for what was evidently an expected caress. Then the young man walked forward, with more of an air of grace than characterized his companions. Evidently, though used to a horse, he was not so saddle-bound as were his mates.

As he walked up to the ranch house he was met by Mr. Carson and Pocus Pete, both of whom looked at him rather eagerly and anxiously.

"Well, son," began the ranch owner, "how did you make out?"

"Pretty fair, Dad," was the answer. "There were more cattle than you led us to expect, and there were more strays than we calculated on. In fact we didn't get near all of them."

"Is that so, Dave?" asked Pocus Pete, quickly. "Whereabouts do you reckon them strays is hidin'?"

"The indications are they're up Forked Branch way. That's where we got some, and we saw more away up the valley, but we didn't have time to go for them, as we had a little trouble; and Tubby and the others thought we'd better come on, and go back for the strays to-morrow."

"Trouble, Dave?" asked Mr. Carson, looking up suddenly.

"Well, not much, though it might have been. We saw some men we took to be rustlers heading for our bunch of cattle, but they rode off when we started for them. Some of the boys wanted to follow but it looked as though it might storm, and Tubby said we'd better move the bunch while we could, and look after the rustlers and strays later."

"Yes, I guess that was best," the ranch owner agreed. "But where were these rustlers from, Dave?"

"Hard to say, Dad. Looked to be Mexicans."

"I reckon that'd be about right," came from Pocus Pete. "We'll have to be on th' watch, Mr. Carson."

"I expect so, Pete. Things aren't going so well that I can afford to lose any cattle. But about these strays, Dave. Do you think we'd better get right after them?"

"I should say so, Dad."

"Think there are many of them?"

"Not more than two of us could drive in. I'll go to-morrow with one of the men. I know just about where to look for them."

"All right, Dave. If you're not too much done out I'd like to have you take a hand."

"Done out, Dad! Don't you think I'm making a pretty good cowpuncher?"

"That's what he is, Mr. Carson, for a fact!" broke in Pete, with admiration. "I'd stake Cowboy Dave ag'in' any man you've got ridin' range to-day. That's what I would!"

"Thanks, Pete," said the youth, with a warm smile.

"Well, that's the truth, Dave. You took to this business like a duck takes to water, though the land knows there ain't any too much water in these parts for ducks."

"Yes, we could use more, especially at this season," Mr. Carson admitted. "Rolling River must be getting pretty dry; isn't it, Dave?"

"I've seen it wetter, Dad. And there's hardly any water in Forked Branch. I don't see how the stray cattle get enough to drink."

"It is queer they'd be off up that way," observed Pete. "But that might account for it," he went on, as though communing with himself.

"Account for what?" asked Dave, as he sat down in a chair on the porch.

"Th' rustlers. If they were up Forked Branch way they'd stand between th' strays and th' cattle comin' down where they could get plenty of water in Rolling River. That's worth lookin' into. I'll ride up that way with you to-morrow, Dave, an' help drive in them cattle."

"Will you, Pete? That will be fine!" the young cowboy exclaimed. Evidently there was a strong feeling of affection between the two. Dave looked to Mr. Carson for confirmation.

"Very well," the ranch owner said, "you and Pete may go, Dave. But don't take any chances with the rustlers if you encounter them."

"We're not likely to," said Pocus Pete, significantly.

From the distant cook house came the appetizing odor of food and Dave sniffed the air eagerly.

"Hungry?" asked Mr. Carson.

"That's what I am, Dad!"

"Well, eat heartily, get a good rest, and tomorrow you can try your hand at driving strays."

Evening settled down over the Bar U ranch; a calm, quiet evening, in spite of the earlier signs of a storm. In the far west a faint intermittent light showed where the elements were raging, but it was so far off that not even the faintest rumble of thunder came over Rolling River, a stream about a mile distant, on the banks of which were now quartered the cattle which the cowboys had recently rounded up for shipment.

The only sounds that came with distinctness were the occasional barking and baying of a dog, as he saw the rising moon, and the dull shuffle of the shifting cattle, which were being guarded by several cowboys who were night-riding.

Very early the next morning Dave Carson and Pocus Pete, astride their favorite horses, and carrying with them a substantial lunch, set off after the strays which had been dimly observed the day before up Forked Branch way.

This was one of the tributaries of Rolling River, the valley of which was at one time one of the most fertile sections of the larges of our Western cattle states. The tributary divided into two parts, or branches, shortly above its junction with Rolling River. Hence its name. Forked Branch came down from amid a series of low foot-hills, forming the northern boundary of Mr. Randolph Carson's ranch.

"We sure have one fine day for ridin'," observed Pocus Pete, as he urged his pony up alongside Dave's.

"That's right," agreed the youth.

For several miles they rode on, speaking but seldom, for a cowboy soon learns the trick of silence—it is so often forced on him.

As they turned aside to take a trail that led to Forked Branch, Dave, who was riding a little ahead, drew rein. Instinctively Pocus Pete did the same, and then Dave, pointing to the front, asked:

"Is that a man or a cow?"

* * * * *

Pocus Pete shaded his eyes with his hand and gazed long and earnestly in the direction indicated by Dave Carson. The two cow-ponies, evidently glad of the little rest, nosed about the sun-baked earth for some choice morsel of grass.

"It might be either—or both," Peter finally said.

"Either or both?" repeated Dave. "How can that be?"

"Don't you see two specks there, Dave? Look ag'in."

Dave looked. His eyes were younger and perhaps, therefore, sharper than were those of the foreman of Bar U ranch, but Dave lacked the training that long years on the range had given the other.

"Yes, I do see two," the youth finally said, "But I can't tell which is which."

"I'm not altogether sure myself," Pete said, quietly and modestly. "We'll ride a little nearer," he suggested, "an' then we can tell for sure. I guess we're on th' track of some strays all right."

"Some strays, Pete? You mean our strays; don't you?" questioned Dave.

"Well, some of 'em 'll be, probably," was the quiet answer. "But you've got t'remember, Dave, that there's a point of land belongin't' Centre O ranch that comes up here along the Forked Branch trail. It may be some of Molick's strays."

"That's so. I didn't think of that, Pete. There's more to this business than appears at first sight."

"Yes, Dave; but you're comin' on first-rate. I was a leetle opposed to th' Old Man sendin' you East to study, for fear it would knock out your natural instincts. But when you picked up that man as soon as you did," and he waved his hand toward the distant specks, "when you did that, I know you've not been spoiled, an' that there's hope for you."

"That's good, Pete!" and Dave laughed.

"Yes, I didn't agree with th' Old Man at first," the foreman went on, "but I see he didn't make any mistake."

Mr. Carson was the "Old Man" referred to, but it was not at all a term of disrespect as applied to the ranch owner. It was perfectly natural to Pete to use that term, and Dave did not resent it.

"Yes, I'm glad Dad did send me East," the young man went on, as they continued on their way up the trail. "I was mighty lonesome at first, and I felt— well, cramped, Pete. That's the only way to express it."

"I know how you felt, Dave. There wasn't room to breathe in th' city."

"That's the way I felt. Out here it—it's different."

He straightened up in the saddle, and drew in deep breaths of the pure air of the plains; an air so pure and thin, so free from mists, that the very distances were deceiving, and one would have been positive that the distant foot-hills were but half an hour's ride away, whereas the better part of a day must be spent in reaching them.

"Yes, this is livin'—that's what it is," agreed Pocus Pete. "You can make them out a little better now, Dave," and he nodded his head in the direction of the two distant specks. They were much larger now.

"It's a chap on a horse, and he's going in the same direction we are," Dave said, after a moment's observation.

"That's right. And it ain't every cowpuncher on Bar U who could have told that."

"I can see two—three—why, there are half a dozen cattle up there, Pete."

"Yes, an' probably more. I reckon some of th' Centre O outfit has strayed, same as ours. That's probably one of Molick's men after his brand," Pete went on.

The Bar U ranch (so called because the cattle from it were branded with a large U with a straight mark across the middle) adjoined, on the north, the range of Jason Molick, whose cattle were marked with a large O in the centre of which was a single dot, and his brand consequently, was known as Centre O.

"Maybe that's Len," suggested Dave, naming a son of the adjoining ranch owner.

"It may be. I'd just as soon it wouldn't be, though. Len doesn't always know how to keep a civil tongue in his head.

"That's right, Pete. I haven't much use for Len myself."

"You an' he had some little fracas; didn't you?"

"Oh, yes, more than once."

"An' you tanned him good and proper, too; didn't you Dave?" asked the foreman with a low chuckle.

"Yes, I did." Dave did not seem at all proud of his achievement. "But that was some time ago," he added. "I haven't seen Len lately."

"Well, you haven't missed an awful lot," said Pete, dryly.

The two rode on in silence again, gradually coming nearer and nearer to the specks which had so enlarged themselves, by reason of the closing up of the intervening distance, until they could be easily distinguished as a number of cattle and one lone rider. The latter seemed to be making his way toward the animals.

"Is he driving them ahead of him?" asked Dave, after a long and silent observation.

"That's the way it looks," said Pocus Pete. "It's Len Molick all right," he added, after another shading of his eyes with his hand.

"Are you sure?" Dave asked.

"Positive. No one around here rides a horse in that sloppy way but him."

"Then he must have found some of his father's strays, and is taking them to the ranch."

"I'm not so sure of that," Pete said.

"Not so sure of what?"

"That the cattle are all his strays. I wouldn't be a bit surprised but what some of our had got mixed up with 'em. Things like that have been known to happen you know."

"Do you think—" began Dave.

"I'm not goin' to take any chances thinkin'," Pete said significantly. "I'm going to make sure."

"Look here, Dave," he went on, spurring his pony up alongside of the young cowboy's. "My horse is good and fresh an' Len's doesn't seem to be in such good condition. Probably he's been abusin' it as he's done before. Now I can take this side trail, slip around through the bottom lands, an' get ahead of him."

"But it's a hard climb up around the mesa, Pete."

"I know it. But I can manage it. Then you come on up behind Len, casual like. If he has any of our cattle—by mistake," said Pete, significantly, "we'll be in a position to correct his error. Nothin' like correctin' errors right off the reel, Dave. We'll have him between two fires, so to speak."

"All right, Pete. I'll ride up behind him, as I'm doing now, and you'll head him off; is that it?"

"That's it. You guessed it first crack out of th' box. If nothin's wrong, why we're all right; we're up this way to look after our strays. And if somethin' is wrong, why we'll be in a position to correct it—that's all."

"I see." There was a smile on Dave's face as his cowboy partner, with a wave of his hand, turned his horse into a different trail, speeding the hardy little pony up so as to get ahead of Len Molick.

Dave rode slowly on, busy with many thought, some of which had to do with the youth before him. Len Molick was about Dave's own age, that is apparently, for, strange as it may seem, Dave was not certain of the exact number of years that had passed over his head.

It was evident that he was about eighteen or nineteen. He had recently felt a growing need of a razor, and the hair on his face was becoming wiry. But once, when he asked Randolph Carson, about a birthday, the ranch owner had returned an evasive answer.

"I don't know exactly when your birthday does come, Dave," he had said. "Your mother, before she—before she died, kept track of that. In fact I sometimes forget when my own is. I think yours is in May or June, but for the life of me I can't say just which month. It doesn't make a lot of difference, anyhow."

"No, Dad, not especially. But just how old am I?"

"Well, Dave, there you've got me again. I think it's around eighteen. But your mother kept track of that, too. I never had the time. Put it down at eighteen, going on nineteen, and let it go at that. Now say, about that last bunch of cattle we shipped—"

Thus the ranchman would turn the subject. Not that Dave gave the matter much thought, only now, somehow or other, the question seemed to recur with increased force.

"Funny I don't know just when my birthday is," he mused. "But then lots of the cowboys forget theirs."

The trail was smooth at this point, and Dave soon found himself close to Len, who was driving ahead of him a number of cattle. With a start of surprise Dave saw two which bore the Bar U brand.

"Hello, Len," he called.

Len Molick turned with a start. Either he had not heard Dave approach, or he had pretended ignorance.

"Well, what do you want?" demanded the surly bully.

"Oh, out after strays, as you are," said Dave, coolly. "Guess your cattle and ours have struck up an acquaintance," he added, with assumed cheerfulness.

"What do you mean?"

"I mean they're traveling along together just as if they belonged to the same outfit."

"Huh! I can't help it, can I, if your cows tag along with our strays?" demanded Len with a sneer.

"That's what I'm here for—to help prevent it," Dave went on, and his voice was a trifle sharp. "The Bar U ranch can't afford to lose any strays these days," he resumed. "The Carson outfit needs all it can get, and, as representative of the Carson interests I'll just cut out those strays of ours, Len, and head them the other way."

"Huh! What right have you got to do it?"

"What right? Why my father sent me to gather up our strays. I saw some of them up here yesterday."

"Your father?" The sneer in Len's voice was unmistakable.

"Yes, of course," said Dave, wondering what was the matter with Len. "My father, Randolph Carson."

"He isn't your father!" burst out Len in angry tones. "And you aren't his son! You're a nameless picked-up nobody, that's what you are! A nobody! You haven't even a name!"

And with this taunt on his lips Len spurred his horse away from Dave's.

* * * * *

Something seemed to strike Dave Carson a blow in the face. It was as though he had suddenly plunged into cold water, and, for the moment, he could not get his breath. The sneering words of Len Molick rang in his ears:

"You're a nameless, picked-up nobody!"

Having uttered those cruel words, Len was riding on, driving before him some of his father's stray cattle, as well as some belonging to the Bar U ranch. The last act angered Dave, and anger, at that moment, was just what was needed to arouse him from the lethargy in which he found himself. It also served, in a measure, to clear away some of the unpleasant feeling caused by the taunt.

"Hold on there a minute, Len Molick!" called Dave, sharply.

Len never turned his head, and gave no sign of hearing.

A dull red spot glowed in each of Dave's tanned cheeks. With a quick intaking of his breath he lightly touched the spurs to his horse—lightly, for that was all the intelligent beast needed. Dave passed his taunting enemy on the rush, and planting himself directly in front of him on the trail, drew rein so sharply that his steed reared. The cows, scattered by the sudden rush, ambled awkwardly on a little distance, and then stopped to graze.

"What do you mean by getting in my way?" growled Len.

"I mean to have you stop and answer a few questions," was the calm retort.

"If it's about these cattle I tell you I'm not trying to drive off any of yours," said Len, in whining tones. He knew the severe penalty attached to this in a cow country, and Dave was sufficiently formidable, as he sat easily on his horse facing the bully, to make Len a little more respectful.

"I'm not going to ask you about these cattle—at least not right away," Dave went on. "This is about another matter. You said something just now that needs explaining."

"I say a good many things," Len admitted, and again there sounded in his voice a sneer. "I don't have to explain to you everything I say; do I?"

"You do when it concerns me," and Dave put his horse directly across the trail, which, at this point narrowed and ran between two low ranges of hills. "You said something about me just now—you called me a nameless, picked-up nobody!"

Dave could not help wincing as he repeated the slur.

"Well, what if I did?" demanded the bully.

"I want to know what you mean. You insinuated that Mr. Carson was not my father."

"He isn't!"

"Why do you say that, and how do you know?" Dave asked. In spite of his dislike of Len, and the knowledge that the bully was not noted for truth-telling, Dave could not repress a cold chill of fear that seemed to clutch his heart.

"I say that because it's so, and how I know it is none of your affair," retorted Len.

"Oh yes, it is my affair, too!" Dave exclaimed. He was fast regaining control of himself. "It is very much my affair. I demand an explanation. How do you know Mr. Carson isn't my father?"

"Well, I know all right. He picked you up somewhere. He doesn't know what your name is himself. He just let you use his, and he called you Dave. You're a nobody I tell you!"

Dave spurred his horse until it was close beside that of Len's. Then leaning over in the saddle, until his face was very near to that of the bully's, and with blazing eyes looking directly into the shrinking ones of the other rancher's son, Dave said slowly, but with great emphasis:

"Who—told—you?"

There was menace in his tone and attitude, and Len shrank back.

"Oh, don't be afraid!" Dave laughed mirthlessly. "I'm not going to strike you—not now."

"You—you'd better not," Len muttered.

"I want you first to answer my questions," Dave went on. "After that I'll see what happens. It's according to how much truth there is in what you have said."

"Oh, it's true all right," sneered the bully.

"Then I demand to know who told you!"

Dave's hand shot out and grasped the bridle of the other's horse, and Len's plan of flight was frustrated.

"Let me go!" he whiningly demanded.

"Not until you tell me who said I am a nobody—that Mr. Carson is not my father," Dave said, firmly.

"I—I—" began the shrinking Len, when the sound of another horseman approaching caused both lads to turn slightly in their saddles. Dave half expected to see Pocus Pete, but he beheld the not very edifying countenance of Whitey Wasson, a tow-headed cowpuncher belonging to the Centre O outfit. Whitey and Len were reported to be cronies, and companions in more than one not altogether pleasant incident.

"Oh, here you are; eh; Len?" began Whitey. "And I see you've got the strays."

"Yes, I've got 'em," said Len, shortly.

"Any trouble?" went on Whitey, with a quick glance at Dave. The position of the two lads—Dave with his hand grasping Len's bridle—was too significant to be overlooked.

"Trouble?" began Len. "Well, he—he—"

"He made a certain statement concerning me," Dave said, quietly, looking from Len to Whitey, "and I asked him the source of his information. That is all."

"What did he say?"

"He said I was a nameless, picked-up nobody, and that Mr. Carson was not my father. I asked him how he knew, and he said some one told him that."

"So he did!" exclaimed Len.

"Then I demand to know who it was!" cried Dave.

For a moment there was silence, and then Whitey Wasson, with a chuckle said:

"I told Len myself!"

"You did?" cried Dave.

"Yes, he did! Now maybe you won't be so smart!" sneered Len. "Let go my horse!" he cried, roughly, as he swung the animal to one side. But no force was needed; as Dave's nerveless hand fell away from the bridle. He seemed shocked—stunned again.

"You—you—how do you know?" he demanded fiercely, raising his sinking head, and looking straight at Whitey.

"Oh, I know well enough. Lots of the cowboys do. It isn't so much of a secret as you think. If you don't believe me ask your father—no, he ain't your father—but ask the Old Man himself. Just ask him what your name is, and where you came from, and see what he says."

Whitey was sneering now, and he chuckled as he looked at Len. Dave's face paled beneath his tan, and he did not answer.

A nameless, picked-up nobody! How the words stung! And he had considered himself, proudly considered himself, the son of one of the best-liked, best-known and most upright cattle raisers of the Rolling River country. Now who was he?

"Come on, Len," said Whitey. "If you've got the strays we'll drive them back. Been out long enough as 'tis."

He wheeled his horse, Len doing the same, and they started after the straying cattle.

"Hold on there, if you please," came in a drawling voice. "Jest cut out them Bar U steers before you mosey off any farther, Whitey," and riding around a little hillock came Pocus Pete.

"Um!" grunted Whitey.

"Guess you'll be needin' a pair of specks, won't you, Whitey?" went on the Bar U foreman, without a glance at Len or Dave. "A Centre O brand an' a Bar U looks mighty alike to a feller with poor eyes, I reckon," and he smiled meaningly.

"Oh, we can't help it, if some of the Randolph cattle get mixed up with our strays," said Len.

"Who's talkin' to you?" demanded Pocus Pete, with such fierceness that the bully shrank back.

"Now you cut out what strays belong to you, an' let ours alone, Mr. Wasson," went on Pocus Pete with exaggerated politeness. "Dave an' I can take care of our own I reckon. An' move quick, too!" he added menacingly.

Whitey did not answer, but he and Len busied themselves in getting together their own strays. Pocus Pete and Dave, with a little effort, managed to collect their own bunch, and soon the two parties were moving off in opposite directions. Dave sat silent on his horse. Pete glanced at him from time to time, but said nothing. Finally, however, as they dismounted to eat their lunch, Pete could not help asking:

"Have any trouble with them, Dave?"

"Trouble? Oh, no."

Dave relapsed into silence, and Pete shook his head in puzzled fashion. Something had happened, but what, he could not guess.

In unwonted silence Dave and Pete rode back to the Bar U ranch, reaching it at dusk with the bunch of strays. They were turned in with the other cattle and then Dave, turning his horse into the corral, walked heavily to the ranch house. All the life seemed to have gone from him.

"Well, son, did you get the bunch?" asked Mr. Carson as he greeted the youth.

"Yes—I did," was the low answer. Mr. Carson glanced keenly at the lad, and something he saw in his face caused the ranch owner to start.

"Was there any trouble?" he asked. It was the same question Pocus Pete had propounded.

"Well, Len Molick and Whitey Wasson had some of our cattle in with theirs."

"They did?"

"Yes, but Pete and I easily cut 'em out. But—Oh, Dad!" The words burst from Dave's lips before he thought. "Am I your son?" he blurted out. "Len and Whitey said I was a picked-up nobody! Am I? Am I not your son?"

He held out his hands appealingly.

A great and sudden change came over Mr. Carson. He seemed to grow older and more sorrowful. A sigh came from him.

Gently he placed on arm over the youth's drooping shoulders.

"Dave," he said gently. "I hoped this secret would never come out—that you would never know. But, since it has, I must tell you the truth. I love you as if you were my own son, but you are not a relative of mine."

The words seemed to cut Dave like a knife.

"Then if I am not your son, who am I?" Dave asked in a husky voice.

The ticking of the clock on the mantle could be plainly, yes, loudly heard, as Mr. Carson slowly answered in a low voice:

"Dave, I don't know!"

HOPALONG NURSES A GROUCH

CLARENCE E. MULFORD

After the excitement incident to the affair at Powers' shack had died down and the Bar-20 outfit worked over its range in the old, placid way, there began to be heard low mutterings, and an air of peevish discontent began to be manifested in various childish ways. And it was all caused by the fact that Hopalong Cassidy had a grouch, and a big one. It was two months old and growing worse daily, and the signs threatened contagion. His foreman, tired and sick of the snarling, fidgety, petulant atmosphere that Hopalong had created on the ranch, and driven to desperation, eagerly sought some chance to get rid of the "sore-thumb" temporarily and give him an opportunity to shed his generous mantle of the blues. And at last it came.

No one knew the cause for Hoppy's unusual state of mind, although there were many conjectures, and they covered the field rather thoroughly; but they did not strike on the cause. Even Red Connors, now well over all ill effects of the wounds acquired in the old ranch house, was forced to guess; and when Red had to do that about anything concerning Hopalong he was well warranted in believing the matter to be very serious.

Johnny Nelson made no secret of his opinion and derived from it a great amount of satisfaction, which he admitted with a grin to his foreman.

"Buck," he said, "Hoppy told me he went broke playing poker over in Grant with Dave Wilkes and them two Lawrence boys, an' that shore explains it all. He's got pack sores from carrying his unholy licking. It was due to come for him, an' Dave Wilkes is just the boy to deliver it. That's the whole trouble, an' I know it, an' I'm damned glad they trimmed him. But he ain't got no right of making us miserable because he lost a few measly dollars."

"Yo're wrong, son; dead, dead wrong," Buck replied. "He takes his beatings with a grin, an' money never did bother him. No poker game that ever was played could leave a welt on him like the one we all mourn, an' cuss. He's been doing something that he don't want us to know—made a fool of hisself some way, most likely, an' feels so ashamed that he's sore. I've knowed him too long an' well to believe that gambling had anything to do with it. But this little trip he's taking will fix him up all right, an' I couldn't 'a' picked a better man—or one that I'd rather get rid of just now."

"Well, lemme tell you it's blamed lucky for him that you picked him to go," rejoined Johnny, who thought more of the woeful absentee than he did of his own skin. "I was going to lick him, shore, if it went on much longer. Me an' Red an' Billy was going to beat him up good till he forgot his dead injuries an' took more interest in his friends."

Buck laughed heartily. "Well, the three of you might 'a' done it if you worked hard an' didn't get careless, but I have my doubts. Now look here—you've been hanging around the bunk house too blamed much lately. Henceforth an' hereafter you've got to earn your grub. Get out on that west line an' hustle."

"You know I've had a toothache!" snorted Johnny with a show of indignation, his face as sober as that of a judge.

"An' you'll have a stomach ache from lack of grub if you don't earn yore right to eat purty soon," retorted Buck. "You ain't had a toothache in yore whole life, an' you don't know what one is. G'wan, now, or I'll give you a backache that'll ache!"

"Huh! Devil of a way to treat a sick man!" Johnny retorted, but he departed exultantly, whistling with much noise and no music. But he was sorry for one thing: he sincerely regretted that he had not been present when Hopalong met his Waterloo. It would have been pleasing to look upon.

While the outfit blessed the proposed lease of range that took him out of their small circle for a time, Hopalong rode farther and farther into the northwest, frequently lost in abstraction which, judging by its effect upon him, must have been caused by something serious. He had not heard from Dave Wilkes about that individual's good horse which had been loaned to Ben Ferris, of Winchester. Did Dave think he had been killed or was still pursuing the man whose neck-kerchief had aroused such animosity in Hopalong's heart? Or had the horse actually been returned? The animal was a good one, a successful contender in all distances from one to five miles, and had earned its owner and backers much money—and Hopalong had parted with it as easily as he would have borrowed five dollars from Red. The story, as he had often reflected since, was as old as lying—a broken-legged horse, a wife dying forty miles away, and a horse all saddled which needed only to be mounted and ridden.

These thoughts kept him company for a day and when he dismounted before Stevenson's "Hotel" in Hoyt's Corners he summed up his feelings for the enlightenment of his horse.

"Damn it, bronc! I'd give ten dollars right now to know if I was a jackass or not," he growled. "But he was an awful slick talker if he lied. An' I've got to go up an' face Dave Wilkes to find out about it!"

Mr. Cassidy was not known by sight to the citizens of Hoyt's Corners, however well versed they might be in his numerous exploits of wisdom and folly. Therefore the habitues of Stevenson's Hotel did not recognize him in the gloomy and morose individual who dropped his saddle on the floor with a crash and stamped over to the three-legged table at dusk and surlily demanded shelter for the night.

"Gimme a bed an' something to eat," he demanded, eyeing the three men seated with their chairs tilted against the wall. "Do I get 'em?" he asked, impatiently.

"You do," replied a one-eyed man, lazily arising and approaching him. "One dollar, now."

"An' take the rocks outen that bed—I want to sleep."

"A dollar per for every rock you find," grinned Stevenson, pleasantly. "There ain't no rocks in my beds," he added.

"Some folks likes to be rocked to sleep," facetiously remarked one of the pair by the wall, laughing contentedly at his own pun. He bore all the ear-marks of being regarded as the wit of the locality—every hamlet has one; I have seen some myself.

"Hee, hee, hee! Yo're a droll feller, Charley," chuckled Old John Ferris, rubbing his ear with unconcealed delight. "That's a good un."

"One drink, now," growled Hopalong, mimicking the proprietor, and glaring savagely at the "droll feller" and his companion. "An' mind that it's a good one," he admonished the host.

"It's better," smiled Stevenson, whereat Old John crossed his legs and chuckled again. Stevenson winked.

"Riding long?" he asked.

"Since I started."

"Going fur?"

"Till I stop."

"Where do you belong?" Stevenson's pique was urging him against the ethics of the range, which forbade personal questions.

Hopalong looked at him with a light in his eye that told the host he had gone too far. "Under my sombrero!" he snapped.

"Hee, hee, hee!" chortled Old John, rubbing his ear again and nudging Charley. "He ain't no fool, hey?"

"Why, I don't know, John; he won't tell," replied Charley.

Hopalong wheeled and glared at him, and Charley, smiling uneasily, made an appeal: "Ain't mad, are you?"

"Not yet," and Hopalong turned to the bar again, took up his liquor and tossed it off. Considering a moment he shoved the glass back again, while Old John tongued his lips in anticipation of a treat. "It is good—fill it again."

The third was even better and by the time the fourth and fifth had joined their predecessors Hopalong began to feel a little more cheerful. But even the liquor and an exceptionally well-cooked supper could not separate him from his persistent and set grouch. And of liquor he had already taken more than his limit. He had always boasted, with truth, that he had never been drunk, although there had been two occasions when he was not far from it. That was one doubtful luxury which he could not afford for the reason that there were men who would have been glad to see him, if only for a few seconds, when liquor had dulled his brain and slowed his speed of hand. He could never tell when and where he might meet one of these.

He dropped into a chair by a card table and, baffling all attempts to engage him in conversation, reviewed his troubles in a mumbled soliloquy, the liquor gradually making him careless. But of all the jumbled words his companions' diligent ears heard they recognized and retained only the bare term "Winchester"; and their conjectures were limited only by their imaginations.

Hopalong stirred and looked up, shaking off the hand which had aroused him. "Better go to bed, stranger," the proprietor was saying. "You an' me are the last two up. It's after twelve, an' you look tired and sleepy."

"Said his wife was sick," muttered the puncher. "Oh, what you saying?"

"You'll find a bed better'n this table, stranger—it's after twelve an' I want to close up an' get some sleep. I'm tired myself."

"Oh, that all? Shore I'll go to bed—like to see anybody stop me! Ain't no rocks in it, hey?"

"Nary a rock," laughingly reassured the host, picking up Hopalong's saddle and leading the way to a small room off the "office," his guest stumbling after him and growling about the rocks that lived in Winchester. When Stevenson had dropped the saddle by the window and departed, Hopalong sat on the edge of the bed to close his eyes for just a moment before tackling the labor of removing his clothes. A crash and a jar awakened him and he found himself on the floor with his back to the bed. He was hot and his head ached, and his back was skinned a little—and how hot and stuffy and choking the room had become! He thought he had blown out the light, but it still burned, and three-quarters of the chimney was thickly covered with soot. He was stifling and could not endure it any longer. After three attempts he put out the light, stumbled against his saddle and, opening the window, leaned out to breathe the pure air. As his lungs filled he chuckled wisely and, picking up the saddle, managed to get it and himself through the window and on the ground without serious mishap. He would ride for an hour, give the room time to freshen and cool off, and come back feeling much better. Not a star could be seen as he groped his way unsteadily towards the rear of the building, where he vaguely remembered having seen the corral as he rode up.

"Huh! Said he lived in Winchester an' his name was Bill—no, Ben Ferris," he muttered, stumbling towards a noise he knew was made by a horse rubbing against the corral fence. Then his feet got tangled up in the cinch of his saddle, which he had kicked before him, and after great labor he arose, muttering savagely, and continued on his wobbly way. "Goo' Lord, it's darker'n cats in—oof!" he grunted, recoiling from forcible contact with the fence he sought. Growling words unholy he felt his way along it and finally his arm slipped through an opening and he bumped his head solidly against the top bar of the gate. As he righted himself his hand struck the nose of a horse and closed mechanically over

it. Cow-ponies look alike in the dark and he grinned jubilantly as he complimented himself upon finding his own so unerringly.

"Anything is easy, when you know how. Can't fool me, ol' cayuse," he
beamed, fumbling at the bars with his free hand and getting them down with
a fool's luck. "You can't do it—I got you firs', las', an' always; an' I got you good.
Yessir, I got you good. Quit that rearing, you ol' fool! Stan' still, can't you?" The
pony sidled as the saddle hit its back and evoked profane abuse from the indignant puncher as he risked his balance in picking it up to try again, this time successfully. He began to fasten the girth, and then paused in wonder and thought
deeply, for the pin in the buckle would slide to no hole but the first. "Huh!
Getting fat, ain't you, piebald?" he demanded with withering sarcasm. "You blow
yoreself up any more'n I'll bust you wide open!" heaving up with all his might
on the free end of the strap, one knee pushing against the animal's side. The
"fat" disappeared and Hopalong laughed. "Been learnin' new tricks, ain't you?
Got smart since you been travellin', hey?" He fumbled with the bars again and
got two of them back in place and then, throwing himself across the saddle as
the horse started forward as hard as it could go, slipped off, but managed to save
himself by hopping along the ground. As soon as he had secured the grip he
wished he mounted with the ease of habit and felt for the reins. "G'wan now, an'
easy—it's plumb dark an' my head's bustin'."

When he saddled his mount at the corral he was not aware that two of
the three remaining horses had taken advantage of their opportunity and had
walked out and made off in the darkness before he replaced the bars, and he was
too drunk to care if he had known it.

The night air felt so good that it moved him to song, but it was not long
before the words faltered more and more and soon ceased altogether and a
subdued snore rasped from him. He awakened from time to time, but only for a
moment, for he was tired and sleepy.

His mount very quickly learned that something was wrong and that it was
being given its head. As long as it could go where it pleased it could do nothing
better than head for home, and it quickened its pace towards Winchester. Some
time after daylight it pricked up its ears and broke into a canter, which soon
developed signs of irritation in its rider. Finally Hopalong opened his heavy eyes
and looked around for his bearings. Not knowing where he was and too tired and
miserable to give much thought to a matter of such slight importance, he glanced
around for a place to finish his sleep. A tree some distance ahead of him looked
inviting and towards it he rode. Habit made him picket the horse before he lay

down and as he fell asleep he had vague recollections of handling a strange picket rope some time recently. The horse slowly turned and stared at the already snoring figure, glanced over the landscape, back to the queerest man it had ever met, and then fell to grazing in quiet content. A slinking coyote topped a rise a short distance away and stopped instantly, regarding the sleeping man with grave curiosity and strong suspicion. Deciding that there was nothing good to eat in that vicinity and that the man was carrying out a fell plot for the death of coyotes, it backed away out of sight and loped on to other hunting grounds.

* * * * *

Stevenson, having started the fire for breakfast, took a pail and departed towards the spring; but he got no farther than the corral gate, where he dropped the pail and stared. There was only one horse in the enclosure where the night before there had been four. He wasted no time in surmises, but wheeled and dashed back towards the hotel, and his vigorous shouts brought Old John to the door, sleepy and peevish. Old John's mouth dropped open as he beheld his habitually indolent host marking off long distances on the sand with each falling foot.

"What's got inter you?" demanded Old John.

"Our broncs are gone! Our broncs are gone!" yelled Stevenson, shoving Old John roughly to one side as he dashed through the doorway and on into the room he had assigned to the sullen and bibulous stranger. "I knowed it! I knowed it!" he wailed, popping out again as if on springs. "He's gone, an' he's took our broncs with him, the measly, low-down dog! I knowed he wasn't no good! I could see it in his eye; an' he wasn't drunk, not by a darn sight. Go out an' see for yoreself if they ain't gone!" he snapped in reply to Old John's look. "Go on out, while I throw some cold grub on the table—won't have no time this morning to do no cooking. He's got five hours' start on us, an' it'll take some right smart riding to get him before dark; but we'll do it, an' hang him, too!"

"What's all this here rumpus?" demanded a sleepy voice from upstairs. "Who's hanged?" and Charley entered the room, very much interested. His interest increased remarkably when the calamity was made known and he lost no time in joining Old John in the corral to verify the news.

Old John waved his hands over the scene and carefully explained what he had read in the tracks, to his companion's great irritation, for Charley's keen eyes and good training had already told him all there was to learn; and his reading did not exactly agree with that of his companion.

"Charley, he's gone and took our cayuses; an' that's the very way he came—'round the corner of the hotel. He got all tangled up an' fell over there, an' here he bumped inter the palisade, an' dropped his saddle. When he opened the bars he took my roan gelding because it was the best an' fastest, an' then he let out the others to mix us up on the tracks. See how he went? Had to hop four times on one foot afore he could get inter the saddle. An' that proves he was sober, for no drunk could hop four times like that without falling down an' being drug to death. An' he left his own critter behind because he knowed it wasn't no good. It's all as plain as the nose on your face, Charley," and Old John proudly rubbed his ear. "Hee, hee, hee! You can't fool Old John, even if he is getting old. No, sir, b'gum."

Charley had just returned from inside the corral, where he had looked at the brand on the far side of the one horse left, and he waited impatiently for his companion to cease talking. He took quick advantage of the first pause Old John made and spoke crisply.

"I don't care what corner he came 'round, or what he bumped inter; an' any fool can see that. An' if he left that cayuse behind because he thought it wasn't no good, he was drunk. That's a Bar-20 cayuse, an' no hoss-thief ever worked for that ranch. He left it behind because he stole it; that's why. An' he didn't let them others out because he wanted to mix us up, neither. How'd he know if we couldn't tell the tracks of our own animals? He did that to make us lose time; that's what he did it for. An' he couldn't tell what bronc he took last night—it was too dark. He must 'a' struck a match an' seen where that Bar-20 cayuse was an' then took the first one nearest that wasn't it. An' now you tell me how the devil he knowed yourn was the fastest, which it ain't," he finished, sarcastically, gloating over a chance to rub it into the man he had always regarded as a windy old nuisance.

"Well, mebby what you said is—"

"Mebby nothing!" snapped Charley. "If he wanted to mix the tracks would he 'a' hopped like that so we couldn't help telling what cayuse he rode? He knowed we'd pick his trail quick, an' he knowed that every minute counted; that's why he hopped—why, yore roan was going like the wind afore he got in the saddle. If you don't believe it, look at them toe-prints!"

"H'm; reckon yo're right, Charley. My eyes ain't nigh as good as they once was. But I heard him say something 'bout Winchester," replied Old John, glad to change the subject. "Bet he's going over there, too. He won't get through that town on no critter wearing my brand. Everybody knows that roan, an'—"

"Quit guessing!" snapped Charley, beginning to lose some of the tattered remnant of his respect for old age. "He's a whole lot likely to head for a town on a stolen cayuse, now ain't he! But we don't care where he's heading; we'll foller the trail."

"Grub pile!" shouted Stevenson, and the two made haste to obey.

"Charley, gimme a chaw of yore tobacker," and Old John, biting off a generous chunk, quietly slipped it into his pocket, there to lay until after he had eaten his breakfast.

All talk was tabled while the three men gulped down a cold and uninviting meal. Ten minutes later they had finished and separated to find horses and spread the news; in fifteen more they had them and were riding along the plain trail at top speed, with three other men close at their heels. Three hundred yards from the corral they pounded out of an arroyo, and Charley, who was leading, stood up in his stirrups and looked keenly ahead. Another trail joined the one they were following and ran with and on top of it. This, he reasoned, had been made by one of the strays and would turn away soon. He kept his eyes looking well ahead and soon saw that he was right in his surmise, and without checking the speed of his horse in the slightest degree he went ahead on the trail of the smaller hoof-prints. In a moment Old John spurred forward and gained his side and began to argue hot-headedly.

"Hey! Charley!" he cried. "Why are you follering this track?" he demanded.

"Because it's his; that's why."

"Well, here, wait a minute!" and Old John was getting red from excitement. "How do you know it is? Mebby he took the other!"

"He started out on the cayuse that made these little tracks," retorted Charley, "an' I don't see no reason to think he swapped animules. Don't you know the prints of yore own cayuse?"

"Lawd, no!" answered Old John. "Why, I don't hardly ride the same cayuse the second day, straight hand-running. I tell you we ought to foller that other trail. He's just cute enough to play some trick on us."

"Well, you better do that for us," Charley replied, hoping against hope that the old man would chase off on the other and give his companions a rest.

"He ain't got sand enough to tackle a thing like that singlehanded," laughed Jed White, winking to the others.

Old John wheeled. "Ain't, hey! I am going to do that same thing an' prove that you are a pack of fools. I'm too old to be fooled by a common trick like that. An' I don't need no help—I'll ketch him all by myself, an' hang him, too!"

And he wheeled to follow the other trail, angry and outraged. "Young fools," he muttered. "Why, I was fighting all round these parts afore any of 'em knowed the difference between day an' night!"

"Hard-headed old fool," remarked Charley, frowning, as he led the way again.

"He's gittin' old an' childish," excused Stevenson. "They say warn't nobody in these parts could hold a candle to him in his prime."

Hopalong muttered and stirred and opened his eyes to gaze blankly into those of one of the men who were tugging at his hands, and as he stared he started his stupefied brain sluggishly to work in an endeavor to explain the unusual experience. There were five men around him and the two who hauled at his hands stepped back and kicked him. A look of pained indignation slowly spread over his countenance as he realized beyond doubt that they were really kicking him, and with sturdy vigor. He considered a moment and then decided that such treatment was most unwarranted and outrageous and, further more, that he must defend himself and chastise the perpetrators.

"Hey!" he snorted, "what do you reckon yo're doing, anyhow? If you want to do any kicking, why kick each other, an' I'll help you! But I'll lick the whole bunch of you if you don't quit mauling me. Ain't you got no manners? Don't you know anything? Come 'round waking a feller up an' man-handling—"

"Get up!" snapped Stevenson, angrily.

"Why, ain't I seen you before? Somewhere? Sometime?" queried Hopalong, his brow wrinkling from intense concentration of thought. "I ain't dreaming; I've seen a one-eyed coyote som'ers, lately, ain't I?" he appealed, anxiously, to the others.

"Get up!" ordered Charley, shortly.

"An' I've seen you, too. Funny, all right."

"You've seen me, all right," retorted Stevenson. "Get up, damn you! Get up!"

"Why, I can't—my han's are tied!" exclaimed Hopalong in great wonder, pausing in his exertions to cogitate deeply upon this most remarkable phenomenon. "Tied up! Now what the devil do you think—"

"Use yore feet, you thief!" rejoined Stevenson roughly, stepping forward and delivering another kick. "Use yore feet!" he reiterated.

"Thief! Me a thief! Shore I'll use my feet, you yaller dog!" yelled the prostrate man, and his boot heel sank into the stomach of the offending Mr. Stevenson with sickening force and laudable precision. He drew it back slowly, as if debating shoving it farther. "Call me a thief, hey! Come poking 'round kicking honest punchers an' calling 'em names! Anybody want the other boot?" he inquired with grave solicitation.

Stevenson sat down forcibly and rocked to and fro, doubled up and gasping for breath, and Hopalong squinted at him and grinned with happiness. "Hear him sing! Reg'lar ol' brass band. Sounds like a cow pulling its hoofs outen the mud. Called me a thief, he did, just now. An' I won't let nobody kick me an' call me names. He's a liar, just a plan, squaw's dog liar, he—"

Two men grabbed him and raised him up, holding him tightly, and they were not over careful to handle him gently, which he naturally resented. Charley stepped in front of him to go to the aid of Stevenson and caught the other boot in his groin, dropping as if he had been shot. The man on the prisoner's left emitted a yell and loosed his hold to sympathize with a bruised shinbone, and his companion promptly knocked the bound and still intoxicated man down. Bill Thomas swore and eyed the prostrate figure with resentment and regret. "Hate to hit a man who can fight like that when he's loaded an' tied. I'm glad, all the same, that he ain't sober an' loose."

"An' you ain't going to hit him no more!" snapped Jed White, reddening with anger. "I'm ready to hang him, 'cause that's what he deserves, an' what we're here for, but I'm damned if I'll stand for any more mauling. I don't blame him for fighting, an' they didn't have no right to kick him in the beginning."

"Didn't kick him in the beginning," grinned Bill. "Kicked him in the ending. Anyhow," he continued seriously, "I didn't hit him hard—didn't have to. Just let him go an' shoved him quick."

"I'm just naturally going to clean house," muttered the prisoner, sitting up and glaring around. "Untie my han's an' gimme a gun or a club or anything, an' watch yoreselves get licked. Called me a thief! What you you fellers, then?—sticking me up an' busting me for a few measly dollars. Why didn't you take my money an' lemme sleep 'stead of waking me up an' kicking me? I wouldn't 'a' cared then."

"Come on, now; get up. We ain't through with you yet, not by a whole lot," growled Bill, helping him to his feet and steadying him. "I'm plumb glad you kicked 'em; it was coming to 'em."

"No, you ain't; you can't fool me," gravely assured Hopalong. "Yo're lying, an' you know it. What you going to do now? Ain't I got money enough? Wish I had an even break with you fellers! Wish my outfit was here!"

Stevenson, on his feet again, walked painfully up and shook his fist at the captive, from the side. "You'll find out what we want of you, you damned hoss-thief!" he cried. "We're going to tie you to that there limb so yore feet'll swing above the grass, that's what we're going to do."

Bill and Jed had their hands full for a moment and as they finally mastered the puncher, Charley came up with a rope. "Hurry up—no use dragging it out this way. I want to get back to the ranch some time before next week."

"Why I ain't no hoss-thief, you liar!" Hopalong yelled. "My name's Hopalong Cassidy of the Bar-20, an' when I tell my friends about what you've gone an' done they'll make you hard to find! You gimme any kind of a chance an' I'll do it all by myself, sick as I am, you yaller dogs!"

"Is that yore cayuse?" demanded Charley, pointing.

Hopalong squinted towards the animal indicated. "Which one?"

"There's only one there, you fool!"

"That so?" replied Hopalong, surprised. "Well, I never seen it afore. My cayuse is—is—where the devil is it" he asked, looking around anxiously.

"How'd you get that one, then, if it ain't yours?"

"Never had it—'t ain't mine, nohow," replied Hopalong, with strong conviction. "Mine was a hoss."

"You stole that cayuse last night outen Stevenson's corral," continued Charley, merely as a matter of form. Charley believed that a man had the right to be heard before he died—it wouldn't change the result and so could not do any harm.

"Did I? Why—" his forehead became furrowed again, but the events of the night before were vague in his memory and he only stumbled in his soliloquy. "But I wouldn't swap my cayuse for that spavined, saddle-galled, ring-boned bone-yard! Why, it interferes, an' it's got the heaves something awful!" he finished triumphantly, as if an appeal to common sense would clinch things. But he made no headway against them, for the rope went around his neck almost before he had finished talking and a flurry of excitement ensued. When the dust settled he was on his back again and the rope was being tossed over the limb.

The crowd had been too busily occupied to notice anything away from the scene of their strife and were greatly surprised when they heard a hail and saw a stranger sliding to a stand not twenty feet from them. "What's this?" demanded the newcomer, angrily.

Charley's gun glinted as it swung up and the stranger swore again. "What you doing?" he shouted. "Take that gun off'n me or I'll blow you apart!"

"Mind yore business an' sit still!" Charley snapped. "You ain't in no position to blow anything apart. We've got a hoss-thief an' we're shore going to hang him regardless."

"An' if there's any trouble about it we can hang two as well as we can one," suggested Stevenson, placidly. "You sit tight an' mind yore own affairs, stranger," he warned.

Hopalong turned his head slowly. "He's a liar, stranger; just a plain, squaw's dog of a liar. An' I'll be much obliged if you'll lick hell outen 'em an' let—why hullo, hoss-thief!" he shouted, at once recognizing the other. It was the man he had met in the gospel tent, the man he had chased for a horse-thief and then swapped mounts with. "Stole any more cayuses?" he asked, grinning, believing that everything was all right now. "Did you take that cayuse back to Grant?" he finished.

"Han's up!" roared Stevenson, also covering the stranger. "So yo're another one of 'em, hey? We're in luck to-day. Watch him, boys, till I get his gun. If he moves, drop him quick."

"You damned fool!" cried Ferris, white with rage. "He ain't no thief, an' neither am I! My name's Ben Ferris an' I live in Winchester. Why, that man you've is Hopalong Cassidy—Cassidy, of the Bar-20!"

"Sit still—you can talk later, mebby," replied Stevenson, warily approaching him. "Watch him, boys!"

"Hold on!" shouted Ferris, murder in his eyes. "Don't you try that on me! I'll get one of you before I go; I'll shore get one! You can listen a minute, an' I can't get away."

"All right; talk quick."

Ferris pleaded as hard as he knew how and called attention to the condition of the prisoner. "If he did take the wrong cayuse he was too blind drunk to know it! Can't you see he was!" he cried.

"Yep; through yet?" asked Stevenson, quietly.

"No! I ain't started yet!" Ferris yelled. "He did me a good turn once, one that I can't never repay, an' I'm going to stop, this murder or go with him. If I go I'll take one of you with me, an' my friends an' outfit'll get the rest."

"Wait till Old John gets here," suggested Jed to Charley. "He ought to know this feller."

"For the Lord's sake!" snorted Charley. "He won't show up for a week. Did you hear that, fellers?" he laughed, turning to the others.

"He knows me all right; an' he'd like to see me hung," replied the stranger. "I won't give up my guns, an' you won't lynch Hopalong Cassidy while I can pull a trigger. That's flat!" He began to talk feverishly to gain time and his eyes lighted suddenly. Seeing that Jed White was wavering, Stevenson ordered them to go on with the work they had come to perform, and he watched Ferris as a cat watches a mouse, knowing that he would be the first man hit if the stranger got a chance to shoot. But Ferris stood up very slowly in his stirrups so as not to alarm the five with any quick movement, and shouted at the top of his voice, grabbing off his sombrero and waving it frantically. A faint cheer reached his ears and made the lynchers turn quickly and look behind them. Nine men were tearing towards them at a dead gallop and had already begun to forsake their bunched-up formation in favor of an extended line. They were due to arrive in a very few minutes and caused Mr. Ferris' heart to overflow with joy.

HOW I BECAME A COWBOY

FRANK HARRIS

Chicago in the early seventies was a city of 350,000 inhabitants. Life there pleased me, but did not impress me greatly. The city was brisk and busy, the houses fine, I thought, and the great lake boundless like the sea; but my reading had taught me to expect all this and more.

Yet my life in Chicago was destined to be the turning point of my existence! I learned to invest the money, most of my salary of $150 a month, knowing I should need it one day, and the day came sooner than I thought.

One day in August, as acting manager of the Fremont Hotel, I received a Spanish family named Vidal. Señor Vidal was like a French Officer of middle height, trim figure; he was very dark with gray mustache waving up at the ends. His wife, motherly but stout, had large dark eyes and small features; a cousin, a man of about thirty, was rather tall with sharp imperious ways. At first I did not notice the girl who was talking to her Indian maid. I understood at once that the Vidals were rich and gave them the best rooms. "All communicating—

except yours," I added, turning to the young man, "it is on the other side of the corridor, but large and quiet." A shrug and a contemptuous nod were all I got for my pains from him.

As I handed the keys to the bell boy, the girl appeared in a black mantilla. "Any letters for us?" she asked quietly. For a minute I stood dumfounded, enthralled. Then, "I'll see," I replied, and went to the rack, but only to give myself a countenance. I knew there were none.

"None, I'm sorry to say," I half-apologized watching the girl as she moved away.

"What's the matter with me?" I said to myself angrily. "She's nothing wonderful, this Miss Vidal; pretty, yes, and dark with fine dark eyes, but nothing extraordinary." But it would not do; I was shaken in a new way and would not admit it even to myself. In fact the shock was so great that my head took sides against heart and temperament at once, as if alarmed.

Next day I found out that the Vidals were on their way to their hacienda near Chihuahua in Northern Mexico. They meant to rest in Chicago for three or four days because Señora Vidal had heart trouble. I discovered besides that Señor Arriga was either courting his cousin or betrothed to her.

In a thousand little ways I took occasion to commend myself to the Vidals. The beauty of the girl grew on me extraordinarily: yet it was the pride and reserve in her face that fascinated me more even that her great dark eyes or her fine features and splendid coloring.

It is to be presumed that the girl saw how it was with me and was gratified. She betrayed herself in no way, but she was always eager to go downstairs to the lounge and missed no opportunity of making some inquiry at the desk.

One little talk I got with my goddess: one morning she came to the office to ask about reserving a Pullman drawing-room for El Paso. I undertook at once to see to everything, and when the dainty little lady added in her funny accent: "We have so many baggage, twenty-six bits," I said as earnestly as if my life depended on it:

"Please trust me. I shall see to everything. I only wish," I added, "I could do more for you."

"That's kind," said the coquette, "very kind," looking full at me. Emboldened by despair at her approaching departure I added: "I'm so sorry you're going. I shall never forget you, never."

Taken aback by my directness, the girl laughed saucily: *"Never* means a week, I suppose!"

"You will see," I went on hurriedly as if driven, as indeed I was. "If I thought I should not see you again, and soon, I should not wish to live."

"Hush, hush," she said gravely. "You are too young to take vows and I must not listen." But seeing my sad face, she added: "You have been very kind. I shall remember my stay in Chicago with pleasure." She stretched out her hand. I took it and held it, treasuring every touch.

Her look and the warmth of her fingers I garnered up in my heart as purest treasure.

As soon as she had gone and the radiance with her, I cudgeled my brains to find some pretext for another talk. "She goes to-morrow," hammered in my brain and my heartache choked me, almost preventing my thinking. Suddenly the idea of flowers came to me. I'd buy a lot. No; every one would notice them and talk. A few would be better. How many? I thought and thought.

When they came into the lounge next day ready to start, I handed her three splendid red rosebuds, prettily tied up with maidenhair fern.

"How kind!" she exclaimed, coloring. "And how pretty," she added, looking at the roses. "Just three?"

"One for your hair," I said with love's cunning, "one for your eyes and one for your heart."

"Will you remember?" I added in a low voice intensely.

She nodded and then looked up sparkling. "As long—as ze flowers last," she laughed, and was back with her mother.

I saw them into the omnibus and got kind words from all the party, even from my rival, Señor Arriga, but cherished most her look and word as she went out of the door.

Holding it open for her, I murmured as she passed, for the others were within hearing: "I shall come soon."

The girl stopped at once, pretending to look at the tag on a trunk the partner was carrying. "El Paso is far away," she sighed, "and the hacienda ten leagues further on. When shall we arrive—when?" she added, glancing up at me.

"When" was the significant word to me for many a month; her eyes had filled it with meaning.

I've told of this meeting with Miss Vidal at length because it marked an epoch in my life; it was the first time that love had cast her glamour over me making beauty superlative, intoxicating. The passion rendered it easier for me to resist ordinary temptation, for it taught me there was a whole gorgeous world in Love's kingdom that I had never imagined, much less explored.

At the back of my mind was the fixed resolve to get to Chihuahua somehow or other in the near future and meet my charmer again and that resolve in due course shaped my life anew.

Some time later that year, three strangers came to the hotel, all cattlemen I was told, but of a new sort. Two of them, Reece and Ford, I was to know well.

Harrel Ford, the "Boss" as he was called, was a Westerner from near Leavenworth, Kansas, who owned, it was said, half a dozen ranches and twenty thousand head of cattle; he had just brought four thousand head into the stock yards to be sold. Reece was his partner. Reece, I soon found out, was an Englishman, a lover of books and so became interesting to me at once.

All three, however, were remarkably quiet and discreet and nothing would have been known about them had they not been attended by a Mexican servant whom every one knew as Bob. Bob was at least as taciturn as his masters when sober, but living in the hotel with nothing to do, the other servants got after him and soon discovered that his weak point was a love of strong drink. When he had got outside half a bottle of Bourbon, Bob would brag to beat the band and had stories innumerable at command which gained in the telling from the curious broken jargon he used for American. He was as small as a dime and as cattle-wise as a cow's mother.

Harrel Ford's quiet resolution made an impression on me from the beginning. In appearance he was like any of a dozen tall, thin lanternjawed Westerners whom I had met; the hawk-like features, sallow skin and careless slangy speech were common, but behind his careless manner were hard, keen, grey eyes and a suggestion of immutable decision—a bad antagonist to bargain or fight with.

Reece, whom I was to know best, was a very different kind of man than either Bob or Ford. He was younger, though even quieter than Ford, rather tall, dark and handsome; a little dandyish in dress and talked like the Englishman he was. Though Reece was a partner, Bob, the Mexican, always called Ford "the Boss." I found out the reason later.

Ford never rode in Chicago; indeed, appeared to be more interested in the stock markets than the stock yards, but Reece, in the daytime, was always in cord breeches and high brown boots, and took my fancy by always riding everywhere. Ford seemed to accept my little kindnesses as usual, but Reece was of richer and more generous blood. He asked me one day to come for a ride, adding that Bob, the Mexican servant, would get me a mount; I confessed I had no breeches, but Reece showed me how to put straps on my ordinary trousers.

And the same afternoon he took me out for a ride and then together we paid a visit to the stock yards, where to my surprise I found that Ford and Reece had still over two thousand head of cattle and nearly two hundred horses which they had driven up on the long trail from New Mexico to Kansas City and thence by train to Chicago.

I found they were all going down again in the spring and the profits were big. Cows could be bought for a dollar a head, "most everywhere near the Rio Grande," and they fetched from twenty to thirty dollars each in Chicago. The profits were enormous but the risks were huge.

"I'd like to go down with you," I confessed, but Reece at once warned me about the risks. Indians took nearly one herd out of every two and a good many cowboys lost their lives on the trail. As 5,000 cattle constituted a herd the loss was heavy.

"What do you do if the Indians get your herd?" I asked.

"Go back and get another," replied Reece carelessly, and then added, seeing that I had made up my mind, "but you must see Ford, he's the chief in this business and I shouldn't like to go against him." So he dismissed the matter from his kindly, careless mind.

Fortunately for me, I made up to Bob before I tackled Ford. I had learned a little Spanish grammar in my spare time and knew a few sentences by heart: I shot off a *"buenos dias, Señor,"* one morning at Bob and was answered with a volubility that surprised and overwhelmed me. I had to explain that I was only just learning, a beginner.

"I understan'," replied Bob with grim contempt, "all American man. He asks *'si habla Español'* and den dat's all he know."

But he found that I knew more than that and meant to know much more and soon we were talking half-Spanish, half-English, and Bob taught me a good deal more than the proper pronunciation of the new tongue.

In one of our talks I told him I thought of going with Ford and Reece into the Southwest.

"Reece good man," said Bob, "at once—*Caballero*—*muy bueno;* but Ford hard, hard as nail: you talk with me, learn ride . . . then speak with Boss."

So I resolved to bide my time and wait. But one day Ford spoke to me. He began by saying: "You want to go down on the trail, Reece tells me. I'm not going down after this next summer. Why don't you take my place and go in partnership with Reece? It would only cost you six or seven thousand dollars."

"I haven't got so much"—I confessed naïvely—"though I could have by next spring. I have only a couple of thousand dollars saved or at most three thousand."

"Come in for what you have got," said the Boss. "I only took a hand to help Reece. If he's willing to let you in for a quarter for three thousand I'll sell you so much of my mortgage. Then you and I'll have a quarter each against Reece's half and perhaps you will be able to teach him to save and be careful. He's too easy, too generous, too Southern—that's what's the matter with him."

I accepted the offer in principle and when the opportunity offered, talked it over with Reece. Reece, it appeared, had taken a great fancy to me, perhaps because I deferred to him and admired him openly. Without any purpose he had begun teaching me to ride and finding me an apt pupil he took a liking to me as we all do to those we help and can mold.

Half unconsciously, too, I had copied Reece in dress, imitated his seat on horseback, modeled myself outwardly at least on him, and this flattered him and increased his liking for me. It must be remembered that I was only seventeen at that time and he was a man of 35. But the hero-worship had an even deeper effect on me. We all grow by imitating our heroes and even when we no longer copy them, something of them remains in us.

At length, on one of our afternoon rides together, it was settled by Reece and myself practically as the Boss had proposed.

Then and not till then did I approach the hotel proprietor; I offered to give up my place before the winter began if he would give me a month's salary as bonus. The chief agreed to my proposal on condition that I shouldn't work for any other hotel in Chicago, and we shook hands on the first of September.

A few days later my new friends—the Boss, Reece, Dell and Bob—and I took train for St. Louis, and from St. Louis to Kansas City, at that time a jumping-off place, so to speak. Here we packed our town clothes carefully away in bags for wagon transport, and then, like school boys released, pulled on chaps, flannel shirts and high boots, buckled on cartridge belts and revolvers, slung rifles along our saddles and started off in true cowboy style to ride the two or three hundred miles to Eureka, Kansas, where the partners had a ranch.

The Boss had left a wagon and half a dozen horses in a stable just outside Kansas City in charge of a colored man named Paul. Charlie Bates, a Kansan, had stayed with Paul on what he called "grub wages." By Reece's advice I picked a young mare out of the bunch for my own use and gave the Boss twenty dollars for her. I hadn't had Moll for an hour when I realized that I had made a good bargain.

* * * * *

That first ride into the Southwest was of the essence of romance: it was a plunge a thousand miles into the unknown; it was like an old border foray, with enough strangeness to interest and enough danger to warm the blood. One's comrades were all new, too, and had to be learned.

With the intensified resolution given to me by my success in Chicago, I set myself to master riding, the chief art of the cowboy. At once, I realized my life would often depend on it, because being near-sighted, I'd never be a good shot. For the first days I suffered tortures; my hips were all raw, but after washing, or rather frying them well with salt water and whiskey every night, I soon got hard and suffered no further inconvenience. I was more than repaid for all my troubles and pains by Reece's approval. Before the week was over, Reece remarked one evening: "If you persevere you'll ride this summer as well as Bob."

"What can he do that I can't do?" I asked Reece.

"Oh," said Reece, "ask him and you will soon see!"

So the next time we met I asked Bob. He looked at me with a little grin and then said: "Drop something on the ground, a handkerchief or a coin or anything you like." So I dropped a dollar. Immediately Bob shouted, tore away on his horse fifty or sixty yards, swung round and came past me at full gallop.

As he neared the dollar he caught the horse's mane in his left hand, swung down and picked up the dollar and swung back again into place without any apparent exertion. I realized at once that it was an extraordinary feat and set myself forthwith to learn it.

If I say it took me at least a fortnight, working every day for two or three hours, my readers may be surprised. But let them try it and they will find out it takes some doing.

Bob was a little man, five feet four in height, weighing perhaps one hundred and twenty-five pounds; he was weather-beaten and dried up so that he looked like leather; but he was very active and strong in spite of the fact that he must have been fifty years of age. From his appearance it would have been impossible to say what age he was; but he had fought with Santa Anna all through the Mexican War, so he could hardly be less than fifty, though his little brown eyes were just as bright and quick as they had been when he was sixteen, and his seat in the saddle just as firm and his wrist just as supple-strong.

The life was enchanting. Our three wagons, each drawn by a pair of good horses, could make their thirty miles a day. Although one man was always detailed to hunt for the pot, very often he would be accompanied by half a dozen, who would race down buffalo and kill perhaps three or four cows or calves with revolvers. In the heat of the day the cowboys would play cards for wages to come or shoot one against the other, or simply skylark about. We took seventy to a hundred ponies for the dozen cowboys, and each man broke three or four of these to his own special requirements.

Every now and then one came across a broncho with some particular and peculiar vice. And these were often the most admired and the best cared for of the whole herd for a very simple reason. It was the custom whenever one gang of cowboys met another immediately to trade a broncho and, of course, the most vicious animal was always the one to be swapped. The trading was conducted in the slow Yankee fashion. The spokesman of gang A would try to get the representative of gang B to give some money to boot:

"I guess my hoss is wuth two o' yourn; look at 'im."

"Looks ain't nuthen: I'll bet you five dollars my hoss'll run (gallop) faster'n yourn."

If it was found impossible to get money to boot, half a dozen curious bets would be made, for none of the bets were allowed to suggest the horse's special trick. Finally the bets were agreed to: everything was settled and the two bronchos were solemnly put forward. Then came the heart of the fun.

One of the A gang mounted the horse of the B gang and proceeded to show his paces. Commonly he found a practiced and extraordinary buckjumper; but aided by a Mexican saddle it was possible to sit the worst bucker, provided the broncho could not buck himself out of his saddle, which, however, occasionally happened. After this trial one of the B gang would mount the horse which the A gang had offered. The broncho itself and money, too, changed hands on the result of this contest. Usually the broncho had some impish or devilish trick.

I remember mounting one which seemed to have no fault of any kind. Fortunately for me I was riding on an English saddle, which is like a racing pad in front. The broncho walked, trotted, loped and galloped to perfection. I began to think that the other gang didn't understand the game, and I turned and cantered carelessly back to the crowd. Suddenly, without warning, the beast tucked its forelegs under it and I went rolling over and over like a shot rabbit.

I got up half dazed and bleeding from nose and mouth amid yells of laughter from both gangs.

"Quiet to ride, ain't he? Pity he put his foot in that prairie dog's hole,"—and another roar of laughter.

The broncho we usually traded was a very good-looking black mare which had been ruined by rough handling when broken in. She would walk or trot or gallop for two or three minutes and then would stand stock still—a confirmed jibber. Nothing could make her move. And at last the rider had to dismount and pack his own saddle and bridle back to the starting point.

We had another horse which was certain to win the game, or at least to draw it, but she was seldom put forward, for we used her for races on account of her speed and bottom, and a broncho which was swapped was sometimes subjected to a good deal of ill treatment. Blue Dick, as this mare was called, was a fleabitten gray, fifteen and a half hands and pure bred, if it is possible to judge breeding from form and pace and courage.

She had been bought cheap because she had broken up a trap in Kansas City and savaged the groom. After a long time we cured her of every vice save one. When ridden by some one she didn't know she used to stretch her head out again and again till she got the reins a little loose: then she would turn round as quick as a snake, get your toe in her mouth and bit like a fiend. The pain was so horrible—excruciating—I have seen a strong man fall from her back fainting with agony.

It was usually arranged that the crowd which won gained both horses; if the result was a draw, each gang took possession again of its own steed.

I tell these stories just to give an idea of the life. The days spent on the trail were, for the first year, at least, of time-consuming interest. Riding tempered the great heat and made the climate absolutely delightful.

The plains varied from 700 to 1,500 feet above sea level; but that was not sufficient to account for the dry lightness of the atmosphere, which exhilarated one like champagne. Shielded on one side by 1,500 miles of plains and on the other by the Rocky Mountains this vast track of country was completely protected from the rain. So dry was the atmosphere that when we killed a buffalo the carcass would dry up to dust without putrefying, and this gave us better jerked meat than was to be found anywhere else in the world, better even than the biltong of South Africa. All you had to do was to take, say, the loin of a buffalo, though the rump was generally used, cut it into strips, sprinkle a little salt on it, and hang it over lines from one wagon to another, or even throw it on the top of the wagon, and leave it there for a day or two, then turn it and leave it another couple of days, and you had beef which looked like strips of mahogany, yet which ate like the best beef slightly salted; for these hard, wood-like strips got soft in the mouth at once.

Another peculiarity of this dry atmosphere on the great plains was that the short buffalo grass used to dry up and cure itself on the ground, becoming, in fact, hay, without the trouble of cutting and stacking.

It was often said thirty years ago that buffalo meat was praised only by Westerners because they were pretty hungry when they ate it. At the time I thought this a reasonable explanation, but on the trail I found it to be simply silly. Buffalo meat, even when one is not hungry, is the best meat I've ever eaten; as much superior to ordinary beef as grouse is superior to the barn-fed fowl, for not only has it greater tenderness and greater juiciness, but also the game flavor: it was, I decided—the first time I ate it as the hundredth—the best food in the world.

Yet unfortunately the buffalo has been wiped out, and his place given to ordinary domestic cattle. He was indeed an easy prey for several reasons: the bulls were just as savage as the African bull buffalo, but the African bull can retreat into forest, or, worse still, into the heavy thorn bush which he alone can pass through without difficulty; he has therefore an immense advantage over the man hunting him. But a herd of buffalo out on the plains had no protection and could be ridden down and shot, from ten or twelve yards distance, almost as easily as cattle. Moreover, the hunters soon found a peculiarity of the buffalo which placed him at their mercy. Near any salt lick, where the buffaloes were wont to congregate at early morning, it was only necessary to conceal one's self in a neighboring hollow and shoot straight. So long as the hunter kept out of sight, buffalo after buffalo could be killed. At every shot the uninjured buffaloes would lift their head and look about; but seeing nothing, would again begin to wallow and roll about as if there was no danger to be feared. One morning a hunter killed a herd of thirty-five at such a lick merely for their hides. The hides, untanned, were worth always about five dollars apiece, and each of them weighed some forty pounds. They were too thick and stiff to make good pelts; the hides of the calves and young cows made the best robes.

* * * * *

Before going down to buy cattle in New Mexico in the Spring, we spent the winter months on Reece's Ranch. I shall never forget the coming to the Ranch.

We did not even stop at the little village of Eureka, but left the trail and rode a bee-line across the prairie for home. After nearly ten miles of hard riding we came to a bridge over a little creek that was perhaps fifteen yards wide and three feet deep, and then Ford and Reece began to race up a long slope. I followed hard on their heels, when suddenly on the very ridge of the slope in front I saw the ranch. It was simply a large one-story frame building lifted about three feet from the ground; all the winds of heaven blew underneath it, and the fowls and dogs used this as a shady resting place.

There was a room in which the Boss, Reece and I slept on bunks, and behind a dining room; across the passage from the chief room there was a great room where all the men slept, and behind it the kitchen ruled over by Peggy, an Indian. He was called Peggy on the theory that cooking was woman's work. There was hardly any furniture in the place; the boys slept on buffalo rugs thrown on bunks round the walls. There was no ornament except pictures from the illustrated papers pasted on the walls. Here and there rifles were hung, and shotguns, revolvers and bowie-knives, a perfect arsenal of modern weapons.

In one corner of the sitting room was a big easy chair, always claimed by any one who was not well, and buffalo rugs were everywhere in heaps.

About three hundred yards from the house was a great stable which Reece had had built of stone. It would hold a hundred horses, had twenty loose boxes for the best horses and immense hay lofts above and enormous corn bins and harness rooms at the side. It was infinitely warmer in winter and cooler in summer and altogether more comfortable than the wooden shanty where the masters lived.

Not a moment of the day on the ranch hung heavy on my hands. The breaking-in of the colts palled a little till an incident took place which taught me that if I had an excellent seat in the saddle I had still a good deal to learn about horses.

An unbroken black mare was brought out one morning, saddled and bridled, and I jumped on her back. Instead of bucking or kicking the animal simply stood stock still as if carved in stone. I played with the bridle and coaxed her; the black took absolutely no notice. One of the men passing by gave her a sharp cut across the hind-quarters with a quirt and an encouraging shout. The mare did not even turn her head or seek to brush the pain away with a switch of her tail. She seemed hypnotized with fear.

The boys began soon to chaff me; but I had sense enough to take no notice, and the noise brought Reece out to see what was the matter. I felt that in sitting still I had Reece's approval, so I smiled at the boys and paid no attention to Charlie, whose chaff was the loudest. At length Reece said:

"Why don't you get on Charlie and show the tenderfoot how to ride?"

"I'd soon make her go," said Charlie, glad to show off; but after ten minutes of useless efforts he altered his tune.

"No one can make that mare stir except Bob," he said viciously as he dismounted. Without a word Reece went over the mare, handled her, pulled her ears gently once or twice, then got on her back, and the mare walked away at once.

"How did you do it?" I asked running alongside.

"Search me," answered Reece laughing, "I don't know."

"How did you get such power?" I persisted.

"When I was young," said Reece, "I used to break-in all our colts and a lot of them were thoroughbreds with any amount of spirit—that taught me. Breakin'-in's the best practice in the world."

"Has Bob got your power?" I asked jealously. Reece nodded his handsome head.

"Really?" I exclaimed.

"Bob knows more about cattle," Reece summed up dispassionately, "than any one I ever saw. He's not so good with horses. For instance, his seat now ain't so good as yours; but he knows all animals, I guess, and what he don't know about steers and bulls ain't worth considering. He's a wonder! You should take Bob as a teacher," he added smiling.

"I was right, wasn't I?" I asked eager for a little praise, "to sit the mare without beating her?"

"Sure, sure!" replied Reece. "She was frightened with all the novel experience. What would you have done if they put a bit in your mouth all of a sudden? To punish her could only make her worse; that's why I came out. These Western men believe too much in brute force—like all young people," he added, as if thinking aloud.

From that moment I resolved to make a friend of Bob and so get the heart of his mystery sooner or later. Meanwhile I went on with my breaking-in persistently morning after morning and soon realized that half the bad temper of horses being pure fear, gentleness and patience were infinitely more effective than whip or spur or rough usage.

One day we were riding in the prairie when we sighted a "coyote" or prairie wolf. It had begun to get warm, and the coyote loped along in front of us apparently unconcerned, as if he knew we had no chance of catching him. A quarter of an hour's riding showed us that we had no chance and just as this impression became dominant, the wolf stopped and turned round to look at his pursuers. A young fellow named Capper, from Wyoming, had got his rifle out at the first halt and now stopped, took a snapshot at the coyote, and as luck would have it, broke his leg, though the coyote must have been six or seven hundred yards away.

"A good shot," cried Reece, pulling his horse to a standstill, "what did you sight for?"

"Seven hundred yards," said the youth casually, "this Winchester is real good," he added modestly. Somehow or other his manner pleased me.

After waiting for the majority of the men who had ridden on eagerly to enjoy the catching of the wounded coyote, we all set off home-ward, and a very tired, excited crew sat down to dinner on the ranch that day: Charlie, of course, the loudest of the bunch. He kept on praising Capper's shot till even I saw purpose in it, and at last he came out flat-footed with the conclusion:—

"Joe Capper's the best shot in this camp," but nobody seemed to pay much attention to him till he said: "I'd like to bet a month's pay on Joe against any of us."

Bob took him up

"I cover your fifty dollars," he squeaked, "Bent's a better shot." Bent, to my astonishment, didn't say a word, in fact, was about the first to leave the table and go about his business. But the money was staked in the Boss' hands and the match fixed for the next Sunday at six in the morning.

The test was a true Western one, and is usually reserved for winter when the snow is on the ground. A turkey was buried, leaving only neck and head above the ground. Perhaps because it was so closely caged, the bird's head was not still for a second. The constantly moving mark, I thought, brought an element of chance into the contest. Capper was there with his Winchester, surrounded by Charlie and others, laughing and joking.

Bent, on the other hand, stood by himself making careful preparation. To my astonishment, he drew the cartridge of his Winchester and refilled it, measuring the powder most carefully in a little steel measure before pouring it into the shell.

"One would think," I remarked, "that good shooting depended on a single grain of powder."

"That's it," said Bent quietly, "that's the fact." I stared at the man.

The men were to shoot alternatively at three turkeys. The shooting line was drawn at first one hundred yards from the turkey, then two and at least three hundred yards. Capper knelt down, fired quickly and missed. His second shot killed the turkey. Another bird was put into the next hole and again he killed it. Charlie was jubilant.

"Go in and beat that if you can," he cried jeeringly to Bent. Another turkey was in position, and Bent knelt down. He aimed, as it seemed to me, an interminable time and then fired. Before the smoke cleared away showing the turkey was killed, Bent had risen as if in no doubt of the result, opened his rifle and cleaned the barrel out with an oiled rag. By that time another turkey was ready, and he knelt and again killed the bird.

"Good, good," I cried almost beside myself with admiration of the man's uncanny skill. "But why do you take so long to aim?".

"There's a little wind," Bent replied simply; "I wait till it's still."

Again quietly he killed his bird and won a hearty cheer from the boys. Charlie insisted that Capper should have another shot, the first shot should not have counted, and so forth. In silence Capper knelt down. This time I noticed he also took a long time to aim—and killed his bird.

Going back to the ranch I stuck close to Bent. I wanted to know how he had learned his markmanship. Was it merely long practice?

"An' the rifle," Bent corrected, "fine shootin' all in the gun. Capper, I guess, is as good a shot as I am or anybody else, if he'd take care and load properly and use his brains. He missed the first time through not taking thought of the wind."

"Do you mean," I questioned, "that anybody could be a first-rate shot?"

"I reckon so," Bent replied, "anybody with good eyes. Anybody," he went on, "can learn to hold straight." Bent's matter-of-fact simplicity and carefulness made a great impression on me. I felt sorry: I could never become a good shot with my poor eyes.

* * * * *

Of course, little by little I got to know every one on the ranch and got to know, too, a good deal of the life that lay before me.

It was in March, I think, the buffalo grass just sprouting, when we resolved to start for the Rio Grande. Reece was to be our boss, Ford not going down, and the men all got $40 a month and a commission on the profits if we succeeded in bringing cattle up to Chicago.

The first days on the trail were not especially exciting. Every one was up about four o'clock, well before daybreak. The first man to awake would throw some buffalo chips (dry dung) on the fire; Peggy, the Indian cook, would soon swing a kettle on it and make the coffee, while some of us went down to the creek and washed our hands and faces, or even had a bath. Then we came fresh and eager to the hot coffee and hot biscuits, with a grill of buffalo steaks and fat bacon.

The air, even in early Spring and before sunrise, was warm, like fresh milk. Suddenly the curtain of the night would be drawn back, opal tints would climb up the eastern heaven, and these would change to mother-of-pearl, and break into streams of rose and crimson; in a moment the sun would show above the horizon, and at once it was day. After breakfast we would wash up and put things away in one of the wagons; Bent and the negroes would generally climb into a wagon and go to sleep again: the wagons would then be harnessed and commence their journey southward, while the rest of us would mount our bronchos and go on in front, detaching two of our number to drive the rest of the horses. In one respect these bronchos were something like Texan cattle—they all followed a leader and were therefore very easy to drive; bar anything unusual, one had simply to ride behind them, and an occasional flick of the whip or even a shout would keep them moving.

Five or six of us used to be perpetually riding together on young, fresh horses, summer day after summer day. Of course, there was all manner of skylarking and playing about. Some one would have mounted a new horse and want to prove it; immediately a bet would be made, and we would have a race to decide whether the new beast could gallop or not. If he turned out very fast, I would generally be sent off to get Shiloh or Blue Dick out of the herd and see how he would shape beside the fastest we had got. Shiloh was a thoroughbred horse, bought by Reece in Kentucky; as a three-year-old he had done a half-mile in forty-nine seconds, and over a mile was almost as fast as a Derby winner—was certainly as fast as good plating form. He could beat Blue Dick in a sprint or a scurry, but stretch the course from two miles to ten and Blue Dick would beat him a long way. I used to think that if you cantered Blue Dick for half a mile or so before you made her gallop, you could gallop until you were tired without tiring her.

I remember one occasion when I had to test her: we had camped about sixteen miles from Albuquerque, New Mexico. The men had been skylarking about with a prairie rattlesnake, trying to lift it on little twigs of sagebrush and throw it at each other. The prairie rattlesnake is very small, three feet or so in length, and thin as a whip-lash, whereas the forest rattlesnake is five or six feet long and as thick as a girl's arm; but the prairie rattlesnake, though small, is just as venomous and ten times as quick and bad-tempered as his larger brother. The play ended, therefore, as might have been expected: the rattlesnake stung one of the men, a half-Indian, half-Greaser.

As one of the lightest of the party, I was immediately called and told by Reece, our chief, to round up Blue Dick and ride into Albuquerque and bring out a bottle of whisky, for it appeared that our small barrel had been allowed to get quite empty, and the poisoned man could only have a glass or so. I put a racing pad on Blue Dick's back and started with the boss's last words in my ears, "Don't spare the horse; Indian Pete is in a bad way." Pete was a silent, sulky creature, but the need was imminent, and though I was filled with anxiety about the mare I was to ride, I intended to do my best. I trotted the two hundred or three hundred yards to the creek and took her through the ford quite quietly. On the opposite bank I let her begin to canter, and I cantered for the next mile or so, till she had got quite dry and warm, and then I began to answer her craving for speed and let her go faster into a sort of hand-gallop. I kept at this for about half an hour, and then loosed her out: in an incredibly short time I found myself on the outskirts of the town. I drew Blue Dick together for the last mile and let her go as hard as she could lay legs to ground. I pulled up at the first saloon in the main street, threw myself from her back, hitched her to the post, rushed in and got a bottle of whisky, stuffed it in my pocket, and buckling my belt round it so as to keep it safe, rushed out, threw myself on Blue Dick's back, and was again racing down the street within two minutes, I should think, from the time I drew rein. Now, I said to myself, I must find out what Blue Dick can do. The heat was tremendous; it must have been quite ninety in the shade, perhaps a hundred and thirty-five in the sun; but the air was light, and though the mare was in a reek of sweat, she was breathing as easily as when she started. Gradually the fear of being late grew upon me, and I let her race as she would: the mare herself seemed to realize that speed was needed, for she settled down to her long stretching gallop, which I always compared to the gallop of a wolf, so tireless it seemed, and long and easy. Mile after mile swept past, and at last I saw the rise in the prairie which was the edge of the creek, and the few, mingy cottonwood trees that showed me I was almost home. Again and again I had strained forward to look at the mare; there seemed no sign of distress in her; and then a sort of exultation in her tireless strength came to me, and wild joy that she was uninjured, and I shook her together with a shout, lifting her in her stride at the same time. At once she got hold of the bit, and before I could do anything had bolted with me at lightning speed. Down to the creek over the steep bank with a plunge into the water; across, up the opposite bank, and away like a mad thing. I had overshot the wagons by a hundred yards before I could pull her up. There were a dozen hands to take the whisky bottle, which was fortunately whole. I threw myself off the mare and gave her to the care of Mexican Bob, to walk about; but almost at once any anxiety I had about Blue Dick vanished, for she set herself to munch some buffalo grass, and I saw that the long, hard gallop had done her no harm.

Strange to say, the whisky didn't cure the Indian; he could not keep it on his stomach. He didn't even seem to try: from the first he believed that he was done for; he said, "I'm a dead 'un," wrapped himself in his blanket and wanted to be left alone. When I saw him he was in a comatose state, and it was impossible to rouse him. We poured some whisky down his throat, but it was thrown up again immediately: a couple of hours later he was dead.

That same night we buried him under one of the dwarf cotton-wood trees near the bank of the creek, and there he probably sleeps quietly enough till this day. Our grief was not deep; none of us knew him well; he was not companionable; he simply disappeared—swept out of sight, like wreckage on a stream.

* * * * *

I shall never forget my comrades: especially Wild Bill, Bent and Charlie—all dead already a long time ago, heroes of a tragic Odyssey.

When I went down on the trail the first time, Wild Bill (Hickok was his real surname) attracted my interest immediately. He was very good looking; about 6 feet in height with broad shoulders in spite of his light waist; the features of his face excellent, long straight nose; heavy mustache, dark and long and fine eyes, now gray, now blue—an extremely good-looking man. He had been made City Marshal of one of the new towns springing up, Wichita or Fort Dodge (I forget the precise place). Within a week of his election he had been called to a saloon where there was a row, and had settled it by shooting three of the most quarrelsome. Coming out of the saloon, Bill met a man who made an incautious gesture; quick as a flash he drew and shot—a popular railway boss. Peace—never much esteemed by cowboys and railway hands—seemed dear at the price: a vigilance committee was formed, and next morning two hundred armed men surrounded the Marshal's house to drive him out of the country or kill him. Suddenly the door opened and Bill appeared on the porch, a revolver in each hand.

"What do you 'uns want?'"

"Get out! Who killed old Bourbon? Git."

The voices were hardly raised; but there was deadly menace in the quiet tones.

"I want my salary before I go."

"You'll get no salary," said one man in front, meditatively. "I'd go quick if I were you; 'taint healthy for you here."

"That's so; that's so"—a score of voices.

"All right," replied Hickok, quietly, "all right. I s'pose I kin git somethin' to eat first"; and he moved to the door and entered the house.

He had not been fired at partly because it would have been awkward for the first man who raised his hand, and partly because his careless hardihood pleased the crowd. The boys dispersed, but Hickok had to find work some distance away, his methods were too brusque to be popular. And so he took a turn with us on the trail as a cowboy at sixty dollars a month and grub.

It was understood that he would only go with us as far as San Anton, where he was said to have friends. He was not a real cowboy, but a friend of Reece.

Wild Bill was such a peculiar product of the border that he deserves a careful study. He deserves study, too, for the same reason that a mountain tells you more of a country than a piece of plain. He was a freak if you will, but a freak only possible in Western America after the great Civil War. On getting to know him well through months of intimacy, it became clear to me that he was a product of the war—a characteristic product of a desperate struggle.

With the curiosity of a boy in a strange country, who in spite of himself was impressed by the sort of unwilling respect which every one showed to Bill Hickok, I attached myself to him and plied him with questions. If ever a man was unwilling to talk about himself, incapable of any conscious self-painting, inarticulate in a peculiar degree, it was this man. Shaw's fighters, and Conan Doyle's, and, of course, Shakespeare's have all the glib tongue of trained talkers; but the real fighting men are sometimes wholly inarticulate. Again and again I tried to get out of Hickok how he became so great a revolver shot, the deadest shot in all the Winning of the West. At one time I found out that he always had "a sort of liking for it"; at another, that he practised a great deal as a boy: and again that his father was a "mighty good shot," that "everybody round us thought a lot of it." Mere hints for the picture, but the picture came one day when I chanced to ask him to tell me about his first row, the first time he killed a man. For some reason or other his guard of secretiveness seemed to break down before this direct assault, or perhaps what I took for secretiveness was merely constitutional silence or reticence bred of slow speech. The reader must judge, but in any case, this is what I gathered bit by bit from him.

Bill Hickok had been brought up in Missouri, near Pleasant Hill. Just before the war he was a boy of eighteen or nineteen, his father was a Yankee and Abolitionist, and they lived in the very hottest center of a slave State when feeling ran at its highest. The father seems to have been a sort of John Brown, with perhaps less piety but more pugnacity, who spoke his mind against slavery in season and out of season, and was willing at any time to put his life on the block. "Why the old man didn't get killed," Wild Bill said, "I don't know: he was always shootin' off his mouth even when he hadn't no need to."

"Didn't he bring you up strictly," I asked, and seeing that he did not understand, I added, "religiously?"

"I should smile," Bill answered. "He was always taking me to the old Methodist Chapel, and he used to pray so loud I was clean ashamed of him. The only thing he ever showed me was how to swing an ax and use a revolver. I could shoot better than the old man from the start," he added.

"But how did you get into your first row?" I asked.

"Well," he said, "it was just before the war and I was kind o' sore. None of the boys about that I used to go to school with would speak to me. They used to shout 'Abolitionist!' after me. So I got mad, and when the girls tossed their heads too and wouldn't look at me, I sort of took it that I *would* be an Abolitionist, though I didn't care nuthin' about the slaves; I always thought niggers should be made to work for white folks anyway. But being forced into defendin' them I did a good job of it and soon the country proved mighty unpleasant for me, so I got out of town. I found work in Pleasant Hill and as I never talked much I got on pretty well. But they were red hot Southerners, all of them, and I was kind o' marked as a black Abolitionist on account of my father. They even tried to tar and feather the old man one night, but some of them got hurt. He got shot twice, but he was very tough—sort of wiry—and he warn't in bed more'n a week."

Again I came back to the subject. "But how about your first row?" I asked, and after numberless attempts I got him to confess it.

It seems as a sort of outcast, Bill had taken to gambling at Pleasant Hill, and used perpetually to haunt a gambling saloon. He felt he was not wanted and was not liked, but sometimes in the heat of the game the ill-feeling used tbe forgotten, just as at other times it became more pronounced.

The spice of danger tempted the reckless spirit of the youth. "Sometimes I was rich and could enjoy myself," he explained, "and that was great as I hadn't had much fun in my life. Sometimes I lost all and it was hell. But even then I was better off than on the farm. I always did like cussin' better than preachin', and a handout at cards seemed to me then better than preachin' any day.

"I had got a gold watch that I froze on to. I had won it fair and square, but one night I had no money and I asked Ned Tomlin, the son of the banker (I knew him at school) to lend me fifty dollars on the watch: I wanted to play. He didn't seem to want to; was mighty cool in fact: told me I didn't ought to play there anyway. I said nuthin', but I laid it up for him, and at last he gave me the money. I soon lost it all; one always does lose borrowed money, and I have noticed one generally loses when one wants most to win—a sort of contrary spirit in the damned pips. About that time there was a great fuss about Abe Lincoln's election, and all slave-owners got spoutin' round and raisin' hell. I got a letter tellin' me I had better get out: Pleasant Hill warn't no place for Abolitionists. I paid no attention. Then I got a letter from Tomlin tellin' me I had better pay back the fifty dollars and take my watch: he had no use for it. I just paid no attention.

"One night I was up in the gamblin' saloon and they began talkin' about watches, and one of'em up and said Ned Tomlin was going to carry my watch across the square at Pleasant Hill and auction it off as an Abolitionist's watch who did not pay his debts. I saw it was up to me, so I asked when Tomlin was goin' to do this. It was a Wednesday I remember, and they said, 'Saturday at twelve o'clock, when all the farmers would be in town.' That made me mad, and I just up and said, 'If dead men can carry watches across a public square, Tomlin may carry my watch,' an' I went off to bed.

"On the Saturday morning I got my horse and hitched it up fifty yards down Fremont Street, so as to give me a chance if the crowd did turn on me, as I sort of expected they might. I knew in any case I would have to leave Pleasant Hill: I had felt for sometime it was getting rather warm. On the mornin' I went into the square, and sure enough about twelve o'clock Tomlin left the Planter's House and came down with a hull crowd about him; he had a revolver in his right hand, my watch in his left, and I went out to meet him. I was willin' to give him a chance, so when we got pretty near together I called out pleasant-like:

"'I guess you have got my watch, Ned, and I want it.' He said: 'I want my fifty dollars. I never did see an Abolitionist that would pay what he owed,' and he kind o' lifted his hand. I drew at once and fired, and as he dropped it came to me that I would have my watch, so I ran in and grabbed it and crowded it in my pocket and turned to go; but they just leapt me. I must have shot the first one, because he let go, and then I started to run as hard as I could lick for Fremont Street, where my broncho was hitched. As I went, everybody seemed to run and have a shot at me; they must have been excited, for none of 'em hit me till I got to the pony and loosed him and threw myself into the saddle; then I got it in the shoulder—bored me right through. And as I went down the street lickety split I got it again in the left leg—poor shootin' eh?"

"But did Tomlin shoot at you?" I asked.

"I guess so," was the reply.

"Why didn't he hit you?"

"The fellow who gits there fust is generally safe," was the answer.

"And afterwards," I asked, "what did you do?"

"I went off to St. Louis, and from there I wrote to my father, and I got the first letter from the old man I ever read. He told me I had witnessed for the faith, and he was proud of me, and he had put a mortgage on the farm because he saw he would not need it long, and he sent me the five hundred dollars he had raised. I had a good time in St. Louis on it and won nearly five thousand. While I was playin' round, the war broke out, and then I heard my father had been killed—they got him at last. I joined the Northern Army and was made a scout. That is how it began: that's all there's to it . . ."

Every one spoke of Wild Bill as being a dead shot, but I had no idea how good he was till on the trail.

We had all been skylarking, and some one proposed to shoot for money. A piece of paper was plastered up on one of the fence posts, perhaps four inches wide by five long. We stood about 40 yards away from the post and paid a dollar for a shot; whoever hit the paper got five dollars; but there were a great many more misses than hits.

Suddenly some one proposed to ride past the paper and see if he could hit it from the galloping horse. We had missed twenty times, every one had missed, when I suddenly saw Wild Bill passing on his horse. I ran over to him and asked him if he would try. None of us had been able to ride past and hit the mark.

"How often do you want hits?" asked Bill.

"Three or four times, if it would be possible," was my answer, "please do it."

He smiled, rode away a few yards and then turned round and came at full speed past the post, perhaps thirty yards away. As he came he whipped out two revolvers and fired right and left, two shots from each and then went on and disappeared. When we got to the paper we found four bullets in it; they could be covered by the palm of one's hand. Such markmanship put an end to the game. We all realized that such skill was beyond our hoping. He was the surest shot, as the kids say, since a horse-pistol was raised from a Colt.

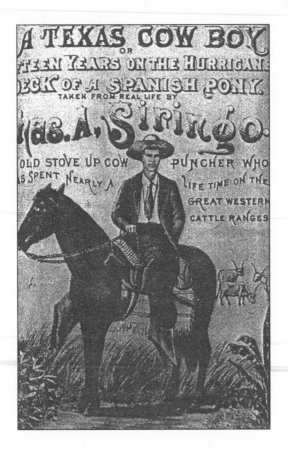

A TRIP TO CHICAGO AS COW-PUNCHER.
MY FIRST ACQUAINTANCE WITH OUTLAW "BILLY THE KID"

CHARLES A. SIRINGO

Towards spring mr. Moore put a cowboy in my place, to camp with Roberson, and I was sent out with a scouting outfit to drift over the South

Staked Plains in search of stray cattle. Our outfit consisted of a cook, Owl-head Johnson, and three riders, Jack Ryan, Van Duzen and myself. After starting on this trip we experienced a touch of hardship. Camp was pitched after dark one evening on the edge of a "dry" lake, or basin. Enough buffalo-chips were gathered to cook supper.

After retiring under our tarpaulins, spread over the beds on the ground, a severe snowstorm sprang up. By daylight our beds were covered with a foot of snow.

Crawling out of these warm beds into the deep snow made it anything but pleasant. We had no buffalo-chips to build a fire—hence had to cut up the bed of the mess-wagon.

There we were afoot on these snowy plains, as the pony staked out the evening before had pulled up the stake-pin and drifted south with the hobbled ponies. They were not found until late that evening, about ten miles from camp.

It was on this trip that I saw the piles of bones from thousands of ponies killed by orders from General McKinzie. They were at the head of Tule Canyon, which empties into Canyon Paliduro.

It was here that General McKinzie and his United States soldiers rounded up the 7,000 Comanche Indians, in 1874, when they broke away from Ft. Sill, Indian Territory, on the war-path—killing hundreds of white men.

The Indian ponies were shot and killed to prevent another break on horseback, the reds being made to walk back to Ft. Sill.

One forenoon 3,000 Comanche Indians gave us a "scaring up," as we didn't know whether they were on the war-path or not. On Mulberry Creek they came pouring down the hills from the eastward, on a gallop. We were completely surrounded.

The chief made inquiry about buffalos to the westward. They were from Ft. Sill, Indian Territory, on a big buffalo hunt. The chief showed us a letter from the commanding officer at Ft. Sill stating that they were peaceable, and friendly toward the white men.

Before reaching Ft. Elliot we ran into thousands of Cheyenne and Pawnee Indians on hunting trips.

After an absence of several weeks we arrived back at the LX ranch with a small bunch of steers.

About the last of March all the cowboys were called in from the outside line-camps to prepare for the spring round-up.

Mr. Moore hired every renegade outlaw and cowboy passing through the country for this big spring round-up.

One evening before bed-time the sky became red from a big prairie fire off to the south-eastward.

The fire was being driven by a strong south-east wind, down into the Canadian River Breaks, from the Staked Plains.

Now the headquarter ranch became a busy place. Saddle ponies were rounded up and a start made for the big fire, by the dozens of cowboys.

In a swift gallop Moore led the crowd in the pitchy darkness, over all kinds of rough places.

A ride of about fifteen miles brought us to the fire. Then we became fire-fighters in dead earnest.

Large droves of cattle were running ahead of the fire. Some of these largest animals were shot and killed.

Then the carcasses were split open. Now two cowboys would fasten their ropes to each hind leg of the dead animal, and by the saddle-horn drag it to the blaze.

If the fire was down in an arroya, where the blue-stem grass grows tall, it was allowed to burn its way onto a level flat covered with short buffalo grass. Here the two cowboys dragging a carcass would straddle the blaze—the one on the burnt side close up, with his rope shortened, while the other, on the hot smoky side, would be at the extreme end of his rope.

Now the wet carcass was dragged slowly along the blaze. This would put out the fire, all but small spots. These being whipped out by cowboys following afoot with wet saddle blankets, or pieces of fresh cow-hide.

A few miles of dragging in a hot blaze would wear a carcass into a frazzle. Then another animal was killed to take its place.

Without a bite to eat, except broiled beef without salt, this strenuous work was kept up until about three o'clock the following evening, when the fire was under control, and our range saved.

We arrived back at the ranch about sun-down—a smoky, dirty, tired and hungry crowd.

Soon after this fire excitement Mr. Moore lost nearly half of his crew of cowboys. They "hit the trail for tall timber," in New Mexico and Arizona—some on stolen ponies.

The cause of this cowboy outlaw stampede was the arrival of E. W. Parker—now a respected citizen of El Paso, Texas—and his large, well armed crew of Government Star-route mail surveyors. But they kept their mission a secret, hence the boys had them spotted as Texas Rangers in disguise.

A few months later the first mail route in the Panhandle of Texas was established. It ran from Ft. Elliot, Texas, to Las Vegas, New Mexico, a distance of about three hundred miles. Our home ranch was made Wheeler post-office.

Previous to this all our mail came from Ft. Bascom, New Mexico, two hundred and twenty-five miles west, on the upper Canadian River. It came by private conveyance, and each letter sent, or received, cost us twenty-five cents—news-papers the same.

By the middle of April our range was crowded with buffalo again. They were migrating north. But there was no great herd like the one going south in the early winter.

Not over half of the wooly beasts which went south ever returned. They had been slaughtered for their hides, worth one dollar each, at the south edge of the Llano Estacado. It was estimated that, during the winter, there were 7,000 buffalo hunters along the Texas Pacific Railway—then building west to El Paso.

Now these buffalo were going north through Kansas and Nebraska to their summer feeding ground in Dakota, to be killed by the northern hunters.

The following fall only a few scattering herds passed through the Canadian River Breaks, on their way south. Most of these met their doom that winter by the southern hunters. Thus were the millions of buffalo wiped from the face of the earth in a few years.

About the middle of April Moore took all his cowboys, about twenty-five with two well filled mess-wagons, and went to Tascosa, there to meet other outfits from different parts of the country. Many of these cattle outfits came from the Arkansas River in southeastern Colorado, and south-western Kansas.

When we pulled out of Tascosa for the upper Canadian River, there were dozens of mess-wagons, and hundreds of riders.

This gereral round-up, the first ever pulled off in the Texas Panhandle, started work near Ft. Bascom, New Mexico, and continued down the river almost to the Indian Territory line.

During the winter thousands of northern cattle had drifted south and lodged in the Canadian River Breaks. These were all driven north after the general round-up.

While these round-up crews were at Tascosa, that little burg saw the need of saloons and dance-halls to relieve the wild and wooly cowboy of his loose change. For the supply of liquors, sardines and crackers in Howard & Reinhart's store melted away like a snow-ball would if dropped into Hades.

In June, after the spring round-ups, our cattle were all shoved onto the summer range, on Blue Creek, north of the river.

I and another cowboy were placed at the extreme head of the Blue, to ride line. Our camp was pitched at a spring.

Every morning and evening I had to ride past a plum-thicket, which was a few miles west of our camp, at the edge of which lay the bodies of three murdered Mexican buffalo hunters. They were badly swollen, and the sight of them made me nervous.

Strange to relate these corpses were never devoured by the many lobos and coyotes around them. This fact convinces me that there is truth in the theory that wolves won't eat a dead Mexican—possibly on account of his system being impregnated with chilli, (red peppers).

A short time previous, these three men were murdered by Nelson and three companions, in order to get their ox-teams to haul buffalo hides to Dodge City, Kansas.

These murderers were never arrested, as there was no law in the country—and not a law-officer nearer than Ft. Elliot.

While camped at the head of the Blue, several herds of "Jingle-bob" cattle passed near our camp.

These thousands of cattle had belonged to cattle king John Chisum, of the Pecos River, in New Mexico, until Colonel Hunter, of the firm of Hunter and Evans in southern Kansas, had played a "Dirty Irish" trick on him.

In the early '70s John Chisum had bought thousands of she cattle from the old battle-scarred Confederate soldiers in middle Texas, giving his notes as pay.

These cattle were driven across the Staked Plains to the Horse-head crossing of the Pecos river—thence up the river over two hundred miles into New Mexico, where they were turned loose.

Then Mr. Chisum introduced fine-blooded shorthorn bulls to breed out the long horns on these Texas cattle.

The notes given by Chisum for these cattle were finally outlawed, as they couldn't be collected in New Mexico.

In the winter of 1877 and '78 Col. Hunter and his flowing grey beard hiked from Medicine Lodge, Kansas, to middle Texas and bought up these outlawed notes for five and ten cents on the dollar.

These notes were tucked into a satchel, and in the early spring of '78 taken to Las Vegas, New Mexico, and placed in a bank.

Now Col. Hunter went overland down the Pecos to South Spring River, where Mr. Chisum had established his "Jingle-bob" headquarter ranch.

There a deal was made for about 20,000 head of his picked cattle, at a fancy price.

Now Jesse Evans, Col. Hunter's partner, went to Dodge City, Kansas, and hired fifty fighting cowboys to go to New Mexico after these cattle.

As soon as the Chisum outfit got a herd "put up" they were turned over to the Hunter and Evans cowboys.

When the last herd was gathered, and headed north-eastward, for the line of Texas, Col. Hunter and John Chisum went overland to Las Vegas to settle up.

Among cattle-men Col. Hunter's word was as good as his bond, hence Mr. Chisum had no fear about getting his pay.

The curtain of this "dirty Irish" play goes down when, in the bank, the old satchel was opened and Mr. Chisum was paid for the cattle in his own notes, with the years of accumulated interest.

As fast as a team could travel, John Chisum went back to his ranch. Then he tried to make up a fighting crowd to follow up these Hunter and Evans herds, and recover them. He offered "Billy the Kid" and his warriors big inducements to do the job, but they knew the Hunter and Evans cowboys were armed to the teeth, and being already over the line in Texas, they declined.

In the middle of June Mr. Moore sent for me to take charge of a herd of steers containing 2500 head. I was told to take them out onto the south Staken Plains and fatten them. My crew consisted of four riders, and a cook to drive the mess-wagon, with five ponies to the man.

Soon after this three more herds of steers were sent to the South Plains and I was put in charge of the four herds. This made me feel of some importance. I had nothing to do but ride from one camp to the other—sometimes twenty miles apart—to see that the steers were kept on fresh range so as to put on fat by the time cold weather set in.

The summer of 1878 was a wet one—hence the "dry" lakes, or basins, were full of rain water.

During the summer Mr. David T. Beals paid me a visit. He brought a young man, Burkley Howe, from Massachusetts, and turned him over to me to be taught the cow-business.

The first lesson I dished out to Burkley Howe was on mustang meat.

I shot and killed a young mustang from a band of 300 head. Then a young buffalo was killed. Some of the meat from each animal was taken to camp. I instructed the cook to prepare each kind the same, but to have it in separate vessels.

When we squatted down on the grass to eat our supper, the cook pointed out the vessel containing the mustang meat, which in reality was the buffalo meat. Of course the other boys had been posted.

Burkley Howe could not be induced to even taste the horse meat. Instead he filled up on the supposed buffalo beef, which he declared was the finest he had ever eaten. When told of the trick, after supper, he was mad all over, and tried to vomit. This goes to show that the mind controls the taste.

About the first of October 800 fat steers were cut out of my four herds and started for Dodge City, Kansas.

The balance of the steers being turned loose on the winter range, along the Canadian river.

Now I secured permission from Mr. Moore to overtake the fat steer herd and accompany them to Chicago.

Mounted on my own pony, Whiskey-Pete, I started in company with a cowboy named John Farris. We kept on the Bascom trail.

After crossing the Cimarron river we saw a band of about two hundred Indians, off to our left, in a deep arroyo, traveling westward, single file. Being hungry we concluded to gallop over to them and get something to eat.

On seeing us coming they all bunched up and showed great excitement. This didn't look good to Ferris and me, so we galloped back to the Bascom trail and continued north.

About sundown we reached Mead City, a new town started a few months previous. Here there were a half dozen new frame buildings, their insides being turned "topsy turvy," showing that the Indians had run the occupants off and ransacked the dwellings. There were Indian moccasin tracks everywhere.

Now we hurried on to the store, on Crooked Creek, arrived there after dark. Here we found the same conditions as at Mead City, showing that the Indians had looted the store. Hearing some ox-bells down the creek we rode to them, about a mile distant. Here we found several yoke of oxen and a log cabin, the door of which was locked.

Being hungry the lock on the door was broken, and we entered. A playful puppy inside gave us a hearty welcome.

After the lamps were lighted we found sacks of grain for our tired ponies, and a cupboard full of nice food.

Hanging over the still warm ashes in the fire-place was a pot of fresh beef stew. This proved a treat, and we filled up to the bursting point.

About midnight we started on the last lap of our 225 mile journey.

A twenty-five mile ride brought us to the toughest town on earth, Dodge City.

It was now daylight, and the first man met on the main street was Cape Willingham, who at this writing is a prosperous cattle broker in El Paso, Texas.

Cape gave us our first news of the great Indian outbreak. He told of the many murders committed by the reds south of Dodge City the day previous—one man being killed at Mead City, and another near the Crooked Creek store.

Riding up the main street Ferris and I saw twenty-five mounted cowboys, holding rifles in their hands, and facing one of the half dozen saloons, adjoining each other, on that side of the street.

In passing this armed crowd one of them recognized me. Calling me by name he said: "Fall in line quick, h—l is going to pop in a few minutes".

We jerked our Winchester rifles from the scabbards and fell in line, like most any other fool cowboys would have done.

In a moment Clay Allison, the man-killer, came out of one of the saloons holding a pistol in his hand. With him was Mr. McNulty, owner of the large Panhandle "Turkey-track" cattle outfit.

Clay, who was about half drunk, remarked to the boys in line that none of the S——b's were in that saloon."

Then a search was made in the next saloon. He was hunting for some of the town policemen, or the city marshall, so as to wipe them off the face of the earth. His twenty-five cowboy friends had promised to help him clean up Dodge City.

After all the saloons had been searched Mr. McNulty succeeded in getting Clay to bed at the Bob Wright Hotel. Then we all dispersed.

Soon after, the city law-officers began to crawl out of their hiding places, and appear on the streets.

Clay Allison had sworn to kill the first officer found—and no doubt he would have done so.

I found Mr. Erskine Clement, a partner of Mr. Beals, at the Wright Hotel, greatly worried over the non-arrival of the steer herd, which Mr. Moore had written him had started two weeks previous. He was surprised when told that I had seen no sign of them having come over the Bascom trail.

Telegrams kept pouring in from the west, of the bloody deeds committed by the Indians, on their way to Dakota. They were Northern Cheyennes, who had broken away from the Cheyenne Agency in the Indian Territory.

That evening at the Wright Hotel I heard a captain from Ft. Dodge, five miles east of Dodge City, say that he would round up this tribe of reds or leave his dead body on the ground. He and his company of soldiers were waiting for a west bound train. A week later he was killed in a battle which took place.

In passing through western Nebraska these Indians murdered many settlers. At one ranch-house they captured a widow woman and her two daughters. After a days march they turned the mother loose on the prairie, stark naked, keeping her two daughters with them.

After much hardship this woman found the cabin of a "fool hoe-man," who was living alone. He wrapped the robe of Charity and his overcoat around her, and took her to civilization.

About midnight my chum, John Ferris, was flat broke, and borrowed twenty-five dollars of my accumulated wages, amounting to over $300. He had in this short time "blowed in" his $114.00. By morning he had borrowed $50.00 from the livery man on his pony and saddle, and I had to get these out of "soak" for him, before he could hit the road again.

He went direct to Ft. Sumner, New Mexico, where he was shot and killed by Barney Mason, one of "Billy the Kid's" gang, and a brother-in-law of the fearless New Mexico sheriff, Pat Garrett.

The next morning after my arrival in Dodge City, Erskine Clement and I struck south to look up the lost herd of steers.

We found the outfit traveling up Crooked Creek very slowly. They had quit the Bascom trail to avoid long drives between watering places. This, no doubt, had saved them from running into the Indians.

In Dodge City the herd was split in two, 400 head being put aboard of a train for Chicago. I went in charge of this first shipment, and Mr. Clement followed with the next.

Two of the cowboys went with me, one of them being A. M. Melvin, who now, after forty years, lives with a happy family at No. 11, Blackinton Street, Orient Heights, East Boston, Mass.

Now for the first time in my life I became a cow-puncher, carrying a lantern and a long pole with a spike in the end, to keep the steers punched up, when they got down in the crowded cars.

In a few years the name, Cow-puncher, became attached to all cowboys.

At Burlington, Iowa, we crossed the Mississippi River into Illinois, and there on the east bank of the great river unloaded to feed the steers.

During our two days stay we three cow-punchers made a dozen or more trips on the ferry boat to Burlington, a swift city. Our trips were free, and everything in the way of liquor, cigars, meals, candy, etc. bought in Burlington were free.

The fact of us wearing our cowboy outfits, including chaparejos, pistol and spurs may have had something to do with the people refusing to take money from us. But is was said that their object was to encourage cattle-men to ship by way of Burlington.

On the first night after leaving Burlington I came within an ace of being ground to death by the train. The thoughts of my narrow escape cause my flesh to creep, even to this day.

A sleet storm was raging. The train stopped to take on coal. We three cow punchers left the caboose and ran up towards the engine, peeping through the cracks to see if any of the steers were down.

About the time we reached the engine the train started. Then we climbed onto the first car and started back to the caboose, on the run. I was in the rear. In making a spring from the top of one car to the other—the space between being about two feet—my high-heel boots slipped on the icy boards. There I lay flat on my back with my head and shoulders over the open space. I had grabbed the edge of the footplank with my right hand. This is all that saved me from sliding down between the cars.

Mr. Beals met us on our arrival in Chicago. After unloading at the stock yards he took me to dine with him at the Palmer House. He wanted me to take a room in his hotel, but I told him that the food and price, five to ten dollars a day, were too rich for my blood. Therefore I went to the Irvine House where the price was only $2.00 a day.

That night I turned myself loose in the toughest part of the city, spending all the money I had, about $200.00.

Towards daylight I managed to find my way back to the Irvine House, where a nap was taken.

About ten a. m. I struck out for the Palmer House to borrow some money from Mr. Beals. On the way there, while gazing up at the signs, I saw the name of Dr. Bruer, Dentist. This put me in mind of the teeth which needed filling, so up the stairs I went, not realizing that my pockets were empty of cash.

In the dentist office I found Mr. Bruer and his handsome young lady assistant.

After seating myself in the dentist chair, the doctor asked me what kind of filling I wanted for the two teeth. I told him to fill them with gold.

In those days the filling had to be done by hand. The doctor used the punch and the young lady the mallet. They didn't stop for lunch. It was three p. m. when the job was finished.

Now I got down off the chair, and for the first time realized that I didn't have a cent to pay for the work.

I asked the amount of my bill, and was told that it was $45.00. I told the doctor that I would drop around in the morning and pay him. He turned pale, and so did his assistant. The large pistol and bowie-knife buckled around my waist may have caused them to turn pale.

Finally the doctor asked the name of my hotel. I told him. Then he said: "Now you wont forget to come up in the morning and pay me?" I answered him that he could depend upon it.

I found Mr. David T. Beals at the Palmer House and borrowed $100.00. Then I started out to see more of the sights of a great city. But I took the precaution to tuck the dentist's $45.00 down in the watch pocket of my pants, so that it wouldn't be spent.

The next morning at nine o'clock I was in the dentist's office and paid over the $45.00. The doctor and his assistant were happily surprised.

The doctor had me go to lunch with him. Then we spent the afternoon driving over the city in his buggy, drawn by a fine pair of black horses.

We visited the water-works and climbed up to the top of the tall, round tower, from the inside. On reaching the top I looked over the edge, to the ground below, just once. That was enough. I was afraid the thing would topple over from my weight. The dentist laughed at me, but he couldn't induce me to look over the edge again.

After the drive was over I hunted up Mr. Beals to get more money for the night's sight-seeing.

I can look back now and see that I was an "easy mark" for the city people. Of course they knew at a glance by my bowlegs and high-heel boots where I was from, and they charged be accordingly, for what was purchased.

After a few days sight-seeing I boarded a train for Dodge City, Kansas. Mr. Beals and Erskine Clement accompanied me.

Shortly after leaving Chicago I became very angry towards my employer, for not giving a poor blind beggar some loose change.

This old blind man had passed through our car leaving each passenger a slip of poetry, to be returned if a donation was not given.

When the old man returned through the car gathering up his little sheets of poetry, I waited to se how much money Millionaire Beals would give him. Not a cent did he give. This caused me to boil over with rage, although nothing was said. Reaching my hand in my pants pocket all the loose change therein was grabbed and handed to the poor blind beggar. It amounted to two or three dollars.

After the blind man had passed on, Mr. Beals said: "You are foolish Charlie to throw your money away. That old cuss is rich. "You ask the conductor when he comes through about him." I did so, and the conductor told me that this blind beggar lived in one of the swell residences of Chicago, and was considered wealthy. This caused my anger to flop from Mr. Beals to my own fool self.

On our way west Mr. Beals "harked back" to his early life, telling me of how he struggled at a shoe-makers bench, in Massachusetts, to accumulate his first $500.00.

With this sum in his pocket he drifted to Dead-wood, Dakota.

In a mining camp, across a range of mountains from Deadwood, he opened a boot and shoe store, ordering his stock of goods on credit, from his home town in the east.

After one year in business, his profits footed up $60.00. The next year it amounted to $60,000, partly in gold dust. He then sold out the business and walked with two hired men, carrying the gold dust, to Salt Lake City, Utah, there taking a stagecoach for Denver, Colorado, where he located, building the first iron-front store building ever put up in Denver.

Arriving in Dodge City, Whiskey-Pete was mounted early one morning for my 225 mile lonely ride to the LX ranch.

I arrived at the headquarter ranch late in the evening.

A crowd of strangers were playing cards under a cottonwood tree near by. The cook informed me that they were "Billy the Kid" and his Lincoln County, New Mexico, warriors.

When the cook rang the supper bell these strangers ran for the long table. After being introduced, I found myself seated by the side of good-natured "Billy the Kid". Henry Brown, Fred Waite and Tom O'Phalliard are the only names of this outlaw gang that I can recall.

When supper was over I produced a box of fine Havana cigars, brought from Chicago as a treat for the boys on the ranch. They were passed around.

Then one was stuck into my new $10 meerschaum cigar holder, and I began to puff smoke towards the ceiling.

Now "Billy the Kid" asked for a trial of my cigar-holder. This was granted. He liked it so well that he begged me to present it to him, which I did. In return he presented me with a finely bound novel which he had just finished reading. In it he wrote his autograph, giving the date that it was presented to me.

During the next few weeks "Billy the Kid" and I became quite chummy.

After selling out the band of ponies, which he and his gang had stolen from the Seven River warriors, in New Mexico, he left the Canadian river country, and I never saw him again.

Two of his gang, Henry Brown, and Fred Waite—a half-breed Chicasaw Indian—quit the outfit and headed for the Indian Territory.

During his long stay around the LX ranch, and Tascosa, "Billy the Kid" made one portly old capitalist from Boston, Mass., sweat blood for a few minutes.

Mr. Torey owned a large cattle ranch above Tascosa. On arriving from the east he learned that "Billy the Kid" and gang had made themselves at home on his ranch, for a few days—hence he gave the foreman orders not to feed them, if they should make another visit. This order reached the "Kid's" ears.

While in Tascosa "Billy the Kid" saw old man Torey ride up to the hitching rack in front of Jack Ryan's saloon. He went out to meet him, and asked if he had ordered his foreman not to feed them.

Mr. Torey replied, yes, that he didn't want to give his ranch a bad name by harboring outlaws.

Then the "Kid" jerked his Colts pistol and jabbed the old man several times in his portly stomach, at the same time telling him to say his prayers, as he was going to pump him full of lead.

With tears in his voice Mr. Torey promised to countermand the order. Then war was declared off.

Thus did Mr. Torey, a former sea captain, get his eye-teeth cut in the ways of the wild and wooly west.

This story was told to me by "Billy the Kid," and Steve Arnold, who was an eye witness to the affair. But the "Kid" said he had no intention of shooting Mr. Torey—that he just wanted to teach him a lesson.

THE KID

WALTER NOBLE BURNS

Billy the kid's legend in New Mexico seems destined to a mellow and genial immortality like that which gilds the misdeeds and exaggerates the virtues of such ancient rogues as Robin Hood, Claude Duval, Dick Turpin, and Fra Diavolo. From the tales you hear of him everywhere, you might be tempted to fancy him the best-loved hero in the state's history. His crimes are forgotten or condoned, while his loyalty, his gay courage, his superman adventures are treasured in affectionate memory. Men speak of him with admiration; women extol his gallantry and lament his fate. A rude balladry in Spanish and English has grown up about him, and in every *placeta* in New Mexico, Mexican girls sing to their guitars songs of Billy the Kid. A halo has been clapped upon his scapegrace brow. The boy who never grew old has become a sort of symbol of frontier knight-errantry, a figure of eternal youth riding for ever through a purple glamour of romance.

Gray-beard skald at boar's-head feast when the foaming goblets of mead went round the board in the gaunt hall of vikings never sang to his wild harp saga more thrilling than the story of Billy the Kid. A boy is its hero: a boy when the tale begin, a boy when it ends; a boy born to battle and vendetta, to hatred and murder, to tragic victory and tragic defeat, and who took it all with a smile.

Fate set a stage. Out of nowhere into the drama stepped this unknown boy. Opposite him played Death. It was a drama of Death and the Boy. Death dogged his trail relentlessly. It was for ever clutching at him with skeleton hands. It lay in ambush for him. It edged him to the gallows' stairs. By bullets, conflagration, stratagems, every lethal trick, it sought to compass his destruction. But the boy was not to be trapped. He escaped by apparent miracles; he was saved as if by necromancy. He laughed at Death. Death was a joke. He waved Death a jaunty good-bye and was off to new adventures. But again the inexorable circle closed. Now life seemed sweet. It beckoned to love and happiness. A golden vista opened before him. He set his foot upon the sunlit road. Perhaps for a moment the boy dreamed this drama was destined to a happy ending. But no. Fate prompted from the wings. The moment of climax was at hand. The boy had had his hour. It was Death's turn. And so the curtain.

Billy the Kid was the Southwest's most famous desperado and its last great outlaw. He died when he was twenty-one years old and was credited with having killed twenty-one men—a man for every year of his life. Few careers in pioneer annals have been more colourful; certain of his exploits rank among the classic adventures of the West. He lived at a transitional period of New Mexican history. His life closed the past; his death opened the present. His destructive and seemingly futile career served a constructive purpose: it drove home the lesson that New Mexico's prosperity could be built only upon a basis of stability and peace. After him came the great change for which he involuntarily had cleared the way. Law and order came in on the flash and smoke of the six-shooter that with one bullet put an end to the outlaw and to outlawry.

That a boy in a brief life-span of twenty-one years should have attained his sinister preëminence on a lawless and turbulent frontier would seem proof of a unique and extraordinary personality. He was born for his career. The mental and physical equipment that gave his genius for depopulation effectiveness and background and enabled him to survive in a tumultuous time of plots and murders was a birthright rather than an accomplishment. He had the desperado complex which, to endure for any appreciable time in his environment, combined necessarily a peculiarly intricate and enigmatic psychology with a dextrous trigger-finger.

Billy the Kid doubtless would fare badly under the microscope of psycho-analysis. Weighed in the delicate balance of psychiatry, he would be dropped, neatly labelled, into some category of split personality and abnormal psychosis. The desperado complex, of which he was an exemplar, may perhaps be defined as frozen egoism plus recklessness and minus mercy. It its less aggravated forms it is not uncommon. There are desperadoes of business, the pulpit, the drawing room. The business man who plots the ruin of his rival; the minister who consigns to eternal damnation all who disbelieve in his personal creed; the love pirate, who robs another woman of her husband; the speed-mad automobilist who disregards life and limb, are all desperado types. The lynching mob is a composite desperado. Among killers there are good and bad desperadoes; both equally deadly, one killing lawlessly and the other to uphold the law. Wild Bill won his reputation as an officer of the law, killing many men to establish peace. The good "bad man" had a definite place in the development of the West.

But in fairness to Billy the Kid he must be judged by the standards of his place and time. The part of New Mexico in which he passed his life was the most murderous spot in the West. The Lincoln County war, which was his background, was a culture-bed of many kinds and degrees of desperadoes. There were the embryo desperado whose record remained negligible because of lack of excuse or occasion for murder; the would-be desperado who loved melodrama and felt called upon, as an artist, to shed a few drops of blood to maintain the prestige of his melodrama; and the desperado of genuine spirit but mediocre craftsmanship whose climb toward the heights was halted abruptly by some other man an eighth of a second quicker on the trigger. All these men were as ruthless and desperate as Billy the Kid, but they lacked the afflatus that made him the finished master. They were journeymen mechanics laboriously carving notches on the handles of their guns. He was a genius painting his name in flaming colours with a six-shooter across the sky of the Southwest.

With his tragic record in mind, one might be pardoned for visualizing Billy the Kid as an inhuman monster revelling in blood. But this conception would do him injustice. He was a boy of bright, alert mind, generous, not unkindly, of quick sympathies. The steadfast loyalty of his friendships was proverbial. Among his friends he was scrupulously honest. Moroseness and sullenness were foreign to him. He was cheerful, hopeful, talkative, given to laughter. He was not addicted to swagger or braggadocio. He was quiet, unassuming, courteous. He was a great favourite with women, and in his attitude toward them he lived up to the best traditions of the frontier.

But hidden away somewhere among these pleasant human qualities was a hiatus in his character—a sub-zero vacuum—devoid of all human emotions. He was upon occasion the personification of merciless, remorseless deadliness. He placed no value on human life, least of all upon his own. He killed a man as nonchalantly as he smoked a cigarette. Murder did not appeal to Billy the Kid as tragedy; it was merely a physical process of pressing a trigger. If it seemed to him necessary to kill a man, he killed him and got the matter over with as neatly and with as little fuss as possible. In his murders, he observed no rules of etiquette and was bound by no punctilios of honour. As long as he killed a man he wanted to kill, it made no difference to him how he killed him. He fought fair and shot it out face to face if the occasion demanded but under other circumstances he did not scruple at assassination. He put a bullet through a man's heart as coolly as he perforated a tin can set upon a fence post. He had no remorse. No memories haunted him.

His courage was beyond question. It was a static courage that remained the same under all circumstances, a noon or at three o'clock in the morning. There are yellow spots in the stories of many of the West's most famous desperadoes. We are told that in certain desperate crises with the odds against them, they weakened and were no braver than they might have been when, for instance, the other man got the drop on them and they looked suddenly into the blackness of forty-four calibre death. But no tale has come down that Billy the Kid ever showed the "yellow streak." Every hour in his desperate life was the zero hour, and he was never afraid to die. "One chance in a million" was one of his favourite phrases, and more than once he took that chance with the debonair courage of a cavalier. Even those who hated him and the men who hunted him to his death admitted his absolute fearlessness.

But courage alone would not have stamped him as extraordinary in the Southwest where courage is a tradition. The quality that distinguished his courage from that of other brave men lay in a nerveless imperturbability. Nothing excited him. He had nerve but no nerves. He retained a cool, unruffled poise in the most thrilling crises. With death seemingly inevitable, his face remained calm; his steady hands gave no hint of quickened pulses; no unusual flash in his eyes—and eyes are accounted the Judas Iscariots of the soul—betrayed his emotions or his plans.

The secrets of Billy the Kid's greatness as a desperado—and by connoisseurs in such matters he was rated as an approach to the ideal desperado type—lay in a marvellous coordination between mind and body. He not only had the will but the skill to kill. Daring, coolness, and quick-thinking would not have served unless they had been combined with physical quickness and a marksmanship which enabled him to pink a man neatly between the eyes with a bullet at, say, thirty paces. He was not pitted against six-shooter amateurs but against experienced fighters adept themselves in the handling of weapons. The men he killed would have killed him if he had not been their master in a swifter deadliness. In times of danger, his mind was not only calm but singularly clear and nimble, watching like a hawk for an advantage and seizing it with incredible celerity. He was able to translate an impulse into action with the suave rapidity of a flash of light. While certain other men were a fair match for him in target practice, no man in the Southwest, it is said, could equal him in the lightning-like quickness with which he could draw a six-shooter from its holster and with the same movement fire with deadly accuracy. It may be remarked incidentally that shooting at a target is one thing and shooting at a man who happens to be blazing away at you is something entirely different; and Billy the Kid did both kinds of shooting equally well.

His appearance was not unprepossessing. He had youth, health, good nature, and a smile—a combination which usually results in a certain sort of good looks. His face was long and colourless except for the deep tan with which it had been tinted by sun, wind, and weather, and was of an asymmetry that was not unattractive. His hair was light brown, worn usually rather long and inclined to waviness. His eyes were gray, clear and steady. His upper front teeth were large and slightly prominent, and to an extent disfigured the expression of a well-formed mouth. His hands and feet were remarkably small. He was five feet eight inches tall, slender and well proportioned. He was unusually strong for his inches, having for a small man quite powerful arms and shoulders. He weighed, in condition, one hundred and forty pounds. When out on the range, he was as rough-looking as any other cowboy. In towns, among the quality-folk of the frontier, he dressed neatly and took not a little care in making himself personable. Many persons, especially women, thought him handsome. He was a great beau at fandangos and was considered a good dancer.

He had an air of easy, unstudied, devil-may-care insuociance which gave no hint of his dynamic energy. His movements were ordinarily deliberate and unhurried. But there was a certain element of calculation in everything he did. Like a billiardist who "plays position," he figured on what he might possibly have to do next. This foresightedness and forehandedness even in inconsequential matters provided him with a sort of subconscious mail armour. He was forearmed even when not forewarned; for ever on guard.

Like all the noted killers of the West, Billy the Kid was of the blond type. Wild Bill Hickok, Ben Thompson, King Fisher, Henry Plummer, Clay Allison, Wyatt Earp, Doc Holliday, Frank and Jesse James, the Youngers, the Daltons— the list of others is long—were all blond. There was not a pair of brown eyes among them. It was the gray and blue eye that flashed death in the days when the six-shooter ruled the frontier. This blondness of desperadoes is a curious fact, contrary to popular imagination and the traditions of art and the stage. The theatre immemorially has portrayed its unpleasant characters as black-haired and black-eyed. The popular mind associates swarthiness with villainy. Blue eyes and golden hair are, in the artistic cannon, a sort of heavenly hall mark. No artist has yet been so daring as to paint a winged cherub with raven tresses, and a search of the world's canvases would discover no brown-eyed angel. It may be remarked further, as a matter of incidental interest, that the West's bad men were never heavy, stolid, lowering brutes. Most of them were good-looking, some remarkably so. Wild Bill Hickok, beau ideal of desperadoes, was considered the handsomest man of his day on the frontier, and with his blue eyes and yellow hair falling on his shoulders, he moved through his life of tragedies with something of the beauty of a Greek god. So much for fact versus fancy. Cold deadliness in Western history seems to have run to frosty colouring in eyes, hair, and complexion.

Though it is possible that the record of twenty-one killings attributed to Billy the Kid is exaggerated, there is strong reason to believe it true. He was remarkably precocious in homicide; he is said to have killed his first man when he was only twelve years old. He is supposed to have killed about twelve men before he appeared in Lincoln County. This early phase of his life is vague. From the outbreak of the Lincoln County war, his career is easily traceable and clearly authentic.

It is impossible now to name twenty-one men that he killed, though, if Indians be included, it is not difficult to cast up the ghastly total. It may be that in his record were secret murders of which only he himself knew. There are rife in New Mexico many unauthenticated stories in which the names of his victims are not given. One tale credits him with having killed five Mexicans in camp near Seven Rivers. Another has it that a number of the twenty or more unmarked graves on the banks of the Pecos at the site of John Chisum's old Bosque Grande ranch contain the dust of men the Kid sent to their long sleep.

The Kid himself claimed to have killed twenty-one. He made this statement unequivocally a number of times to a number of men and he was never regarded as a braggart or a liar.

"I have killed twenty-one men and I want to make it twenty-three before I die," he said a little before his death to Pete Maxwell at Fort Sumner. "If I live long enough to kill Pat Garrett and Barney Mason, I'll be satisfied.

Sheriff Pat Garrett, who for several years was the Kid's close friend—and who killed him—placed the Kid's record at eleven. John W. Poe, who was with Garrett at the Kid's death, accepted the Kid's own statement. In a letter written to me shortly before his death in 1923, Poe said:

Billy the Kid had killed more men than any man I ever knew or heard of during my fifty years in the Southwest. I cannot name the twenty-one men he killed; nor can any man alive to-day. I doubt if there ever was a man who could name them all except the Kid himself. He was the only man who knew exactly. He said he had killed twenty-one and I believe him.

Poe, who succeeded Pat Garrett as sheriff of Lincoln County and was at the time of his death president of the Citizens National Bank of Roswell, was a veteran man-hunter and knew the criminal element of the Southwest as few men did. If Poe, with his first-hand knowledge of the Kid, had faith in the Kid's own statement, it would seem fair grounds for presumption that the statement is true.

So the matter stands. With most of the actors in the old drama now dead and gone, it is safe to say the tragic conundrum of how many men fell before Billy the Kid's six-shooters will never be definitely answered. Certainly the list was long. And it is worth remembering that the Kid was only a boy when he died and, however his record is itemized, each item is a grave.

To realize the bizarre quality of Billy the Kid's character try to fancy yourself in his place. Suppose, if you please, that under stress of circumstances you had killed several men. Assume that you felt justified in these homicides. Very well. Would an easy conscience bring you peace of mind? No. If you did not regret the killings, you would regret profoundly the necessity for them. The thought of blood on your soul would for ever haunt you. Your spirit would be shaken and shadowed by remorse.

But that would not be all. The relatives and friends of those you had killed would hate you. They would hound you everywhere with their hatred. They would dog your footsteps and lie in wait to take your life. They would watch with jungle eyes for an opportunity for revenge.

Nor would this fill the cup of your misery. You would have achieved the sinister reputation of a fighter and a killer. Men who had no cause of quarrel against you, to whom your killings had meant nothing, would look upon you as they might upon a dangerous beast, a menace to society, a being outside the pale of human sympathy and law. The pack would be ready at any time to fall upon you without mercy and tear you to pieces. You would approach every rock and tree with caution lest some hidden foe fire upon you. You would not dare sleep in the same bed twice. You would suspect every man of treachery. When you sat at meat, you would feel that Death sat across the table with hollow eyes fixed upon you. Any minute you might expect a bullet or the plunge of a knife driven by unutterable hatred. Fear would walk hand in hand with you and lie down with you at night. You could not smile; peace and happiness would be denied you; there would be no zest, no joy for you this side of the grave. In your despair, you would welcome death as an escape from the hopeless hell of your hunted, haunted life.

But Billy the Kid was not of the stuff of ordinary men. There must have been in him a remarkable capacity for forgetfulness; he might seem to have drunk every morning a nepenthe that drowned in oblivion all his yesterdays. For him there was no past. He lived in the present from minute to minute, yet he lived happily. He killed without emotion and he accepted the consequences of his killings without emotion. His murders were strong liquor that left no headache. Surrounded by enemies who would have killed him with joy, breathing an atmosphere of bitter hatred, in danger of violent death every moment, he went his way through life without remorse, unracked by nerves or memories, gay, light-hearted, fearless, always smiling.

If you would learn in what affectionate regard the people of New Mexico cherish the memory of Billy the Kid to-day, you have but to journey in leisurely fashion through the Billy the Kid country. Every one will have a story to tell you of his courage, generosity, loyalty, light-heartedness, engaging boyishness. More than likely you yourself will fall under the spell of these kindly tales and, before you are aware, find yourself warming with romantic sympathy to the idealized picture of heroic and adventurous youth.

Sit, for instance, on one of the benches under the shade trees in the old square at Santa Fé where the wagon caravans used to end their long journey across the plains. Here the rich and poor of this ancient capital of the land of mañana and sunshine come every day to while away an hour and smoke and talk politics. Mention Billy the Kid to some leisurely burgher. Instantly his face will light up; he will cease his tirade against graft and corruption in high places and go off into interminable anecdotes. Yes Billy the Kid lived here in Santa Fé when he was a boy. Many a time when he was an outlaw with a price on his head, he rode into town and danced all night at the dance hall over on Gallisteo Street. The house is still there; the pink adobe with the blue door and window shutters. Did the police attempt to arrest him? Not much. Those blue-coated fellows valued their hides. Why, that boy wasn't afraid of the devil. Say, once over at Anton Chico . . .

Or drop into some little adobe home in Puerta de Luna. Or in Santa Rosa. Or on the Hondo. Or anywhere between the Ratons and Seven Rivers. Perhaps the Mexican housewife will serve you with frijoles and tortillas and coffee with goat's milk. If you are wise in the ways of Mexicans, you will tear off a fragment of tortilla and, cupping it between your fingers, use it as a spoon to eat your frijoles that are red with chili pepper and swimming in soup rich with fat bacon grease. But between mouthfuls of these beans of the gods—and you will be ready to swear they are that, else you are no connoiseur in beans—don't forget to make some casual reference to Billy the Kid. Then watch the face of your hostess. At mention of the magic name, she will smile softly and dream-light will come into her eyes.

"Billee the Keed? Ah, you have hear of heem? He was one gran' boy, señor. All Mexican pepul his friend. You nevair hear a Mexican say one word against Billee the Keed. Everybody love that boy. He was so kind-hearted, so generous, so brave. And so 'andsome. *Nombre de Dios!* Every leetle señorita was crazy about heem. They all try to catch that Billee the Keed for their sweetheart. Ah, many a pretty *muchacha* cry her eyes out when he is keel; and when she count her beads at Mass, she add a prayer for good measure for his soul to rest in peace. Poor Billee the Keed! He was good boy—*muy valiente, muy caballero.*"

Or ask Frank Coe about him. You will find him a white-haired old man now on his fruit ranch in Ruidoso Cañon. He fought in the Lincoln County war by the Kid's side and as he tells his story you may sit in a rocking chair under the cottonwoods while the Ruidoso River sings its pleasant tune just back of the rambling, one-story adobe ranch house.

"Billy the Kid," says Coe, "lived with me for a while soon after he came to Lincoln County in the fall of 1877. Just a little before he went to work for Tunstall on the Feliz. No, he didn't work for me. Just lived with me. Riding the chuck line. Didn't have anywhere else special to stay just then. He did a lot of hunting that winter. Billy was a great hunter, and the hills hereabouts were full of wild turkey, deer, and cinnamon bear. Billy could hit a bear's eye so far away I could hardly see the bear.

"He was only eighteen years old, as nice-looking a young fellow as you'd care to meet, and certainly mighty pleasant company. Many a night he and I have sat up before a pine-knot fire swapping yarns. Yes, he had killed quite a few men even then, but it didn't seem to weigh on him. None at all. Ghosts, I reckon, never bothered Billy. He was about as cheerful a little hombre as I ever ran across. Not the grim, sullen kind; but full of talk, and it seemed to me he was laughing half his time.

"You never saw such shooting as that lad could do. Not a dead shot. I've heard about these dead shots but I never happened to meet one. Billy was the best shot with a six-shooter I ever saw, but he missed sometimes. Jesse Evans, who fought on the Murphy side, used to brag that he was as good a shot as the Kid, but I never thought so, and I knew Jesse and have seen him shoot. Jesse, by the way, used to say, too that he wasn't afraid of Billy the Kid. Which was just another one of his brags. He was scared to death of the Kid, and once when they met in Lincoln, Billy made him take water and made him like it. Billy used to do a whole lot of practice shooting around the ranch, and had the barn peppered full of holes. I have heard people say they have seen him empty his shooter at a hat tossed about twenty feet into the air and hit it six times before it struck the ground. I won't say he couldn't do it, but I never saw him do it. One of his favourite stunts was to shoot at snowbirds sitting on fence posts along the road as he rode by with his horse at a gallop. Sometimes he would kill a half-a-dozen birds one after the other; and then he would miss a few. His average was about one in three. And I'd say that was mighty good shooting.

"Billy had had a little schooling, and he could read and write as well as anybody else around here. I never saw him reading any books, but he was a great hand to read newspapers whenever he could get hold of any. He absorbed a lot of education from his newspaper reading. He didn't talk like a back-woodsman. I don't suppose he knew much about the rules of grammar, but he didn't make the common, glaring mistakes of ignorant people. His speech was that of an intelligent and fairly well-educated man. He had a clean mind; his conversation was never coarse or vulgar; and while most of the men with whom he associated swore like pirates, he rarely used an oath.

"He was a free-hearted, generous boy. He'd give a friend the shirt off his back. His money came easy when it came; but sometimes it didn't come. He was a gambler and, like all gamblers, his life was chicken one day and feathers the next, a pocketful of money to-day and broke to-morrow. Monte was his favourite game; he banked the game or bucked it, depending on his finances. He was as slick a dealer as ever threw a card, and as a player, he was shrewd, usually lucky, and bet 'em high—the limit on every turn. While he stayed with me, he broke a Mexican monte bank every little while down the cañon at San Patricio. If he happened to lose, he'd take it like a good gambler and, like as not, crack a joke and walk away whistling with his hands rammed in his empty pockets. Losing his money never made him mad. To tell the truth, I never saw Billy the Kid mad in my life, and I knew him several years.

"Think what you please, the Kid had a lot of principle. He was about as honest a fellow as I ever knew outside of some loose notions about rustling cattle. This was stealing, of course, but I don't believe it struck him exactly that way. It didn't seem to have any personal element in it. There were the cattle running loose on the plains without any owner in sight or sign of ownership, except the brands, seeming like part of the landscape. Billy, being in his fashion a sort of potentate ruling a large portion of the landscape with his six-shooter, felt, I suppose, like he had a sort of proprietary claim on those cattle, and it didn't seem to him like robbery—not exactly—to run them off and cash in on them at the nearest market. That's at least one way of figuring it out. But as for other lowdown kinds of theft like sticking up a lonely traveller on the highway, or burglarizing a house, or picking pockets, he was just as much above that sort of thing as you or me. I'd have trusted him with the last dollar I had in the world. One thing is certain, he never stole a cent in his life from a friend."

The history of Billy the Kid already has been clouded by legend. Less than fifty years after his death, it is not always easy to differentiate fact from myth. Historians have been afraid of him, as if this boy of six-shooter deadliness might fatally injure their reputations if they set themselves seriously to write of a career of such dime-novel luridness. As a consequence, history has neglected him. Fantastic details have been added as the tales have been told and retold. He is already in process of evolving into the hero of a Southwestern Niebelungenlied. Such a mass of stories has grown about him that it seems safe to predict that in spite of anything history can do to rescue the facts of his life, he is destined eventually to be transformed by popular legend into the Robin Hood of New Mexico—a heroic out-law endowed with every noble quality fighting the battle of the common people against the tyranny of wealth and power.

Innumerable stories in which Billy the Kid figures as a semimythical hero are to be picked up throughout New Mexico. They are told at every camp fire on the range; they enliven the winter evenings in every Mexican home. There is doubtless a grain of truth in every one, but the troubadour touch is upon them all. You will not find them in books, and their chief interest perhaps lies in the fact that they are examples of oral legend kept alive in memory and passed on by the story-tellers of one generation to the story-tellers of the next in Homeric succession. They are folklore in the making. As each narrative adds a bit of drama here an a picturesque detail there, one wonders what form these legends will assume as time goes by, and in what heroic proportions Billy the Kid will appear in fireside fairy tales a hundred years or so from now.

A RODEO AT LOS OJOS

FREDERIC REMINGTON

The sun beat down on the dry grass, and the punchers were squatting about in groups in front of the straggling log and *adobe* buildings which constituted the outlying ranch of Los Ojos.

Mr. Johnnie Bell, the *capitan* in charge, was walking about in his heavy *chaparras*, a slouch hat, and a white "biled" shirt. He was chewing his long yellow mustache, and gazing across the great plain of Bavicora with set and squinting eyes. He passed us and repassed us, still gazing out, and in his long Texas drawl said, "That's them San Miguel fellers."

I looked, but I could not see any San Miguel fellows in the wide expanse of land.

"Hyar, crawl some horses, and we'll go out and meet 'em," continued Mr. Bell; and, suiting the action, we mounted our horses and followed him. After a time I made out tiny specks in the atmospheric wave which rises from the heated land, and in half an hour could plainly make out a cavalcade of horsemen. Presently breaking into a gallop, which movement was imitated by the other party, we bore down upon each other, and only stopped when near enough to shake hands, the half-wild ponies darting about and rearing under the excitement. Greetings were exchanged in Spanish, and the peculiar shoulder tap, or abbreviated embrace, was indulged in. Doubtless a part of our outfit was as strange to Governor Terraza's men—for he is the *patron* of San Miguel—as they were to us.

My imagination had never before pictured anything so wild as these leather-clad *vaqueros*. As they removed their hats to greet Jack, their unkempt locks blew over their faces, back off their foreheads, in the greatest disorder. They were clad in terracotta buckskin, elaborately trimmed with white leather, and around their lower legs wore heavy cowhide as a sort of legging. They were fully armed, and with their jingling spurs, their flapping ropes and buckskin strings, and with their gay *serapes* tied behind their saddles, they were as impressive a cavalcade of desert-scamperers as it has been my fortune to see. Slowly we rode back to the corrals, where they dismounted.

Shortly, and unobserved by us until at hand, we heard the clatter of hoofs, and, leaving in their wake a cloud of dust, a dozen punchers from another outfit bore down upon us as we stood under the *ramada* of the ranch-house, and pulling up with a jerk, which threw the ponies on their haunches, the men dismounted and approached, to be welcomed by the master of the *rodeo*.

A few short orders were given, and three mounted men started down to the springs, and, after charging about, we could see that they had roped a steer, which they led, bawling and resisting, to the ranch, where it was quickly thrown and slaughtered. Turning it on its back, after the manner of the old buffalo hunters, it was quickly disrobed and cut up into hundreds of small pieces, which is the method practised by the Mexican butchers, and distributed to the men.

In Mexico it is the custom for the man who gives the "round-up" to supply fresh beef to the visiting cow-men; and on this occasion it seemed that the pigs, chickens, and dogs were also embraced in the bounty of the *patron*, for I noticed one piece which hung immediately in front of my quarters had two chickens roosting on the top of it, and a pig and a dog tugging vigorously at the bottom.

The horse herds were moved in from the *llano* and rounded up in the corral, from which the punchers selected their mounts by roping, and as the sun was westering they disappeared, in obedience to orders, to all points of the compass. The men took positions back in the hills and far out on the plain; there, building a little fire, they cook their beef, and, enveloped in their *serapes*, spend the night. At early dawn they converge on the ranch, driving before them such stock as they may.

In the morning we could see from the ranch-house a great semicircle of gray on the yellow plains. It was the thousands of cattle coming to the *rodeo*. In an hour more we could plainly see the cattle, and behind them the *vaqueros* dashing about, waving their *serapes*. Gradually they converged on the *rodeo* ground, and, enveloped in a great cloud of dust and with hollow bellowings, like the low pedals of a great organ, they begin to mill, or turn about a common centre, until gradually quieted by the enveloping cloud of horsemen. The *patron* and the captains of the neighboring ranches, after an exchange of long-winded Spanish formalities, and accompanied by ourselves, rode slowly from the ranch to the herd, and, entering it, passed through and through and around in solemn procession. The cattle part before the horsemen, and the dust rises so as to obscure to unaccustomed eyes all but the silhouettes of the moving thousands. This is an important function in a cow country, since it enables the owners or their men to estimate what numbers of the stock belong to them, to observe the brands, and to inquire as to the condition of the animals and the numbers of calves and "mavericks," and to settle any dispute which may arise therefrom.

All controversy, if there be any, having been adjusted, a part of the punchers move slowly into the herd, while the rest patrol the outside, and hold it. Then a movement soon begins. You see a figure dash at about full speed through an apparently impenetrable mass of cattle; the stock becomes uneasy and moves about, gradually beginning the milling process, but the men select the cattle bearing their brand, and course them through the herd; all becomes confusion, and the cattle simply seek to escape from the ever-recurring horsemen. Here one sees the matchless horsemanship of the punchers. Their little ponies, trained to the business, respond to the slightest pressure. The cattle make every attempt to escape, dodging in and out and crowding among their kind; but right on their quarter, gradually forcing them to the edge of the herd, keeps the puncher, until finally, as a last effort, the cow and the calf rush through the supporting line, when, after a terrific race, she is turned into another herd, and is called "the cut."

One who finds pleasure in action can here see the most surprising manifestations of it. A huge bull, wild with fright, breaks from the herd, with lowered head and whitened eye, and goes charging off indifferent to what or whom he may encounter, with the little pony pattering in his wake. The cattle run at times with nearly the intensity of action of a deer, and whip and spur are applied mercilessly to the little horse. The process of "tailing" is indulged in, although it is a dangerous practice for the man, and reprehensible from its brutality to the cattle. A man will pursue a bull at top speed, will reach over and grasp the tail of the animal, bring it to his saddle, throw his right leg over the tail, and swing his horse suddenly to the left, which throws the bull rolling over and over. That this method has its value I have seen in the case of pursuing "mavericks," where an unsuccessful throw was made with the rope, and the animal was about to enter the thick timber; it would be impossible to coil the rope again, and an escape would follow but for the wonderful dexterity of these men in this accomplishment. The little calves become separated from their mothers, and go bleating about; their mothers respond by bellows, until pandemonium seems to reign. The dust is blinding, and the puncher becomes grimy and soiled; the horses lather; and in the excitement the desperate men do deeds which convince you of their faith that "a man can't die till his time comes." At times a bull is found so skilled in these contests that he cannot be displaced from the herd; it is then necessary to rope him and drag him to the point desired; and I noticed punchers ride behind recalcitrant bulls and, reaching over, spur them. I also saw two men throw simultaneously for an immense creature, when, to my great astonishment, he turned tail over head and rolled on the ground. They had both sat back on their ropes together.

The whole scene was inspiring to a degree, and well merited Mr. Yorick's observation that "it is the sport of kings; the image of war, with twenty-five per cent of its danger."

Fresh horses are saddled from time to time, but before high noon the work is done, and the various "cut-offs" are herded in different directions. By this time the dust had risen until lost in the sky above, and as the various bands of cowboys rode slowly back to the ranch, I observed their demoralized condition. The economy *per force* of the Mexican people prompts them to put no more cotton into a shirt than is absolutely necessary, with the consequence that, in these cases, their shirts had pulled out from their belts and their *serapes*, and were flapping in the wind; their mustaches and their hair were perfectly solid with dust, and one could not tell a bay horse from a black.

Now come the cigarettes and the broiling of beef. The bosses were invited to sit at our table, and as the work of cutting and branding had yet to be done, no time was taken for ablutions. Opposite me sat a certain individual who, as he engulfed his food, presented a grimy waste of visage only broken by the rolling of his eyes and the snapping of his teeth.

We then proceeded to the corrals, which were made in stockaded form from gnarled and many-shaped posts set on an end. The cows and calves were bunched on one side in fearful expectancy. A fire was built just outside of the bars, and the branding-irons set on. Into the corrals went the punchers, with their ropes coiled in their hands. Selecting their victims, they threw their ropes, and, after pulling and tugging, a bull calf would come out of the bunch, whereat two men would set upon him and "rastle" him to the ground. It is a strange mixture of humor and pathos, this mutilation of calves—humorous when the calf throws the man, and pathetic when the man throws the calf. Occasionally an old cow takes an unusual interest in her offspring, and charges boldly into their midst. Those men who cannot escape soon enough throw dust in her eyes, or put their hats over her horns. And in this case there were some big steers which had been "cut out" for purposes of work at the plough and turned in with the young stock; one old grizzled veteran manifested an interest in the proceedings, and walked boldly from the bunch, with his head in the air and bellowing; a wild scurry ensued, and hats and *serapes* were thrown to confuse him. But over all this the punchers only laugh, and go at it again. In corral roping they try to catch the calf by the front feet, and in this they become so expert that they rarely miss. As I sat on the fence, one of the foremen, in play, threw and caught my legs as they dangled.

When the work is done and the cattle are again turned into the herd, the men repair to the *casa* and indulge in games and pranks. We had shooting-matches and hundred-yard dashes; but I think no records were broken, since punchers on foot are odd fish. They walk as though they expected every moment to sit down. Their knees work outward, and they have a decided "hitch" in their gait; but once let them get a foot in a stirrup and a grasp on the horn of the saddle, and a dynamite cartridge alone could expel them from their seat. When loping over the plain the puncher is the epitome of equine grace, and if he desires to look behind him he simply shifts his whole body to one side and lets the horse go as he pleases. In the pursuit of cattle at a *rodeo* he leans forward in his saddle, and with his arms elevated to his shoulders he "plugs" in his spurs and makes his pony fairly sail. While going at this tremendous speed he turns his pony almost in his stride, and no matter how a bull may twist and swerve about, he is at his tail as true as a magnet to the pole. The Mexican punchers all use the "ring bit," and it is a fearful contrivance. Their saddle-trees are very short, and as straight and quite as shapeless as a "saw-buck pack-saddle." The horn is as big as a dinner plate, and taken altogether it is inferior to the California tree. It is very hard on horses' backs, and not at all comfortable for a rider who is not accustomed to it.

They all use hemp ropes which are imported from some of the southern states of the republic, and carry a lariat of hair which they make themselves. They work for from eight to twelve dollars a month in Mexican coin, and live on the most simple diet imaginable. They are mostly *peoned*, or in hopeless debt to their *patrons*, who go after any man who deserts the range and bring him back by force. A puncher buys nothing but his gorgeous buckskin clothes, and his big silver-mounted straw hat, his spurs, his riata, and his *cincha* rings. He makes his *teguas* or buckskin boots, his heavy leggings, his saddle, and the *patron* furnishes his arms. On the round-up, which lasts about half of the year, he is furnished beef, and also kills game. The balance of the year he is kept in an outlying camp to turn stock back on the range. These camps are often the most simple things, consisting of a pack containing his "grub," his saddle, and *serape*, all lying under a tree, which does duty as a house. He carries a flint and steel, and has a piece of sheet-iron for a stove, and a piece of pottery for boiling things in. This part of their lives is passed in a long siesta, and a man of the North who has a local reputation as a lazy man should see a Mexican puncher loaf, in order to comprehend that he could never achieve distinction in the land where *poco tiempo* means forever. Such is the life of the *vaquero*, a brave fellow, a fatalist, with less wants than the pony he rides, a rather thoughtless man, who lacks many virtues, but when he mounts his horse or casts his riata all men must bow and call him master.

The *baile*, the song, the man with the guitar—and under all this *dolce far niente* are their little hates and bickerings, as thin as cigarette smoke and as enduring as time. They reverence their parents, they honor their *patron*, and love their *compadre*. They are grave, and grave even when gay; they eat little, they think less, they meet death calmly, and it's a terrible scoundrel who goes to hell from Mexico.

The Anglo-American foremen are another type entirely. They have all the rude virtues. The intelligence which is never lacking and the perfect courage which never fails are found in such men as Tom Bailey and Johnnie Bell—two Texans who are the superiors of any cow-men I have ever seen. I have seen them chase the "mavericks" at top speed over a country so difficult that a man could hardly pass on foot out of a walk. On one occasion Mr. Bailey, in hot pursuit of a bull, leaped a tremendous fallen log at top speed, and in the next instant "tailed" and threw the bull as it was about to enter the timber. Bell can ride a pony at a gallop while standing up on his saddle, and while Cossacks do this trick they are enabled to accomplish it easily from the superior adaptability of their saddles to the purpose. In my association with these men of the frontier I have come to greatly respect their moral fibre and their character. Modern civilization, in the process of educating men beyond their capacity, often succeeds in vulgarizing them; but these natural men possess minds which, though lacking all embellishment, are chaste and simple, and utterly devoid of a certain flippancy which passes for smartness in situations where life is not so real. The fact that a man bolts his food or uses his table-knife as though it were a deadly weapon counts very little in the game these men play in their lonely range life. They are not complicated, these children of nature, and they never think one thing and say another. Mr. Bell was wont to squat against a fireplace—*à la* Indian—and dissect the peculiarities of the audience in a most ingenuous way. It never gave offence either, because so guileless. Mr. Bailey, after listening carefully, to a theological tilt, observed that "he believed he'd be religious if he knowed how."

The jokes and pleasantries of the American puncher are so close to nature often, and so generously veneered with heart-rending profanity, as to exclude their becoming classic. The cow-men are good friends and virulent haters, and, if justified in their own minds, would shoot a man instantly, and regret the necessity, but not the shooting, afterwards.

Among the dry, saturnine faces of the cow punchers of the Sierra Madre was one which beamed with human instincts, which seemed to say, "Welcome, stranger!" He was the first impression my companion and myself had of Mexico, and as broad as are its plains and as high its mountains, yet looms up William on a higher pinnacle of remembrance.

We crawled out of a Pullman in the early morning at Chihuahua, and fell into the hands of a little black man, with telescopic pantaloons, a big sombrero with the edges rolled up, and a grin on his good-humored face like a yawning *barranca*.

"Is you frens of Mista Jack's?"

"We are."

"Gimme your checks. Come dis way," he said; and without knowing why we should hand ourselves and our property over to this uncouth personage, we did it, and from thence on over the deserts and in the mountains, while shivering in the snow by night and by day, there was Jack's man to bandage our wounds, lend us tobacco when no one else had any, to tuck in our blankets, to amuse us, to comfort us in distress, to advise and admonish, until the last *adios* were waved from the train as it again bore us to the border-land.

On our departure from Chihuahua to meet Jack out in the mountains the stage was overloaded, but a proposition to leave William behind was beaten on the first ballot; it was well vindicated, for without William the expedition would have been a "march from Moscow." There was only one man in the party with a sort of bass-relief notion that he could handle the Spanish language, and the relief was a very slight one—almost imperceptible—the politeness of the people only keeping him from being mobbed. But William could speak German, English, and Spanish, separately, or all at once.

William was so black that he would make a dark hole in the night, and the top of his head was not over four and a half feet above the soles of his shoes. His legs were all out of drawing, but forty-five winters had not passed over him without leaving a mind which, in its sphere of life, was agile, resourceful, and eminently capable of grappling with any complication which might arise. He had personal relations of various kinds with every man, woman, and child whom we met in Mexico. He had been thirty years a cook in a cow camp, and could evolve banquets from the meat on a bull's tail, and was wont to say, "I don' know so much 'bout dese yar stoves, but gie me a camp-fire an' I can make de bes' thing yo' ever threw your lip ober."

When in camp, with his little cast-off English tourist cap on one side of his head, a short black pipe tipped at the other angle to balance the effect, and two or three stripes of white corn-meal across his visage, he would move round the camp-fire like a cub bear around a huckleberry bush, and in a low, authoritative voice have the Mexicans all in action, one hurrying after water, another after wood, some making *tortillas*, or cutting up venison, grinding coffee between two stones, dusting bedding, or anything else. The British Field-Marshal air was lost in a second when he addressed "Mister Willie" or "Mister Jack," and no fawning courtier of the Grand Monarch could purr so low.

On our coach ride to Bavicora, William would seem to go up to any ranch-house on the road, when the sun was getting low, and after ten minutes' conversation with the grave Don who owned it, he would turn to us with a wink, and say: "Come right in, gemmen. Dis ranch is yours." Sure enough, it was. Whether he played us for major-generals or governors of states I shall never know, but certainly we were treated as such.

On one occasion William had gotten out to get a hat blown off by the wind, and when he came up to view the wreck of the turn-over of the great Concord coach, and saw the mules going off down the hill with the front wheels, the ground littered with boxes and débris, and the men all lying about, groaning or fainting in agony, William scratched his wool, and with just a suspicion of humor on his face he ventured, "If I'd been hyar, I would be in two places 'fore now, shuah," which was some consolation to William, if not to us.

In Chihuahua we found William was in need of a clean shirt, and we had got one for him in a shop. He had selected one with a power of color enough to make the sun stand still, and with great glass diamonds in it. We admonished him that when he got to the ranch the punchers would take it away from him.

"No, sah; I'll take it off 'fore I get thar."

William had his commercial instincts developed in a reasonable degree, for he was always trying to trade a silver watch, of the Captain Cuttle kind, with the Mexicans. When asked what time it was, William would look at the sun and then deftly cant the watch around, the hands of which swung like compasses, and he would show you the time within fifteen minutes of right, which little discrepancy could never affect the value of a watch in the land of *mañana*.

That he possessed tact I have shown, for he was the only man at Bavicora whose relations with the *patron* and the smallest, dirtiest Indian "kid," were easy and natural. Jack said of his popularity, "He stands 'way in with the Chinese cook; gets the warm corner behind the stove." He also had courage, for didn't he serve out the ammunition in Texas when his "outfit" was in a life-and-death tussle with the Comanches? did he not hold a starving crowd of Mexican teamsters off the grub-wagon until the boys came back?

There was only one feature of Western life with which William could not assimilate, and that was the horse. He had trusted a bronco too far on some remote occasion, which accounted partially for the kinks in his legs; but after he had recovered fully his health he had pinned his faith to *burros*, and forgotten the glories of the true cavalier.

"No, sah, Mister Jack, I don' care for to ride dat horse. He's a good horse, but I jes hit de flat for a few miles 'fore I rides him," he was wont to say when the cowboys gave themselves over to an irresponsible desire to see a horse kill a man. He would then go about his duties, uttering gulps of suppressed laughter, after the negro manner, safe in the knowledge that the *burro* he affected could "pack his freight."

One morning I was taking a bath out of our wash-basin, and William, who was watching me and the coffeepot at the same time, observed that "if one of dese people down hyar was to do dat dere, dere'd be a funeral 'fo' twelve o'clock."

William never admitted any social affinity with Mexicans, and as to his own people he was wont to say: "Never have went with people of my own color. Why, you go to Brazos to-day, and dey tell you dere was Bill, he go home come night, an' de balance of 'em be looking troo de grates in de morning." So William lives happily in the "small social puddle," and always reckons to "treat any friends of Mister Jack's right." So if you would know William, you must do it through Jack.

It was on rare occasions that William, as master of ceremonies, committed any indiscretion, but one occurred in the town of Guerrero. We had gotten in rather late, and William was sent about the town to have some one serve supper for us. We were all very busy when William "blew in" with a great sputtering, and said, "Is yous ready for dinner, gemmen?" "Yes, William," we answered, whereat William ran off. After waiting a long time, and being very hungry, we concluded to go and "rustle" for ourselves, since William did not come back and had not told us where he had gone. After we had found and eaten a dinner, William turned up, gloomy and dispirited. We inquired as to his mood. "I do declar', gemmen, I done forget dat you didn't know where I had ordered dat dinner; but dere's de dinner an' nobody to eat it, an' I's got to leave dis town 'fore sunup, pay for it, or die." Unless some one had advanced the money, William's two other alternatives would have been painful.

The romance in William's life even could not be made mournful, but it was the "mos' trouble" he ever had, and it runs like this: Some years since William had saved up four hundred dollars, and he had a girl back in Brazos to whom he had pinned his faith. He had concluded to assume responsibilities, and to create a business in a little mud town down the big road. He had it arranged to start a travellers' eating-house; he had contracted for a stove and some furniture; and at about that time his dishonest employer had left Mexico for parts unknown, with all his money. The stove and furniture were yet to be paid for, so William entered into hopeless bankruptcy, lost his girl, and then, attaching himself to Jack, he bravely set to again in life's battle. But I was glad to know that he had again conquered, for before I left I overheard a serious conversation between

William and the *patron*. William was cleaning a frying-pan by the camp-fire light, and the *patron* was sitting enveloped in his *serape* on the other side.

"Mist' Jack, I's got a girl. She's a Mexican."

"Why, William, how about that girl up in the Brazos?" inquired the *patron*, in surprise.

"Don't care about her now. Got a new girl."

"Well, I suppose you can have her, if you can win her," replied the *patron*.

"Can I, sah? Well, den, I's win her already, sah—dar!" chuckled William.

"Oh! very well, then, William, I will give you a wagon, with two yellow ponies, to go down and get her; but I don't want you to come back to Bavicora with an empty wagon."

"No, sah; I won't, sah," pleasedly responded the lover.

"Does that suit you, then?" asked the *patron*.

"Yes, sah; but, sah, wonder, sah, might I have the two old whites?"

"All right! You can have the two old white ponies;" and, after a pause, "I will give you that old *adobe* up in La Pinta, and two speckled steers; and I don't want you to come down to the ranch except on *baile* nights, and I want you to slide in then just as quiet as any other outsider," said the *patron*, who was testing William's loyalty to the girl.

"All right! I'll do that."

"William, do you know that no true Mexican girl will marry a man who don't know how to ride a charger?" continued the *patron*, after a while.

"Yes; I's been thinking of dat; but dar's dat Timborello, he's a good horse what a man can 'pend on," replied William, as he scoured at the pan in a very wearing way.

"He's yours, William; and now all you have got to do is to win the girl."

After that William was as gay as a robin in the spring; and as I write this I suppose William is riding over the pass in the mountains, sitting on a board across his wagon, with his Mexican bride by his side, singing out between the puffs of his black pipe, "Go on, dar, you muchacos; specks we ever get to Bavicora dis yar gait?"

JACK HILDRETH AMONG THE INDIANS

KARL MAY

TOWARD THE SETTING SUN

It is not necessary to say much about myself. First of all because there is not very much to tell of a young fellow of twenty-three, and then because I hope what I have done and seen will be more interesting than I am, for, between you and me, I often find Jack Hildreth a dull kind of person, especially on a rainy day when I have to sit in the house alone with him.

When I was born three other children has preceded me in the world, and my father's dreamy blue eyes saw no way of providing suitably for this superfluous fourth youngster. And then my uncle John came forward and said: "Name the boy after me, and I'll be responsible for his future." Now Uncle John was rich and unmarried, and though my father could never get his mind down to anything more practical than deciphering cuneiform inscriptions, even he saw that this changed the unflattering prospects of his latest-born into unusually smiling ones.

So I became Jack Hildreth secundus, and my uncle nobly fulfilled his part of the contract. He kept me under his own eye, gave me a horse before my legs were long enough to bestride him, nevertheless expecting me to sit him fast, punished me well if I was quarrelsome or domineering with other boys, yet punished me no less surely if when a quarrel was forced upon me, I showed the white feather or failed to do my best to whip my enemy.

"Fear God, but fear no man. Never lie, or sneak, or truckle for favor. Never betray a trust. Never be cruel to man or beast. Never inflict pain deliberately, but never be afraid to meet it if you must. Be kind, be honest, be daring. Be a man, and you will be a gentleman." This was my uncle's simple code; and as I get older, and see more of life, I am inclined to think there is none better.

My uncle sent me to the Jesuit college, and I went through as well as I could, because he trusted me to do so. I did not set the college world afire, but I stood fairly in my classes, and was first in athletics, and my old soldier uncle cared for that with ill-concealed pride.

When I left the student's life, and began to look about on real life and wonder where to take hold of it, I was so restless and overflowing with health and strength that I could not settle down to anything, and the fever for life on the plains came upon me. I longed to be off to the wild and woolly West—the wilder and woollier the better—before I assumed the shackles of civilization forever.

"Go if you choose, Jack," my uncle said. "Men are a better study than books, after you've been grounded in the latter. Begin the studying the primer of an aboriginal race, if you like; indeed it may be the best. There's plenty of time to decide on your future, for, as you're to be my heir, there's no pressing need of beginning labor."

My uncle had the necessary influence to get me appointed as an engineer with a party which was to survey for a railroad among the mountains of New Mexico and Arizona—a position I was competent to fill, as I had chosen civil engineering as my future profession, and had studied it thoroughly.

I scarcely realised that I was going till I found myself in St. Louis, where I was to meet the scouts of the party, who would take me with them to join the surveyors at the scene of our labors. On the night after my arrival I invited the senior scout, Sam Hawkins, to sup with me, in order that I might make his acquaintance before starting in the morning.

I do not know whether the Wild West Show was unconsciously in my mind, but when Mr. Hawkins appeared at the appointed time I certainly felt disappointed to see him clad in ordinary clothes and not in the picturesque costume of Buffalo Bill, till I reflected that in St. Louis even a famous Indian scout might condescend to look like every-day mortals.

"So you're the young tenderfoot; glad to make your acquaintance, sir," he said, and held out his hand, smiling at me from an extraordinary face covered with a bushy beard of many moons' growth and shadowed by a large nose a trifle awry, above which twinkled a pair of sharp little eyes.

My guest surprised me not a little, after I had responded to his greeting, by hanging his hat on the gas-fixture, and following it with his hair.

"Don't be shocked," he said calmly, seeing, I suppose, that this was unexpected. "You will excuse me, I hope, for the Pawnees have taken my natural locks. It was a mighty queer feeling, but fortunately I was able to stand it. I went to Tacoma and bought myself a new scalp, and it cost me a roll of good dollars. It doesn't matter; the new hair is more convenient than the old, especially on a warm day, for I never could hang my own wig up like that."

He had a way of laughing inwardly, and his shoulders shook as he spoke, though he made no sound.

"Can you shoot?" asked my queer companion suddenly.

"Fairly," I said, not so much, I am afraid, because I was modest as because I wanted to have the fun of letting him find out that I was a crack marksman.

"And ride?"

"If I have to."

"If you have to! Not as well as you shoot, then?"

"Pshaw! what is riding? The mounting is all that is hard; you can hang on somehow if once you're up."

He looked at me to see whether I was joking or in earnest; but I looked innocent, so he said: "There's where you make a mistake. What you should have said is that mounting is hard because you have to do that yourself, while the horse attends to your getting off again."

"The horse won't see to it in my case," I said with confidence—born of the fact that my kind uncle had accustomed me to clinging to high-strung beasts before I had lost my milk-teeth.

"A kicking broncho is something to try the nettle of a tenderfoot," remarked Hawkins dryly.

I suppose you know what a tenderfoot is. He is one who speaks good English, and wears gloves as if he were used to them. He also has a prejudice in favor of nice handkerchiefs and well-kept finger-nails; he may know a good deal about history, but he is liable to mistake turkey-tracks for bear-prints, and, though he has learned astronomy, he could never find his way by the stars. The tenderfoot sticks his bowie-knife into his belt in such a manner that it runs into his thigh when he bends; and when he builds a fire on the prairie he makes it so big that it flames as high as a tree, yet feels surprised that the Indians notice it. But many a tenderfoot is a daring, strong-bodied and strong-hearted fellow; and though there was no doubt that I was a tenderfoot fast enough, I hoped to convince Sam Hawkins that I had some qualities requisite for success on the plains.

By the time our supper was over there was a very good understanding established between me and the queer little man to whose faithful love I was to owe so much. He was an eccentric fellow, with a pretence of crustiness covering his big, true heart; but it was not hard to read him by the law of contraries, and our mutual liking dated from that night of meeting.

We set out in the early dawn of the following morning, accompanied by the other two scouts, Dick Stone and Will Parker, whom I then saw for the first time, and whom I learned to value only less than Sam as the truest of good comrades. Our journey was as direct and speedy as we could make it to the mountain region of New Mexico, near the Apache Indian reservation, and I was welcomed by my fellow-workers with a cordiality that gave rise to hopes of pleasant relations with them which were never realised. The party consisted of the head engineer, Bancroft, and three men under him. With them were twelve men intended to serve as our protectors, a sort of standing army, and for whom, as hardworking pioneers, I, a new-comer, had considerable respect until I discovered that they were men of the lowest moral standards.

Although I had entered the service only for experience, I was in earnest and did my duty conscientiously; but I soon found out that my colleagues were genuine adventurers, only after money, and caring nothing for their work except as a means of getting it.

Bancroft was the most dishonest of all. He loved his bottle too well and got private supplies for it from Santa Fe, and worked harder with the brandy-flask than with his surveying instruments. Riggs, Marcy, and Wheeler, the three surveyors, emulated Bancroft in this unprofitable pursuit; and as I never touched a drop of liquor, I naturally was the laborer, while the rest alternated between drinking and sleeping off the effects.

It goes without saying that under such circumstances our work did not progress rapidly, and at the end of the glorious autumn and three months of labor we found ourselves with our task still unaccomplished, while the section with which ours was to connect was almost completed. Besides our workmen being such as they were, we had to work in a region infested with Comanches, Kiowas, and Apaches, who objected to a road through their territory, and we had to be constantly on our guard, which made our progress still slower.

Personally my lot was not a bed of roses, for the men disliked me, and called me "tenderfoot" ten times a day, and took a special delight in thwarting my will, especially Rattler, the leader of our so-called guard, and as big a rascal as ever went unhanged. I durst not speak to them in an authoritative manner, but had to manage them as a wise woman manages a tyrannical husband without his perceiving it.

But I had allies in Sam Hawkins and his two companion scouts, Dick Stone and Will Parker. They were friendly to me, and held off from the others, in whom Sam Hawkins especially managed to inspire respect in spite of his droll peculiarities. There was an alliance formed between us silently, which I can best describe as a sort of feudal relation; he had taken me under his protection like a man who did not need to ask if he were understood. I was the "tenderfoot," and he the experienced frontiersman whose words and deeds had to be infallible to me. As often as he had time and opportunity he gave me practical and theoretical instruction in everything necessary to know and do in the Wild West; and though I graduated from the high school later, so to speak, with Winneotu as master, Sam Hawkins was my elementary teacher.

He made me expert with a lasso, and let me practise with that useful weapon on his own little person and his horse. When I had reached the point of catching them at every throw he was delighted, and cried out: "Good, my young sir! That's fine. But don't be set up with this praise. A teacher must encourage his stupid scholars when they make a little progress. I have taught lots of young frontiersmen, and they all learned much easier and understood me far quicker than you have, but perhaps it's possible that after eight years or so you may not be called a tenderfoot. You can comfort yourself with the thought that sometimes a stupid man gets on as well as or even a little better than a clever one."

He said this as if in sober earnest, and I received it in the same way, knowing well how differently he meant it. We met at a distance from the camp, where we could not be observed. Sam Hawkins would have it so; and when I asked why, he said: "For mercy's sake, hide yourself, sir. You are so awkward that I should be ashamed to have these fellows see you, so that's why I keep you in the shade—that's the only reason; take it to heart."

The consequence was that none of the company suspected that I had any skill in weapons, or special muscular strength—an ignorance that I was glad to foster.

One day I gave Rattler an order; it was some trifling thing, too small for me to remember now, and he would have been willing to carry it out had not his mood been rather uglier than usual.

"Do it yourself," he growled. "You impudent greenhorn, I'll show you I'm as good as you are any day."

"You're drunk," I said, looking him over and turning away.

"I'm drunk, am I?" he replied, glad of a chance to get at me, whom he hated.

"Very drunk, or I'd knock you down," I answered.

Rattler was a big, brawny fellow, and he stepped up in front of me, rolling up his sleeves. "Who, me? Knock me down? Well, I guess not, you blower, you kid, you greenhorn—"

He said no more. I hit him square in the face, and he dropped like an ox. Fearing mischief from Rattler's followers, and realising that now or never was my authority to be established, I drew my pistol, crying: "If one of you puts his hand to a weapon I'll shoot him on the spot." No one stirred. "Take your friend away, and let him sober up, and when he comes to his senses he may be more respectful," I remarked.

As the men obeyed me, Wheeler, the surveyor, whom I thought the best of the lot, stepped from the others and came up to me. "That was a great blow," he said. "Let me congratulate you. I never saw such strength. They'll call you Shatterhand out here."

This seemed to suit little Sam exactly. He threw up his hat, shouting joyously: "Shatterhand! Good! A tenderfoot, and already won a name, and what a name! Shatterhand; Old Shatterhand. It's like Old Firehand, who is a frontiersman as strong as a bear. I tell you, boy, it's great, and you're christened for good and all in the Wild West."

And so I found myself in a new and strange life, and beginning it with a new name, which became as familiar and as dear to me as my own.

MY FIRST BUFFALO

Three days after the little disciplining I had given Rattler, Mr. White, the head engineer of the next section, rode over to us to report that their work was finished, and to inquire what our prospects were for making speedy connection. When he set out on his return he invited Sam Hawkins and me to accompany him part of the way through the valley.

We found him a very agreeable companion; and when we came to the point where we were to turn back we shook hands cordially, leaving him with regret. "There's one thing I want to warn you of," Mr. White said in parting. "Look out for redskins."

"Have you seen them?" Sam asked.

"Not them, but their tracks. Now is the time when the wild mustangs and the buffaloes go southward, and the Indians follow in the chase. The Kiowas are all right, for we arranged with them for the road, but the Apaches and Comanches know nothing of it, and we don't dare let them see us. We have finished our part, and are ready to leave this region; hurry up with yours, and do likewise. Remember there's danger, and good-by."

Sam looked gravely after his retreating form, and pointed to a footprint near the spring where we had paused for parting. "He's quite right to warn us of Indians," he said.

"Do you mean this footprint was made by an Indian?"

"Yes, an Indian's moccasin. How does that make you feel?"

"Not at all."

"You must feel or think something."

"What should I think except that an Indian has been here?"

"Not afraid?"

"Not a bit."

"Oh," cried Sam, "you're living up to your name of Shatterhand; but I tell you that Indians are not so easy to shatter; you don't know them."

"But I hope to understand them. They must be like other men, enemies to their enemies, friends to their friends; and as I mean to treat them well, I don't see why I should fear them."

"You'll find out," said Sam, "or you'll be a greenhorn for eternity. You may treat the Indians as you like, and it won't turn out as you expect, for the results don't depend on your will. You'll learn by experience, and I only hope the experience won't cost you your life."

This was not cheering, and for some time we rode through the pleasant autumn air in silence.

Suddenly Sam reined up his horse, and looked ahead earnestly through half-closed lids. "By George," he cried excitedly, "there they are! Actually there they are, the very first ones."

"What?" I asked. I saw at some distance ahead of us perhaps eighteen or twenty dark forms moving slowly.

"What!" repeated Sam, bouncing up and down in his saddle. "I'd be ashamed to ask such a question; you are indeed a precious greenhorn. Can't you guess, my learned sir, what those things are before your eyes there?"

"I should take them for deer if I didn't know there were none about here; and though those animals look so small from here, I should say they were larger than deer."

"Deer in this locality! That's a good one! But your other guess is not so bad; they certainly are larger than deer."

"O Sam, they surely can't be buffaloes?"

"They surely can. Bisons they are, genuine bisons beginning their travels, and the first I have seen. You see Mr. White was right: buffaloes and Indians. We saw only a footprint of the red men, but the buffaloes are there before our eyes in all their strength. What do you say about it?"

"We must go up to them."

"Sure."

"And study them."

"Study them? Really study them?" he asked glancing at me sidewise in surprise.

"Yes; I never saw a buffalo, and I'd like to watch them."

I felt the interest of a naturalist, which was perfectly incomprehensible to little Sam. He rubbed his hands together, saying: "Watch them, only watch them! Like a child putting his eye to a rabbit's hole to see the little bunnies! O you young tenderfoot, what I must put up with in you! I don't want to watch them or study them, I tell you, but hunt them. They mean meat—meat, do you understand? and such meat! A buffalo-steak is more glorious than ambrosia, or ambrosiana, or whatever you call the stuff the old Greeks fed their gods with. I must have a buffalo if it costs me my life. The wind is towards us; that's good. The sun's on the left, towards the valley, but it's shady on the right, and if we keep in the shade the animals won't see us. Come on."

He looked to see if his gun, "Liddy," as he called it, was all right, and I hastily overhauled my own weapon. Seeing this, Sam held up his horse and asked: "Do you want to take a hand in this?"

"Of course."

"Well, you let that thing alone if you don't want to be trampled to jelly in the next ten minutes. A buffalo isn't a canary bird for a man to take on his finger and let it sing."

"But I will –"

"Be silent, and obey me," he interrupted in a tone he had never used before. "I won't have your life on my conscience, and you would ride into the jaws of certain death. You can do what you please at other times, but now I'll stand no opposition."

Had there not been such a good understanding between us I would have given him a forcible answer; but as it was, I rode after him in the shadow of the hills without speaking, and after a while Sam said in his usual manner: "There are twenty head, as I reckon. Once a thousand or more browsed over the plains. I have seen early herds numbering a thousand and upward. They were the Indians' food, but the white men have taken it from them. The redskin hunted to live, and only killed what he needed. But the white man has ravaged countless herds, like a robber who for very lust of blood keeps on slaying when he is well supplied. It won't be long before there are no buffaloes, and a little longer and there'll be no Indians, God help them! And it's just the same with the herds of horses. There used to be herds of a thousand mustangs, and even more. Now a man is lucky if he sees two together."

We had come within four hundred feet of the buffaloes unobserved, and Hawkins reined in his horse. In the van of the herd was an old bull whose enormous bulk I studied with wonder. He was certainly six feet high and ten long; I did not then know how to estimate the weight of a buffalo, but I should now say that he must have weighed sixteen hundred pounds—an astounding mass of flesh and bone.

"That's the leader, whispered Sam, "the most experienced of the whole crowd. Whoever tackles him had better make his will first. I will take the young cow right back of him. The best place to shoot is behind the shoulder-blade into the heart; indeed it's the only sure place except the eyes, and none but a madman would go up to a buffalo and shoot into his eyes. You stay here, and hide yourself and your horse in the thicket. When they see me they'll run past here; but don't you quit your place unless I come back or call you."

He waited until I had hidden between two bushes, and then rode slowly forward. It seemed to me this took great courage. I had often read how buffaloes were hunted, and knew all about it; but there is a great difference between a printed page and the real thing. To-day I had seen buffaloes for the first time in my life; and though at first I only wished to study them, as I watched Sam I felt an irresistible longing to join in the sport. He was going to shoot a young cow. Pshaw! that, I thought, required no courage; a true man would choose the strongest bull.

My horse was very restless; he, too, had never seen buffaloes before, and he pawed the ground, frightened and so anxious to run that I could scarcely hold him. Would it not be better to let him go, and attack the old bull myself? I debated this question inwardly, divided between desire to go and regard for Sam's command, meantime watching his every movement.

He had approached within a hundred feet of the buffaloes, when he spurred his horse and galloped into the herd, past the mighty bull, up to the cow which he had selected. She pricked up her ears, and started to run. I saw Sam shoot. She staggered, and her head dropped, but I did not know whether or not she fell, for my eyes were chained to another spot.

The great bull, which had been lying down, was getting up, and turned toward Sam Hawkins. What a mighty beast! The thick head with the enormous skull, the broad forehead with its short, strong horns, the neck and breast covered with the coarse mane, made a picture of the greatest possible strength. Yes, it was a marvellous creature, but the sight of him aroused a longing to measure human strength with this power of the plains. Should I or should I not? I could not decide, nor was I sure that my roan would take me towards him; but just then my frightened horse sprang forth from our cover, and I resolved to try, and spurred him towards the bull. He heard me coming, and turned to meet me, lowering his head to receive horse and rider on his horns. I heard Sam cry out something with all his might, but had no time even to glance at him. It was impossible to shoot the buffalo, for in the first place he was not in the right position, and in the second place my horse would not obey me, but for very fear ran straight towards the threatening horns. The buffalo braced his hind legs to toss us, and raised his head with a mighty bellow. Exerting all my strength, I turned my horse a little, and he leaped over the bull, while the horns grazed my leg.

My course lay directly towards a mire in which the buffalo had been sleeping. I saw this, and fortunately drew my feet from the stirrups; my horse slipped and we both fell.

How it all happened so quickly is incomprehensible to me now, but the next moment I stood upright beside the morass, my gun still in my hand. The buffalo turned on the horse, which had also risen quickly, and came on him in ungainly leaps, and this brought his flank under my fire. I took aim. One more bound and the buffalo would reach my horse. I pulled the trigger; he stopped, whether from fear or because he was hit I did not know, but I fired again, two shots in rapid succession. He slowly raised his head, froze my blood with a last awful roar, swayed from side and side and fell where he stood.

I might have rejoiced over this narrow escape, but I had something else to attend to. I saw Sam Hawkins galloping for dear life across the valley, followed by a steer not much smaller than my bull had been.

When the bison is aroused his speed is as great as that of a horse; he never gives up his object, and shows a courage and perseverance one would not have expected of him. So this steer was pressing the rider hard, and in order to escape him Sam had to make many turns, which so wearied his horse that he could not hold out as long as the buffalo, and it was quite time that help arrived.

I did not stop to see whether or not my bull was dead. I quickly reloaded both chambers of my gun, and ran across the grass towards Sam. He saw me, and turned his horse in my direction. This was a great mistake, for it brought the horse's side towards the steer behind him. I saw him lower his horns, and in an instant horse and rider were tossed in the air, and fell to the ground with a dreadful thud. Sam cried for help as well as he could. I was a good hundred and fifty feet away, but I dared not delay, though the shot would have been surer at shorter range. I aimed at the steer's left shoulder-blade and fired. The buffalo raised his head as if listening, turned slowly, then ran at me with all his might. Luckily for me, his moment of hesitation had given me time to reload, and therefore I was ready for him by the time the beast had made thirty paces towards me. He could no longer run; his steps became slow, but with deep-hanging head and protruding, bloodshot eyes he came nearer and nearer to me, like some awful, unavoidable fate. I knelt down and brought my gun into position. This movement made the buffalo halt and raise his head a little to see me better, thus bringing his eyes just in range of both barrels. I sent one shot into the right, and another into the left eye; a quick shudder went through his body, and the beast fell dead.

Springing to my feet, I rushed toward Sam; but it was not necessary, for I saw him approaching.

"Hallo!" I cried, "are you alive?"

"Very much so, only my left hip pains me, or the right; I'm sure I can't tell which."

"And your horse?"

"Done for; he's still alive, but he's torn past help. We'll have to shoot him to put him out of his misery, poor fellow. Is the buffalo dead?"

I was not able to answer this question positively, so we made sure that there was no life in my former foe, and Hawkins said: "He treated me pretty badly, this old brute; a cow would have been gentler, but I suppose you can't expect such an old soldier to be lady-like. Let us go to my poor horse."

We found him in a pitiable condition, torn so that his entrails protruded, and groaning with agony. Sam loaded, and gave the poor creature the shot that ended his suffering, and then he removed the saddle and bridle, saying: "I'll be my own horse, and put these on my back."

"Where will you get another horse?" I asked.

"That's the least of my trouble; I'll find one unless I'm mistaken."

"A mustang?"

"Yes. The buffaloes are here; they've begun travelling southward, and soon we'll see the mustangs, I'm sure of that."

"May I go with you when you catch one?"

"Sure; you'll have to learn to do it. I wonder if that old bull is dead; such Mathusalas are wonderfully tough."

But the beast was dead, as we found on investigation; and as he lay there I realized more fully what a monster he was. Sam looked him over, shook his head, and said: "It is perfectly incredible. Do you know what you are?"

"What?"

"The most reckless man on earth."

"I've never been accused of recklessness before."

"Well, now you know that 'reckless' is the word for you. I forbade you meddling with a buffalo or leaving your hiding-place; but if you were going to disobey me, why didn't you shoot a cow?"

"Because this was more knightly."

"Knightly! Great Scott! This tenderfoot wants to play knight!" He laughed till he had to take hold of the bushes for support, and when he got his breath he cried: "The true frontiersman does what is most expedient, not what's more knightly."

"And I did that, too."

"How do you make that out?"

"That big bull has much more flesh on him than a cow."

Sam looked at me mockingly. "Much more flesh!" he cried. "And this youngster shot a bull for his flesh! Why, boy, this old stager had surely eighteen or twenty years on his head, and his flesh is as hard as leather, while the cow's flesh is fine and tender. All this shows again what a greenhorn you are. Now go get your horse, and we'll load him with all the meat he can carry."

In spite of Sam's mocking me, that night as I stood unobserved in the door of the tent where he and Stone and Parker sat by their fire I heard Sam say: "Yes, sir, he's going to be a genuine Westerner; he's born one. And how strong he is! Yesterday he drew our great oxcart alone and single-handed. Now to-day I owe him my life. But we won't let him know what we think of him."

"Why not?" asked Barker.

"It might swell his head," replied Sam. "Many a good fellow has been spoiled by praise. I suppose he'll think I'm an ungrateful old curmudgeon, for I never even thanked him for saving my life. But to-morrow I'll give him a treat; I'll take him to catch a mustang, and, no matter what he thinks, I know how to value him."

I crept away, pleased with what I had heard, and touched by the loving tone of my queer friend's voice as he spoke of me.

WILD MUSTANGS AND LONG-EARED NANCY

The next morning as I was going to work Sam came to me, saying: "Put down your instruments; we have something on hand more interesting than surveying."

"What is it?"

"You'll see. Get your horse ready; we're going to ride."

"And how about the work?"

"Nonsense! You've done your share. However, I expect to be back by noon, and then you can measure as much as you will."

After arranging with Bancroft for my absence, we started; and as Sam made a mystery of the object of our expedition, I said nothing to show that I suspected what it was.

We went back of the ravine where we were surveying to a stretch of prairie which Sam had pointed out the day before. It was two good miles broad, and surrounded by woody heights, from which flowed a brook irrigating the plain. We rode to the westerly boundary, where the grass was freshest, and here Sam securely tied his horse—his borrowed horse—and let him graze. As he looked about him an expression of satisfaction shone on his rugged face, like sunshine on rocks. "Dismount, sir," he said, "and tie your horse strong; we'll wait here."

"Why tie him so strongly?" I asked, though I knew well.

"Because you might lose him. I have often seen horses go off with such companions."

"Such companions as what?" I asked.

"Try to guess."

"Mustangs?"

"How did you know?"

"I've read that if domestic horses weren't well tied they'd join the wild ones when a herd came along."

"Confound it! you've read so much a man can't get the best of you."

"Do you want to get the best of me?"

"Of course. But look, the mustangs have been here."

"Are those their tracks?"

"Yes; they went through here yesterday. It was a scouting party. Let me tell you that these beasts are uncommonly sharp. They always send out little advance-parties, which have their officers exactly like soldiers, and the commander is the strongest and most experienced horse. They travel in circular formation, stallions outside, mares next them inside, and the foals in the middle, in order that the males may protect the mares and young. I have already shown you how to catch a mustang with a lasso; do you remember? Would you like to capture one?"

"Certainly I would."

"Well, you'll have a chance before noon to-day."

"Thanks, but I don't intend to catch one."

"The dickens you don't! And why not?"

"Because I don't need a horse."

"But a real frontiersman never asks whether he needs a horse or not."

"Now look here, Sam; only yesterday you were speaking of the brutal way the white men, though they do not need meat, kill the buffaloes in masses, depriving the Indians of their food. We agreed that was a crime against beasts and men."

"Assuredly."

"This is a similar case. I should do wrong to rob one of these glorious fellow of his freedom unless I needed a horse."

"That's well said, young man; bravely said. Any man, any Christian worth calling so, would feel thus; but who said anything about robbing him of his freedom? Just put your education in lasso-throwing to the proof, that's all."

"That's a different thing; I'll do that."

"All right; and I'll use one in earnest, for I do need a horse. I've often told you, and now I'll say again: Sit strong in your saddle, control your horse well when you feel the lasso tighten, and pull; for if you don't you'll be unseated, and the mustang will gallop off, taking your horse and lasso with him. then you'll lose your mount and be, like me, only a common foot soldier."

He was about to give more advice, but stopped suddenly, and pointed to the northern end of the prairie. There stood a horse, one single solitary horse. He walked slowly forward, not stopping to graze, turning his head first to one side, then to the other, snuffing the air as he came.

"Do you see?" whispered Sam. "Didn't I tell you they'd come? That's the scout come on ahead to see if all's safe. He's a wise beast! See how he looks in all directions! He won't discover us, though, for we have the wind towards us."

The mustang broke into a trot, running to the right, then to the left, and finally turned and disappeared as we had seen him come.

"Did you see him?" cried Sam admiringly. "How wise he is! An Indian scout could not have done better."

"That's so; I'm surprised at him."

"Now he's gone back to tell his general the air is pure. How we fooled him! They'll all be here shortly. You ride back to the other end of the prairie, and wait there, while I go towards them and hide in the trees. When they come I'll chase them, and they'll fly in your direction; then you show yourself, and they'll turn back towards me. So we'll drive them back and forth till we've picked out the two best horses, and we'll catch them and choose between them. Do you agree?"

"How can you ask? I know nothing of the art of mustangcatching, of which you are past master, and I've nothing to do but follow your directions."

"All right. I have caught mustangs before to-day, and I hope you're not far wrong in calling me a 'master' of that trade. Now let's take our places."

We turned and rode in opposite directions, he northward, I southward to the spot where we had entered the prairie. I got behind some little trees, made one end of the lasso fast, and coiled the other ready for use. The further end of the prairie was so far off that I could not see the mustangs when they first appeared, but after I had been waiting a quarter of an hour I saw what looked like a dark cloud rapidly increasing in size and advancing in my direction. At first it seemed to be made up of objects about as big as sparrows, then they seemed like cats, dogs, calves, and at last I saw them in their own proportions. They were the mustangs in wild gallop, coming towards me. What a sight these lordly beasts were, with their manes flying about their necks, and their tails streaming like plumes in the wind! There were at least three hundred head, and the earth seemed to tremble beneath the pounding of their hoofs. A white stallion led them, a noble creature that any man might be glad to capture, only no prairie hunter would ride a white horse, for he would be too conspicuous to his enemies.

Now was the time to show myself. I came out, and the startled leader sprang back as though an arrow had pierced him. The herd halted; one loud, eager whinny from the white stallion which plainly meant: Wheel, squadron! and the splendid fellow turned, followed by all his companions, and tore back whence they had come. I followed slowly; there was no hurry, for I knew Sam Hawkins would drive them back to me. I wanted to make sure I was right in which I had seen, for in the brief instant the herd had halted it seemed to me that one of them was not a horse, but a mule. The animal that I thought a mule had been in the front ranks, immediately behind the leader, and so seemed not merely to be tolerated by its companions, but to hold honorable rank among them.

Once again the herd came towards me, and I saw that I was not mistaken, but that a mule really was among them, a mule of a delicate light brown color, with dark back-stripe, and which I thought had the biggest head and the longest ears I had ever seen. Mules are more suitable for rough mountain-riding than horses, are surer-footed, and less likely to fall into abysses—a fact worth consideration. To be sure they are obstinate, and I have known a mule be beaten half to death rather than take another step, not because it was overladen or the way was hard, but simply because it would not. It seemed to me that this mule showed more spirit than the horses, and that its eyes gleamed brighter and more intelligently than theirs, and I resolved to capture it. Evidently it had escaped from its former owner and joined the mustangs.

Now once more Sam turned the herd, and we had approached each other till I could see him. The mustangs could no longer run back and forth; they turned to the side, we following them. The herd had divided, and I saw that the mule was with the more important part, still keeping beside the white horse, and proving itself an unusually strong and swift animal. I pursued this band, and Sam seemed to have the same design.

"Get around them; I left, you right," he shouted.

We spurred our horses, and not only kept up with the mustangs, but rode so swiftly that we headed them off from the woods. They began to scatter to all sides like chickens when a hawk swoops down among them; and as we both chased the white stallion and the mule, Sam cried: "You'll always be a greenhorn. Who else would pick out a white horse?"

I answered him, but his loud laugh drowned my reply, and if he thought I was after the white horse it did not much matter. I left the mule to his tender care, and in a moment he had come so near her that he threw the lasso.

The noose encircled the beast's neck, and now Sam had to hold on as he had directed me to do, and throw himself backward to make the lasso hold when it tautened. This he did, but a moment too late; his horse did not obey on the instant, and was thrown by the force of the jerk. Sam flew through the air, and landed on the ground with a thump. The horse shook himself free, and was up and off in a moment, and the mule with him, since the lasso was fast to the saddle-bow.

I hastened to see if Sam was hurt, and found him standing, much shaken, but not otherwise the worse. He said to me in mournful tones: "There go Dick Stone's chestnut and the mule without saying good-by."

"Are you hurt?"

"No. Jump down and give me your horse."

"What for?"

"To catch them, of course. Hurry up."

"Not much; you might turn another somersault, and then both our horses would be gone to the four winds." With these words I put my horse after the mule and Dick's horse. Already they were in trouble, one pulling one way, the other another, and held together by the lasso, so I could easily come up with them. It never entered my head to use my lasso, but I grabbed the one holding them, wound it around my hand, and felt sure the day was won. I drew the noose tighter and tighter, thus easily controlling the mule, and brought her back, together with the horse, in apparent subjection to where Sam stood.

Then I suddenly pulled the noose taut, when the mule lost her breath and fell to the ground.

"Hold on fast till I have the rascal, and then let go," shouted Sam, springing to the side of the prostrate beast. "Now!" he cried.

I let go the lasso, and the mule instantly jumped up, but not before Sam was on her back. She stood motionless a moment in surprise, then rushed from side to side, then stood first on her hind legs, then on her fore legs, and finally jumped into the air with all four bunched together, and her back arched like a cat's. but still little Sam sat fast.

"Don't get near; she's going to try her last hope and run away, but I'll bring her back tamed," shouted Sam.

He proved to be mistaken, however; she only ran a little way, and then deliberately lay down and rolled. This was too much for Sam's ribs; he had to get out of the saddle. I jumped from my horse, seized the lasso, and wound it around some tough roots near at hand. The mule, finding she had no rider, got up and started to run off; but the roots were strong, the noose drew tight, and again the animal fell. Sam had retired to one side, feeling his legs and ribs, and making a face as if he had eaten sauerkraut and marmalade.

"Let the beast go," he said. "I believe nobody can conquer her."

"Well, I guess not," said I. "No animal whose father was no gentleman, but a donkey, is going to shame me. She's got to mind me. Look out."

I unwound the lasso from the bushes, and stood astride the mule, which at once got up, feeling herself freed. Now it was a question of strength of legs, and in this I far surpassed Sam. If a rider presses his beast's ribs with strong knees it causes intense pain. As the mule began to try to throw me as she had Sam, I caught up the lasso, half hanging on the ground, and fastened it tight behind the noose. This I drew whenever she began any of her tricks, and by this means and pressure of the knees I contrived to keep her on all fours.

It was a bitter struggle, strength against strength. I began to sweat from every pore, but the mule was dripping, and foam fell from her lips in great flakes. Her struggles grew more and more feeble, her heavy breathing became short gasps, till at last she gave in altogether, not willing, but because she was at her last limit, and stood motionless with bulging eyes. I drew long, deep breaths; it seemed to me as if every bone and sinew in my body were broken.

"Heavens! what a man you are!" cried Sam. "You're stronger than the brute! If you could see your face you would be scared; your eyes are staring, your lips are swollen, your cheeks are actually blue."

"I suppose so; that comes of being a tenderfoot who won't be beaten, while his teacher gives in and lets a horse and a mule conquer him."

Sam made a wry face. "Now let up, young fellow. I tell you the best hunter gets whipped some times."

"Very likely. How are your ribs and other little bones?"

"I don't know; I'll have to count 'em to find out. That's a fine beast you have under you there."

"She is indeed. See how patiently she stands; one feels sorry for her. Shall we saddle and bridle her and go back?"

The poor mule stood quiet, trembling in every limb; nor did she try to resist when we put saddle and bridle on her, but obeyed the bit like a well-broken horse. "She's had a master before," said Sam. "I'm going to call her Nancy, for I once had a mule by that name, and it's too much trouble to get used to another. And I'm going to ask you to do me a favor."

"Gladly; what is it?"

"Don't tell at the camp what has happened this morning, for they'd have nine days' sport with me."

"Of course I won't; you're my teacher and friend, so I'll keep your secrets."

His queer face lighted up with pleasure. "Yes, I'm your friend, and if I knew you had a little liking for me, my old heart would be warmed and rejoiced."

I stretched out my hand to him, surprised and touched. "I can easily give you that pleasure, dear Sam," I said. "You may be sure I honestly care for you with real respect and affection."

He shook my hand, looking so delighted that even my young self-sufficiency could perceive how lonely this rough, cranky old frontiersman was, and how great was his yearning for human sympathy.

I fastened Dick Stone's horse with the lasso, and mounting mine, as Sam got on Nancy, we rode away.

"She's been educated, this new Nancy, in a very good school," Sam remarked presently. "I see at every step she is going to be all right, and is regaining the old knowledge which she had forgotten among the mustangs. I hope she has not only temperament but character."

"We've had two good days, Sam," I said.

"Bad ones for me, except in getting Nancy; and bad for you, too, in one way, but mighty honorable."

"Oh, I've done nothing; I came West to get experience. I hope to have a chance at other sport."

"Well, I hope it will come more easily; yesterday your life hung by a hair. You risked too much. Never forget you're a greenhorn tenderfoot. The idea of creeping up to shoot a buffalo in the eye! Did ever any one hear the like? But though hunting buffaloes is dangerous, bear-hunting is far more so."

"Black bear?"

"Nonsense! The grizzly. You've read of him?"

"Yes."

"Well, be glad you don't know him outside of books; and take care you don't for you might have a chance to meet him. He sometimes comes about such places as this, following the rivers even as far as the prairie. I'll tell you more of him another time; here we are at the camp."

"A mule, a mule! Where did you get her, Hawkins?" cried all the men.

"By special delivery from Washington, for a ten-cent stamp. Would you like to see the envelope?" asked Sam, dismounting.

Though they were curious, none asked further questions, for, like the beast he had captured, when Sam wouldn't he wouldn't, and that was the end of it.

A GRIZZLY AND A MEETING

The morning after Sam and I had caught Miss Nancy we moved our camp onward to begin labor on the next section of the road. Hawkins, Stone, and Parker did not help in this, for Sam was anxious to experiment further with Nancy's education, and the other two accompanied him to the prairie, where they had sufficient room to carry out this purpose. We surveyors transferred our instruments ourselves, helped by one of Rattler's men, while Rattler himself loafed around doing nothing.

We came to the spot where I had killed the two buffaloes, and to my surprise I saw that the body of the old bull was gone, leaving a broad trail of crushed grass that led to the adjoining thicket.

"I thought you had made sure both bulls were dead," Rattler exclaimed. "The big one must have had some life in him."

"Think so?" I asked.

"Of course, unless you think a dead buffalo can take himself off."

"Must he have taken himself off? Perhaps it was done for him."

"Yes, but who did it?"

"Possibly Indians, we saw an Indian's footprint over yonder."

"You don't say! How well a greenhorn can explain things!" sneered Rattler. "If it was done by Indians, where do you think they came from? Dropped from the skies? Because if they came from anywhere else we'd see their tracks. No, there was life in that buffalo, and he crawled into the thicket, where he must have died. I'm going to look for him."

He started off, followed by his men. He may have expected me to go, too, but it was far from my thoughts, for I did not like the way he had spoken. I wanted to work, and did not care a button what had become of the old bull.

So I went back to my employment, and had only just taken up the measuring-rod, when a cry of horror rang from the thicket, two, three shots echoed, and then I heard Rattler cry: "Up the tree, quick! up the tree, or you're lost! he can't climb."

Who could not climb? One of Rattler's men burst out of the thicket, writhing like one in mortal agony.

"What is it? What's happened?" I shouted.

"A bear, a tremendous grizzly bear!" he gasped, as I ran up to him.

And within the thicket an agonised voice cried: "Help, help! He's got me!" in the tone of a man who saw the jaws of death yawning before him.

Evidently the man was in extreme danger, and must be helped quickly, but how? I had left my gun in the tent, for in working it hindered me; nor was this an oversight, since we surveyors had the frontiersmen purposely to guard us at our work. If I went to the tent to get the gun, the bear would have torn the man to shreds before I could get back; I must go to him as I was with a knife and two revolvers stuck in my belt, and what were these against a grizzly bear?

The grizzly is a near relation of the extinct cave-bear, and really belongs more to primeval days than to the present. It grows to a great size, and its strength is such that it can easily carry off a deer, a colt, or a young buffalo cow in its jaws. The Indians hold the killing of a grizzly a brilliant feat, because of its absolute fearlessness and inexhaustible endurance.

So it was to meet such a foe that I sprang into the thicket. The trail led further within, where the trees began, and where the bear had dragged the buffalo. It was a dreadful moment. Behind me I could hear the voices of the engineers; before me were the frontiersmen screaming, and between them and me, in indescribable agony, was their companion whom the bear had seized.

I pushed further in, and heard the voice of the bear; for, though this mighty beast differs from others of the bear family in not growling, when in pain or anger it utters something like a loud, harsh breathing and grunting.

And now I was on the scene. Before me lay the torn body of the buffalo, to right and left were the men, who were comparatively safe, having taken to the trees, which a grizzly bear seldom has been known to climb, if ever. One of the men had tried to get up a tree like the others, but had been overtaken by the bear. He hung by both arms hooked to the lowest limb, while the grizzly reached up and held him fast with its fore paws around the lower part of his body.

The man was almost dead; his case was hopeless. I could not help him, and no one could have blamed me if I had gone away and saved myself. But the desperation of the moment seemed to impel me onward. I snatched up a discarded gun, only to find it already emptied. Taking it by the muzzle I sprang over the buffalo, and dealt the bear a blow on the skull with all my might. The gun shattered like glass in my hand; even a blow with a battle-axe would have no effect on such a skull but I had the satisfaction of distracting the grizzly's attention from its victim.

It turned its head toward me, not quickly, like a wild beast of the feline or canine family, but slowly, as if wondering at my stupidity. It seemed to measure me with its little eyes, decided between going at me or sticking to its victim; and to this slight hesitation I owe my life, for in that instant the only possible way to save myself came to me. I drew a revolver, sprang directly at the bear, and shot it, once, twice, thrice, straight in the eyes, as I had the buffalo.

Of course this was rapidly done, and at once I jumped to one side, and stood still with my knife drawn. Had I remained where I was, my life would have paid for my rashness, for the blinded beast turned quickly from the tree, and threw itself on the spot where I had stood a moment before. I was not there, and the bear sought mine with angry mutterings and heavy breathing. It wheeled around like a mad thing, hugged itself, rose on its hind legs, reaching and springing all around to find me, but fortunately I was out of reach. Its sense of smell would have guided it to me, but it was mad with rage and pain, and this prevented its instinct from serving it.

At last it turned its attention more to its misfortune than to him who had caused it. It sat down, and with sobs and gnashing of teeth laid its fore paws over its eyes. I was sorry that necessity for saving human life was causing the big fellow such pain, and, with pity for it, as well as desire for my own safety, tried to make it short. Quietly I stood beside it and stabbed it twice between the ribs. Instantly it grabbed for me, but once more I sprang out of the way. I had not pierced its heart, and it began seeking me with redoubled fury. This continued for fully ten minutes. It had lost a great deal of blood, and evidently was dying; it sat down again to mourn its poor lost eyes. This gave me a chance for two rapidly repeated knife-thrusts, and this time I aimed better; it sank forward, as again I sprang aloof, made a feeble step to one side, then back, tried to rise, but had not sufficient strength, swayed back and forth in trying to get on its feet, and then stretched out and was still.

"Thank God!" cried Rattler from his tree, "the beast is dead. That was a close call we had."

"I don't see that it was a close call for you," I replied. "You took good care of your own safety. Now you can come down."

"Not yet; you make sure it's truly dead."

"It is dead."

"You don't know; you haven't an idea how tough such a creature is. Go examine it."

"If you doubt me, examine it yourself; you're an experienced frontiersman, and I'm a tenderfoot, you know."

So saying I turned to his comrade, who still hung on the tree in an awful plight. His face was torn, and his wide-open eyes were glassy, the flesh was stripped from the bones of his legs, and he was partly disembowelled. I conquered the horror of the sight enough to say: "Let go, my poor fellow; I will take you down." He did not answer, or show any sign of having heard me, and I called his comrades to help me. Only after I had made sure the bear was dead would the courageous gang come down from their trees, when we gently removed the wounded man. This required strength to accomplish, for his arms had wound tightly around the tree, and stiffened there: he was dead.

This horrible end did not seem to affect his companions in the least, for they turned from him to the bear, and their leader said: "Now things are reversed; the bear meant to eat us, but we will eat it. Quick, you fellows, take its pelt, and let us get at the paws and steak."

He drew his knife and knelt down to carry out his words, but I checked him. "It would have been more fitting if you had used your knife when it was alive. Now it's too late; don't give yourself the trouble."

"What!" he cried. "Do you mean to hinder me?"

"Most emphatically I do, Mr. Rattler."

"By what right?"

"By the most indisputable right. I killed that bear."

"That's not so. Maybe you think a greenhorn can kill a grizzly with a knife! As soon as we saw it we shot it."

"And immediately got up a tree! Yes, that's very true."

"You bet it's true, and our shots killed it, not the two little needle-pricks of your knife. The bear is ours, and we'll do with it what we like. Understand?"

He started to work again, but I said coolly: "Stop this minute, Rattler. I'll teach you to respect my words; do you understand?" And as he bent forward to stick the knife into the bear's hide I put both arms around his hips and, raising him, threw him against the next tree so hard that it cracked. I was too angry just then to care whether he or the tree broke, and as he flew across the space I drew my second and unused revolver, to be ready for the next move.

He got up, looked at me with eyes blazing with rage, drew his knife, and cried: "You shall pay or this. You knocked me down once before; I'll see it doesn't happen a third time." He made a step towards me, but I covered him with my pistol, saying: "One step more and you'll have a bullet in your head. Drop that knife. When I say 'three' I'll shoot you if you still hold it. Now: One, two –" He held the knife tight, and I should have shot him, not in the head, but in the hand, for he had to learn to respect me; but luckily I did not get so far for at this moment a loud voice cried: "Men, are you mad? What reason have the whites to tear out one another's eyes? Stop!"

We looked in the direction whence the voice came, and saw a man appearing from behind the trees. He was small, thin, and hunchbacked, clad and armed like a red man. One could not tell whether he was an Indian or a white; his sharp-cut features indicated the former, while the tint of his face, although sunburned, was that of a white man. He was bareheaded, and his dark hair hung to his shoulders. He wore leather trousers, a hunting-shirt of the same material, and moccasins, and was armed with a knife and gun. His eyes shone with unusual intelligence, and there was nothing ridiculous in his deformity. Indeed, none but stupid and brutal men ever laugh at bodily defects; but Rattler was of this class, for as soon as he looked at the new-comer he cried:

"Hallo! What kind of a freak comes here? Do such queer things grow in the big West?"

The stranger looked at him calmly, and answered quietly: "Thank God that your limbs are sound. It is by the heart and soul that men are judged, and I should not fear a comparison with you in those respects."

He made a gesture of contempt, and turned to me, saying: "You are strong, young sir; it is not every one can send a man flying through the air as you did just now; it was wonderful to see." Then touching the grizzly with his foot, he added: "And this is the game we wanted, but we came too late. We discovered its tracks yesterday, and followed over hill and dale, through thick and thin, only to find the work done when we came up with it."

"You speak in the plural; you are not alone?" I asked.

"No; I have two companions with me. But before I tell you who they are, will you introduce yourselves? You know one cannot be too cautious here, where we meet more bad men than good ones." He glanced significantly at Rattler and his followers, but instantly added in a friendly tone: "However, one can tell a gentleman that can be trusted. I heard the last part of your discussion, and know pretty well where I stand."

"We are surveyors, sir," I explained. "We are locating a railroad to go through here."

"Surveyors! Have you purchased the right to build your road?"

His face became stern as he asked the question, for which he seemed to have some reason; so I replied: "I have occupied myself with my task, and never thought of asking."

"Ah, yes; but you must know where you are. Consider these lands whereon we stand are the property of the Indians; they belong to the Apaches of the Mascaleros tribe. I am sure, if you are sent to survey, the ground is being marked out by the whites for some one else."

"What is that to you?" Rattler cried. "Don't bother yourself with the affairs of others. Any one can see you are a white man."

"I am an Apache, one of the Mascaleros," the stranger said quietly. "I am Kleki-Petrah."

This name in the Apache tongue is equivalent to White Father, and Rattler seemed to have heard it before. He bowed with mock deference, and said: "Ah, Kleki-Petrah, the venerated school-master of the Apaches! It's a pity you are deformed, for it must annoy you to be laughed at by the braves."

"They never do that, sir. Well-bred people are not amused by such things, and the braves are gentlemen. Since I know who you are and why you are here, I will tell you who my companions are, or perhaps you had better meet them."

He called in the Indian tongue, and two extraordinarily interesting figures appeared, and came slowly towards us. They were Indians, father and son, as one could see at the first glance. The elder was a little above medium height, very strongly built. His air was truly noble; his earnest face was of pure Indian type but not so sharp and keen as that of most red men. His eyes had a calm gentle expression, like one much given to contemplation. His head was bare, his hair worn in a knot in which was stuck an eagle's feather, the badge of chieftainship. His dress consisted of moccasins, leather leggings, and hunting-jacket, very simple and unadorned. From his belt, in which a knife was thrust, hung all the appointments necessary to a dweller on the plains. A medicine-charm with sacred inscriptions cut around its face hung from his neck, and in his hand he carried a double-barrelled gun, the handle adorned with silver nails.

The younger man was clad like his father, except that his garments were showier; his leggings were beautifully fringed, and his hunting-shirt was embellished with scarlet needlework. He also wore a medicine-charm around his neck, and a calumet; like his father he was armed with a knife and a double-barrelled gun. He, too, was bareheaded, his hair bound in a knot, but without the feather; it was so long that the end below the knot fell thick and heavy on his shoulders, and many a fine lady might have coveted it. His face was even nobler than his father's, its color a light brown with a touch of bronze. He seemed to be, as I afterwards learned he was, of the same age as myself, and his appearance made as profound an impression on me then, when I saw him first, as his character has left upon me today, after our long friendship.

We looked at one another long and searchingly, and I thought I saw for a moment in his earnest dark eyes a friendly light gleam upon me.

"These are my friends and companions," said Kleki-Petrah, introducing first the father, then the son. "This is Intschu-Tschuna Good Sun, the chief of the Mascaleros, whom all Apaches acknowledge as their head. And here stands his son Winnetou, who already in his youth has accomplished more deeds of renown than any ten old warriors have in all their lives. His name will be known and honored as far as the prairies and Rockies extend."

This sounded like exaggeration, but later I found that he had spoken only the truth.

Rattler laughed insultingly, and said: "So young a fellow, and committed such deeds? I say committed purposely, for every one knows they are only deeds of robbery and cruelty. The red men steal from every one."

This was an outrageous insult, but the Indians acted as though they had not heard it. Stooping down over the bear, Kleki-Petrah admired it, calling Winnetou's attention to its size and strength. "It was killed by a knife and not a bullet," he said as he rose.

Evidently, I thought, he had heard the dispute and wished me to have justice.

"What does a school-master know of bear-hunting?" said Rattler. "When we take the skin off we can see what killed him. I won't be robbed of my rights by a greenhorn."

Then Winnetou bent down, touched the bloody wound, and asked me in good English: "Who stabbed the beast?"

"I did," I replied.

"Why did not my young white brother shoot him?"

"Because I had no gun with me."

"Yet here are guns."

"They are not mine; they were thrown away by these men when they climbed the trees shrieking with terror."

"Ugh! the low cowards and dogs, to fly like tissuepaper! A man should make resistance, for if he has courage he may conquer the strongest brute. My young white brother has such courage."

"My son speaks truly," added the father in as perfect English. "This brave young pale-face is no longer a greenhorn. He who kills a grizzly in this manner is a hero; and he who does it to save those who climb trees deserves thanks, not insults. Let us go to visit the pale-faces that have come into our dominion."

They were but three, and did not know how many we numbered, but that never occurred to them. With slow and dignified strides they went out of the thicket, we following.

Then for the first time Intschu-Tschuna saw the surveying instruments standing as we had left them, and, stopping suddenly, he turned to me, demanding: "What is this? Are the pale-faces measuring the land?"

"Yes," I answered.

"Why?"

"For a railroad."

His eyes lost their calmness, and he asked sternly: "Do you obey these people, and measure with them?"

"Yes."

"And are paid for it?"

"Yes."

He threw a scornful glance upon me, and in a contemptuous tone he said to Kleki-Petrah: "Your teachings sound well, but they do not often agree with what I see. Christians deceive and rob the Indians. Here is a young pale-face with a brave heart, open face, honorable eyes, and when I ask what he does here he tells me he has come to steal our land. The faces of the white men are good and bad, but inside they are all alike."

To be honest, his words filled me with shame. Could I well be proud of my share in this matter—I, a Catholic, who had been taught so early: "Thou shalt not covet thy neighbor's goods"? I blushed for my race and for myself before this fine savage; and before I could rally enough even to try to reply, the head engineer, who had been watching us through a hole in the tent, came forth to meet us, and my thoughts were diverted by what then took place.

THE SPEECH OF THE APACHE CHIEF

The first question the head engineer asked us as we came up, although he was surprised to see the Indians with us, was what had become of the bear.

Rattler instantly replied: "We've shot him, and we'll have bear-paws for dinner, and bear-steak to-night for supper."

Our three guests looked at me as if to see whether I would let this pass, and I said: "I claim to have stabbed the bear. Here are three witnesses who have corroborated my statement; but we'll wait till Hawkins, Stone, and Parker come, and they will give their opinion, by which we will be guided. Till then the bear must lie untouched."

"Not much will I leave it to the scouts," growled Rattler. "I'll go with my men and cut up the bear, and whoever tries to hinder us will be driven off with a dozen shots in his body."

"Hold on, Mr. Rattler," said I. "I'm not as much afraid of your shots as you were of the bear. You won't drive me up a tree with your threats. I recommend you to bury your dead comrade; I would not leave him lying thus."

"Is some one dead?" asked Bancroft, startled.

"Yes, Rollins," Rattler replied. "The poor fellow had jumped for a tree, like the rest of us, and would have been all right, but this greenhorn came up, excited the bear, and it tore Rollins horribly."

I stood speechless with amazement that he should dare go so far. It was impossible to endure such lying, and in my very presence. I turned on Rattler and demanded: "Do you mean to say Rollins was escaping and I prevented it?"

"Yes," he nodded, drawing his revolver.

"And I say the bear had seized him before I came."

"That's a lie," said Rattler.

"Very well; here's a truth for you," and with these words I knocked his revolver from his hand with my left, and with the right gave him such a blow on the ear that he staggered six or eight feet away, and fell flat on the ground.

He sprang up, drew his knife, and came at me raging like a wild beast. I parried the knife-thrust with my left hand, and with my right laid him senseless at my feet.

"Ugh! ugh!" grunted Intschu-Tschuna, surprised into admiration, which his race rarely betray.

"That was Shatterhand again," said Wheeler, the surveyor.

I kept my eye on Rattler's comrades; they were angry but no one dared attack me, and though they muttered among themselves they did no more.

"You must send Rattler away, Mr. Bancroft," I said. "I have done nothing to him, yet he constantly seeks a quarrel with me. I am afraid he'll make serious trouble in the camp. Send him away, or, if you prefer, I'll go myself."

"Oh, things aren't as bad as that," said Bancroft easily.

"Yes, they are, just as bad as that. Here are his knife and revolver; don't let him have them, for I warn you they'd not be in good hands."

Just as I spoke these words our three scouts joined us, and having heard the story of Rattler's lying claim, and my counter-statement, they set off at once to examine the bear's carcass to settle the dispute. They returned in a short time, and as soon as he was within hailing distance Sam called out: "What idiocy it was to shoot a grizzly and then run! If a man doesn't intend making a fight, then what on earth does he shoot for? Why doesn't he leave the bear in peace? You can't treat grizzlies like poodle-dogs. Poor Rollins paid dear for it though. Now, who killed that bear did you say?

"I did," cried Rattler, who had come to. "I killed him with my gun."

"Well, that agrees; that's all right. The bear was shot."

"Do you hear that, men? Sam Hawkins has decided for me," cried Rattler triumphantly

"Yes, for you," said Sam. "You shot him, and took off the tip of his ear, and such a loss naturally ended the grizzly, ha! ha! ha! If you shot again it went wide of the mark, for there's no other gun-shot on him. But there are four true knife-thrusts, two above the heart and two in it; who gave him those?"

"I did," I said.

"You alone?"

"No one else."

"Then the bear belongs to you. That is, the pelt is yours; the flesh belongs to all, but you have the right to divide it. This is the custom of the West. Have you anything to say, Mr. Rattler?"

Rattler growled something that condemned us to a much warmer climate, and turned sullenly to the wagon where the liquor was stored. I saw him pour down glass after glass, and knew he would drink till he could drink no more.

The Indians had listened to our discussion, and watched us in silent interest; but now, our affairs being settled, the chief, Intschu-Tschuna, turned to the head engineer, saying: "My ear has told me that among these palefaces you are chief; is this so?"

"Yes," Bancroft replied.

"Then I have something to say to you."

"What is it?"

"You shall hear. But you are standing, and men should sit in conference."

"Will you be our guest?" asked Bancroft.

"No, for it is impossible. How can I be your guest when you are on my lands, in my forests, my valleys, my prairies? Let the white men be seated."

"Tell me what you wish of me," said Bancroft.

"It is not a wish, but a command," answered Intschu-Tschuna proudly.

"We will take no command," responded the head engineer with equal pride.

A look of anger passed over the chief's face, but he controlled himself, and said mildly: "My white brother will answer me one question truthfully. Have you a house?"

"Yes."

"With a garden?"

"Yes."

"If a neighbor would cut a path through that garden would my brother submit to it?"

"No."

"The lands beyond the Rocky Mountains and east of the Mississippi belong to the pale-faces. What would they say if the Indians came to build a railroad there?"

"They would drive them away."

"My white brother has answered truly. But the palefaces come here on these lands of ours, and drive away our mustangs and kill our buffaloes; they seek among us for gold and precious stones, and now they will build a long, long road on which their fire-horses can run. Then more pale-faces will follow this road, and settle among us, and take the little we have left us. What are we to say to this?"

Bancroft was silent.

"Have we fewer rights than they? You call yourselves Christians, and speak of love, yet you say: We can rob and cheat you, but you must be honest with us. Is that love? You say your God is the Good Father of all men, red and white. Is He only our stepfather, and are you His own sons? Did not all the land belong to the red man? It has been taken from us, and what have we instead? Misery, misery, misery. You drive us ever farther and farther back, and press us closer and closer together, and in a little time we shall be suffocated. Why do you do this?

Is it because you have not room enough? No, for there is room in your lands still for many, many millions. Each of your tribes can have a whole State, but the red man, the true owner, may not have a place to lay his head. Kleki-Petrah, who sits here before me, has taught me your Holy Book. There it says that the first man had two sons, and one killed the other, and his blood cried to Heaven. How is it with the two brothers, the red and the white? Are you not Cain, and are we not Abel, whose blood cries to Heaven? And when you try to destroy us you vanish us to make no defence. But we will defend ourselves, will defend ourselves. We have been driven from place to place, ever farther away; now we collide here, where we believed ourselves at rest, but you come to build your railroad. Have we not the same rights you have over your house and garden? If we followed our own laws we should kill you; but we only wish your laws to be fulfilled towards us: are they? No! Your laws have two faces, and you turn them to us as it suits your advantage. Have you asked our permission to build this road?"

"No," said Bancroft. "It was not necessary."

"Have you bought the land, or have we sold it?"

"Not to me."

"Nor to any other. Were you an honest man sent here to build a way for the fire-horse, you would first have asked the man who sent you whether he had a right to do this thing, and made him prove it. But this you have not done. I forbid you to measure further."

These last words were spoken in a tone of most bitter earnest.

I had read much of the red man, but never had found in any book such a speech from an Indian, and I wondered if he owed his fluent English and forcible logic to Kleki-Petrah.

The head engineer found himself in an awkward predicament. If he was honest and sincere he could not gainsay what Intschu-Tschuna had spoken; but there were considerations more weighty with Bancroft than honesty, so the chief had to wait his answer, looking him straight in the eyes.

Seeing that Bancroft was shifting about in his mind for a way out of his difficulty, Intschu-Tschuna rose, saying decidedly: "There is no need of further speech. I have spoken. My will is that you leave here to-day, and go back whence you came. Decide whether you will obey or not. I will now depart with my son Winnetou, and will return at the end of that time which the pale-faces call an hour, when you will give me your answer. If you go, we are brothers; if you stay, it shall be deadly enmity between you and me. I am Intschu-Tschuna, the chief of all the Apaches. I have spoken."

Winnetou followed him as he went out from among us, and they were soon lost to sight down the valley.

Kleki-Petrah remained seated, and Bancroft turned to him and asked his advice. He replied: "Do as you will, sir. I am of the chief's opinion. The red race has been cruelly outraged and robbed. But as a white man I know that the Indian must disappear. If you are an honest man and go to-day, to-morrow another will come to carry on your work. I warn you, however, that the chief is in earnest."

He, too, rose, as if to put an end to further questioning. I went up to him and said: "Sir, will you let me go with you? I promise to do or say nothing that will annoy you. It is only because I feel extraordinary interest in Intschu-Tsc-huna, and even more in Winnetou."

That he himself was included in this interest I dared not say.

"Yes, come with me a little way," he replied. "I have withdrawn from my race, and must know them no more; but since you have crossed my path, there can be no harm in our meeting, and some good may result from it. We will walk a little together. You seem to me the most intelligent of these men; am I right?"

"I am the youngest, and not clever, and I should be honored if you allowed me to go with you," I answered respectfully.

"Come, then," said Kleki-Petrah kindly, and we walked slowly away from the camp.

THE DRIVE

STEWART EDWARD WHITE

A cry awakened me. It was still deep night. The moon sailed overhead, the stars shone unwavering like candles, and a chill breeze wandered in from the open spaces of the desert. I raised myself on my elbow, throwing aside the blankets and the canvas tarpaulin. Forty other indistinct, formless bundles on the ground all about me were sluggishly astir. Four figures passed and repassed between me and a red fire. I knew them for the two cooks and the horse wranglers. One of the latter was grumbling.

"Didn't git in till moon-up last night," he growled. "Might as well trade my bed for a lantern and be done with it."

Even as I stretched my arms and shivered a little, the two wranglers threw down their tin plates with a clatter, mounted horses and rode away in the direction of the thousand acres or so known as the pasture.

I pulled on my clothes hastily, buckled in my buckskin shirt, and dove for the fire. A dozen others were before me. It was bitterly cold. In the east the sky had paled the least bit in the world, but the moon and stars shone on bravely and undiminished. A band of coyotes was shrieking desperate blasphemies against the new day, and the stray herd, awakening, was beginning to bawl and bellow.

Two crater-like dutch ovens, filled with pieces of fried beef, stood near the fire; two galvanised water buckets, brimming with soda biscuits, flanked them; two tremendous coffee pots stood guard at either end. We picked us each a tin cup and a tin plate from the box at the rear of the chuck wagon; helped ourselves from a dutch oven, a pail, and a coffee pot, and squatted on our heels as close to the fire as possible. Men who came too late borrowed the shovel, scooped up some coals, and so started little fires of their own about which new groups formed.

While we ate, the eastern sky lightened. The mountains under the dawn looked like silhouettes cut from slate-coloured paper; those in the west showed faintly luminous. Objects about us became dimly visible. We could make out the windmill, and the adobe of the ranch houses, and the corrals. The cowboys arose one by one, dropped their plates into the dishpan, and began to hunt out their ropes. Everything was obscure and mysterious in the faint grey light. I watched Windy Bill near his tarpaulin. He stooped to throw over the canvas. When he bent, it was before daylight; when he straightened his back, daylight had come. It was just like that, as though someone had reached out his hand to turn on the illumination of the world.

The eastern mountains were fragile, the plain was ethereal, like a sea of liquid gases. From the pasture we heard the shoutings of the wranglers, and made out a cloud of dust. In a moment the first of the remuda came into view, trotting forward with the free grace of the unburdened horse. Others followed in procession: those near sharp and well defined, those in the background more or less obscured by the dust, now appearing plainly, now fading like ghosts. The leader turned unhesitatingly into the corral. After him poured the stream of the remuda—two hundred and fifty saddle horses—with an unceasing thunder of hoofs.

Immediately the cook-camp was deserted. The cowboys entered the corral. The horses began to circle around the edge of the enclosure as around the circumference of a circus ring. The men, grouped at the centre, watched keenly, looking for the mounts they had already decided on. In no time each had recognised his choice, and, his loop trailing, was walking toward that part of the revolving circumference where his pony dodged. Some few whirled the loop, but most cast it with a quick flip. It was really marvellous to observe the accuracy with which the noose would fly, past a dozen tossing heads, and over a dozen backs, to settle firmly about the neck of animal perhaps in the very centre of the group. But again, if the first throw failed, it was interesting to see how the selected pony would dodge, double back, twist, turn, and hide to escape a second cast. And it was equally interesting to observe how his companions would help him. They seemed to realise that they were not wanted, and would push themselves between the cowboy and his intended mount with the utmost boldness. In the thick dust that instantly arose, and with the bewildering thunder of galloping, the flashing change of grouping, the rush of the charging animals, recognition alone would seem almost impossible, yet in an incredibly short time each had his mount, and the others, under convoy of the wranglers, were meekly wending their way out over the plain. There, until time for a change of horses, they would graze in a loose and scattered band, requiring scarcely any supervision. Escape? Bless you, no, that thought was the last in their minds.

In the meantime the saddles and bridles were adjusted. Always in a cowboy's "string" of from six to ten animals the boss assigns him two or three broncos to break in to the cow business. Therefore, each morning we could observe a half dozen or so men gingerly leading wicked looking little animals out to the sand "to take the pitch out of them." One small black, belonging to a cowboy called the Judge, used more than to fulfil expectations of a good time.

"Go to him, Judge!" someone would always remark.

"If he ain't goin' to pitch, I ain't goin' to make him," the Judge would grin, as he swung aboard.

The black would trot off quite calmly and in a most matter of fact way, as though to shame all slanderers of his lamb-like character. Then, as the bystanders would turn away, he would utter a squeal, throw down his head, and go at it. He was a very hard bucker, and made some really spectacular jumps, but the trick on which he based his claims to originality consisted in standing on his hind legs at so perilous an approach to the perpendicular that his rider would conclude he was about to fall backwards, and then suddenly springing forward in a series of stifflegged bucks. The first manoeuvre induced the rider to loosen his seat in order to be ready to jump from under, and the second threw him before he could regain his grip.

"And they say a horse don't think!" exclaimed an admirer.

But as these were broken horses—save the mark!—the show was all over after each had had his little fling. We mounted and rode away, just as the mountain peaks to the west caught the rays of a sun we should not enjoy for a good half hour yet.

I had five horses in my string, and this morning rode "that C S horse Brown Jug." Brown Jug was a powerful and well-built animal, about fourteen two in height, and possessed of a vast enthusiasm for cow-work. As the morning was frosty, he felt good.

At the gate of the water corral we separated into two groups. The smaller, under the direction of Jed Parker, was to drive the mesquite in the wide flats; the rest of us, under the command of Homer, the round-up captain, were to sweep the country even as far as the base of the foothills near Mount Graham. Accordingly we put our horses to the full gallop.

Mile after mile we thundered along at a brisk rate of speed. Sometimes we dodged in and out among the mesquite bushes, alternately separating and coming together again; sometimes we swept over grassy plains apparently of illimitable extent; sometimes we skipped and hopped and buck-jumped through and over little gullies, barrancas, and other sorts of malpais—but always without drawing rein. The men rode easily, with no thought to the way nor care for the footing. The air came back sharp against our faces. The warm blood stirred by the rush flowed more rapidly. We experienced a delightful glow. Of the morning cold only the very tips of our fingers and the ends of our noses retained a remnant. Already the sun was shining low and level across the plains. The shadows of the cañons modelled the hitherto flat surfaces of the mountains.

After a time we came to some low hills helmeted with the outcrop of a rock escarpment. Hitherto they had seemed a termination of Mount Graham, but now, when we rode around them, we discovered them to be separated from the range by a good five miles of sloping plain. Later we looked back and would have sworn them part of the Dos Cabesas system, did we not know them to be at least eight miles' distant from that rocky rampart. It is always that way in Arizona. Spaces develop of whose existence you had not the slightest intimation. Hidden in apparently plane surfaces are valleys and prairies. At one sweep of the eye you embrace the entire area of an eastern State; but nevertheless the reality as you explore it foot by foot proves to be infinitely more than the vision has promised.

Beyond the hill we stopped. Here our party divided again, half to the right and half to the left. We had ridden, up to this time, directly away from camp, now we rode a circumference of which headquarters was the centre. The country was pleasantly rolling and covered with grass. Here and there were clumps of soapweed. Far in a remote distance lay a slender dark line across the plain. This we knew to be mesquite; and once entered, we knew it, too, would seem to spread out vastly. And then this grassy slope, on which we now rode, would show merely as an insignificant streak of yellow. It is also like that in Arizona. I have ridden in succession through grass land, brush land, flower land, desert. Each in turn seemed entirely to fill the space of the plains between the mountains.

From time to time Homer halted us and detached a man. The business of the latter was then to ride directly back to camp, driving all cattle before him. Each was in eight of his right- and left-hand neighbour. Thus was constructed a drag-net whose meshes contracted as home was neared.

I was detached, when of our party only the Cattleman and Homer remained. They would take the outside. This was the post of honour, and required the hardest riding, for as soon as the cattle should realise the fact of their pursuit, they would attempt to "break" past the end and up the valley. Brown Jug and I congratulated ourselves on an exciting morning in prospect.

Now, wild cattle know perfectly well what a drive means, and they do not intend to get into a round-up if they can help it. Were it not for the two facts, that they are afraid of a mounted man, and cannot run quite so fast as a horse, I do not know how the cattle business would be conducted. As soon as a band of them caught sight of any one of us, they curled their tails and away they went at a long, easy lope that a domestic cow would stare at in wonder. This was all very well; in fact we yelled and shrieked and otherwise uttered cow-calls to keep them going, to "get the cattle started," as they say. But pretty soon a little band of the many scurrying away before our thin line, began to bear farther and farther to the east. When in their judgment they should have gained an opening, they would turn directly back and make a dash for liberty. Accordingly the nearest cowboy, clapped spurs to his horse and pursued them.

It was a pretty race. The cattle ran easily enough, with long, springy jumps that carried them over the ground faster than appearances would lead one to believe. The cow-pony, his nose stretched out, his ears slanted, his eyes snapping with joy of the chase, flew fairly "belly to earth." The rider sat slightly forward, with the cowboy's loose seat. A whirl of dust, strangely insignificant against the immensity of a desert morning, rose from the flying group. Now they disappeared in a ravine only to scramble out again the next instant, pace undiminished. The rider merely rose slightly and threw up his elbows to relieve the jar of the rough gully. At first the cattle seemed to hold their own, but soon the horse began to gain. In a short time he had come abreast of the leading animal. The latter stopped short with a snort, dodged back, and set out at right angles to his former course. From a dead run the pony came to a stand in two fierce plunges, doubled like a shot, and was off on the other tack. An unaccustomed rider would here have lost his seat. The second dash was short. With a final shake of the head, the steers turned to the proper course in the direction of the ranch. The pony dropped unconcernedly to the shuffling jog of habitual progression.

Far away stretched the arc of our cordon. The most distant rider was a speck, and the cattle ahead of him were like maggots endowed with a smooth, swift onward motion. As yet the herd had not taken form; it was still too widely scattered. Its units, in the shape of small bunches, momently grew in numbers. The distant plains were crawling and alive with minute creatures making toward a common tiny centre.

Immediately in our front the cattle at first behaved very well. Then far down the long gentle slope I saw a break for the upper valley. The manikin that represented Homer at once became even smaller as it departed in pursuit. The Cattleman moved down to cover Homer's territory until he should return, and I in turn edged farther to the right. Then another break from another bunch. The Cattleman rode at top speed to head it. Before long he disappeared in the distant mesquite. I found myself in sole charge of a front three miles long.

The nearest cattle were some distance ahead, and trotting along at a good gait. As they had not yet discovered the chance left open by unforeseen circumstance, I descended and took in on my cinch while yet there was time. Even as I mounted, an impatient movement on the part of experienced Brown Jug told me that the cattle had seen their opportunity.

I gathered the reins and spoke to the horse. He needed no further direction, but set off at a wide angle, nicely calculated, to intercept the truants. Brown Jug was a powerful beast. The spring of his leap was as whalebone. The yellow earth began to stream past like water. Always the pace increased with a growing thunder of hoofs. It seemed that nothing could turn us from the straight line, nothing check the headlong momentum of our rush. My eyes filled with tears from the wind of our going. Saddle strings streamed behind. Brown Jug's mane whipped my bridle hand. Dimly I was conscious of soapweed, sacatone, mesquite, as we passed them. They were abreast and gone before I could think of them or how they were to be dodged. Two antelope bounded away to the left; birds rose hastily from the grasses. A sudden *chirk, chirk, chirk*, rose all about me. We were in the very centre of a prairie-dog town, but before I could formulate in my mind the probabilities of holes and broken legs, the *chirk, chirk, chirk*ing had fallen astern. Brown Jug had skipped and dodged successfully.

We were approaching the cattle. They ran stubbornly and well, evidently unwilling to be turned until the latest possible moment. A great rage at their obstinacy took possession of us both. A broad shallow wash crossed our way, but we plunged through its rocks and boulders recklessly, angered at even the slight delay they necessitated. The hard land on the other side we greeted with joy. Brown Jug extended himself with a snort.

Suddenly a jar seemed to shake my very head loose. I found myself staring over the horse's head directly down into a deep and precipitous gully, the edge of which was so cunningly concealed by the grasses as to have remained invisible to my blurred vision. Brown Jug, however, had caught sight of it at the last instant, and had executed one of the wonderful stops possible only to a cow-pony.

But already the cattle had discovered a passage above, and were scrambling down and across. Brown Jug and I, at more sober pace, slid off the almost per-pendicular bank, and out the other side.

A moment later we had headed them. They whirled, and without the necessity of any suggestion on my part Brown Jug turned after them, and so quickly that my stirrup actually brushed the ground. After that we were masters. We chased the cattle far enough to start them well in the proper direction, and then pulled down to a walk in order to get a breath of air.

But now we noticed another band, back on the ground over which we had just come, doubling through in the direction of Mount Graham. A hard run set them to rights. We turned. More had poured out from the hills. Bands were crossing everywhere, ahead and behind. Brown Jug and I set to work.

Being an indivisible unit, we could chase only one bunch at a time; and, while we were after one, a half dozen others would be taking advantage of our preoccupation. We could not hold our own. Each run after an escaping bunch had to be on a longer diagonal. Gradually we were forced back, and back, and back; but still we managed to hold the line unbroken. Never shall I forget the dash and clatter of that morning. Neither Brown Jug nor I thought for a moment of sparing horseflesh, nor of picking a route. We made the shortest line, and paid little attention to anything that stood in the way. A very fever of resistance possessed us. It was like beating against a head wind, or fight-ing fire, or combating in any other way any of the great forces of nature. We were quite alone. The Cattleman and Homer had vanished. To our left the men were fully occupied in marshalling the compact brown herds that had gradually massed—for these antagonists of mine were merely the outlying remnants.

I suppose Brown Jug must have run nearly twenty miles with only one check. Then we chased a cow some distance and into the dry bed of a stream, where she whirled on us savagely. By luck her horn hit only the leather of my saddle skirts, so we left her; for when a cow has sense enough to "get on the peck," there is no driving her farther. We gained nothing, and had to give ground, but we succeeded in holding a semblance of order, so that the cattle did not break and scatter far and wide. The sun had by now well risen, and was beginning to shine hot. Brown Jug still ran gamely and displayed as much interest as ever, but he was evidently tiring. We were both glad to see Homer's grey showing in the fringe of mesquite.

Together we soon succeeded in throwing the cows into the main herd. And, strangely enough, as soon as they had joined a compact band of their fellows, their wildness left them and, convoyed by outsiders, they set themselves to plodding energetically toward the home ranch.

As my horse was somewhat winded, I joined the "drag" at the rear. Here by course of natural sifting soon accumulated all the lazy, gentle, and sickly cows, and the small calves. The difficulty now was to prevent them from lagging and dropping out. To that end we indulged in a great variety of the picturesque cow-calls peculiar to the cowboy. One found an old tin can which by the aid of a few pebbles he converted into a very effective rattle.

The dust rose in clouds and eddied in the sun. We slouched easily in our saddles. The cowboys compared notes as to the brands they had seen. Our ponies shuffled along, resting, but always ready for a dash in chase of an occasional bull calf or yearling with independent ideas of its own.

Thus we passed over the country, down the long gentle slope to the "sink" of the valley, whence another long gentle slope ran to the base of the other ranges. At greater or lesser distances we caught the dust, and made out dimly the masses of the other herds collected by our companions, and by the party under Jed Parker. They went forward toward the common centre, with a slow ruminative movement, and the dust they raised went with them.

Little by little they grew plainer to us, and the home ranch, hitherto merely a brown shimmer in the distance, began to take on definition as the group of buildings, windmills, and corrals we knew. Miniature horsemen could be seen galloping forward to the open white plain where the herd would be held. Then the mesquite enveloped us; and we knew little more, save the anxiety lest we overlook laggards in the brush, until we came out on the edge of that same white plain.

Here were more cattle, thousands of them, and billows of dust, and a great bellowing, and dim, mounted figures riding and shouting ahead of the herd. Soon they succeeded in turning the leaders back. These threw into confusion those that followed. In a few moments the cattle had stopped. A cordon of horsemen sat at equal distances holding them in.

"Pretty good haul," said the man next to me; a good five thousand head."

It was somewhere near noon by the time we had bunched and held the herd of some four or five thousand head in the smooth, wide flat, free from bushes and dog holes. Each sat at ease on his horse facing the cattle, watching lazily the clouds of dust and the shifting beasts, but ready at any instant to turn back the restless or independent individuals that might break for liberty.

Out of the haze came Homer, the round-up captain, on an easy lope. As he passed successively the sentries he delivered to each a low command, but without slacking pace. Some of those spoken to wheeled their horses and rode away. The others settled themselves in their saddles and began to roll cigarettes.

"Change horses; get something to eat," said he to me; so I swung after the file trailing at a canter over the low swells beyond the plain.

The remuda had been driven by its leaders to a corner of the pasture's wire fence and there held. As each man arrived he dismounted, threw off his saddle, and turned his animal loose. Then he flipped a loop in his rope and disappeared in the eddying herd. The discarded horse, with many grunts, indulged in a satisfying roll, shook himself vigorously, and walked slowly away. His labour was over for the day, and he knew it, and took not the slightest trouble to get out of the way of the men with the swinging ropes.

Not so the fresh horses, however. They had no intention of being caught, if they could help it, but dodged and twisted, hid and doubled behind the moving screen of their friends. The latter, seeming as usual to know they were not wanted, made no effort to avoid the men, which probably accounted in great measure for the fact that the herd as a body remained compact, in spite of the cowboys threading it, and in spite of the lack of an enclosure.

Our horses caught, we saddled as hastily as possible; and then at the top speed of our fresh and eager ponies we swept down on the chuck wagon. There we fell off our saddles and descended on the meat and bread like ravenous locusts on a cornfield. The ponies stood where we left them, "tied to the ground" in the cattle-country fashion.

As soon as a man had stoked up for the afternoon he rode away. Some finished before others, so across the plain formed an endless procession of men returning to the herd, and of those whom they replaced coming for their turn at the grub.

We found the herd quiet. Some were even lying down, chewing their cuds as peacefully as any barnyard cows. Most, however, stood ruminative, or walked slowly to and fro in the confines allotted by the horsemen, so that the herd looked from a distance like a brown carpet whose pattern was constantly changing—a dusty brown carpet in the process of being beaten. I relieved one of the watchers, and settled myself for a wait.

At this close inspection the different sorts of cattle showed more distinctly their characteristics. The cows and calves generally rested peacefully enough, the calf often lying down while the mother stood guard over it. Steers, however, were more restless. They walked ceaselessly, threading their way in and out among the standing cattle, pausing in brutish amazement at the edge of the herd, and turning back immediately to endless journeyings. The bulls, excited by so much company forced on their accustomed solitary habit, roared defiance at each other until the air fairly trembled. Occasionally two would clash foreheads. Then the powerful animals would push and wrestle, trying for a chance to gore. The decision of supremacy was a question of but a few minutes, and a bloody topknot the worst damage. The defeated one side-stepped hastily and clumsily out of reach, and then walked away.

Most of the time all we had to do was to sit our horses and watch these things, to enjoy, the warm bath of the Arizona sun, and to converse with our next neighbours. Once in a while some enterprising cow, observing the opening between the men, would start to walk out. Others would fall in behind her until the movement would become general. Then one of us would swing his leg off the pommel and jog his pony over to head them off. They would return peacefully enough.

But one black muley cow, with a calf as black and muley as herself, was more persistent. Time after time, with infinite patience, she tried it again the moment my back was turned. I tried driving her far into the herd. No use; she always returned. Quirtings and stones had no effect on her mild and steady persistence.

"She's a San Simon cow," drawled my neighbour. "Everybody knows her. She's at every round-up, just naturally raisin' hell."

When the last man had returned from chuck, Homer made the dispositions for the cut. There were present probably thirty men from the home ranches round about, and twenty representing owners at a distance, here to pick up the strays inevitable to the season's drift. The round-up captain appointed two men to hold the cow-and-calf cut, and two more to hold the steer cut. Several of us rode into the herd, while the remainder retained their positions as sentinels to hold the main body of cattle in shape.

Little G and I rode slowly among the cattle looking everywhere. The animals moved sluggishly aside to give us passage, and closed in as sluggishly behind us, so that we were always closely hemmed in wherever we went. Over the shifting sleek backs, through the eddying clouds of dust, I could make out the figures of my companions moving slowly, apparently aimlessly, here and there.

Our task for the moment was to search out the unbranded J H calves. Since in ranks so closely crowded it would be physically impossible actually to see an animal's branded flank, we depended entirely on the ear-marks.

Did you ever notice how any animal, tame or wild, always points his ears inquiringly in the direction of whatever interests or alarms him? Those ears are for the moment his most prominent feature. So when a brand is quite indistinguishable because, as now, of press of numbers, or, as in winter, from extreme length of hair, the cropped ears tell plainly the tale of ownership. As every animal is so marked when branded, it follows that an uncut pair of ears means that its owner has never felt the iron.

So, now we had to look first of all for calves with uncut ears. After discovering one, we had to ascertain his ownership by examining the ear-marks of his mother, by whose side he was sure, in this alarming multitude, to be clinging faithfully.

Calves were numerous, and J H cows everywhere to be seen, so in somewhat less than ten seconds I had my eye on a mother and son. Immediately I turned Little G in their direction. At the slap of my quirt against the stirrup, all the cows immediately about me shrank suspiciously aside. Little G stepped forward daintily, his nostrils expanding, his ears working back and forth, trying to the best of his ability to understand which animals I had selected. The cow and her calf turned in toward the centre of the herd. A touch of the reins guided the pony. At once he comprehended. From that time on he needed no further directions. Cautiously, patiently, with great skill, he forced the cow through the press toward the edge of the herd. It had to be done very quietly, at a foot pace, so as to alarm neither the objects of pursuit nor those surrounding them. When the cow turned back, Little G somehow happened always in her way. Before she knew it she was at the outer edge of the herd. There she found herself, with a group of three or four companions, facing the open plain. Instinctively she sought shelter. I felt Little G's muscles tighten beneath me. The moment for action had come. Before the cow had a chance to dodge among her companions the pony was upon her like a thunderbolt. She broke in alarm, trying desperately to avoid the rush. There ensued an exciting contest of dodgings, turnings, and doublings. Wherever she turned Little G was before her. Some of his evolutions were marvellous. All I had to do was to sit my saddle, and apply just that final touch of judgment denied even the wisest of the lower animals. Time and again the turn was so quick that the stirrup swept the ground. At last the cow, convinced of the uselessness of further effort to return, broke away on a long lumbering run to the open plain. She was stopped and held by the men detailed, and so formed the nucleus of the new cut-herd. Immediately Little G, his ears working in conscious virtue, jog-trotted back into the herd, ready for another.

After a dozen cows had been sent across to the cut-herd, the work simplified. Once a cow caught sight of this new band, she generally made directly for it, head and tail up. After the first short struggle to force her from the herd, all I had to do was to start her in the proper direction and keep her at it until her decision was fixed. If she was too soon left to her own devices, however, she was likely to return. An old cowman knows to a second just the proper moment to abandon her.

Sometimes in spite of our best efforts a cow succeeded in circling us and plunging into the main herd. The temptation was then strong to plunge in also, and to drive her out by main force; but the temptation had to be resisted. A dash into the thick of it might break the whole band. At once, of his own accord, Little G dropped to his fast, shuffling walk, and again we addressed ourselves to the task of pushing her gently to the edge.

This was all comparatively simple—almost any pony is fast enough for the calf cut—but now Homer gave orders for the steer cut to begin, and steers are rapid and resourceful and full of natural cussedness. Little G and I were relieved by Windy Bill, and betook ourselves to the outside of the herd.

Here we had leisure to observe the effects that up to this moment we had ourselves been producing. The herd, restless by reason of the horsemen threading it, shifted, gave ground, expanded, and contracted, so that its shape and size were always changing in the constant area guarded by the sentinel cowboys. Dust arose from these movements, clouds of it, to eddy and swirl, thicken and dissipate in the currents of air. Now it concealed all but the nearest dimly-out lined animals; again it parted in rifts through which mistily we discerned the riders moving in and out of the fog; again it lifted high and thin, so that we saw in clarity the whole herd and the outriders and the mesas far away. As the afternoon waned, long shafts of sun slanted through this dust. It played on men and beasts magically, expanding them to the dimensions of strange genii, appearing and effacing themselves in the billows of vapour from some enchanted bottle.

We on the outside found our sinecure of hot noontide filched from us by the cooler hours. The cattle, wearied of standing, and perhaps somewhat hungry and thirsty, grew more and more impatient. We rode continually back and forth, turning the slow movement in on itself. Occasionally some particularly enterprising cow would conclude that one or another of the cut-herds would suit her better than this mill of turmoil. She would start confidently out, head and tail up, find herself chased back, get stubborn on the question, and lead her pursuer a long, hard run before she would return to her companions. Once in a while one would even have to be roped and dragged back. For know, before something happens to you, that you can chase a cow safely only until she gets hot and winded. Then she stands her ground and gets emphatically "on the peck."

I remember very well when I first discovered this. It was after I had had considerable cow work, too. I thought of cows as I had always seen them—afraid of a horseman, easy to turn with the pony, and willing to be chased as far as necessary to the work. Nobody told me anything different. One day we were making a drive in an exceedingly broken country. I was bringing in a small bunch I had discovered in a pocket of the hills, but was excessively annoyed by one old cow that insisted on breaking back. In the wisdom of further experience, I now conclude that she probably had a calf in the brush Finally she got away entirely. After starting the bunch well ahead, I went after her.

Well, the cow and I ran nearly side by side for as much as half a mile at top speed. She declined to be headed. Finally she fell down and was so entirely winded that she could not get up.

"Now, old girl, I've got you!" said I, and set myself to urging her to her feet.

The pony, acted somewhat astonished, and suspicious of the job. Therein he knew a lot more than I did. But I insisted, and, like a good pony, he obeyed. I yelled at the cow, and slapped my hat, and used my quirt. When she had quite recovered her wind, she got slowly to her feet—and charged me in a most determined manner.

Now, a bull, or a steer, is not difficult to dodge. He lowers his head, shuts his eyes, and comes in on one straight rush. But a cow looks to see what she is doing; her eyes are open every minute, and it overjoys her to take a side hook at you even when you succeed in eluding her direct charge.

The pony I was riding did his best, but even then could not avoid a sharp prod that would have ripped him up had not my leather bastos intervened. Then we retired to a distance in order to plan further, but we did not succeed in inducing that cow to revise her ideas, so at last we left her. When, in some chagrin, I mentioned to the round-up captain the fact that I had skipped one animal, he merely laughed.

"Why, kid," said he, "you can't do nothin' with a cow that gets on the prod that away 'thout you ropes her; and what could you do with her out there if you *did* rope her?"

So I learned one thing more about cows.

After the steer cut had been finished, the men representing the neighbouring ranges looked through the herd for strays of their brands. These were thrown into the stray-herd, which had been brought up from the bottom lands to receive the new accessions. Work was pushed rapidly, as the afternoon was nearly gone.

In fact, so absorbed were we that until it was almost upon us we did not notice a heavy thunder-shower that arose in the region of the Dragoon Mountains, and swept rapidly across the zenith. Before we knew it the rain had begun. In ten seconds it had increased to a deluge, and in twenty we were all to leeward of the herd striving desperately to stop the drift of the cattle down wind.

We did everything in our power to stop them, but in vain. Slickers waved, quirts slapped against leather, six-shooters flashed, but still the cattle, heads lowered, advanced with a slow and sullen persistence that would not be stemmed. If we held our ground, they divided around us. Step by step we were forced to give way—the thin line of nervously plunging horses sprayed before the dense mass of the cattle.

"No, they won't stampede, "shouted Charley to my question. "There's cows and calves in them. If they was just steers or grown critters, they might."

The sensations of those few moments were very vivid—the blinding beat of the storm in my face, the unbroken front of horned heads bearing down on me, resistless as fate, the long slant of rain with the sun shining in the distance beyond it.

Abruptly the downpour ceased. We shook our hats free of water, and drove the herd back to the cutting grounds again.

But now the surface of the ground was slippery, and the rapid manoeuvring of horses had become a matter precarious in the extreme. Time and again the ponies fairly sat on their haunches and slid when negotiating a sudden stop, while quick turns meant the rapid scramblings that only a cow-horse could accomplish. Nevertheless the work went forward unchecked. The men of the other outfits cut their cattle into the stray-herd. The latter was by now of considerable size, for this was the third week of the round-up.

Finally everyone expressed himself as satisfied. The largely diminished main herd was now started forward by means of shrill cowboy cries and beating of quirts. The cattle were only too eager to go. From my position on a little rise above the stray-herd I could see the leaders breaking into a run, their heads thrown forward as they snuffed their freedom. On the mesa side the sentinel riders quietly withdrew. From the rear and flanks the horsemen closed in. The cattle poured out in a steady stream through the opening thus left on the mesa side. The fringe of cowboys followed, urging them on. Abruptly the cavalcade turned and came loping back. The cattle continued ahead on a trot, gradually spreading abroad over the landscape, losing their

integrity as a herd. Some of the slower or hungrier dropped out and began to graze. Certain of the more wary disappeared to right or left.

Now, after the day's work was practically over, we had our first accident. The horse ridden by a young fellow from Dos Cabesas slipped, fell, and rolled quite over his rider. At once the animal lunged to his feet, only to be immediately seized by the nearest rider. But the Dos Cabesas man lay still, his arms and legs spread abroad, his head doubled sideways in a horribly suggestive manner. We hopped off. Two men straightened him out, while two more looked carefully over the indications on the ground.

"All right," sang out one of these, "the horn didn't catch him."

He pointed to the indentation left by the pommel. Indeed five minutes brought the man to his senses. He complained of a very twisted back. Homer sent one of the men in after the bed-wagon, by means of which the sufferer was shortly transported to camp. By the end of the week he was again in the saddle. How men escape from this common accident with injuries so slight has always puzzled me. The horse rolls completely over his rider, and yet it seems to be the rarest thing in the world for the latter to be either killed or permanently injured.

Now each man had the privilege of looking through the J H cuts to see if by chance strays of his own had been included in them. When all had expressed themselves as satisfied, the various bands were started to the corrals.

From a slight eminence where I had paused to enjoy the evening I looked down on the scene. The three herds, separated by generous distances one from the other, crawled leisurely along; the riders, their hats thrust back, lolled in their saddles, shouting conversation to each other, relaxing after the day's work; through the clouds strong shafts of light belittled the living creatures, threw into proportion the vastness of the desert.

FORTY ISLANDS FORD

ANDY ADAMS

After securing a count on the herd that morning and finding nothing
short, we trailed out up the North Platte River. It was an easy country
in which to handle a herd; the trail in places would run back from the river as

far as ten miles, and again follow close in near the river bottoms. There was an abundance of small creeks putting into this fork of the Platte from the south, which afforded water for the herd and good camp grounds at night. Only twice after leaving Ogalalla had we been compelled to go to the river for water for the herd, and with the exception of thunderstorms and occasional summer rains, the weather had been all one could wish. For the past week as we trailed up the North Platte, some one of us visited the river daily to note its stage of water, for we were due to cross at Forty Islands, about twelve miles south of old Fort Laramie. The North Platte was very similar to the South Canadian,—a wide sandy stream without banks; and our experience with the latter was fresh in our memories. The stage of water had not been favorable, for this river also had its source in the mountains, and as now mid-summer was upon us, the season of heavy rainfall in the mountains, augmented by the melting snows, the prospect of finding a fordable stage of water at Forty Islands was not very encouraging.

We reached this well-known crossing late in the afternoon the third day after leaving the Wyoming line, and found one of the Prairie Cattle Company's herds waterbound. This herd had been wintered on one of that company's ranges on the Arkansaw River in southern Colorado, and their destination was in the Bad Lands near the mouth of the Yellowstone, where the same company had a northern range. Flood knew the foreman, Wade Scholar, who reported having been waterbound over a week already with no prospect of crossing without swimming. Scholar knew the country thoroughly, and had decided to lie over until the river was fordable at Forty Islands, as it was much the easiest crossing on the North Platte, though there was a wagon ferry at Fort Laramie. He returned with Flood to our camp, and the two talked over the prospect of swimming it on the morrow.

"Let's send the wagons up to the ferry in the morning," said Flood, "and swim the herds. If you wait until this river falls, you are liable to have an experience like we had on the South Canadian,—lost three days and bogged over a hundred cattle. When one of these sandy rivers has had a big freshet, look out for quicksands; but you know that as well as I do. Why, we've swum over half a dozen rivers already, and I'd much rather swim this one than attempt to ford it just after it has fallen. We can double our outfits and be safely across before noon. I've got nearly a thousand miles yet to make, and have just *got* to get over. Think it over to-night, and have your wagon ready to start with ours."

Scholar rode away without giving our foreman any definite answer as to what he would do, though earlier in the evening he had offered to throw his herd well out of the way at the ford, and lend us any assistance at his command. But when it came to the question of crossing his own herd, he seemed to dread the idea of swimming the river, and could not be induced to say what he would do, but said that we were welcome to the lead. The next morning Flood and I accompanied our wagon up to his camp, when it was plainly evident that he did not intend to send his wagon with ours, and McCann started on alone, though our foreman renewed his efforts to convince Scholar of the feasibility of swimming the herds. Their cattle were thrown well away from the ford, and Scholar assured us that his outfit would be on hand whenever we were ready to cross, and even invited all hands of us to come to his wagon for dinner. When returning to our herd, Flood told me that Scholar was considered one of the best foremen on the trail, and why he should refuse to swim his cattle was unexplainable. He must have time to burn, but that didn't seem reasonable, for the earlier through cattle were turned loose on their winter range the better. We were in no hurry to cross, as our wagon would be gone all day, and it was nearly high noon when we trailed up to the ford.

With the addition to our force of Scholar and nine or ten of his men, we had an abundance of help, and put the cattle into the water opposite two islands, our saddle horses in the lead as usual. There was no swimming water between the south shore and the first island, though it wet our saddle skirts for some considerable distance, this channel being nearly two hundred yards wide. Most of our outfit took the water, while Scholar's men fed our herd in from the south bank, a number of their men coming over as far as the first island. The second island lay down the stream some little distance; and as we pushed the cattle off the first one we were in swimming water in no time, but the saddle horses were already landing on the second island, and our lead cattle struck out, and, breasting the water, swam as proudly as swans. The middle channel was nearly a hundred yards wide, the greater portion of which was swimming, though the last channel was much wider. But our saddle horses had already taken it, and when within fifty yards of the farther shore, struck solid footing. With our own outfit we crowded the leaders to keep the chain of cattle unbroken, and before Honeyman could hustle his horses out of the river, our lead cattle had caught a foothold, were heading up stream and edging out for the farther shore.

I had one of the best swimming horses in our outfit, and Flood put me in the lead on the point. As my horse came out on the farther bank, I am certain I never have seen a herd of cattle, before or since, which presented a prettier sight when swimming than ours did that day. There was fully four hundred yards of water on the angle by which we crossed, nearly half of which was swimming, but with the two islands which gave them a breathing spell, our Circle Dots were taking the water as steadily as a herd leaving their bed ground. Scholar and his men were feeding them in, while half a dozen of our men on each island were keeping them moving. Honeyman and I pointed them out of the river; and as they grazed away from the shore, they spread out fan-like, many of them kicking up their heels after they left the water in healthy enjoyment of their bath. Long before they were half over, the usual shouting had ceased, and we simply sat in our saddles and waited for the long train of cattle to come up and cross. Within less than half an hour from the time our saddle horses entered the North Platte, the tail end of our herd had landed safely on the farther bank.

As Honeyman and I were the only ones of our outfit on the north side of the river during the passage, Flood called to us from across the last channel to graze the herd until relieved, when the remainder of the outfit returned to the south side to recover their discarded effects and to get dinner with Scholar's wagon. I had imitated Honeyman, and tied my boots to my cantle strings, so that my effects were on the right side of the river; and as far as dinner was concerned,—well, I'd much rather miss it than swim the Platte twice in its then stage of water. There is a difference in daring in one's duty and in daring out of pure venturesomeness, and if we missed our dinners it would not be the first time, so we were quite willing to make the sacrifice. If the Quirk family never achieve fame for daring by field and flood, until this one of the old man's boys brings the family name into prominence, it will be hopelessly lost to posterity.

We allowed the cattle to graze of their own free will, and merely turned in the sides and rear, but on reaching the second bottom of the river, where they caught a good breeze, they lay down for their noonday siesta, which relieved us of all work but keeping watch over them. The saddle horses were grazing about in plain view on the first bottom, so Honeyman and I dismounted on a little elevation overlooking our charges. We were expecting the outfit to return promptly after dinner was over, for it was early enough in the day to have trailed eight or ten miles farther. It would have been no trouble to send some one up the river to meet our wagon and pilot McCann to the herd, for the trail left on a line due north from the river. We had been lounging about for an hour while the cattle were resting, when our attention was attracted by our saddle horses in the bottom. They were looking at the ford, to which we supposed their attention had been attracted by the swimming of the outfit, but instead only two of the boys showed up, and on sighting us nearly a mile away, they rode forward very leisurely. Before their arrival we recognized them by their horses as Ash Borrow-stone and Rod Wheat, and on their riding up the latter said as he dismounted,—

"Well, they're going to cross the other herd, and they want you to come back and point the cattle with that famous swimming horse of yours. You'll learn after a while not to blow so much about your mount, and your cutting horses, and your night horses, and your swimming horses. I wish every horse of mine had a nigger brand on him, and I had to ride in the wagon, when it comes to swimming these rivers. And I'm not the only one that has a distaste for a wet proposition, for I wouldn't have to guess twice as to what's the matter with Scholar. But Flood has pounded him on the back ever since he met him yesterday evening to swim his cattle, until it's either swim or say he's afraid to,—it's 'Shoot, Luke, or give up the gun' with him. Scholar's a nice fellow, but I'll bet my interest in goose heaven that I know what's the matter with him. And I'm not blaming him, either; but I can't understand why our boss should take such an interest in having him swim. It's none of his business if he swims now, or fords a month hence, or waits until the river freezes over in the winter and crosses on the ice. But let the big augers wrangle it out; you noticed, Ash, that not one of Scholar's outfit ever said a word one way or the other, but Flood poured it into him until he consented to swim. So fork that swimming horse of yours and wet your big toe again in the North Platte."

As the orders had come from the foreman, there was nothing to do but obey. Honeyman rode as far as the river with me, where after shedding my boots and surplus clothing and secreting them, I rode up above the island and plunged in. I was riding the gray which I had tried in the Rio Grande the day we received the herd, and now that I understood handling him better, I preferred him to Nigger Boy, my night horse. We took the first and second islands with but a blowing spell between, and when I reached the farther shore, I turned in my saddle and saw Honeyman wave his hat to me in congratulation. On reaching their wagon, I found the herd was swinging around about a mile out from the river, in order to get a straight shoot for the entrance at the ford. I hurriedly swallowed my dinner, and as we rode out to meet the herd, asked Flood if Scholar were not going to send his wagon up to the ferry to cross, for there was as yet no indication of it. Flood replied that Scholar expected to go with the wagon, as he needed some supplies which he thought he could get from the sutler at Fort Laramie.

Flood ordered me to take the lower point again, and I rode across the trail and took my place when the herd came within a quarter of a mile of the river, while the remainder of the outfit took positions near the lead on the lower side. It was a slightly larger herd than ours,—all steers, three-year-olds that reflected in their glossy coats the benefits of a northern winter. As we came up to the water's edge, it required two of their men to force their *remuda* into the water, though it was much smaller than ours,—six horses to the man, but better ones than ours, being northern wintered. The cattle were well trail-broken, and followed the leadership of the saddle horses nicely to the first island, but they would have balked at this second channel, had it not been for the amount of help at hand. We lined them out, however, and they breasted the current, and landed on the second island. The saddle horses gave some little trouble on leaving for the farther shore, and before they were got off, several hundred head of cattle had landed on the island. But they handled obediently and were soon trailing out upon terra firma, the herd following across without a broken link in the chain. There was nothing now to do but keep the train moving into the water on the south bank, see that they did not congest on the islands, and that they left the river on reaching the farther shore. When the saddle horses reached the farther bank, they were thrown up the river and turned loose, so that the two men would be available to hold the herd after it left the water. I had crossed with the first lead cattle to the farther shore, and was turning them up the river as fast as they struck solid footing on that side. But several times I was compelled to swim back to the nearest island, and return with large bunches which had hesitated to take the last channel.

The two outfits were working promiscuously together, and I never knew who was the directing spirit in the work; but when the last two or three hundred of the tail-enders were leaving the first island for the second, and the men working in the rear started to swim the channel, amid the general hilarity I recognized a shout that was born of fear and terror. A hushed silence fell over the riotous riders in the river, and I saw those on the sand bar nearest my side rush down the narrow island and plunge back into the middle channel. Then it dawned on my mind in a flash that some one had lost his seat, and that terrified cry was for help. I plunged my gray into the river and swam to the first bar, and from thence to the scene of the trouble. Horses and men were drifting with the current down the channel, and as I appealed to the men I could get no answer but their blanched faces, though it was plain in every countenance that one of our number was under water if not drowned. There were not less than twenty horsemen drifting in the middle channel in the hope that whoever it was would come to the surface, and a hand could be stretched out in succor.

About two hundred yards down the river was an island near the middle of the stream. The current carried us near it, and, on landing, I learned that the unfortunate man was none other than Wade Scholar, the foreman of the herd. We scattered up and down this middle island and watched every ripple and floating bit of flotsam in the hope that he would come to the surface, but nothing but his hat was seen. In the disorder into which the outfits were thrown by this accident, Flood first regained his thinking faculties, and ordered a few of us to cross to either bank, and ride down the river and take up positions on the other islands, from which that part of the river took its name. A hundred conjectures were offered as to how it occurred; but no one saw either horse or rider after sinking. A free horse would be hard to drown, and on the nonappearance of Scholar's mount it was concluded that he must have become entangled in the reins or that Scholar had clutched them in his death grip, and horse and man thus met death together. It was believed by his own outfit that Scholar had no intention until the last moment to risk swimming the river, but when he saw all the others plunge into the channel, his better judgment was overcome, and rather than remain behind and cause comment, he had followed and lost his life.

We patrolled the river until darkness without result, the two herds in the mean time having been so neglected that they had mixed. Our wagon returned along the north bank early in the evening, and Flood ordered Priest to go in and make up a guard from the two outfits and hold the herd for the night. Some one of Scholar's outfit went back and moved their wagon up to the crossing, within hailing distance of ours. It was a night of muffled conversation, and every voice of the night or cry of waterfowl in the river sent creepy sensations over us. The long night passed, however, and the sun rose in Sabbath benediction, for it was Sunday, and found groups of men huddled around two wagons in silent contemplation of what the day before had brought. A more broken and disconsolate set of men than Scholar's would be hard to imagine.

Flood inquired of their outfit if there was any sub-foreman, or *segundo* as they were generally called. It seemed there was not, but their outfit was unanimous that the leadership should fall to a boyhood acquaintance of Scholar's by the name of Campbell, who was generally addressed as "Black" Jim. Flood at once advised Campbell to send their wagon up to Laramie and cross it, promising that we would lie over that day and make an effort to recover the body of the drowned foreman. Campbell accordingly started his wagon up to the ferry, and all the remainder of the outfits, with the exception of a few men on herd, started out in search of the drowned man. Within a mile and a half below the ford, there were located over thirty of the forty islands, and at the lower end of this chain of sand bars we began and searched both shores, while three or four men swam to each island and made a vigorous search.

The water in the river was not very clear, which called for a close inspection; but with a force of twenty-five men in the hunt, we covered island and shore rapidly in our search. It was about eight in the morning, and we had already searched half of the islands, when Joe Stallings and two of Scholar's men swam to an island in the river which had a growth of small cottonwoods covering it, while on the upper end was a heavy lodgment of driftwood. John Officer, The Rebel, and I had taken the next island above, and as we were riding the shallows surrounding it we heard a shot in our rear that told us the body had been found. As we turned in the direction of the signal, Stallings was standing on a large driftwood log, and signaling. We started back to him, partly wading and partly swimming, while from both sides of the river men were swimming their horses for the brushy island. Our squad, on nearing the lower bar, was compelled to swim around the driftwood, and some twelve or fifteen men from either shore reached the scene before us. The body was lying face upward, in about eighteen inches of eddy water. Flood and Campbell waded out, and taking a lariat, fastened it around his chest under the arms. Then Flood, noticing I was riding my black, asked me to tow the body ashore. Forcing a passage through the driftwood, I took the loose end of the lariat and started for the north bank, the double outfit following. On reaching the shore, the body was carried out of the water by willing hands, and one of our outfit was sent to the wagon for a tarpaulin to be used as a stretcher.

Meanwhile, Campbell took possession of the drowned foreman's watch, six-shooter, purse, and papers. The watch was as good as ruined, but the leather holster had shrunk and securely held the gun from being lost in the river. On the arrival of the tarpaulin, the body was laid upon it, and four mounted men, taking the four corners of the sheet, wrapped them on the pommels of their saddles and started for our wagon. When the corpse had been lowered to the ground at our camp, a look of inquiry passed from face to face which seemed to ask, "What next?" But the inquiry was answered a moment later by Black Jim Campbell, the friend of the dead man. Memory may have dimmed the lesser details of that Sunday morning on the North Platte, for over two decades have since gone, but his words and manliness have lived, not only in my mind, but in the memory of every other survivor of those present. "This accident," said he in perfect composure, as he gazed into the calm, still face of his dead friend, "will impose on me a very sad duty. I expect to meet his mother some day. She will want to know everything. I must tell her the truth, and I'd hate to tell her we buried him like a dog, for she's a Christian woman. And what makes it all the harder, I know that this is the third boy she has lost by drowning. Some of you may not have understood him, but among those papers which you saw me take from his pockets was a letter from his mother, in which she warned him to guard against just what has happened. Situated as we are, I'm going to ask you all to help me give him the best burial we can. No doubt it will be crude, but it will be some solace to her to know we did the best we could."

Every one of us was eager to lend his assistance. Within five minutes Priest was galloping up the north bank of the river to intercept the wagon at the ferry, a well-filled purse in his pocket with which to secure a coffin at Fort Laramie. Flood and Campbell selected a burial place, and with our wagon spade a grave was being dug on a near-by grassy mound, where there were two other graves. There was not a man among us who was hypocrite enough to attempt to conduct a Christian burial service, but when the subject came up, McCann said as he came down the river the evening before he noticed an emigrant train of about thirty wagons going into camp at a grove about five miles up the river. In a conversation which he had had with one of the party, he learned that they expected to rest over Sunday. Their respect for the Sabbath day caused Campbell to suggest that there might be some one in the emigrant camp who could conduct a Christian burial, and he at once mounted his horse and rode away to learn.

In preparing the body for its last resting-place we were badly handicapped, but by tearing a new wagon sheet into strips about a foot in width and wrapping the body, we gave it a humble bier in the shade of our wagon, pending the arrival of the coffin. The features were so ashened by having been submerged in the river for over eighteen hours, that we wrapped the face also, as we preferred to remember him as we had seen him the day before, strong, healthy, and buoyant. During the interim, awaiting the return of Campbell from the emigrant camp and of the wagon, we sat around in groups and discussed the incident. There was a sense of guilt expressed by a number of our outfit over their hasty decision regarding the courage of the dead man. When we understood that two of his brothers had met a similar fate in Red River within the past five years, every guilty thought or hasty word spoken came back to us with tenfold weight. Priest and Campbell returned together; the former reported having secured a coffin which would arrive within an hour, while the latter had met in the emigrant camp a superannuated minister who gladly volunteered his services. He had given the old minister such data as he had, and two of the minister's granddaughters had expressed a willingness to assist by singing at the burial services. Campbell had set the hour for four, and several conveyances would be down from the emigrant camp. The wagon arriving shortly afterward, we had barely time to lay the corpse in the coffin before the emigrants drove up. The minister was a tall, homely man, with a flowing beard, which the frosts of many a winter had whitened, and as he mingled amongst us in the final preparations, he had a kind word for every one. There were ten in his party; and when the coffin had been carried out to the grave, the two granddaughters of the old man opened the simple service by singing very impressively the first three verses of the Portuguese Hymn. I had heard the old hymn sung often before, but the impression of the last verse rang in my ears for days afterward.

"When through the deep waters I call thee to go,

The rivers of sorrow shall not overflow;

For I will be with thee thy troubles to bless,

And sanctify to thee thy deepest distress."

As the notes of the hymn died away, there was for a few moments profound stillness, and not a move was made by any one. The touching words of the old hymn expressed quite vividly the disaster of the previous day, and awakened in us many memories of home. For a time we were silent, while eyes unused to weeping filled with tears. I do not know how long we remained so. It may have been only for a moment, it probably was; but I do know the silence was not broken till the aged minister, who stood at the head of the coffin, began his discourse. We stood with uncovered heads during the service, and when the old minister addressed us he spoke as though he might have been holding family worship and we had been his children. He invoked Heaven to comfort and sustain the mother when the news of her son's death reached her, as she would need more than human aid in that hour; he prayed that her faith might not falter and that she might again meet and be with her loved ones forever in the great beyond. He then took up the subject of life,—spoke of its brevity, its many hopes that are never realized, and the disappointments from which no prudence or foresight can shield us. He dwelt at some length on the strange mingling of sunshine and shadow that seemed to belong to every life; on the mystery everywhere, and nowhere more impressively than in ourselves. With his long bony finger he pointed to the cold, mute form that lay in the coffin before us, and said, "But this, my friends, is the mystery of all mysteries." The fact that life terminated in death, he said, only emphasized its reality; that the death of our companion was not an accident, though it was sudden and unexpected; that the difficulties of life are such that it would be worse than folly in us to try to meet them in our own strength. Death, he said, might change, but it did not destroy; that the soul still lived and would live forever; that death was simply the gateway out of time into eternity; and if we were to realize the high aim of our being, we could do so by casting our burdens on Him who was able and willing to carry them for us. He spoke feelingly of the Great Teacher, the lowly Nazarene, who also suffered and died, and he concluded with an eloquent description of the blessed life, the immortality of the soul, and the resurrection of the body. After the discourse was ended and a brief and earnest prayer was offered, the two young girls sang the hymn, "Shall we meet beyond the river?" The services being at an end, the coffin was lowered into the grave.

Campbell thanked the old minister and his two granddaughters on their taking leave, for their presence and assistance; and a number of us boys also shook hands with the old man at parting.

THE ROUND-UP

THEODORE ROOSEVELT

During the winter-time there is ordinarily but little work done among the cattle. There is some line riding, and a continual lookout is kept for the very weak animals,—usually cows and calves, who have to be driven in, fed, and housed; but most of the stock are left to shift for themselves, undisturbed. Almost every stock-growers' association forbids branding any calves before the spring round-up. If great bands of cattle wander off the range, parties may be fitted out to go after them and bring them back; but this is only done when absolutely necessary, as when the drift of the cattle has been towards an Indian reservation or a settled granger country, for the weather is very severe, and the horses are so poor that their food must be carried along.

The bulk of the work is done during the summer, including the late spring and early fall, and consists mainly in a succession of round-ups, beginning, with us, in May and ending towards the last of October.

But a good deal may be done in the intervals by riding over one's range. Frequently, too, herding will be practiced on a large scale.

Still more important is the "trail" work: cattle, while driven from one range to another, or to a shipping point for beef, being said to be "on the trail." For years, the over-supply from the vast breeding ranches to the south, especially in Texas, has been driven northward in large herds, either to the shipping towns along the great railroads, or else to the fattening ranges of the North-west; it having been found, so far, that while the calf crop is larger in the South, beeves become much heavier in the North. Such cattle, for the most part, went along tolerably well-marked routes or trails, which became for the time being of great importance, flourishing—and extremely lawless—towns growing up along them; but with the growth of the railroad system, and above all with the filling-up of the northern ranges, these trails have steadily become of less and less consequence, though many herds still travel them on their way to the already crowded ranges of western Dakota and Montana, or to the Canadian regions beyond. The trail work is something by itself. The herds may be on the trail several months, averaging fifteen miles or less a day. The cowboys accompanying each have to undergo much hard toil, of a peculiarly same and wearisome kind, on account of the extreme slowness with which everything must be done, as trail cattle should never be hurried. The foreman of a trail outfit must be not only a veteran cowhand, but also a miracle of patience and resolution.

Round-up work is far less irksome, there being an immense amount of dash and excitement connected with it; and when once the cattle are on the range, the important work is done during the round-up. On cow ranches, or wherever there is breeding stock, the spring round-up is the great event of the season, as it is then that the bulk of the calves are branded. It usually lasts six weeks, or thereabouts; but its end by no means implies rest for the stockman. On the contrary, as soon as it is over, wagons are sent to work out-of-the-way parts of the country that have been passed over, but where cattle are supposed to have drifted; and by the time these have come back the first beef round-up has begun, and thereafter beeves are steadily gathered and shipped, at least from among the larger herds, until cold weather sets in; and in the fall there is another round-up, to brand the late calves and see that the stock is got back on the range. As all of these round-ups are of one character, a description of the most important, taking place in the spring, will be enough.

In April we begin to get up the horses. Throughout the winter very few have been kept for use, as they are then poor and weak, and must be given grain and hay if they are to be worked. The men in the line camps need two or three apiece, and each man at the home ranch has a couple more; but the rest are left out to shift for themselves, which the tough, hardy little fellows are well able to do. Ponies can pick up a living where cattle die; though the scanty feed, which they may have to uncover by pawing off the snow, and the bitter weather often make them look very gaunt by spring-time. But the first warm rains bring up the green grass, and then all the live-stock gain flesh with wonderful rapidity. When the spring round-up begins the horses should be as fat and sleek as possible. After running all winter free, even the most sober pony is apt to betray an inclination to buck; and, if possible, we like to ride every animal once or twice before we begin to do real work with him. Animals that have escaped for any length of time are almost as bad to handle as if they had never been broken. One of the two horses mentioned in a former chapter as having been gone eighteen months has, since his return, been suggestively dubbed "Dynamite Jimmy," on account of the incessant and eruptive energy with which he bucks. Many of our horses, by the way, are thus named from some feat or peculiarity. Wire Fence, when being broken, ran into one of the abominations after which he is now called; Hackamore once got away and remained out for three weeks with a hackamore, or breaking-halter, on him; Macaulay contracted the habit of regularly getting rid of the huge Scotchman to whom he was intrusted; Bulberry Johnny spent the hour or two after he was first mounted in a large patch of thorny bulberry bushes, his distracted rider unable to get him to do anything but move round sidewise in a circle; Fall Back would never get to the front; Water Skip always jumps mud-puddles; and there are a dozen others with names as purely descriptive.

The stock-growers of Montana, of the western part of Dakota, and even of portions of extreme northern Wyoming,—that is, of all the grazing lands lying in the basin of the Upper Missouri,—have united, and formed themselves into the great Montana Stockgrowers' Association. Among the countless benefits they have derived from this course, not the least has been the way in which the various round-ups work in with and supplement one another. At the spring meeting of the association, the entire territory mentioned above, including perhaps a hundred thousand square miles, is mapped out into round-up districts, which generally are changed but slightly from year to year, and the times and places for the round-ups to begin refixed so that those of adjacent districts may be run with a view to the best interests of all. Thus the stockmen along the Yellowstone have one round-up; we along the Little Missouri have another; and the country lying between, through which the Big Beaver flows, is almost equally important to both. Accordingly, one spring, the Little Missouri round-up, beginning May 25, and working down-stream, was timed so as to reach the mouth of the Big Beaver about June 1, the Yellowstone round-up beginning at that date and place. Both then worked up the Beaver together to its head, when the Yellowstone men turned to the west and we bent back to our own river; thus the bulk of the strayed cattle of each were brought back to their respective ranges. Our own round-up district covers the Big and Little Beaver creeks, which rise near each other, but empty into the Little Missouri nearly a hundred and fifty miles apart, and so much of the latter river as lies between their mouths.

The captain or foreman of the round-up, upon whom very much of its efficiency and success depends, is chosen beforehand. He is, of course, an expert cowman, thoroughly acquainted with the country; and he must also be able to command and to keep control of the wild rough-riders he has under him—a feat needing both tact and firmness.

At the appointed day all meet at the place from which the round-up is to start. Each ranch, of course, has most work to be done in its own round-up district, but it is also necessary to have representatives in all those surrounding it. A large outfit may employ a dozen cowboys, or over, in the home district, and yet have nearly as many more representing its interest in the various ones adjoining. Smaller outfits generally club together to run a wagon and send outside representatives, or else go along with their stronger neighbors, they paying part of the expenses. A large outfit, with a herd of twenty thousand cattle or more, can, if necessary, run a round-up entirely by itself, and is able to act independently of outside help; it is therefore at a great advantage compared with those that can take no step effectively without their neighbors' consent and assistance.

If the starting-point is some distance off, it may be necessary to leave home three or four days in advance. Before this we have got everything in readiness; have overhauled the wagons, shod any horse whose forefeet are tender,—as a rule, all our ponies go barefooted,—and left things in order at the ranch. Our outfit may be taken as a sample of every one else's. We have a stout four-horse wagon to carry the bedding and the food; in its rear a mess-chest is rigged to hold the knives, forks, cans, etc. All our four team-horses are strong, willing animals, though of no great size, being originally just "broncos," or unbroken native horses, like the others. The teamster is also cook: a man who is a really first-hand at both driving and cooking—and our present teamster is both—can always command his price. Besides our own men, some cowboys from neigh-boring ranches and two or three representatives from other round-up districts are always along, and we generally have at least a dozen "riders," as they are termed,—that is, cowboys, or "cowpunchers," who do the actual cattle-work,—with the wagon. Each of these has a string of eight or ten ponies; and to take charge of the saddle-band, thus consisting of a hundred odd head, there are two herders, always known as "horse-wranglers"—one for the day and one for the night. Occasionally there will be two wagons, one to carry the bedding and one the food, known, respectively, as the bed and the mess wagon; but this is not usual.

While traveling to the meeting point the pace is always slow, as it is an object to bring the horses on the ground as fresh as possible. Accordingly we keep at a walk almost all day, and the riders, having nothing else to do, assist the wranglers in driving the saddle-band, three or four going in front, and others on the side, so that the horses shall keep on a walk. There is always some trouble with the animals at the starting out, as they are very fresh and are restive under the saddle. The herd is likely to stampede, and any beast that is frisky or vicious is sure to show its worst side. To do really effective cow-work a pony should be well broken; but many even of the old ones have vicious traits, and almost every man will have in his string one or two young horses, or broncos, hardly broken at all. Thanks to the rough methods of breaking in vogue on the plains many even of the so called broken animals retain always certain bad habits, the most common being that of bucking. Of the sixty odd horses on my ranch all but half a dozen were broken by ourselves; and though my men are all good riders, yet a good rider is not necessarily a good horse-breaker, and indeed it was an absolute impossibility properly to break so many animals in the short time at our com-mand—for we had to use them almost immediately after they were bought. In consequence, very many of my horses have to this day traits not likely to set a timid or a clumsy rider at his ease. One or two run away and cannot be held by even the strongest bit; others can hardly be bridled or saddled until they have been thrown; two or three have a tendency to fall over backward; and half of them buck more or less, some so hard that only an expert can sit them; several I never ride myself, save from dire necessity.

In riding these wild, vicious horses, and in careering over such very bad ground, especially at night, accidents are always occurring. A man who is merely an ordinary rider is certain to have a pretty hard time. On my first round-up I had a string of nine horses, four of them broncos, only broken to the extent of having each been saddled once or twice. One of them it was an impossibility to bridle or to saddle single-handed; it was very difficult to get on or off him, and he was exceedingly nervous if a man moved his hands or feet; but he had no bad tricks. The second soon became perfectly quiet. The third turned out to be one of the worst buckers on the ranch: once, when he bucked me off, I managed to fall on a stone and broke a rib. The fourth had a still worse habit, for he would balk and then throw himself over backward: once, when I was not quick enough, he caught me and broke something in the point of my shoulder, so that it was some weeks before I could raise the arm freely. My hurts were far from serious, and did not interfere with my riding and working as usual through the round-up; but I was heartily glad when it ended, and ever since have religiously done my best to get none but gentle horses in my own string. However, every one gets falls from or with his horse now and then in the cow country; and even my men, good riders though they are, are sometimes injured. One of them once broke his ankle; another a rib; another was on one occasion stunned, remaining unconscious for some hours; and yet another had certain of his horses buck under him so hard and long as finally to hurt his lungs and make him cough blood. Fatal accidents occur annually in almost every district, especially if there is much work to be done among stampeded cattle at night; but on my own ranch none of my men have ever been seriously hurt, though on one occasion a cowboy from another ranch, who was with my wagon, was killed, his horse falling and pitching him heavily on his head.

For bedding, each man has two or three pairs of blankets, and a tarpaulin or small wagon-sheet. Usually, two or three sleep together. Even in June the nights are generally cool and pleasant, and it is chilly in the early mornings; although this is not always so, and when the weather stays hot and mosquitoes are plenty, the hours of darkness, even in midsummer, seem painfully long. In the Bad Lands proper we are not often bothered very seriously by these winged pests; but in the low bottoms of the big Missouri, and beside many of the reedy ponds and great sloughs out on the prairie, they are a perfect scourge. During the very hot nights, when they are especially active, the bedclothes make a man feel absolutely smothered, and yet his only chance for sleep is to wrap himself tightly up, head and all; and even then some of the pests will usually force their way in. At sunset I have seen the mosquitoes rise up from the land like a dense cloud, to make the hot, stifling night one long torture; the horses would neither lie down nor graze, traveling restlessly to and fro till daybreak, their bodies streaked and bloody, and the insects settling on them so as to make them all one color, a uniform gray; while the men, after a few hours' tossing about in the vain attempt to sleep, rose, built a little fire of damp sage brush, and thus endured the misery as best they could until it was light enough to work.

But if the weather is fine, a man will never sleep better nor more pleasantly than in the open air after a hard day's work on the round-up; nor will an ordinary shower or gust of wind disturb him in the least, for he simply draws the tarpaulin over his head and goes on sleeping. But now and then we have a wind-storm that might better be called a whirlwind and has to be met very differently; and two or three days or nights of rain insure the wetting of the blankets, and therefore shivering discomfort on the part of the would-be sleeper. For two or three hours all goes well; and it is rather soothing to listen to the steady patter of the great raindrops on the canvas. But then it will be found that a corner has been left open through which the water can get in, or else the tarpaulin will begin to leak somewhere; or perhaps the water will have collected in a hollow underneath and have begun to soak through. Soon a little stream trickles in, and every effort to remedy matters merely results in a change for the worse. To move out of the way insures getting wet in a fresh spot; and the best course is to lie still and accept the evils that have come with what fortitude one can. Even thus, the first night a man can sleep pretty well; but if the rain continues, the second night, when the blankets are already damp, and when the water comes through more easily, is apt to be most unpleasant.

Of course, a man can take little spare clothing on a round-up; at the very outside two or three clean handkerchiefs, a pair of socks, a change of under-clothes, and the most primitive kind of washing-apparatus, all wrapped up in a stout jacket which is to be worn when nightherding. The inevitable "slicker," or oil-skin coat, which gives complete protection from the wet, is always carried behind the saddle.

At the meeting-place there is usually a delay of a day or two to let every one come in; and the plain on which the encampment is made becomes a scene of great bustle and turmoil. The heavy four-horse wagons jolt in from different quarters, the horse-wranglers rushing madly to and fro in the endeavor to keep the different saddle-bands from mingling, while the "riders," or cowboys, with each wagon jog along in a body. The representatives from outside districts ride in singly or by twos and threes, every man driving before him his own horses, one of them loaded with his bedding. Each wagon wheels out of the way into some camping-place not too near the others, the bedding is tossed out on the ground, and then every one is left to do what he wishes, while the different wagon bosses, or foremen, seek out the captain of the round-up to learn what his plans are.

There is a good deal of rough but effective discipline and method in the way in which a round-up is carried on. The captain of the whole has as lieutenants the various wagon foremen, and in making demands for men to do some special service he will usually merely designate some foreman to take charge of the work and let him parcel it out among his men to suit himself. The captain of the round-up or the foreman of a wagon may himself be a ranchman; if such is not the case, and the ranchman nevertheless comes along, he works and fares precisely as do the other cowboys.

While the head men are gathered in a little knot, planning out the work, the others are dispersed over the plain in every direction, racing, breaking rough horses, or simply larking with one another. If a man has an especially bad horse, he usually takes such an opportunity, when he has plenty of time, to ride him; and while saddling he is surrounded by a crowd of most unsympathetic associates who greet with uproarious mirth any misadventure. A man on a bucking horse is always considered fair game, every squeal and jump of the bronco being hailed with cheers of delighted irony for the rider and shouts to "stay with him." The antics of a vicious bronco show infinite variety of detail, but are all modeled on one general plan. When the rope settles round his neck the fight begins, and it is only after much plunging and snorting that a twist is taken over his nose, or else a hackamore—a species of severe halter, usually made of plaited hair—slipped on his head. While being bridled he strikes viciously with his fore feet, and perhaps has to be blindfolded or thrown down; and to get the saddle on him is quite as difficult. When saddled, he may get rid of his exuberant spirits by bucking under the saddle, or may reserve all his energies for the rider. In the last case, the man keeping tight hold with his left hand of the cheek-strap, so as to prevent the horse from getting his head down until he is fairly seated, swings himself quickly into the saddle. Up rises the bronco's back into an arch; his head, the ears laid straight back, goes down between his forefeet, and, squealing savagely, he makes a succession of rapid, stiff-legged, jarring bounds. Sometimes he is a "plunging" bucker, who runs forward all the time while bucking; or he may buck steadily in one place, or "sun-fish,"—that is, bring first one shoulder down almost to the ground and then the other,—or else he may change ends while in the air. A first-class rider will sit throughout it all without moving from the saddle, quirting[1] his horse all the time, though his hat may be jarred off his head and his revolver out of its sheath. After a few jumps, however, the average man grasps hold of the horn of the saddle—the delighted onlookers meanwhile earnestly advising him not to "go to leather"—and is contented to get through the affair in any shape provided he can escape without being thrown off. An accident is of necessity borne with a broad grin, as any attempt to resent the raillery of the bystanders—which is perfectly good-humored—would be apt to result disastrously. Cowboys are certainly extremely good riders. As a class they have no superiors. Of course, they would at first be at a disadvantage in steeple-chasing or fox-hunting, but their average of horsemanship is without doubt higher than that of the men who take part in these latter amusements. A cow-boy would learn to ride across country in a quarter of the time it would take a cross-country rider to learn to handle a vicious bronco or to do good cow-work round and in a herd.

On such a day, when there is no regular work, there will often also be horse-races, as each outfit is pretty sure to have some running pony which it believes can outpace any other. These contests are always short-distance dashes, for but a few hundred yards. Horse-racing is a mania with most plainsmen, white or red. A man with a good racing pony will travel all about with it, often winning large sums, visiting alike cow ranches, frontier towns, and Indian encampments. Sometimes the race is "pony against pony," the victor taking both steeds. In racing the men ride bareback, as there are hardly any light saddles in the cow country. There will be intense excitement and very heavy betting over a race between two well-known horses, together with a good chance of blood being shed in the attendance quarrels.

Indians and whites often race against each other as well as among them-selves. I have seen several such contests, and in every case but one the white man happened to win. A race is usually run between two thick rows of spectators, on foot and on horseback, and as the racers pass, these rows close in behind them, every man yelling and shouting with all the strength of his lungs, and all waving their hats and cloaks to encourage the contestants, or firing off their revolvers and saddle guns. The little horses are fairly maddened, as is natural enough, and

---

1   *Quirt is the name of the short flexible riding-whip used throughout cowboy land. The term is a Spanish one.*

run as if they were crazy: were the distances longer some would be sure to drop in their tracks.

Besides the horse-races, which are, of course, the main attraction, the men at a round-up will often get up wrestling matches or footraces. In fact, every one feels that he is off for a holiday; for after the monotony of a long winter, the cowboys look forward eagerly to the round-up, where the work is hard, it is true, but exciting and varied, and treated a good deal as a frolic. There is no eight-hour law in cowboy land: during round-up time we often count ourselves lucky if we get off with much less than sixteen hours; but the work is done in the saddle, and the men are spurred on all the time by the desire to out do one another in feats of daring and skillful horsemanship. There is very little quarreling or fighting; and though the fun often takes the form of rather rough horseplay, yet the practice of carrying dangerous weapons makes cowboys show far more rough courtesy to each other and far less rudeness to strangers than is the case among, for instance, Eastern miners, or even lumbermen. When a quarrel may very probably result fatally, a man thinks twice before going into it: warlike people or classes always treat one another with a certain amount of consideration and politeness. The moral tone of a cow-camp, indeed, is rather high: than otherwise. Meanness, cowardice, and dishonesty are not tolerated. There is a high regard for truthfulness and keeping one's word, intense contempt for any kind of hypocrisy, and a hearty dislike for a man who shirks his work. Many of the men gamble and drink, but many do neither; and the conversation is not worse than in most bodies composed wholly of male human beings. A cowboy will not submit tamely to an insult, and is ever ready to avenge his own wrongs; nor has he an overwrought fear of shedding blood. He possesses, in fact, few of the emasculated, milk-and-water moralities admired by the pseudo-philanthropists; but he does possess, to a very high degree, the stern, manly qualities that are invaluable to a nation.

The method of work is simple. The mess-wagons and loose horses, after breaking camp in the morning, move on in a straight line for some few miles, going into camp again before midday; and the day herd, consisting of all the cattle that have been found far off their range, and which are to be brought back there, and of any others that it is necessary to gather, follows on afterwards. Meanwhile the cowboys scatter out and drive in all the cattle from the country round about, going perhaps ten or fifteen miles back from the line of march, and meeting at the place where camp has already been pitched. The wagons always keep some little distance from one another, and the saddle-bands do the same, so that the horses may not get mixed. It is rather picturesque to see the four-horse teams filing down at a trot through a pass among the buttes—the saddle-bands being driven along at a smart pace to one side or behind, the teamsters cracking their whips, and the horse-wranglers calling and shouting as they ride rapidly from side to side behind the horses, urging on the stragglers by dexterous touches with the knotted ends of their long lariats that are left trailing from the saddle. The country driven over is very rough, and it is often necessary to double up teams and put on eight horses to each wagon in going up an unusually steep pitch, or hauling through a deep mud-hole, or over a river crossing where there is quicksand.

The speed and thoroughness with which a country can be worked depends, of course, very largely upon the number of riders. Ours is probably about an average roundup as regards size. The last spring I was out, there were half a dozen wagons along; the saddle-bands numbered about a hundred each; and the morning we started, sixty men in the saddle splashed across the shallow ford of the river that divided the plain where we had camped from the valley of the long winding creek up which we were first to work.

In the morning the cook is preparing breakfast long before the first glimmer of dawn. As soon as it is ready, probably about 3 o'clock, he utters a long-drawn shout, and all the sleepers feel it is time to be up on the instant, for they know there can be no such thing as delay on the round-up, under penalty of being set afoot. Accordingly they bundle out, rubbing their eyes and yawning, draw on their boots and trousers,—if they have taken the latter off,—roll up and cord their bedding, and usually without any attempt at washing crowd over to the little smoldering fire, which is placed in a hole dug in the ground, so that there may be no risk of its spreading. The men are rarely very hungry at breakfast, and it is a meal that has to be eaten in shortest order, so it is perhaps the least important. Each man, as he comes up, grasps a tin cup and plate from the mess-box, pours out his tea or coffee, with sugar, but, of course, no milk, helps himself to one or two of the biscuits that have been baked in a Dutch oven, and perhaps also to a slice of the fat pork swimming in the grease of the frying-pan, ladles himself out some beans, if there are any, and squats down on the ground to eat his breakfast. The meal is not an elaborate one; nevertheless a man will have to hurry if he wishes to eat it before hearing the foreman sing out, "Come, boys, catch your horses"; when he must drop everything and run out to the wagon with his lariat. The night wrangler is now bringing in the saddle-band, which he has been up all night guarding. A rope corral is rigged up by stretching a rope from each wheel of one side of the wagon, making a V-shaped space, into which the saddle-horses are driven. Certain men stand around to keep them inside, while the others catch the horses: many outfits have one man to do all the roping. As soon as each has caught his horse—usually a strong, tough animal, the small, quick ponies being reserved for the work round the herd in the afternoon—the band, now in charge of the day wrangler, is turned loose, and every one saddles up as fast as possible. It still lacks some time of being sunrise, and the air has in it the peculiar chill of the early morning. When all are saddled, many of the horses bucking and dancing about, the riders from the different wagons all assemble at the one where the captain is sitting, already mounted. He waits a very short time—for laggards receive but scant mercy—before announcing the proposed camping-place and parceling out the work among those present. If, as is usually the case, the line of march is along a river or creek, he appoints some man to take a dozen others and drive down (or up) it ahead of the day herd, so that the latter will not have to travel through other cattle; the day herd itself being driven and guarded by a dozen men detached for that purpose. The rest of the riders are divided into two bands, placed under men who know the country, and start out, one on each side, to bring in every head for fifteen miles back. The captain then himself rides down to the new camping-place, so as to be there as soon as any cattle are brought in.

Meanwhile the two bands, a score of riders in each, separate and make their way in opposite directions. The leader of each tries to get such a "scatter" on his men that they will cover completely all the land gone over. This morning work is called circle riding, and is peculiarly hard in the Bad Lands on account of the remarkably broken, rugged nature of the country. The men come in on lines that tend to a common center—as if the sticks of a fan were curved. As the band goes out, the leader from time to time detaches one or two men to ride down through certain sections of the country, making the shorter, or what was called inside, circles, while he keeps on; and finally, retaining as companions the two or three whose horses are toughest, makes the longest or outside circle himself, going clear back to the divide, or whatever the point may be that marks the limit of the round-up work, and then turning and working straight to the meeting-place. Each man, of course, brings in every head of cattle he can see.

These long, swift rides in the glorious spring mornings are not soon to be forgotten. The sweet, fresh air, with a touch of sharpness thus early in the day, and the rapid motion of the fiery little horse combine to make a man's blood thrill and leap with sheer buoyant light-heartedness and eager, exultant pleasure in the boldness and freedom of the life he is leading. As we climb the steep sides of the first range of buttes, wisps of wavering mist still cling in the hollows of the valley; when we come out on the top of the first great plateau, the sun flames up over its edge, and in the level, red beams the galloping horsemen throw long fantastic shadows. Black care rarely sits behind a rider whose pace is fast enough; at any rate, not when he first feels the horse move under him.

Sometimes we trot or pace, and again we lope or gallop; the few who are to take the outside circle must needs ride both hard and fast. Although only grass-fed, the horses are tough and wiry; and, moreover, are each used but once in four days, or thereabouts, so they stand the work well. The course out lies across great grassy plateaus, along knife-like ridge crests, among winding valleys and ravines, and over acres of barren, sun-scorched buttes, that look grimly grotesque and forbidding, while in the Bad Lands the riders unhesitatingly go down and over places where it seems impossible that a horse should even stand. The line of horsemen will quarter down the side of a butte, where every pony has to drop from ledge to ledge like a goat, and will go over the shoulder of a soapstone cliff, when wet and slippery, with a series of plunges and scrambles which if unsuccessful would land horses and riders in the bottom on the cañon-like washout below. In descending a clay butte after a rain, the pony will put all four feet together and slide down to the bottom almost or quite on his haunches. In very wet weather the Bad Lands are absolutely impassable; but if the ground is not slippery, it is a remarkable place that can shake the matter-of-course confidence felt by the rider in the capacity of his steed to go anywhere.

When the men on the outside circle have reached the bound set them,—whether it is a low divide, a group of jagged hills, the edge of the rolling, limitless prairie, or the long, waste reaches of alkali and sage brush,—they turn their horses' heads and begin to work down the branches of the creeks, one or two riding down the bottom, while the others keep off to the right and the left, a little ahead and fairly high up on the side hills, so as to command as much of a view as possible. On the level or rolling prairies the cattle can be seen a long way off, and it is an easy matter to gather and drive them; but in the Bad Lands every little pocket, basin, and coulée has to be searched, every gorge or ravine entered, and the dense patches of brushwood and spindling, wind-beaten trees closely examined. All the cattle are carried on ahead down the creek; and it is curious to watch the different behavior of the different breeds. A cowboy riding off to one side of the creek, and seeing a number of long-horned Texans grazing in the branches of a set of coulées, has merely to ride across the upper ends of these, uttering the drawn-out "ei-koh-h-h," so familiar to the cattlemen, and the long-horns will stop grazing, stare fixedly at him, and then, wheeling, strike off down the coulées at a trot, tails in air, to be carried along by the center riders when they reach the main creek into which the coulées lead. Our own range cattle are not so wild, but nevertheless are easy to drive; while Eastern-raised beasts have little fear of a horseman, and merely stare stupidly at him until he rides directly towards them. Every little bunch of stock is thus collected, and all are driven along together. At the place where some large fork joins the main creek another band may be met, driven by some of the men who have left earlier in the day to take one of the shorter circles; and thus, before coming down to the bottom where the wagons are camped and where the actual "round-up" itself is to take place, this one herd may include a couple of thousand head; or, on the other hand, the longest ride may not result in the finding of a dozen animals. As soon as the riders are in, they disperse to their respective wagons to get dinner and change horses, leaving the cattle to be held by one or two of their number. If only a small number of cattle have been gathered, they will all be run into one herd; if there are many of them, however, the different herds will be held separate.

A plain where a round-up is taking place offers a picturesque sight. I well remember one such. It was on a level bottom in a bend of the river, which here made an almost semicircular sweep. The bottom was in shape a long oval, hemmed in by an unbroken line of steep bluffs so that it looked like an amphitheater. Across the faces of the dazzling white cliffs there were sharp bands of black and red, drawn by the coal seams and the layers of burned clay: the leaves of the trees and the grass had the vivid green of spring-time. The wagons were camped among the cottonwood trees fringing the river, a thin column of smoke rising up from beside each. The horses were grazing round the outskirts, those of each wagon by themselves and kept from going too near the others by their watchful guard. In the greater circular corral, towards one end, the men were already branding calves, while the whole middle of the bottom was covered with lowing herds of cattle and shouting, galloping cowboys. Apparently there was nothing but dust, noise, and confusion; but in reality the work was proceeding all the while with the utmost rapidity and certainty.

As soon as, or even before, the last circle riders have come in and have snatched a few hasty mouthfuls to serve as their midday meal, we begin to work the herd—or herds, if the one herd would be of too unwieldy size. The animals are held in a compact bunch, most of the riders forming a ring outside, while a couple from each ranch successively look the herds through and cut out those marked with their own brand. It is difficult, in such a mass of moving beasts,—for they do not stay still, but keep weaving in and out among each other,—to find all of one's own animals: a man must have natural gifts, as well as great experience, before he becomes a good brand-reader and is able really to "clean up a herd"—that is, be sure he has left nothing of his own in it.

To do good work in cutting out from a herd, not only should the rider be a good horseman, but he should also have a skillful, thoroughly trained horse. A good cutting pony is not common, and is generally too valuable to be used anywhere but in the herd. Such an one enters thoroughly into the spirit of the thing, and finds out immediately the animal his master is after; he will then follow it closely of his own accord through every wheel and double at top speed. When looking through the herd, it is necessary to move slowly; and when any animal is found it is taken to the outskirts at a walk, so as not to alarm the others. Once at the outside, however, the cowboy has to ride like lightning; for as soon as the beast he is after finds itself separated from its companions it endeavors to break back among them, and a young, range-raised steer or heifer runs like a deer. In cuffing out a cow and a calf two men have to work together. As the animals of a brand are cut out they are received and held apart by some rider detailed for the purpose, who is said to be "holding the cut."

All this time the men holding the herd have their hands full, for some animal is continually trying to break out, when the nearest man flies at it at once and after a smart chase brings it back to its fellows. As soon as all the cows, calves, and whatever else is being gathered have been cut out, the rest are driven clear off the ground and turned loose, being headed in the direction contrary to that in which we travel the following day. Then the riders surround the next herd, the men holding cuts move them up near it, and the work is begun anew.

If it is necessary to throw an animal, either to examine a brand or for any other reason, half a dozen men will have their ropes down at once; and then it is spur and quirt in the rivalry to see which can outdo the other until the beast is roped and thrown. A first-class hand will, unaided, rope, throw, and tie down a cow or steer in wonderfully short time; one of the favorite tests of competitive skill among the cowboys is the speed with which this feat can be accomplished. Usually, however, one man ropes the animal by the head and another at the same time gets the loop of his lariat over one or both its hind legs, when it is twisted over and stretched out in a second. In following an animal on horseback the man keeps steadily swinging the rope round his head, by a dexterous motion of the wrist only, until he gets a chance to throw it; when on foot, especially if catching horses in a corral, the loop is allowed to drag loosely on the ground. A good roper will hurl out the coil with marvelous accuracy and force; it fairly whistles through the air, and settles round the object with almost infallible certainty. Mexicans make the best ropers; but some Texans are very little behind them. A good horse takes as much interest in the work as does his rider, and the instant the noose settles over the victim wheels and braces himself to meet the shock, standing with his legs firmly planted, the steer or cow being thrown with a jerk. An unskillful rider and untrained horse will often themselves be thrown when the strain comes.

Sometimes an animal—usually a cow or steer, but, strangely enough, very rarely a bull—will get fighting mad, and turn on the men. If on the drive, such a beast usually is simply dropped out; but if they have time, nothing delights the cowboys more than an encounter of this sort, and the charging brute is roped and tied down in short order. Often such an one will make a very vicious fight, and is most dangerous. Once a fighting cow kept several of us busy for nearly an hour; she gored two ponies, one of them, which was luckily, hurt but slightly, being my own pet cutting horse. If a steer is hauled out of a mud-hole, its first act is usually to charge the rescuer.

As soon as all the brands of cattle are worked, and the animals that are to be driven along have been put in the day herd, attention is turned to the cows and calves, which are already gathered in different bands, consisting each of all the cows of a certain brand and all the calves that are following them. If there is a corral, each band is in turn driven into it; if there is none, a ring of riders does duty in its place. A fire is built, the irons heated, and a dozen men dismount to, as it is called, "wrestle" the calves. The best two ropers go in on their horses to catch the latter; one man keeps tally, a couple put on the brands, and the others seize, throw, and hold the little unfortunates, A first-class roper invariably catches the calf by both hind feet, and then, having taken a twist with his lariat round the horn of the saddle, drags the bawling little creature, extended at full-length, up to the fire, where it is held before it can make a struggle. A less skillful roper catches round the neck, and then, if the calf is a large one, the one who seizes it has his hands full, as the bleating, bucking animal develops astonishing strength, cuts the wildest capers, and resists frantically and with all its power. If there are seventy or eighty calves in a corral, the scene is one of the greatest confusion. The ropers, spurring and checking the fierce little horses, drag the calves up so quickly that a dozen men can hardly hold them;

the men with the irons, blackened with soot, run to and fro; the calf-wrestlers, grimy with blood, dust, and sweat, work like beavers; while with the voice of a stentor the tallyman shouts out the number and sex of each calf. The dust rises in clouds, and the shouts, cheers, curses, and laughter of the men unite with the lowing of the cows and the frantic bleating of the roped calves to make a perfect babel. Now and then an old cow turns vicious and puts every one out of the corral. Or a *maverick* bull,—that is, an unbranded bull,—a yearling or a two-years-old, is caught, thrown, and branded; when he is let up there is sure to be a fine scatter. Down goes his head, and he bolts at the nearest man, who makes out of the way at top speed, amidst roars of laughter from all of his companions; while the men holding down calves swear savagely as they dodge charging mavericks, trampling horses, and taut lariats with frantic, plunging little beasts at the farther ends.

Every morning certain riders are detached to drive and to guard the day herd, which is most monotonous work, the men being on from 4 in the morning till 8 in the evening, the only rest coming at dinner-time, when they change horses. When the herd has reached the camping ground there is nothing to do but to loll listlessly over the saddle-bow in the blazing sun watching the cattle feed and sleep, and seeing that they do not spread out too much. Plodding slowly along on the trail through the columns of dust stirred up by the hoofs is not much better. Cattle travel best and fastest strung out in long lines; the swiftest taking the lead in single file, while the weak and the lazy, the young calves and the poor cows, crowd together in the rear. Two men travel along with the leaders, one on each side, to point them in the right direction; one or two others keep by the flanks, and the rest are in the rear to act as "drag-drivers" and hurry up the phalanx of reluctant weaklings. If the foremost of the string travels too fast, one rider will go along on the trail a few rods ahead, and thus keep them back so that those in the rear will not be left behind.

Generally all this is very tame and irksome; but by fits and starts there will be little flurries of excitement. Two or three of the circle riders may unexpectedly come over a butte near by with a bunch of cattle, which at once start for the day herd, and then there will be a few minutes' furious riding hither and thither to keep them out. Or the cattle may begin to run, and then get "milling"—that is, all crowd together into a mass like a ball, wherein they move round and round, trying to keep their heads towards the center, and refusing to leave it. The only way to start them is to force one's horse in among them and cut out some of their number, which then begin to travel off by themselves, when the others will probably follow. But in spite of occasional incidents of this kind, day-herding has a dreary sameness about it that makes the men dislike and seek to avoid it.

From 8 in the evening till 4 in the morning the day herd becomes a night herd. Each wagon in succession undertakes to guard it for a night, dividing the time into watches of two hours apiece, a couple of riders taking each watch. This is generally chilly and tedious; but at times it is accompanied by intense excitement and danger, when the cattle become stampeded, whether by storm or otherwise. The first and the last watches are those chosen by preference; the others are disagreeable, the men having to turn out cold and sleepy, in the pitchy darkness, the two hours of chilly wakefulness completely breaking the night's rest. The first guards have to bed the cattle down, though the day-herders often do this themselves; it simply consists in hemming them into as small a space as possible, and then riding round them until they lie down and fall asleep. Often, especially at first, this takes some time—the beasts will keep rising and lying down again. When at last most become quiet, some perverse brute of a steer will deliberately hook them all up; they keep moving in and out among one another, and long strings of animals suddenly start out from the herd at a stretching walk, and are turned back by the nearest cowboy only to break forth at a new spot. When finally they have lain down and are chewing their cud or slumbering, the two night guards begin riding round them in opposite ways, often, on very dark nights, calling or singing to them, as the sound of the human voice on such occasions seems to have a tendency to quiet them. In inky black weather, especially when rainy, it is both difficult and unpleasant work; the main trust must be placed in the horse, which, if old at the business, will of its own accord keep pacing steadily round the herd, and head off any animals that, unseen by the rider's eyes in the darkness, are trying to break out. Usually the watch passes off without incident, but on rare occasions the cattle become restless and prone to stampede. Anything may then start them—the plunge of a horse, the sudden approach of a coyote, or the arrival of some outside steers or cows that have smelt them and come up. Every animal in the herd will be on its feet in an instant, as if by an electric shock, and off with a rush, horns and tail up. Then, no matter how rough the ground nor how pitchy black the night, the cowboys must ride for all there is in them and spare neither their own nor their horses' necks. Perhaps their charges break away and are lost altogether; perhaps by desperate galloping, they may head them off, get them running in a circle, and finally stop them. Once stopped, they may break again, and possibly divide up, one cowboy, perhaps, following each band. I have known six such stops and renewed stampedes to take place in one night, the cowboy staying with his ever-diminishing herd of steers until daybreak, when he managed to get them under control again, and, by careful humoring of his jaded, staggering horse, finally brought those there were left back to the camp, several miles distant. The riding in these night stampedes is wild and dangerous to a degree, especially if the man gets caught in the rush of the beasts. It also frequently necessitates an immense amount of work in collecting the scattered animals. On one such occasion a small party of us were thirty-six hours in the saddle, dismounting only to change horses or to eat. We were almost worn out at the end of the time; but it must be kept in mind that for a long spell of such work a stock-saddle is far less tiring then the ordinary Eastern or English one, and in every way superior to it.

By very hard riding, such a stampede may sometimes be prevented. Once we were bringing a thousand head of young cattle down to my lower ranch, and as the river was high were obliged to take the inland trail. The third night we were forced to make a dry camp, the cattle having had no water since the morning. Nevertheless, we got them bedded down without difficulty, and one of the cowboys and myself stood first guard. But very soon after nightfall, when the darkness had become complete, the thirsty brutes of one accord got on their feet and tried to break out. The only salvation was to keep them close together, as, if they once got scattered, we knew they could never be gathered; so I kept on one side, and the cowboy on the other, and never in my life did I ride so hard. In the darkness I could but dimly see the shadowy outlines of the herd, as with whip and spurs I ran the pony along its edge, turning back the beasts at one point barely in time to wheel and keep them in at another. The ground was cut up by numerous little gullies, and each of us got several falls, horses and riders turning complete somersaults. We were dripping with sweat, and our ponies quivering and trembling like quaking aspens when, after more than an hour of the most violent exertion, we finally got the herd quieted again.

On another occasion while with the round-up we were spared an excessively unpleasant night only because there happened to be two or three great corrals not more than a mile or so away. All day long it had been raining heavily, and we were well drenched; but towards evening it lulled a little, and the day herd, a very large one, of some two thousand head, was gathered on an open bottom. We had turned the horses loose, and in our oilskin slickers cowered, soaked and comfortless, under the lee of the wagon, to take a meal of damp bread and lukewarm tea, the sizzling embers of the fire having about given up the ghost after a fruitless struggle with the steady downpour. Suddenly the wind began to come in quick, sharp gusts, and soon a regular blizzard was blowing, driving the rain in stinging level sheets before it. Just as we were preparing to turn into bed, with the certainty of a night of more or less chilly misery ahead of us, one of my men, an iron-faced personage, whom no one would ever have dreamed had a weakness for poetry, looked towards the plain where the cattle were, and remarked, "I guess there's 'racing and chasing on Cannobie Lea' now, sure." Following his gaze, I saw that the cattle had begun to drift before the storm, the night guards being evidently unable to cope with them, while at the other wagons riders were saddling in hot haste and spurring off to their help through the blinding rain. Some of us at once ran out to our own saddle-band. All of the ponies were standing huddled together, with their heads down and their tails to the wind. They were wild and restive enough usually; but the storm had cowed them, and we were able to catch them without either rope or halter. We made quick work of saddling; and the second each man was ready, away he loped through the dusk, splashing and slipping in the pools of water that studded the muddy plain. Most of the riders were already out when we arrived. The cattle were gathered in a compact, wedge-shaped, or rather fan-shaped mass, with their tails to the wind—that is, towards the thin end of the wedge or fan. In front of this fan-shaped mass of frightened, maddened beats was a long line of cowboys, each muffled in his slicker and with his broad hat pulled down over his eyes, to shield him from the pelting rain. When the cattle were quiet for a moment every horseman at once turned round with his back to the wind, and the whole line stood as motionless as so many sentries. Then, if the cattle began to spread out and overlap at the ends, or made a rush and broke through at one part of the lines, there would be a change into wild activity. The men, shouting and swaying in their saddles, darted to and fro with reckless speed, utterly heedless of danger—now racing to the threatened point, now checking and wheeling their horses so sharply as to bring them square on their haunches, or even throw them flat down, while the hoofs plowed long furrows in the slippery soil, until, after some minutes of this mad galloping hither and thither, the herd, having drifted a hundred yards or so, would be once more brought up standing. We always had to let them drift a little to prevent their spreading out too much. The din of the thunder was terrific, peal following peal until they mingled in one continuous, rumbling roar; and at every thunder-clap louder than its fellows the cattle would try to break away. Darkness had set in, but each flash of lightning showed us a dense array of tossing horns and staring eyes. It grew always harder to hold in the herd; but the drift took us along to the corrals already spoken of, whose entrances were luckily to windward. As soon as we reached the first we cut off part of the herd, and turned it within; and after again doing this with the second, we were able to put all the remaining animals into the third. The instant the cattle were housed five-sixth of the horsemen started back at full speed for the wagons; the rest of us barely waited to put up the bars and make the corrals secure before galloping after them. We had to ride right in the teeth of the driving storm; and once at the wagons we made small delay in crawling under our blankets, damp though the latter were, for we were ourselves far too wet, stiff, and cold not to hail with grateful welcome any kind of shelter from the wind and the rain.

All animals were benumbed by the violence of this gale of cold rain: a prairie chicken rose from under my horse's feet so heavily that, thoughtlessly striking at it, I cut it down with my whip; while when a jack rabbit got up ahead of us, it was barely able to limp clumsily out of our way.

But though there is much work and hardship, rough fare, monotony, and exposure connected with the round-up, yet there are few men who do not look forward to it and back to it with pleasure. The only fault to be found is that the hours of work are so long that one does not usually have enough time to sleep. The food, if rough, is good; beef, bread, pork, beans, coffee or tea, always canned tomatoes, and often rice, canned corn, or sauce made from dried apples. The men are good-humored, bold and thoroughly interested in their business, continually vying with one another in the effort to see which can do the work best. It is superbly health-giving, and is full of excitement and adventure, calling for the exhibition of pluck, self-reliance, hardihood, and dashing horsemanship; and of all forms of physical labor the earliest and pleasantest is to sit in the saddle.

THE RACE

STEWART EDWARD WHITE

This story is most blood-and-thundery, but, then, it is true. It is one of the stories of Alfred; but Alfred is not the hero of it at all—quite another man, not nearly so interesting in himself as Alfred.

At the time, Alfred and this other man, whose name was Tom, were convoying a band of Mexican vaqueros over to the Circle-X outfit. The Circle-X was in the heat of a big round-up, and had run short of men. So Tom and Alfred had gone over to Tucson and picked up the best they could find, which best was enough to bring tears to the eyes of an old-fashioned, straight-riding, swift-roping Texas cowman. The gang was an ugly one: it was sullen, black-browed, sinister. But it, one and all, could throw a rope and cut out stock, which was not only the main thing—it was the whole thing.

Still, the game was not pleasant. Either Alfred or Tom usually rode night-herd on the ponies—merely as a matter of precaution—and they felt just a trifle more shut off by themselves and alone than if they had ridden solitary over the limitless alkali of the Arizona plains. This feeling struck in the deeper because Tom had just entered one of his brooding spells. Tom and Alfred had been chums now for close on two years, so Alfred knew enough to leave him entirely alone until he should recover.

The primary cause of Tom's abstraction was an open-air preacher, and the secondary cause was, of course, a love affair. These two things did not connect themselves consciously in Tom's mind, but they blended subtly to produce a ruminative dissatisfaction.

When Tom was quite young he had fallen in love with a girl back in the Dakota country. Shortly after a military-post had been established near by, and Ann Bingham had ceased to be spoken of by mayors' daughters and officers' wives. Tom, being young, had never quite gotten over it. It was still part of his nature, and went with a certain sort of sunset, or that kind of star-lit evening in which an imperceptible haze dims the brightness of the heavens.

The open-air preacher had chosen as his text the words, "passing the love of woman," and Tom, wandering idly by, had caught the text. Somehow ever since the words had run in his mind. They did not mean anything to him, but merely repeated themselves over and over, just as so many delicious syllables which tickled the ear and rolled succulently under the tongue. For, you see, Tom was only an ordinary battered Arizona cow-puncher, and so, of course, according to the fireside moralists, quite incapable of the higher feelings. But the words reacted to arouse memories of black-eyed Anne, and the memories in turn brought one of his moods.

Tom, and Alfred, and the ponies, and the cook-wagon, and the cook, and the Mexican vaqueros had done the alkali for three days. Underfoot has been an exceedingly irregular plain; overhead an exceedingly bright and trying pol-ished sky; around about an exceedingly monotonous horizon-line and dense clouds of white dust. At the end of the third day everybody was feeling just a bit choked up and tired, and, to crown a series of petty misfortunes, the fire failed to respond to Black Sam's endeavours. This made supper late.

Now at one time in this particular locality Arizona had not been dry and full of alkali. A mighty river, so mighty that in its rolling flood no animal that lives to-day would have had the slightest chance, surged down from the sharp-pointed mountains on the north, pushed fiercely its way through the southern plains, and finally seethed and boiled in eddies of foam out into a southern sea which has long since disappeared. On its banks grew strange, bulbous plants. Across its waters swam uncouth monsters with snake-like necks. Over it alternated storms so savage that they seem to rend the world, and sunshine so hot that it seemed that were it not for the bulbous plants all living things would perish as in an oven.

In the course of time conditions changed, and the change brought the Arizona of to-day. There are now no turbid waters, no bulbous plants, no uncouth beasts, and, above all, no storms. Only the sun and one other thing remain: that other thing is the bed of the ancient stream.

On one side—the concave of the curve—is a long easy slope, so gradual that one hardly realizes where it shades into the river-bottom itself. On the other—the convex of the curve—where the swift waters were turned aside to a new direction, is a high, perpendicular cliff running in an almost unbroken breastwork for a great many miles, and baked as hard as iron in this sunny and almost rainless climate. Occasional showers have here and there started to eat out little transverse gullies, but with a few exceptions have only gone so far as slightly to nick the crest. The exceptions, reaching to the plain, afford steep and perilous ascents to the level above. Anyone who wishes to pass the barrier made by the primeval river must hunt out himself one of these narrow passages.

On the evening in question the cowmen had made camp in the hollow beyond the easy slope. On the rise, sharply silhouetted against the west, Alfred rode wrangler to the little herd of ponies. Still farther westward across the plain was the clay-cliff barriers, looking under the sunset like a narrow black ribbon. In the hollow itself was the camp, giving impression in the background of a scattering of ghostly mules, a half-circle of wagons, ill-defined forms of recumbent vaqueros, and then in the foreground of Sam with his gleaming semicircle of utensils, and his pathetic little pile of fuel which would not be induced to gleam at all.

For, as has been said, Black Sam was having great trouble with his fire. It went out at least six times, and yet each time it hung on in a flickering fashion so long that he had felt encouraged to arrange his utensils and distribute his provisions. Then it had expired, and poor Sam had to begin all over again. The Mexicans smoked yellow-paper cigarettes and watched his off-and-on movements with sullen distrust; they were firmly convinced that he was indulging in some sort of a practical joke. So they hated him fervently and wrapped themselves in their serapes. Tom sat on a wagon-tongue swinging a foot and repeating vaguely to himself in a sing-song inner voice, "passing the love of woman, passing the love of woman," over and over again. His mind was a dull blank of grayness. From time to time he glanced at Sam, but with no impatience: he was used to going without. Sam was to him a matter of utter indifference.

As to the cook himself, he had a perplexed droop in every curve of his rounded shoulders. His kinky gray wool was tousled from perpetual undecided scratching, and his eyes had something of the dumb sadness of the dog as he rolled them in despair. Life was not a matter of indifference to him. Quite the contrary. The problem of *damp wood* + *matches* = *cooking-fire* was the whole tangle of existence. There was something pitiable in it. Perhaps this was because there is something more pathetic in a comical face grown solemn than in the most melancholy countenance in the world.

At last the moon rose and the fire decided to burn. With the seventh attempt to flared energetically; then settled to a steady glow of possible flap-jacks.

But its smoke was bitter, and the evening wind fitful. Bitter smoke on an empty stomach might be appropriately substituted for the last straw of the proverb—when the proverb has to do with hungry Mexicans. Most of the recumbent vaqueros merely cursed a little deeper and drew their serapes closer, but José Guiterrez grunted, threw off his blanket, and approached the fire.

Sam rolled the whites of his eyes up at him for a moment, grinned in a half-perplexed fashion, and turned again to his pots and pans. José, being sulky and childish, wanted to do something to somebody, so he insolently flicked the end of his long quirt through a mess of choice but still chaotic flap-jacks. The quirt left a narrow streak across the batter. Sam looked up quickly.

"Doan you done do dat!" he said, with indignation.

He looked upon the turkey-like José for a heavy moment, and then turned back to the cooking. In rescuing an unstable coffeepot a moment later, he accidentally jostled against José's leg. José promptly and fiercely kicked the whole outfit into space. The frying-pan crowned a sage-brush; the coffee-pot rolled into a hollow, where it spouted coffee-grounds and water in a diminishing stream; the kettle rolled gently on its side; flap-jacks distributed themselves impartially and moistly; and, worst of all, the fire was drowned out altogether.

Black Sam began stiffly to arise. The next instant he sank back with a gurgle in his throat and a knife thrust in his side.

The murderer stood looking down at his victim. The other Mexicans stared. The cowboy jumped up from the tongue of the wagon, drew his weapon from the holster at his side, took deliberate aim, and fired twice. Then he turned and began to run toward Alfred on the hill.

A cowboy cannot run so very rapidly. He carries such a quantity of dunnage below in the shape of high boots, spurs, chaps, and cartridgebelts that his gait is a waddling single-foot. Still, Tom managed to get across the little stony ravine before the Mexicans recovered from their surprise and became disentangled from their ponchos. Then he glanced over his shoulder. He saw that some of the vaqueros were running toward the arroya, that some were busily unhobbling the mules, and that one or two had kneeled and were preparing to shoot. At the sight of these last, he began to jump from side to side as he ran. This decreased his speed. Half-way up the hill he was met by Alfred on his way to get in the game, whatever it might prove to be. The little man reached over and grasped Tom's hand. Tom braced his foot against the stirrup, and in an instant was astride behind the saddle. Alfred turned up the hill again, and without a word began applying his quirt vigorously to the wiry shoulders of his horse. At the top of the hill, as they passed the grazing ponies, Tom turned and emptied the remaining four chambers of his revolver into the herd. Two ponies fell kicking; the rest scattered in every direction. Alfred grunted approvingly, for this made pursuit more difficult, and so gained them a little more time.

Now both Alfred and Tom knew well enough that a horse carrying two men cannot run away from a horse carrying one man, but they also knew the country, and this knowledge taught them that if they could reach the narrow passage through the old clay bluff, they might be able to escape to Peterson's, which was situated a number of miles beyond. This would be possible, because men climb faster when danger is behind them than when it is in front. Besides, a brisk defence could render even an angry Mexican a little doubtful as to just when he should begin to climb. Accordingly, Alfred urged the pony across the flat plain of the ancient river-bed toward the nearest and only break in the cliff. Fifteen miles below was the regular passage. Otherwise the upper mesa was as impregnable as an ancient fortress. The Mexicans had by this time succeeded in roping some of the scattered animals, and were streaming over the brow of the hill, shouting wildly. Alfred looked back and grinned. Tom waved his wide sombrero mockingly.

When they approached the ravine, they found the sides almost perpendicular and nearly bare. Its bed was V-shaped, and so cut up with miniature gullies, fantastic turrets and spires, and so undermined by former rains as to be almost impassable. It sloped gently at first, but afterward more rapidly, and near the top was straight up and down for two feet or more. As the men reached it, they threw themselves from the horse and commenced to scramble up, leading the animal by the bridle-rein. From riding against the sunset their eyes were dazzled, so this was not easy. The horse followed gingerly, his nose close to the ground.

It is well known that quick, short rains followed by a burning sun tend to undermine the clay surface of the ground and to leave it with a hard upper shell, beneath which are cavities of various depths. Alfred and Tom as experienced men, should have foreseen this, but they did not. Soon after entering the ravine the horse broke through into one of the underground cavities and fell heavily on his side. When he had scrambled somehow to his feet, he stood feebly panting, his nostrils expanded.

"How is it, Tom?" called Alfred, who was ahead.

"Shoulder out," said Tom briefly.

Alfred turned back without another word, and putting the muzzle of his pistol against the pony's forehead just above the line of the eyes he pulled the trigger. With the body the two men improvised a breastwork across a little hummock. Just as they dropped behind it the Mexicans clattered up, riding bareback. Tom coolly reloaded his pistol.

The Mexicans, too, were dazzled from riding against the glow in the west, and halted a moment in a confused mass at the mouth of the ravine. The two cowboys within rose and shot rapidly. Three Mexicans and two ponies fell. The rest in wild confusion slipped rapidly to the right and left beyond the Americans' line of sight. Three armed with Winchesters made a long detour and dropped quietly into the sagebrush just beyond accurate pistol-range. There they lay concealed, watching. Then utter silence fell.

The rising moon shone full and square into the ravine, illuminating every inch of the ascent. A very poor shot could hardly miss in such a light and with such a background. The two cowmen realized this and settled down more comfortably behind their breastwork. Tom cautiously raised the pony's head with a little chunk of rock, thus making a loophole through which to keep tab on the enemy, after which he rolled on his belly and began whittling in the hard clay, for Tom had the carving habit—like many a younger boy. Alfred carefully extracted a short pipe from beneath his chaparejos, pushed down with his blunt forefinger the charge with which it was already loaded, and struck a match. He poised this for a moment above the bowl of the pipe.

"What's the row anyway!" he inquired, with pardonable curiosity.

"Now, it's jest fifteen mile to th' cut," said Tom, disregarding Alfred's question entirely, "an' of co'se they's goin' to send a posse down thar on th' keen jump.

That'll take clost onto three hours in this light. Then they'll jest pot us a lot from on top."

Alfred puffed three times toward the moonlight, and looked as though the thing were sufficiently obvious without wasting so much breath over it.

"We've jest *got* to git out!" concluded Tom, earnestly.

Alfred grunted.

"An' how are we goin' to do it?"

Alfred paused in the act of blowing a cloud.

"Because, if we makes a break, those Greasers jest nat'rally plugs us from behind th' minute we begins to climb."

Alfred condescended to nod. Tom suspended his whittling for a reply.

"Well," said Alfred, taking his pipe from his mouth—Tom contentedly took up whittling again—"there's only one way to do it, and that's to keep them so damn busy in front that they *can't* plug us."

Tom looked perplexed.

"We just got to take our chances on the climbing. Of course, there's bound to be th' risk of accident. But when I give th' word, *you mosey*, and if one of them pots you, it'll be because my six-shooter's empty"

"But you can't expec' t' shoot *an'* climb!" objected Tom.

"Course not," replied Alfred, calmly, "Division of labour: you climb; I shoot."

A light dawned in Tom's eyes, and his shut his jaws with a snap.

"I guess not!" said he, quietly.

"Yo' laigs is longer," Alfred urged, in his gentle voice, "and yo'll get to Peterson's quicker;" and then he looked in Tom's eyes and changed his tone. "All right!" he said, in a business-like manner. "I'll toss you for it."

For reply, Tom fished out an old pack of cards.

"I tell you," he proposed, triumphantly, "I'll turn you fer it. First man that gits a jack in th' hand-out stays."

He began to manipulate the cards, lying cramped on his side, and in doing so dropped two or three. Alfred turned to pick them up. Tom deftly slipped the jack of diamonds to the bottom of the pack. He inserted in the centre those Alfred handed him, and began at once to deal.

"Thar's yore's," he said, laying out the four of clubs, "an' yere's mine," he concluded, producing the jack of diamonds. "Luck's ag'in me early in th' game," was his cheerful comment.

For a minute Alfred was silent, and a decided objection appeared in his eyes. Then his instinct of fair play in the game took the ascendant. He kicked off his chaps in the most business-like manner, unbuckled his six-shooter and gave it to Tom, and perched his hat on the end of his quirt, which he then raised slowly above the pony's side for the purpose of drawing the enemy's fire. He did these things quickly and without heroics, because he was a plainsman. Hardly had the bullets from three Winchesters spatted against the clay before he was up and climbing for dear life.

The Mexicans rushed to the opening from either side, fully expecting to be able either to take wing-shots at close range, or to climb so fast as to close in before the cowboys would have time to make a stand at the top. In this they shut off their most effective fire—that of the three men with the Winchesters-and, instead of getting wing-shots themselves, they received an enthusiastic battering from Tom at the range of six yards. Even a tenderfoot cannot over-shoot at six yards. What was left of the Mexicans disappeared quicker than they had come, and the three of the Winchesters scuttled back to cover like a spent covey of quail.

Tom then lit Alfred's pipe, and continued his excellent sculpture in the bed of hard clay. He knew nothing more would happen until the posse came. The game had passed out of his hands. It had become a race between a short-legged man on foot and a band of hard riders on the backs of very good horses. Viewing the matter dispassionately, Tom would not have cared to bet on the chances.

As has been stated, Alfred was a small man and his legs were short—and not only short, but unused to exertion of any kind, for Alfred's daylight hours were spent on a horse. At the end of said legs were tight boots with high French heels, which most Easterners would have considered a silly affectation, but which all Westerners knew to be purposeful in the extreme—they kept his feet from slipping forward through the wide stirrups. In other respects, too, Alfred was handicapped. His shoulders were narrow and sloping and his chest was flat. Indoors and back East he would probably have been a consumptive; out here, he was merely short-winded.

So it happened that Alfred lost the race.

The wonder was not that he lost but that he succeeded in finishing at Peterson's at all. He did it somehow, and even made a good effort to ride back with the rescuing party, but fell like a log when he tried to pick up his hat. So someone took off his boots, also, and put him to bed.

As to the rescuing party, it disbanded less than an hour later. Immediately afterward it reorganized into a hunting party—and its game was men. The hunt was a long one, and the game was bagged even unto the last, but that is neither here nor there.

Poor Tom was found stripped to the hide, and hacked to pieces. Mexicans are impulsive, especially after a few of them have been killed. His equipment had been stolen. The naked horse and the naked man, bathed in the light of gray dawn, that was all—except that here and there fluttered bits of paper that had once been a pack of cards. The clay slab was carved deeply—a man can do much of that sort of thing with two hours to waste. Most of the decorative effects were arrows, or hearts, or brands, but in one corner were the words, "passing the love of woman," which was a little impressive after all, even though Tom had not meant them, being, as I said, only an ordinary battered Arizona cow-puncher incapable of the higher feelings.

How do I know he played the jack of diamonds on purpose? Why, I knew Tom, and that's enough.

CHARLIE RUSSELL

BOB KENNON

I WAS REPPING for the 79 at the Big State wagon in the Judith Basin when Charlie Russell was a night-hawk. He had held this same job for eleven years. Pete Vann, Bill Skelton, and Teddy Blue Abbott were also there. In later years Vann and Skelton became well-to-do cattlemen in the Geyser country, and Abbott ran cattle below Fort Maginnis.

We had camped on a high divide west of Judith River, about fifteen miles from the river, where there were a number of big springs. Charlie Russell was as lousy as a pet coon. Pete Vann and Bill Skelton told him to pull off all his clothes and lay them on some anthills near by.

"Will that take care of the situation?" asked Charlie.

"Yes, the ants will eat all the lice," Bill Skelton answered.

Charlie pondered over this a second or two, then began undressing, putting his clothes on the anthills. The first thing he pulled off was his hat, then his coat and shirt, then off went his pants, lastly his boots. The ants sure had a feast and devoured all the lice. Bill Skelton and Pete Vann walked down to the roundup wagon, bringing back some cottonwood sticks and boards. They drove the stakes into the ground, tied the boards to the sticks with some rawhide strings, took a piece of charcoal from the fire, and printed this sign:

Louse Creek Bench

This bench is known by that name to this day.

Shortly after I became acquainted with Charlie, he quit riding for a living. Ma Nature seemed to have it planned that he was to make his big pile with his brushes and palette.

He left his mark of friendship and the touch of his genius in many places, and of course in the saloons all over the range country. Every little cow town had his wonderful buffalo, his Indians, his bears, and the pictures of us cowpokes. Dozens of times we found these pictures which he had given to his old friends to decorate their homes and their saloons. Almost everyone knew Charlie, and he visited a lot during the active times of the year and when the weather was good. You could usually locate him every summer at some of his old stomping grounds. The roping and cutting range, the branding corral, and the chuck wagon—these were the things he painted in winter at home in his studio, but in the summer he liked to visit around and take back again these fresh memory pictures of all he loved.

I'll never forget the night I first met Charlie. It happened in Lewistown, and as well as I remember it was in 1897. It seems to me this was the year we had so many good times in Lewistown, when we would come in for a fight with those gold miners from Gilt Edge. I'll certainly always remember that this was the year I met Charlie, and the night when all the drinking went on at the bar next to the stage station, a plenty popular bar for fellows who waited for the usually late stage.

We cowboys came in from Kendall and at this time we were flush with money and with spare time to enjoy ourselves. It was late summer and just before fall roundup. We were itching to try our luck at a few games and have a few drinks before the fellows from Gilt Edge would get into town. There were some among us who would never rest until they could beat up some of these cooty miners, who were due in town this Saturday night. They had been paid off, and were anxious for some poker and whiskey.

Charlie was a great lover of animals, especially the wild ones, so we did a lot of trapping that night over the bar. Looking back to that night, he seemed no different from the rest of us, for he was jolly and full of the devil. He was dressed just like other riders except for that old red sash he always wore. He asked repeatedly how this or that range was, who had sold out their spreads, how the water and grass were, and all those things a range man's always interested in. I'm sure that, though we all liked his pictures, he hadn't the faintest idea of their worth, nor did we appreciate the genius who sat that night laughing and exchanging stories of the Judith and the Musselshell roundups with us.

It was very hot inside, so Charlie and I strolled outside. He pointed up the road and remarked that the dust being stirred up must be the stage coming in. But he was wrong, for it was a buck-board coming in at a good trot. As the vehicle pulled to a stop, we recognized the driver as a rancher who lived not very far from town. He was a good fellow, but had a reputation for getting drunk and staying on a spree for weeks at a time when he got to town. Tonight, though, he refused to be drawn inside the saloon and declared he had come in to meet a friend who was due on the stage from Great Falls.

His name was Hugh McIver and it was whispered around by the hangers-on at the bar that he was waiting for a lady whom he had never met but to whom he had been writing all winter and spring, getting her name and address from one of those "mailorder bride" papers. He was dressed up in a new brown suit, white shirt, green tie, and new hat. His boots were polished to a gloss. He seemed nervous and kept asking about the stage from Great Falls. I was told that he had driven in from his homestead near Lewistown to meet his mailorder bride, whom he had found through that magazine called *Heart and Hand*.

Charlie got quite a kick out of this story, and the homesteader took on a new importance and interest for all of us you may be sure. In spite of his extreme nervousness, we couldn't persuade him to take a drink. I think it might have been all right if it hadn't been for those miners, who now began to arrive in ore wagons, buggies, and on horseback. As soon as these roughnecks found out that Hughie was waiting for a new bride, he didn't have a chance to stay sober. They dragged him inside bodily and started filling him with whiskey. As soon as he got a little too much, he started giving all his secrets away, and soon he pulled out the lady's picture and these miners were having a regular picnic with him.

Meanwhile, where was the Great Falls to Lewistown stage?

Now perhaps I should tell you that at any season of the year it was a long, hard trip. It had been a wet spring and during the summer we had had a lot of rain in the early part, so that when we did get the hot weather, the sun baked these deep ruts and chuckholes into a mighty rough road. It took a good twenty-four hours to make the trip with a six-horse team. Of course the teams were changed at the relay stations, which were really ranches or very small cow towns. From Great Falls to Lewistown the stopping places, as I remember, were Belt, Cora Creek, Spion Kop, Old Geyser, Old Stanford, and then, I believe, some ranch halfway between Stanford and Lewistown. Anyway, when travelers got that far, they were pretty sore from the bumps of the road and strangers always asked: "My God, how much farther to Lewistown?"

On this night at the saloon in Lewistown, Charlie tried to talk Hughie into leaving the boys and taking a walk out in the air, but Hughie refused to do so. He showed Charlie and me the lady's picture, though it was now much the worse for the handling and grabbing of the miners, who were bent on pestering the bridegroom. After looking at the photo, which had been done in St. Jo in big-city style, we could see that the lady was certainly a "good looker," to quote Charlie. We both had our doubts, though, as to whether this was the girl Hughie would actually get. This had happened before and it wasn't the first time that a lady sent some beauty's picture instead of her own.

This one was dark haired, with flashing white teeth and large, dark eyes which gazed somewhat boldly at us. "A very flashy sort of gal"—that was what we all agreed. She was dressed fit to kill in white flounces and laces and ribbons, which was the fashion of city ladies at this time. Upon her curls was perched a big white hat, and she carried an umbrella—I think they called it a parasol.

On the back of the photo, Hughie told us, were the full instructions as to how she was to be met at Lewistown and they stated she would be wearing this same outfit and carrying in the other hand a bird cage with her pet canary in it. We later had reason to recall this parasol and bird-cage arrangement.

Now the part about meeting her made Charlie laugh, as he could see that this girl thought she might get lost or the crowd would be so large that Hughie would have a time finding her. We decided that it was time to do something drastic before this lady arrived, for the least we could do would be to see that she was given a decent reception, no matter how things turned out afterward for Hughie. Charlie and the bartender cooked up a plan, and after everyone had a round of drinks the bar was closed and we all went outside to cool off and wait for the stage. There was less objection to this arrangement than we feared, and we hoped we could sober Hughie up out there. To tell the truth, I was for taking him over to the hotel where I had gotten a room earlier in the day and putting him to bed, but Charlie was against this and someone went out promising to get back with some black coffee. Then Charlie spied the water trough where we tended the horses and stage teams and declared that a dip in this cold spring water would be just the thing, but we had to act quick for the stage was due any time. We had Hughie between us, and he refused to even take a drink of the water, though we set a good example by drinking freely of it as it trickled down into the trough. At a sign from Charlie, we gave him a good push and he sprawled into the trough, choking and blubbering.

If we had not gotten him out when we did, he would surely have drowned. We tried to dry him off, but it was so hot this didn't take much effort. Lord, was he mad! It was getting dark by now and all of us went into the stage station and left him outside raving. Charlie said he felt a sort of kinship with anyone coming from Missouri and he was going to see that this lady was treated well.

At last a yell went up as the stage was coming in, with great clouds of dust whirling along the horizon. We rushed out and could hear the rumble of the vehicle and the rattle of the harness on the six-horse team.

Lanterns were brought out and hung up, as was the custom when the passengers were to get out. Of course there was so much pushing and so much chatter and noise that Charlie and I were left way back in the crowd. We craned our necks and pushed too, so we at least could see that a man was helping a lady down. She had on light clothes, and sure enough, Hughie was being called up front. He was there and you must know that he was beyond any sensible conversation.

Soon everyone was going into the station and here we saw that she was indeed the same gal as in the photo. I must state that a lot of fellows lost their bets, as some had bet for sure that she would not show up at all and some others that it would be a different gal. Though it was the same girl, she didn't look as fresh as her picture, for her dress was wrinkled and she seemed wilted all over. She had no hat nor parasol, and indeed no bird cage.

She saw Charlie and rushed to meet him and cuddled in his arms. She kissed him smack on the lips and knocked his Stetson off into the dust. The crowd hooted and hollered, and as Charlie tried to free himself from this unwanted situation, here came the worst-looking spectacle it has been my lot to behold. There stood Hughie, wet and very angry as he clutched the photo. He was pushed forward and introduced to the girl, but she seemed to think it was some joke and still clung to Charlie's arm. Hughie refused to claim her and demanded to see the bird cage, the hat, and the parasol. He seemed to think that he had been cheated. He was just sobering up and at that unhappy stage which makes a man really mean. It took some talking to convince both of them.

Charlie told some bystanders that she should be taken over to Ma Murphy's, who kept a respectable boarding house, and we promised her that we would see what could be done with Hughie when he became more sober. She was a swell-looking girl and no shrinking violet, but now she seemed to have a crush on Charlie and would have traded in Hughie for sure, but we told her Charlie was a married man.

The stage driver even tried to explain to Hughie that he didn't let her bring the bird cage and that it was still up in Great Falls, and that she had nearly been left behind at the halfway station near Lewistown and there she had left her hat and parasol in the rush.

Hughie finally sobered up and came to his senses, and he and his mail-order bride were married by a preacher in Ma Murphy's parlor. Often in later years Charlie would ask me how Hughie's bargain turned out. Her name was Dolly and she was known for miles around, as she bought herself a fancy top buggy and a team of matched bays which she named Granger and Rowdy. They were put up at the livery barn many times when I was there in Lewistown, and many would have paid her a top price for that fine team.

For many years Charlie's path and mine crossed often, but I didn't have the pleasure of meeting his wife until we attended the big Calgary Stampede. I could see then why he had taken up a different life from his earlier and wilder cowboy days, for she was a fine little lady. She was not only pretty, but she had wit and sparkle, often crossing us both in a good argument.

One day Charlie and I were sitting along the bank of the Missouri River where the Milwaukee Railroad depot now stands in Great Falls. As we carried on a lazy sort of general conversation, Charlie picked up a handful of adobe with his left hand and from this he fashioned a perfect image of a bear. He modeled this without even seeming to be looking at what he was doing, and when it was finished he handed it to me. I couldn't help but wonder at such genius, and I wish now I had kept it.

Another time, Charlie and I were at a cigar store, one of his favorite hangouts, next door to the Mint Saloon. Late in the afternoon his wife, Nancy, drove down in their one-horse buggy to take him home. She was sitting in the buggy, near the curb, looking at a fellow standing on the edge of the sidewalk. He had all sorts of tobacco tags on his hat. Charlie drew a picture of this character. In about a week I saw him again and he handed me this picture. It was a perfect likeness. I thanked him, and put the picture in my vest pocket, little knowing how very valuable that sketch would become as time passed. I suppose the picture just wore out there in my pocket.

Sid Willis, owner of the famous Mint Saloon in Great Falls, and Charlie were very close friends. For years the walls of the Mint were lined on either side with large Russell paintings, many of them gifts to Sid from his artist friend, many of them to pay for drinks for other friends. People from all over the United States, as well as foreign lands, paid visits to the Mint to view these paintings. Actually this place was more like an art gallery than a saloon, and here, too, were many of Charlie's finest models done in wax.

Sid was acquainted with many famous people. He and Jaycox, the Milner Livestock Company range boss, went to Texas from Arkansas on horseback. They then decided to come north with a Texas trail herd, the N Bar N outfit. Jaycox secured a job with the Milner Livestock Company, and Sid stayed on with the N Bar N, both of Glasgow, Montana. Later on he became a United States marshal, holding this job for many years. Sid passed away in the early fifties, leaving a void in the friendship of many years which cannot be easily filled. He never ceased grieving for Charlie, who had passed on many years earlier.

Charlie had come back from the Mayo Clinic and was pretty weak. He had suffered a long time from sciatic rheumatism, and now, as he said, his "old pump was givin' out." Before he died on October 24, 1926, he told his wife he wanted to be carried to the cemetery behind horses. Horse-drawn hearses had gone out of style by then and they had to search a long time before they found one in Cascade that had been stored away for years. But his wife saw that his wish was carried out.

As I stood there with the rest of Charlie's friends—which numbered into the hundreds—and watched his riderless horse and the old hearse carry his mortal remains to the cemetery, I felt a sadness that, like many another cowman's, was too deep to be put into any language. He had indeed joined the old trail riders on the "Other Side."

WHISKEY

CHARLES M. RUSSELL

Whiskey has been blamed for lots it didn't do. It's a brave-maker. All men know it. If you want to know a man, get him drunk and he'll tip his hand. If I like a man when I'm sober, I kin hardly keep from kissing him when I'm drunk. This goes both ways. If I don't like a man when I'm sober, I don't want him in the same town when I'm drunk.

Remember, I ain't saying that booze is good for men, but it boils what's in him to the top. A man that beats his wife when he's drunk ain't a good man when he's sober. I've knowed drunks that would come home to mama loaded down with flowers, candy, and everything that they thought their wife would like. Other men that wouldn't take a drink never brought home nothing but laundry soap. The man that comes home drunk and licks his wife wouldn't fight a chickadee when he's sober. The drunk that brings home presents knows he's wrong and is sorry. He wants to square himself. The man that licks his wife ain't sorry for nobody but himself, and the only way to make him real sorry is to beat him near to death.

There's a difference in whiskey—some's worse than others. Me and a friend drops into a booze parlor on the Canadian line. The man that runs this place is a friend of ours. I ain't mentioning no names but his front name's Dick. He's an old-time cowpuncher. He's bought a lot of booze in his day but right now he's selling it.

When me and my friend name our drink we notice there's about ten men in this joint. Their actions tells us they've been using some of Dick's goods, but there ain't no loud talk. They are all paired off, talking low like they're at a funeral. I get curious and ask Dick if these gents are pallbearers that's spreading sorrow on his joint.

"No," says Dick, looking wise. "This ain't no cow-town no more. It's one of the coming farmer-cities of this country, and the sellers of all this rich land don't want nothing that'll scare away farmers, and I'm here to please the folks. Most of these tillers of the soil come from prohibition states where men do their drinkin' alone in the cellar. When you drink that way, it don't cost so much. The old-timer that you knew was generally on the square. When he got drunk he wanted everybody to know it and they did, if they were in the same town. Folks to-day ain't been able to sweep all this old stuff out but, like some old bachelors I know, they've swept the dirt under the bed, and what you don't see don't look bad.

"The gent that sold me this brand of booze told me there ain't a cross word in a barrel of it, and he told the truth. All these gents you see in here are pleasant without the noise. This bunch, if they stay to the finish, will whisper themselves to sleep. This booze would be safe for a burglar. I call it," says Dick, "whisperin' booze."

But as I said before, there's different kinds. I knowed a old Injun trader on the Missouri River that sold another kind. Back in the '80s the cowmen of Judith country was throwing their cattle north of the river. This old trader had a place on the river right where we crossed the cattle. All summer we were swimming herds.

I never knowed what made an Injun so crazy when he drunk till I tried this booze. I always was water shy and this old stream has got many a man, but with a few drinks of this trade whiskey the Missouri looked like a creek and we spur off in it with no fear. It was sure a brave-maker, and if a man had enough of this booze you couldn't drown him. You could even shoot a man through the brain or heart and he wouldn't die till he sobered up.

When Injuns got their hides full of this they were bad and dangerous. I used to think this was because an Injun was a wild man, but at this place where we crossed the herds there's about ten lodges of Assiniboines, and we all get drunk together. The squaws, when we started, got mighty busy caching guns and knives. In an hour we're all, Injuns and whites, so disagreeable that a shepherd dog couldn't have got along with us. Some wise cowpuncher had persuaded all the cowpunchers to leave their guns in camp. This wise man could see ahead an' knowed things was going to be messy. Without guns either cowpunchers or Injuns are harmless—they can't do nothing but pull hair. Of course the Injun, wearing his locks long, gets the worst of it. We were so disagreeable that the Injuns had to move camp.

It used to be agin the law to sell an Injun whiskey, but the law has made Injuns out of all of us now. Most new booze is worse than trade whiskey. Whiskey made all men brave. If nobody got drunk the East Coast would be awful crowded by this time. Maybe the leaders of the exploring party didn't drink, but the men that went with them did. It's a safe bet there wasn't a man in Columbus' crew that knowed what a maple-nut sundae was.

In the old times, when the world had lots of wild countries and some brave explorer wanted men to go up agin danger and maybe starvation, he don't go to the fireside of home lovers; he finds the toughest street in a town where there's music, booze, and lots of fighters—he ain't lookin' for pets. When he steps in this joint, he walks to the bar and asks them all up. He don't bar nobody, not even the bartender. He starts with making a good feller of himself. This sport don't ask nobody who he is, but while he's buyin' drinks he's telling about others that has gone to these countries and come back with gold in every pocket, an' it ain't long till all have signed up and joined. If there's any danger of them weakening, he keeps them drunk. There's been many a man that got drunk in St. Louis, and when he comes to out of this debauch he's hundreds of miles up the Missouri, on a line dragging a boat loaded with trade goods for the Injun country. If he turns back he's liable to bump into war parties, so he stays. This game is played on sailor, woods and river men. Cowpunchers were of the same kind of goods—all careless, homeless, hard-drinking men.

Fur traders were the first and real adventurers. They went to countries unknown—every track they made was dangerous. On every side were unseen savages. Such people as Colter, Bridger, and men of their stamp, these fellers were not out for gold or great wealth—they asked for little but life and adventure. They had no dreams of palaces. Few of them ever returned. The gold-hunter who came later loved the mountains for the gold he found in them, and some when they got it returned to the city, where they spent it and died in comfort. But most trappers kissed good-bye to civilization and their birth-place—took an Injun woman, and finished, nobody knowed how or where.

The cowboy was the last of this kind, and he's mighty near extinct. He came from everywhere—farms, big cities, and some of them from colleges. Most of them drank when they could get it.

As I said before, they're all Injuns now since the Volstead law. Just the other day I'm talking to a friend. Says he, "It's funny how crazy an Injun is for whiskey. A few days ago I'm riding along—I got a quart of booze in my saddle pocket. I meet an Injun. He sees what I got, and offers me the hoss he's riding for the quart. To a man that wants a saddle hoss, this one is worth a hundred dollars. I paid six for this moonshine."

"Did you make the trade?" says I.

"Hell, no!" says he. "It's all the booze I got!"

TWENTY STRAIGHT ON THE PRAIRIE

EMERSON HOUGH

The great herd, scattered over a mile of grazing ground, by now was well quieted. Wearied by their own exertions, some of the animals were lying down, as though aware that the end of their journey was at hand; the remainder scattered, grazing contentedly. Men were on guard here and there at the edges of the herd; others were at the fire, eating. A sudden excitement arose among the cow hands when word passed that a buyer was on the scene, for so they interpreted the advent of Nabours and his companions. Nabours waved a hand with genuine cowman enthusiasm.

"Look at them!" he exclaimed. "Did you ever see a finer outfit of cows in your borned days, Mr. Pattison?"

The face of the trader remained expressionless, though his eyes were busy as he rode.

"You've got some she-stock in here," said he at length; "some yearlings in too. I should say, too, that you've got several sorts of brands."

"Well, maybe we have," said Nabours. "I'd have a damned sight more if we had not hit so much country where there wasn't no cows coming north. This here herd belongs to a orphant, Mr. Pattison, and in our country they ain't no questions asked about orphants. We put up this herd in our own country. Our road brand is a Fishhook, and when you buy a Fishhook steer you are buying our support of the brand—twenty good men that can shoot. I got to sell these cows straight too."

Pattison reined up, still dubious.

"Let me tell you something. I know beef—that's my trade. You've got maybe three or four hundred of light stuff and shes. They don't pack well. Still, here I am with a good ranch over on the Smoky Hill. It hasn't got a head of stock on it yet.

"I just took in the land and water and trusted to God for the cattle. I know where the real money is, and it isn't in buying lean fours. If I had any way to handle these stockers over on my ranch I'd take your herd straight."

"I can't split no cows," said Jim Nabours. "It's all or none. I got to sell all these cows afore dark. We both allowed that five minutes was plenty."

"Well, it is," said Pattison quietly. "I trade as quick as anybody, and I don't go to the saloon first, as two or three other men have, whom I happen to know, that came on that train. Now I'll tell you what I'll do: If you'll hold out that stuff below the fours I'll give you twenty straight for your fours, right here on the prairie. Five thousand cash down, balance in draft on the First National of Kansas City."

Suddenly Dan McMasters turned to Nabours.

"The herd is sold," said he. "Twenty a head, straight through."

"How do you mean, Dan?"

"I am taking all the she-stuff and stockers for myself. Let Mr. Pattison have the fours."

"But what're you going to do?"

"I am thinking of starting a Northern ranch for myself. It don't take me long to decide either. I believe Mr. Pattison is right. There's where the money is. Besides, I'm leaving Texas before long."

Pattison turned toward him with his quizzical smile, estimating him after his own fashion.

"You bid me up, young man," said he; "but you've sold this herd, yearlings and all, at twenty straight on the prairie.

"Now, we've got plenty time left—two minutes by the watch. I'll give you just a minute and a half to think of me as your partner in my ranch on the Smoky Hill, myself to own half this stuff you've just bought in, you to trail a fresh herd up to us next year and to run this upper ranch for me—all dependent on your investigation of me back East, preferably by telegraph to-night. I've got the land, you've got the cows.

"I'll show you how to get three-four-five cents a pound for beef on the hoof. What do you say?"

McMasters turned his own cool gray eyes upon the other, regarding him with a like smile as their eyes met, and their hands.

"We have traded," said he quietly.

Nabours looked from one to the other, scratching his head.

"Then is my cows sold?" he demanded. "Do we get twenty straight?"

"You heard us," said Pattison. "There is a new company on the new northern range—the PM brand. Mr. McMasters is my partner; you see, I know something about him already. And I want to say to you, sir, you are on the road to more money than you could ever make in Texas. We'll cut this stuff and tally out to-morrow if it pleases you. Come on over to the fire, partner; let's light down."

Each in his mood, Nabours somewhat chastened as he endeavored to figure out how much the five minutes' work had meant to him, they moved to where the giant cart of Buck the cook loomed on the level prairie. Pattison reached into the pocket of his coat and drew out a great package of folded bills, which he tossed on the ground before him as he reached for his coffee cup.

"I think that's five thousand dollars," said he. "I can't carry much cash with me, of course. In town, I'll give you a draft on the First National of Kansas City for fifty-five thousand more if the herd tallies out three thousand head. I am almost ready to take your own tally."

"No," said Jim Nabours, "we haven't tallied out since the last run; I been scared to. If we hadn't had no bad luck down the trail there wouldn't 'a' been money enough in Kansas City to buy all them cows we started with. Do you mean to say to me that you're going to give me sixty thousand dollars for them cows?"

"I certainly am if you don't object too much about it. And I call this a good day's work. I have bought the first northern-trail herd. Besides, I have got a partner and a manager for my ranch, and a line of supply for the ranch, too. Yes, I call it a good five minutes' work.

"You shall have all the time you want to put up your half for these stockers, Mr. McMasters," he added.

"I don't want any time," replied Dan McMasters. "I can raise a little money. You see, I know the history of this herd. I'd almost have been ready to buy it straight through at twenty a head myself."

"I was afraid you would," said Pattison. "But I wanted the cows and a partner too. All right, take your pleasure as to your half of the northern ranch ante. I tell you, I am going to make you more money than either of us ever made in our lives. Lord, this is just the beginning of things! What a fine world it is out here!"

He turned to the others as he went on, tin cup of coffee in hand.

"You see, I am banking on two things that you Texas men didn't know anything about. One is the stockyards at Kansas City. The other is a packing business in Kansas City. There's going to be the market for this range stuff. Meantime I'll have to get some of your boys to drive these fours over to Junction City for me. I'll buy all your ponies except what you need to get back home. My partner and I will need some horses for the PM outfit on the Smoky Hill.

"Oh, I don't blame you for not seeing the game very far ahead up here," he went on. "This is a colder country than you are used to. But if I can hire some of your men to run the herd for us, they can build dugouts in a few days like those you saw in town, and hole up warm and snug for the winter. After a while you'll begin to make hay, but you'll need a whole lot less than you think right now.

"We are going to start the first winter ranch on the heels of the first herd north of thirty-six. I am going to show you that cows will do a heap better when you fatten them north of the edge of winter and north of the tick line.

"Is our five minutes up? I don't like to waste time here. Let's go back to town."

"When do we deliver, then?" asked Nabours.

"You've sold and delivered right now and right here, on the prairie, replied Pattison. "I am hiring all the men that will go in with Mr. McMasters and me; we'd like at least six or eight. Mr. McMasters will come out to help tally to-morrow if that suits you. I never knew a Texas cowman to falsify a count, and I never knew one that didn't go broke trying to pack his own cattle. It takes big men to do big business, and you will have to pardon me if I say it never was in the cards to pack cattle in Texas, by Texas or for Texas. The South needs the

North in this thing. It's going to take both the North and the South to make this country out here." He swept a wide arm. "The West! Oh, by golly!"

"Well," sighed Jim Nabours, still unable to credit his sudden good fortune, "my boss is the richest girl in Texas right now, if she was in Texas. I'll have to admit she owes part to a damn Yankee, same as part to us Texans."

He turned earnestly to the Northern trader.

"You've got to see our boss when you get in town," said he. "You'll be glad to see where all your money went to. She shore is prettier than a spotted pup."

"Well, let's ride," laughed Pattison. "We'll have a look at Abilene and the Texas orphan."

"On our way!" said Nabours, and they mounted. Nabours rode off to accost one of his men. "We've sold the herd, Len," said he. "I'll pay off to-morrow in town. All you fellows that wants to hire out to these folks can do it. You split the men to-night, Len, and half of you come to town if you feel like it.

"Oh, yes," he added, turning, as he started off, "I forgot to tell you. I forgot to tell you that Cal Dalhart got killed in town a little while ago. I heard it just when I left. Del Williams done shot him, looks like."

"The hell he did!" remarked Hersey. "Well, it was plain enough the last three months they had it in for each other—both allowing to marry Miss Taisie."

"And now they won't neither of them will," nodded Nabours. "Ain't it hell how men fuss over a woman? Now Del's gone somewheres. Both good cow hands as ever rid. That's the fourth man I've lost since we left home, not mentioning several hundred cows. I'm the onluckiest man in the world.

"Yet," he went on as he joined McMasters and Pattison, addressing the former, "I call this a good day's work. We've brung our brand through, and we've done sold her out. I reckon Mr. Sim Rudabaugh has played in hard luck. He didn't keep us out of Aberlene, now did he?"

"He did his best," replied Dan McMasters. "He got here just a little too late. He came to town on the train just a little while ago. There are two or three of his men here already, maybe more."

Nabours looked at him narrowly, suddenly serious.

"Some of us boys'll be in town to-night," said he.

As they rode by the jumbled heap of the camp-cart goods a very exact observer might have noted that the pair of wide horns carefully cherished by Len Hersey had disappeared since the first passing of the group from town. No one had particularly noticed Len as he rode up near the cart with a stubborn little yearling dogy on his rope; it was thought the cook had requisitioned beef. But now, as the party turned to leave the herd, the keen eye of Pattison caught sight of an astonishing creature, scarce larger than a calf, but bearing so enormous a spread of horns as would have graced any immemorial steer of the Rio Grande.

"My Lord!" he exclaimed. "What on earth is that? Is that the way cattle grow down in your country?"

"Yes, sir," replied Len gravely, still holding the animal on his reata. "He's a nice little yearling. Give him time, an' he'll raise right smart o'horn. O'course, he's still young. Texas, she sort of runs to horn, in some spots, special seems like."

"Spots? Spots? What spots?" demanded Pattison. "Where'd that critter come from?"

"He come from our range, sir," replied Len. "He range over with a bunch near the Laguna Del Sol. They all watered in there, at the Laguna. Near's we could tell there must be something in the water in the Laguna sort of makes the cows in there run to horn, like."

"Well, I should say so! But still, you can't make me believe that any steer less than four could ever grow horns like that."

"Oh, yes, they kin." Rejoined this artless child of the range. "My pap used to drive down to Rockport, on the coast—I've helped drive south, to ship cows on the Plant steamers. I reckon they was going to Cuby. We had to rope every steer and throw him down and take a ax and chop off his horns, they was so wide. That was to give more room on the boats. Some steers didn't like to have their horns chopped off thataway. Well, here we got plenty of room for horns anyhow." He swept an arm over the field of waving grass reaching on to the blue horizon. "Give me three years more on this dogy and I promise you he'll have horns.

"Speaking of horns, Jim," he resumed; "once when we were driving in a coast drive we turned in a lot of dogies, of course claimin' a cow was a cow, an' nache'l, four years old even if it was only a yearling. Well, the damn Yankee who was buying our cows he kicked on so many dogies. Of course, none of us fellers'd ever heard of a thing like that; a buyer allus taken the run o' the delivery, head for head. Says he, 'I ain't buyin' yearlin's, I'm buyin' fours.'

"Well, we driv in another dogy right then, on of them Lagunies, an' he had horns big as this one here. The damn little fool he put on more airs than any Uvalde mossy horn about his headworks. It was just like he said, 'Look at me! I done riz these her horns in one year, where it taken you maybe a hunderd.' Cows was their pride, mister, same as us. Uh-huh.

"But do you believe me? That damn Yankee wouldn't take my word that the horns of them Lagunies gets their growth early sometimes. I says, 'Mister, I'll bet you a hundred dollars that's a four.' 'Well, maybe it is,' says he. He scratch his haid. But he couldn't git over it. When we come to load in at the boat he says, 'Well I be damned ef that ain't the littlest cow I ever seen fer a four.' I was sort o'hot by then, and I says, 'Boss, you're right—that ain't a four, it's a yearlin'.'

"Well, then he swung around the other way. Says he, 'It kain't noways be a yearlin', not with them horns. I bought too many cows not to know that much. It don't stand to reason that no yearlin' can raise no horns more'n five foot acrost.' You see, mister, that yearlin' was carryin' horns about like this one—one of our Lagunies. O'course, I don't say that all Texas cows has horns like that as yearlin's; you can see that fer yore own self right here. Only way we could convince that gentleman was to show him."

"Well, that may all be," said Pattison, nettled, "Anyhow, I always take my own judgment in cattle, ages and all. I've known buyers who couldn't tell long twos from threes. I've studied cattle.

"I never did much," said Len Hersey; "I never had time. But my folks couldn't never break me of gamblin'—monte, you know. Sometimes I win a shirt, and then agin I'd lose one. Right now"—he looked ruefully at his elbow—"I'd like fer to win one. I'll gamble that critter's a yearlin', now. I'd hate to take a man's money on a cinch; but ef you, now, was feelin' you'd like to peel off a couple of hundred against my hawse an' saddle, an' what's left of my shirt, why, I'd hate to rob you—I'd bet that that's a yearlin'. I was goin' to kill it fer beef. We don't eat the horns, mister, but them Lagunies is special tender on account of that something in the water around there."

"You foolTexans deserve to be trimmed," said Pattison; "a boy like you putting your judgment up against that of one of the oldest buyers that ever saw Kansas City."

"I know it—I know I'm foolish," nodded Len Hersey, "I was borned thataway. I allus hatter be bettin' on monte er somethin'. Still I'll bet thataway on this here yearlin' ef you insist. Does you?"

"I certainly do, just to teach you a lesson. Here, Mr. Nabours"—he pulled out his roll of bills once more—"take this couple hundred, against this man's horse and saddle. You be the judge. He bets that's a yearling. That suit you?" He turned to Len Hersey, who still was holding the mooted animal on his reata.

"Yes, all right," humbly replied that youth.

"Throw him, Len," commanded Nabours; "then we'll all look him over and decide." He was as solemn as his man.

Len sunk a spur and with a leap his pony crossed in front of the quarry, swept its feet from under it. It was thrown with such violence that one of its horns was knocked off and lay entirely free on the grass. Jim Nabours, dismounting, gravely held up the remaining horn, easily detachable from the normal stubby yearling growth on the dogy's head. He looked at Pattison dubiously, none too sure how he would take this range jest. But the Northern man was a sportsman. He broke into a roar of laughter, which for hours he renewed whenever the thought again came to his mind.

"Give him his money, Nabours," said he. "He's won it fair and I've had a lesson, and when your boys come to town the treat's on me. Keep those horns for me," he added. "If I don't sell old Mitch or young Phil Armour at Kansas City with those horns I'll eat them both!" Again he went off into gusty laughter, in which all could join.

"Sho, now." said Len Hersey. "Now look at that! He must of got his horns jarred loose, like, in some night run in the timber. I've knowed that to happen."

"Len," commanded Nabours, "I don't want no more of this damned foolishness. Here's ten dollars, and that's enough to buy you a shirt, and I want to see you do it. He'll only play the rest at monte or faro or something," turning to Pattison.

"No, give it all to him." The latter rejoined. "It's his. Let him play it. I've done as much myself when I was younger. And monte's a cinch compared to buying and packing and shipping cattle to the East."

They turned and rode toward town, young in the youth of the open range, where to-morrow did not yet loom.

THE QUEST BEGINS

MAX BRAND

"You know the old place on the other side of the range?"

"Like a book. I got pet names for all the trees."

"There's a man there I want."

"Logan?"

"No. His name is Bard."

"H-m! Any relation to the old bird that was partners with you back about the year one?"

"I want Anthony Bard brought here," said Drew, entirely overlooking the question.

"Easy. I can make the trip in a buckboard and I'll dump him in the back of it."

"No. He's got to *ride* here, understand?"

"A dead man," said Nash calmly, "ain't much good on a hoss."

"Listen to me," said Drew, his voice lowering to a sort of musical thunder, "if you harm a hair of this lad's head I'll—I'll break you in two with my own hands."

And he made a significant gesture as if he were snapping a twig between his fingers. Nash moistened his lips, then his square, powerful jaw jutted out.

"Which the general idea is me doing baby talk and sort of hypnotizing this Bard feller into coming along?"

"More than that. He's got to be brought here alive, untouched, and placed in that chair tied so that he can't move hand or foot for ten minutes while I talk."

"Nice, quiet day you got planned for me, Mr. Drew."

The grey man considered thoughtfully.

"Now and then you've told me of a girl at Eldara—I think her name is Sally Fortune?"

"Right. She begins where the rest of the calico leaves off."

"H-m! that sounds familiar, somehow. Well, Steve, you've said that if you had a good start you think the girl would marry you."

"I think she *might*."

"She pretty fond of you?"

"She knows that if I can't have her I'm fast enough to keep everyone else away."

"I see. A process of elimination with you as the eliminator. Rather an odd courtship, Steve?"

The cowpuncher grew deadly serious.

"You see, I love her. There ain't no way of bucking out of that. So do nine out of ten of all the boys that've seen her. Which one will she pick? That's the question we all keep askin', because of all the contrary, freckle-faced devils with the heart of a man an' the smile of a woman, Sally has 'em all beat from the drop of the barrier. One feller has money; another has looks; another has a funny line of talk. But I've got the fastest gun. So Sally sees she's due for a complete outfit of black mournin' if she marries another man while I'm alive; an' that keeps her thinkin'. But if I had the price of a start in the world—why, maybe she'd take a long look at me."

"Would she call one thousand dollars in cash a start in the world—and your job as foreman of my place, with twice the salary you have now?"

Steve Nash wiped his forehead.

He said huskily: "A joke along this line don't bring no laugh from me, governor."

"I mean it, Steve. Get Anthony Bard tied hand and foot into this house so that I can talk to him safely for ten minutes, and you'll have everything I promise. Perhaps more. But that depends."

The blunt-fingered hand of Nash stole across the table.

"If it's a go, shake, Mr. Drew."

A mighty hand fell in his, and under the pressure he set his teeth. Afterward he covertly moved his fingers and sighed with relief to see that no permanent harm had been done.

"Me speakin' personal, Mr. Drew, I'd of give a lot to seen you when you was ridin' the range. This Bard—he'll be here before sunset to-morrow."

"Don't jump to conclusions, Steve. I've an idea that before you count your thousand you'll think that you've been underpaid. That's straight."

"This Bard is something of a man?"

"I can say that without stopping to think."

"Texas?"

"No. He's a tenderfoot, but he can ride a horse as if he was sewed to the skin, and I've an idea that he can do other things up to the same standard. If you can find two or three men who have silent tongues and strong hands, you'd better take them along. I'll pay their wages, and big ones. You can name your price."

But Nash was frowning.

"Now and then I talk to the cards a bit, Mr. Drew, and you'll hear fellers say some pretty rough things about me, but I've never asked for no odds against any man. I'm not going to start now."

"You're a hard man, Steve, but so am I; and hard men are the kind I take to. I know that you're the best foreman who ever rode this range and I know that when you start things you generally finish them. All that I ask is that you bring Bard to me in this house. The way you do it is your own problem. Drunk or drugged, I don't care how, but get him here unharmed. Understand?"

"Mr. Drew, you can start figurin' what you want to say to him now. I'll get him here—safe! And then Sally—"

"If money will buy her you'll have me behind you when you bid."

"When shall I start?"

"Now."

"So-long, then."

He rose and passed hastily from the room, leaning forward from the hips like a man who is making a start in a foot-race.

Straight up the stairs he went to his room, for the foreman lived in the big house of the rancher. There he took a quantity of equipment from a closet and flung it on the bed. Over three selections he lingered long.

The first was the cartridge belt, and he tried over several with conscientious care until he found the one which received the cartridges with the greatest ease. He could flip them out in the night, automatically as a pianist fingers the scale in the dark.

Next he examined lariats painfully, inch by inch, as though he were going out to rope the stanchest steer that ever roamed the range. Already he knew that those ropes were sound and true throughout, but he took no chances now. One of the ropes he discarded because one or two strands in it were, or might be, a trifle frayed. The other he took alternately and whirled with a broad loop, standing in the centre of the room. Of the set one was a little more supple, a little more durable, it seemed. This he selected and coiled swiftly.

Last of all he lingered—and longest—over his revolvers. Six in all, he set them in a row along the bed and without delay threw out two to begin with. Then he fingered the others, tried their weight and balance, slipped cartridges into the cylinders and extracted them again, whirled the cylinders, and examined the minutest parts of the actions.

They were all such guns as an expert would have turned over with shining eyes, but finally he threw one aside into the discard; the cylinder revolved just a little too hard. Another was abandoned after much handling of the remaining three because to the delicate touch of Nash it seemed that the weight of the barrel was a gram more than in the other two; but after this selection it seemed that there was no possible choice between the final two.

So he stood in the centre of the room and went through a series of odd gymnastics. Each gun in turn he placed in the holster and then jerked it out, spinning it on the trigger guard around his second finger, while his left hand shot diagonally across his body and "fanned" the hammer. Still he could not make his choice, but he would not abandon the effort. It was an old maxim with him that there is in all the world one gun which is the best of all and with which even a novice can become a "killer."

He tried walking away, whirling as he made his draw, and levelling the gun on the door-knob. Then without moving his hand, he lowered his head and squinted down the sights. In each case the bead was drawn to a centre shot. Last of all he weighed each gun; one seemed a trifle lighter—the merest shade lighter than the other. This he slipped into the holster and carried the rest of his apparatus back to the closet from which he had taken it.

Still the preparation had not ended. Filling his cartridge belt, every cartridge was subject to a rigid inspection. A full half hour was wasted in this manner. Wasted, because he rejected not one of the many he examined. Yet he seemed happier after having made his selection, and went down the stairs, humming softly.

Out to the barn he went, lantern in hand. This time he made no comparison of horses but went directly to an ugly-headed roan, long of leg, vicious of eye, thin-shouldered, and with hips that slanted sharply down. No one with a knowledge of fine horse-flesh could have looked on this brute without aversion. It did not have even size in its favour. A wild, free spirit, perhaps, might be the reason; but the animal stood with hanging head and pendant lower lip. One eye was closed and the other only half opened. A blind affection, then, made him go to this horse first of all.

No, his greeting was to jerk his knee sharply into the ribs of the roan, which answered with a grunt and swung its head around with bared teeth, like an angry dog. "Damn your eyes!" roared the hoarse voice of Steve Nash, "stand still or I'll knock you for a goal!"

The ears of the mustang flattened close to its neck and a devil of hate came up in its eyes, but it stood quiet, while Nash went about at a judicious distance and examined all the vital points. The hooves were sound, the backbone prominent, but not a high ridge from famine or much hard riding, and the indomitable hate in the eyes of the mustang seemed to please the cowpuncher.

It was a struggle to bridle the beast, which was accomplished only by grinding the points of his knuckles into a tender part of the jowl to make the locked teeth open.

In saddling, the knee came into play again, rapping the ribs of the brute repeatedly before the wind, which swelled out the chest to false proportions, was expelled in a sudden grunt, and the cinch whipped up taut. After that Nash dodged the flying heels, chose his time, and vaulted into the saddle.

The mustang trotted quietly out of the barn. Perhaps he had had his fill of bucking on that treacherous, slippery wooden floor, but once outside he turned loose the full assortment of the cattle-pony's tricks. It was only ten minutes, but while it lasted the cursing of Nash was loud and steady, mixed with the crack of his murderous quirt against the roan's flanks. The bucking ended as quickly as it had begun, and they started at a long canter over the trail.

* * * * *

Mile after mile of the rough trail fell behind him, and still the pony shambled along at a loose trot or a swinging canter; the steep upgrades it took at a steady jog and where the slopes pitched sharply down, it wound among the rocks with a faultless sureness of foot.

Certainly the choice of Nash was well made. An Eastern horse of blood over a level course could have covered the same distance in half the time, but it would have broken down after ten miles of that hard trail.

Dawn came while they wound over the crest of the range, and with the sun in their faces they took the downgrade. It was well into the morning before Nash reached Logan. He forced from his eye the contempt which all cattlemen feel for sheepherders.

"I s'pose you're here askin' after Bard?" began Logan without the slightest prelude.

"Bard? Who's he?"

Logan considered the other with a sardonic smile.

"Maybe you been ridin' all night jest for fun?"

"If you start usin' your tongue on me, Logan, you'll wear out the snapper on it. I'm on my way to the A Circle Y."

"Listen; I'm all for old man Drew. You know that. Tell me what Bard has on him?"

"Never heard the name before. Did he rustle a couple of your sheep?"

Logan went on patiently: "I knew something was wrong when Drew was here yesterday but I didn't think it was as bad as this."

"What did Drew do yesterday?"

"Came up as usual to potter around the old house, I guess, but when he heard about Bard bein' here he changed his mind sudden and went home."

"That's damn queer. What sort of a lookin' feller is this Bard?"

"I don't suppose you know, eh?" queried Logan ironically. "I don't suppose the old man described him before you started, maybe?"

"Logan, you poor old hornless maverick, d'you think I'm on somebody's trail? Don't you know I've been through with that sort of game for a hell of a while?"

"When rocks turn into ham and eggs I'll trust you, Steve. I'll tell you what I done to Bard, anyway. Yesterday, after he found that Drew had been here and gone he seemed sort of upset; tried to keep it from me, but I'm too much used to judin' changes of weather to be fooled by any tenderfoot that ever used school English. Then he hinted around about learnin' the way to Eldara, because he knows that town is pretty close to Drew's place, I guess. I told him; sure I did. He should of gone due west, but I sent him south. There *is* a south trail, only it takes about three days to get to Eldara."

"Maybe you think that interests me. It don't."

Logan overlooked this rejoinder, saying: "Is it his scalp you're after?"

"Your ideas are like nest-eggs, Logan, an' you set over 'em like a hen. They look like eggs; they feel like eggs; but they don't never hatch. That's the way with your ideas. They look all right; they sound all right; but they don't mean nothin'. So-long."

But Logan merely chuckled wisely. He had been long on the range.

As Nash turned his pony and trotted off in the direction of the A Circle Y ranch, the sheepherder called after him: "What you say cuts both ways, Steve. This feller Bard looks like a tenderfoot; he sounds like a tenderfoot; but he ain't a tenderfoot."

Felling that this parting shot gave him the honours of the meeting, he turned away whistling with such spirit that one of his dogs, overhearing, stood still and gazed at his master with his head cocked wisely to one side.

His eastern course Nash pursued for a mile or more, and then swung sharp to the south. He was weary, like his horse, and he made no attempt to start a sudden burst of speed. He let the pony go on at the same tireless jog, clinging like a bulldog to the trail.

About midday he sighted a small house cuddled into a hollow of the hills and made toward it. As he dismounted, a tow-headed, spindling boy lounged out of the doorway and stood with his hands shoved carelessly into his little overall pockets.

"Hello, young feller."

"'Lo, stranger."

"What's the chance of bunking here for three or four hours and gettin' a good feed for the hoss?"

"Never better. Gimme the hoss; I'll put him up in the shed. Feed him grain?"

"No, you won't put him up. I'll tend to that."

"Looks like a bad 'un."

"That's it."

"But a sure goer, eh?"

"Yep."

He led the pony to the shed, unsaddled him, and gave him a small feed. The horse first rolled on the dirt floor and then started methodically on his fodder. Having made sure that his mount was not "off his feed," Nash rolled a cigarette and strolled back to the house with the boy.

"Where's the folks?" he asked.

"Ma's sick, a little, and didn't get up to-day. Pa's down to the corral, cussing mad. But I can cook you up some chow."

"All right son. I got a dollar here that'll buy you a pretty good store knife."

The boy flushed so red that by contrast his straw coloured hair seemed positively white.

"Maybe you want to pay me?" he suggested fiercely. "Maybe you think we're squatters that run a hotel?"

Recognizing the true Western breed even in this small edition, Nash grinned.

"Speakin' man to man, son, I didn't think that, but I thought I'd sort of feel my way."

"Which I'll say you're lucky you didn't try to feel your way with pa; not the way he's feelin' now."

In the shack of the house he placed the best chair for Nash and set about frying ham and making coffee. This with crackers, formed the meal. He watched Nash eat for a moment of solemn silence and then the foreman looked up to catch a meditative chuckle from the youngster.

"Let me in on the joke, son."

"Nothin'. I was just thinkin' of pa."

"What's he sore about? Come out short at poker lately?"

"No; he lost a hoss. Ha, ha, ha!"

He explained: "He's lost his only standin' joke, and now the laugh's on pa!"

Nash sipped his coffee and waited. On the mountain desert one does not draw out a narrator with questions.

"There was a feller come along early this mornin' on a lame hoss," the story began. "He was a sure enough tenderfoot—leastways he looked it an' he talked it, but he wasn't."

The familiarity of this description made Steve sit up a trifle straighter.

"Was he a ringer?"

"Maybe. I dunno. Pa meets him at the door and asks him in. What d'you think this feller comes back with?"

The boy paused to remember and then with twinkling eyes he mimicked: "'That's very good of you, sir, but I'll only stop to make a trade with you—this horse and some cash to boot for a durable mount out of your corral. The brute has gone lame, you see.'

"Pa waited and scratched his head while these here words sort of sunk in. Then says very smooth: 'I'll let you take the best hoss I've got, an' I won't ask much cash to boot.'

"I begin wonderin' what pa was drivin' at, but I didn't say nothin'—jest held myself together and waited.

"'Look over there to the corral,' says pa, and pointed. 'They's a hoss that ought to take you wherever you want to go. It's the best hoss I've ever had.'

"It *was* the best horse pa ever had, too. It was a piebald pinto called Jo, after my cousin Josiah, who's jest a plain bad un and raises hell when there's any excuse. The piebald, he didn't even need an excuse. You see, he's one of them hosses that likes company. When he leaves the corral he likes to have another hoss for a runnin' mate and he was jest as tame as anything. I could ride him; anybody could ride him. But if you took him outside the bars of the corral without company, first thing he done was to see if one of the other hosses was comin' out to join him. When he seen that he was all laid out to make a trip by himself he jest nacherally started in to raise hell. Which Jo can raise more hell for his size than any hoss I ever seen.

"He's what you call an eddicated bucker. He don't fool around with no pauses. He jest starts in and figgers out a situation and then he gets busy slidin' the gent that's on him off'n the saddle. An' he always used to win out. In fact, he was known for it all around these parts. He begun nice and easy, but he worked up like a fiddler playin' a favourite piece, and the end was the rider lyin' on the ground.

"Whenever the boys around here wanted any excitement they used to come over and try their hands with Jo. We used to keep a pile of arnica and stuff like that around to rub them up with and tame down the bruises after Jo laid 'em cold on the ground. There wasn't never anybody could ride that hoss when he was started out alone.

"Well, this tenderfoot, he looks over the hoss in the corral and says: 'That's a pretty fine mount, it seems to me. What do you want to boot?'

"'Aw, twenty-five dollars in enough,' says pa.

"'All right,' says the tenderfoot, 'here's the money.'

"And he counts it out in pa's hand.

"He says: 'What a little beauty! It would be a treat to see him work on a polo field.'

"Pa says: 'It'd be a treat to see this hoss work anywhere.'

"Then he steps on my foot to make me wipe the grin off'n my face.

"Down goes the tenderfoot and takes his saddle and flops it on the piebald pinto, and the piebald was jest as nice as milk. Then he leads him out'n the corral and gets on.

"First the pinto takes a look over his shoulder like he was waiting for one of his pals among the hosses to come along, but he didn't see none. Then the circus started. An' b'lieve me, it was some circus. Jo hadn't had much action for some time, an' he must have used the wait thinkin' up new ways of raisin' hell.

"There ain't enough words in the Bible to describe what he done. Which maybe you sort of gather that he *had* to keep on performin', because the tenderfoot was still in the saddle. He was. An' he never pulled leather. No, sir, he never touched the buckin' strap, but jest sat there with his teeth set and his lips twistin' back—the same smile he had when he got into the saddle. But pretty soon I s'pose Jo had a chance to figure out that it didn't do him no particular harm to be alone.

"The minute he seen that he stopped fightin' and started off at a gallop the way the tenderfoot wanted him to go, which was over there.

"'Damn my eyes!' says pa, an' couldn't do nuthin' but just stand there repeatin' that with variations because with Jo gone there wouldn't be no drawin' card to get the boys around the house no more. But you're lookin' sort of sleepy, stranger?"

"I am," answered Nash.

"Well, if you'd seen that show you wouldn't be thinkin' of sleep. Not for some time."

"Maybe not, but the point is I didn't see it. D'you mind if I turn in on that bunk over there?"

"Help yourself," said the boy. "What time d'you want me to wake you up?"

"Never mind; I wake up automatic. S'long, Bud."

He stretched out on the blankets and was instantly asleep.

* * * * *

At the end of three hours he awoke as sharply as though an alarm were clamouring at his ear. There was no elaborate preparation for renewed activities. A single yawn and stretch and he was again on his feet. Since the boy was not in sight he cooked himself an enormous meal, devoured it, and went out to the mustang.

The roan greeted him with a volley from both heels that narrowly missed the head of Nash, but the cowpuncher merely smiled tolerantly.

"Feelin' fit agin, eh, damn your soul?" he said genially, and picking up a bit of board, fallen from the side of the shed, he smote the mustang mightily along the ribs. The mustang, as if it recognized the touch of the master, pricked up one ear and side-stepped. The brief rest had filled it with all the old, vicious energy.

For once more, as soon as they rode clear of the door, there ensued a furious struggle between man and beast. The man won, as always, and the roan, dropping both ears flat against its neck, trotted sullenly out across the hills.

In that monotony of landscape, one mile exactly like the other, no landmarks to guide him, no trail to follow, however faintly worn, it was strange to see the cowpuncher strike out through the vast distances of the mountain-desert with as much confidence as if he were travelling on a paved street in a city. He had not even a compass to direct him but he seemed to know his way as surely as the birds know the untracked paths of the air in the seasons of migration.

Straight on through the afternoon and during the long evening he kept his course at the same unvarying dog-trot until the flush of the sunset faded to a stern grey and the purple hills in the distance turned blue with shadows. Then, catching the glimmer of a light on a hillside, he turned toward it to put up for the night.

In answer to his call a big man with a lantern came to the door and raised his light until it shone on a red, bald head and a portly figure. His welcome was neither hearty nor cold; hospitality is expected in the mountain-desert. So Nash put up his horse in the shed and came back to the house.

The meal was half over, but two girls immediately set a plate heaped with fried potatoes and bacon and flanked by a mighty cup of jet-black coffee on one side and a pile of yellow biscuits on the other. He nodded to them, grunted by way of expressing thanks, and sat down to eat.

Beside the tall father and the rosy-faced mother, the family consisted of the two girls, one of them with her hair twisted severely close to her head, wearing a man's blue cotton shirt with the sleeves rolled up to a pair of brown elbows. Evidently she was the boy of the family and to her fell the duty of performing the innumerable chores of the ranch, for her hands were thick with work and the tips of the fingers blunted. Also she had that calm, self-satisfied eye which belongs to the workingman who knows that he has earned his meal.

Her sister monopolized all the beauty and the grace, not that she was either very pretty or extremely graceful, but she was instinct with the challenge of femininity like a rare scent. It lingered about her, it enveloped her ways; it gave a light to her eyes and made her smile exquisite. Her clothes were not of much finer material than her sister's, but they were cut to fit, and a bow of crimson ribbon at her throat was as effective in that environment as the most costly orchids on an evening gown.

She was armed in pride this night, talking only to her mother, and then in monosyllables alone. At first it occurred to Steve that his coming had made her self-conscious, but he soon discovered that her pride was directed at the third man at the table. She at least maintained a pretence of eating, but he made not even a sham, sitting miserably, his mouth hard set, his eyes shadowed by a tremendous frown. At length he shoved back his chair with such violence that the table trembled.

"Well," he rumbled, "I guess this lets me out. S'long."

And he strode heavily from the room; a moment later his cursing came back to them as he rode into the night.

"Takes it kind of hard, don't he?" said the father.

And the mother murmured: "Poor Ralph!"

"So you went an' done it?" said the mannish girl to her sister.

"What of it?" snapped the other.

"He's too good for you, that's what of it."

"Girls!" exclaimed the mother anxiously. "Remember we got a guest!"

"Oh," said she of the strong brown arms, "I guess we can't tell him nothin'; I guess he had eyes to be seein' what's happened."

She turned calmly to Steve.

"Lizzie turned down Ralph Boardman—poor feller!"

"Sue!" cried the other girl.

"Well, after you done it, are you ashamed to have it talked about? You make me sore, I'll tell a man!"

"That's enough, Sue," growled the father.

"What's enough?"

"We ain't goin' to have no more show about this. I've had my supper spoiled by it already."

"I say it's a rotten shame," broke out Sue, and she repeated, "Ralph's too good for her. All because of a city dude—a tenderfoot!"

In the extremity of her scorn her voice drawled in a harsh murmur.

"Then take him yourself, if you can get him!" cried Lizzie. "I'm sure I don't want him!"

Their eyes blazed at each other across the table, and Lizzie, having scored an unexpected point, struck again.

"I think you've always had a sort of hankerin' after Ralph—oh, I've seen your eyes rollin' at him."

The other girl coloured hotly through her tan.

"If I was fond of him I wouldn't be ashamed to let him know, you can tell the world that. And I wouldn't keep him trottin' about like a little pet dog till I got tired of him and give him up for the sake of a greenhorn who"—her voice lowered to a spiteful hiss—"kissed you the first time he even seen you!"

In vain Lizzie fought for her control; her lip trembled and her voice shook.

"I hate you, Sue!"

"Sue, ain't you ashamed of yourself?" pleaded the mother.

"No, I ain't! Think of it; here's Ralph been sweet on Liz for two years an' now she gives him the go-by for a skinny, affected dude like that feller that was here. And *he's* forgot you already, Liz, the minute he stopped laughing at you for bein' so easy."

"Ma, are you goin' to let Sue talk like this—right before a stranger?"

"Sue, you shut up!" commanded the father.

"I don't see nobody that can make me," she said, surly as a grown boy. "I can't make any more of a fool out of Liz than that tenderfoot made her!"

"Did he," asked Steve, "ride a piebald mustang?"

"D'you know him?" breathed Lizzie, forgetting the tears of shame which had been gathering in her eyes.

"Nope. Jest heard a little about him along the road."

"What's his name?"

Then she coloured, even before Sue could say spitefully: "Didn't he even have to tell you his name before he kissed you?"

"He did! His name is—Tony!"

"Tony!"—in deep disgust. "Well, he's dark enough to be a dago! Maybe he's a foreign count, or something, Liz, and he'll take you back to live in some castle or other."

But the girl queried, in spite of this badinage: "Do you know his name?"

"His name," said Nash, thinking that it could do no harm to betray as much as this, "is Anthony Bard, I think."

"And you don't know him?"

"All I know is that the feller who used to own that piebald mustang is pretty mad and cusses every time he thinks of him."

"He didn't steal the hoss?"

This with more bated breath than if the question had been: "He didn't kill a man?" for indeed horse-stealing was the greater crime.

Even Nash would not make such an accusation directly, and therefore he fell back on an innuendo almost as deadly.

"I dunno," he said non-committally, and shrugged his shoulders.

With all his soul he was concentrating on the picture of the man who conquered a fighting horse and flirted successfully with a pretty girl the same day; each time riding on swiftly from his conquest. The clues on this trail were surely thick enough, but they were of such a nature that the pleasant mind of Steve grew more and more thoughtful.

* * * * *

In fact, so thoughtful had Nash become, that he slept with extraordinary lightness that night and was up at the first hint of day. Sue appeared on the scene just in time to witness the last act of the usual drama of bucking on the part of the roan, before it settled down to the mechanical dog-trot with which it would wear out the ceaseless miles of the mountain-desert all day and far into the night, if need be.

Nash now swung more to the right, cutting across the hills, for he presumed that by this time the tenderfoot must have gotten his bearings and would head straight for Eldara. It was a stiff two-day journey, now, the whole first day's riding having been a worse than useless detour; so the bulldog jaw set harder and harder, and the keen eyes squinted as if to look into the dim future.

Once each day, about noon, when the heat made even the desert and the men of the desert drowsy, he allowed his imagination to roam freely, counting the thousand dollars over and over again, and tasting again the joys of a double salary. Yet even his hardy imagination rarely rose to the height of Sally Fortune. That hour of dreaming, however, made the day of labour almost pleasant.

This time, in the very middle of his dream, he reached the cross-roads saloon and general merchandise store of Flanders; so he banished his visions with a compelling shrug of the shoulders and rode for it at a gallop, a hot dryness growing in his throat at every stride. Quick service he was sure to get, for there were not more than half a dozen cattle-ponies standing in front of the little building with its rickety walls guiltless of paint save for the one great sign inscribed with uncertain letters.

He swung from the saddle, tossed the reins over the head of the mustang, made a stride forward—and then checked himself with a soft curse and reached for his gun.

For the door of the bar dashed open and down the steps rushed a tall man with light yellow moustache, so long that it literally blew on either side over his shoulders as he ran; in either hand he carried a revolver—a two-gun man, fleeing, perhaps, from another murder.

For Nash recognized in him a character notorious through a thousand miles of the range, Sandy Ferguson, nicknamed by the colour of that famous moustache, which was envied and dreaded so far and so wide. It was not fear that made Nash halt, for otherwise he would have finished the motion and whipped out his gun; but at least it was something closely akin to fear.

For that matter, there were unmistakable signs in Sandy himself of what would have been called arrant terror in any other man. His face was so bloodless that the pallor showed even through the leathery tan; one eye stared wildly, the other being sheltered under a clumsy patch which could not quite conceal the ugly bruise beneath. Under his great moustache his lips were as puffed and swollen as the lips of a negro.

Staggering in his haste, he whirled a few paces from the house and turned, his guns levelled. At the same moment the door opened and the perspiring figure of little fat Flanders appeared. Scorn and anger rather than hate or any bloodlust appeared in his face. His right arm, hanging loosely at his side, held a revolver, and he seemed to have the greatest unconcern for the leveled weapons of the gunman.

He made a gesture with that armed hand, and Sandy winced as though a whiplash had flicked him.

"Steady up, damn your eyes!" bellowed Flanders, "and put them guns away. Put 'em up; hear me?"

To the mortal astonishment of Nash, Sandy obeyed, keeping the while a fascinated eye upon the little Dutchman.

"Now climb your hoss and beat it, and if I ever find you in reach again, I'll send my kid out to rope you and give you a hoss-whippin'."

The gun fighter lost no time. A single leap carried him into his saddle and he was off over the sand with a sharp rattle of the beating hoofs.

"Well," breathed Nash, "I'll be hanged."

"Sure you will," suggested Flanders, at once changing his frown for a smile of somewhat professional good nature, as one who greeted an old customer, "sure you will unless you come in an' have a drink on the house. I want something myself to forget what I been doin'. I feel like the dog-catcher."

Steve, deeply meditative, strode into the room.

"Partner," he said gravely to Flanders, "I've always prided myself on having eyes a little better than the next one, but just now I guess I must have been seein' double. Seemed to me that that was Sandy Ferguson that you hot-footed out of that door—or has Sandy got a double?"

"Nope," said the bartender, wiping the last of the perspiration from his forehead, "that's Sandy, all right."

"Then gimme a big drink. I need it."

The bottle spun expertly across the bar, and the glasses tinkled after.

"Funny about him, all right," nodded Flanders, "but then it's happened the same way with others I could tell about. As long as he was winnin' Sandy was the king of any roost. The minute he lost a fight he wasn't worth so many pounds of salt pork. Take a hoss; a fine hoss is often jest the same. Long as it wins nothin' can touch some of them blooded boys. But let 'em go under the wire second, maybe jest because they's packing twenty pounds too much weight, and they're never any good any more. Any second-rather can lick 'em. I lost five hundred iron boys on a hoss that laid down like that."

"All of which means," suggested Nash, "that Sandy has been licked?"

"Licked? No, he ain't been licked, but he's been plumb annihilated, washed off the map, cleaned out, faded, rubbed into the dirt; if there was some stronger way of puttin' it, I would. Only last night, at that, but now look at him. A girl that never seen a man before could tell that he wasn't any more dangerous now than if he was made of putty; but if the fool keeps packin' them guns he's sure to get into trouble."

He raised his glass.

"So here's to the man that Sandy was and ain't no more."

They drank solemnly.

"Maybe you took the fall out of him yourself, Flanders?"

"Nope. I ain't no fighter, Steve. You know that. The feller that downed Sandy was—a tenderfoot. Yep, a greenhorn."

"Ah-h-h," drawled Nash softly, "I thought so."

"You did?"

"Anyway, let's hear the story. Another drink—on me, Flanders."

"It was like this. Along about evening of yesterday Sandy was in here with a couple of other boys. He was pretty well lighted—the glow was circulatin' promiscuous, in fact—when in comes a feller about your height, Steve, but lighter. Good lookin', thin face, big dark eyes like a girl. He carried the signs of a long ride on him. Well, sir, he walks up to the bar and says: 'Can you make me a very sour lemonade, Mr. Bartender?'

"I grabbed the edge of the bar and hung on tight.

"'A which?' says I.

"'Lemonade, if you please.'

"I rolled an eye at Sandy, who was standin' there with his jaw falling, and then I got busy with lemons and the squeezer, but pretty soon Ferguson walks up to the stranger.

"'Are you English?' he asks.

"I knew by his tone what was comin', so I slid the gun I keep behind the bar closer and got prepared for a lot of damaged crockery.

"'I?' says the tenderfoot. 'Why, no. What makes you ask?'

"'Your damned funny way of talkin',' says Sandy.

"'Oh,' says the greenhorn, nodding as if he was thinkin' this over and discovering a little truth in it. 'I suppose the way I talk is a little unusual.'

"'A little rotten,' says Sandy. 'Did I hear you askin' for a lemonade?'

"'You did.'

"'Would I seem to be askin' too many questions,' says Sandy, terrible polite, 'if I inquires if bar whisky ain't good enough for you?'

"The tenderfoot, he stands there jest as easy as you an' me stand here now, and he laughed.

"He says: 'The bar whisky I've tasted around this country is not very good for any one, unless, perhaps, after a snake has bitten you. Then it works on the principle of poison fight poison, eh?'

"Sandy says after a minute: 'I'm the most quietest, gentle, innercent cowpuncher that ever rode the range, but I'd tell a man that it riles me to hear good bar whisky insulted like this. Look at me! Do I look as if whisky ain't good for a man?'

"'Why,' says the tenderfoot, 'you look sort of funny to me.'

"He said it as easy as if he was passin' the morning with Ferguson, but I seen that it was the last straw with Sandy. He hefted out both guns and trained 'em on the greenhorn.

"I yelled: 'Sandy, for God's sake, don't be killin' a tenderfoot!'

"'If whisky will kill him he's goin' to die,' says Sandy. 'Flanders, pour out a drink of rye for this gent.'

"I did it, though my hand was shaking a lot, and the chap takes the glass and raises it polite, and looks at the colour of it. I thought he was goin' to drink, and starts wipin' the sweat off'n my forehead.

"But this chap, he sets down the glass and smiles over to Sandy.

"'Listen,' he says, still grinnin', 'in the old days I suppose this would have been a pretty bluff, but it won't work with me now. You want me to drink this glass of very bad whisky, but I'm sure that you don't want it badly enough to shoot me.

"'There are many reasons. In the old days a man shot down another and then rode off on his horse and was forgotten, but in these days the telegraph is faster than any horse that was ever foaled. They'd be sure to get you, sir, though you might dodge them for a while. And I believe that for a crime such as you threaten, they have recently installed a little electric chair which is a perfectly good inducer of sleep—in fact, it is better than a cradle. Taking these things all into consideration, I take it for granted that you are bluffing, my friend, and one of my favourite occupations is calling a bluff. You look dangerous, but I've an idea that you are as yellow as your moustache.'

"Sandy, he sort of swelled up all over like a poisoned dog.

"He says: 'I begin to see your style. You want a clean man-handlin', which suits me uncommon well.'

"With that, he lays down his guns, soft and careful, and puts up his fists, and goes for the other gent.

"He makes his pass, which should have sent the other gent into kingdom come. But it didn't. No, sir, the tenderfoot, he seemed to evaporate. He wasn't there when the fist of Ferguson come along. Ferguson, he checked up short and wheeled around and charged again like a bull. And he missed again. And so they kept on playin' a sort of a game of tag over the place, the stranger jest side-steppin' like a prize-fighter, the prettiest you ever seen, and not developin' when Sandy started on one of his swings.

"At last one of Sandy's fists grazed him on the shoulder and sort of peeved him, it looked like. He ducks under Sandy's next punch, steps in, and wallops

Sandy over the eye—that punch didn't travel more'n six inches. But it slammed Sandy down in a corner like he's been shot.

"He was too surprised to be much hurt, though, and drags himself up to his feet, makin' a pass at his pocket at the same time. Then he came again, silent and thinkin' of blood, I s'pose, with a knife in his hand.

"This time the tenderfoot didn't wait. He went in with a sort of hitch step, like a dancer. Ferguson's knife carved the air beside the tenderfoot's head, and then the skinny boy jerked up his right and his left—one, two—into Sandy's mouth. Down he goes again—slumps down as if all the bones in his body was busted—right down on his face. The other feller grabs his shoulder and jerks him over on his back.

"He stands lookin' down at him for a moment, and then he says, sort of thoughtful: 'He isn't badly hurt, but I suppose I shouldn't have hit him twice.'

"Can you beat that, Steve? You can't!

"When Sandy come to he got up to his feet, wobbling—seen his guns—went over and scooped 'em up, with the eye of the tenderfoot on him all the time—scooped 'em up—stood with 'em all poised—and so he backed out through the door. It wasn't any pretty thing to see. The tenderfoot, he turned to the bar again.

"'If you don't mind,' he says, 'I think I'll switch my order and take that whisky instead. I seem to need it.'

"'Son!' says I, 'there ain't nothin' in the house you can't have for the askin'. Try some of this!'

"And I pulled out a bottle of my private stock—you know the stuff; I've had it twenty-five years, and it was ten years old when I got it. That ain't as much of a lie as it sounds.

"He takes a glass of it and sips it, sort of suspicious, like a wolf scentin' the wind for an elk in winter. Then his face lighted up like a lantern had been flashed on it. You'd of thought that he was lookin' his long-lost brother in the eye from the way he smiled at me. He holds the glass up and lets the light come through it, showin' the little traces and bubbles of oil.

"'May I know your name?' he says.

"It made me feel like Rockerbilt, hearin' him say that, in *that* special voice.

"'Me,' says I, 'I'm Flanders.'

"'It's an honour to know you, Mr. Flanders,' he says. 'My name is Anthony Bard.'

"We shook hands, and his grip was three fourths man, I'll tell the world.

"'Good liquor,' says he, 'is like a fine lady. Only a gentleman can appreciate it. I drink to you, sir.'

"So that's how Sandy Ferguson went under the sod. To-day? Well, I couldn't let Ferguson stand in a barroom where a gentleman had been, could I?"

* * * * *

Even the stout roan grew weary during the third day, and when they topped the last rise of hills, and looked down to darker shadows in Eldara in the black heart of the hollow, the mustang stood with hanging head, and one ear flopped forward. Cruel indeed had been the pace which Nash maintained, yet they had never been able to overhaul the flying piebald of Anthony Bard.

As they trotted down the slope, Nash looked to his equipment, handled his revolver, felt the strands of the lariat, and resting only his toes in the stirrups, eased all his muscles to make sure that they were uncramped from the long journey. He was fit; there was no doubt of that.

Coming down the main street—for Eldara boasted no fewer than three thoroughfares—the first houses which Nash passed showed no lights. As far as he could see, the blinds were all drawn; not even the glimmer of a candle showed, and the voices which he heard were muffled and low.

He thought of plague or some other disaster which might have overtaken the little village and wiped out nine tenths of the populace in a day. Only such a thing could account for silence in Eldara. There should have been bursts and roars of laughter here and there, and now and then a harsh stream of cursing. There should have been clatter of kitchen tins; there should have been neighing of horses; there should have been the quiver and tingle of children's voices at play in the dusty streets. But there was none of this. The silence was as thick and oppressive as the unbroken dark of the night. Even Butler's saloon was closed!

This, however, was something which he would not believe, no matter what testimony his eyes gave him. He rode up to a shuttered window and kicked it with his heel.

Only the echoes of that racket replied to him from the interior of the place. He swore, somewhat touched with awe, and kicked again.

A faint voice called: "Who's there?"

"Steve Nash. What the devil's happened to Eldara?"

The boards of the shutter stirred, opened, so that the man within could look out.

"Is it Steve, honest?"

"Damn it, Butler, don't you know my voice? What's turned Eldara into a cemetery?"

"Cemetery's right. 'Butch' Conklin and his gang are going to raid the place to-night."

"Butch Conklin?"

And Nash whistled long and low.

"But why the devil don't the boys get together if they know Butch is coming with his gunmen?"

"That's what they've done. Every able-bodied man in town is out in the hills trying to surprise Conklin's gang before they hit town with their guns going."

Butler was a one-legged man, so Nash kept back the question which naturally formed in his mind.

"How do they know Conklin is coming? Who gave the tip?"

"Conklin himself."

"What? Has he been in town?"

"Right. Came in roaring drunk."

"Why'd they let him get away again?"

"Because the sheriff's a bonehead and because our marshal is solid ivory. That's why."

"What happened?"

"Butch came in drunk, as I was saying, which he generally is, but he wasn't giving no trouble at all, and nobody felt particular called on to cross him and ask questions. He was real sociable, in fact, and that's how the mess was started."

"Go on. I don't get your drift."

"Everybody was treatin' Butch like he was the king of the earth and not passin' out any backtalk, all except one tenderfoot——"

But here a stream of tremendous profanity burst from Nash. It rose, it rushed on, it seemed an exhaustless vocabulary built up by long practice on mustangs and cattle.

At length: "Is that damned fool in Eldara?"

"D'you know him?"

"No. Anyway, go on. What happened?"

"I was sayin' that Butch was feelin' pretty sociable. It went all right in the bars. He was in here and didn't do nothin' wrong. Even paid for all the drinks for everybody in the house, which nobody could ask more even from a white man. But then Butch got hungry and went up the street to Sally Fortune's place."

A snarl came from Nash.

"Did they let that swine go in there?"

"Who'd stop him? Would you?"

"I'd try my damnedest."

"Anyway, in he went and got the centre table and called for ten dollars' worth of bacon and eggs—which there hasn't been an egg in Eldara this week. Sally, she told him, not being afraid even of Butch. He got pretty sore at that and said that is was a frame-up and everyone was ag'in' him. But finally he allowed that if she'd sit down to the table and keep him company he'd manage to make out on whatever her cook had ready to eat."

"And Sally done it?" groaned Nash.

"Sure; it was like a dare—and you know Sally. She'd risk her whole place any time for the sake of a bet."

"I know it, but don't rub it in."

"She fetched out a steak and served Butch as if he'd been a king and then sat down beside him and started kiddin' him along, with all the gang of us sittin' or standin' around and laughin' fit to bust, but not loud for fear Butch would get annoyed.

"Then two things come in together and spoiled the prettiest little party that was ever started in Eldara. First was that player piano which Sally got shipped in and paid God-knows-how-much for; the second was this greenhorn I was tellin' you about."

"Go on," said Nash, the little snarl coming back in his voice. "Tell me how the tenderfoot walked up and kicked Butch out of the place."

"Somebody been tellin' you?"

"No; I just been readin' the mind of Eldara."

"It was a nice play, though. This Bard—we found out later that was his name—walks in, takes a table, and not being served none too quick, he walks over and slips a nickel in the slot of the piano. Out she starts with a piece of rippin' ragtime—you know how loud it plays? Butch, he kept on talkin' for a minute, but couldn't hear himself think. Finally he bellers: 'Who turned that damned tin-pan loose?'

"This Bard walks up and bows. He says: 'Sir, I came here to find food, and since I can't get service, I'll take music as a substitute.'

"Them was the words he used, Steve, honest to God. Used them to Butch!

"Well, Conklin was too flabbergasted to budge, and Bard, he leaned over and says to Sally: 'This floor is fairly smooth. Suppose you and I dance till I get a chance to eat?'

"We didn't know whether to laugh or to cheer, but most of us compromised by keeping an eye on Butch's gun.

"Sally says, 'Sure I'll dance,' and gets up.

"'Wait!' hollers Butch; 'are you leavin' me for this wall-eyed galoot?'

"There ain't nothin' Sally loves more'n a fight—we all know that. But this time I guess she took pity on the poor tenderfoot, or maybe she jest didn't want to get her floor all messed up.

"'Keep your hat on, Butch,' she says, 'all I want to do is to give him some motherly advice.'

"'If you're acting that part,' says Bard, calm as you please, 'I've got to tell mother that she's been keeping some pretty bad company.'

"'Some what?' bellers Butch, not believin' his ears.

"And young Bard, he steps around the girl and stands over Butch.

"'Bad company is what I said,' he repeats, 'but maybe I can be convinced.'

"'Easy,' says Butch, and reaches for his gun.

"We all dived for the door, but me being held up on account of my missing leg, I was slow an' couldn't help seein' what happened. Butch was fast, but the young feller was faster. He had Butch by the wrist before the gun came clear—just gave a little twist—and there he stood with the gun in his hand pointin' into Butch's face, and Butch sittin' there like a feller in a trance or wakin' up out of a bad dream.

"Then he gets up, slow and dignified, though he had enough liquor in him to float a ship.

"'I been mobbed,' he says, 'it's easy to see that. I come here peaceful and quiet, and here I been mobbed. But I'm comin' back, boys, and I ain't comin' alone.'

"There was our chance to get him, while he was walking out of that place without a gun, but somehow nobody moved for him. He didn't look none too easy, even without his shootin' irons. Out he goes into the night, and we stood around starin' at each other. Everybody was upset, except Sally and Bard.

"He says: 'Miss Fortune, this is our dance, I think.'

"'Excuse me,' says Sally, 'I almost forgot about it.'

"And they started to dance to the piano, waltzin' around among the tables; the rest of us lit out for home because we knew that Butch would be on his way with his gang before we got very far under cover. But hey, Steve, where you goin'?"

"I'm going to get in on that dance," called Nash, and was gone at a racing gallop down the street.

CATTLE DETECTIVE

TOM HORN

Early in april of 1887, some of the boys came down from the Pleasant Valley, where there was a big rustler war going on and the rustlers were getting the best of the game. I was tired of the mine and willing to go, and so away we went. Things were in a pretty bad condition. It was war to the knife between cowboys and rustlers, and there was a battle every time the two outfits ran together. A great many men were killed in the war. Old man Blevins and his three sons, three of the Grahams, a Bill Jacobs, Jim Payne, Al Rose, John Tewkesbury, Stolt, Scott, and a man named "Big Jeff" were hung on the Apache and Gila County line. Others were killed, but I do not remember their names now. I was the mediator, and was deputy sheriff under Bucky O'Neil, of Yavapai County, under Commodore Owens, of Apache County, and Glenn Reynolds, of Gila County. I was still a deputy for Reynolds a year later when he was killed by the Apache Kid, in 1888.

After this war in the Pleasant Valley I again went back to my mine and went to work, but it was too slow, and I could not stay at it. I was just getting ready to go to Mexico and was going down to clean out the spring at the mine one evening. I turned my saddle horse loose and let him graze up the cañon. After I got the spring cleaned out, I went up the cañon to find my horse and I saw a moccasin track covering the trail made by the rope my horse was dragging. That meant to go back, but I did not go back. I cut up the side of the mountain and found the trail where my horse had gone out. It ran into the trail of several more horses, and they were all headed south. I went down to the ranch, got another horse and rode over to the Agency, about twenty miles, to get an Indian or two to go with me to see what I could learn about this bunch of Indians.

I got to the Agency about two o'clock in the morning and found that there had been an outbreak and mutiny among Sieber's police. It was like this: Sieber had raised a young Indian he always called "the Kid," and now known as the "Apache Kid." This kid was the son of old Chief Toga-de-chuz, a San Carlos Apache. At a big dance on the Gila at old Toga-de-chuz's camp everybody got drunk and when morning came old Toga was found dead from a knife thrust. An old hunter belonging to another tribe of Indians and called "Rip" was accused of doing the job, but from what Sieber could learn, as he afterwards told me, everybody was too drunk to know how the thing did happen. The wound was given in a very skillful manner and as it split open old Toga's heart it was supposed to be given by one who knew where the heart lay.

Toga and old Rip had had a row over a girl about forty years before (they were both about sixty at this time), and Toga had gotten the best of the row and the girl to boot. Some say that an Indian will forget and forgive the same as a white man. I say no. Here had elapsed forty years between the row and the time old Toga was killed.

Rip had not turned his horse loose in the evening before the killing, so it was supposed he had come there with express intention of killing old Toga.

Anyway the Kid was the oldest son Toga-de-chuz and he must revenge the death of his father. He must, according to all Indian laws and customs, kill old Rip. Sieber knew this and cautioned the Kid about doing anything to old Rip. The Kid never said a word to Sieber as to what he would do. The Kid was first sergeant of the Agency scouts. The Interior Department had given the Agency over to the military and there were no more police, but scouts instead.

Shortly after this killing, Sieber and Captain Pierce, the agent, went up to Camp Apache to see about the distribution of some annuities to the Indians there, and the Kid, as first sergeant of the scouts, was left in charge of the peace of the Agency.

No sooner did Sieber and Captain Pierce get started than the Kid took five of his men and went over on the Aravaipo, where old Rip lived, and shot him. That evened up their account, and the Kid went back to where his band was living up above the Agency. Sieber heard of this and he and Pierce immediately started to San Carlos.

When they got there, they found no one in command of the scouts. Sieber sent word up to the camp where the Kid's people lived to tell the Kid to come down. This he did, escorted by the whole band of bucks.

Sieber, when they drew up in front of his tent, went out and spoke to the Kid and told him to get off his horse, and this the Kid did. Sieber then told him to take the arms of the other four or five men who had government rifles. This also the Kid did. He took their guns and belts and then Sieber told him to take off his own belt and put down his gun and take the other deserters and go to the guardhouse.

Some of the bucks with the Kid (those who were not soldiers) said to the Kid to fight, and in a second they were at it—eleven bucks against Sieber alone. It did not make any particular difference to Sieber about being outnumbered. His rifle was in his tent. He jumped back and got it, and at the first shot he killed one Indian. All the others fired at him as he came to the door of his tent, but only one bullet struck him; that hit him on the shin and shattered his leg all to pieces. He fell, and the Indian ran away.

This was what Sieber told me when I got to the Agency. And then I knew it was the Kid who had my horse and outfit. Soldiers were already on his trail.

From where he had stolen my horse, he and his band crossed over the mountain to the Table Mountain district, and there stole a lot of Bill Atchley's saddle horses. A few miles further on they killed Bill Dihl, then headed on up through the San Pedro country, turned down the Sonoita River, and there they killed Mike Grace; then they were turned back north again by some of the cavalry that was after them.

They struck back north, and Lieutenant Johnson got after them about Pontaw, overtook them in the Rincon Mountains, and had a fight, killing a couple of them, and put all the rest of them afoot. My horse was captured unwounded, and as the soldiers knew him, he was taken to the San Pedro and left there; they sent word to me, and eventually I got him, though he was pretty badly used up.

That was the way the Kid came to break out. He went back to the Reservation, and later on he surrendered. He was tried for desertion, and given a long time by the federal courts, but was pardoned by President Cleveland, after having served a short term.

During the time the Kid and his associates were hiding around on the Reservation, previous to his first arrest, he and his men had killed a freighter, or he may have been only a whisky peddler. Anyway, he was killed twelve miles above San Carlos, on the San Carlos River, by the Kid's outfit, and when the Kid returned to the Agency after he had done his short term and had been pardoned by the President, he was rearrested by the civil authorities of Gila County, Arizona, to be tried for the killing of this man at the Twelve Mile Pole.

This was in the fall of 1888. I was deputy sheriff of Gila County at that time, and as it was a new county, Reynolds was the first sheriff. I was to be the interpreter at the Kid's trial, but on July 4, 1888, I had won the prize at the Globe for tying down a steer, and there was a county rivalry among the cowboys all over the Territory as to who was the quickest man at that business. One Charley Meadows (whose father and brother were before mentioned as being killed by the Cibicus on their raid) was making a big talk that he could beat me tying at the Territorial Fair, at Phoenix. Our boys concluded I must go to the fair and make a trial for the Territorial prize, and take it out Meadows. I had known Meadows for years, and I thought I could beat him, and so did my friends.

The fair came off at the same time as did court in our new county, and since I could not very well be at both places, and, as they said, could not miss the fair, I was not at the trial.

While I was at Phoenix, the trial came off and several of the Indians told about the killing. There were six on trial, and they were all sentenced to the penitentiary at Yuma, Arizona, for life. Reynolds and "Hunky Dory" Holmes started to take them to Yuma. There were the six Indians and a Mexican sent up for one year, for horse stealing. The Indians had their hands coupled together, so that there were three in each of the two bunches.

Where the stage road from Globe to Casa Grande (the railroad station on the Southern Pacific Railroad) crosses the Gila river there is a very steep sand wash, up which the stage road winds. Going up this, Reynolds took his prisoners out and they were all walking behind the stage. The Mexican was handcuffed and inside the stage. Holmes got ahead of Reynolds some little distance. Holmes had three Indians and Reynolds three.

Just as Holmes turned a short bend in the road and got behind a point of rocks and out of sight of Reynolds, at a given signal, each bunch of prisoners turned on their guard and grappled with him. Holmes was soon down and they killed him. The three that had tackled Reynolds were not doing so well, but the ones that had killed Holmes got his rifle and pistol and went to the aid of the ones grappling Reynolds. These three were holding his arms so he could not get his gun. The ones that came up killed him, took his keys, unlocked the cuffs, and they were free.

Gene Livingston was driving the stage, and he looked around the side of the stage to see what the shooting was about. One of the desperadoes took a shot at him, striking him over the eye, and down he came. The Kid and his men then took the stage horses and tried to ride them, but there was only one of the four that they could ride.

The Kid remained an outlaw after that, till he died a couple of years ago of consumption. The Mexican, after the Kid and his men left the stage (they had taken off his handcuffs), struck out for Florence and notified the authorities. The driver was only stunned by the shot over the eye and is a resident and business man of Globe.

Had I not been urged to go to the fair at Phoenix, this would never have happened, as the Kid and his comrades just walked along and put up the job in their own language, which no one there could understand but themselves. Had I not gone to the fair, I would have been with Reynolds and could have understood what they said and it would never have happened. I won the prize roping at the fair, but it was at a very heavy cost.

In the winter I again went home, and in the following spring I went to work on my mine. Worked along pretty steady on it for a year, and in 1890 we sold it to a party of New Yorkers. We got $8,000 for it.

We were negotiating for this sale, and at the same time the Pinkerton National Detective Agency at Denver, Colorado, was writing to me to get me to come to Denver and to go to work for them. I thought it would be a good thing to do, and as soon as all the arrangements for the sale of the mine were made, I came to Denver and was initiated into the mysteries of the Pinkerton institution.

My work for them was not the kind that exactly suited my disposition; too tame for me. There were a good many instructions and a good deal of talk given the operative regarding the things to do and the things that had been done.

James McParland, the superintendent, asked me what I would do if I were put on a train robbery case. I told him if I had a good man with me I could catch up to them.

Well, on the last night of August, that year, at about midnight, a train was robbed on the Denver & Rio Grande Railway, between Cotopaxi and Texas

Creek. I was sent out there, and was told that C.W. Shores would be along in a day or so. He came on time and asked me how I was getting on. I told him I had struck the trail, but there were so many men scouring the country that I, myself, was being held up all the time; that I had been arrested twice in two days and taken in to Salida to be identified!

Eventually all the sheriff's posses quit, and then Mr. W. A. Pinkerton and Mr. McParland told Shores and me to go at 'em. We took up the trail where I had left it several days before and we never left it till we got the robbers.

They had crossed the Sangre de Cristo range, come down by the Villa Grove iron mines, and crossed back to the east side of the Sangre de Cristos at Mosca Pass, then on down through the Huerfano Cañon, out by Cucharas, thence down east of Trinidad. They had dropped into Clayton, N.M., and got into a shooting scrape there in a gin mill. They then turned east again toward the "Neutral Strip" and close to Beaver City, then across into the "Pan Handle" by a place in Texas called Ochiltree, the county seat of Ochiltree County. They then headed toward the Indian Territory, and crossed into it below Canadian City. They then swung in on the head of the Washita River in the Territory, and kept down this river for a long distance.

We finally saw that we were getting close to them, as we got in the neighborhood of Paul's Valley. At Washita station we located one of them in the house of a man by the name of Wolfe. The robber's name was Burt Curtis. Shores took this one and came on back to Denver, leaving me to get the other one if ever he came back to Wolfe's.

After several days of waiting on my part, he did come back, and as he came riding up to the house I stepped out and told him someone had come! He was "Peg Leg" Watson, and considered by everyone in Colorado as a very desperate character. I had no trouble with him.

We had an idea that Joe McCoy, also, was in the robbery, but "Peg" said he was not, and gave me information enough so that I located him. He was wanted very badly by the sheriff of Fremont County, Colorado, for a murder scrape. He and his father had been tried previous to this for murder, had been found guilty, and were remanded to jail to wait sentence, but before Joe was sentenced he had escaped. The old man McCoy got a new trial, and at the new trial was sentenced to eighteen years in the Cañon City, Colorado, penitentiary.

When I captured my man, got to a telegraph station and wired Mr. McParland that I had the notorious "Peg," the superintendent wired back: "Good! Old man McCoy got eighteen years today!" This train had been robbed in order to get money to carry McCoy's case up to the Supreme Court, or rather to pay the attorneys (Macons & Son), who had carried the case up.

Later on I told Mr. McParland that I could locate Joe McCoy, and he communicated with Stewart, the sheriff, who came to Denver and made arrangements for me to go with him and try to get McCoy.

We left Denver on Christmas Eve and went direct to Rifle, from there to Meeker, and on down White River. When we got to where McCoy had been, we learned that he had gone to Ashley, in Utah, for the Christmas festivities. We pushed on over there, reaching the town late at night and could not locate our man. Next morning I learned where he got his meals, and as he went in to get his breakfast, I followed him in and arrested him. He had a big Colt's pistol, but did not shoot me. We took him out by Fort Duchesne, Utah, and caught the D. & R. G. train at Price station.

The judge under whom he had been tried had left the bench when McCoy finally was landed back in jail, and it would have required a new trial before he could be sentenced by another judge; he consented to plead guilty to involuntary manslaughter, and took six years in the Cañon City pen. He was pardoned out in three years, I believe.

Peg Leg Watson and Burt Curtis were tried in the United States court for robbing the United States mails on the highway, and were sentenced for life in the Detroit federal prison. In robbing the train they had first made the fireman break into the mail compartment of the compartment car. They then saw their mistake, and did not even take the amount of a one-cent postage stamp, but went and made the fireman break into the rear compartment, where they found the express matter, and took it. But the authorities proved that it was mail robbery and their sentence was life.

While Pinkerton's is one of the greatest institutions of the kind in existence, I never did like the work, so I left them in 1894.

I then came to Wyoming and went to work for the Swan Land and Cattle Company, since which time everybody else has been more familiar with my life and business than I have been myself.

And I think that since my coming here the yellow journal reporters are better equipped to write my history than am I, myself!

Respectfully,

TOM HORN

* * * * *

"In Arizona and New Mexico, roping contests used to be held as a kind of annual tournament, in August, to the fair, or else as a special entertainment, often comprising, among other features, horse racing, a bull fight, baile and fiesta. Roping contests are generally held in a large field or enclosure—such as the interior of a race course. Inside this compound is built a small corral, in which are confined wild beef cattle, usually three-year-old steers, just rounded up off the range.

"The contest is a time race, to see who can overtake, lasso, throw and tie hard and fast the feet of a steer in the shortest period. The record was made at Phoenix, Arizona, in 1891. The contestants were, Charlie Meadows, Bill McCann, George Iago, Ramon Barca and Tom Horn, all well-known vaqueros of the Mexican-Arizona border. Tom Horn won the contest. Time, 49 ½ seconds, which I do not think has since been lowered.

"Two parallel lines, about as far apart as the ends of a polo court, were marked by banderoles or guidons. A steer was let out of the corral and driven at a run in a direction at right angles to the lines marked. As the steer crossed the second line, a banderole was dropped, which was the signal for a vaquero to start from the first line, thus giving the beef a running start of 250 yards. The horses used were all large, fleet animals, wonderfully well trained, and swooped for their prey at full speed and by the shortest route, turning without a touch of the rein to follow the steer, often anticipating his turns by a shorter cut. When the vaquero got within fifty yards of his beef the loop of his riata was swinging in a sharp, crisp circle about his right arm, raised high to his right and rear, and when twenty yards closer, it shot forward, hovered for an instant, and then descended above the horns of its victim, which a moment later would land a somersault. Before the beef could recover his surprise or wind he would have a half hitch about his fore legs, a second about his hind legs, and a third found all four a snug little bunch, hard and fast.

"The rope, of course, is not taken from the head; it is all one rope, the slack being successively used. Sometimes the vaqueros used foot-roping instead of head. It requires more skill and is practiced more by the Mexicans, who think it is a good method with large-horned cattle while in herd, where heads are so little separated that a lasso would fall on horns not wanted. In foot-roping the noose is thrown lower and a bit in front of the beef, so that at his next step he will put his foot into the noose before it strikes the ground. If the noose falls too quickly for this, it is jerked sharply upward just as the foot is raised above it.

"I have seen men so skillful at this that they would bet even money on rop-ing an animal on a single throw, naming the foot that they would secure, as right hind, left fore, and so forth. As regards the lash end of the riata, two methods in this contest were also used. In the 'Texas style' the lash of the riata is made hard and fast to the horn of the saddle. The instant the rope 'holds,' a pony who understands his work plants his fore feet forward and checks suddenly, giving the steer a header. His rider dismounts quickly, runs to the beef, which the pony keeps down by holding the rope taut.

"As soon as the vaquero faces the pony and grasps the rope near the beef, the pony moves forward, and with the slack of the rope the beef is secured. While the beef is plunging or wheeling on the rope the pony is careful to keep his head toward the beef, or, as the sailor would say, he goes 'bow on.'

"The Texas method is best adapted to loose ground, where it is much easier on the vaquero, but it is utterly unsuited for mountain work or steep hillsides, as the pony would lose his footing and land up in the bottom of a cañon.

"For such country, the California style is used. Here the lash is not made fast; a few frapping turns are made about the horn, and the rider uses his weight and a checking of the pony to throw the beef. When he dismounts, he carries the lash end forward, keeping it taut, toward the beef, taking up the slack and coils it as he goes, and with it secures the beef. The pony is free after the steer is thrown. It is the more rapid method. Tom Horn used it in the contest won, when he made his record. With it the vaquero has free use of his riata for secur-ing the beef. But it is a hard method, and plainsmen prefer letting Mr. Bronco take the brunt of it.

"Tom Horn is well known all along the border. He served as government guide, packer, scout and as chief of Indian scouts, which latter position he held with Captain Crawford at the time the Mexicans killed him in the Sierra Madre Mountains. He is the hero referred to in the story of 'The Killing of the Cap-tain,' by John Heard, Sr., published some months ago in the Cosmopolitan Magazine."

—Philadelphia TIMES 1895

A PAIR OF OUTLAWS

CHARLES M. RUSSELL

The worst hoss I ever rode," said Bowlegs, "I rode because I had to. It was a case of ride or lose my locks, an' I'm still wearin' hair.

"I was born in a cow-country an' raised with a hoss under me. I've been ridin' 'em ever since, an' come pretty near savvyin' the animal. Of course I'm a has-been now, but there was a time when I feared nothin' that wore hair, an' I've rode some bad ones. This snaky hoss is one I pick up on the range one time I'm makin' a get-away.

"I ain't goin' into no details, but I'm with a trail outfit when I get into this jackpot. It's at a dance-house where we've been long enough for the red-eye they're handin' us to get action, an' durin' an' between quadrilles we're sure givin' full vent to our joy. I'm gettin' pretty well salivated an' it ain't no wonder, 'cause one drink of this booze would make a jackrabbit spit in a rattlesnake's eye.

"But we're all peaceful enough till the sport that runs this hog-ranch objects to the noise I'm makin'. There's a little back talk an' he tells me if I don't take my gun off he'll make me eat it. He's a bad 'ombry, already packin' notches on his gun, an' I'm not so drunk but what I can see the butt of a forty-five peepin' from his waistband.

"Knowin' this feller's back history, I ain't takin' no chances. I see his right hand drop; the next thing I know he's on the floor with a bunch of screamin' women over him, an' I'm backin' for the door with a smokin' gun.

"It's night, an' goin' from light into darkness that way blinds me for a second or two, but it ain't long till I got my hoss from a snortin', whistlin' bunch at the rack. An' the way that old cow-pony pushes the country behind him, it looks like he savvies there's trouble.

"Our wagon's camped about a mile from this burg, an' it ain't long till I hear the bell of the remuda. This saddle bunch is pretty well trail-worn, but I've one tough, long-winded hoss in my string, an' as the one I'm on won't stand a hard ride, I'm thinkin' of changin'. So when I locate the hoss-wrangler, after tellin' him my troubles, he bunches the remuda till I drop the loop on my top hoss. This wrangler's righter than a rabbit, 'cause when he shakes goodbye, he forks over all his cattridges an' what loose money he's got.

"I know the country south of me well enough, but it ain't healthy hangin' too close to the old trail, so ridin' wide of that, I travel the lonesome places. There ain't no wire in the country them days an' it's smooth sailin'. Cattle's plentiful, an' by the use of my six-gun it's no trouble to get beef. Three days later I'm crossin' the Cheyenne country. These people are pretty warlike, they've been havin' considerable trouble with the cowmen an' there's been some killin' done. You bet all you got they'd make it interestin' for any lonesome puncher they bump into. Knowin' this, I'm mighty cautious.

"What's troublin' me most is my hoss. I've covered anyway two hundred miles, an' he's gone tender. His feet's so wore down that once, lookin' back, I notice blood in his track, an' I can't help thinkin' what a snap these savages would have if they'd run onto me ridin' this leg-weary pony.

"About this time I sight a bunch of hosses trailin' in to water. They're all Injun stock, mostly mares, barrin' one big, high-headed roan. If I can only get my string on him I'll be all right, but with this dead-head between my legs, how am I goin' to do it?

"The creek they're headin' for is pretty broken, an' there's a chance to cut-bank him, so droppin' in behind, I trail along easy, like I'm one of 'em. None of 'em notice me much but the roan; he keeps eyein' me over his shoulder, kind of suspicious. He's a rangy hoss with four white feet an' a bald face, one glass eye givin' him a snaky look. His tail's been trimmed out, an' saddle-marks tells me he's been rode.

"The only thing I don't like about him is his brands. He wears an iron everywhere you can burn a hoss—even his neck an' both jaws. He's burnt till he resembles a brand-book. I don't have to tell you fellers that's a bad sign. Whenever you see a hoss worked over this way, it's a cinch he's changed hands a lot of times an' none of his owners loved him. But then, again, if I'm pickin' a hoss for a long ride, give me a bad one. If he's an outlaw, he ain't got me beat none—there's a pair of us.

"When we drop down on the water I'm plenty pleased. It couldn't have been better if I'd had it made to order. She's cut-banked an' rim-rocked up an' down as far as I can see. But the minnit we start down the slope, Mister Roan gets nervous. With his head higher than ever he starts circlin'. He's seen me makin' my loop, an' it looks like he's on to my hole-card. Right here the creek makes a half-circle, with walls on the opposite side from eight to ten feet high.

"These hosses act pretty dry, for the minnit their feet hit the wet, their muzzles go to the water; all but the roan—he's too busy watchin' me. I've got him cut-banked an' he knows it, but's figurin' on breakin' back. The minnit my rope hits the air, he starts for the open, head an' tail up, but the hum of my swingin' rope turns him, an' back he goes through the mares. With one jump, clearin' the creek, he's agin the bank an' tryin' to climb out, but it's too many for him. He's back with a bull rush, knockin' one mare down an' jumpin' over another. He comes out of there like a bat out of hell an's got the whole bunch stirred up now. Reefin' my tired hoss from shoulder to flank, we jump to the gap. I ain't takin' no chances; my rope's tied hard an' fast, an' with one backhand swing my loop settles on his shoulders, but grabbin' the slack quick, I jerk her up his jaws. Then throwin' all my weight in my left stirrup, with my right spur hooked under the cantle to help my hoss, I wait for the jar.

"This old hoss I'm ridin''s one of the kind that holds with his hindquarters towards the animal. He's spread out an' braced, but bein' weak, when the roan goes to the end of the rope, he's jerked down. The roan's in the air when the rope tightens, an' he goes plumb over, turnin' a summerset an' hittin' the ground with a thud that stuns him, givin' my hoss time to get to his feet.

"'Tain't two seconds till the roan's up and comin' at me through the dust, with his head an' ears up an' tail flagged; he sure looks warlike. Trottin' up within twenty-five feet of me he stops with all feet braced an' whistles long an' loud. He's tryin' to buffalo me. It's the first hoss I ever see that I'm plumb scared of. From looks he's a man-eater; he's got me pretty near bluffed.

"But sizin' up the hoss under me, it's a groundhog case—climb the tree or the dog'll get you. So slidin' from the saddle I start walkin' up on the rope. He stands braced till I reach his nose; then strikes like a flash of lightnin' with both front feet, just touchin' the rim of my hat. By the way his hoofs cut the air, it wouldn't have been healthy for me if I'd-a-been under 'em.

"'If that's yer game, I'll head it off,' thinks I, so goin' to my saddle hoss I unloop the McCarthy from my hackamore. An' buildin' another loop, 'tain't long till I got him by the front feet. When I get him hobbled good, I unsaddle my old friend an' start fixin' for high ridin'. From the looks of the roan's hindquarters an' the way he's muscled an' strung up it's a safe bet he'll go in the air some. When I'm bridlin' him he tries to reach me with his front feet, but bein' hobbled, can't do much. He stands humped, but quiet enough when I'm bridlin' him. He can't fool me; by the way his left ear's dropped down an' the look he's givin' me with that glass eye, I savvy he's layin' for me.

"Of a sudden he swings his head a little to the right an' straightens his ears. Lookin' between 'em, I spy a band of about as nasty a-lookin' Cheyennes as I ever see. One look's a plenty; the way they're stripped an' painted, I know they ain't friendly. These Injuns have sighted me now; I can tell that by their yelpin'. They ain't more'n half a mile off, every pony runnin' an' every rider kickin' him in the belly.

"It's sure a case of hurry up, so tightenin' the cinch till the roan grunts, an' loosenin' the footrope, I grab the cheekpiece of the bridle an' pull the roan's head close 'round to me. Grippin' the horn of the saddle an' chuckin' my foot into the stirrup to the heel, I step across him. The minnit he feels my weight, the ball opens.

"Mister Outlaw squats an' then shoots up straight as a rocket —so straight I'm afraid he's comin' back over, but he don't. He lands all spraddled out. The next jump he catches his head, weaves an' sunfishes, hittin' the ground one leg at a time, all stiffened, givin' me four separate jolts. This mighty near loosens me, but hookin' my right spur in his shoulder an' grabbin' leather with all hands, I get back. When he goes up again he shakes himself like a dog leavin' water, an' the saddle pops an' rattles, causin' me to lose my left stirrup. As I never did get the right one, I'm sittin' on his ribs. He'd a-unloaded me all right, but I hear shots from the Cheyennes an' it scares me so you couldn't a-chopped me loose from him with an axe. If he turned summersets in the air he couldn't pile me now. I've made my brags before this that nothin' that wore hair could make me go to leather, but this time I damn near pull the horn out by the roots, an' it's a Visalia steel fork at that. I've heard many a hoss bawl before, but this one roared, an' I believe if he'd a-loosened me he'd a-eat me up. I'm scareder of him than I am of the Injuns, 'cause there ain't a man on earth, white or red, that could hit me with a scattergun while I'm goin' through these motions. The work I'm doin' would make a professional trapeze performer look like a green hand. Sometimes I'm behind the cantle, then I move over in front of the horn. Finally he kicks my hat off—either that or he makes me kick it off.

"I don't know how long this lasts, but I'm gettin' mighty dizzy when the roan raises his head from where he's had it hid, an' straightenin' his back, starts runnin'. Talk about swift hosses—in two jumps I'm goin' the fastest I ever rode; it looks like he's tryin' to run from under me.

"He's sure bustin' a hole in the breeze. Once there's a Cheyenne ball tears the dust off to one side, but it don't scare me none. At the gait we're goin', if a ball did hit me it wouldn't break the hide. It wouldn't no more'n catch up with us. When I look back over my shoulder there's a chain of dust a mile long, an' it appears like the Cheyennes 're backin' up. The wind roarin' in my ears finally brings me to my senses, an' shakin' the hair out of my hands I get the reins an' start lookin' over my layout. The roan's mane's pretty well pulled out from his ears back. My hat an' six-shooter's missin' an' there's one cantle-string tore out, but barrin' these trimmin's we're all right an' there's no kick comin'. The hoss under me can beat these Injun cavayos any distance from a squirrel's jump to the Rocky Mountains, so I bid farewell to the Cheyennes.

"Yes, fellers, that's the worst hoss I ever forked, but that same roan packed me many a hundred miles to safety, an' as I said before, gentle hosses is all right, but give me a snaky one for a hard ride."

DEADWOOD DICK

NAT LOVE

In the spring of 1876 orders were received at the home ranch for three thousand head of three-year-old steers to be delivered near Deadwood, South Dakota. This being one of the largest orders we had ever received at one time, every man around the ranch was placed on his mettle to execute the order in record time.

Cow boys mounted on swift horses were dispatched to the farthest limits of the ranch with orders to round up and run in all the three-year-olds on the place, and it was not long before the ranch corrals began to fill up with the long horns as they were driven by the several parties of cow boys; as fast as they came in we would cut out, under the bosses' orders such cattle as were to make up our herd.

In the course of three days we had our herd ready for the trail and we made our preparations to start on our long journey north. Our route lay through New

Mexico, Colorado and Wyoming, and as we had heard rumors that the Indians were on the war path and were kicking up something of a rumpus in Wyoming, Indian Territory and Kansas, we expected trouble before we again had the pleasure of sitting around our fire at the home ranch. Quite a large party was selected for this trip owing to the size of the herd and the possibility of trouble on the trail from the Indians. We, as usual, were all well armed and had as mounts the best horses our ranch produced, and in taking the trail we were perfectly confident that we could take care of our herd and ourselves through anything we were liable to meet. We had not been on the trail long before we met other outfits, who told us that General Custer was out after the Indians and that a big fight was expected when the Seventh U. S. Cavalry, General Custer's command, met the Crow tribe and other Indians under the leadership of Sitting Bull, Rain-in-the-Face, Old Chief Joseph, and other chiefs of lesser prominence, who had for a long time been terrorizing the settlers of that section and defying the Government.

As we proceeded on our journey it became evident to us that we were only a short distance behind the soldiers. When finally the Indians and soldiers met in the memorable battle or rather massacre in the Little Big Horn Basin on the Little Big Horn River in northern Wyoming, we were only two days behind them, or within 60 miles, but we did not know that at the time or we would have gone to Custer's assistance. We did not know of the fight or the outcome until several days after it was over. It was freely claimed at the time by cattle men who were in a position to know and with whom I talked that if Reno had gone to Custer's aid as he promised to do, Custer would not have lost his entire command and his life.

It was claimed Reno did not obey his orders, however that may be, it was one of the most bloody massacres in the history of this country. We went on our way to Deadwood with our herd, where we arrived on the 3rd of July, 1876, eight days after the Custer massacre took place.

The Custer Battle was June 25, '76, the battle commenced on Sunday afternoon and lasted about two hours. That was the last of General Custer and his Seventh Cavalry. How I know this so well is because we had orders from one of the Government scouts to go in camp, that if we went any farther North we were liable to be captured by the Indians.

We arrived in Deadwood in good condition without having had any trouble with the Indians on the way up. We turned our cattle over to their new owners at once, then proceeded to take in the town. The next morning, July 4th, the gamblers and mining men made up a purse of $200 for a roping contest between the cow boys that were then in town, and as it was a holiday nearly all the cow boys for miles around were assembled there that day. It did not take long to arrange the details for the contest and contestants, six of them being colored cow boys, including myself. Our trail boss was chosen to pick out the mustangs from a herd of wild horses just off the range, and he picked out twelve of the most wild and vicious horses that he could find.

The conditions of the contest were that each of us who were mounted was to rope, throw, tie, bridle and saddle and mount the particular horse picked for us in the shortest time possible. The man accomplishing the feat in the quickest time to be declared the winner.

It seems to me that the horse chosen for me was the most vicious of the lot. Everything being in readiness, the "45" cracked and we all sprang forward together, each of us making for our particular mustang.

I roped, threw, tied, bridled, saddled and mounted my mustang in exactly nine minutes from the crack of the gun. The time of the next nearest competitor was twelve minutes and thirty seconds. This gave me the record and championship of the West, which I held up to the time I quit the business in 1890, and my record has never been beaten. It is worthy of passing remark that I never had a horse pitch with me so much as that mustang, but I never stopped sticking my spurs in him and using my quirt on his flanks until I proved his master. Right there the assembled crowd named me Deadwood Dick and proclaimed me champion roper of the western cattle country.

The roping contest over, a dispute arose over the shooting question with the result that a contest was arranged for the afternoon, as there happened to be some of the best shots with rifle and revolver in the West present that day. Among them were Stormy Jim, who claimed the championship; Powder Horn Bill, who had the reputation of never missing what he shot at; also White Head, a half breed, who generally hit what he shot at, and many other men who knew how to handle a rifle or 45-colt.

The range was measured off 100 and 250 yards for the rifle and 150 for the Colt 45. At this distance a bulls eye about the size of an apple was put up. Each man was to have 14 shots at each range with the rifle and 12 shots with the Colts 45.

I placed every one of my 14 shots with the rifle in the bulls eye with ease, all shots being made from the hip; but with the 45 Colts I missed it twice, only placing 10 shots in the small circle, Stormy Jim being my nearest competitor, only placing 8 bullets in the bulls eye clear, the rest being quite close, while with the 45 he placed 5 bullets in the charmed circle. This gave me the championship of rifle and revolver shooting as well as the roping contest, and for that day I was the hero of Deadwood, and the purse of $200 which I had won on the roping contest went toward keeping things moving, and they did move, as only a large crowd of cattle men can move things. This lasted for several days when most of the cattle men had to return to their respective ranches, as it was the busy season, accordingly our outfit began to make preparations to return to Arizona.

In the meantime news had reached us of the Custer massacre, and the indignation and sorrow was universal, as General Custer was personally known to a large number of the cattle men of the West. But we could do nothing now, as the Indians were out in such strong force. There was nothing to do but let Uncle Sam revenge the loss of the General and his brave command, but it is safe to say not one of us would have hesitated a moment in taking the trail in pursuit of the blood thirsty red skins had the opportunity offered.

Everything now being in readiness with us we took the trail homeward bound, and left Deadwood in a blaze of glory. On our way home we visited the Custer battle field in the Little Big Horn Basin.

There was ample evidence of the desperate and bloody fight that had taken place a few days before. We arrived home in Arizona, in a short time without further incident, except that on the way back we met and talked with many of the famous Government scouts of that region, among them Buffalo Bill (William F. Cody), Yellow Stone Kelley, and many others of that day, some of whom are now living, while others lost their lives in the line of duty, and a finer or braver body of men never lived than these sccouts of the West. It was my pleasure to meet Buffalo Bill often in the early 70s, and he was as fine a man as one could wish to meet, kind, generous, true and brave.

Buffalo Bill got his name from the fact that in the early days he was engaged in hunting buffalo for their hides and furnishing U. P. Railroad graders with meat, hence the name Buffalo Bill. Buffalo Bill, Yellowstone Kelley, with many others were at this time serving under Gen. C. C. Miles.

The name of Deadwood Dick was given to me by the people of Deadwood, South Dakota, July 4, 1876, after I had proven myself worthy to carry it, and after I had defeated all comers in riding, roping, and shooting, and I have always carried the name with honor since that time.

We arrived at the home ranch again on our return from the trip to Deadwood about the middle of September, it taking us a little over two months to make the return journey, as we stopped in Cheyenne for several days and at other places, where we always found a hearty welcome, especially so on this trip, as the news had preceded us, and I received enough attention to have given me the big head, but my head had constantly refused to get enlarged again ever since the time I sampled the demijohn in the sweet corn patch at home.

Arriving at home, we received a send off from our boss and our comrades of the home ranch, every man of whom on hearing the news turned loose his voice and his artillery in a grand demonstration in my honor.

But they said it was no surprise to them, as they had long known of my ability with the rope, rifle and 45 Colt, but just the same it was gratifying to know I had defeated the best men of the West, and brought the record home to the home ranch in Arizona. After a good rest we proceeded to ride the range again, getting our herds in good condition for the winter now at hand.

* * * * *

In the spring of 1877, now fully recovered from the effects of the very serious wounds I had received at the hands of the Indians and feeling my old self again, I joined the boys in their first trip of the season, with a herd of cattle for Dodge City. The trip was uneventful until we reached our destination. This was the first time I had been in Dodge City since I had won the name of "DEAD-WOOD DICK," and many of the boys, who knew me when I first joined the cow boys there in 1869, were there to greet me now. After our herd had been delivered to their new owners, we started out to properly celebrate the event, and for a space of several days we kept the old town on the jump.

And so when we finally started for home all of us had more or less of the bad whiskey of Dodge City under our belts and were feeling rather spirited and ready for anything.

I probably had more of the bad whiskey of Dodge City than any one and was in consequence feeling very reckless, but we had about exhausted our resources of amusement in the town, and so were looking for trouble on the trail home.

On our way back to Texas, our way led past old Fort Dodge. Seeing the soldiers and the cannon in the fort, a bright idea struck me, but a fool one just the same. It was no less than a desire to rope one of the cannons. It seemed to me that it would be a good thing to rope a cannon and take it back to Texas with us to fight Indians with.

The bad whiskey which I carried under my belt was responsible for the fool idea, and gave me the nerve to attempt to execute the idea. Getting my lariat rope ready I rode to a position just opposite the gate of the fort, which was standing open. Before the gate paced a sentry with his gun on his shoulder and his white gloves showing up clean and white against the dusty grey surroundings. I waited until the sentry had passed the gate, then putting spurs to my horse I dashed straight for and through the gate into the yard. The surprised sentry called halt, but I paid no attention to him. Making for the cannon at full speed my rope left my hand and settled square over the cannon, then turning and putting spurs to my horse I tried to drag the cannon after me, but strain as he might my horse was unable to budge it an inch. In the meantime the surprised sentry at the gate had given the alarm and now I heard the bugle sound, boots and saddles, and glancing around I saw the soldiers mounting to come after me, and finding I could not move the cannon, I rode close up to it and got my lariat off then made for the gate again at full speed. The guard jumped in front of me with his gun up, calling halt, but I went by him like a shot, expecting to hear the crack of his musket, but for some reason he failed to fire on me, and I made for the open prairie with the cavalry in hot pursuit.

My horse could run like a wild deer, but he was no match for the big, strong, fresh horses of the soldiers and they soon had me. Relieving me of my arms they placed me in the guard house where the commanding officer came to see me. He asked me who I was and what I was after at the fort. I told him and then he asked me if I knew anyone in the city. I told him I knew Bat Masterson. He ordered two guards to take me to the city to see Masterson. As soon as Masterson saw me he asked me what the trouble was, and before I could answer, the guards told him I rode into the fort and roped one of the cannons and tried to pull it out. Bat asked me what I wanted with a cannon and what I intended doing with it. I told him I wanted to take it back to Texas with me to fight the Indians with; then they all laughed. Then Bat told them that I was all right, the only trouble being that I had too much bad whiskey under my shirt. They said I would have to set the drinks for the house. They came to $15.00, and when I started to pay for them, Bat said for me to keep my money that he would pay for them himself, which he did. Bat said that I was the only cowboy that he liked, and that his brother Jim also thought very much of me. I was then let go and I joined the boys and we continued on our way home, where we arrived safely on the 1st of June, 1877.

We at once began preparing for the coming big round up. As usual this kept us very busy during the months of July and August, and as we received no more orders for cattle this season, we did not have to take the trail again, but after the round up was over, we were kept busy in range riding, and the general all around work of the big cattle ranch. We had at this time on the ranch upwards of 30,000 head of cattle, our own cattle, not to mention the cattle belonging to the many other interests without the Pan Handle country, and as all these immense herds used the range of the country, in common as there was no fences to divide the ranches, consequently the cattle belonging to the different herds often got mixed up and large numbers of them strayed.

At the round ups it was our duty to cut out and brand the young calves, take a census of our stock, and then after the round up was over we would start out to look for possible strays. Over the range we would ride through canyons and gorges, and every place where it was possible for cattle to stray, as it was important to get them with the main herd before winter set in, as if left out in small bunches there was danger of them perishing in the frequent hard storms of the winter. While range riding or hunting for strays, we always carried with us on our saddle the branding irons of our respective ranches, and whenever we ran across a calf that had not been branded we had to rope the calf, tie it, then a fire was made of buffalo chips, the only fuel besides grass to be found on the prairie.

The irons were heated and the calf was branded with the brand of the finder, no matter who it personally belonged to. It now became the property of the finder. The lost cattle were then driven to the main herd. After they were once gotten together it was our duty to keep them together during the winter and early spring. It was while out hunting strays that I got lost, the first and only time I was ever lost in my life, and for four days I had an experience that few men ever went through and lived, as it was a close pull for me.

I had been out for several days looking for lost cattle and becoming separated from the other boys and being in a part of the country unfamiliar to me. It was stormy when I started out from the home ranch and when I had ridden about a hundred miles from home it began to storm in earnest, rain, hail, sleet, and the clouds seemed to touch the earth and gather in their inpenetrable embrace every thing thereon. For a long time I rode on in the direction of home, but as I could not see fifty yards ahead it was a case of going it blind. After riding for many weary hours through the storm I came across a little log cabin on the Palidore river. I rode up to within one hundred yards of it where I was motioned to stop by an old long haired man who stepped out of the cabin door with a long buffalo gun on his arm. It was with this he had motioned me to stop.

I promptly pulled up and raised my hat, which, according to the custom of the cowboy country, gave him to understand I was a cowboy from the western cow ranges. He then motioned me to come on. Riding up to the cabin he asked me to dismount and we shook hands.

He said, when I saw you coming I said to myself that must be a lost cowboy from some of the western cow ranges. I told him I was lost all right, and I told him who I was and where from. Again we shook hands, he saying as we did so, that we were friends until we met again, and he hoped forever. He then told me to picket out my horse and come in and have some supper, which very welcome invitation I accepted.

His cabin was constructed of rough hewn logs, somewhat after the fashion of a Spanish block house. One part of it was constructed under ground, a sort of dug out, while the upper portion of the cabin was provided with many loop holes, commanding every direction.

He later told me these loop holes had stood him in handy many a time when he had been attacked by Indians, in their efforts to capture him. On entering his cabin I was amazed to see the walls covered with all kinds of skins, horns, and antlers. Buffalo skins in great numbers covered the floor and bed, while the walls were completely hidden behind the skins of every animal of that region, including a large number of rattle snakes skins and many of their rattles.

His bed, which was in one corner of the dug out, was of skins, and to me, weary from my long ride through the storm, seemed to be the most comfortable place on the globe just then. He soon set before me a bountious supper, consisting of buffalo meat and corn dodgers, and seldom before have I enjoyed a meal as I did that one. During supper he told me many of his experiences in the western country. His name was Cater, and he was one of the oldest buffalo hunters in that part of Texas, having hunted and trapped over the wild country ever since the early thirties, and during that time he had many a thrilling adventure with Indians and wild animals.

I stayed with him that night and slept soundly on a comfortable bed he made for me. The next morning he gave me a good breakfast and I prepared to take my departure as the storm had somewhat moderated, and I was anxious to get home, as the boys knowing I was out would be looking for me if I did not show up in a reasonable time.

My kind host told me to go directly northwest and I would strike the Calones flats, a place with which I was perfectly familiar. He said it was about 75 miles from his place. Once there I would have no difficulty in finding my way home. Cater put me up a good lunch to last me on my way, and with many expressions of gratitude to him, I left him with his skins and comfortable, though solitary life. All that day and part of the night I rode in the direction he told me, until about 11 o'clock when I became so tired I decided to go into camp and give my tired horse a rest and a chance to eat. Accordingly I dismounted and removed the saddle and bridle from my horse I hobbled him and turned him loose to graze on the luxuriant grass, while I, tired out, laid down with my head on my saddle fully dressed as I was, not even removing my belt containing my 45 pistol from my waist, laying my Winchester close by. The rain had ceased to fall, but it was still cloudy and threatening. It was my intention to rest a few hours then continue on my way; and as I could not see the stars on account of the clouds and as it was important that I keep my direction northwest in order to strike the Flats, I had carefully taken my direction before sundown, and now on moving my saddle I placed it on the ground pointing in the direction I was going when I stopped so that it would enable me to keep my direction when I again started out. I had been laying there for some time and my horse was quietly grazing about 20 yards off, when I suddenly heard something squeal. It sounded like a woman's voice. It frightened my horse and he ran for me. I jumped to my feet with my Winchester in my hand. This caused my horse to rear and wheel and I heard his hobbles break with a sharp snap. Then I heard the sound of his galloping feet going across the Pan Handle plains until the sound was lost in the distance. Then I slowly began to realize that I was left alone on the plains on foot, how many miles from home I did not know. Remembering I had my guns all right, it was my impulse to go in pursuit of my horse as I thought I could eventually catch him after he had got over his scare, but when I thought of my 40 pound saddle, and I did not want to leave that, so saying to myself that is the second saddle I ever owned, the other having been taken by the Indians when I was captured, and this saddle was part of the outfit presented to me by the boys, and so tired and as hungry as a hawk, I shouldered my saddle and started out in the direction I was going when I went into camp, saying to myself as I did so, if my horse could pack me and my outfit day and night, I can at least pack my outfit. Keeping my direction as well as I could I started out over the prairie through the dark, walking all that night and all the next day without anything to eat or drink until just about sundown and when I had begun to think I would have to spend another night on the prairie without food or drink, when I emerged from a little draw on to a raise on the prairie, then looking over on to a small flat I saw a large herd of buffalo. These were the first I had seen since I became lost and the sight of them put renewed life and hope in me as I was then nearly famished, and when I saw them I knew I had something to eat.

Off to one side about 20 yards from the main herd and about 150 yards from me was a young calf. Placing my Winchester to my shoulder I glanced along the shining barrel, but my hands shook so much I lowered it again, not that I was afraid of missing it as I knew I was a dead shot at that distance, but my weakness caused by my long enforced fast and my great thirst made my eyes dim and my hands shake in a way they had never done before, so waiting a few moments I again placed the gun to my shoulder and this time it spoke and the calf dropped where it had stood. Picking up my outfit I went down to where my supper was laying. I took out my jack knife and commenced on one of his hind quarters. I began to skin and eat to my hearts content, but I was so very thirsty. I had heard of people drinking blood to quench their thirst and that gave me an idea, so cutting the calf's throat with my knife I eagerly drank the fresh warm blood.

It tasted very much like warm sweet milk. It quenched my thirst and made me feel strong, when I had eaten all I could, I cut off two large chunks of the meat and tied them to my saddle, then again shouldering the whole thing I started on my way feeling almost as satisfied as if I had my horse with me. I was lost two days, and two nights, after my horse left me and all that time I kept walking packing my 40 pounds saddle and my Winchester and two cattle pistols.

On the second night about daylight the weather became more threatening and I saw in the distance a long column which looked like smoke. It seemed to be coming towards me at the rate of a mile a minute. It did not take it long to reach me, and when it did I struggled on for a few yards but it was no use, tired as I was from packing my heavy outfit for more than 48 hours and my long tramp, I had not the strength to fight against the storm so I had to come alone. When I again came to myself I was covered up head and foot in the snow, in the camp of some of my comrades from the ranch.

It seemed from what I was told afterwards that the boys knowing I was out in the storm and failing to show up, they had started out to look for me, they had gone in camp during the storm and when the blizzard had passed they noticed an object out on the prairie in the snow, with one hand frozen, clenched around my Winchester and the other around the horn of my saddle, and they had hard work to get my hands loose, they picked me up and placed me on one of the horses and took me to camp where they stripped me of my clothes and wrapped me up in the snow, all the skin came off my nose and mouth and my hands and feet had been so badly frozen that the nails came off. After had got thawed out in the mess wagon and took me home in 15 days I was again in the saddle ready for business but I will never forget those few days I was lost and the marks of that storm I will carry with me always.

SOME COOKS I HAVE KNOWN

BOB KENNON

I MUST TELL you about some cooks I've known while working for the 79. Bilious Bill was one of them. He was cooking for the LU when I repped there for the 79. I remember it was in the spring of 1903 when we were on Sunday Creek that an old mule played us a dirty trick. The weather was fine and we had worked the surrounding country until we came to the Big Dry where the town of Jordan now stands. We were camped at what the fellows called Lone Tree.

This outfit had an old mule which used to be worked on the mess wagon but was now on the retired list. But come what may, he'd still follow the outfit faithfully. From dawn till dark, from range to range, there he was, trailing close behind.

A number of outfits were camped near by, among them the 79. The cook for this outfit was the one named Vinegar Jim whom I've just mentioned. Jim always tried to have pies for the boys at every supper. Now at this time it was the finest spring weather anyone could want, and Vinegar Jim decided to take the back flap off the mess tent. He had baked some fine pumpkin pies and thoughtlessly left them on the table. Strolling over to where his friend Bilious Bill was sitting in the shade, he sat down beside him to exchange yarns and comment upon the weather.

Just as Jim glanced up from rolling a cigarette he let out a string of cuss words that'd sizzle bacon. The lounging punchers jerked to attention only to see this old mule sauntering toward the two cooks. Jim and Bill were both on their feet, too, and the war was on, for the old mule had pumpkin pie smeared all over his face.

Needless to say, the two old fellows were sworn enemies thereafter. All the boys laughed and joked and tried to get them in a good humor again, but old Bill became even more bilious and Jim developed an even more vinegary disposition.

Bilious Bill got his name from forever taking soda for his "bilious stomach." One hot summer day the outfit had just butchered a beef and left the remains—paunch, etc.—near the wagon. Bill had a very spirited horse which he called Rocky Mountain Boy. On this particular day he was out riding this animal, whose favorite trick was to shy and buck his rider off.

When Bill came to the wagon to start supper, his horse shied at the beef paunch and off went Bill with the first buck. His head hit the paunch, and he got up plenty mad. "Why in hell can't you butcher someplace besides this mess wagon?" he yelled. The fellows claimed he was so bilious after this experience that he could hardly cook a thing for days.

Bill was very fond of cats. He had a big yellow one and had trained him from a kitten to ride with him in a box on the chuck wagon. He was one of the smartest cats I ever saw. When we started to break camp, he would climb on the seat and get into his little box. Here he would wait for the moving wagon. Upon our arrival at a new camp, he promptly climbed down again and watched Bill as he prepared his meal.

There was one thing that this cat seemed to like better than any other, and that was raw doughnut dough. When Bill would cut his doughnut dough, he would pitch the centers to the cat. One afternoon I watched this until I thought surely that cat would kick the bucket that night. But next morning he was there, big as life, stuffing himself with warmed-up doughnuts. He sure must have had the nine lives which cats are supposed to have or he couldn't have digested all those sinkers. In the winter he always stayed at one of the line-camps, and he was a lucky old cat, for he always had plenty of good beefsteak.

I recall the incident of the French cook and the rattlesnake. I was repping for the 79 at the CK wagon. At that time we were near the Canadian border and around Malta. The CK outfit was the famous Conrad Kohrs spread of which we have heard a great deal in later years. Mr. Kohrs's wife seemed fond of bringing over French cooks from the old country and training them to cook for her, or for the wagons. She tried to train them to speak English and understand American ways.

One day Conrad brought out a great big fellow named Joe. He seemed amazed at the mess-wagon setup and could understand very little English. Supper passed without incident, as our regular cook hadn't left yet. Next morning we eyed the departing cook with misgivings, for somehow the boys seemed to know we were in for some bad cooking.

A fellow by the name of Webb was running the wagon at this time and he and I were just coming in from circle that morning. When we approached the wagon, we could hear Joe threatening someone in broken English. There he stood, over six feet tall, with a chef's cap on his head and wearing a long, white apron that reached his feet. Every once in a while he would back up and down, brandishing a long butcher knife at the big bread box.

"What's wrong, Joe?" yelled Webb as we both dismounted and ran toward the cook. We felt sure he must have been taking too much of the bottle.

There was terror in his face as he shook his fist and cried out: "Buzz—eee, says I. Son-of-a-beech, talk I. Buzz—eee. He son-of-a-beech."

I jumped forward and kicked over the bread box and one of the biggest rattlers I ever saw crawled out. Webb's gun took care of him, but the French cook was so scared he had to have us stay around most of the day looking for more "buzz—eees." He wouldn't use that box again, and one of the boys had to build a rattler-proof box for him and put a padlock on it.

He was never any good as a wagon cook, though some of his dishes were tasty enough. Mrs. Kohrs sent him back to France, but we always laughed when we thought of the stories he must have told the people over there. Maybe they believed him, or maybe they thought he was crazy. At any rate, he took chances of being called the biggest liar in town.

Dirty Dave earned this title, not because he was really dirty, but because he was so particular about the washing of the dishes, the dishcloths, and towels. As one cowhand said: "He's plumb soap-and-water crazy, so damn clean that he's dirty." And from this he got his name. His real name was Dave Rankin. He often quit cooking and drove stage just for a change. Sometimes the chuck-wagon jobs got him down because he was very particular about the supplies allowed him and the utensils and other gear used at the wagon. He was the brother-in-law of the famous Pat O'Hara (mayor, saloonkeeper, and supply merchant of Old Geyser in its roaring days), so he could usually be found playing poker and having a few drinks in Pat's saloon.

One year near the end of the season when the supplies were running low, Dave cooked nothing but great kettles of rice and raisins three times a day for three days. The boys were getting pretty short tempered and threatened to give him a ducking in the creek if he didn't give them a change of diet. This dish is known as spotted pup and it doesn't make a bad pudding when served with cream and sugar, but we were tired of it as a main dish.

Dave was nervous that third night as the boys sat down again to this spotted-pup dish. Sure enough, they raised the devil and told him that if he didn't get out the next morning after breakfast and go to a ranch over the hill and get a change of provender, they'd take care of him good.

So Dave left the next morning to see what he could find. He was a good rider and was leading a good pack horse as he approached this ranch house. He saw no sign of life, and after knocking on the door many times he called out, "Is anyone at home?" but got no answer.

A nice flock of chickens were busily scratching in the hen house. Dave had come with the best intentions, but seeing there was no one around and realizing that time was passing and he was a long way from camp, he decided to shoo a few of the fat chickens into the gunny sacks he carried on his saddle. This he did without any trouble and started off toward the milkhouse, or springhouse. No one was there either so he helped himself to a fine can of buttermilk. Here was Heaven! Fresh cream; butter; rich cream-topped sweet milk. He was sampling this and that and didn't hear footsteps approaching. A shadow darkened the open doorway, then something hit him. The lash of a quirt hit him over the back. He dodged back and got a glimpse of his assailant. She was a big red-faced woman wearing men's shoes and a Mother Hubbard nightgown. Ordinarily this would have been a funny sight, but under the circumstances Dave failed to see anything comical. This woman meant business, for she had caught a thief red handed and she meant to punish him.

"Take dat and dot, you [here a lot of cuss words in broken English], you stealer!"

Dave recognized this woman as the Dutchman's wife, the terror of the Judith, and he really wanted to get away. He knew now why the boys had sent him to this ranch: it was all a part of a joke.

Still dodging that quirt, his eyes fell upon a crock of buttermilk. It was his only chance. He hurled it full into the Dutchwoman's face, and she fell into the corner spluttering. Before she could rise, he dashed out the door, mounted his horse, and was gone. He said afterward that he spurred his horse all the way to camp and got there with the chickens bobbing up and down in the gunny sack. He put them on to cook in record time.

The heavenly aroma of chicken soup was filling the air when the boys came in for supper. At this moment they thought only of their stomachs and asked no questions. Later his explanation was that it had been "sent from Heaven." No amount of torture could have dragged the truth from him. Best of all, they were heading back to the home ranch at dawn the next day and nobody would care any more what he cooked. This was his last roundup, for no matter how much anyone begged him, he never again signed on as a wagon cook.

AN ELEVEN HUNDRED MILE HORSEBACK RIDE DOWN THE CHISHOLM TRAIL

CHARLES A. SIRINGO

After laying around the home ranch a few weeks Mr. Moore put me in charge of a scouting outfit, to drift over the South Staked Plains, in search of any cattle which might have escaped from the line-riders.

While on this trip I went to church several times.

A colony of Illinois Christians, under the leadership of the Reverend Mr. Cahart, had established the town of Clarendon, on the head of Salt Fork, a tributary of Red River, and there built a white church house among the buffalo and wolves.

Clarendon is still on the map, being the county seat of Donnely county, Texas.

When spring came I was called in from the plains and put in charge of a round-up crew, consisting of a cook and twelve riders.

Our first round-up was on the Goodnight range, at the mouth of Mulberry Creek. Here we had the pleasure of a genuine cattle-queen's presence. Mrs. Goodnight, a noble little woman, a dyed in the wool Texan, whose maiden name was Dyer, attended these roundups with her husband.

Mrs. Goodnight touched a soft spot in my heart by filling me up on several occasions, with juicy berries which she had gathered with her own hands.

At this writing Mr. and Mrs. Charlie Goodnight are still alive, and living in the town of Goodnight, Texas, which has been made famous as the home of the largest herd of buffalo in that state, and possibly the whole United States.

The foundation of this herd of buffalo was started on this round-up in the spring of 1879.

In the round-up at the head of Mulberry Creek was a lone buffalo bull. When ready to turn the round-up cattle loose Mr. Buffalo was roped and thrown, and a cow-bell fastened to his neck. When turned loose he stampeded, and so did the thousands of cattle.

In the round-up the following spring the bell-buffalo was with the cattle, and had with him several female buffalos.

During that summer Mr. Goodnight fenced his summer range on Mulberry Creek, and this small herd of buffalo found themselves enclosed with a strong barbed wire fence.

From what I was told Charlie Goodnight increased this buffalo herd by having cowboys rope young animals to be put inside the Mulberry Creek fenced pasture.

Many years afterwards I rode through this tame herd of buffalos, near the town of Goodnight.

We wound up this spring round-up on the Rocking Chair range, at the mouth of McClellan Creek, where I saw about 50,000 cattle in one bunch— more than I had ever seen before in one band.

Now we returned to the home ranch with about 500 LX cattle, which had drifted away from the range during the winter.

Shortly after our return Mr. Moore had us help him brand some large long-horn steers, late arrivals from South Texas.

We did the branding on the open plains, at Amarillo Lake.

While roping and tying down these wild steers we had great sport in see-ing "Center-fire" saddles jerked over sideways from the pony's back, the riders with them.

Mr. Moore had got his cowboy training in California, where they use "cen-ter-fire", high horn saddles and riatas, (ropes) which they wrap around the sad-dle-horn when roping on horseback. The cinchas on these saddles being broad, and in the center of the saddle, which makes it difficult to keep the saddle tight on the pony's back.

Mr. Moore had persuaded many of his cowboys to use these saddles and the long rawhide "riatas"—hence a large order had been sent to California in the early spring. In the order were many silver mounted spurs and Spanish bridle bits. I sent for one of these ten dollar bridle bits, and am still using it to ride with.

I must confess that Moore never got a fall from his "center-fire" saddle, as he had learned his lesson early in life. He was also an expert roper with his 75-foot "riata." He could throw the large loop further and catch his animal oftener than any man in the crowd of about twenty-five riders.

Moore tried his best to persuade me, and such Texas raised cow-boys as Jim East, Steve Arnold and Lee Hall, not to tie our 30-foot ropes hard and fast to the saddle horns when roping large steers. He argued that it was too dangerous. No doubt he was right, but we had been trained that way.

Later poor Lee Hall was gored to death by a wild steer, roped down in the Indian Territory. The steer had jerked his mount over backward, and one of his spurs caught in the flank cinch, preventing him from freeing himself until too late to save his life.

The spur which hung in the cinch and caused his death, was one of the fine silver mounted pair which Moore sent to California for.

After his death I fell heir to Lee Hall's spurs and they are used by me to this day, over 40 years later.

In the latter part of June Mr. Moore put me in charge of 800 fat steers for the Chicago market. My outfit consisted of a well filled mess-wagon, a cook and five riders.

We headed for Nickerson, Kansas, on the Arkansas River, across country through No-Mans-Land—now the 30 mile strip of Oklahoma which butts up against New Mexico on the west, and on the north is bordered by Kansas and Colorado, the Texas Panhandle being the south border.

Late in the fall we arrived in Nickerson, Kansas, and turned the steers over to "Deacon" Bates.

Leaving Whiskey-Pete and a Missouri mare, which I had traded for, with a "fool hoe-man," five miles south of town, "Jingle-bob" Joe Hargraves and I started west across country to meet another herd of fat steers.

As the snow had begun to fly it was thought best to turn this herd towards Dodge City, Kansas—hence we being sent to pilot the outfit to Dodge City.

While on this lonely ride I came within an ace of "passing in my checks." We ran out of grub and for supper one night filled up on canned peaches, without anything else to eat with them. All night these juicy peaches held a war-dance in the pit of my stomach, and before daylight I was all in. "Jingle-bob" Joe wanted me to pray, but I told him that I would wait a little longer, in hopes that I might pull through.

Joe Hargraves was not much on the pray himself, but I believe he has a passport to heaven for one kindly act done the winter previous. He was on his way to Dodge City, over the Bascom trail, when he stopped for the night on the Cimarron River, where a short time previous a small store had been established.

The next morning a "fool hoe-man" and his hungry and ragged family drove up in a covered wagon drawn by two skinny ponies. They were half starved and didn't have a cent of money.

"Jingle-bob" Joe asked the store man what he would take for all the goods in his place. He set the price at $150.00, which was accepted. Then the goods were loaded into the "hoeman's" wagon, and he drove off singing "Home, Sweet Home". He was looking for a free home to settle on.

We finally found the steer outfit and turned them towards Dodge City. There the fat steers were put aboard two trains, and I took charge of one train, thus taking my second lesson in cow-punching, with a spiked pole and lantern.

As on the former trip the steers were unloaded across the Mississippi River from Burlington, Iowa, and fed.

In the city of Burlington we punchers were treated royally. None of the candy and ice-cream merchants would take a penny from us. Everything in that line was free.

On arriving in Chicago Mr. Beals met us. Then at the Palmer House Mr. Beals settled up my wage and expense account. With a few hundred dollars in my pocket I started out to see the sights again.

I had told Mr. Beals of my intention to quit his outfit and spend the winter in Southern Texas. He agreed that if I concluded to go back to work for the XL company in the spring, he would arrange for me to boss a herd of steers up the trail. Said he had already contracted with Charlie Word of Goliad, Texas, for two herds to be delivered on the LX Ranch.

A couple of days and nights sight-seeing put me almost "on the bum," financially. Then a train was boarded for Nickerson, Kansas.

Whiskey-Pete and the bay mare were found hog fat. The "fool hoe-man" had shoved corn to them with a scoop shovel.

After purchasing a pack-saddle, and some grub, I had just six dollars in cash left to make my eleven hundred mile journal down the Chisholm trail to the gulf coast of Texas.

Puck was not far off when he wrote: "What fools these mortals be." For here was a fool cowboy starting out to ride eleven hundred miles, just to be in the saddle, and to get a pony back home.

On the way down the trail I kept myself supplied with cash by swapping saddles, pack pony, watches, and running races with Whiskey-Pete, who was hard to beat in a three hundred yard race.

At one place in middle Texas I laid over a couple of days to rest my ponies, and to make a few dollars picking cotton.

One morning I was sent out by the farmer, with a bunch of bare-footed girls, to pick cotton in a field which had already been picked over. These young damsels gave me the "horse-laugh" for my awkwardness in picking the snowy balls of cotton.

When night came I had earned just thirty cents, while the girls had made more than a dollar each. This was my last stunt as a cotton picker.

On Pecan Creek, near Denton, I put up one night at the home of old man Murphy—the father of Jim Murphy, who was a member of the Sam Bass gang of train robbers, and whose name is mentioned in the Sam Bass song, which was a favorite with trail cowboys.

The old Chisholm trail was lined with negroes, headed for Topeka and Emporia, Kansas, to get a free farm and a span of mules from the state government.

Over my pack there was a large buffalo robe, and on my saddle hung a fine silver-mounted Winchester rifle. These attracted the attention of those green cotton-field negroes, who wore me out asking questions about them.

Some of these negroes were afoot, while others drove donkeys and oxen. The shiny black children and half-starved dogs were plentiful. Many of the outfits turned back when I told them of the cold blizzards and deep snow in Kansas.

My eleven hundred mile journey ended at the old Rancho Grande head-quarter ranch, after being on the trail one month and twelve days.

The balance of the winter was spent on hunting trips after deer and wild hogs, and visiting friends throughout the county of Matagorda.

Early in the spring I mounted Gotch, a pony traded for, and bidding Whiskey-Pete goodbye, he being left with my chum, Horace Yeamans, we headed for Goliad to meet Charlie Word. He was found near Beeville, thirty miles west of Goliad, putting up a herd of long-horn steers for the LX company. He had received a letter from Mr. David T. Beals telling him to put me in charge of one of the herds.

This first herd was to be bossed "up the trail" by Liash Stevens.

The outfit was up to their ankles in sticky mud, in a large round corral, putting the road-brand on the steers, when I found them. I pitched in and helped, and was soon covered with mud from head to feet. Each steer had to be roped and thrown afoot, which made it a disagreeable job in the cold drizzling rain. And to finish out the days work, after my thirty mile ride from Goliad, I stood guard over the steers until after midnight.

Mr. Word had just purchased a band of "wet" ponies from old Mexico, and I showed my skill in riding some of the wildest ones.

One large iron-grey gelding, which the Mexicans said was a man-killer, broke my cinchas and dumped me and the saddle into the mud. Then he pawed the saddle with his front feet until it was ruined. I had to buy a new saddle to finish breaking this man-killing broncho. But he proved to be a dandy cow pony when tamed.

After the herd had been road-branded and turned over to Mr. Stevens and his crew of trail cowboys, Charlie word asked me to help him get the herd started on the trail.

Our first night out proved a strenuous one. Mr. Stevens had taken a fool notion to arm his cowboys with bulls-eye lanterns, so that they could see the location of each other on dark nights. He had ordered a few extra ones and insisted on me trying one that night, which I did.

About ten o'clock a severe storm came up and we were all in the saddle ready for stampede.

While I was running at break-neck speed, to reach the lead of the herd, my pony went head over heels over a rail fence. The light from the lantern had blinded him, so that he failed to see it in time.

The pony was caught and mounted and the new-fangled bulls-eye lantern was left on the ground.

Strange to relate, this lantern is prized today as a souvenir of by-gone days. It was picked up next day by a young rancher, who, at this writing lives near Kingston, Sierra County, New Mexico.

I finally reached the lead of the herd, and from that time 'till day-light it was one stampede after another.

Daylight found young Glass and me alone with about half the herd of 3700 head. We were jammed into the foot of a lane, down which the cattle had drifted during the last hour of darkness.

This lane was built with five strands of new barbed wire, and was cut off by a cross fence. Here the herd was jammed together so tightly that it was impossible to ride to the rear.

There we had to wait and pray that another stampede wouldn't start while hemmed in on three sides by a high wire fence. A stampede would have, no doubt, sent us to the happy hunting ground.

It required two days hard work to gather up steers lost during the night. They had become mixed up with range cattle.

In that camp the price of bulls-eye lanterns took a tumble. It was almost impossible to give one away.

After the herd was strung out again on the trail I went to Goliad to meet Charlie Word.

Here he made up a crew of twelve riders, a cook and mess-wagon, with five ponies to the rider, and turned them over to me. With this crew I drifted northwesterly to the crooked-street, straggling town of San Antonio,—now one of the leading cities of Texas.

In San Antonio we had all of our ponies shod, as we were going into a rocky country.

When out of San Antonio about fifty miles a bucking broncho "busted" a blood vessel in my bread basket. Being in great misery, and unable to sit up straight in the saddle, I concluded to ride back to the Alamo City and consult that great German doctor, Herff. The crew were instructed to lay over until my return.

In San Antonio I made inquiry as to where Doctor Herff could be found.

Riding up to a large, old-fashioned, stone residence I found this noted doctor—more than ninety years of age—hoeing in his garden. He informed me that he had turned his practice over to his son.

I found Dr. Herff, Jr. living in a fine two-story stone mansion. He laid me on a couch and examined the seat of pain. He pronounced a blood vessel stretched out of shape, so that the blood was not flowing through it—hence the great pain.

He told me to go back to camp, and on rising every morning, for a couple of weeks, to drink all the water I could possibly hold, and then, immediately afterwards, to drink that much more. He said this was all the medicine I needed. His charge was fifty cents for the examination and advice.

The next morning after reaching camp I took a half-gallon coffee-pot down to the creek and filling it drank it empty. It seemed impossible to drink any more, but by a great effort the coffee pot was emptied again.

After the first morning it was no trick at all to drink a gallon of water at one siting.

In a few days I was completely cured, and the memory of Doctor Herff and his half-dollar fee will stay with me to the grave.

Now we continued the journey up the Llano River.

On reaching Kimble County we laid over in a new village called Junction City, now the prosperous seat of government of Kimble county, to load up our mess-wagon with grub, etc.

Farther up the river we came to the end of our journey, at the Joe, and Creed Taylor ranches. We established camp on Paint Creek, in a very rough, rocky country.

Charlie Word had bought 2500 head of cattle from Joe Taylor, and it was our duty to gather them from this range.

Mr. Creed Taylor had raised a son, "Buck" who was a reckless, daredevil. He was buried with his boots on—that is, shot and killed.

In the beginning of the '70s, around Quero, in Victoria County, Texas, a bloody feud raged between the Taylor and Sutton gangs.

In one of their bloody battles in the town of Quero, it was reported that nine men were killed.

About thirty-five years later I tried to obtain the truth of this report.

In the little city of Las Cruces, New Mexico, lives one of these noted feudists. He is a highly respected banker and cattle raiser. It is said that he lay in jail, on account of the Taylor-Sutton feud, seven long years before being freed by the higher courts.

About the year 1914 I happened to be in Las Cruces, and concluded to find out the truth about this bloody battle in Quero.

I was stopping at the Park Hotel, owned by the president of the First National Bank of that town. This gentleman had been brought up in the neighborhood of Quero, and believed the story was correct, about nine men being killed in one battle, when the Taylor and Sutton gangs met. This didn't satisfy me, so I told the gentleman that I was going to visit this noted feudist at his bank and find out the truth.

He advised me not to do it, as it would result in me being kicked out of the bank, if I mentioned the subject.

On walking into the feudist's bank, he met me with out-stretched hand, and conducted me to his private desk in the rear.

I introduced myself as an early day Texas cowboy who had worked for "Shangai" Pierce. He knew "Shanghai" well, and had much to say in his favor.

After we had talked about different subjects, I finally said: "Oh, by the way, is it true that there were nine men killed in Quero one night when the Taylor and Sutton crowds met?"

In all my long life I never saw a man change so suddenly from a smiling, good-natured man to a scowling demon. His black eyes shot sparks of fire and he straightened up in his chair, striking the desk with his fist, saying: "You bet it is true, we killed them knee-deep that night!"

Just then three men came into the bank and told him to hurry up, as they were waiting for him.

Here he begged my pardon for having to leave me, but he said he had to go out in the country to look at some cattle.

When he uttered the above expression I felt relieved, for it seemed that he was getting ready to kick me out of the bank.

I met the gentleman many times afterwards, but never alone, so as to renew the subject.

About the same time that the Taylor-Sutton feud was raging, there was another bloody feud being enacted in Jackson and Colorado counties, between the Stafford and Townsend gangs. "Tuck" Townsend was the leader on one side and Bob Stafford on the other.

Bob Stafford was a wealthy cattle owner, of Columbus, on the Colorado river.

Only a few of Bob Stafford's warmest friends knew the secret of how he became crippled in the left hand. It happened thus:

Stafford was riding along the road on a skittish horse. On the ground near by sat a twelve year old German boy eating his noonday lunch. Near by grazed his small band of sheep, which he was herding.

The boy's dog ran out and scared Mr. Stafford's mount. Then he drew his pistol and killed the dog.

Now the boy sprang to his feet, and pulling his powder and ball pistol, opened fire on Stafford, who at once began shooting at the boy. But his horse jumping around made his aim untrue.

Bob Stafford had emptied his pistol, while the boy had only shot twice, and was taking aim for the third shot.

Here Stafford threw up his right hand, which held the pistol, saying: "Don't shoot, I'm empty."

The boy replied: "Alright, load up." Then he squatted down on the ground, and taking his powder horn from his shoulder proceeded to load the two empty chambers of his six-shooter.

Stafford replied, as he rode away: "No, I've got enough!" He was wounded in the left hand from one of the boy's shots.

Later Mr. Stafford rewarded the boy for his cool bravery.

Now, on the Creed and Joe Taylor range, we began gathering 2500 head of wild cattle. It was the hardest job of my life, working from daylight 'till dark, and then standing night-guard half the night.

As a rule bosses don't stand guard at night, excepting when there is danger of a stampede. But in order to keep my crew in a good humor I took my regular turn. The boys were worn out, and were almost on the eve of striking, from having to work twenty-six hours out of every twenty-four, as they expressed it.

Finally we got the herd "broke in," and started "up the trail," but not "up the Chisholm trail," which lay to the eastward about 100 miles.

During that spring of 1880 the Chisholm trail was impassible for large herds, as "fool hoe-men" had squatted all over it, and were turning its hard packed surface into ribbons with plows.

When about fifty miles west of Ft. Worth, Charlie Word, who had come around by rail, drove out in a buggy to see how we were getting along, and to supply me with more expense money.

At Doan's store, on Red River, we found Liash Stevens waiting for us. We swapped herds, as it had been decided to drive the herd I was with up into Wyoming.

I arrived at the LX ranch with 3700 head of steers on the first day of July.

Now part of my crew were paid off, and with the balance, six riders, I took the herd onto the South Staked Plains to fatten the steers.

Shortly afterwards I rode into Tascosa, and saw the great changes which had taken place since my last visit, a year previous.

Now there were three saloons and two dance-halls running full blast. Also the foundation laid for a new Court House.

The county of Oldham, with Tascosa as the County-seat, had been organized, and twelve unorganized counties attached to Oldham County.

My cowboy friend, Cape Willingham, had been appointed sheriff of these thirteen counties.

One of the first things I did after riding into Tascosa was to step into Mr. Turner's restaurant to see his pretty daughter, Miss Victoria Turner. I was not hungry, but to have the pleasure of this pretty miss waiting on me I was ordering all the good things in the restaurant. Just then a gang of cowboys came charging through the main street shooting off pistols.

As this was no uncommon thing for a live cow-town, I didn't even get up from the table.

In a moment Sheriff Willingham came running into the cafe with a double-barrel shot-gun in his hand. He asked me to help him arrest some drunken cow-boys who had just dismounted and gone into Jack Ryan's saloon, near by.

Just as we reached the Ryan saloon these cowboys came out. One of them sprang onto his horse, when the sheriff told him to throw up his hands. Instead of throwing up his hands he drew his pistol. Then Willingham planted a charge of buckshot in his heart, and he tumbled to the ground dead.

The dead cowboy was the one the sheriff was after, as he had seen him empty his pistol at a flock of ducks, which a lady was feeding out of her hand, as she sat in a door-way.

In galloping down the street this cowboy remarked to his companions: "Watch me kill some of those ducks." He killed them alright, and the woman fainted.

These nine cowboys had just arrived "up the trail" with a herd of long-horn cattle, and were headed for the north. For fear they might make a raid on him that night, which they threatened to do, the sheriff had me stay with him till morning.

Thus did Tascosa bury her first man with his boots on, which gave her the reputation of being a genuine cow-town.

From now on Tascosa's "Boot-hill" cemetery began to show new-made graves. The largest killing in one night being six. At that time my cowboy friend, James H. East, now a well-to-do citizen of Douglas, Arizona, was sheriff. He held the office for four terms, and helped to lay many wild and wooly cowboys under the sod, with their boots on.

Before the court house and jail were finished Tascosa had a bad murder case to try. The District Judge, and attorney, came from Mobeta to try the case.

Jack Ryan was foreman of the jury, and the upstairs part of his saloon was selected as the jury room.

When the prisoner's case was finished the jury were locked up over the saloon.

About midnight Jack Ryan and some of the jury men were holding out for murder in the first degree.

About that time Frank James, Ryan's gambling partner, got a ladder and climbed up to the outside window of the jury-room. He then called for Ryan, and told him that there was a big poker game going on in the saloon, and that he needed $300.00.

Jack gave him the money from the bank-roll, which he carried in his pocket, at the same time telling him to keep the game going until he could get down there, and take a hand.

Now Ryan called the jury men together and told them about the big poker game down in the saloon. He said it was necessary for him to be there and help

Frank James out—hence he had come to the conclusion that the prisoner was innocent, and had no evil intentions of murdering his victim.

In a few moments Ryan had the few stubborn jury-men on his side, and the prisoner was declared innocent. At least this is the story told to me by men who claimed to know the facts of the case. This added another laurel to Tascosa's brow as a wide-open cow-town.

The following year Tascosa put on city airs by the arrival of a young lawyer by the name of Lucius Dills, who hung out a shingle as Attorney at Law.

During that fall the first election of Oldham County was held and Mr. Dills was elected the first County Judge. He was appointed District Attorney for the whole Panhandle district, comprising twenty-four counties, before his term as judge expired. Then he tore down his shingle as Attorney at Law, and moved to Mobeta, thus Tascosa lost her first lawyer.

In the spring of 1885 Mr. Lucius Dills quit the Panhandle country and moved to Lincoln County, New Mexico, finally setting down in Roswell as editor of the Roswell Record. Here he married the lovely daughter of Judge Frank Lea, Miss Gertrude, and at the present writing has two pretty daughters. He is now Surveyor General for the State of New Mexico, and lives in Santa Fe, where his friends are counted by the hundreds.

STYLE ON THE RANCH

W. S. JAMES

If there is any one thing that has engaged the mind of the majority of the human family more than another in the past, it is the question of their personal appearance and style or fashion has been as changeable as Texas weather, and I dare say the locality and peculiar people that never change style are the exception. If one should wish to know anything about the rural districts of Old Mexico, they would have to go back four or five thousand years and read in Genesis, but only give them time and they too will change.

In the mountains of eastern Tennessee and the swamps of Louisiana and Arkansas, as well as the piney woods of eastern Texas, they have changed from the old flint-lock to the cap and ball gun, and some of them have quit making their own clothing and wear store clothes, because it is stylish now to wear brown duck instead of "jeans." The cow-boy is no exception to the rule. He has his flights of fancy as clearly defined as the most fashionable French belle.

In 1867, I remember distinctly the style that prevailed, flowing toefenders, narrow stirrup, and the rider stood on his toe. The saddle at that time was almost anything that could be had, but preferably the broad horn standing at an angle of forty-five degrees, pointing heavenward. The bridle was hardly to be called a creation of fancy, as it was all they had, and was made from the hide of a cow, rubbed and grained until it was pliable.

Some men broke the monotony by adopting the Mexican plan of making them of hair, which was a very popular article of which to make ropes. Some made their bridles of rawhide by platting, which made quite an artistic one, some would plait the quirt on the end of the rein. The rope used for catching and handling horses and cattle was a platted one and was one of the best ropes for the purpose I ever used. I have seen a few ropes that were very good, made of rawhide, of three strands twisted and run together. In fact, during, and for several years after the war, long after reconstruction days in Texas, it was said—and not without some foundation—that a Texan could take a butcher knife and rawhide and make a steamboat, of course he could not have made the boiler, but when it came to the top part he would have been at home. One thing certain, if the thing had broken to pieces, he could have tied it up.

During the war his clothing was made from homespun cloth, he had no other, home-made shoes or boots, even his hat was home-made, the favorite hat material being straw. Rye straw was the best. Sometimes a fellow would get hold of a Mexican hat, and then he was sailing.

The popular way for protecting the clothing, was to make a leather cap for the knee and seat of the pants, the more enterprising would make leggins of calf-skin, hair out, and sometimes buckskin with fringe down the side.

By 1872 most everything on the ranch had undergone a change, even some of the boys had changed their range headquarters for sunnier climes, because they had to, some had sold out to a lawyer and had taken a contract from the State; others had changed their spurs and leggins for a crown, harp and wings, and gone to pastures green, perhaps. But especially had style changed, the wool hat, the leather leggins, leather bridle and the broad stirrup; the invention of an old fellow who lived on the Llano river had become so popular that one who was not provided with them was not in the style.

The stirrup was from six to eight inches broad, and the rider drew his leathers so as to ride with legs crooked up considerably. The saddle used was one with a broad flat horn, much higher in front than behind, adorned with saddle pockets, covered with either goat or bear skin. The spur too was another article that changed, the long shank with bells had taken the place of the little straight shank and sharp rowel, the long ones making a curve downward and having long teeth rowel. In this age of the cow-man they wore buckskin gloves with long gauntlets.

The style changed again by '77. The John B. Stetson hat with a deeper crown and not so broad a rim, and the ten-ounce hat took the cake. Up to this date, the high-heeled boots were the rage, and when it was possible to have them, the heel was made to stand under the foot, for what reason I never knew, unless it was the same motive that prompts the girls to wear the opera heel in order to make a small track, thus leaving the impression that a number ten was only a six, this I am guessing at and will leave it open for the reader to draw to. By the last named date, '77 or '78, the cow-man had in many places adopted the box-toed boot with sensible heels, and the California saddle was taking the place of all others. This was an extremely heavy saddle, with a small horn but very strong and the most comfortable saddle to be found for steady use, and as a rule, the easiest one on a horse.

There was another saddle, a Texas production, closely allied to the Bucharia, but not so heavy, that was, and is to this day, a very popular saddle. The slicker and tarpaulin were two of the most valuable accessions to the cow-man's outfit that ever came into the business. They were made of good cotton stuff, and a preparation of linseed oil filled every pore so completely that they were as thoroughly waterproof as a shingle roof, and became the cow-boy's right bower.

A cow-boy's outfit is never complete except he has a good supply of hopples on hand. After sea-grass ropes became so plentiful and cheap, the good old rawhide hopples and platted lariettes were relegated to the rear, and if the cow-pony could talk, unless he was a good, religious pony, he would curse the day when sea-grass hopples were introduced. His feelings toward the inventor of that article would be something like those of the native toward the barbed-wire manufacturer, for the poor little fellows sometimes wore a very sore pair of legs by the use of the strand of a rope for a hopple.

There has been much said about pack-ponies, and that method of working a range, by taking the grub on a pack. Some very amusing things will occur with the pack. I remember once, while driving through Waco, the pack-pony became a little unruly, and was running up and down street after street, when the pack slipped and turned under. This put the little gentlemen to kicking. The result was that flour, bacon, beans, tincups and plates, coffee-pot, sugar, onions and bedding were strewn over about five acres of ground. Some of the boys suggested that we hire the ground broke and harrowed before it rained and thus secure a good crop of grub.

The pack-pony was very handy, but the greatest trouble of any one thing in the outfit, and it was the most cruel thing imaginable to fasten the pack on so as to make it secure, even with a saddle, and fasten it well, let the pony or donkey, as the case might be, run into a pond of water and get the ropes wet; it was terrible on him. When an outfit had to resort to a pack, they usually hired their bread made, or made it sometimes, when they couldn't find a woman, not infrequently making it up in the mouth of the sack, and if they had no skillet would either fry it or cook it hoe-cake fashion, but I have seen it cooked by rolling the dough round a stick and holding it over the fire, turning it until cooked.

The change in the styles of saddles brought the change, also, in the stirrup. Since '78, and the introduction of the California saddle, the narrow stirrup has been used, and has been found to be the most comfortable. The change in position of the legs, too, accompanied this change in the fashion. The foot is thrust through the stirrup until the stirrup rests in the hollow of the foot, or the foot rests thus in the stirrup, just as you like, and when the rider sits in his saddle the straps are lengthened so as to let him rest his weight just comfortably in the stirrup, while at the same time he is not removed from the saddle-seat.

It has been fully demonstrated that the man who rides thus, and sits straight on his horse, is capable of riding farther, and with less fatigue to himself and his horse, than one who is all the time changing.

The methods of handling cattle change as well as the paraphernalia. I remember it was a rare thing ever to see a man branding cattle on horseback. If they did, they usually threw the rope on the animal's head, and then tied them to a tree and heeled them, or threw the rope round their hind legs and simply stretched them out. In branding yearlings or calves on the range, they would make a run, toss the tug on the animal; one man would hold while another would dismount, catch it by the tail, jerk it down, draw its tail between its hind legs, place his knee against its back while it would be lying on its side, and thus hold it while the first man would brand and mark it. In the way described above, one man could hold the largest animal on the range, if he understood his business. Range-branding was a very popular method of branding mavericks. The necessary outfit usually was a sharp knife, a straight bar and half circle; the ring end of a wagon-rod, or common iron rings, were good. In the case of using rings, one needed a pair of pincers. However, one used to such work could very successfully run a brand with them by using a couple of sticks, with which to hold them.

For many years, however, the custom was to drive the cattle to some pen, many of which were located over each range, and then brand up all those that belonged to any one in the outfit, or those they knew and sometimes a miracle would be performed by branding all those left in the brand of the cows they followed, and if any were left whose owner was not known, and was too old to claim a mother, they were—well, I can't exactly say, as I was not always by, but usually those whose mothers were strays were turned out and left to run until they were too old to be known. In after years they were usually dealt with differently.

The style changed to catching cattle as well as horses by the front feet or fore feet, as we called them, which was a much better method of throwing them.

The horse when roped by the head if wild, will choke himself down and the best method of holding him when once down is to take him by the ear with one hand, nose with the other. To illustrate, if the horse falls on his left side you want to take hold of his ear with your right hand and nose with the left hand, raising it until his mouth is at an angle of forty five degrees, placing one knee on his neck near his head. In this way a small man can hold a large horse on the ground.

The difference in holding a horse and cow down is that you must hold the horse's front legs or head on the ground because he never gets up behind first but throws his front feet out and then gets up: the cow on the contrary gets up directly the reverse, gets up on her hind feet first, therefore you must hold her down by the tail. The horse is easily choked down but it is almost an impossibility to choke a cow down. It is a noted fact that a colt that is handled when sucking, being staked and becoming used to a rope between the time he is two months and a year old, is never very wild. He may be hard to drive when allowed to run with wild horses but when once in hand is easily managed. The cow on the other hand may be raised perfectly gentle and if allowed to run out and become wild, may become the most vicious of any other.

Speaking of the method of holding cattle and horses down calls to mind a little incident that came under my observation. A cattleman employed a Swede who was a very stout fellow, he was as willing as he was green, and was green enough to make up for all his other virtues. This cattleman was not over-sensitive about what another had to perform. One day they roped a wild horse of good size and when they choked him until he fell to the ground, the cow-man called to the Swede "Jump on his head," meaning, of course, for him to catch the horse as before described but instead of that the ignorant fellow jumped right astride the horse's head and the rope being slacked the horse made a lunge and threw the poor fellow his length on the ground and ran over him. It seemed a miracle if he came out alive but he only received a few bruises.

At another time when handling a bad cow, the same parties being engaged, the cow made a run at the Swede when his boss called him to catch her by the horns which he did and the cow simply lifted him a double somersault over her back. He eventually got tired and quit the cattle business, went to farming and as a good story book would say, "did well and lived happy ever afterward."

Those who think the cow-boy is not stylish simply let them hunt him up, study his character, note his fancy, and while it is true that like poor Yorick of old he is "a fellow of infinite jest, of most peculiar fancy," still he is stylish after a fashion of his own.

To say that any law of fashion does or could wield an influence over him, I think, would be a mistake. I don't think one could be induced to wear a plug hat. If he did at all it would be for the novelty of the thing. If you see him in New York or Chicago you see him wearing the same sort of hat and boots he wears at home.

He is looked upon by some as a law breaker. It is true in some cases, but is it not equally true of all classes? I maintain that it is not more universal with this than any other class of men in any one vocation of life. It may be a little more out-breaking but of the same kind. His wild free range and constant association with nature and natural things makes him more sensitive to restraint than he otherwise would be. Under the influences of a free wild life he has grown to be self-reliant and like Davie Crocket, "he asks no favors and shuns no responsibilities;" he, however, measures his responsibilities by rule of his own construction which is oftener the outgrowth of personal inclination than a well balanced consciousness of moral responsibility, like his brother of more favorable surroundings who is prone to reject the moral teaching of God's word and fall back for a refuge to the unreliable guidance of conscience; when this moral guide has been so educated as to be like the material of which he makes his hopples which, by a little dampening and working becomes pliable, has a tendency to stretch and thus meet the demands of its environments.

The cow-boy's outfit of clothing, as a rule, is of the very best from hat to boots, he may not have a dollar in the world, but he will wear good, substantial clothing, even if he has to buy it on a credit, and he usually has plenty of that,

that is good. I once heard a minister in a little Northern town, in using the cow-boy as an illustration, say "The cow-boy with an eighteen dollar hat and a two dollar suit of clothing is as happy as a king on his throne," or words to that effect.

With those who knew no better the illustration perhaps held good, but to a crowd of the boys it would have been very ridiculous and amusing. In fact extravagance is one of the cow-boy's failing. The inventory of his wardrobe could be very correctly summed up as follows: Hat, five to ten dollars; pants, five to ten dollars; coat and vest, from eight to twenty dollars; overshirt, from three to five dollars, and everything else to match. They may be cheated in buying, but are never beat by the same man the second time, they at least think they are getting the best, and always make the best of their bargain.

The days of free grass are gone. If you wish to arouse recollections of by-gones that will make the old timer in the cattle business heave a sigh of regret, just mention the good old days of free range when the grass was as free as the air they breathed and when the "Wo hau come" of the horny handed son of the granger was never heard in the sacred precincts of the land of free grass and water.

The man who came to Texas when the wild cayote and the lion of the tribe of Mexico were his most intimate neighbors, when the hiss of the rattle-snake and the unearthly yell of the panther were by far the most familiar sounds to his ear, and after years of toil and scratching shins, breaking the briers mixed with fighting the blood-thirsty savage thief, the red child of the desert, is it strange that he should think it an infringement on his natural rights for people to come in and begin to plow up the land, thus limiting his cattle range? He had enjoyed this unalloyed bliss of living as "monarch of all he surveyed" so long that he felt almost as though it was his by the statute of limitation.

There was never any contention worth naming among the cattle men. It is true they didn't wish to be crowded. In illustration of their ideas of what that meant I recite a little incident in connection with one of the old residenters. He lived out perhaps a hundred miles from our little country town and seventy-five miles from the nearest trading point except the government post. While down in the settlement with his teams after bread my grandfather asked him how he was getting on. "Very well, very well, thank you, Bill. I've got to move, though." "Why?" said grandfather. "O, because they are crowding me out there, the nest-ers are settling all 'round me and I will not be crowded. One of the impudent varmints has settled right down in my back yard."

Upon close inquiry we found the location of the obnoxious nester referred to, to be twenty-eight miles below him on the opposite side of the river. Of course, it was more of a jest than earnest; the real fact, however, is there were none who enjoyed the presence of the nester, he was held in somewhat the same contempt that a physician of the old school looks upon patent medicine men, or a sheep-man would a wolf.

The cattlemen looked upon the country as being fit for nothing but pasture and the man that presumed to squat down and attempt to dig his living out of the ground by the sweat of his brow as being in very small business. In fact they went on the principle that they had put no grubs in the ground and didn't propose to take any out and, as I once heard a cow man say, that "God had discriminated in favor of the stock man when he had respect unto Abel in his offering and despised the offering of Cain, consequently the cattleman had a right to his range." This gentleman reminds one very much of the theologians of today who simply construe God's word to mean that which meets the demands of their own inclination. This is clearly proven by their antagonism of the sheep-man a few years later. Of all the despicable characters to the cattlemen it was the sheep-man. They then quoted the passage portraying the churlishness of Nabal, the son of folly, and fain would assume the character of an insulted and outraged David and further would have wiped him off the face of the earth with all his coolies but for the reconciling influences of "Abigal," though not so graciously polite as the Abigal of old, yet quite as effective, the great strong arm of the law.

One discrimination this modern Abigal made, however, and that was the sheep-man must keep his stock on his own land while the "King of the Kow" was allowed to turn his cattle loose to roam at will. As there is not an event in history without its forerunner or prophecy so the coming of the sheep-man and the attending results was a prophecy of the eventual downfall of the reign of free grass, and if one will stop and think for a moment, as some men did think, it was an inevitable result, the discrimination against the sheep-man in favor of the cow-puncher was enough to bring it about.

The snoozer was not allowed to herd or turn his sheep loose on the range that he didn't own. The cow-man could with impunity locate on the line of the sheep-man's range, though the snoozer owned his miles of range, the cattle of a dozen ranches were allowed to roam at will on his land. This would naturally drive him to fence. Other sheep-men seeing the prosperity of one would come in and buy up large tracts of land and say to Mr. cow-puncher "move your ranch;" then he "had to" and in order to protect himself he was forced to buy or lease and fence. So the ball began to roll and accumulate until the trouble precipitated between the pasture men and the free grass fellows.

The weather class, of course, could buy up larger tracts and lease more land than the little fellow, and when it once began to be a fixed rule for each man to get all he could and keep all he had, the demon of avarice that goes to make up the leaven of so many of our lives, stepped in as the initiator of schemes for swindling and prompted many men to buy up and lease land on all sides of large bodies of individual property that was not likely for years to be molested, fence all together and thus utilize thousands of acres of land that they had no right to.

This had the natural tendency to bring out all the rough points of antagonism in the little fellow, who was thus cheated out of what he conceived to be his legitimate heritage, and the consequence was that he bought a pair of nippers and went to cutting or hired some enterprising fellow to do it for him.

There was at one time a law passed in favor of the cattleman, allowing one man to take up seven sections of State school land on certain conditions, giving a certain time in which to pay it out. A cattleman of means would take up seven sections and then have as many of his hands as he wished to take seven sections each, and thus enable one man to control whole counties. This brought about a state of affairs that culminated in the repeal of that law and the passage of a new one allowing but one section to each man and opening all land to actual settlers, not leased or legitimately held by former claimants; this resulted in a more relentless war between the big pasture men and the squatter, or the man with the hoe, than had ever been waged between any two classes in the state, making litigation almost endless and causing the larger cattle owners to combine, forming cattle companies and syndicates sufficiently powerful to crush out of existence the smaller frey.

The advent of barbed wire into Texas brought with it a reign of lawlessness and terror, such as has no parallel in the State's eventful history.

Then there were decidedly two classes, free grass and pasture men, and never in any land has there been greater bitterness and eternal hatred than existed between those two factions. It was to be heard on the range, at home 'round the fireside, in the courts, in the legislative halls, every election was carried or lost on this issue, the best men of the country were on one or the other side of this question. If a man was a pasture man, he was favoring the wealthy, when in reality neither charge was necessarily true. It is useless for me to enter into the arguments on the two sides of the question as it has been thoroughly "cussed and discussed" by writers better qualified than I am to do the subject justice, besides it is not my object to deal in theory but facts, and this I shall do as far as in me lies.

From my knowledge of the true state of affairs wire-cutting was merely another or new form of mob law; the beginning of such work was, to some who never stopped to reason, a justifiable act of self-defense, but to a thinking man lawlessness is never justifiable.

An outraged community unable to bring to justice a known criminal, takes the law into its own hands and metes out to the offender summary punishment; they argue that "this is the only way to deal with him" never looking to their own crime. If a man is hanged without a trial, the perpetrators in the eyes of the law are murderers and instead of lessening crime they have increased the criminal class. A man fenced up land he had no legal right to, he was criminal; his neighbors band together and cut his fence and there are more criminals.

The first thing that especially aroused the indignation of the stockman relative to barbed wire was the terrible destruction to stock caused from being torn first on the wire, and the screw worm doing the rest—this was especially the case with horses. When the first fences were made, the cattle never having had experience with it, would run full till right into it and many of them got badly hurt, and when one got a scratch sufficient to draw the blood, the worms would take hold of it. Some man would come into a range, where the stock had regular rounds or beaten way, and fence up several hundred acres right across the range and thus endanger thousands of cattle and horses. After the first three years of wire fences, I have seen horses and cattle that could hardly drive between two posts, and if there was a line of posts running across the prairie, I have seen a bunch of range horses follow the line out to the end and then turn, but in a few years the old tough hided cow found a way to crawl through into a cornfield if the wire was not well stretched and the posts close together. The man who had horses cut up and killed by the wire, often felt like cutting it down all of it, and in many instances did; but like every other class of lawlessness it ran to extremes and before it had gotten very far, was taken up by the more vicious, and such a time one would hardly dream of, who has never had the misfortune to witness it. It became so common that whole pastures would fall in one night and it made no difference who owned them, the presence of the dread enemy was sufficient evidence, and down she came. The men who cut the wire with a very few exceptions were men who owned but few if any horses or cattle; many of them owned nothing at all, they came out to find room and grass and that class was the most rabid of all others.

I once met one of those fellows, who was working a little East Texas dogy stag and a little bull to an old human wagon (wood axle). He had seven dogs, nine children, a wife, a cob pipe and a roll of home-spun tobacco stuck down in his hip pocket. I mean the tobacco was in his pocket—not the family. I asked him where he was from: "I am from Arkansaw, Whoa Bully." "Where are you going?" "Going West to find grass and room. Ike-lep." He was a regular copperas-breeches and one-gallus sort of a character; had just as soon live as to die; fight one man as two, and would spend more time twisting a rabbit out of a hollow tree than he would to secure a shelter for his family in time of a storm. He could afford to have one or two children blown away, but rabbits were too scarce to take the chances on losing one.

There would seem to be some excuse for the man who had stock injured by the wire, but for the man who had nothing on earth to lose or gain, who just did it from pure unadulterated cussedness there can be no mitigation of his crime. Doubtless many good men for the lack of better judgment on the impulse of the moment, when they came face to face with the evidence of their loss were led to cut fences, but the cutting offences made them no better citizens, but had the direct tendency to lead them into other evils. "Evil communications corrupt good manners." One starts out down the stream of wrongdoing, and soon he finds its water growing deeper, the cause being that every little rivulet of evil wends it way on downward to the River of Crime and the man who once allows himself launched upon this dangerous stream is too apt to drift with the tide of evil, until at last he is disrobed of his power to battle with the awful current, and is help-lessly swept out into the whirlpool of ruin, irretrievably sinking at last into the ocean of eternity, where he receives his wages for "The wages of sin is death."

The legislature eventually made it a felony to cut a fence, with punish-ment at "State Contract." Many men, both good and bad, lost their lives in the conflict and a bitterness engendered of neighbor against neighbor that will tend to chill the blood of good citizenship for years to come. Free grass has gone and nothing to show for its usefulness but the fact that the country was opened and the way made possible for our present development and growth, by men who had iron nerve and will to brave the difficulties of a frontier life, all for the ben-efits offered by free range, and that, that was good.

Suffice to say that the old fellows who came, saw and conquered, were not the wire cutters, and, to their credit be it said, almost to a man they condemned it. I mean the older settlers, those men who came in the early days and carved out of the wilderness a home for themselves. Many of the dear old "diamonds in the rough" have gone to answer the summons of the great pioneer of the universe and those who are still with us and witnessing the advancement of civilization as a rule are not appropriating to themselves the credit due them for the patient toil and hardships that have given to many a poor man a home in the land of milk and honey, and very few of those who are enjoying the fruits of their labors properly appreciate their real worth, plodding along as they do their chief occupation gone, often looking as they do with an eye of longing toward the setting sun that so often in early life marked the course of their journey, taking delight in nothing now so much as the privilege of recounting their experiences of more exciting times.

But some day the eye that was so keen to discover the presence of his inveterate foe, the red man, and draw so fine a bead along the barrel of an old "Human rifle" as to make it extremely unhealthy for the varmint or game that came within the range of his trusty piece, that eye will look for the last time upon the accoutrements that were once his trusty companions in the times that tried men's hearts, and then the soul will take its place in the phantom bark that will bear it across the River of Death to the "better shores of the spiritland," where there will be no more heartaches, no more Indians to encounter in deadly strife, no more wild beasts to trouble the peacefulness of that home of delight, no more struggles between free grass advocates and pasture men.

Nearly all of the old frontiersmen of my knowledge are soldiers of King Emanuel, many of those who took part in the struggles recorded in this chapter have since laid down the sword and taken up the cross, many of the thoughtless youths who were led into lawlessness are now living in a way that bids fair to render them useful. Let us hope that the gospel of peace will yet reach many more who are yet on the "broad trail," may be as a pointer to the herd, may be as a common hustler keeping up the drags fet on the "broad trail" that leads to eternal condemnation, for "Wide is the gate and broad the way that leads to destruction and many there be which go in thereat."

Yes, the great free grass struggles are over, the people have as a rule buried the tomahawk. Barbed wire, like the Johnson grass, came to stay, and the people of Texas have decided to make it a blessing instead of wrestling with it. It is bad medicine when a fellow fools with it, and no sadder plight can be imagined than one in which a man is described as being between a mad Texas steer and a good wire fence the only thing possible for him to do is to drop to the ground and roll under, leaving the steer to interview the fence.

The experience of the free grass men wrestling with barbed wire reminds me of a story told on an old frontiersman which occurred in an early day. He lived out on the Colorado river not far from the mouth of the Concho. While out hunting one day with one or two of his boys, they became separated and were on opposite sides of the creek, the water hole, unfortunately, was swimming for some distance up and down from where they were, the old gentleman discovered a young wildcat, and it being small, he decided to take it prisoner, so he caught it, but it was large enough to make him regret the rash act, so he decided to turn the thing loose, but when he pulled its fore feet loose, it would catch him with its hind feet, it was simply making sausage meat of him, when he called for help. His boy ran down to the bank opposite to where he was and being unable to reach him called out to know what the trouble was. "I have caught a wildcat and it is tearing me all to pieces," said the father. "Turn it loose," said the boy. "Turn it loose that is just what I have been trying to do," said the father, "but I can't turn it loose." So with the wire cutter, he caught a wildcat and could not turn it loose.

I shall never forget the first wire fence I ever saw. I took a trip to Fannin county with my grandfather to buy some cow horses. While passing through Tarrant county we stopped near his old ranch on Deer Creek to see about some stock horses of his that ranged near the old place. While there, I saw a horse that had been cut across the knee, and we were told that the wire fence we had just passed was the cause. When I saw a barbed-wire machine at work manufacturing it and was told that there were thousands of them at the same work, I went home and told the boys they might just as well put up their cutters and quit splitting rails and use barbed-wire instead. I was as confident than as I am to-day that wire would win and just as confident when we landed the first train-load of cattle at Forth Worth, Texas, that between wire and railroads the cow-boy's days were numbered, as I am that he is now almost a thing of the past.

SOME PRANKS

BOB KENNON

When i was stock inspector, I had to pass on a bunch of horses that were being shipped from Square Butte to the Miles City yards. It so happened that these horses got loose from the riders and got over into the brakes and badlands. We had to ride out and hunt them down and then rope them. We necked a wild one with a gentle one to drive them in. Finally we got them loaded for Miles City and saw them pull out. We were a happy bunch after fighting those jugheads for several days. One of the owners gave me a twenty-dollar bill to treat the fellows.

Two fellows ran a saloon there in Square Butte. They called it Bob and Jack's Place. It wasn't much and had a floor made of two-by-fours with a cellar below in which they stored the jugs and bottles of booze. We got pretty drunk celebrating and I noticed that an old farmer had tied a big work horse outside at the hitchrail. This gave me an idea. I went out, got on this plug, and rode him into the saloon onto those two-by-four floor boards. Bob and Jack were so sore they went after the town marshal. When he came, I was sitting out in the middle of the street. "I'm after you," yelled this marshal when he got within about thirty feet of me.

I fired a shot or two over his head, and he began to run. The faster I shot, the faster he ran for home, and the neighbors said that when he got there he locked himself in. He sent his wife downtown two days later to see if I'd left town. The bartenders told her I'd gone back to Fort Benton. He then very bravely went about town and said he'd arrest me if I ever returned. He made this boast in the presence of a crowd in this same saloon, but some wise guy laughed and said: "If ever you do arrest him, it'll have to be on the run."

One day in the early spring we heard about a big dance being planned down on Highwood Creek. After the long winter, George Jeffries and I felt like going over and making a night of it. The dances in Highwood Valley always were a lot of fun, as the people came from far and near to attend them. They were noted for the wonderful suppers and for the pretty girls. Sometimes a good-looking schoolmarm would cause a big stir and give us the thrill of dancing with her. The word went out that there was to be a prize given the best-looking man and one for the prettiest girl.

We were over on Arrow Creek at the time and it would be a sixty-mile ride into Highwood Valley. We rode hard, but were late, as the music was pouring forth from the open windows and the dancers were having a good time when we got there. The yard was filled with top buggies, wagons, saddle horses, buckboards, and all sorts of ranch vehicles. We were getting off our horses when some friends yelled to us: "Hello, Kickin'! Hurry up! They're goin' to give out the prizes soon!"

We got into the big log hall and found it jammed with people all clapping and laughing. Pretty soon, George, who had sandy-red hair and freckles, was called up by the prettiest gal in the whole room. She presented him with a beautiful cake, all frosted and fixed up fancy. It was his prize, but being so flustered and embarrassed, he laid it back on the table. The rest of the night was spent eating a wonderful chicken supper, with cake and all the fixin's.

The party broke up at daylight, and George got his cake, put it in the box, and we saddled for our trip home. We planned to eat the cake when we got hungry along the road to the Arrow Creek Ranch. It was getting on toward midmorning when we decided to get off the horses at a small creek, water them, and eat some of the cake. Our mouths were just watering as George took the box of cake out of the flour sack in which he had been carrying it behind the cantle of his saddle.

I got out my pocketknife and cut two big slices while George was getting some water from the creek above the saddle horses. As I cut into the cake I found a slip of paper, but paid no attention, just tossing it off on the grass.

George came up, grabbed his piece of cake, and took an enormous bite. He let out a yell, then almost strangled as he gulped down some water.

"God-a-mighty! Taste that cake, Kickin'," he said with his eyes watering and his tongue burning.

I did, and found that the frosting was made with salt instead of sugar. Then I remembered the paper, and picking it up, I read: "First prize for April Fool."

Just then we realized that last night had been the first of April.

Once I was repping for the P Lazy N outfit and we were just about finished with the shipping of the beef at Big Sandy. At this time, over by the stockyards, there were some women's tipis which belonged to a bunch of dames who had come down from Great Falls. We called these gals "tipi gals." They were there to get all the boys' pay, as we were paid off here. Everyone was drunk the night we finished and still celebrating the next day. McNamara and Marlow just about owned the TL outfit and they had a foreman named Sam Miller. A pal of mine named Harry was with me and he was a devil for pranks. We were up to our usual tricks on each other, and just dying to get a good joke on Miller. We watched to see if he would go into one of these tents by the stockyards. We were riding around roping everything in sight when Harry spied old Sam go into one of these tents. They were strongly made, with double doors which could be locked from inside or outside.

"Get your rope, Bob," yelled Harry.

We roped and dragged out this tent, and down the street we went. Now old Sam had no chance to get out those doors, and besides, they were on the ground side.

Ike Rogers was then running a saloon in Sandy, and he came out betting on who was in that tipi. He was followed by a bunch of yelling, whooping cowboys, who were now wilder than Indians. This brought McNamara himself out of his store to see what was going on. When we got down in front of his store, we stopped and took the rope from the tent and old Sam came crawling out just madder than hell. He swore to kill us sure. What made it worse was the fact that this woman came crawling out after him, looking like a porcupine. McNamara's face was purple with rage. "You're fired, you s.o.b.!" he yelled. "You ain't no foreman of mine."

When we got the cattle shipped out, we went back to the P Lazy N. We had a lot of fire-water along with us even when we got to the home ranch. The boys were sure feeling wild and reckless, and were just about ready to pull off any kind of stunt. The ranch house itself was made of rock, and on one of the walls in the dining room hung a big photograph of the owner's former ranch and a big herd of cattle. He prized it highly. He also had another article which he valued very much, an old buffalo gun which always stood in the corner.

It's a coincidence that this old buffalo gun had formerly belonged to John Madden, an uncle of my wife, Marie. This old gun hadn't been fired for years, but was loaded just the same. Unfortunately, I picked it up and pulled the trigger. The bullet took out the picture and a square block of rock from the wall.

After I had done this damage I said I would go see Mr. Norris. Now when you went into his office from the store, you had to step down. I missed the step and went headlong and hit Mr. Norris in the belly with my head. "Drunk again" was all he could say.

Bill Norris was half-owner of a ranch on the Judith River. One time Bill and I were subpoenaed as witnesses in a shooting scrape which took place on the Judith, so we had to take the stagecoach at Claggett to Big Sandy, then go on to Fort Benton the next morning. It was necessary to stay overnight in Big Sandy and we put up at the old Spokane House. This was a two-story log building, and a deathtrap for cowpunchers who came in late or were lit up.

Next morning I got up quite early, long before Bill was astir, and I couldn't for the life of me remember just how I got up to my room the night before. Instead of turning left when I came out of my room, I turned right. Then I saw a door, opened it, and stepped out quickly. Straight down I went, seven or eight feet, landing right in front of the barroom door. It was a wonder I didn't break a leg or so. I gave a bloodcurdling yell when I took off toward the ground. The bartender heard me and came out.

"What the hell you practicin' for? The circus?" he yelled.

When I'd picked myself up and found I was still whole, Bill came running down, tripping over his pants and with his suspenders down.

"Why the devil don't you fix them steps," he raged.

"They been that way for years, and we ain't aimin' to fix any new ones—too damned much work."

I remember an incident which happened down at Suffolk, on the Milwaukee Railroad, where we liked to camp for the spring roundup. The Circle

C, the 2 Bar, which was Frank Stevens' outfit, and the 72 Bar—all these brands were represented here. The P Lazy N had a foreman named Milsap, Horace Brewster was there for the Circle C, Frank Stevens for the 2 Bar, and Hamilton for the 72 Bar.

For three springs in a row a very odd thing had taken place here. Three men, all from the Circle C, had died, one each year, when we had camped here at Dog Creek. One died in his sleep, one was dragged to death by his horse, and one had his neck broken in a fall over a cliff. Brewster was more than a little annoyed and couldn't seem to understand it any more than we could.

We had been coming in all day, the different reps and cow-punchers, but still no Brewster. Along about sundown I saw the Circle C outfit pull in way up on a hill some distance from the rest of us, so I decided to ride up there and ask some questions. Old Horace didn't take kindly to my joking, and got a little huffy when I asked him what he was doing up on this hill. "Hell, Bob," he said, "Coburn ain't aimin' to start no private cemetery down in that coulee."

Brewster was a very superstitious man. He was the man, when foreman of the roundup on the Judith in 1881, who gave Charlie Russell his first job as horse wrangler.

At another time when this same wagon boss, Horace Brewster, was still at the Circle C, we started taking a herd across the Missouri at Rocky Point. It was in the fall of the year and they were to be put over on the north side for the winter range. Then in the spring we would throw the cattle on the south side of the river again.

Coburn, owner of the Circle C, had a breed fellow who spoke only broken French and English and was called Parley Voo by all the boys. If he had any real name I never heard it, but he was a good fellow and helped the cook, did errands, and such. At this particular time, Bill Coburn was with us and was working the cattle not too far from me. I looked back and there crossing with the steers was this young breed Parley Voo. I tell you I was about to faint, for he was already up to his waist in water and we were sure getting into some real swimming water.

I yelled to Bill and pointed to Parley Voo, but Bill couldn't hear me or see this fellow. Somehow we got that breed across, but I just knew something awful was happening to him. We got over and I rode back on the bank of the stream and saw Parley Voo wringing out his pants and grinning. Bill rode up then, too, and we gave him the devil for this stunt. "I not drown—I got the gum boots on," he kept reminding us.

An Indian boy rode with us that day and remembered this incident well. He is now my close neighbor. His name is Jack Gardipee, and we often sit and relive some of the old range days of the past. His father was killed in a bear's den, and it worried him because his father and mother were not buried side by side, for his mother was buried in the Lewistown cemetery. One day he dug up his father's bones, put them in a sack, and buried them beside his mother's grave. "Now they sleep there happy for always," he said.

LIFE IN THE CATTLE COUNTRY

FREDERIC REMINGTON

The "cattle country" of the West comprises the semi-arid belt lying between the Rocky Mountains and the arable lands of the Missouri and Mississippi Rivers, and extending from Mexico to British America. The name has been given it not because there are more cattle there than elsewhere, but because the land in its present condition is fit for little or nothing but stock raising. One who for the first time traverses the territory known abroad for its cattle, naturally expects to find the broad plains dotted with browsing herds standing knee-deep in lush pasturage; but, in fact, if he travels in the summer season, he sees the brown earth showing through a sparse covering of herbage equally brown, while he may go many miles before he comes upon a straggling bunch of gaunt, long-horned steers picking gingerly at the dry vegetation. In the humid farming regions, where corn and tame grasses can be grown for feeding, the amount of land necessary for the support of a cow is small; but upon the great plains, which lie desolate and practically dead for half the year, the conservative stockman finds it necessary to allow twenty or thirty acres for each head of his herd. No grain is raised there, and none is fed save in great emergency; the only food for the cattle is the wild grass native to the plains. This grass makes its growth in the spring; and when the rains of spring cease it is cured where it stands by the glowing sunlight. This natural hay is scant at the best, and gives little promise to the unpracticed eye; but it is in fact very nutritious, and range cattle will thrive and fatten upon it. Every aspect of the plains suggests the necessity for avoiding the danger of overstocking; the allowance of twenty-five acres for each animal is not extravagant.

For a long time the cattle country of the Northwest was a mere stretch of wild land, wholly unbroken by fences; then the herds ranged freely under semi-occasional oversight from their owners. In that time the "cow-boy" of song and story was in his element. A gradual change has come over that old-time free-dom; for where once the land was the property of the Federal government, and open to all who chose to make legitimate use of it, of late years the owners of the herds—the "cattle kings"—have acquired title to their lands, and the individual ranch has taken the place of Nature's range. Railway lines have multiplied; and with individual ownership of land has come the wire fence to mark the bounds of each man's possessions. To the wire fence more than to any other cause is due the passing of the traditional "cow-boy." Of course the fencing of the ranges is not yet universal; but every year sees a nearer approach to that end.

In former time the "round-up" was of much more importance than it is to-day; for with nothing to hinder, the cattle belonging to many owners would mix and mingle intimately, and the process of rounding up was the only method of separating them and establishing ownership. It is altogether likely the people of the next generation will see nothing of this picturesque and interesting activity.

In the cattle lands of the North, the work of rounding up begins so soon as spring is well established. During the winter the herds have been suffered to range freely, and in hard winters will often be found to have drifted far from home. The spring round-up in Nebraska and Dakota begins late in April or in May, and has for its purpose the assembling of the herds which belong to the several ranches of a neighborhood, the separation of each man's cattle from the mass, the branding of calves, etc., and the return of each herd to its own range, where the beef animals are to be put in condition for market, pending the summer and fall round-up. Cattle growers' associations have been formed in the Western States, and when the season opens each association designates the times when the several ranges within its jurisdiction shall round up their cattle, and these times are sought to be arranged that when the first round-up is completed, say in District No. 1, District No. 2, which lies adjoining, will take up the work where No. 1 left off, and No. 3 will follow No. 2 in like manner; and in this way the round-up in the entire State consists not so much of a broken series of drives as of one long drive, with the result that practically every head of stock is discovered, identified and claimed by its owner.

Once the date is fixed for the round-up in a given district, the semi-quiescence of the winter gives instant place to hurry, bustle and strenuous activity. The "cow-ponies" which are to be ridden by the men have been upon the range through the winter, and these must be gathered up and put in condition for riding—often a task of no small difficulty, for after their winter's freedom they are not infrequently so wild as to require to be broken anew to the saddle. But, as Kipling is so fond of saying, that is another story.

The "riders" of the round-up—the men upon whom devolves the actual labor of handling the cattle—rely very greatly upon their saddle ponies. These must necessarily be trained to the work which they are to perform, and know not only the ways of men, but also the more erratic ways of the light-headed steers and cows. Ponies untrained to their duties would make endless trouble, to say nothing of greatly endangering the lives of the men. Each rider takes with him upon the round-up his own "string," consisting of ten or a dozen ponies, which are to be used in turn, so as to insure having a fresh, strong animal in instant readiness for the emergencies which are always arising, but which can never be foretold. Cow-ponies are seldom entirely trustworthy in the matter of habits and temper; but they are stout-hearted, sure-footed little beasts, who know how to keep faith in the crises of driving and "cutting out."

Besides the personal equipment of each man, the ranch sends with the party a general outfit, the principal item of which is a strong and heavy four-horse wagon, carrying bedding, food, cooking utensils, etc., and with this wagon is the man in the hollow of whose skilful hand lies the comfort and welfare of every man on the round-up—that is to say, the camp cook. Nowhere is a good cook more appreciated than in those waste places of the West. The bill of fare for the party on round-up duty is not of very great variety; the inevitable beans, salt pork, canned goods, bread and coffee make the sum total of what the men may expect to eat.

It is of great importance that this food should be well and palatably cooked; and quite independent of his abstract skill, it is always possible for the genius presiding over frying-pan and coffee-pot to make life endurable for men situated as these are. Each ranch which takes part in the round-up sends such an outfit with the men who are delegated to represent it and look after its interests, so that when the camp is pitched upon the plains it presents a very bustling and business-like appearance.

The round-up is under the direct charge of one man, known as the captain, who is sometimes selected by the association at the time of appointing the meeting, and is sometimes chosen by the ranchmen themselves when the party assembles for its work. For the time being the authority of the captain is as nearly absolute as one man's authority can be over American citizens. Violations of his orders are punishable in most cases by the assessment of arbitrary fines; but recourse is not often had to this penalty, for as a rule the men know what is expected of them, and take keen pride in doing their work well. The captain has a lieutenant chosen from the representatives of each ranch taking part in the round-up. Thus officered the force of men is ready for its work.

At the appointed time the delegates from the several ranches come straggling to the place of meeting. There is usually some delay in beginning the work, and while the captain and his aids are planning the details, the riders are wont to engage in a variety of activities, some serious, some designed for amusement— breaking unruly ponies, racing, trading, card-playing, and whatever occurs by way of passing the time. This is all put aside, however, when work actually begins; for the round-up is earnest.

With the opening of spring, when the snows have disappeared from the plains, the cattle will naturally have sought the grazing lands in the neighborhood of the water-courses; therefore, as a rule, the line travelled by the round-up lies along the valley of a small stream, extending back so far as may be necessary upon either hand.

The men are awakened in the morning long before daylight. They have probably slept on the ground, rolled in blankets and with saddles or boots for pillows. Toilets are hurriedly made, for tardiness is not tolerated. The camp breakfast is gulped down in the dark, and every man must be instantly ready to mount when the summons comes. A force of twenty or thirty men is chosen for the day's riding, and this force is divided into two parties, one of which is to cover the territory to the right and the other to the left of the line of the riders' march. For the most part, the land which borders the streams of the far Northwest is broken, rocky and ragged, and to ride a horse over it is certainly not a pleasure trip, to say nothing of the necessity for looking out sharply for straggling bunches of cattle, gathering them up and driving them forward; for range cattle are wild as deer and perverse as swine.

So soon as possible the night's camp is struck and the wagons move forward for five miles or so, where the riders are to assemble after the morning's work. The two parties of riders then strike off in opposite directions, those in each party gradually drawing further and further apart, until the dozen men form a line ten or fifteen miles in length, extending from the site of the night's camp back to the foothills bordering the stream; and then this line, with its members a mile or so apart, moves forward in the direction of the new camp, searching every nook and cranny among the rocks and hills for wandering bunches of grazing cattle. These must be assembled and driven to camp. The man on the inner end of the line keeps close to the stream, riding straight forward, while he at the other end will have to ride for perhaps thirty or forty miles, making a long circling sweep to the hills and then back to the stream. This ride is hard and often perilous, for the land is much broken and cut up by ravines and precipitous "buttes." The half-wild cattle will climb everywhere, and wherever they go the ponies must follow. It may be that in the course of the morning's drive the riders will gather many hundreds or perhaps thousands of cattle; or it is possible that no more than a score or two will be found. At any rate, the drive is carried forward with the intention of reaching camp about midday. Dinner is eaten with a ravenous appetite, but with scant ceremony, and there is no allowance of time for an after-dinner nap, for the herd gathered in the morning must be sorted over and the animals given to their several owners. This is the most trying work of the round-up. It requires clean, strong courage to ride a pony of uncertain temper into the heart of a herd of several hundred or thousand wild cattle which are wrought up, as these are, to a pitch of high nervous excitement; but there is no other recourse.

Each ranch has its individual mark or brand, which is put upon its animals—sometimes a letter or combination of letters, and sometimes a geometrical figure.

The brands are protected by State law, somewhat after the fashion of a copyright, and each is the absolute property of the ranch which uses it. The ranches are commonly known among the cattlemen of the neighborhood by the name of the brand which they use—as "Circle-Bar Ranch," "Lazy L Ranch," etc. A lazy L is an L lying upon its side. In the work of "cutting out," a delegate from a ranch rides into the herd gathered in the morning, singles out one at a time those cattle bearing his ranch's brand, and slowly urges them to the edge of the mass, where they are taken in charge by other riders and kept together in a bunch. Great vigilance is necessary in holding out these separated bunches, for they are constantly striving to return to the main herd. The ponies used in cutting out must be the best, thoroughly broken to the work, and wise as serpents; for in case of some maddened cow or steer forming a sudden disposition to stampede, the life of the rider often depends upon the willingness and cool adroitness of his pony in getting out of the way.

Once the herd is apportioned to its owners, there remains the labor of branding. Calves with their mothers are easily identified; but there will always be found some mature animals which have escaped the branding-iron in former round-ups, and which are known as mavericks. It may be imagined that the burning of a brand upon the shoulder, flank or side of a lusty two-year-old bull is fraught with considerable excitement. To do this, it is first necessary that the animal be "roped," or lariated, and thrown down. The skill of men trained to handle the rope is really admirable, and it may be remarked in passing that an expert roper is always in demand. The wildly excited steer or bull will be in full flight over the prairie, diving, dodging, plunging this way and that to escape from the inevitable noose swinging over the head of the shrill-yelling rider in pursuit. The greatest skill lies in throwing the noose so that it will settle upon the ground in such wise as to catch the fore or hind legs of the galloping beast; this is the pride of the adept roper. To throw the noose over the head or horns is a trick held in slight esteem. When the noose has settled to its place, the rider gives to his pony a well-understood signal, and the willing beast settles himself for the shock to come when the captive brings up at the end of the taut rope. The pony goes back upon his haunches, the man takes a few turns with the rope around the high horn of his saddle; then with a jerk and a jar the helpless victim throws a furious summersault, and after that there is nothing for it but to submit to fate. A second rider throws his lariat over the other pair of struggling legs, and with the brute thus pinioned the hot branding-iron is set against his side. Where the iron has touched, the hair may grow no more; or if it grows, it will be so discolored as to leave the brand easily recognizable. When the ropes are loosed the fun is fast; for the infuriated animal seeks vengeance, and will charge blindly at any moving thing with sight. The branding of calves is not child's play, but it is tame as compared with the work upon grown animals.

The work of branding concludes the most serious business of the day, save that the herd requires constant watching throughout the twenty-four hours. When night has fallen and the herd has lain down, riders are detailed to circle continually about to guard against the ever-present danger of a stampede. In the night, cattle will take fright upon very slight alarm, and often quite causelessly. One or two will rise bellowing, and in an instant the entire herd is upon its feet, crazed with fright and desiring nothing but flight. To break a stampede, it is necessary to head off the leaders and turn them back into the herd. If the onward rush can be checked and the herd induced to move around in a circle, the present danger is past; but it is impossible to foretell when another break will occur. The rider who deliberately goes in front of a stampeding herd in the pitchy darkness of a prairie night, thoughtless of everything save his duty, must be a man of fine fibre. And indeed I must say at the last that the "cow-punchers" as a class, maligned and traduced as they have been, possess a quality of sturdy, sterling manhood which would be to the credit of men in any walk of life. The honor of the average "puncher" abides with him continually. He will not lie; he will not steal. He keeps faith with his friends; toward his enemies he bears himself like a man. He has his vices—as who has not?—but I like to speak softly of them when set against his unassailable virtues. I wish that the manhood of the cow-boy might come more into fashion further East.

A MEXICAN PLUG

MARK TWAIN

I resolved to have a horse to ride. I had never seen such wild, free, magnificent horsemanship outside of a circus as these picturesquely-clad Mexicans, Californians and Mexicanized Americans displayed in Carson streets every day. How they rode! Leaning just gently forward out of the perpendicular, easy and nonchalant, with broad slouch-hat brim blown square up in front, and long *riata* swinging above the head, they swept through the town like the wind! The next minute they were only a sailing puff of dust on the far desert. If they trotted, they sat up gallantly and gracefully, and seemed part of the horse; did not go jiggering up and down after the silly Miss-Nancy fashion of the riding-schools. I had quickly learned to tell a horse from a cow, and was full of anxiety to learn more. I was resolved to buy a horse.

While the thought was rankling in my mind, the auctioneer came skurrying through the plaza on a black beast that had as many humps and corners on him as a dromedary, and was necessarily uncomely; but he was "going, going, at twenty-two!—a horse, saddle and bridle at twenty-two dollars, gentlemen!" and I could hardly resist.

A man whom I did not know (he turned out to be the auctioneer's brother) noticed the wistful look in my eye, and observed that that was a very remarkable horse to be going at such a price; and added that the saddle alone was worth the money. It was a Spanish saddle, with ponderous *tapidaros*, and furnished with the ungainly sole-leather covering with the unspellable name. I said I had half a notion to bid. Then this keen-eyed person appeared to me to be "taking my measure"; but I dismissed the suspicion when he spoke, for his manner was full of guileless candor and truthfulness. Said he:

"I know that horse—know him well. You are a stranger, I take it, and so you might think he was an American horse, but I assure you he is not. He is nothing of the kind; but—excuse my speaking in a low voice, other people being near—he is, without the shadow of a doubt, a Genuine Mexican Plug!"

I did not know what a Genuine Mexican Plug was, but there was something abut this man's way of saying it, that made me swear inwardly that I would own a Genuine Mexican Plug, or die.

"Has he any other—er—advantages?" I inquired, suppressing what eagerness I could.

He hooked his forefinger in the pocket of my army-shirt, led me to one side, and breathed in my ear impressively these words:

"He can out-buck anything in America!"

"Going, going, going—at *twenty*-four dollars and a half, gen—"

"Twenty-seven!" I shouted in a frenzy.

"And sold!" said the auctioneer, and passed over the Genuine Mexican Plug to me.

I could scarcely contain my exultation. I paid the money, and put the animal in a neighboring livery-stable to dine and rest himself.

In the afternoon I brought the creature into the plaza, and certain citizens held him by the head, and others by the tail, while I mounted him. As soon as they let go, he placed all his feet in a bunch together, lowered his back, and then suddenly arched it upward, and shot me straight into the air a matter of three or four feet! I came as straight down again, lit in the saddle, went instantly up again, came down almost on the high pommel, shot up again, and came down on the horse's neck—all in the space of three or four seconds. Then he rose and stood almost straight up on his hind feet, and I, clasping his lean neck desperately, slid back into the saddle, and held on. He came down, and immediately hoisted his heels into the air, delivering a vicious kick at the sky, and stood on his forefeet. And then down he came once more, and began the original exercise of shooting me straight up again. The third time I went up I heard a stranger say:

"Oh, *don't* he buck, though!"

While I was up, somebody struck the horse a sounding thwack with a leathern strap, and when I arrived again the Genuine Mexican Plug was not there. A Californian youth chased him up and caught him, and asked if he might have a ride. I granted him that luxury. He mounted the Genuine, got lifted into the air once, but sent his spurs home as he descended, and the horse darted away like a telegram. He soared over three fences like a bird, and disappeared down the road toward the Washoe Valley.

I sat down on a stone, with a sigh, and by a natural impulse one of my hands sought my forehead, and the other the base of my stomach. I believe I never appreciated, till then, the poverty of the human machinery—for I still needed a hand or two to place elsewhere. Pen cannot describe how I was jolted up. Imagination cannot conceive how disjointed I was—how internally, externally and universally I was unsettled, mixed up and ruptured. There was a sympathetic crowd around me, though.

One elderly-looking comforter said:

"Stranger, you've been taken in. Everybody in this camp knows that horse. Any child, any Injun, could have told you that he'd buck; he is the very worst devil to buck on the continent of America. You hear *me*. I'm Curry. *Old* Curry. Old *Abe* Curry. And moreover, he is a simon-pure, out-and-out genuine d—d Mexican plug, and an uncommon mean one at that, too. Why, you turnip, if you had laid low and kept dark, there's chances to buy an *American* horse for mighty little more than you paid for that bloody old foreign relic."

I gave no sign; but I made up my mind that if the auctioneer's brother's funeral took place while I was in the Territory I would postpone all other recreations and attend it.

After a gallop of sixteen miles the Californian youth and the Genuine Mexican Plug came tearing into town again, shedding foam-flakes like the spume-spray that drives before a typhoon, and, with one final skip over a wheelbarrow and a Chinaman, cast anchor in front of the "ranch."

Such panting and blowing! Such spreading and contracting of the red equine nostrils, and glaring of the wild equine eye! But was the imperial beast subjugated? Indeed he was not. His lordship the Speaker of the House thought he was, and mounted him to go down to the Capitol; but the first dash the creature made was over a pile of telegraph poles half as high as a church; and his time to the Capitol—one mile and three quarters—remains unbeaten to this day. But then he took an advantage—he left out the mile, and only did the three quarters. That is to say, he made a straight cut across lots, preferring fences and ditches to a crooked road; and when the Speaker got to the Capitol he said he had been in the air so much he felt as if he had made the trip on a comet.

In the evening the Speaker came home afoot for exercise, and got the Genuine towed back behind a quartz wagon. The next day I loaned the animal to the Clerk of the House to go down to the Dana silver mine, six miles, and *he* walked back for exercise, and got the horse towed. Everybody I loaned him to always walked back; they never could get enough exercise any other way. Still, I continued to loan him to anybody who was willing to borrow him, my idea being to get him crippled, and throw him on the borrower's hands, or killed, and make the borrower pay for him, but somehow nothing ever happened to him. He took chances that no other horse ever took and survived, but he always came out safe. It was his daily habit to try experiments that had always before been considered impossible, but he always got through. Sometimes he miscalculated a little, and did not get his rider through intact, but *he* always got through himself. Of course I had tried to sell him; but that was a stretch of simplicity which met with little sympathy. The auctioneer stormed up and down the streets for four days, dispersing the populace, interrupting business, and destroying children, and never got a bid—at least never any but the eighteen-dollar one he hired a notoriously substanceless bummer to make. The people only smiled pleasantly, and restrained their desire to buy, if they had any. Then the auctioneer brought in his bill, and I withdrew the horse from the market. We tried to trade him off at private vendue next, offering him at a sacrifice for second-hand tombstones, old iron, temperance tracts—any kind of property. But holders were stiff, and we retired from the market again. I never tried to ride the horse any more. Walking was good enough exercise for a man like me, that had nothing the matter with him except ruptures, internal injuries, and such things. Finally I tried to *give* him away. But it was a failure. Parties said earthquakes were handy enough on the Pacific coast—they did not wish to own one. As a last resort I offered him to the Governor for the use of the "Brigade." His face lit up eagerly at first, but toned down again, and he said the thing would be too palpable.

Just then the livery stable man brought in his bill for six weeks' keeping—stall-room for the horse, fifteen dollars; hay for the horse, two hundred and fifty! The Genuine Mexican Plug had eaten a ton of the article, and the man said he would have eaten a hundred if he had let him.

I will remark here, in all seriousness, that the regular price of hay during that year and a part of the next was really two hundred and fifty dollars a ton. During a part of the previous year it had sold at five hundred a ton, in gold, and during the winter before that there was such scarcity of the article that in several instances small quantities had brought eight hundred dollars a ton in coin! The consequence might be guessed without my telling it; people turned their stock loose to starve, and before the spring arrived Carson and Eagle valleys were almost literally carpeted with their carcases! Any old settler there will verify these statements.

I managed to pay the livery bill, and that same day I gave the Genuine Mexican Plug to a passing Arkansas emigrant whom fortune delivered into my hand. If this ever meets his eye, he will doubtless remember the donation.

Now whoever has had the luck to ride a real Mexican plug will recognize the animal depicted in this chapter, and hardly consider him exaggerated—but the uninitiated will feel justified in regarding his portrait as a fancy sketch, perhaps.

SOME GLIMPSES INTO RANCH LIFE

FRANK S. HASTINGS

A ranch in its entirety is known as an "Outfit," and yet in a general way the word "Outfit" suggests the wagon outfit which does the cow-work and lives in the open from April 15th, when work begins, to December 1st, when it ends.

The wagon outfit consists of the "Chuck Wagon" which carries the food, bedding and tents, and from the back of which the food is prepared over an open fire. The "Hoodlum Wagon," which carries the water barrel, wood and branding irons, furnishes the Chuck Wagon with water and wood, the branding crew with wood, and attends all round-ups or branding pens with supply of drinking water.

The Remuda (cow ponies) and Horse Wrangler always travel with the "Wagon." Remuda is the Spanish word for Saddle Horses.

The wagon crew consists of the Wagon Boss, usually foreman of the ranch, Cook, Hoodlum Driver, Horse Wrangler, Straw Boss, next in authority to Wagon Boss, and eight to twelve men as the work may demand. In winter the outfit is reduced to the regular year-around men who are scattered over the different ranch camps.

In almost everything industrial the problem is reduced to "Men," but in the Ranch it is reduced to "Men and horses." One might almost say to horses: since the love of a horse explains why there are cowboys—not rough riders, or the gun-decorated hero of the moving picture, but earnest, everyday, hardworking boys who will sit twenty-four hours in a saddle and never whimper, but who "Hate your guts" if you ask them to plow an acre of land or do anything else "afoot."

Every cowboy has a mount of from eight to fourteen horses regulated by his work, and the class of horses. A line rider can get along with fewer horses than a "wagon" man, and a man with a good many young horses needs more than the man with an older or steadier mount. Every one of these men will claim they are "afoot" and that "There ain't no more good cow ponies," but woe to the "outfit" that tries to take one of the no-accounts away, or, as the saying is, "Monkey with a man's mount."

Horses are assigned and then to all intents and purposes they become the property of the man. Some foremen do not let their men trade horses among themselves, but it is quite generally permitted under supervision that avoids "sharking."

Every horse has a name and every man on the ranch knows every horse by name, and in a general way over all the S. M. S. Ranches with over 500 cow ponies in service the men know all the horses by name, and what horses are in each man's mount. A man who does not love his mount does not last long in the cow business. Very few men are cruel to their horses, and a man who does not treat his mount well is only a "bird of passage" on most ranches, and always on the S. M. S. Ranch. There is an old ranch saying that between the shoulder and the hip belongs to the rider, and the rest to the company. Beating over the head or spurring in the shoulder means "time check." Cowboys' principal topic is their horses or of men who ride, and every night about the camp fire they trade horses, run imaginary horse races, or romance about their pet ponies.

I shall speak of horses in the main as with the wagon. All the saddle horses of an outfit thrown together are called the Remuda—pronounced in Texas "Remoother"—slurring the "ther." The Remuda is in charge of a man, usually a half-grown boy known as the "Horse Wrangler," whose duty it is to have them in a band when wanted to change mounts, and to see that they are watered and grazed and kept from straying. They are always assembled early morning at noon and at night, and at such other times as the work may demand a change, as, for instance, in making a round the boys use their wildest and swiftest horses— usually their youngest—to tame them down. When the round-up is together they use their "cutting" horses, which are as a rule their oldest and best horses.

The Remuda for an ordinary outfit will number from 125 to 150 horses. The Wrangler must know every horse by sight and name, and tell at a glance if one is missing. The Remuda trails with the wagon, but is often sent to some round-up place without the wagon. A horse is a "Hoss" always in a cow camp. Horses ridden on grass may be called upon to be ridden until down and out, but are not hurt as a grain-fed horse would be, and when his turn comes again in a few days is as chipper as ever . . . . The horse breaker or "Bronc Buster" usually names horses as he breaks them; and if the horse has any flesh marks or distinct characteristics, it is apt to come out in the name, and any person familiar with the practical can often glance at a horse and guess his name. For instance, if he has peculiar black stripes toward the tail with a little white in the tail, you are pretty safe to guess "Pole Cat." If his feet are big and look clumsy, "Puddin Foot" is a good first chance. The following names occur in three mounts, and to get the full list I had to dig hard, and both men [he may mean all three] left out several horses until I asked about them, because always the suspicion that something was going to be done that would take a horse:

Red Hell, Tar Baby, Sail Away Brown, Big Henry, Streak, Brown Lina, Hammer Head, Lightning, Apron Face, Feathers, Panther, Chub, Dumbbell, Rambler, Powder, Straight Edge, Scissors, Gold Dollar, Silver City, Julius Caesar, Pop Corn, Talameslie, Louse Cage, Trinidad, Tater Slip, Cannon Ball, Big Enough, Lone Oak, Stocking, Pain, Grey Wonder, Rattler, Whiteman, Monkey Face, Snakey, Slippers, Jesse James, Buttermilk, Hop Ale, Barefoot, Tetotler, Lift Up, Pancho, Boll Weevil, Crawfish, Clabber, Few Brains, Showboy, Rat Hash, Butter-beans, Cigarette, Bull Pup. Feminine names are often used, such as Sweetheart, Baby Mine, or some girl's name.

A "Bronc" is a horse recently broken or about to be broken. The "Bronc Buster" [in some parts he is called also a peeler or a twister] rides him a few saddles. This pony is known as a Bronc the first season and as "Last Year's Bronc" the second season. Most all of the Broncs pitch some, but very few of them long or dangerously. Modern methods of breaking have reduced the percentage of bad horses—many would not pitch at all after the first few times if the rider did not deliberately make them. It is hard to get the old hands to ride anything but a pretty gentle horse, and yet there is always someone in the outfit who glories in mean horses, most of which are really fine animals, except for their "morning's morning" but the rider who likes them usually has no trouble in getting them. Every cowboy must, of course, be able to handle a mean horse if necessary.

An "Outlaw" is a horse which no amount of riding or handling will subdue. He is "turned in" and sold in the "Scalawag" bunch which goes out every year, and includes the horses no longer fit for cow use. They are bought by traders who take them into some of the older Southern States and sell them to the negro tenants for cotton horses.

A "Sunday Hoss" is one with an easy saddle gait—usually a single footer with some style. The boys go "Gallin" Sundays, and in every mount of the younger men there is apt to be such a horse, but not in any sense saved from the regular work for Sunday.

"An Individual" is the private property of a cowboy and not very much encouraged, as it is only natural that he does not get much work, and is an encouragement to go "Gallin" when the foreman holds the boys down on ranch horses more on the boys' account because it is often a long night ride and impairs the boys' capacity for a hard day's work in busy times . . . . The owner of an "Individual" may be the embodiment of general honesty, but seems to feel that oats sneaked out for "his hoss" is at worst a very small venial sin.

A cow horse is trained so that he is tied when the reins are down. He can, of course, drift off and when frightened run, but stepping on the reins seems to intimidate him into standing still as a rule. There are two reasons for this: first, the cowboy frequently has work where it is vital to leap from his horse and do something quick; second, that there is rarely anything to tie him to; though even when tying a horse a fairly even pull will loosen the reins. Cow horses are easily startled and apt to pull back and break the reins.

The regular cowboy gait for pasture riding or line work or ordinary cross-country riding is a "Jiggle"—a sort of fox trot that will make five miles per hour. For the round-up hard running is necessary part of the time and usually a stiff gallop the balance.

Cowboy life is very different from the ideas given by a Wild West Show or the "Movies." It is against Texas law to carry a pistol, and the sale is unlawful. This, however, is evaded by leasing 99 years. Occasionally a rider will carry a Winchester on his saddle for coyotes or Lobo wolves, but in the seventeen years the writer has been intimate with range life he has never seen a cowboy carry a pistol hung about him, and very few instances where one was carried concealed. There is always a gun of some sort with the outfit carried in the wagon.

Every cowboy furnishes his own saddle, bridle, saddle blanket, and spurs; also his bedding, known as "Hot Roll," a 16 to 20 oz. canvas "Tarp" about 18 feet long doubled and bedding in between, usually composed of several quilts known as "suggans" and blankets—rarely a mattress, the extra quilts serving for mattress. The top "Tarp" serves as extra covering and protects against rain.

Working outfits are composed as far as possible of unmarried men, with the exception of the Wagon Boss, who is usually the Ranch foreman. They rarely leave the wagon at night, and as the result of close association an interchange of wit, or "josh," as it is called, has sprung up. There is nothing like the chuck-wagon josh in any other phase of life, and it is almost impossible to describe, because so much of it revolves about or applies to the technical part of ranching. It is very funny, very keen, and very direct, and while the most of it is understood by an outsider, he cannot carry it away with him.

At headquarters a bunk house is always provided which is usually known as "the Dog House" or "the Dive." No gambling is permitted on the ranches, but the cowboys' great game, "Auction Pitch," or dominoes or stag dances or music fill the hours of recreation, divided with the great cowboy occupation of "Quirt" making, in which they are masters. The use of liquor is not permitted on the S. M. S. Ranches or by the men when on duty away from the ranches.

THE CATTLE COUNTRY
OF THE FAR WEST

THEODORE ROOSEVELT

The great grazing lands of the West lie in what is known as the arid belt, which stretches from British America on the north to Mexico on the south, through the middle of the United States. It includes New Mexico, part of Arizona, Colorado, Wyoming, Montana, and the western portion of Texas, Kansas, Nebraska, and Dakota. It must not be understood by this that more cattle are to be found here than elsewhere, for the contrary is true, it being a fact often lost sight of that the number of cattle raised on the small, thick-lying farms of the fertile Eastern States is actually many times greater than that of those scattered over the vast, barren ranches of the far West; for stock will always be most plentiful in districts where corn and other winter food can be grown. But in this arid belt, and in this arid belt only,—save in a few similar tracts on the Pacific slope,—stock-raising is almost the sole industry, except in the mountain districts where there is mining. The whole region is one vast stretch of grazing country, with only here and there spots of farm-land, in most places there being nothing more like agriculture than is implied in the cutting of some tons of wild hay or the planting of a garden patch for home use. This is especially true of the northern portion of the region, which comprises the basin of the Upper Missouri, and with which alone I am familiar. Here there are no fences to speak of, and all the land north of the Black Hills and the Big Horn Mountains and between the Rockies and the Dakota wheat fields might be spoken of as one gigantic, unbroken pasture, where cowboys and branding-irons take the place of fences.

The country throughout this great Upper Missouri basin has a wonderful sameness of character; and the rest of the arid belt, lying to the southward, is closely akin to it in its main features. A traveler seeing it for the first time is especially struck by its look of parched, barren desolation; he can with difficulty believe that it will support cattle at all. It is a region of light rainfall; the grass is short and comparatively scanty; there is no timber except along the beds of the streams, and in many places there are alkali deserts where nothing grows but sage-brush and cactus. Now the land stretches out into level, seemingly endless plains or into rolling prairies; again it is broken by abrupt hills and deep, winding valleys; or else it is crossed by chains of buttes, usually bare, but often clad with a dense growth of dwarfed pines or gnarled, stunted cedars. The muddy rivers run in broad, shallow beds, which after heavy rainfalls are filled to the brim by the swollen torrents, while in droughts the larger streams dwindle into sluggish trickles of clearer water, and the smaller ones dry up entirely, save in occasional deep pools.

All through the region, except on the great Indian reservations, there has been a scanty and sparse settlement, quite peculiar in its character. In the forest the woodchopper comes first; on the fertile prairies the granger is the pioneer; but on the long, stretching uplands of the far West it is the men who guard and follow the horned herds that prepare the way for the settlers who come after. The high plains of the Upper Missouri and its tributary rivers were first opened, and are still held, by the stockmen, and the whole civilization of the region has received the stamp of their marked and individual characteristics. They were from the South, not from the East, although many men from the latter region came out along the great transcontinental railway lines and joined them in their northern migration.

They were not dwellers in towns, and from the nature of their industry lived as far apart from each other as possible. In choosing new ranges, old cowhands, who are also seasoned plainsmen, are invariably sent ahead, perhaps a year in advance, to spy out the land and pick the best places. One of these may go by himself, or more often, especially if they have to penetrate little known or entirely unknown tracts, two or three will go together, the owner or manager of the herd himself being one of them. Perhaps their herds may already be on the border of the wild and uninhabited country: in that case they may have to take but a few days' journey before finding the stretches of sheltered, long-grass land that they seek. For instance, when I wished to move my own elkhorn steer brand on to a new ranch I had to spend barely a week in traveling north among the Little Missouri Bad Lands before finding what was then untrodden ground far outside the range of any of my neighbors' cattle. But if a large outfit is going to shift its quarters it must go much farther; and both the necessity and the chance for long wanderings were especially great when the final overthrow of the northern Horse Indians opened the whole Upper Missouri basin at one sweep to the stockmen. Then the advance-guards or explorers, each on one horse and leading another with food and bedding, were often absent months at a time, threading their way through the trackless wastes of plain, plateau, and river bottom. If possible they would choose a country that would be good for winter and summer alike; but often this could not be done, and then they would try to find a well-watered tract on which the cattle could be summered, and from which they could be driven in fall to their sheltered winter range—for the cattle in winter eat snow, and an entirely waterless region, if broken, and with good pasturage, is often the best possible winter ground, as it is sure not to have been eaten off at all during the summer; while in the bottoms the grass is always cropped down soonest. Many outfits regularly shift their herds every spring and fall; but with us in the Bad Lands all we do, when cold weather sets in, is to drive our beasts off the scantily grassed river-bottom back ten miles or more among the broken buttes and plateaus of the uplands to where the brown hay, cured on the stalk stands thick in the winding coulees.

These lookouts or foreruners having returned, the herds are set in motion as early in the spring as may be, so as to get on the ground in time to let the travel-worn beasts rest and gain flesh before winter sets in. Each herd is accompanied by a dozen, or a score, or a couple of score, of cowboys, according to its size, and beside it rumble and jolt the heavy four-horse wagons that hold the food and bedding of the men and the few implements they will need at the end of their journey. As long as possible they follow the trails made by the herds that have already traveled in the same direction, and when these end they strike out for themselves. In the Upper Missouri basin, the pioneer herds soon had to scatter out and each find its own way among the great dreary solitudes, creeping carefully along so that the cattle should not be overdriven and should have water at the halting-places. An outfit might thus be months on its lonely journey, slowly making its way over melancholy, pathless plains, or down the valleys of the lonely rivers. It was tedious, harassing work, as the weary cattle had to be driven carefully and quietly during the day and strictly guarded at night, with a perpetual watch kept for Indians or white horsethieves. Often they would skirt the edges of the streams for days at a time, seeking for a ford or a good swimming crossing, and if the water was up and the quicksand deep the danger to the riders was serious and the risk of loss among the cattle very great.

At last, after days of excitement and danger and after months of weary, monotonous toil, the chosen ground is reached and the final camp pitched. The footsore animals are turned loose to shift for themselves, outlying camps of two or three men each being established to hem them in. Meanwhile the primitive ranch house, out buildings, and corrals are built, the unhewn cottonwood logs being chinked with moss and mud, while the roofs are of branches covered with dirt, spades and axes being the only tools needed for the work. Bunks, chairs, and tables are all home made, and as rough as the houses they are in. The supplies, of coarse, rude food are carried perhaps two or three hundred miles from the nearest town, either in the ranch-wagons or else by some regular freighting outfit, the huge canvas-topped prairie schooners of which are each drawn by several yoke of oxen, or perhaps by six or eight mules. To guard against the numerous mishaps of prairie travel, two or three of these prairie schooners usually go together, the brawny teamsters, known either as "bull-whackers" or as "mule-skinners," stalking beside their slow moving teams.

The small outlying camps are often tents, or mere dug-outs in the ground. But at the main ranch there will be a cluster of log buildings, including a separate cabin for the foreman or ranchman; often another in which to cook and eat; a long house for the men to sleep in; stables, sheds, a blacksmith's shop etc.,— the whole group forming quite a little settlement, with the corrals, the stacks of natural hay, and the patches of fenced land for gardens or horse pastures. This little settlement may be situated right out in the treeless, nearly level open, but much more often is placed in partly wooded bottom of a creek or river, sheltered by the usual background of somber brown hills.

When the northern plains began to be settled, such a ranch would at first be absolutely alone in the wilderness, but others of the same sort were sure soon to be established within twenty or thirty miles on one side or the other. The lives of the men in such places were strangely cut off from the outside world, and, indeed the same is true to a hardly less extent at the present day. Sometimes the wagons are sent for provisions, and the beef-steers are at stated times driven off for shipment. Parties of hunters and trappers call now and then. More rarely small bands of emigrants go by in search of new homes, impelled by the restless, aimless craving for change so deeply grafted in the breast of the American borderer: the white-topped wagons are loaded with domestic goods, with sallow, dispirited-looking women, and with tow-headed children; while the gaunt, moody frontiersmen slouch alongside, rifle on shoulder, lank, homely, uncouth, and yet with a curious suggestion of grim strength underlying it all. Or cowboys from neighboring ranches will ride over, looking for lost horses, or seeing if their cattle have strayed off the range. But this is all. Civilization seems as remote as if we were living in an age long past. The whole existence is patriarchal in character: it is the life of men in the open, who tend their herds on horseback; who go armed and ready to guard their lives by their own prowess, whose wants are very simple, and who call no man master. Ranching is an occupation like those of vigorous, primitive pastoral peoples, having little in common with the humdrum, workaday business world of the nineteenth century; and the free ranchman in his manner of life shows more kinship to an Arab sheik than to a sleek city merchant or tradesman.

By degrees the country becomes what in a stock-raising region passes for well settled. In addition to the great ranches smaller ones are established, with a few hundred, or even a few score, head of cattle apiece; and now and then miserable farmers straggle in to fight a losing and desperate battle with drought, cold, and grasshoppers. The wheels of the heavy wagons, driven always over the same course from one ranch to another, or to the remote frontier towns from which they get their goods, wear ruts in the soil, and roads are soon formed, perhaps originally following the deep trails made by the vanished buffalo. These roads lead down the river-bottoms or along the crests of the divides or else strike out fairly across the prairie, and a man may sometimes journey a hundred miles along one without coming to a house or a camp of any sort. If they lead to a shipping point whence the beeves are sent to market, the cattle, traveling in single file, will have worn many and deep paths on each side of the wheel-marks; and the roads between important places which are regularly used either by the United States Government, by stage-coach lines, or by freight teams become deeply worn landmarks—as, for instance, near us, the Deadwood and the old Fort Keogh trails.

Cattle-ranching can only be carried on in its present form while the population is scanty; and so in stock-raising regions, pure and simple, there are usually few towns, and these are almost always at the shipping points for cattle.

But, on the other hand, wealthy cattlemen, like miners who have done well, always spend their money freely; and accordingly towns like Denver, Cheyenne, and Helena, where these two classes are the most influential in the community, are far pleasanter places of residence than cities of five times their population in the exclusively agricultural States to the eastward.

A true "cow town" is worth seeing,—such a one as Miles City, for instance, especially at the time of the annual meeting of the great Montana Stock-raisers' Association. Then the whole place is full to overflowing, the importance of the meeting and the fun of the attendant frolics, especially the horse-races, drawing from the surrounding ranch country many hundreds of men of every degree, from the rich stock-owner worth his millions to the ordinary cowboy who works for forty dollars a month. It would be impossible to imagine a more typically American assemblage, for although there are always a certain number of foreigners, usually English, Irish, or German, yet they have become completely Americanized; and on the whole it would be difficult to gather a finer body of men, in spite of their numerous shortcomings. The ranch-owners differ more from each other than do the cowboys; and the former certainly compare very favorably with similar classes of capitalists in the East. Anything more foolish than the demagogic outcry against "cattle kings" it would be difficult to imagine. Indeed, there are very few businesses so absolutely legitimate as stock-raising and so beneficial to the nation at large; and a successful stock-grower must not only be shrewd, thrifty, patient, and enterprising, but he must also possess qualities of personal bravery, hardihood, and self-reliance to a degree not demanded in the least by any mercantile occupation in a community long settled. Stockmen are in the West the pioneers of civilization, and their daring and adventurousness make the after settlement of the region possible. The whole country owes them great debt.

The most successful ranchmen are those, usually South-westerners, who have been bred to the business and have grown up with it; but many Eastern men, including not a few college graduates, have also done excellently by devoting their whole time and energy to their work,—although the Easterners who invest their money in cattle without knowing anything of the business, or who trust all to their subordinates, are naturally enough likely to incur heavy losses. Stockmen are learning more and more to act together; and certainly the meetings of their associations are conducted with a dignity and good sense that would do credit to any parliamentary body.

But the cowboys resemble one another much more and outsiders much less than is the case even with theeir employers, the ranchmen. A town in the cattle country, when for some cause it is thronged with men from the neighborhood, always presents a picturesque sight. On the wooden sidewalks of the broad, dusty streets the men who ply the various industries known only to frontier existence jostle one another as they saunter to and fro or lounge lazily in front of the straggling, cheap-looking board houses. Hunters come in from the plains and the mountains, clad in buckskin shirts and fur caps, greasy and unkempt, but with resolute faces and sullen, watchful eyes, that are ever on the alert. The teamsters, surly and self-contained, wear slouch hats and great cowhide boots; while the stage-drivers, their faces seamed by the hardship and exposure of their long drives with every kind of team, through every kind of country, and in every kind of weather, proud of their really wonderful skill as reinsmen and conscious of their high standing in any frontier community, look down on and sneer at the "skin hunters" and the plodding drivers of the white-topped prairie schooners. Besides these there are trappers, and wolfers, whose business is to poison wolves, with shaggy, knock-kneed ponies to carry their small bales and bundles of furs—beaver, wolf, fox, and occasionally otter; and silent sheep-herders, with cast-down faces, never able to forget the absolute solitude and monotony of their dreary lives, nor to rid their minds of the thought of the woolly idiots they pass all their days in tending. Such are the men who have come to town, either on business or else to frequent the flaunting saloons and gaudy hells of all kinds in search of the coarse, vicious excitement that in the minds of many of them does duty as pleasure—the only form of pleasure they have ever had a chance to know. Indians too, wrapped in blankets, with stolid, emotionless faces, stalk silently round among the whites, or join in the gambling and horseracing. If the town is on the borders of the mountain country, there will also be sinewy lumbermen, rough-looking miners, and packers, whose business it is to guide the long mule and pony trains that go where wagons can not and whose work in packing needs special and peculiar skill; and mingled with and drawn from all these classes are desperadoes of every grade, from the gambler up through the horse-thief to the murderous professional bully, or, as he is locally called, "bad man"—now, however, a much less conspicuous object than formerly.

But everywhere among these plainsmen and mountain-men, and more important than any, are the cowboys,—the men who follow the calling that has brought such towns into being. Singly, or in twos or threes, they gallop their wiry little horses down the street, their lithe, supple figures erect or swaying slightly as they sit loosely in the saddle; while their stirrups are so long that their knees are hardly bent, the bridles not taut enough to keep the chains from clanking. They are smaller and less muscular than the wielders of ax and pick; but they are as hardy and self-reliant as any men who ever breathed—with bronzed, set faces, and keen eyes that look all the world straight in the face without flinching as they flash out from under the broad-brimmed hats. Peril and hardship, and years of long toil broken by weeks of brutal dissipation, draw haggard lines across their eager faces, but never dim their reckless eyes nor break their bearing of defiant self-confidence. They do not walk well, partly because they so rarely do any work out of the saddle, partly because their *chaperajos* or leather overalls hamper them when on the ground; but their appearance is striking for all that, and picturesque too, with their jingling spurs, the big revolvers stuck in their belts, and bright silk handkerchiefs knotted loosely round their necks over the open collars of the flannel shirts. When drunk on the villainous whisky of the frontier towns, they cut mad antics, riding their horses into the saloons, firing their pistols right and left, from boisterous light-heartedness rather than from any viciousness, and indulging too often in deadly shooting affrays, brought on either by the accidental contact of the moment or on account of some long-standing grudge, or perhaps because of bad blood between two ranches or localities; but except while on such sprees they are quiet, rather self-contained men, perfectly frank and simple, and on their own ground treat a stranger with the most whole-souled hospitality, doing all in their power for him and scorning to take any reward in return. Although prompt to resent an injury, they are not at all apt to be rude to outsiders, treating them with what can almost be called a grave courtesy. They are much better fellows and pleasanter companions than small farmers or agricultural laborers; nor are the mechanics and workmen of a great city to be mentioned in the same breath.

The bulk of the cowboys themselves are South-westerners; but there are also many from the Eastern and the Northern States, who, if they begin young, do quite as well as the Southerners. The best hands are fairly bred to the work and follow it from their youth up. Nothing can be more foolish than for an Easterner to think he can become a cowboy in a few months' time. Many a young fellow comes out hot with enthusiasm for life on the plains, only to learn that his clumsiness is greater than he could have believed possible; that the cowboy business is like any other and has to be learned by serving a painful apprenticeship; and that this apprenticeship implies the endurance of rough fare, hard living, dirt, exposure of every kind, no little toil, and month after month of the dullest monotony. For cowboy work there is need of special traits and special training, and young Easterners should be sure of themselves before trying it; the struggle for existence is very keen in the far West, and it is no place for men who lack the ruder, coarser virtues and physical qualities, no matter how intellectual or how refined and delicate their sensibilities. Such are more likely to fail there than in older communities. Probably during the past few years more than half of the young Easterners who have come West with a little money to learn the cattle business have failed signally and lost what they had in the beginning. The West, especially the far West, needs men who have been bred on the farm or in the workshop far more than it does clerks or college graduates.

Some of the cowboys are Mexicans, who generally do the actual work well enough, but are not trustworthy; moreover, they are always regarded with extreme disfavor by the Texans in an outfit, among whom the intolerant caste spirit is very strong. Southern-born whites will never work under them, and look down upon all colored or half-caste races. One spring I had with my wagon a Pueblo Indian, an excellent rider and roper, but a drunken, worthless, lazy devil; and in the summer of 1886 there were with us a Sioux half-breed, a quiet, hard-working, faithful fellow, and a mulatto, who was one of the best cow hands in the whole round-up.

Cowboys, like most Westerners, occasionally show remarkable versatility in their tastes and pursuits. One whom I know has abandoned his regular occupation for the past nine months, during which time he has been in succession a bartender, a school-teacher, and a probate judge! Another, whom I once employed for a short while, had passed through even more varied experiences, including those of a barber, a sailor, an apothecary, and a buffalo-hunter.

As a rule the cowboys are known to each other only by their first names, with, perhaps, as a prefix, the title of the brand for which they are working. Thus I remember once overhearing a casual remark to the effect that "Bar Y Harry" had married "the Seven Open A Girl," the latter being the daughter of a neighboring ranchman. Often they receive nicknames, as, for instance, Dutch Wannigan, Windy Jack, and Kid Williams, all of whom are on the list of my personal acquaintances.

No man traveling through or living in the country need fear molestation from the cowboys unless he himself accompanies them on their drinking-bouts, or in other ways plays the fool, for they are, with us at any rate, very good fellows, and the most determined and effective foes of real law-breakers, such as horse and cattle thieves, murderers, etc. Few of the outrages quoted in Eastern papers as their handiwork are such in reality, the average Easterner apparently considering every individual who wears a broad hat and carries a six-shooter a cowboy. These outrages are, as a rule, the work of the roughs and criminals who always gather on the outskirts of civilization, and who infest every frontier town until the decent citizens become sufficiently numerous and determined to take the law into their own hands and drive them out. The old buffalo-hunters, who formed a distinct class, became powerful forces for evil once they had destroyed the vast herds of mighty beasts the pursuit of which had been their means of livelihood. They were absolutely shiftless and improvident; they had no settled habits; they were inured to peril and hardship, but entirely unaccustomed to steady work; and so they afforded just the materials from which to make the bolder and more desperate kinds of criminals. When the game was gone they hung round the settlements for some little time, and then many of them naturally took to horse-stealing, cattle-killing, and highway robbery, although others, of course, went into honest pursuits. They were men who died off rapidly, however; for it is curious to see how many of these plainsmen, in spite of their iron nerves and thews, have their constitutions completely undermined, as much by the terrible hardships they have endured as by the fits of prolonged and bestial revelry with which they have varied them.

The "bad men," or professional fighters and man-killers, are of a different stamp, quite a number of them being, according to their light, perfectly honest. These are the men who do most of the killing in frontier communities; yet it is a noteworthy fact that the men who are killed generally deserve their fate. These men are, of course, used to brawling, and are not only sure shots, but, what is equally important, able to "draw" their weapons with marvelous quickness. They think nothing whatever of murder, and are the dread and terror of their associates; yet they are very chary of taking the life of a man of good standing, and will often weaken and back down at once if confronted fearlessly. With many of them their courage arises from confidence in their own powers and knowledge of the fear in which they are held; and men of this type often show the white feather when they get in a tight place. Others, however, will face any odds without flinching; and I have known of these men fighting, when mortally wounded, with a cool, ferocious despair that was terrible. As elsewhere, so here, very quiet men are often those who in an emergency show themselves best able to hold their own. These desperadoes always try to "get the drop" on a foe—that is, to take him at a disadvantage before he can use his own weapon. I have known more men killed in this way, when the affair was wholly one-sided, than I have known to be shot in fair fight; and I have known fully as many who were shot by accident. It is wonderful, in the event of a street fight, how few bullets seem to hit the men they are aimed at.

During the last two or three years the stockmen have united to put down all these dangerous characters, often by the most summary exercise of lynch law. Notorious bullies and murderers have been taken out and hung, while the bands of horse and cattle thieves have been regularly hunted down and destroyed in pitched fights by parties of armed cowboys; and as a consequence most of our territory is now perfectly law-abiding. One such fight occurred north of me early last spring. The horse-thieves were overtaken on the banks of the Missouri; two of their number were slain, and the others were driven on the ice, which broke, and two more were drowned. A few months previously another gang, whose headquarters were near the Canadian line, were surprised in their hut; two or three were shot down by the cowboys as they tried to come out, while the rest barricaded themselves in and fought until the great log-hut was set on fire, when they broke forth in a body, and nearly all were killed at once, only one or two making their escape. A little over two years ago one committee of vigilantes in eastern Montana shot or hung nearly sixty—not, however, with the best judgment in all cases.

OUT ON THE RANGE

A stranger in the North-western cattle country is especially struck by the resemblance the settlers show in their pursuits and habits to the Southern people. Nebraska and Dakota, east of the Missouri, resemble Minnesota and Iowa and the States farther east, but Montana and the Dakota cow country show more kinship with Texas; for while elsewhere in America settlement has advanced along the parallels of latitude, on the great plains it has followed the meridians of longitude and has gone northerly rather than westerly. The business is carried on as it is in the South. The rough-rider of the plains, the hero of rope and revolver, is first cousin to the backwoodsman of the southern Alleghanies, the man of the ax and the rifle; he is only a unique offshoot of the frontier stock of the South-west. The very term "round-up" is used by the cowboys in the exact sense in which it is employed by the hill people and mountaineers of Kentucky, Tennessee, and North Carolina, with whom also labor is dear and poor land cheap, and whose few cattle are consequently branded and turned loose in the woods exactly as is done with the great herds on the plains.

But the ranching industry itself was copied from the Mexicans, of whose land and herds, the South-western frontiersmen of Texas took forcible possession; and the traveler in the North-west will see at a glance that the terms and practices of our business are largely of Spanish origin. The cruel curb-bit and heavy stock-saddle, with its high horn and cantle, prove that we have adopted Spanish-American horsegear; and the broad hat, huge blunt spurs, and leather *chaperajos* of the rider, as well as the corral in which the stock are penned, all alike show the same ancestry. Throughout the cattle country east of the Rocky Mountains, from the Rio Grande to the Saskatchewan, the same terms are in use and the same system is followed; but on the Pacific slope, in California, there are certain small differences, even in nomenclature. Thus, we of the great plains all use the double cinch saddle, with one girth behind the horse's fore legs and another farther back, while Californians prefer one with a single cinch, which seems to us much inferior for stock-work. Again, Californians use the Spanish word "lasso," which with us has been entirely dropped, no plainsman with pretensions to the title thinking of any word but "rope," either as noun or verb.

The rope, whether leather lariat or made of grass, is the one essential feature of every cowboy's equipment. Loosely coiled, it hangs from the horn or is tied to one side of the saddle in front of the thigh, and is used for every conceivable emergency, a twist being taken round the stout saddle-horn the second the noose settles over the neck or around the legs of a chased animal. In helping pull a wagon up a steep pitch, in dragging an animal by the horns out of a bog-hole, in hauling logs for the fire, and in a hundred other ways aside from its legitimate purpose, the rope is of invaluable service, and dexterity with it is prized almost or quite as highly as good horsemanship, and is much rarer. Once a cowboy is a good roper and rider, the only other accomplishment he values is skill with his great army revolver, it being taken for granted that he is already a thorough plainsman and has long mastered the details of cattlework; for the best roper and rider alive is of little use unless he is hard-working, honest, keenly alive to his employer's interest, and very careful in the management of the cattle.

All cowboys can handle the rope with more or less ease and precision, but great skill in its use is only attained after long practice, and for its highest development needs that the man should have begun in earliest youth. Mexicans literally practice from infancy; the boy can hardly toddle before he gets a string and begins to render life a burden to the hens, goats, and pigs. A really first-class roper can command his own price, and is usually fit for little but his own special work.

It is much the same with riding. The cowboy is an excellent rider in his own way, but his way differs from that of a trained school horseman or cross-country fox-hunter as much as it does from the horsemanship of an Arab or of a Sioux Indian, and, as with all these, it has its special merits and special defects—schoolman, fox-hunter, cowboy, Arab, and Indian being all alike admirable riders in their respective styles, and each cherishing the same profound and ignorant contempt for every method but his own. The flash riders, or horse-breakers, always called "bronco busters," can perform really marvelous feats, riding with ease the most vicious and unbroken beasts, that no ordinary cowboy would dare to tackle. Although sitting seemingly so loose in the saddle, such a rider cannot be jarred out of it by the wildest plunges, it being a favorite feat to sit out the antics of a bucking horse with silver half-dollars under each knee or in the stirrups under each foot. But their method of breaking is very rough, consisting only in saddling and bridling a beast by main force and then riding him, also by main force, until he is exhausted, when he is turned over as "broken." Later on the cowboy himself may train his horse to stop or wheel instantly at a touch of the reins or bit, to start at top speed at a signal, and to stand motionless when left. An intelligent pony soon picks up a good deal of knowledge about the cow business on his own account.

All cattle are branded, usually on the hip, shoulder, and side, or on any one of them, with letters, numbers, or figures in every combination, the outfit being known by its brand. Near me, for instance, are the Three Sevens, The Thistle, the Bellows, the OX, the VI., the Seventy-six Bar (76), and the Quarter Circle Diamond (◊) outfits. The dew-lap and the ears may also be cut, notched, or slit. All brands are registered, and are thus protected against imitators, any man tampering with them being punished as severely as possible. Unbranded animals are called *mavericks*, and when found on the round-up are either branded by the owner of the range on which they are, or else are sold for the benefit of the association. At every shipping point, as well as where the beef cattle are received, there are stock inspectors who jealously examine all the brands on the live animals or on the hides of the slaughtered ones, so as to detect any foul play, which is immediately reported to the association. It becomes second nature with a cowboy to inspect and note the brands of every bunch of animals he comes across.

Perhaps the thing that seems strangest to the traveler who for the first time crosses the bleak plains of this Upper Missouri grazing country is the small number of cattle seen. He can hardly believe he is in the great stock region, where for miles upon miles he will not see a single head, and will then come only upon a straggling herd of a few score. As a matter of fact, where there is no artificial food put up for winter use cattle always need a good deal of ground per head; and this is peculiarly the case with us in the North-west, where much of the ground is bare of vegetation and where what pasture there is is both short and sparse. It is a matter of absolute necessity, where beasts are left to shift for themselves in the open during the bitter winter weather, that they then should have grass that they have not cropped too far down; and to insure this it is necessary with us to allow on the average about twenty-five acres of ground to each animal. This means that a range of country ten miles square will keep between two and three thousand head of stock only, and if more are put on, it is at the risk of seeing a severe winter kill off half or three-quarters of the whole number. So a range may be in reality overstocked when to an Eastern and unpracticed eye it seems hardly to have on it a number worth taking into account.

Overstocking is the great danger threatening the stock-raising industry on the plains. This industry has only risen to be of more than local consequence during the past score of years, as before that time it was confined to Texas and California; but during these two decades of its existence the stockmen in different localities have again and again suffered the most ruinous losses, usually with overstocking as the ultimate cause. In the south the drought, and in the north the deep snows, and everywhere unusually bad winters, do immense damage; still, if the land is fitted for stock at all, they will, averaging one year with another, do very well so long as the feed is not cropped down too close.

But, of course, no amount of feed will make some countries worth anything for cattle that are not housed during the winter; and stockmen in choosing new ranges for their herds pay almost as much attention to the capacity of the land for yielding shelter as they do to the abundant and good quality of the grass. High up among the foot-hills of the mountains cattle will not live through the winter; and an open, rolling prairie land of heavy rainfall, where in consequence the snow lies deep and there is no protection from the furious cold winds, is useless for winter grazing, no matter how thick and high the feed. The three essentials for a range are grass, water, and shelter: the water is only needed in summer and the shelter in winter, while it may be doubted if drought during the hot months has ever killed off more cattle than have died of exposure on shelterless ground to the icy weather, lasting from November to April.

The finest summer range may be valueless either on account of its lack of shelter or because it is in a region of heavy snowfall—portions of territory lying in the same latitude and not very far apart often differing widely in this respect, or extraordinarily severe weather may cause a heavy death-rate utterly unconnected with overstocking. This was true of the loss that visited the few herds which spent the very hard winter of 1880 on the northern cattle plains. These were the pioneers of their kind, and the grass was all that could be desired; yet the extraordinary severity of the weather proved too much for the cattle. This was especially the case with those herds consisting of "pilgrims," as they are called—that is, of animals driven up on to the range from the south, and therefore in poor condition. One such herd of pilgrims on the Powder River suffered a loss of thirty-six hundred out of a total of four thousand, and the survivors kept alive only by browsing on the tops of cottonwoods felled for them. Even seasoned animals fared very badly. One great herd in the Yellowstone Valley lost about a fourth of its number, the loss falling mainly on the breeding cows, calves, and bulls,—always the chief sufferers, as the steers, and also the dry cows, will get through almost anything. The loss here would have been far heavier than it was had it not been for a curious trait shown by the cattle. They kept in bands of several hundred each, and during the time of the deep snows a band would make a start and travel several miles in a straight line, plowing their way through the drifts and beating out a broad track; then, when stopped by a frozen water-course or chain of buttes, they would turn back and graze over the trail thus made, the only place where they could get at the grass.

A drenching rain, followed by a severe snap of cold, is even more destructive than deep snow, for the saturated coats of the poor beasts are turned into sheets of icy mail, and the grass-blades, frozen at the roots as well as above, change into sheaves of brittle spears as uneatable as so many icicles. Entire herds have perished in consequence of such a storm. Mere cold, however, will kill only very weak animals, which is fortunate for us, as the spirit in the thermometer during winter often sinks to fifty degrees below zero, the cold being literally arctic; yet though the cattle become thin during such a snap of weather, and sometimes have their ears, tails, and even horns frozen off, they nevertheless rarely die from the cold alone. But if there is a blizzard blowing at such a time, the cattle need shelter, and if caught in the open, will travel for scores of miles before the storm, until they reach a break in the ground, or some stretch of dense woodland, which will shield them from the blasts. If cattle traveling in this manner come to some obstacle that they cannot pass, as, for instance, a wire fence or a steep railway embankment, they will not try to make their way back against the storm, but will simply stand with their tails to it until they drop dead in their tracks; and, accordingly, in some parts of the country—but luckily far to the south of us—the railways are fringed with countless skeletons of beasts that have thus perished, while many of the long wire fences make an almost equally bad showing. In some of the very open country of Kansas and Indian Territory, many of the herds during the past two years have suffered a loss of from sixty to eighty per cent., although this was from a variety of causes, including drought as well as severe winter weather. Too much rain is quite as bad as too little, especially if it falls after the 1st of August, for then, though the growth of grass is very rank and luxuriant, it yet has little strength and does not cure well on the stalk; and it is only possible to winter cattle at large at all because of the way in which the grass turns into natural hay by this curing on the stalk.

But scantiness of food, due to overstocking, is the one really great danger to us in the north, who do not have to fear the droughts that occasionally devastate portions of the southern ranges. In a fairly good country, if the feed is plenty, the natural increase of a herd is sure shortly to repair any damage that may be done by an unusually severe winter—unless, indeed, the latter should be one such as occurs but two or three times in a century. When, however, the grass becomes cropped down, then the loss in even an ordinary year is heavy among the weaker animals, and if the winter is at all severe it becomes simply appalling. The snow covers the shorter grass much quicker, and even when there is enough, the cattle, weak and unfit to travel around, have to work hard to get it; their exertions tending to enfeeble them and to render them less able to cope with the exposure and cold. The large patches of brushwood, into which the cattle crowd and which to a small number afford ample shelter and some food, become trodden down and yield neither when the beasts become too plentiful. Again, the grass is, of course, soonest eaten off where there is shelter; and, accordingly, the broken ground to which the animals cling during winter may be grazed bare of vegetation though the open plains, to which only the hardiest will at this season stray, may have plenty; and insufficiency of food, although not such as actually to starve them, weakens them so that they succumb readily to the cold or to one of the numerous accidents to which they are liable—as slipping off an icy butte or getting cast in a frozen washout. The cows in calf are those that suffer most, and so heavy is the loss among these and so light the calf crop that it is yet an open question whether our northern ranges are as a whole fitted for breeding. When the animals get weak they will huddle into some nook or corner and simply stay there till they die. An empty hut, for instance, will often in the spring be found to contain the carcasses of a dozen weak cows or poor steers that have crawled into it for protection from the cold, and once in have never moved out.

Overstocking may cause little or no harm for two or three years, but sooner or later there comes a winter which means ruin to the ranches that have too many cattle on them; and in our country, which is even now getting crowded, it is merely a question of time as to when a winter will come that will understock the ranges by the summary process of killing off about half of all the cattle throughout the North-west.* The herds that have just been put on suffer most in such a case; if they have come on late and are composed of weak animals, very few indeed, perhaps not ten per cent., will survive. The cattle that have been double or single wintered do better; while a range-raised steer is almost as tough as a buffalo.

In our northern country we have "free grass"; that is, the stockmen rarely own more than small portions of the land over which their cattle range, the bulk of it being unsurveyed and still the property of the National Government—for the latter refuses to sell the soil except in small lots, acting on the wise principle of distributing it among as many owners as possible. Here and there some ranchman has acquired title to narrow strips of territory peculiarly valuable as giving water-right; but the amount of land thus occupied is small with us,—although the reverse is the case farther south,—and there is practically no fencing to speak of. As a consequence, the land is one vast pasture, and the man who overstocks his own range damages his neighbors as much as himself. These huge northern pastures are too dry and the soil too poor to be used for agriculture until the rich, wet lands to the east and west are occupied; and at present we have little to fear from grangers. Of course, in the end much of the ground will be taken up for small farms, but the farmers that so far have come in have absolutely failed to make even a living, except now and then by raising a few vegetables for the use of the stockmen; and we are inclined to welcome the incoming of an occasional settler, if he is a decent man, especially as, by the laws of the Territories in which the great grazing plains lie, he is obliged to fence in his own patch of cleared ground, and we do not have to keep our cattle out of it.

At present we are far more afraid of each other. There are always plenty of men who for the sake of the chance of gain they themselves run are willing to jeopardize the interests of their neighbors by putting on more cattle than the land will support—for the loss, of course, falls as heavily on the man who has

* *Written in the fall of 1886; the ensuing winter exactly fulfilled the prophecy.*

put on the right number as on him who has put on too many; and it is against these individuals that we have to guard so far as we are able. To protect ourselves completely is impossible, but the very identity of interest that renders all of us liable to suffer for the fault of a few also renders us as a whole able to take some rough measures to guard against the wrong-doing of a portion of our number; for the fact that the cattle wander intermixed over the ranges forces all the ranchmen of a locality to combine if they wish to do their work effectively. Accordingly, the stockmen of a neighborhood, when it holds as many cattle as it safely can, usually unitedly refuse to work with any one who puts in another herd. In the cow country a man is peculiarly dependent upon his neighbors, and a small outfit is wholly unable to work without their assistance when once the cattle have mingled completely with those of other brands. A large outfit is much more master of its destiny, and can do its own work quite by itself; but even such a one can be injured in countless ways if the hostility of the neighboring ranchmen is incurred.

The best days of ranching are over; and though there are many ranchmen who still make money, yet during the past two or three years the majority have certainly lost. This is especially true of the numerous Easterners who went into the business without any experience and trusted themselves entirely to their Western representatives; although, on the other hand, many of those who have made most money at it are Easterners, who, however, have happened to be naturally fitted for the work and who have deliberately settled down to learning the business as they would have learned any other, devoting their whole time and energy to it. Stock-raising, as now carried on, is characteristic of a young and wild land. As the country grows older, it will in some places die out, and in others entirely change its character; the ranches will be broken up, will be gradually modified into stock-farms, or, if on good soil, may even fall under the sway of the husbandman.

In its present form stock-raising on the plains is doomed, and can hardly outlast the century. The great free ranches, with their barbarous, picturesque, and curiously fascinating surroundings, mark a primitive stage of existence as surely as do the great tracts of primeval forests, and like the latter must pass away before the onward march of our people; and we who have felt the charm of the life, and have exulted in its abounding vigor and its bold, restless freedom, will not only regret its passing for our own sakes, but must also feel real sorrow that those who come after us are not to see, as we have seen, what is perhaps the pleasantest, healthiest, and most exciting phase of American existence.

COMING OFF THE TRAIL IN '82

JACK POTTER

In the spring of 1882, the New England Livestock Co. bought three thousand short horns in Southwest Texas, cut them into four herds and started them on the trail to Colorado, with King Hennant of Corpus Christi in charge of the first herd, Asa Clark of Legarta the second herd, Billie Burke the third herd, and John Smith of San Antonio in charge of the fourth. When they reached a point near San Antonio Smith asked me to go with the herd at $30 a month and transportation back. Now, friends, it will not take long to tell my experiences going up the trail, but it will require several pages to recount what I had to endure coming back home.

There was no excitement whatever on this drive. It was to me very much like a summer's outing in the Rocky Mountains. We went out by way of Fredericksburg, Mason and Brady City, and entered the Western trail at Cow Gap, going through Albany near Fort Griffin, where we left the Western trail and selected a route through to Trinidad, Colorado, via Double Mountain Fork of the Brazos, Wichita and Pease Rivers to the Charles Goodnight ranch on the Staked Plains. We had several stampedes while crossing the plains.

En route we saw thousands of antelope crossing the trail in front of the herd. We crossed the Canadian at Tuscosa. This was a typical cowboy town, and at this time a general roundup was in progress, and 1 believe there were a hundred and fifty cow-punchers in the place. They had taken a day off to celebrate, and as there were only seven saloons in Tuscosa they were all doing a flourishing business. We had trouble in crossing the river with our herd, as those fellows were riding up and down the streets yelling and shooting.

Our next point was over the Dim Trail and freight road to Trindad, Colorado, where we arrived the tenth of July. Here the manager met us and relieved two of the outfits, saying the country up to the South Platte was easy driving and that they would drift the horses along with two outfits instead of four. The manager and King Hennant made some medicine and called for the entire crews of John Smith and Asa Clark, and told Billie Burke to turn his crew over to Hennant, who was to take charge of the whole drive. I was disappointed, for I did not want to spoil the summer with a two months' drive. They called the men up one at a time and gave them their checks. However, King Hennant arranged with the manager for me to remain with them, and then it was agreed to send me with some of the cow ponies to the company's cattle ranch in the Big Horn Basin later on.

The drive up the South Platte was fine. We traveled for three hundred miles along the foothills of the Rockies, where we were never out of sight of the snowy ranges. We went out by way of La Junta, Colorado, on the Santa Fe, and then to Deer Trail. We would throw our two herds together at night and the next morning again cut them into two herds for the trail. We arrived at the South Platte River near Greeley, Colorado, about the tenth of August.

The itch or ronia had broken out on the trail and in those days people did not know how to treat it successfully. Our manager sent us a wagon load of kerosene and sulphur with which to fight the disease.

When we reached Cow Creek we turned the herds loose and began building what is known as the Crow Ranch. I worked here thirty days and it seemed like thirty years. One day the manager came out and gave instructions to shape up a herd of one hundred and fifty select cow ponies to be taken to the Big Horn Ranch, and I was chosen to go with the outfit. This was the first time I had seen an outfit fixed up in the North. I supposed we would get a pack horse and fit up a little outfit and two of us hike out with them. It required two days to get started. The outfit consisted of a wagon loaded with chuck, a big wall tent, cots to sleep on, a stove, and a number one cook. We hit the trail, and it was another outing for me, for this time we were traveling in new fields.

After leaving Cheyenne we pulled out for Powder River and then up to Sheridan. The weather was getting cold and I began to get homesick. When we reached the Indian country I was told that it was only one day's drive to Custer's battleground. I was agreeably surprised the next morning as we came down a long slope into the Little Big Horn Valley to the battleground. I was under the impression that Sitting Bull had hemmed Custer up in a box canyon and came up from behind and massacred his entire army. But that was a mistake, as Sitting Bull with his warriors was camped in the beautiful valley when Custer attacked him in the open. It seems that the Indians retreated slowly up a gradual slope to the east and Custer's men followed. The main fight took place at the top of the rise, as there is a headstone where every soldier fell, and a monument where Custer was killed.

The balance of that day we passed thousands of Indians who were going the same direction we were traveling. When they go to the agency to get their monthly allowance they take along everything with them, each family driving their horses in a separate bunch. When we arrived at the Crow Agency the boss received a letter from the manager instructing him to send me back to Texas, as the company were contracting for cattle for spring delivery, and I would be needed in the trail drives. The next morning I roped my favorite horse and said to the boys: "Good-bye, fellows, I am drifting south where the climate suits my clothes." That day I overtook an outfit on the way to Ogallala, and traveled with them several days, and then cut out from them and hiked across the prairie one hundred and fifty miles to the Crow ranch, where I sold my two horses and hired a party to take me and my saddle to Greeley, where I expected to set out for home.

Now, reader, here I was, a boy not yet seventeen years old, two thousand miles from home. I had never been on a railroad train, had never slept in a hotel, never taken a bath in a bath house, and from babyhood I had heard terrible stories about ticket thieves, money-changers, pickpockets, three-card monte, and other robbing schemes, and I had horrors about this, my first railroad trip. The first thing I did was to make my money safe by tying it up in my shirt tail. I had a draft for $150 and some currency. I purchased a second-hand trunk and about two hundred feet of rope with which to tie it. The contents of the trunk were one apple-horn saddle, a pair of chaps, a Colt's 45, one sugan, a hen-skin blanket, and a change of dirty clothes. You will see later that this trunk and its contents caused me no end of trouble.

My cowboy friends kindly assisted me in getting ready for the journey. The company had agreed to provide me with transportation, and they purchased a local ticket to Denver for me and gave me a letter to deliver to the general ticket agent at this point, instructing him to sell me a reduced ticket to Dodge City, Kansas, and enable me to secure a cowboy ticket from there to San Antonio for twenty-five dollars. Dodge City was the largest delivering point in the Northwest, and by the combined efforts of several prominent stockmen a cheap rate to San Antonio had been perfected for the convenience of the hundreds of cowboys returning home after the drives.

About four PM the Union Pacific train came pulling into Greeley. Then it was a hasty handshake with the boys. One of them handed me my trunk check, saying, "Your baggage is loaded. Good-bye, write me when you get home," and the train pulled out. It took several minutes for me to collect myself, and then the conductor came through and called for the tickets. When I handed him my ticket he punched a hole in it, and then pulled out a red slip, punched it, too, and slipped it into my hatband. I jumped to my feet and said, "You can't come that on me. Give me back my ticket," but he passed out of hearing, and as I had not yet learned how to walk on a moving train, I could not follow him. When I had become fairly settled in my seat again the train crossed a bridge, and as it went by I thought the thing was going to hit me on the head. I dodged those bridges all the way up to Denver. When I reached there I got off at the Union Station and walked down to the baggage car, and saw them unloading my trunk. I stepped up and said: "I will take my trunk." A man said, "No; we are handling this baggage." "But," said I, "that is my trunk, and has my saddle and gun in it." They paid no attention to me and wheeled the trunk off to the baggage room, but I followed right along, determined that they were not going to put anything over me. Seeing that I was so insistent one of the men asked me for the check. It was wrapped up in my shirt tail, and I went after it, and produced the draft I had been given as wages. He looked at it and said, "This is not your trunk check. Where is your metal check with numbers on it?" Then it began to dawn on me what the darn thing was, and when I produced it and handed it to him he asked me where I was going. I told him to San Antonio, Texas, if I could get there. I then showed him my letter to the general ticket agent, and he said: "Now, boy, you leave this trunk right here and we will recheck it and you need not bother about it." That sounded bully to me.

I followed the crowd down Sixteenth and Curtiss Streets and rambled around looking for a quiet place to stop. I found the St. Charles Hotel and made arrangements to stay all night. Then I went off to a barber shop to get my hair cut and clean up a bit. When the barber finished with me he asked if I wanted a bath, and when I said yes, a negro porter took me down the hallway and into a side room. He turned on the water, tossed me a couple of towels and disappeared. I commenced undressing hurriedly, fearing the tub would fill up before I could get ready. The water was within a few inches of the top of the tub when I plunged in. Then I gave a yell like a Comanche Indian, for the water was boiling hot! I came out of the tub on all fours, but when I landed on the marble floor it was so slick that I slipped and fell backwards with my head down. I scrambled around promiscuously, and finally got my footing with a chair for a brace. I thought: "Jack Potter, you are scalded after the fashion of a hog." I caught a lock of my hair to see if it would "slip," at the same time fanning myself with my big Stetson hat. I next examined my toe nails, for they had received a little more dipping than my hair, but I found them in fairly good shape, turning a bit dark, but still hanging on.

That night I went to the Tabor Opera House and saw a fine play. There I found a cowboy chum, and we took in the sights until mid-night, when I returned to the St. Charles. The porter showed me up to my room and turned on the gas. When he had gone I undressed to go to bed, and stepped up to blow out the light. I blew and blew until I was out of breath, and then tried to fan the flame out with my hat, but I had to go to bed and leave the gas burning. It was fortunate that I did not succeed, for at that time the papers were full of accounts of people gassed just that way.

The next morning I started out to find the Santa Fe ticket office, where I presented my letter to the head man there. He was a nice appearing gentleman, and when he had looked over the letter he said, "So you are a genuine cowboy? Where is your gun and how many notches have you on its handle? I suppose you carry plenty of salt with you on the trail for emergency? I was just reading in a magazine a few days ago about a large herd which stampeded and one of the punchers mounted a swift horse and ran up in front of the leaders and began throwing out salt, and stopped the herd just in time to keep them from running off a high precipice." I laughed heartily when he told me this and said, "My friend, you can't learn the cow business out of books. That yarn was hatched in the brain of some fiction writer who probably never saw a cow in his life. But I am pleased to find a railroad man who will talk, for I always heard that a railroad man only used two words, Yes and No." Then we had quite a pleasant conversation. He asked me if I was ever in Albert's Buckhorn saloon in San Antonio and saw the collection of fine horns there. Then he gave me an emigrant cowboy ticket to Dodge City and a letter to the agent at that place stating that I was eligible for a cowboy ticket to San Antonio.

As it was near train time I hunted up the baggage crew and told them I was ready to make another start. I showed them my ticket and asked them about my trunk. They examined it, put on a new check, and gave me one with several numbers on it. I wanted to take the trunk out and put it on the train, but they told me to rest easy and they would put it on. I stood right there until I saw them put it on the train, then I climbed aboard.

This being my second day out, I thought my troubles should be over, but not so, for I couldn't face those bridges. They kept me dodging and fighting my head. An old gentleman who sat near me said, "Young man, I see by your dress that you are a typical cowboy, and no doubt you can master the worst bronco or rope and tie a steer in less than a minute, but in riding on a railway train you seem to be a novice. Sit down on this seat with your back to the front and those bridges will not bother you." And sure enough it was just as he said.

We arrived at Coolidge, Kansas, one of the old landmarks of the Santa Fe Trail days, about dark. That night at twelve o'clock we reached Dodge City, where I had to lay over for twenty-four hours. I thought everything would be quiet in the town at that hour of the night, but I soon found out that they never slept in Dodge. They had a big dance hall there which was to Dodge City what Jack Harris' Theater was to San Antonio. I arrived at the hall in time to see a gambler and a cowboy mix up in a six-shooter duel. Lots of smoke, a stampede, but no one killed. I secured a room and retired. When morning came I arose and fared forth to see Dodge City by daylight. It seemed to me that the town was full of cowboys and cattle owners. The first acquaintance I met here was George W. Saunders, now the president and chief remudero of the Old Trail Drivers. I also found Jesse Pressnall and Slim Johnson there, as well as several others whom I knew down in Texas. Pressnall said to me: "Jack, you will have lots of company on your way home. Old 'Dog Face' Smith is up here from Cotulla and he and his whole bunch are going back tonight. Old 'Dog Face' is one of the best trail men that ever drove a cow, but he is all worked up about having to go back on a train. I wish you would help them along down the line in changing cars." That afternoon I saw a couple of chuck wagons coming in loaded with punchers, who had on the same clothing they wore on the trail, their pants stuck in their boots and their spurs on. They were bound for San Antonio. Old "Dog Face" Smith was a typical Texan, about thirty years of age, with long hair and three months' growth of whiskers. He wore a blue shirt and a red cotton handkerchief around his neck. He had a bright, intelligent face that bore the appearance of a good trail hound, which no doubt was the cause of people calling him "Dog Face."

It seemed a long time that night to wait for the train and we put in time visiting every saloon in the town. There was a big stud poker game going on in one place, and I saw one Texas fellow, whose name I will not mention, lose a herd of cattle at the game. But he might have won the herd back before daylight.

I will never forget seeing that train come into Dodge City that night. Old "Dog Face" and his bunch were pretty badly frightened and we had considerable difficulty in getting them aboard. It was about 12:30 when the train pulled out. The conductor came around and I gave him my cowboy ticket. It was almost as long as your arm, and as he tore off a chunk of it I said: "What authority have you to tear up a man's ticket?" He laughed and said, "You are on my division. I simply tore off one coupon and each conductor between here and San Antonio will tear off one for each division." That sounded all right, but I wondered if that ticket would hold out all the way down.

Everyone seemed to be tired and worn out and the bunch began bedding down. Old "Dog Face" was out of humor, and was the last one to bed down. At about three o'clock our train was sidetracked to let the west-bound train pass. This little stop caused the boys to sleep the sounder. Just then the westbound train sped by traveling at the rate of about forty miles an hour, and just as it passed our coach the engineer blew the whistle. Talk about your stampedes! That bunch of sleeping cowboys arose as one man, and started on the run with old "Dog Face" Smith in the lead. I was a little slow in getting off, but fell in with the drags. I had not yet woke up, but thinking I was in a genuine cattle stampede, yelled out, "Circle your leaders and keep up the drags." Just then the leaders circled and ran into the drags, knocking some of us down. They circled again and the news butcher crawled out from under foot and jumped through the window like a frog. Before they could circle back the next time, the train crew pushed in the door and caught old "Dog Face" and soon the bunch quieted down. The conductor was pretty angry and threatened to have us transferred to the freight department and loaded into a stock car.

We had breakfast at Hutchinson, and after eating and were again on our way, speeding through the beautiful farms and thriving towns of Kansas, we organized a kangaroo court and tried the engineer of that westbound train for disturbing the peace of passengers on the eastbound train. We heard testimony all morning, and called in some of the train crew to testify. One of the brakemen said it was an old trick for that engineer to blow the whistle at that particular siding and that he was undoubtedly the cause of a great many stampedes. The jury brought in a verdict of guilty and assessed the death penalty. It was ordered that he be captured, taken to some place on the western trail, there to be hog-tied like a steer, and then have the road brand applied with a good hot iron and a herd of not less than five thousand long-horn Texas steers made to stampede and trample him to death.

We had several hours lay-over at Emporia, Kansas, where we took the M., K. & T. for Parsons, getting on the main line through Indian Territory to Denison, Texas. There was a large crowd of punchers on the through train who were returning from Ogallala by way of Kansas City and Omaha.

As we were traveling through the Territory old "Dog Face" said to me: "Potter, I expect it was me that started that stampede up there in Kansas, but I just couldn' help it. You see, I took on a scare once and since that time I have been on the hair trigger when suddenly awakened. In the year 1875 me and Wild Horse Jerry were camped at a water hole out west of the Nueces River, where we were snaring mustangs. One evening a couple of peloncias pitched camp nearby, and the next morning our remuda was missing, all except our night horses. I told Wild Horse Jerry to hold down the camp and watch the snares, and I hit the trail of those peloncias which headed for the Rio Grande. I followed it for about forty miles and then lost all signs. It was nightfall, so I made camp, prepared supper and rolled up in my blanket and went to sleep. I don't know how long I slept, but I was awakened by a low voice saying: "Dejarle desconsar bien por que en un rato el va a comenzar su viaje por el otro mundo." (Let him rest well, as he will soon start on his journey to the other world.) It was the two Mexican horse thieves huddled around my campfire smoking their cigarettes and taking it easy, as they thought they had the drop on me. As I came out of my bed two bullets whizzed near my head, but about that time my old Colt's forty-five began talking, and the janitor down in Hades had two more peloncias on his hands. Ever since that night, if I am awakened suddenly I generally come out on my all fours roaring like a buffalo bull. I never sleep on a bedstead, for it would not be safe for me, as I might break my darn neck, so I always spread down on the floor."

It was a long ride through the Territory, and we spent the balance of the day singing songs and making merry. I kept thinking about my trunk, and felt grateful that the railroad people had sent along a messenger to look out for it. At Denison we met up with some emigrant families going to Uvalde, and soon became acquainted with some fine girls in the party. They entertained us all the way down to Taylor, where we changed cars. As we told them good-bye one asked me to write a line in her autograph album. Now I was sure enough "up a tree." I had been in some pretty tight places, and had had to solve some pretty hard problems, but this was a new one for me. You see, the American people go crazy over some new fad about once a year, and in 1882 it was the autograph fad. I begged the young lady to excuse me, but she insisted, so I took the album and began writing down all the road brands that I was familiar with. But she told me to write a verse of some kind. I happened to think of a recitation I had learned at school when I was a little boy, so I wrote as follows: "It's tiresome work says lazy Ned, to climb the hill in my new sled, and beat the other boys. Signed, Your Bulliest Friend, JACK POTTER."

We then boarded the I. & G. N. for San Antonio, and at Austin a lively bunch joined us, including Hal Gosling, United States Marshal, Captain Joe Sheeley and Sheriff Quigley of Castroville. Pretty soon the porter called out "San Antonio, Santonnie-o," and that was music to my ears. My first move on getting off the train was to look for my trunk and found it had arrived. I said to myself, "Jack Potter, you're a lucky dog. Ticket held out all right, toe nails all healed up, and trunk came through in good shape." After registering at the Central Hotel, I wrote to that general ticket agent at Denver as follows:

San Antonio, Texas Oct. 5th, 1882.

Gen. Ticket Agt. A. T. & S. F.,

1415 Lamar St., Denver, Colo.:

Dear Sir—I landed in San Antonio this afternoon all O. K. My trunk also came through without a scratch. I want to thank you very much for the man you sent along to look after my trunk. He was very accommodating, and would not allow me to assist him in loading it on at Denver. No doubt he will want to see some of the sights of San Antonio, for it is a great place, and noted for its chili con carne. When he takes a fill of this food, as every visitor does, you can expect him back in Denver on very short notice, as he will be seeking a cooler climate. Did you ever eat any chili con carne? I will send you a dozen cans soon, but tell your wife to keep it in the refrigerator as it might set the house on fire. Thank you again for past favors.

Your Bulliest Friend,

JACK POTTER.

END OF THE TRAIL
(COWBOY LOGIC AND FROLIC)

EDGAR BEECHER BRONSON

We were jogging along in the saddle across the divide between the Rawhide and the Niobrara, Concho Curly and I, *en route* from Cheyenne to the ranch to begin the spring calf round-up.

Travelling the lower trail, we had slept out on our saddle-blankets the night before, beside the sodden wreck of a fire in a little cottonwood grove on Rawhide.

While the night there passed was wretched and comfortless to the last degree, for even our slickers were an insufficient protection against the torrents of warm rain that fell upon us hour after hour, the curtain of gray morning mists that hedged us round about was scarce lifted at bidding of the new day's sun, before eyes, ears, and nostrils told us Nature had wrought one of her great miracles while we slept.

All seed life, somnolent so long in whatever earthly cells the winds and rains had assisted to entomb it, had awakened and arisen into a living force; tree vitality, long hibernating invisible, even in sorely wounded, lightning-riven, gray cottonwood torsos, was asserting itself; voices long still, absent God alone knows where, were gladly hailing the return of the spring.

We had lain down in a dull gray dead world, to awaken in a world pulsing with the life and bright with the colour of sprouting seed and revivifying sap.

Our eyes had closed on tree trunks gaunt and pale, a veritable spectral wood; on wide stretches of buffalo grass, withered yellow and prone upon the ground, the funereal aspect of the land heightened by the grim outlines of two Sioux warriors lashed on pole platforms for their last resting-place in the branches above our heads, fragments of a faded red blanket pendent and flapping in the wind beneath one body, a blue blanket beneath the other, grisly neighbours who appeared to approach or recede as our fire alternately blazed and flickered—both plainly warriors, for beneath each lay the whitening bones of his favourite war pony, killed by his tribesmen to provide him a mount in the Spirit Land.

It was a voiceless, soundless night before the storm came, bar the soughing of the wind, the weary creaking of bare branches, the feeble murmur of the brook (drunk almost dry by the thirsty land), and the flap-flap of our neighbours' last raiment.

Our eyes opened upon trees crowned with the pale green glory of bursting buds, upon valley and hill slopes verdant as the richest meadow; our ears were greeted with the sweet voices of birds chanting a welcome to the spring, and the rollicking song of a brimful stream, merry over the largess it now bore for man and beast and bird and plant, while the sweet, humid scents of animate, palpitant nature had driven from our nostrils the dry, horrid odours of the dead.

So comes the spring on the plains—in a single night!

Concho Curly was a raw, unlettered, freckled product of a Texas pioneer's cabin isolated in a nook of the west slope of the hills about the head of the Concho River, near where they pitch down to the waterless, arid reaches of the staked plains.

But the miracle of the spring, appealing to the universal love of the mysterious, had set even Curly's untrained brain questioning and philosophising.

After riding an hour or more silent, his chin buried in the loose folds of his neckerchief, Curly sighed deeply and then observed:

"Ol' man, hit shore 'pears to me Ol' Mahster hain't never strained Hisself none serious tryin' to divide up even the good things o' this yere world o' ourn.

Looks like He never tried none, an' ef He did, He's shore made a pow'ful pore job!"

"Why, Curley," I asked, "what makes you think so?"

"Some fellers has so dod-blamed much an' some so dod-burned little," he replied. "Why, back whar you-all comes from, thar's oodles o' grass an' fodder an' water the hull year, ain't they, while out here frequent hit's so fur from grass to water th' critters goes hungry to drink an' dry to graze—don't they?"

"Quite true, Curly," I admitted.

"Wall, back thar, then, 'most every feller must be rich, an' have buggies an' ambulances plenty, an' a big gallery round his *jacal*, an' nothin' to do but set on her all day studdyin' what new bunch o' prittys he'll buy for his woman, an' wettin' his whistle frequent with rot-gut to he'p his thinker *select* new kinds o' throat-ticklin' grub to feed his face an' new kinds o' humany quilts an' goose-hair pillers to git to lay on, while out here a hull passle o' fellers is so dod-burned pore they don't even own a name, an' hull families lives 'n' dies 'thout ever gittin' to set in a buggy or to eat anythin' but co'n pone an' sow belly, 'thout no fixin's or dulces to chase them, like th' puddin's an' ice cream you gits to town ef you've got th' spondulix an' are willin' to blow yourse'f reckless.

"On th' level, you cain't make me believe Ol' Mahster had anythin' to do with th' makin' o' these yere parts out yere—ef He had, He'd a shore give us fellers a squarer deal; 'pears to me like when His job was nigh done an' He was sorta tired an' restin', the boys musta got loose an' throwed this part o' th' country together, kinda careless-like, outen th' leavin's."

And on and on he monologued, plucking an occasional "yes" or "no" from me, till apparently a new line of reflection diverted him and he fell silent to study where it might lead him.

Presently, when I was lolling comfortably in the saddle, half dozing, he nudged me in the ribs with the butt of his quirt and remarked:

"Say, ol' man! I reckon I musta been sleep-walkin' an' eatin' loco weed, for I been arguin' plumb wrong.

"Come to think o' hit, while we-all that's pore has to work outrageous to make a skimp of a livin', you-all that's rich has to work a scandalous sight harder to git to keep what you got.

"An' then there's ice! Jest think o' ice! Th' rich has her in th' summer, but d—n me ef th' pore don't get her in th' winter, good an' plenty—makin' hit look like th' good things o' this world is whacked up mighty nigh even, after all, an' that we-all hain't got no roar comin' to us."

Thus happily settled his recent worries, Curly himself dropped into a contented doze, and left me to resume mine.

The season opening promised to be an unusually busy one. It was obvious we were nearing the crest of a three-years' boom. Wild range cattle were selling at higher prices than ever before or since. The Chicago beef-market was correspondingly strong. But there were signs of a reaction that made me anxious to gather and ship my fat beeves soon as possible, before the tide turned.

Every winter two thirds of my herd drifted before the bitter blizzards southeast into the sand hills lying between the sink of Snake Creek and the head of the Blue, a splendid winter range where snow never lay long, and out of which cattle came in the spring in unusually good condition.

Thus, at the end of the spring round-up, I was able to cut fifteen hundred beef steers that, after being grazed under close herd a few weeks on the better-cured, stronger feed on the divide between the Niobrara and Snake Creek, were fit for market, and with them we arrived at our shipping point—Ogallala—July 2, 1882.

Leaving the outfit camped, luckily, on a bench twenty feet above the main valley of the Platte, I rode two miles into town to make shipping arrangements.

A wonderful sight was the Platte Valley about Ogallala in those days, for it was the northern terminus of the great Texas trail of the late '70s and early '80s, where trail-drivers brought their herds to sell and northern ranchmen came to bargain.

That day, far as the eye could see up, down, and across the broad, level valley were cattle by the thousand—thirty or forty thousand at least—a dozen or more separate outfits, grazing in loose, open order so near each other that, at a distance, the valley appeared carpeted with a vast Persian rug of intricate design and infinite variety of colours.

Approached nearer, where individual riders and cattle began to take form, it was a topsy-turvy scene I looked down upon.

The day was unusually, tremendously hot—probably 112° in the shade—so hot the shimmering heat-waves developed a mirage that turned town, herds, and riders upside down—all sprung in an instant to gigantic height, the squat frame houses tall as modern skyscrapers, cattle and riders big as elephants, while here and there deep blue lakes lay placidly over broad expanses that a few moments before were a solid field of variegated, brilliant colours.

Arrived at the Spofford House, the one hotel of the town, I found a familiar bunch of famous Texas cattle kings—Seth Mayberry, Shanghai Pierce, Dillon

Fant, Jim Ellison, John Lytle, Dave Hunter, Jess Presnall, etc.—each with a string of long horns for sale.

The one store and the score of saloons, dance-halls, and gambling joints that lined up south of the railway track and formed the only street Ogallala could boast, were packed with wild and woolly, long-haired and bearded, rent and dusty, lusting and thirsty, red-sashed brush-splitters in from the trail outfits for a frolic.

And every now and then a chorus of wild, shrill yells and a fusillade of shots rent the air that would make a tenderfoot think a battle-royal was on.

But there was nothing serious doing, then; it was only cowboy frolic.

The afternoon's fierce heat proved a weather breeder, as some had predicted.

Shortly after supper, but long before sundown, a dense black cloud suddenly rose in the north, swept swiftly above and around us till it filled the whole zenith—an ominous, low-hanging pall that brought upon us in a few minutes the utter darkness of a starless night.

Quite as suddenly as the coming of the cloud, the temperature fell 40° or 50°, and drove us into the hotel.

And we were little more than sheltered behind closed doors before torrents of rain descended, borne on gusts of hurricane force that blew open the north door of the dining-room, picked up a great pin-pool board standing across a biscuit-shooting opening in the partition, swept it across the breadth of the office, narrowly missing Mayberry and Fant, and dashed it to splinters against the opposite wall.

Ten minutes later the violence of rain and downpour slackened, almost stopped.

Shanghai went to the door and looked out, shivered, and shut it with the remark:

"By cripes, fellers! 'pears like Ol' Mahster plumb emptied His tanks that clatter; the hull flat's under water."

"Maybe so He's stackin' us up agin' a swimmin' match," was Fant's cheerful comment.

And within another ten minutes it certainly seemed Fant had called the turn.

A tremendous crash of thunder came, with lightning flashes that illumined the room till our oil lamps looked like fireflies, followed by another tornado-driven downpour it seemed hopeless to expect the house could survive.

And while our ears were still stunned by its first roar, suddenly there came flood waters pouring in over door-sills and through floor cracks, rising at a rate that instantly drove us all to refuge on the second floor of the hotel.

We were certainly in the track, if not the centre, of a waterspout!

But barely were we upstairs before the aerial flood-gates closed, till no more than an ordinary heavy soaking of rain was falling, and the wind slackened sufficiently to permit us to climb out on the roof of the porch and take stock of the situation.

Our case looked grave enough—grave past hope of escape, or even help.

"Fellers," quietly remarked Shanghai, "here's a game where passin' don't go—leastwise till it's cash in an' pass out o' existence. Here's where I'd sell my chance o' seein' to-morrow's sun at a dollar a head, an' agree not to tally more'n about five head. I've been up agin' Yankee charges, where the air was full of lead and the cold steel 'peared to hide all the rest of the scenery; I've laid in a buffalo wallow two days and nights surrounded by Comanches, and been bush-whacked by Kiowas on the Palo Pinto, but never till now has Shanghai been up agin' a game he couldn't figure out a way to beat."

And so, in truth, it looked.

The whole world was afloat, a raging, tossing flood—our world, at least.

To us a universal flood could mean no more.

Far as the eye could see rolled waters.

And the waters were rising all the time, ever rising, higher and higher; not creeping, but rising, leaping up the pillars of the porch!

It seemed only a matter of moments before the hotel must collapse, or be swept from its foundations.

Already the flood beneath us was dotted thick with drifting flotsam—wrecks of houses, fences, stables, sidewalks.

Men, women, and children were afloat upon the wreckage, drifting they knew not where, safe they knew not how long, shrieking for aid no one could lend.

Dumb beasts and fowls drifted by us, their inarticulate terror cries rising shrill above the piping of the wind—cattle bawling, pigs squealing, dogs howling, horses neighing, chickens clucking madly, and even the ducks and geese quacking notes of alarm.

It seemed the end of the world, no less—at least, of our little corner of it.

However the old Spofford House held to her foundations was a mystery, unless she stood without the line of the strongest current.

But hold she stoutly did until, perhaps fifteen minutes after we were driven upstairs, word was passed out to us by watchers within upon the staircase that the rise had stopped—stopped just about half-way between floor and ceiling of the first story.

And right then, just as we were catching our breath to interchange congratulations, a new terror menaced us—a terror even more appalling than the remorseless flood that still held us in its grip.

An inky-black pall of cloud still shut out the stars and shrouded all the earth, but a pall so riven and torn by constantly recurring flashes of sheet-lightning that our entire field of view was lit almost as bright as by a midday sun.

Suddenly, off in the south, over the divide between the Platte and the Republican, an ominous shape uprose like magic from below the horizon—a balloon-shaped cloud of an ashen-gray that, from reflection of the lightning or other cause, had a sort of phosphorescent glow that outlined its form against the inky background and made plain to our eyes, as the hand held before one's face, that we confronted an approaching cyclone.

Nearing us it certainly was at terrific speed, for it grew and grew as we looked till its broad dome stood half up to the zenith, while its narrow tail was lashing viciously about near and often apparently upon the earth.

On it came, head-on for us, for a space of perhaps four minutes—until, I am sure, any onlooker who had a prayer loose about him was not idle.

And perhaps (who knows?) one or another such appeal prevailed, for just as it seemed no earthly power could save us, off eastward it switched and sped swiftly out of our sight.

It was near midnight before the waters began to fall, and morning before the house was free of them.

And when about eight o'clock horses were brought us, we had to wade and swim them about a quarter of a mile to reach the dry uplands.

From the roof of the hotel we could see that even the trail herds were badly scattered and commingled, and it was the general opinion my herd of un-trail-broke wild beef steers were probably running yet, somewhere.

But when I got out to the benchland where I had left them, there they were, not a single one missing. This to my infinite surprise, for usually an ordinary thunderstorm will drift beef herds more or less, if not actually stampede them.

The reason was quickly explained: the storm had descended upon them so suddenly and with such extraordinary violence that they were stunned into immobility.

Apparently they had been directly beneath the very centre of the water-spout, for the boys told me the rain fell in such solid sheets that they nearly smothered, drowned while mounted and sitting their saddles about the trembling, bellowing herd; came down in such torrents they had to hold their hands in shape of an inverted cup above nose and mouth to get their breath!

Miles of the U.P. track were destroyed that laid us up for three days, awaiting repairs.

The first two days the little village was quiet, trail men out bunching and separating their herds, townsmen taking stock of their losses.

But the third day hell popped good and plenty.

Tempers were so fiery and feelings so tindery that it seemed the recent violence of the very elements themselves had got into men's veins and made them bent to destroy and to kill.

All day long street and saloon swarmed with shouting, quarrelling, shooting punchers, owners and peace officers were alike powerless to control.

About noon the town marshal and several deputies made a bold try to quell the turmoil—and then had to mount and ride for their lives, leaving two of Hunter & Evans's men dead in front of The Cowboys' Rest, and a string of wounded along the street.

This incident stilled the worst of the tumult for two or three hours, for many took up pursuit of the marshal, while the rest were for a time content to quietly talk over the virtues of the departed in the intervals between quadrille-sets—for, of course, the dancing went on uninterrupted.

Toward evening, notwithstanding the orgy had again resumed a fast and furious pace, Fant, Mayberry, and myself were tempted to join the crowd in The Cowboys' Rest, tempted by glimpses of a scene caught from our perch on a corner of the depot platform opposite.

"That *is* blamed funny!" remarked Mayberry. "Come along over and let's see her good. We're no more liable to get leaded there than anywhere else."

So over we went.

"The Rest" belied its name sadly, for rest was about the only thing Jim Tucker was not prepared to furnish his wild and woolly patrons.

Who entered there left coin behind—and was lucky if he left no more.

Stepped within the door, a rude pine "bar" on the right invited the thirsty; on the left, noisy "tin horns," whirring wheels, clicking faro "cases," and rattling chips lured the gamblers; while away to the rear of the room stretched a hundred feet or more of dance-hall, on each of whose rough benches sat enthroned a temptress—hard of eye, deep-lined of face, decked with cheap gauds, sad wrecks of the sea of vice here lurching and tossing for a time.

As we entered, Mayberry's foreman met us and whispered to his boss:

"You-all better stan' back a little, colonel, out o' line o' th' door. Ol' one-eyed John Graham, o' th' Hunter outfit, settin' thar in th' corner's layin' fo' th' sheriff—allows 'twas him sot up th' marshal to shell us up this mo'nin'—an' ol' John's shore pizen when he starts."

So back we moved to the rear end of the bar.

The room was packed: a solid line of men and women before the bar, every table the centre of a crowding group of players, the dance-hall floor and benches jam-full of a roistering, noisy throng.

At the moment all were happy and peace reigned.

But there was one obvious source of discord—there were "not enough gals to go round"; not enough, indeed, if those present had been multiplied by ten, a situation certain to stir jealousies and strife among a lot of wild nomads for whom this was the first chance in four months to gaze into a woman's eyes.

To be sure, one resourceful and unselfish puncher—a foreman of one of the trail outfits—was doing *his* best to relieve the prevailing deficiency in feminine dancers, and it was a distant glimpse of his efforts that had brought us over.

Bearing, if not boasting, the proud old Dutch name of Jake De Puyster, this rollicking six-foot-two blond giant had heard Buck Groner growl:

"Hain't had airy show for a dance yet. Nairy heifer's throwed her eye my way 'fore she's been roped and tied in about a second. Reckon it's shoot for one or pull my freight for camp, and I ain't sleepy none."

"You stake you'self out, son, a few minutes, and I'll git you a she-pardner you'll be glad of a chance to dance with and buy prittys for," reassured Jake, and then disappeared.

Ten minutes later he returned, bringing Buck a partner that stopped drinking, dance, and play—the most remarkably clad figure that ever entered even a frontier dance-hall.

Still wearing his usual costume—wide chaps, spurred heels, and belt—having removed nothing but his tall-crowned Mexican sombrero, Jake had mavericked three certain articles of feminine apparel and contrived to get himself into them.

Cocked jauntily over his right eye he wore a bright red toque crowned with a faded wreath of pale blue flowers, from which a bedraggled green feather drooped wearily over his left ear; about his waist wrinkled a broad pink sash, tied in a great double bow-knot set squarely in front, while fastened also about his waist, pendent no more than midway of his long thighs, hung a garment white of colour, filmy of fabric, bifurcated of form, richly ruffled of extremity—so habited came Jake, and, with a broad grin lurking within the mazes of his great bushy beard and monstrous moustache, sidled mincing to his mate and shyly murmured a hint he might have the privilege of the next quadrille.

At first Buck was furious, growled, and swore to kill Jake for the insult, until, infected by the gales of laughter that swept the room, he awkwardly offered his arm and led his weird partner to an unfilled set.

And a sorry hour was this to the other ladies; for, while there were better dancers and prettier, that first quadrille made "Miss De Puyster" the belle of the ball for the rest of the day and night, and not a few serious affrays over disputes for an early chance of a "round" or "square" with her were narrowly avoided.

Just as we reached the rear end of the bar, the fiddles stopped their cruel liberties with the beautiful measures of "*Sobre las Olas*," and Buck led his panting partner up to our group and courteously introduced us thus:

"Miss De Puyster, here's two mighty slick ol'long-horn mossbacks you wants to be pow'ful shy of, for they'd maverick off their own daddy, an' a little short-horn Yankee orfun I wants to ax you to adopt an' try to make a good mother to. Fellers, this yere's Miss De Puyster; she ain't much for pretty, but she's hell for active on th' floor—so dod-burned active I couldn't tell whether she was waltzin' or tryin' to throw me side-holts."

But before we had time to properly make our aknowledgements, a new figure in the dance was called—a figure which, though familiar enough in Ogallala dance-halls, distracted and held the attention of all present for a few minutes.

Later we learned that, early in the day, a local celebrity—Bill Thompson by name, a tin horn by trade, and a desperado by pretence—had proffered some insult to Big Alice, the leading lady of the house, for which Jim Tucker had "called him down good and plenty," but under such circumstances that to resent it then would have been to court a fairer fight than Bill's kind ever willingly took on.

But, remembering he was brother to Ben Thompson, the then most celebrated man-killer in the State of Texas (who himself was to fall to King Fisher's pistol in Jack Harris's San Antonio variety theatre a few years later), brooding Tucker's abuse of him, figuring what Ben would do in like circumstances illumining his view of the situation by frequent resorts to red eye, Bill by evening had rowled himself ready for action.

So it happened that at the very moment Buck finished our introduction to "Miss De Puyster," Bill suddenly stepped within the door of the saloon and took a quick snapshot at Tucker, who was directly across the bar from us and in the act of passing Fant a glass of whisky with his left hand.

The ball cut off three of Tucker's fingers and the tip of the fourth, and, the bar being narrow, spattered us with his blood.

Tucker fell, momentarily, from the shock.

Supposing from Tucker's quick drop he had made an instant kill, Bill stuck his pistol in his waistband and started leisurely out of the door and down the street.

But no sooner was he out of the house than Jim sprang up, seized a sawed-off ten-gauge shotgun, ran to the door, leveled the gun across the stump of his maimed left hand, and emptied into Bill's back at about six paces, a trifle more No. 4 duckshot than his system could assimilate.

Perhaps altogether ten minutes were wasted on this incident and the time taken to tourniquet and tie up Jim's wound and to pack Bill inside and stow him in a corner behind the faro lookout's chair; and then Jim's understudy called, "Pardners fo' th' next dance!" the fiddlers bravely tackled but soon got hopelessly beyond their depth in "The Blue Danube," and dancing and frolic were resumed, with "Miss De Puyster" still the belle of the ball.

JUSTICE IN THE SADDLE

ANDY ADAMS

It was an hour after the usual time when we bedded down the cattle. The wagon had overtaken us about sunset, and the cooks' fire piloted us into a camp fully two miles to the right of the trail. A change of horses was awaiting us, and after a hasty supper Tupps detailed two young fellows to visit Ogalalla. It required no urging; I outlined clearly what was expected of their mission, requesting them to return by the way of Flood's wagon, and to receive any orders which my employer might see fit to send. The horse-wrangler was pressed in to stand the guard of one of the absent lads on the second watch, and I agreed to take the other, which fell in the third. The boys had not yet returned when our guard was called, but did so shortly afterward, one of them hunting me up on night-herd.

"Well," said he, turning his horse and circling with me, "we caught onto everything that was adrift. The Rebel and Sponsilier were both in town, in charge of two deputies. Flood and your brother went in with us, and with the lads from the other outfits, including those across the river, there must have been twenty-five of Lovell's men in town. I noticed that Dave and The Rebel were still wearing their six-shooters, while among the boys the arrests were looked upon as quite a joke. The two deputies had all kinds of money, and wouldn't allow no one but themselves to spend a cent. The biggest one of the two—the one who gave you the cigar—would say to my boss: 'Sponsilier, you're a trail foreman from Texas—one of Don Lovell's boss men—but you're under arrest; your cattle are in my possession this very minute. You understand that, don't you? Very well, then; everybody come up and have a drink on the sheriff's office.' That was about the talk in every saloon and dancehall visited. But when we proposed starting back to camp, about midnight, the big deputy said to Flood: 'I want you to tell Colonel Lovell that I hold a warrant for his arrest; urge him not to put me to the trouble of coming out after him. If he had identified himself to me this afternoon, he could have slept on a goose-hair bed to-night instead of out there on the mesa, on the cold ground. His reputation in this town would entitle him to three meals a day, even if he was under arrest. Now, we'll have one more, and tell the damned old rascal that I'll expect him in the morning."

We rode out the watch together. On returning to Flood's camp, they had found Don Lovell awake. The old man was pleased with the report, but sent me no special word except to exercise my own judgement. The cattle were tired after their long tramp of the day before, the outfit were saddle weary, and the first rays of the rising sun flooded the mesa before men or animals offered to arise. But the duties of another day commanded us anew, and with the cook calling us, we rose to meet them. I was favorably impressed with Tupps as a segundo, and after breakfast suggested that he graze the cattle over to the North Platte, cross it, and make a permanent camp. This was agreed to, half the men were excused for the day, and after designating, beyond the river, a clump of cottonwoods where the wagon could be found, seven of us turned and rode back for Ogalalla. With picked mounts under us, we avoided the other cattle which could be seen grazing northward, and when fully halfway to town, there before us on the brink of the mesa loomed up the lead of a herd. I soon recognized Jack Splann on the point, and taking a wide circle, dropped in behind him, the column stretching back a mile and coming up the bluffs, forty abreast like an army in loose marching order. I was proud of those "Open A's;" they were my first herd, and though in a hurry to reach town, I turned and rode back with them for fully a mile.

Splann was acting under orders from Flood, who had met him at the ford that morning. If the cattle were in the possession of any deputy sheriff, they had failed to notify Jack, and the latter had already started for the North Platte of his own accord. The "Drooping T" cattle were in the immediate rear under Forrest's segundo, and Splann urged me to accompany him that forenoon, saying: "From what the boys said this morning, Dave and Paul will not be given a hearing until two o'clock this afternoon. I can graze beyond the north ford by that time, and then we'll all go back together. Flood's right behind here with the 'Drooping T's,' and I think it's his intention to go all the way to the river. Drop back and see him."

The boys who were with me never halted, but had ridden on towards town. When the second herd began the ascent of the mesa, I left Splann and turned back, waiting on the brink for its arrival. As it would take the lead cattle some time to reach me, I dismounted, resting in the shade of my horse. But my rest was brief, for the clattering hoofs of a cavalcade of horsemen were approaching, and as I arose, Quince Forrest and Bob Quirk with a dozen or more men dashed up and halted. As their herds were intended for the Crow and Fort Washakie agencies, they would naturally follow up the south side of the North Platte, and an hour or two of grazing would put them in camp. The Buford cattle, as well as Flood's herd, were due to cross this North Fork of the mother Platte within ten miles of Ogalalla, their respective routes thenceforth being north and northeast. Forrest, like myself, was somewhat leary of entering the town, and my brother and the boys passed on shortly, leaving Quince behind. We discussed every possible phase of what might happen in case we were recognized, which was almost certain if Tolleston or the Dodge buyers were encountered. But an overweening hunger to get into Ogalalla was dominant in us, and under the excuse of settling for our supplies, after the herd passed, we remounted our horses, Flood joining us, and rode for the hamlet.

There was little external and no moral change in the town. Several new saloons had opened, and in anticipation of the large drive that year, the Dew-Drop-In dance-hall had been enlarged, and employed three shifts of bartenders. A stage had been added with the new addition, and a special importation of ladies had been brought out from Omaha for the season. I use the term *ladies* advisedly, for in my presence one of the proprietors, with marked courtesy, said to an Eastern stranger, "Oh, no, you need no introduction. My wife is the only woman in town; all the balance are ladies." Beyond a shave and a hair-cut, Forrest and I fought shy of public places. But after the supplies were settled for, and some new clothing was secured, we chambered a few drinks and swaggered about with considerable ado. My bill of supplies amounted to one hundred and twenty-six dollars, and when, without a word, I drew a draft for the amount, the proprietor of the outfitting store, as a pelon, made me a present of two fine silk handkerchiefs. Forrest was treated likewise, and having invested ourselves in white shirts, with flaming red ties, we used the new handkerchiefs to otherwise decorate our persons. We had both chosen the brightest colors, and with these knotted about our necks, dangling from pistol-pockets, or protruding from ruffled shirt fronts, our own mothers would scarcely have known us. Jim Flood, whom we met casually on a back street, stopped, and after circling us once, said, "Now if you fellows just keep perfectly sober, your disguise will be complete."

Meanwhile Don Lovell had reported at an early hour to the sheriff's office. The legal profession was represented in Ogalalla by several firms, criminal practice being their specialty; but fortunately Mike Sutton, an attorney of Dodge, had arrived in town the day before on a legal errand for another trail drover. Sutton was a frontier advocate, alike *popular* with the Texas elements and the gambling fraternity, having achieved laurels in his home town as a criminal lawyer. Mike was born on the little green isle beyond the sea, and, gifted with the Celtic wit, was also in logic clear as the tones of a bell, while his insight into human motives was almost superhuman. Lovell had had occasion in other years to rely on Sutton's counsel, and now would listen to no refusal of his services. As it turned out, the lawyer's mission in Ogalalla was so closely in sympathy with Lovell's trouble that they naturally strengthened each other. The highest tribunal of justice in Ogalalla was the county court, the judge of which also ran the stock-yards during the shipping season, and was banker for two monte games at the Lone Star saloon. He enjoyed the reputation of being an honest, fearless jurist, and supported by a growing civic pride, his decisions gave satisfaction. A sense of crude equity governed his rulings, and as one of the citizens remarked, "Whatever the judge said, *went*." It should be remembered that this was in '84, but had a similar trouble occurred five years earlier, it is likely that Judge Colt would have figured in the preliminaries, and the coroner might have been called on to impanel a jury. But the rudiments of civilization were sweeping westward, and Ogalalla was nerved to the importance of the occasion; for that very afternoon a hearing was to be given for the possession of two herds of cattle, valued at over a quarter-million dollars.

The representatives of The Western Supply Company were quartered in the largest hotel in town, but seldom appeared on the streets. They had employed a firm of local attorneys, consisting of an old and a young man, both of whom evidently believed in the justice of their client's cause. All the cattle-hands in Lovell's employ were anxious to get a glimpse of Tolleston, many of them patronizing the bar and table of the same hostelry, but their efforts were futile until the hour arrived for the hearing. They probably have a new court-house in Ogalalla now, but at the date of this chronicle the building which served as a temple of justice was poorly proportioned, its height being entirely out of relation to its width. It was a two-story affair, the lower floor being used for county offices, the upper one as the court-room. A long stairway ran up the outside of the building, landing on a gallery in front, from which the sheriff announced the sitting of the honorable court of Keith County. At home in Texas, lawsuits were so rare that though I was a grown man, the novelty of this one absorbed me. Quite a large crowd had gathered in advance of the hour, and while awaiting the arrival of Judge Mulqueen, a contingent of fifteen men from the two herds in question rode up and halted in front of the court-house. Forrest and I were lying low, not caring to be seen, when the three plaintiffs, the two local attorneys, and Tolleston put in an appearance. The cavalcade had not yet dismounted, and when Dorg Seay caught sight of Tolleston, he stood up in his stirrups and sang out, "Hello there, Archibald! my old college chum, how goes it?"

Judge Mulqueen had evidently dressed for the occasion, for with the exception of the plaintiffs, he was the only man in the court-room who wore a coat. The afternoon was a sultry one; in that first bottom of the Platte there was scarcely a breath of air, and collars wilted limp as rags. Neither map nor chart graced the unplastered walls, the unpainted furniture of the room was sadly in need of repair, while a musty odor permeated the room. Outside the railing the seating capacity of the court-room was rather small, rough, bare planks serving for seats, but the spectators gladly stood along the sides and rear, eager to catch every word, as they silently mopped the sweat which oozed alike from citizen and cattleman. Forrest and I were concealed in the rear, which was packed with Lovell's boys, when the judge walked in and court opened for the hearing. Judge Mulqueen requested counsel on either side to be as brief and direct as possible, both in their pleadings and testimony, adding: "If they reach the stock-yards in time, I may have to load out a train of feeders this evening. We'll bed the cars, anyhow." Turning to the sheriff, he continued: "Frank, if you happen outside, keep an eye up the river; those Lincoln feeders made a deal yesterday for five hundred three-year-olds.—Read your complaint."

The legal document was read with great fervor and energy by the younger of the two local lawyers. In the main it reviewed the situation correctly, every point, however, being made subservient to their object,—the possession of the cattle. The plaintiffs contended that they were the innocent holders of the original contract between the government and The Western Supply company, properly assigned; that they had purchased these two herds in question, had paid earnest-money to the amount of sixty-five thousand dollars on the same, and concluded by petitioning the court for possession. Sutton arose, counseled a moment with Lovell, and borrowing a chew of tobacco from Sponsilier, leisurely addressed the court.

"I shall not trouble your honor by reading our reply in full, but briefly state its contents," said he, in substance. "We admit that the herds in question, which have been correctly described by road brands and ages, are the property of my client. We further admit that the two trail foremen here under arrest as accessories were acting under the orders of their employer, who assumes all responsibility for their acts, and in our pleadings we ask this honorable court to discharge them from further detention. The earnest-money, said to have been paid on these herds, is correct to a cent, and we admit having the amount in our possession. But," and the little advocate's voice rose, rich in its Irish brogue, "we deny any assignment of the original contract. The Western Supply Company is a corporation name, a shield and fence of thieves. The plaintiffs here can claim no assignment, because they themselves constitute the company. It has been decided that a man cannot steal his own money, neither can he assign from himself to himself. We shall prove by a credible witness that The Western Supply Company is but another name for John C. Fields, Oliver Radcliff, and the portly gentleman who was known a year ago as 'Honest' John Griscom, one of his many aliases. If to these names you add a few moneyed confederates, you have The Western Supply Company, one and the same. We shall also prove that for years past these same gentlemen have belonged to a ring, all brokers in government contracts, and frequently finding it necessary to use assumed names, generally that of a corporation."

Scanning the document in his hand, Sutton continued: "Our motive in selling and accepting money on these herds in Dodge demands a word of explanation. The original contract calls for five million pounds of beef on foot to be delivered at Fort Buford. My client is a sub-contractor under that award. There are times, your honor, when it becomes necessary to resort to questionable means to attain an end. This is one of them. Within a week after my client had given bonds for the fulfillment of his contract, he made the discovery that he was dealing with a double-faced set of scoundrels. From that day until the present moment, secret-service men have shadowed every action of the plaintiffs. My client has anticipated their every move. When beeves broke in price from five to seven dollars a head, Honest John, here, made his boasts in Washington City over a champagne supper that he and his associates would clear one hundred thousand dollars on their Buford contract. Let us reason together how this could be done. The Western Supply Company refused, even when offered a bonus, to assign their contract to my client. But they were perfectly willing to transfer it, from themselves as a corporation, to themselves as individuals, even though they had previously given Don Lovell a subcontract for the delivery of the beeves. The original award was made seven months ago, and the depreciation in cattle since is the secret of why the frog ate the cabbage. My client is under the necessity of tendering his cattle on the day of delivery, and proposes to hold this earnest-money to indemnify himself in case of an adverse decision at Fort Buford. It is the only thing he can do, as The Western Supply Company is execution proof, its assets consisting of some stud-horse office furniture and a corporate seal. On the other hand, Don Lovell is rated at half a million, mostly in pasture lands; is a citizen of Medina County, Texas, and if these gentlemen have any grievance, let them go there and sue him. A judgement against my client is good. Now, your honor, you have our side of the question. To be brief, shall these old Wisinsteins come out here from Washington City and dispossess any man of his property? There is but one answer—not in the Republic of Keith."

All three of the plaintiffs took the stand, their testimony supporting the complaint, Lovell's attorney refusing even to cross-examine any one of them. When they rested their case Sutton arose, and scanning the audience for some time, inquired, "Is Jim Reed here?" In response, a tall, one-armed man worked his way from the outer gallery through the crowd and advanced to the rail. I knew Reed by sight only, my middle brother having made several trips with his trail cattle, but he was known to every one by reputation. He had lost an arm in the Confederate service, and was recognized by the gambling fraternity as the gamest man among all trail drovers, while every cowman from the Rio Grande to the Yellowstone knew him as a poker-player. Reed was asked to take the stand, and when questioned if he knew either of the plaintiffs, siad:

"Yes, I know that fat gentleman, and I'm powerful glad to meet up with him again," replied the witness, designating Honest John. "That man is so crooked that he can't sleep in a bed, and it's one of the wonders of this country that he hasn't stretched hemp before this. I made his acquaintance as manager of The Federal Supply Company, and delivered three thousand cows to him at the Washita Indian Agency last fall. In the final settlement, he drew on three different banks, and one draft of twenty-eight thousand dollars came back, indorsed, *drawee unknown*. I had other herds on the trail to look after, and it was a month before I found out that the check was bogus, by which time Honest John had sailed for Europe. There was nothing could be done but put my claim in a judgement and lay for him. But I've got a grapevine twist on him now, for no sooner did he buy a herd here last week than Mr. Sutton transferred the judgment to this jurisdiction, and his cattle will be attached this afternoon. I've been on his trail for nearly a year, but he'll come to me now, and before he can move his beeves out of this county, the last cent must come, with interest, attorney's fees, detective bills, and remuneration for my own time and trouble. That's the reason that I'm so glad to meet him. Judge, I've gone to the trouble and expense to get his record for the last ten years. He's so snaky he sheds his name yearly, shifting for a nickname from Honest John to The Quaker. In '80 he and his associates did business under the name of The Army & Sutler Supply Company, and I know of two judgments that can be brought very reasonable against that corporation. His record would convince any one that he despises to make an honest dollar."

The older of the two attorneys for the plaintiffs asked a few questions, but the replies were so unsatisfactory to their side, that they soon passed the witness. During the cross-questioning, however, the sheriff had approached the judge and whispered something to his honor. As there were no further witnesses to be examined, the local attorneys insisted on arguing the case, but Judge Mulqueen frowned them down saying:

"This court sees no occasion for any argument in the present case. You might spout until you were black in the face and it wouldn't change my opinion any; besides I've got twenty cars to send and a train of cattle to load out this evening. This court refuses to interfere with the herds in question, at present the property of and in possession of Don Lovell, who, together with his men are discharged from custody. If you're in town tonight, Mr. Reed, drop into the Lone Star. Couple of nice monte games running there; hundred-dollar limit, and if you feel lucky, there's a nice bank roll behind them. Adjourn court, Mr. Sheriff."

TURNING THE TABLES

"Keep away from me, you common cow-hands," said Sponsilier, as a group of us waited for him at the foot of the court-house stairs. But Dave's gravity soon turned to a smile as he continued: "Did you fellows notice The Rebel and me sitting inside the rail among all the big augers? Paul, was it a dream, or did we sleep in a bed last night and have a sure-enough pillow under our heads? My memory is kind of hazy to-day, but I remember the drinks and the cigars all right, and saying to some one that his luck was too good to last. And here we are turned out in the cold world again, our fun all over, and now must go back to those measly cattle. But it's just what I expected."

The crowd dispersed quietly, though the sheriff took the precaution to accompany the plaintiffs and Tolleston back to their hotel. The absence of the two deputies whom we had met the day before was explained by the testimony of the one-armed cowman. When the two drovers came downstairs, they were talking very confidentially together, and on my employer noticing the large number of his men present, he gave orders for them to meet him at once at the White Elephant saloon. Those who had horses at hand mounted and dashed down the street, while the rest of us took it leisurely around to the appointed rendezvous, some three blocks distant. While on the way, I learned from The Rebel that the cattle on which the attachment was to be made that afternoon were then being held well up the North Fork. Sheriff Phillips joined us shortly after we entered the saloon, and informed my employer that the firm of Fields, Radcliff & Co. had declared war. They had even denounced him and the sheriff's office as being in collusion against them, and had dispatched Tolleston with orders to refuse services.

"Let them get on the prod all they want to," said Don Lovell to Reed and the sheriff. "I've got ninety men here, and you fellows are welcome to half of them, even if I have to go out and stand a watch on nightherd myself. Reed, we can't afford to have our business ruined by such a set of scoundrels, and we might as well fight it out here and now. Look at the situation I'm in. A hundred thousand dollars wouldn't indemnify me in having my cattle refused as late as the middle of September at Fort Buford. And believing that I will be turned down, under my contract, so Sutton says, I must tender my beeves on the appointed day of delivery, which will absolve my bondsmen and me from all liability. A man can't trifle with the government—the cattle must be there. Now in my case, Jim, what would you do?"

"That's a hard question, Don. You see we're strangers up in this North-west country. Now, if it was home in Texas, there would be only one thing to do. Of course I'm no longer handy with a shotgun, but you've got two good arms."

"Well, gentlemen," said the sheriff, "you must excuse me for interrupting, but if my deputies are to take possession of that herd this afternoon, I must saddle and go to the front. If Honest John and associates try to stand up any bluffs on my office, they'll only run on the rope once. I'm much obliged to you, Mr. Lovell, for the assurance of any help I may need, for it's quite likely that I may have to call upon you. If a ring of government speculators can come out here and reuse service, or dictate to my office, then old Keith County is certainly on the verge of decadence. Now, I'll be all ready to start for the North Fork in fifteen minutes, and I'd admire to have you all go along."

Lovell and Reed both expressed a willingness to accompany the sheriff. Phillips thanked them and nodded to the force behind the mahogany, who dexterously slid the glasses up and down the bar, and politely inquired of the double now confronting them as to their tastes. As this was the third round since entering the place, I was anxious to get away, and summoning Forrest, we started for our horses. We had left them at a barn on a back street, but before reaching the livery, Quince concluded that he needed a few more cartridges. I had ordered a hundred the day before for my own personal use, but they had been sent out with the supplies and were then in camp. My own belt was filled with ammunition, but on Forrest buying fifty, I took an equal number, and after starting out of the store, both turned back and doubled our purchases. On arriving at the stable, whom should I meet but the Wyoming cowman who had left us at Grinnell. During the few minutes in which I was compelled to listen to his troubles, he informed me that on his arrival at Ogalalla, all the surplus cow-hands had been engaged by a man named Tolleston for the Yellowstone country. He had sent to his ranch, however, for an outfit who would arrive that evening, and he expected to start his herd the next morning. But without wasting any words, Forrest and I swung into our saddles, waved a farewell to the wayfaring acquaintance, and rode around to the White Elephant. The sheriff and quite a cavalcade of our boys had already started, and on reaching the street which terminated in the only road leading to the North Ford, we were halted by Flood to await the arrival of the others. Jim Reed and my employer were still behind, and some little time was lost before they came up, sufficient to give the sheriff a full half-mile start. But under the leadership of the two drovers, we shook out our horses, and the advance cavalcade was soon overtaken.

"Well, Mr. Sheriff," said old man Don, as he reined in beside Phillips, "how do you like the looks of this for a posse? I'll vouch that they're all good cow-hands, and if you want to deputize the whole works, why, just work your rabbit's foot. You might leave Reed and me out, but I think there's some forty odd without us. Jim and I are getting a little too old, but we'll hang around and run errands and do the clerking. I'm perfectly willing to waste a week, and remember that we've got the chuck and nearly a thousand saddle horses right over here on the North Fork. You can move your office out to one of my wagons if you wish, and whatever's mine is yours, just so long as Honest John and his friends pay the fiddler. If he and his associates are going to make one hundred thousand dollars on their Buford contract, one thing is certain—I'll lose plenty of money on this year's drive. If he refuses service and you take possession, your office will be perfectly justified in putting a good force of men with the herd. And at ten dollars a day for a man and horse, they'll soon get sick and Reed will get his pay. If I have to hold the sack in the end, I don't want any company."

The location of the beeves was about twelve miles from town and but a short distance above the herds of The Rebel and Bob Quirk. It was nearly four o'clock when we left the hamlet, and by striking a free gait, we covered the intervening distance in less than an hour and a half. The mesa between the two rivers was covered with through cattle, and as we neared the herd in question, we were met by the larger one of the two chief deputies. The under-sheriff was on his way to town, but on sighting his superior among us, he halted and a conference ensured. Sponsilier and Priest made a great ado over the big deputy on meeting, and after a few inquiries were exchanged, the latter turned to Sheriff Phillips and said:

"Well, we served the papers and left the other two boys in temporary possession of the cattle. It's a badly mixed-up affair. The Texas foreman is still in charge, and he seems like a reasonable fellow. The terms of the sale were to be half cash here and the balance at the point of delivery. But the buyers only paid forty thousand down, and the trail boss refuses to start until they make good their agreement. From what I could gather from the foreman, the buyers simply buffaloed the young fellow out of his beeves, and are not hanging back for more favorable terms. He accepted service all right and assured me that our men would be welcome at his wagon until further notice, so I left matters just as I found them. But as I was on the point of leaving, that segundo of the buyers arrived and tried to stir up a little trouble. We all sat down on him rather hard, and as I left he and the Texas foreman were holding quite a big pow-wow."

"That's Tolleston all right," said old man Don, "and you can depend on him stirring up a muss if there's any show. It's a mystery to me how I tolerated that fellow as long as I did. If some of you boys will corner and hold him for me, I'd enjoy reading his title to him in a few plain words. It's due him, and I want to pay everything I owe. What's the programme, Mr. Sheriff?"

"The only safe thing to do is to get full possession of the cattle," replied Phillips. "My deputies are all right, but they don't thoroughly understand the situation. Mr. Lovell, if you can lend me ten men, I'll take charge of the herd at once and move them back down the river about seven miles. They're entirely too near the west line of the county to suit me, and once they're in our custody the money will be forthcoming, or the expenses will mount up rapidly. Let's ride."

The under-sheriff turned back with us. A swell of the mesa cut off a view of the herd, but under the leadership of the deputy we rode to its summit, and there before and under us were both camp and cattle. Arriving at the wagon, Phillips very politely informed the Texas foreman that he would have to take full possession of his beeves for a few days, or until the present difficulties were adjusted. The trail boss was a young fellow of possibly thirty, and met the sheriff's demand with several questions, but, on being assured that his employer's equity in the herd would be fully protected without expense, he offered no serious objection. It developed that Reed had some slight acquaintance with the seller of the cattle, and lost no time in informing the trail boss of the record of the parties with whom his employer was dealing. The one-armed drover's language was plain, the foreman knew Reed by reputation, and when Lovell assured the young man that he would be welcome at any of his wagons, and would be perfectly at liberty to see that his herd was properly cared for, he yielded without a word. My sympathies were with the foreman, for he seemed an honest fellow, and deliberately to take his herd from him, to my impulsive reasoning looked like an injustice. But the sheriff and those two old cowmen were determined, and the young fellow probably acted for the best in making a graceful surrender.

Meanwhile the two deputies in charge failed to materialize, and on inquiry they were reported as out at the herd with Tolleston. The foreman accompanied us to the cattle, and while on the way he informed the sheriff that he wished to count the beeves over to him and take a receipt for the same. Phillips hesitated, as he was no cowman, but Reed spoke up and insisted that it was fair and just, saying: "Of course, you'll count the cattle and give him a receipt in numbers, ages, and brands. It's not this young man's fault that his herd must undergo all this trouble, and when he turns them over to an officer of the law he ought to have something to show for it. Any of Lovell's foremen here will count them to a hair for you, and Don and I will witness the receipt, which will make it good among cowmen."

Without loss of time the herd was started east. Tolleston kept well out of reach of my employer, and besought every one to know what this movement meant. But when the trail boss and Jim Flood rode out to a swell of ground ahead, and the point-men began filling the column through between the two foremen, Archie was sagacious enough to know that the count meant something serious. In the mean time Bob Quirk had favored Tolleston with his company, and when the count was nearly half over, my brother quietly informed him that the sheriff was taking possession. Once the atmosphere cleared, Archie grew uneasy and restless, and as the last few hundred beeves were passing the counters, he suddenly concluded to return to Ogalalla. But my brother urged him not to think of going until he had met his former employer, assuring Tolleston that the old man had made inquiry about and was anxious to meet him. The latter, however, could not remember anything of urgent importance between them, and pleaded the lateness of the hour and the necessity of his immediate return to town. The more urgent Bob Quirk became, the more fidgety grew Archie. The last of the cattle were passing the count as Tolleton turned away from my brother's entreaty, and giving his horse the rowel, started off on a gallop. But there was a scattering field of horsemen to pass, and before the parting guest could clear it, a half-dozen ropes circled in the air and deftly settled over his horse's neck and himself, one of which pinioned his arms. The boys were expecting something of this nature, and fully half the men in Lovell's employ galloped up and formed a circle around the captive, now livid with rage. Archie was cursing by both note and rhyme, and had managed to unearth a knife and was trying to cut the lassos which fettered himself and horse, when Dorg Seay rode in and rapped him over the knuckles with a six-shooter, saying, "Don't do that, sweetheart; those ropes cost thirty-five cents apiece."

Fortunately, the knife was knocked from Tolleston's hand and his six-shooter secured, rendering him powerless to inflict injury to any one. The cattle count had ended, and escorted by a cordon of mounted men, both horse and captive were led over to where a contingent had gathered around to hear the result of the count. I was merely a delighted spectator, and as the other men turned from the cattle and met us, Lovell languidly threw one leg over his horse's neck, and, suppressing a smile, greeted his old foreman.

"Hello, Archie," said he; "it's been some little time since last we met. I've been hearing some bad reports about you, and was anxious to meet up and talk matters over. Boys, take those ropes off his horse and give him back his irons; I raised this man and made him the cow-hand he is, and there's nothing so serious between us that we should remain strangers. Now, Archie, I want you to know that you are in the employ of my enemies, who are as big a set of scoundrels as ever missed a halter. You and Flood, here, were the only two men in my employ who knew all the facts in regard to the Buford contract. And just because I wouldn't favor you over a blind horse, you must hunt up the very men who are trying to undermine me on this drive. No wonder they gave you employment, for you're a valuable man to them; but it's at a serious loss,—the loss of your honor. You can't go home to Texas and again be respected among men. This outfit you are with will promise you the earth, but the moment that they're through with you, you won't cut any more figure than a last year's bird's nest. They'll throw you aside like an old boot, and you'll fall so hard that you'll hear the clock tick in China. Now, Archie, it hurts me to see a young fellow like you go wrong, and I'm willing to forgive the past and stretch out a hand to save you. If you'll quit those people, you can have Flood's cattle from here to the Rosebud Agency, or I'll buy you a ticket home and you can help with the fall work at the ranch. You may have a day or two to think this matter over, and whatever you decide on will be final. You have shown little gratitude for the opportunities that I've given you, but we'll break the old slate and start all over with a new one. Now, that's all I wanted to say to you, except to do your own thinking. If you're going back to town, I'll ride a short distance with you."

The two rode away together, but halted within sight for a short conference, after which Lovell returned. The cattle were being drifted east by the deputies and several of our boys, the trail boss having called off his men on an agreement of the count. The herd had tallied out thirty-six hundred and ten head, but in making out the receipt, the fact was developed that there were some six hundred beeves not in the regular road brand. These had been purchased extra from another source, and had been paid for in full by the buyers, the seller of the main herd agreeing to deliver them along with his own. This was fortunate, as it increased the equity of the buyers in the cattle, and more than established a sufficient interest to satisfy the judgment and all expenses.

Darkness was approaching, which hastened our actions. Two men from each outfit present were detailed to hold the cattle that night, and were sent on ahead to Priest's camp to secure their suppers and a change of mounts. The deposed trail boss accepted an invitation to accompany us and spend the night at one of our wagons, and we rode away to overtake the drifting herd. The different outfits one by one dropped out and rode for their camps; but as mine lay east and across the river, the course of the herd was carrying me home. After passing The Rebel's wagon fully a half mile, we rounded in the herd, which soon lay down to rest on the bed-ground. In the gathering twilight, the camp-fires of nearly a dozen trail wagons were gleaming up and down the river, and while we speculated with Sponsilier's boys which one was ours, the guard arrived and took the bedded herd. The two old cowmen and the trail boss had dropped out opposite my brother's camp, leaving something like ten men with the attached beeves; but on being relieved by the first watch, Flood invited Sheriff Phillips and his deputies across the river to spend the night with him.

"Like to, mighty well, but can't do it," replied Phillips. "The sheriff's office is supposed to be in town, and not over on the North Fork, but I'll leave two of these deputies with you. Some of you had better ride in to-morrow, for there may be overtures made looking towards a settlement; and treat those beeves well, so that there can be no charge of damage to the cattle. Good-night, everybody."

TOLLESTON BUTTS IN

Morning dawned on a scene of pastoral grandeur. The valley of the North Platte was dotted with cattle from hill and plain. The river, well confined within its low banks, divided an unsurveyed domain of green-swarded meadows like a boundary line between vast pastures. The exodus of cattle from Texas to the new Northwest was nearing flood-tide, and from every swell and knoll the solitary figure of the herdsman greeted the rising sun.

Sponsilier and I had agreed to rejoin our own outfits at the first opportunity. We might have exchanged places the evening before, but I had a horse and some ammunition at Dave's camp and was just contentious enough not to give up a single animal from my own mount. On the other hand, Mr. Dave Sponsilier would have traded whole remudas with me; but my love for a good horse was strong, and Fort Buford was many a weary mile distant. Hence there was no surprise shown as Sponsilier rode up to his own wagon that morning in time for breakfast. We were good friends when personal advantages did not conflict, and where our employer's interest were at stake we stood shoulder to shoulder like comrades. Yet Dave gave me a big jolly about being daffy over my horses, well knowing that there is an indescribable nearness between one of our craft and his own mount. But warding off his raillery, just the same and in due time, I cantered away on my own horse.

As I rode up the North Fork towards my outfit, the attached herd was in plain view across the river. Arriving at my own wagon, I saw a mute appeal in every face for permission to go to town, and consent was readily granted to all who had not been excused on a similar errand the day before. The cook and horse-wrangler were included, and the activities of the outfit in saddling and getting away were suggestive of a prairie fire or a stampede. I accompanied them across the river, and then turned upstream to my brother's camp, promising to join them later and make a full day of it. At Bob's wagon they had stretched a fly, and in its shade lounged half a dozen men, while an air of languid indolence pervaded the camp. Without dismounting, I announced myself as on the way to town, and invited any one who wished to accompany me. Lovell and Reed both declined; half of Bob's men had been excused and started an hour before, but my brother assured me that if I would wait until the deposed foreman returned, the latter's company could be counted on. I waited, and in the course of half an hour the trail boss came back from his cattle. During the interim, the two old cowmen reviewed Grant's siege of Vicksburg, both having been participants, but on opposite sides. While the guest was shifting his saddle to a loaned horse, I inquired if there was anything that I could attend to for any one at Ogalalla. Lovell could think of nothing; but as we mounted to start, Reed aroused himself, and coming over, rested the stub of his armless sleeve on my horse's neck, saying:

"You boys might drop into the sheriff's office as you go in and also again as you are starting back. Report the cattle as having spent a quiet night and ask Phillips if he has any word for me."

Turning to the trail boss he continued: "Young man, I would suggest that you hunt up your employer and have him stir things up. The cattle will be well taken care of, but we're just as anxious to turn them back to you as you are to receive them. Tell the seller that it would be well worth his while to see Lovell and myself before going any farther. We can put him in possession of a few facts that may save him time and trouble. I reckon that's about all. Oh, yes, I'll be at this wagon all evening."

My brother rode a short distance with us and introduced the stranger as Hugh Morris. He proved a sociable fellow, had made three trips up the trail as foreman, his first two herds having gone to the Cherokee Strip under contract. By the time we reached Ogalalla, as strong a fraternal level existed between us as though we had known each other for years. Halting for a moment at the sheriff's office, we delivered our messages, after which we left our horses at the same corral with the understanding that we would ride back together. A few drinks were indulged in before parting, then each went to attend to his own errands, but we met frequently during the day. Once my boys were provided with funds, they fell to gambling so eagerly that they required no further thought on my part until evening. Several times during the day I caught glimpses of Tolleston, always on horseback, and once surrounded by quite a cavalcade of horsemen. Morris and I took dinner at the hotel where the trio of government jobbers were stopping. They were in evidence, and amongst the jolliest of the guests, commanding and receiving the best that the hostelry afforded. Sutton was likewise present, but quiet and unpretentious, and I thought there was a false, affected note in the hilarity of the ringsters, and for effect. I was known to two of the trio, but managed to overhear any conversation which was adrift. After dinner and over fragrant cigars, they reared their feet high on an outer gallery, and the inference could be easily drawn that a contract, unless it involved millions, was beneath their notice.

Morris informed me that his employer's suspicions were aroused, and that he had that morning demanded a settlement in full or the immediate release of the herd. They had laughed the matter off as a mere incident that would right itself at the proper time, and flashed as references a list of congressmen, senators, and bankers galore. But Morris's employer had stood firm in his contentions, refusing to be overawed by flattery or empty promises. What would be the result remained to be seen, and the foreman and myself wandered aimlessly around town during the afternoon, meeting other trail bosses, nearly all of whom had heard more or less about the existing trouble. That we had the sympathy of the cattle interests on our side goes without saying, and one of them, known as "the kidgloved foreman," a man in the employ of Shanghai Pierce, invoked the powers above to witness what would happen if he were in Lovell's boots. This was my first meeting with the picturesque trail boss, though I had heard of him often and found him a trifle boastful but not a bad fellow. He distinguished himself from others on his station on the trail by always wearing white shirts, kid gloves, riding-boots, inlaid spurs, while a heavy silver chain was wound several times round a costly sombrero in lieu of a hatband. We spent an hour or more together, drinking sparingly, and at parting he begged that I would assure my employer that he sympathized with him and was at his command.

The afternoon was waning when I hunted up my outfit and started them for camp. With one or two exceptions, the boys were broke and perfectly willing to go. Morris and I joined them at the livery where they had left their horses, and together we started out of town. Ordering them to ride on to camp, and saying that I expected to return by way of Bob Quirk's wagon, Morris and myself stopped at the court-house. Sheriff Phillips was in his office and recognized us both at a glance. "Well, she's working," said he, "and I'll probably have some word for you late this evening. Yes, one of the local attorneys for your friends came in and we figured everything up. He thought that if this office would throw off a certain percent of its expense, and Reed would knock off the interest, his clients would consent to a settlement. I told him to go right back and tell his people that as long as they thought that way, it would only cost them one hundred and forty dollars every twenty-four hours. The lawyer was back within twenty minutes, bringing a draft, covering every item, and urged me to have it accepted by wire. The bank was closed, but I found the cashier in a poker-game and played his hand while he went over to the depot and sent the message. The operator has orders to send a duplicate of the answer to this office, and the moment I get it, if favorable, I'll send a deputy with the news over to the North Fork. Tell Reed that I think the check's all right this time, but we'll stand pat until we know for a certainty. We'll get an answer by morning sure."

The message was hailed with delight at Bob Quirk's wagon. On nearing the river, Morris rode by way of the herd to ask the deputies in charge to turn the cattle up the river towards his camp. Several of the foreman's men were waiting at my brother's wagon, and on Morris's return he ordered his outfit to meet the beeves the next morning and be in readiness to receive them back. Our foremen were lying around temporary headquarters, and as we were starting for our respective camps for the night, Lovell suggested that we hold our outfits all ready to move out with the herds on an hour's notice. Accordingly the next morning, I refused every one leave of absence, and gave special orders to the cook and horse-wrangler to have things in hand to start on an emergency order. Jim Flood had agreed to wait for me, and we would recross the river together and hear the report from the sheriff's office. Forrest and Sponsilier rode up about the same time we arrived at his wagon, and all four of us set out for headquarters across the North Fork. The sun was several hours high when we reached the wagon, and learned that an officer had arrived during the night with a favorable answer, that the cattle had been turned over to Morris without a count, and that the deputies had started for town at daybreak.

"Well, boys," said Lovell, as we came in after picketing our horses, "Reed, here, wins out, but we're just as much at sea as ever. I've looked the situation over from a dozen different viewpoints, and the only thing to do is graze across country and tender our cattle at Fort Buford. It's my nature to look on the bright side of things, and yet I'm old enough to know that justice, in a world so full of injustice, is a rarity. By allowing the earnest-money paid at Dodge to apply, some kind of a compromise might be effected, whereby I could get rid of two of these herds, with three hundred saddle horses thrown back on my hands at the Yellowstone River. I might dispose of the third herd here and give the remuda away, but at a total loss of at least thirty thousand dollars on the Buford cattle. But then there's my bond to The Western Supply Company, and if this herd of Morris's fails to respond on the day of delivery, I know who will have to make good. An Indian uprising, or the enforcement of quarantine against Texas fever, or any one of a dozen things might tie up the herd, and September the 15th come and go and no beef offered on the contract. I've seen outfits start out and never get through with the chuck-wagon, even. Sutton's advice is good; we'll tender the cattle. There is a chance that we'll get turned down, but if we do, I have enough indemnity money in my possession to temper the wind if the day of delivery should prove a chilly one to us. I think you had all better start in the morning."

The old man's review of the situation was a rational one, in which Jim Reed and the rest of us concurred. Several of the foremen, among them myself, were anxious to start at once, but Lovell urged that we kill a beef before starting and divide it up among the six outfits. He also proposed to Flood that they go into town during the afternoon and freely announce our departure in the morning, hoping to force any issue that might be smouldering in the enemy's camp. The outlook for an early departure was hailed with delight by the older foremen, and we younger and more impulsive ones yielded. The cook had orders to get up something extra for dinner, and we played cards and otherwise lounged around until the midday meal was announced as ready. A horse had been gotten up for Lovell to ride and was on picket, all the relieved men from the attached herd were at Bob's wagon for dinner, and jokes and jollity graced the occasion. But near the middle of the noon repast, some one sighted a mounted man coming at a furious pace for the camp, and shortly the horseman dashed up and inquired for Lovell. We all arose, when the messenger dismounted and handed my employer a letter. Tearing open the missive, the old man read it and turned ashy pale. The message was from Mike Sutton, stating that a fourth member of the ring had arrived during the forenoon, accompanied by a United States marshal from the federal court at Omaha; that the officer was armed with an order of injunctive relief; that he had deputized thirty men whom Tolleston had gathered, and proposed taking possession of the two herds in question that afternoon.

"Like hell they will," said Don Lovell, as he started for his horse. His action was followed by every man present, including the one-armed guest, and within a few minutes thirty men swung into saddles, subject to orders. The camps of the two herds at issue were about four and five miles down and across the river, and no doubt Tolleston knew of their location, as they were only a little more than an hour's ride from Ogalalla. There was no time to be lost, and as we hastily gathered around the old man, he said: "Ride for your outfits, boys, and bring along every man you can spare. We'll meet north of the river about midway between Quince's and Tom's camps. Bring all the cartridges you have, and don't spare your horses going or coming."

Priest's wagon was almost on a line with mine, though south of the river. Fortunately I was mounted on one of the best horses in my string, and having the farthest to go, shook the kinks out of him as old Paul and myself tore down the mesa. After passing The Rebel's camp, I held my course as long as the footing was solid, but on encountering the first sand, crossed the river nearly opposite the appointed rendezvous. The North Platte was fordable at any point, flowing but a midsummer stage of water, with numerous wagon crossings, its shallow channel being about one hundred yards wide. I reined in my horse for the first time near the middle of the stream, as the water reached my saddle-skirt; when I came out on the other side, Priest and his boys were not a mile behind me. As I turned down the river, casting a backward glance, squads of horsemen were galloping in from several quarters and joining a larger one which was throwing up clouds of dust like a column of cavalry. In making a cut-off to reach my camp, I crossed a sand dune from which I sighted the marshal's posse less than two miles distant. My boys were gambling among themselves, not a horse under saddle, and did not notice my approach until I dashed up. Three lads were on herd, but the rest, including the wrangler, ran for their mounts on picket, while Parent and myself ransacked the wagon for ammunition. Fortunately the supply of the latter was abundant, and while saddles were being cinched on horses, the cook and I divided the ammunition and distributed it among the men. The few minutes' rest refreshed my horse, but as we dashed away, the boys yelling like Comanches, the five-mile ride had bested him and he fell slightly behind. As we turned into the open valley, it was a question if we or the marshal would reach the stream first; he had followed an old wood road and would strike the river nearly opposite Forrest's camp. The horses were excited and straining every nerve, and as we neared our crowd the posse halted on the south side and I noticed a conveyance among them in which were seated four men. There was a moment's consultation held, when the posse entered the water and began ford-ing the stream, the vehicle and its occupants remaining on the other side. We had halted in a circle about fifty yards back from the river-bank, and as the first two men came out of the water, Don Lovell rode forward several lengths of his horse, and with his hand motioned to them to halt. The leaders stopped within easy speaking distance, the remainder of the posse halting in groups at their rear, when Lovell demanded the meaning of this demonstration.

An inquiry and answer followed identifying the speakers. "In pursuance of an order from the federal court of this jurisdiction," continued the marshal, "I am vested with authority to take into my custody two herds, numbering nearly seven thousand beeves, now in your possession, and recently sold to Field, Radcliff & Co. for government purposes. I propose to execute my orders peaceably, and any interference on your part will put you and your men in contempt of government authority. If resistance is offered, I can, if necessary, have a company of United States cavalry here from Fort Logan within forty-eight hours to enforce the mandates of the federal court. Now my advice to you would be to turn these cattle over without further controversy."

"And my advice to you," replied Lovell, "is to go back to your federal court and tell that judge that as a citizen of these United States, and one who has borne arms in her defense, I object to having snap judgment rendered against me. If the honorable court which you have the pleasure to represent is willing to dispossess me of my property in favor of a ring of government thieves, and on only hearing one side of the question, then consider me in contempt. I'll gladly go back to Omaha with you, but you can't so much as look at a hoof in my pos-session. Now call your troops, or take me with you for treating with scorn the orders of your court."

Meanwhile every man on our side had an eye on Archie Tolleston, who had gradually edged forward until his horse stood beside that of the marshal. Before the latter could frame a reply to Lovell's ultimatum, Tolleston said to the federal officer: "Didn't my employers tell you that the old ———— would defy you without a demonstration of soldiers at your back? Now, the laugh's on you, and —"

"No, it's on you," interrupted a voice at my back, accompanied by a pistol report. My horse jumped forward, followed by a fusillade of shots behind me, when the hireling deputies turned and plunged into the river. Tolleston had wheeled his horse, joining the retreat, and as I brought my six-shooter into action and was in the act of leveling on him, he reeled from the saddle, but clung to the neck of his mount as the animal dashed into the water. I held my fire in the hope that he would right in the saddle and afford me a shot, but he struck a swift current, released his hold, and sunk out of sight. Above the din and excitement of the moment, I heard a voice which I recognized as Reed's, shouting, "Cut loose on that team, boys! Blaze away at those harness horses!" Evidently the team had been burnt by random firing, for they were rearing and plunging, and as I fired my first shot at them, the occupants sprang out of the vehicle and the team ran away. A lull occurred in the shooting to eject shells and refill cylinders, which Lovell took advantage of by ordering back a number of impulsive lads, who were determined to follow up the fleeing deputies.

"Come back here, you rascals, and stop this shooting!" shouted the old man. "Stop it, now, or you'll land me in a federal prison for life! Those horsemen may be deceived. When federal courts can be deluded with sugar coated blandishments, ordinary men ought to be excusable."

Six-shooters were returned to their holsters. Several horses and two men on our side had received slight flesh wounds, as there had been a random return fire. The deputies halted well out of pistol range, covering the retreat of the occupants of the carriage as best they could, but leaving three dead horses in plain view. As we dropped back towards Forrest's wagon, the team in the mean time having been caught, those on foot were picked up and given seats in the conveyance. Meanwhile a remuda of horses and two chuck-wagons were sighted back on the old wood road, but a horseman met and halted them and they turned back for Ogalalla. On reaching our nearest camp, the posse south of the river had started on their return, leaving behind one of their number in the muddy waters of the North Platte.

Late that evening, as we were preparing to leave for our respective camps, Lovell said to the assembled foremen: "Quince will take Reed and me into Ogalalla about midnight. If Sutton advises it, all three of us will go down to Omaha and try and square things. I can't escape a severe fine, but what do I care as long as I have their money to pay it with? The killing of that fool boy worried me more than a dozen fines. It was uncalled for, too, but he would butt in, and you fellows were all itching for the chance to finger a trigger. Now the understanding is that you all start in the morning."

THE TROUBLE MAN

EUGENE MANLOVE RHODES

I

Billy beebe did not understand. There was no disguising the unpalatable fact: Rainbow treated him kindly. It galled him. Ballinger, his junior in Rainbow, was theme for ridicule and biting jest, target for contumely and abuse; while his own best efforts were met with grave, unfailing courtesy.

Yet the boys liked him; Billy was sure of that. And so far as the actual work was concerned, he was at least as good a roper and brand reader as Ballinger, quicker in action, a much better rider.

In irrelevant and extraneous matters—brains, principle, training, acquirements—Billy was conscious of unchallenged advantage. He was from Ohio, eligible to the Presidency, of family, rich, a college man; yet he had abandoned laudable moss-gathering, to become a rolling, bounding, riotous stone. He could not help feeling that it was rather noble of him. And then to be indulgently sheltered as an honored guest, how beloved soever! It hurt.

Not for himself alone was Billy grieved. Men paired on Rainbow. "One stick makes a poor fire"—so their word went. Billy sat at the feet of John Wesley Pringle—wrinkled, wind-brown Gamaliel. Ballinger was the disciple of Jeff Bransford, gay, willful, questionable man. Billy did not like him. His light banter, lapsing unexpectedly from broad Doric to irreproachable New English, carried in solution audacious, glancing disrespect of convention, established institutions, authorities, axioms, "accepted theories of irregular verbs"—too elusive for disproof, too intolerably subversive to be ignored. That Ballinger, his shadow, was accepted man of action, while Billy was still an outsider, was, in some sense, a reflection on Pringle. Vicarious jealousy was added to the pangs of wounded self-love.

Billy was having ample time for reflection now, riding with Pringle up the Long Range to the Block roundup. Through the slow, dreamy days they threaded the mazed ridges and cañons falling eastward to the Pecos from Guadalupe, Sacramento and White Mountain. They drove their string of thirteen horses each; tough circlers, wise cutting-hoses, sedate night horses and patient old Steamboat, who, in the performance of pack duty, dropped his proper designation to be injuriously known as "the Wagon."

Their way lay through the heart of the Lincoln County War country—on winding trails, by glade and pine-clad mesa; by clear streams, bell-tinkling, beginning, with youth's eager haste, their journey to the far-off sea; by Seven Rivers, Bluewater, the Feliz, Penasco and Silver Spring.

Leisurely they rode, with shady halt at midday—leisurely, for an empire was to be worked. It would be months before they crossed the divide at Nogal, "threw in" with Bransford and Ballinger, now representing Rainbow with the Bar W, and drove home together down the west side.

While Billy pondered his problem Pringle sang or whistled tirelessly—old tunes of amazing variety, ranging from Nancy Lee and Auld Robin Gray to La Paloma Azul or the Nogal Waltz. But ever, by ranch house or brook or pass, he paused to tell of deeds there befallen in the years of old war, deeds violent and bloody, yet half redeemed by hardihood and unflinching courage.

Pringle's voice was low and unemphatic; his eyes were ever on the long horizon. Trojan nor Tyrian he favored, but as he told the Homeric tale of Buckshot Roberts, while they splashed through the broken waters of Ruidoso and held their winding way through the cutoff of Cedar Creek, Billy began dimly to understand.

Between him and Rainbow the difference was in kind, not in degree. The shadow of old names lay heavy on the land; these resolute ghosts yet shaped the acts of men. For Rainbow the Roman *virtus* was still the one virtue. Whenever these old names had been spoken, Billy remembered, men had listened. Horse-shoers had listened at their shoeing; card-players had listened while the game went on; by campfires other speakers had ceased their talk to listen without comment. Not ill-doers, these listeners, but quiet men, kindly, generous; yet the tales to which they gave this tribute were too often of ill deeds. As if they asked not "Was this well done?" but rather "Was this done indeed—so that no man could have done more?" Were the deed good or evil, so it were done utterly it commanded admiration—therefore, imitation.

Something of all this he got into words. Pringle nodded gravely. "You've got it sized up, my son," he said. "Rainbow ain't strictly up to date and still holds to them elder ethics, like Norval on the Grampian Hills, William Dhu Tell, and the rest of them neck-or-nothing boys. This Mr. Rolando, that Eusebio sings about, give our sentiments to a T-Y-ty. He was scrappy and always blowin' his own horn, but, by jings, he delivered the goods as per invoice and could take a major league lickin' with no whimperin'. This Rolando he don't hold forth about gate money or individual percentages. 'Get results for your team,' he says. 'Don't flinch, don't foul, hit the line hard, here goes nothin'!'

"That's a purty fair code. And it's all the one we got. Pioneerin' is trouble-some—pioneer is all the same word as pawn, and you throw away a pawn to gain a point. When we drive in a wild bunch, when we top off the boundin' bronco, it may look easy, but it's always a close thing. Even when we win we nearly lose; when we lose we nearly win. And that forms the stay-with-it-Bill-you're doin'-well habit. See?

"So, we mostly size a fellow up by his abilities as a trouble man. Any kind of trouble—not necessarily the fightin' kind. If he goes the route, if he sets no limit, if he's enlisted for the war—why, you naturally depend on him.

"Now, take you and Jeff. Most ways you've got the edge on him. But you hold by rules and formulas and laws. There's things you must do or mustn't do—because somebody told you so. You go into a project with a mental reserva-tion not to do anything indecorous or improper; also, to stop when you've taken a decent lickin'. But Jeff don't aim to stop while he can wiggle; and he makes up new rules as he goes along, to fit the situation. Naturally, when you get in a tight place you waste time rememberin' what the authorities prescribe as the neat thing. Now, Jeff consults only his own self, and he's mostly unanimous. Mebbe so you both do the same thing, mebbe not. But Jeff does it first. You're a good boy, Billy, but there's only one way to find out if you're a square peg or a round one."

"How's that?" demanded Billy, laughing, but half vexed.

"Get in the hole," said Pringle.

II

"Aw, stay all night! What's the matter with you fellows? I haven't seen a soul for a week. Everybody's gone to the round-up."

Wes' shook his head: "Can't do it, Jimmy. Got to go out to good grass. You're all eat out here."

"I'll side you," said Jimmy decisively. "I got a lot of stored-up talk I've got to get out of my system. I know a bully place to make camp. Box cañon to hobble your horses in, good grass, and a little tank of water in the rocks for cookin'. Bring along your little old Wagon, and I'll tie on a hunk of venison to feed your faces with. Get there by dark."

"How come you didn't go to the work your black self?" asked Wes', as Beebe tossed his rope on the Wagon and led him up.

Jimmy's twinkling eyes lit up his beardless face. "They left me here to play shinny-on-your-own-side," he explained.

"Shinny?" echoed Billy.

"With the Three Rivers sheep," said Jimmy. "I'm to keep them from crossing the mountain."

"Oh, I see. You've got an agreement that the east side is for cattle and the west side for sheep."

Jimmy's face puckered. "Agreement? H'm yes, leastways, I'm agreed. I didn't ask them, but they've got the general idea. When I ketch 'em over here I drive them back. As I don't ever follow 'em beyond the summit they ought to savvy my the'ries by this time."

Pringle opened the gate. "Let's mosey along—they've got enough water. Which way, kid?"

"Left-hand trail," said Jimmy, falling in behind.

"But why don't you come to an understanding with them and fix on a dividing line?" insisted Beebe.

Jimmy lolled sidewise in his saddle, cocking an impish eye at his inquisitor. "Reckon ye don't have no sheep down Rainbow way? Thought not. Right there's the point exactly. They have a dividing line. They carry it with 'em wherever they go. For the cattle won't graze where sheep have been. Sheep pertects their own range, but we've got to look after ours or they'd drive us out. But the under-standing's all right, all right. They don't speak no English, and I don't know no *paisano* talk, but I've fixed up a signal code they savvy as well's if they was all college aluminums."

"Oh, yes—sign talk," said Billy. "I've heard of that." Wes' turned his head aside.

"We-ell, not exactly. Sound talk'd be nearer. One shot means 'Git!' two means 'Hurry up!' and three—"

"But you've no right to do that," protested Billy warmly. "They've got just as much right here as your cattle, haven't they?"

"Surest thing they have—if they can make it stick," agreed Jimmy cordially. "And we've got just as much right to keep 'em off if we can. And we can. There ain't really no right to it. It's Uncle Sam's land we both graze on, and Unkie is some busy with conversation on natural resources, and keepin' republics up in South America and down in Asia, and selectin' texts for coins and infernal revenue stamps, and upbuildin' Pittsburgh, and keepin' up the price of wool, and fightin' all the time to keep the laws from bein' better'n the Constitution, like a Bawston puncher trimmin' a growin' colt's foot down to fit last year's shoes. Shucks! *He* ain't got no time to look after us. We just got to do our own regulatin' or git out."

"How would you like it yourself?" demanded Billy.

Jimmy's eyes flashed. "If my brain was to leak out and I subsequent took to sheep-herdin', I'd like to see any dern puncher drive me out," he declared belligerently.

"Then you can't complain if—"

"He don't," interrupted Pringle. "None of us complain—nary a murmur. If the sheep men want to go they go, an' a little shootin' up the contagious vicinity don't hurt 'em none. It's all over oncet the noise stops. Besides, I think they mostly sorter enjoy it. Sheepherdin' is might dull business, and a little excitement is mighty welcome. It gives 'em something to look forward to. But if they feel hostile they always get the first shot for keeps. That's a mighty big percentage in their favor, and the reports on file with the War Department shows that they generally get the best of it. Don't you worry none, my son. This ain't no new thing. It's been goin' on ever since Abra-ham's outfit and the L O T boys got to scrappin' on the Jordan range, and then some before that. After Abraham took to the hill country, I remember, somebody jumped one of his wells and two of Isaac's. It's been like that, in the shortgass countries ever since. Human nature's not changed much. By jings! There they be now!"

Through the twilight the winding trail climbed the side of a long ridge. To their left was a deep, impassable cañon; beyond that a parallel ridge; and from beyond that ridge came the throbbing, drumming clamor of a sheep herd.

"The son of a gun!" said Jimmy. "He means to camp in our box cañon. I'll show him!" He spurred by the grazing horses and clattered on in the lead, striking fire from the stony trail.

On the shoulder of the further ridge heaved a gray fog, spreading, rolling slowly down the hillside. The bleating, the sound of myriad trampling feet, the multiplication of bewildering echoes, swelled to a steady, unchanging, ubiquitous tumult. A dog suddenly topped the ridge; another; then a Mexican herder bearing a long rifle. With one glance at Jimmy beyond the blackshadowed gulf he began turning the herd back, shouting to the dogs. They ran in obedient haste to aid, sending the stragglers scurrying after the main bunch.

Jimmy reined up, black and gigantic against the skyline. He drew his gun. Once, twice, thrice, he shot. The fire streamed out against the growing dark. The bullets, striking the rocks, whined spitefully. The echoes took up the sound and sent it crashing to and fro. The sheep rushed huddling together, panic-stricken. Herder and dogs urged them on. The herder threw up a hand and shouted.

"That boy's shootin' mighty close to that *paisano*," muttered Pringle. "He orter quit now. Reckon he's showin' off a leetle." He raised his voice in warning. "Hi! you Jimmy!" he called. "He's a-goin'! Let him be!"

"*Vamos! Hi-i!*" shrilled Jimmy gayly. He fired again. The Mexican clapped his hand to his leg with an angry scream. With the one movement he sank to his knees, his long rifle fell to a level, cuddled to his shoulder, spitting fire. Jimmy's hand flew up; his gun dropped; he clutched at the saddle-horn, missed it, fell heavily to the ground. The Mexican dropped out of sight behind the ridge. It had been but a scant minute since he first appeared. The dogs followed with the remaining sheep. The ridge was bare. The dark fell fast.

Jimmy lay on his face. Pringle turned him over and opened his shirt.

He was quite dead.

III

From Malagra to Willow Spring, the next available water, is the longest jump on the Bar W range. Working the "Long Lane" fenced by Malpais and White Mountain is easy enough. But after cutting out and branding there was the long wait for the slow day herd, the tedious holding to water from insufficient troughs. It was late when the day's "cut" was thrown in with the herd, sunset when the bobtail had caught their night horses and relieved the weary day herders.

The bobtail moves the herd to the bed ground—some distance from camp, to avoid mutual annoyance and alarm—and holds it while night horses are caught and supper eaten. A thankless job, missing the nightly joking and banter over the day's work. Then the first guard comes on and the bobtail goes, famished, to supper. It breakfasts by starlight, relieves the last guard, and holds cattle while breakfast is eaten, beds rolled and horses caught, turning them over to the day herders at sunup.

Bransford and Ballinger were two of the five bobtailers, hungry, tired, dusty and cross. With persuasive, soothing song they trotted around the restless cattle, with hasty, envious glances for the merry groups around the chuck wagon. The horse herd was coming in; four of the boys were butchering a yearling; beds were being dragged out and unrolled. Shouts of laughter arose; they were baiting the victim of some mishap by making public an exaggerated version of his discomfiture.

Turning his back on the camp, Jeff Bransford became aware of a man riding a big white horse down the old military road from Nogal way. The horse was trotting, but wearily; passing the herd he whinnied greeting, again wearily.

The cattle were slow to settle down. Jeff made several circlings before he had time for another campward glance. The horse herd was grazing off, and the boys were saddling and staking their night horses; but the stranger's hose, still saddled, was tied to a soapweed.

Jeff sniffed. "Oh, Solomon was sapient and Solomon was wise!" he crooned, keeping time with old Summersault's steady fox-trot. "And Solomon was marvelously wide between the eyes!" He sniffed again, his nose wrinkled, one eyebrow arched, one corner of his mouth pulled down; he twisted his mustache and looked sharply down his nose for consultation, pursing his lips. "H'm! That's funny!" he said aloud. "That horse is some tired. Why don't he turn him loose? Bransford, you old fool, sit up and take notice! 'Eternal vigilance is the price of liberty.'"

He had been a tired and a hungry man. He put his weariness by as a garment, keyed up the slackened strings, and rode on with every faculty on the alert. It is to be feared that Jeff's conscience was not altogether void of offense toward his fellows.

A yearling pushed tentatively from the herd. Jeff let her go, fell in after her and circled her back to the bunch behind Clay Cooper. Not by chance. Clay was from beyond the divide.

"Know the new man, Clay?" Jeff asked casually, as he fell back to preserve the proper interval.

Clay turned his head. "Sure. Clem Littlefield, Bonita man."

When the first guard came at last Jeff was on the farther side and so the last to go in. A dim horseman overtook him and waved a sweeping arm in dismissal.

"We've got 'em! Light a rag, you hungry man!"

Jeff turned back slowly, so meeting all the relieving guard and noting that Squatty Robinson, of the VV, was not of them, Ollie Jackson taking his place.

He rode thoughtfully into camp. Staking his horse in the starlight he observed a significant fact. Squatty had not staked his regular night horse, but Alizan, his favorite. He made a swift investigation and found that not a man from the east had caught his usual night horse. Clay Cooper's horse was not staked, but tied short to a mesquit, with the bridle still on.

Pete Johnson, the foreman, was just leaving the fire for bed. Beyond the fire the east-side men were gathered, speaking in subdued voices. Ballinger, with loaded plate, sat down near them. The talking ceased. It started again at once. This time their voices rose clear and distinct in customary badinage.

"Why, this is face up," thought Jeff. "Trouble. Trouble from beyond the divide. They're going to hike shortly. They've told Pete that much, anyhow. Serious trouble—for they've kept it from the rest of them. Is it to my address? Likely. Old Wes' and Beebe are over there somewhere. If I had three guesses the first two'd be that them Rainbow chasers was in a tight."

He stumbled into the firelight, carrying his bridle, which he dropped by the wagon wheel. "This day's sure flown by like a week," he grumbled, fumbling around for cup and plate. "My stomach was just askin' was my throat cut."

As he bent over to spear a steak the tail of his eye took in the group beyond and intercepted a warning glance from Squatty to the stranger. There was an almost imperceptible thrusting motion of Squatty's chin and lips; a motion which included Jeff and the unconscious Ballinger. It was enough. Surmise, suspicion flamed to certainty. "My third guess," reflected Jeff sagely, "is just like the other two. Mr. John Wesley Pringle has been doing a running high jump or some such stunt, and has plumb neglected to come down."

He seated himself cross-legged and fell upon his supper vigorously, bandying quips and quirks with the bobtail as they ate. At last he jumped up, dropped his dishes clattering in the dishpan, and drew a long breath.

"I don't feel a bit hungry," he announced plaintively. "Gee! I'm glad I don't have to stand guard. I do hate to work between meals."

He shouldered his roll of bedding. "Good-by, old world—I'm going home!" he said, and melted into the darkness. Leo following, they unrolled their bed. But as Leo began pulling off his boots Jeff stopped him.

"Close that aperture in your face and keep it that way," he admonished guardedly. "You and me has got to do a ghost dance. Project around and help me find them Three Rivers men."

The Three Rivers men, Crosby and Os Hyde, were sound asleep. Awakened, they were disposed to peevish remonstrance.

"Keep quiet!" said Jeff, "Al, you slip on your boots and go tell Pete you and Os is goin' to Carrizo and that you'll be back in time to stand your guard. Tell him out loud. Then you come back here and you and Os crawl into our bed. I'll show him where it is while you're gone. You use our night horses. Me and Leo want to take yours."

"If there's anything else don't stand on ceremony," said Crosby. "Don't you want my toothbrush?"

"You hurry up," responded Jeff. "D'ye think I'm doin' this for fun? We're It. We got to prove an alibi."

"Oh!" said Al.

A few minutes later, the Three Rivers men disappeared under the tarp of the Rainbow bed, while the Rainbow men, on Three Rivers horses, rode silently out of camp, avoiding the firelit circle.

Once over the ridge, well out of sight and hearing from camp, Jeff turned up the draw to the right and circled back toward the Nogal road on a long trot.

"Beautiful night," observed Leo after an interval. "I just love to ride. How far is it to the asylum?"

"Leo," said Jeff, "you're a good boy—a mighty good boy. But I don't believe you'd notice it if the sun didn't go down till after dark." He explained the situation. "Now, I'm going to leave you to hold the horses just this side of the Nogal road, while I go on afoot and eavesdrop. Them fellows'll be makin' big medicine when they come along here. I'll lay down by the road and get a line on their play. Don't you let them horses nicker."

Leo waited an interminable time before he heard the eastside men coming from camp. They passed by, talking, as Jeff had prophesied. After another small eternity Jeff joined him.

"I didn't get all the details, he reported. "But it seems that the Parsons City people has got it framed up to hang a sheepman some. Wes' is dead set against it—I didn't make out why. So there's a deadlock and we've got the casting vote.

Call up your reserves, old man. We're due to ride around Nogal and beat that bunch to the divide."

It was midnight by the clock in the sky when they stood on Nogal divide. The air was chill. Clouds gathered blackly around Capitan, Nogal Peak and White Mountain. There was steady, low muttering of thunder; the far lightnings flashed pale and green and rose.

"Hustle along to Lincoln, Leo," commanded Jeff, "and tell the sheriff they state, positive, that the hangin' takes place prompt after breakfast. Tell him to bring a posse—and a couple of battleships if he's got 'em handy. Meantime, I'll go over and try what the gentle art of persuasion can do. So long! If I don't come back the mule's yours."

He turned up the right-hand road.

IV

"Well?" said Pringle.

"Light up!" said Uncle Pete. "Nobody's goin' to shoot at ye from the dark. We don't do business that way. When we come we'll come in day-light, down the big middle of the road. Light up. I ain't got no gun. I come over for one last try to make you see reason. I knowed thar weren't use talkin' to you when you was fightin' mad. That's why I got the boys to put it off till mawnin'. And I wanted to send to Angus and Salado and the Bar W for Jimmy's friends. He ain't got no kinnery here. They've come. They all see it the same way. Chavez killed Jimmy, and they're goin' to hang him. And, since they've come, there's too many of us for you to fight."

Wes' lit the candle. "Set down. Talk all you want, but talk low and don't wake Billy," he said as the flame flared up.

That he did not want Billy waked up, that there was not even a passing glance to verify Uncle Pete's statement as to being unarmed, was, considering Uncle Pete's errand and his own position, a complete and voluminous commentary on the men and ethics of that time and place.

Pete Burleson carefully arranged his frame on a bench, and glanced around.

On his cot Billy tossed and moaned. His fevered sleep was tortured by a phantasmagoria of broken and hurried dreams, repeating with monstrous exaggeration the crowded hours of the past day. The brainstunning shock and horror of sudden, bloody, death, the rude litter, the night-long journey with their awful burden, the doubtful aisles of pine with star 'galazies' wheeling beyond, the gaunt, bare hill above, the steep zigzag to the sleeping town, the flaming wrath of violent men—in his dream they came and went. Again, hasty messengers flashed across the haggard dawn; again, he shared the pursuit and capture of the sheepherder. Sudden clash of unyielding wills; black anger; wild voices for swift death, quickly backed by wild, strong hands; Pringle's cool and steady defiance; his own hot, resolute protest; the prisoner's unflinching fatalism; the hard-won respite—all these and more—the lights, the swaying crowd, fierce faces black and bitter with inarticulate wrath—jumbled confusedly in shifting, unsequenced combinations leading ever to some incredible, unguessed catastrophe.

Beside him, peacefully asleep, lay the manslayer, so lately snatched from death, unconscious of the chain that bound him, oblivious of the menace of the coming day.

"He takes it pretty hard," observed Uncle Pete, nodding at Billy.

"Yes. He's never seen any sorrow. But he don't weaken one mite. I tried every way I could think of to get him out of here. Told him to sidle off down to Lincoln after the sheriff. But he was dead on to me."

"Yes? Well, he wouldn't 'a' got far, anyway," said Uncle Pete dryly. "We're watching every move. Still, it's pity he didn't try. We'd 'a' got him without hurtin' him, and he'd' a' been out o' this."

Wes' made no answer. Uncle Pete stroked his grizzled beard reflectively. He filled his pipe with cut plug and puffed deliberately.

"Now, look here," he said slowly: "Mr. Procopio Chavez killed Jimmy, and Mr. Procopio Chavez is going to hang. It wa'n't no weakenin' or doubt on my part that made me call the boys off yesterday evenin'. He's got to hang. I just wanted to keep you fellers from gettin' killed. There might 'a' been some sense in your fighting then, but there ain't now. There's too many of us."

"Me and Billy see the whole thing," said Wes', unmoved. "It was too bad Jimmy got killed, but he was certainly mighty brash. The sheep-herder was goin' peaceable, but Jimmy kept shootin', and shootin' close. When that splinter of rock hit the Mexican man he thought he was shot, and he turned loose. Reckon it hurt him like sin. There's a black-and-blue spot on his leg big as the palm of your hand. You'd 'a' done the same as he did.

"I ain't much enthusiastic about sheep-herders. In fact, I jerked my gun at the time; but I was way down the trail and he was out o' sight before I could shoot. Thinkin' it over careful, I don't see where this Mexican's got any hangin' comin'. You know, just as well as I do, no court's goin' to hang him on the testimony me and Billy's got to give in."

"I do," said Uncle Pete. "That's exactly why we're goin' to hang him our-selves. If we let him go it's just encouragin' the *pastores* to kill up some more of the boys. So we'll just stretch his neck. This is the last friendly warnin', my son. If you stick your fingers between the anvil and the hammer you'll get 'em pinched. 'Tain't any of your business, anyway. This ain't Rainbow. This is the White Mountain and we're strictly home rulers. And, moresoever, that war talk you made yesterday made the boys plumb sore."

"That war talk goes as she lays," said Pringle steadily. "No hangin' till after the shootin'. That goes."

"Now, now—what's the use?" remonstrated Uncle Pete. "Ye'll just get your-self hurted and 'twon't do the greaser any good. You might mebbe so stand us off in a good, thick 'dobe house, but not in this old shanty. If you want to swell up and be stubborn about it, it just means a grave apiece for you all and likely for some few of us."

"It don't make no difference to me," said Pringle, "if it means diggin' a grave in a hole in the cellar under the bottomless pit. I'm goin' to make my word good and do what I think's right."

"So am I, by Jupiter! Mr. Also Ran Pringle, it is a privilege to have known you!" Billy, half awake, covered Uncle Pete with a gun held in a steady hand. "Let's keep him here for a hostage and shoot him if they attempt to carry out their lynching," he suggested.

"We can't Billy. Put it down," said Pringle mildly. "He's here under flag of truce."

"I was tryin' to save your derned fool hides," said Uncle Pete benignantly.

"Well—'tain't no use. We're just talkin' round and round in a circle, Uncle Pete. Turn your wolf loose when you get ready. As I said before, I don't noways dote on sheepmen, but I seen this, and I've got to see that this poor devil gets a square deal. I got to!"

Uncle Pete sighed. "It's a pity!" he said; "a great pity! Well, we're comin' quiet and peaceful. If there's any shootin' done you all have got to fire the first shot. We'll have the last one."

"Did you ever stop to think that the Rainbow men may not like this?" inquired Pringle. "If they're anyways dissatisfied they're liable to come up here and scratch your eyes out one by one."

"Jesso. That's why you're goin' to fire the first shot," explained Uncle Pete patiently. "Only for that—and likewise because it would be a sorter mean trick to do—we could get up on the hill and smoke you out with rifles at long range, out o' reach of your six-shooters. You all might get away, but the sheepherder's chained fast and we could shoot him to kingdom come, shack and all, in five minutes. But you've had fair warnin' and you'll get an even break. If you want to begin trouble it's your own lookout. That squares us with Rainbow."

"And you expect them to believe you?" demanded Billy.

"Believe us? Sure! Why shouldn't they!" said Uncle Pete simply. "Of course they'll believe us. It'll be so." He stood up and regarded them wistfully. "There don't seem to be any use o' sayin' any more, so I'll go. I hope there ain't no hard feelin's?"

"Not a bit!" said Pringle; but Billy threw his head back and laughed angrily. "Come, I like that! By Jove, if that isn't nerve for you! To wake a man up and announce that you're coming presently to kill him, and then expect to part the best of friends!"

"Ain't I doin' the friendly part?" demanded Uncle Pete stiffly. He was both nettled and hurt. "If I hadn't thought well of you fellers and done all I could for you, you'd 'a' been dead and done forgot about it by now. I give you all credit for doin' what you think is right, and you might do as much for me."

"Great Caesar's ghost! Do you want us to wish you good luck?" said Billy, exasperated almost to tears. "Have it your own way, by all means—you gentle-hearted old assassin! For my part, I'm going to do my level best to shoot you right between the eyes, but there won't be any hard feeling about it. I'll just be dong what I think is right—a duty I owe to the world. Say! I should think a gentleman of your sportsmanlike instincts would send over a gun for our prisoner. Twenty to one is big odds."

"Twenty to one is a purty good reason why you could surrender without no disgrace," rejoined Uncle Pete earnestly. "You can't make nothin' by fightin', cause you lose your point, anyway. And then, a majority of twenty to one—ain't that a good proof that you're wrong?"

"Now, Billy, you can't get around that. That's your own argument," cried Pringle, delighted. "You've stuck to it right along that you Republicans was dead right because you always get seven votes to our six. *Nux vomica*, you know."

Uncle Pete rose with some haste. "Here's where I go. I never could talk politics without gettin' mad," he said.

"Billy, you're certainly making good. You're a square peg. All the same, I wish," said Wes' Pringle plaintively, as Uncle Pete crunched heavily through the gravel, "that I could hear my favorite tune now."

Billy stared at him. "Does your mind hurt your head?" he asked solicitously.

"No, no—I'm not joking. It would do me good if I could only hear him sing it."

"Hear who sing what?"

"Why, hear Jeff Bransford sing The Little Eohippus—right now. Jeff's got the knack of doing the wrong thing at the right time. Hark! What's that?"

It was a firm footstep at the door, a serene voice low chanting:

"There was once a little animal
No bigger than a fox,
And on five toes he scampered—"

"Good Lord!" said Billy. "It's the man himself."

Questionable Bransford stepped through the half-open door, closed it and set his back to it.

"That's my cue! Who was it said eavesdroppers never heard good of themselves?"

V

He was smiling, his step was light, his tones were cheerful, ringing. His eyes had looked on evil and terrible things. In this desperate pass they wrinkled to pleasant, sunny warmth. He was unhurried, collected, confident. Billy found himself wondering how he had found this man loud, arbitrary, distasteful.

Welcome, question, answer; daybreak paled the ineffectual candle. The Mexican still slept.

"I crawled around the opposition camp like a snake in the grass," said Jeff. "There's two things I observed there that's mightily in our favor. The first thing is, there's no whisky goin'. And the reason for that is the second thing—our one best big chance. Mister Burleson won't let 'em. Fact! Pretty much the entire population of the Pecos and tributary streams had arrived. Them that I know are mostly bad actors, and the ones I don't know looked real horrid to me; but your Uncle Pete is the bell mare. 'No booze!' he says, liftin' one finger; and that settled it. I reckon that when Uncle Simon Peter says 'Thumbs up!' those digits'll be elevated accordingly. If I can get him to see the gate the rest will only need a little gentle persuasion."

"I see you persuading them now," said Billy. "This is a plain case of the irresistible force and the immovable body."

"You will," said Jeff confidently. "You don't know what a jollier I am when I get down to it. Watch me! I'll show you a regular triumph of mind over matter."

"They're coming now," announced Wes' placidly. "Two by two, like the animals out o' the ark. I'm glad of it. I never was good at waitin'. Mr. Bransford will now oblige with his monologue entitled 'Givin' a bull the stop signal with a red flag.' Ladies will kindly remove their hats."

It was a grim and silent cavalcade. Uncle Pete rode at the head. As they turned the corner Jeff walked briskly down the path, hopped lightly on the fence, seated himself on the gatepost and waved an amiable hand.

"Stop, look, and listen!" said this cheerful apparition.

The procession stopped. A murmur, originating from the Bar W contingent, ran down the ranks. Uncle Pete reined up and demanded of him with marked disfavor: "Who in merry hell are you?"

Jeff's teeth flashed white under his brown moustache. "I'm Ali Baba," he said, and paused expectantly. But the allusion was wasted on Uncle Pete. Seeing that no introduction was forthcoming, Jeff went on:

"I've been laboring with my friends inside, and I've got a proposition to make. As I told Pringle just now, I don't see any sense of us gettin' killed, and killin' a lot of you won't bring us alive again. We'd put up a pretty fight—a very pretty fight. But you'd lay us out sooner or later. So what's the use?"

"I'm mighty glad to see some one with a leetle old horse-sense," said Uncle Pete. "Your friends is dead game sports all right, but they got mighty little judgment. If they'd only been a few of us I wouldn't 'a' blamed 'em a mite for not givin' up. But we got too much odds of 'em."

"This conversation is taking an unexpected turn," said Jeff, making his eyes round. "I ain't named giving up that I remember of. What I want to do is to rig up a compromise."

"If there's any halfway place between a hung Mexican and a live one," said Uncle Pete, "mebbe we can. And if not, not. This ain't no time for triflin', young fellow."

"Oh, shucks! I can think of half a dozen compromises," said Jeff blandly. "We might play seven-up and not count any turned-up jacks. But I was thinking of something different. I realize that you outnumber us, so I'll meet you a good deal more than half way. First, I want to show you something about my gun. Don't anybody shoot, 'cause I ain't going to. Hope I may die if I do!"

"You will if you do. Don't worry about that," said Uncle Pete. "And maybe so, anyhow. You're delayin' the game."

Jeff took this for permission. "Everybody please watch and see there is no deception."

Holding the gun, muzzle up, so all could see, he deliberately extracted all the cartridges but one. The audience exchanged puzzled looks.

Jeff twirled the cylinder and returned the gun to its scabbard. "Now!" he said, sparkling with enthusiasm. "You all see that I've only got one cartridge. I'm in no position to fight. If there's any fighting I'm already dead. What happens to me has no bearing on the discussion. I'm out of it.

"I realize that there's no use trying to intimidate you fellows. Any of you would take a big chance with odds against you, and here the odds is for you. So, as far as I'm concerned, I substitute a certainty for chance. I don't want to kill up a lot of rank strangers—or friends, either. There's nothing in it.

"Neither can I go back on old Wes' and Billy. So I take a half-way course. Just to manifest my entire disapproval, if any one makes a move to go through that gate I'll use my one shot—and it won't be on the man goin' through the gate, either. Nor yet on you, Uncle Pete. You're the leader. So, if you want to give the word, go it! I'm not going to shoot you. Nor I ain't going to shoot any of the Bar W push. They're free to start the ball rolling."

Uncle Pete, thus deprived of the initiatory power, looked helplessly around the Bar W push for confirmation. They nodded in concert. "He'll do whatever he says," said Clay Cooper.

"Thanks," said Jeff pleasantly, "for this unsolicited testimonial. Now, boys, there's no dare about this. Just cause and effect. All of you are plumb safe to make a break—but one. To show you that there's nothing personal about it, no dislike or anything like that, I'll tell you how I picked that one. I started at some place near both ends or the middle and counted backward, or forward, sayin' to myself, 'Intra, mintra, cutra, corn, apple seed and brier thorn,' and when I got to 'thorn' that man was stuck. That's all. Them's the rules."

That part of Uncle Pete's face visible between beard and hat was purple through the brown. He glared at Jeff, opened his mouth, shut it tightly, and breathed heavily through his nose. He looked at his horse's ears, he looked at the low sun, he looked at the distant hills; his gaze wondered disconsolately back to the twinkling indomitable eyes of the man on the gatepost. Uncle Pete sighed deeply.

"That's good! I'll just about make the wagon by noon," he remarked gently. He took his quirt from his saddle-horn. "Young man," he said gravely, flicking his horse's flank, "any time you're out of a job come over and see me." He waved his hand, nodded, and was gone.

Clay Cooper spurred up and took his place, his black eyes snapping. "I like a damned fool," he hissed; "but you suit me too well!"

The forty followed; some pausing for quip or jest, some in frowning silence. But each, as he passed that bright, audacious figure, touched his hat in salute to a gallant foe.

Squatty Robinson was the last. He rode close up and whispered confidentially:

"I want you should do me a favor, Jeff. Just throw down on me and take my gun away. I don't want to go back to camp with any such tale as this."

"You see, Billy," explained Jeff, "you mustn't dare the denizens—never! They dare. They're uncultured; their lives ain't noways valuable to society and they know it. If you notice, I took pains not to dare anybody. Quite otherhow. I merely stated annoyin' consequences to some other fellow, attractive as I could, but impersonal. Just like I'd tell you: 'Billy, I wouldn't set the oil can on the fire—it might boil over.'

"Now, if I'd said: 'Uncle Pete, if anybody makes a break I'll shoot your eye out, anyhow,' there'd 'a' been only one dignified course open to him. Him and me would now be dear Alphonsing each other about payin' the ferryman.

"Spose I'd made oration to shoot the first man through the gate. Every man Jack would have come 'a-snuffin'—each one tryin' to be first. The way I put it up to 'em, to be first wasn't no graceful act—playin' safe at some one else's expense—and then they seen that some one else wouldn't be gettin' an equitable vibration. That's all there was to it. If there wasn't any first there couldn't conveniently be any second, so they went home. B-r-r-! I'm sleepy. Let's go by-by. Wake that dern lazy Mexican up and make him keep watch till the sheriff comes!"

BIT BY BIT

CLARENCE E. MULFORD

The sun was near the meridian when Johnny rode into Gunsight, a town which he took as a matter of course. They were all alike, he reflected. If it were not for the names they scarcely could be told apart—and it would have been just as well to have numbered them. A collection of shacks, with the overplayed brave names. The shack he was riding for was the "Palace," which only rubbed it in. Out of a hundred towns, seventy-five would have their Palace saloon and fifty would have a Delmonico hotel. Dismounting before the door, he went in and saw the proprietor slowly arising from a chair, and he was the fattest man Johnny ever had seen. The visitor's unintentional stare started the conversation for him.

"Well, don't you like my looks?" bridled the proprietor.

Johnny's expression was one of injured innocence. "Why, I wasn't seein' you," he explained. "I was thinkin'—but now that you mention it, I don't see noth-in' th' matter with your looks. Should there be?"

The other grunted something, becoming coherent only when the words concerned business. "What's yourn?"

"A drink with you, an' some information."

"Th' drink goes; but th' information don't."

"I take it all back," soliloquized Johnny. "This town don't need a number; it don't even need a name. It's different. It's th' only one this side of Montanny where the barkeeper was hostile at th' start. I'm peaceful. My han's are up, palm out. If you won't give me information, will you tell me where I can eat an' sleep? Which of th' numerous hotels ain't as bad as th' rest of 'em?"

Davis Lee Beauregard Green slid a bottle across the bar, sent a glass spinning after it, leaned against the back bar and grinned. "Gunsight ain't impressin' you a hull lot?" he suggested.

"Why not? It's got all a man needs, which is why towns are made, ain't it?" Johnny tasted the liquor and downed it. "I allus size up a town by th' liquor it sells. I say Gunsight is a d—d sight better than I thought from a superficial examination."

Dave Green, wise in the psychology of the drinking type, decided that the stranger was not and never had been what he regarded as a drinking man; and even went so far in a quick, spontaneous flash of thought, as to tell himself that the stranger never had been drunk. Now, in his opinion, a hard-drinking, two-gun man was "bad;" but a coldly sober, real two-gun man was worse, although possibly less quarrelsome. He was certain that they lived longer. Dave was a good man with a short gun, despite his handicap; but a stirring warning instinct had told him that this stranger was the best who ever had entered his place. This impression came, was recognized, tabbed, and shoved back in his memory, all in a mechanical way. It was too plain to be overlooked by a man who, perhaps without realizing it, studied humanity, although he could not lay a finger on a single thing and call it by name.

Dave put the bottle back and washed the glass. "Well," he remarked, "every man sizes things up accordin' to his own way of thinkin', which is why there are so many different opinions about th' same thing." Letting this ponderous nugget sink in, he continued: "I reckon th' bottom of it all is a man's wants. You want good liquor, so a town's good, or bad. Which is as good a way as any other, for it suits you. But, speakin' about eatin'-houses, there's a hotel just around th' corner. It's th' only one in town. It butts up agin' th' corner of my rear wall. Further than sayin' I've et there, I got no remarks to make. I cook my own, owin' to th' pressure of business, an' choice."

"It ain't run by no woman, is it?" asked Johnny.

"No; why?"

Johnny grinned. "I'm ridin' clear of wimmin. It was wimmin that sent me roamin' over th' face of th' earth, a wanderer. My friends all got married, an'—oh, well, I drifted. Th' first section I come to where there ain't none, I'll tie fast; an' this country looks like a snubbin' post, to me."

"You lose," chuckled Dave. "There's one down here, an' some folks think she's considerable. What's more, she's lookin' for a good man to run her dad's ranch, an' get an outfit together, as will stay put. But if you don't like 'em, that loses th' job for you. An' I reckon yo're right lucky at that."

"Shore; I know th' kind of a 'good' man they want," said Johnny, reminiscently. "'Good,' meanin' habits only. A man that don't smoke, chew, drink, cuss, get mad, or keep his hat on in th' house. Losin' th' job ain't bendin' my shoulders. I ain't lookin' for work; I'm dodgin' it. Goin' to loaf till my money peters out, which won't be soon. You'd be surprised if you knowed how many people between here an' Montanny think they can play poker. Just now I'm a eddicator. I'm peddlin' knowledge to th' ignorant, an' I ain't no gambler, at that!"

Dave chuckled. "There's some around here, too. Now, me; I'm different. I can't play, an' I know it; but, of course, I'll set in, just for th' excitement of it, once in a while, if there ain't nothin' else to do. Come to think of it, I got a deck of cards around here some'rs, right now."

The rear door opened and closed. Johnny looked up and saw the worst-looking tramp of his experience. The newcomer picked up a sand-box cuspidor and started with it for the street.

"Hi, stranger!" called Johnny. "Ain't that dusty work?"

The tramp stiffened. He hardly could believe his ears. The tones which had assailed them were so spontaneously friendly that for a moment he was stunned. It had been a long time since he had been hailed like that—far too long a time. He turned his head slowly and looked and believed, for the grin which met his eyes was as sincere as the voice. It made him honest in his reply.

"No," he said, "this here's sand."

"But ain't yore throat dusty?"

Two-Spot put the box down. "Seems like it allus is. If these boxes *get* dusty, I'll know how it come about, me bendin' over 'em like I do, an' breathin' on 'em."

Johnny laughed. "I take it we're all dusty." He turned to Dave. "Got three left?"

Two-Spot walked up to the bar. Usually he sidled. He picked up his glass and held it up to the light, and drank it in three swallows. Usually it was one gulp. Wiping his lips on a sleeve, he pushed back the glass, dug down into a pocket and brought up a silver dollar, which he tossed onto the bar. "Fill 'em again, Dave," he said, quietly.

At this Dave's slowly accumulating wonder leaped. He looked at the coin and from it to Two-Spot. Sensing the situation, Johnny pushed it farther along towards the proprietor. "Our friend is right, Dave," he said, "two *is* company. Make mine th' same."

Two-Spot put down his empty glass and grinned. "I'll now go on from where I was interrupted, Gents," and, picking up the box, went towards the door. As he was about to pass through he saw Pepper, and he stopped. "Good, Lord!" he muttered. "What a hoss! I've seen passels of hosses, but never one like that. Midnight her name oughter be, or Thunderbolt." He turned. "Stranger, what name do you call that hoss?"

Johnny looked around. "That's Pepper."

Two-Spot grinned. "Did you see that?" he demanded, tilting the box until the sand ran out. "Did you *see* it? She knows her name like a child. Well, it's a good name—a fair name," he hedged. "But, shucks! There ain't *no* name fit for that hoss! How fur has she come today?"

"Near forty miles," answered Johnny.

"I say it ag'in—there ain't *no* name fit for that hoss. She looks like she come five," and he passed out.

"Don't mind him," said Dave. "But where did he git that dollar? Steal it? Find it? Reckon he found it I near dropped dead. Pore devil—he come here last winter an' walks in, cleans my boxes an' sweeps. Then he goes 'round to th' hotel an' mops an' cleans th' pans better than they ever was before. He was so handy an' useful that we let him stay. An' I've never seen him more than half drunk—it's amazin' th' liquor he can hold."

"Sleep here?"

"No; an' nobody knows where he does sleep. He's cunnin' as a fox, an' fooled 'em every time. But wherever it is, it's dry."

Johnny produced a Sharps single-shot cartridge. "Where can I get some of these Specials?" he asked.

Dave looked at it. "'.45-120-550'—you won't get none of 'em down in this country."

"Post office in town?"

"Not yet. Th' nearest is Rawlins, thirty mile east, with th' worst trail a man ever rode. Th' next is High-bank, forty mile south. We use that, for th' trail's good. We get mail about twice a month. Th' Bar H an' th' Triangle take turns at it."

"Then I'll write for some of these after I feed. Ill tell 'em to send 'em to you, at Highbank. What name will I give?"

"Dave Green, Highbank-Gunsight mail. But you better write before you eat. This is goin' away day, an' th' Bar H will be in any minute now."

Johnny arose. "Not before I eat. I ain't had nothin' since daybreak, an' it's afternoon now. I hate letter writin'; an' if I don't eat soon I'll get thin."

"Then don't eat—'though I wasn't thinkin' of you when I spoke," growled Dave. "Wish I was in danger of gettin' thin."

"What you care?" demanded Johnny. "Yo're healthy, an' yore job don't call for a man bein' light."

"That's th' way you fellers talk," said Dave. "I'm short-winded, I'm in my own way, an' the joke of th' country. I can't ride a hoss—why, cuss it, I can't even get a gun out quick enough to get a hop-toad before he's moved twenty feet!"

"Pullin' a gun has its advantages, I admits," replied Johnny, who had his own ideas about Dave's ability in that line. Dave, he thought, could get a gun out quick enough for the average need—being a bartender, and still alive, was proof enough of that. He walked toward the door. "If you was to get a big hoss—a single-footer, you could ride, all right."

He went around and entered the hotel, mentally numbering it. Arranging for a week's board and bed for himself and Pepper, he hurried out to the wash bench just outside the dining-room door, where he found two tin basins, a bucket of water, a cake of yellow soap, a towel, and two men using them all. Taking his turn he in turn followed them into the dining-room and chose the fourth and last table, which was next to a window. The meal was better than he had expected but, hungry as he was, he did not eat as hurriedly as was his habit. Fragments of the conversation of the two punchers in the corner reached and interested him. It had to do with the SV ranch, as near as he could judge, and helped him to build the skeleton upon which he hoped to hang a body by dint of investigation and questioning. The episode of that morning had occurred on the SV ranch if the brands on the cattle he had seen meant anything. The woman's name was Arnold, and she had a father and a brother, the latter a boy. There was a fragment about "th' Doc," but just what it was he did not hear, except that it was coupled to the Bar H. Also, something was afoot, but it was so cautiously mentioned that he gained no information about it. Finishing before him, the two men went out, and soon rode past the window, mounted on Triangle horses.

He rattled his cup and ordered it refilled, and when the waiter slouched back with it, Johnny slid a perfectly good cigar across the table and waved his hand. "Sit down, an' smoke. You ought to rest while you got th' chance."

The waiter lost some of his slouch and obeyed, nodding his thanks. "Are you punchin'?" he asked.

"When I'm broke," answered Johnny. "Just now I'm ridin' around lookin' at th' scenery. Never knowed we had any out here till I heard some Easterners goin' mad about it. I've been tryin' to find it ever since. But, anyhow, punchin' is shore monotonous."

"If you can show me anythin' monotoner than *this* job, I'll eat it," growled the waiter. "It's hell on wheels for me."

"Oh, this whole range is monotonous," grunted Johnny. "Reckon nothin' interestin' has happened down here since Moses got lost. But there's one thing I like about it—there ain't no woman in thirty miles."

"You foiler Clear River into Green Valley, which is SV, an' you'll change yore mind," chuckled the waiter. "She'll chase you off, too."

"I'll be cussed. An' she's suspicious of strangers?"

"Don't put no limit on it like that; she's suspicious of everythin' that wears pants."

"How's that?"

"Well, her cows has been wanderin' off, lookin' for better grass, I reckon, an' she thinks they're bein' 'drove."

Johnny pictured the valley, but hid his smile. "Oh, well; you can't blame the cows. They'll find th' best., Any ranches 'round here run by men?"

"Shore; three of 'em. There's th' Bar H, an' th' Triangle, an' over west is th' Double X, but it's ranch-house is so fur from here that it's a sort of outsider. It's th' biggest, th' Bar H is next, an' then comes th' Triangle. Th' Triangle don't hardly count, neither, 'though it's close by."

"What about th' SV you mentioned? An' what's yore name?"

"My name's George. Th' SV has gone to th' dogs since it was sold. It ain't a ranch no more. Of course, it's got range, an' water, an' some cows, an' a couple of buildin's—but it ain't got no outfit. Old Arnold, his gal, an* his kid—all tenderfeet—are tryin' to run it."

"But they've got to have punchers," objected Johnny.

"They can't keep 'em, though I ain't sayin' why," replied George mysteriously.

"Does th' Doc own th' Bar H?" asked Johnny.

"Lord, no! It owns him—but, say; you'll have to excuse me. I got work to do. See you at supper. So long."

Johnny left and rode back the way he had come that morning, lost in meditation. Reaching the rim of the valley he looked down over the rolling expanse of vivid green, here and there broken by shallow draws, with their brush and trees. He noticed an irregular circle of posts just south of him and close to the river. Experience told him what they meant, and he frowned. Here was a discordant note—that enclosure, small as it was, was a thing sinister, malevolent, to him almost possessing a personality. Turning from the quicksands he sat and gazed at the nest of rocks below him until Pepper, well trained though she was, became restless and thought it time to move. Stirring, he smiled and pressed a knee against her and as he rode away he shook his head. "Yes, girl, I'm still a-rollin'—an' I 'don't know where to."

After supper he talked with George until they heard the creaking of wheels and harness. Looking up they saw four heavy horses slowly passing the window, followed by a huge, covered wagon with great, heavy wheels having four-inch tires. A grizzled, whiskered, weather-beaten patriarch handled the lines and talked to his horses as though they were children.

"Now I got to make a new fire an' cook more grub," growled George, arising. "Why can't he get here in time for supper? He's allus late, goin' an' comin'.'"

"Who is he, an' where's he from?"

"Ol' Buffaler Wheatley from Highbank. He's goin' up to Juniper an' Sherman."

"He come from Highbank today?" demanded Johnny, surprised.

"Shore—an' he must 'a' come slow."

"Slow? Forty miles with *that* in a day, an' he come *slow?*" retorted Johnny. "He was lucky to get here before midnight. If you'd 'a' done what that old feller has today, you'd not think much of anybody as wanted you on hand at supper time."

"Mebby yo're right," conceded George, dubiously, as he went into the kitchen.

Johnny arose and went out to the shed where the driver was flexing his muscles. "Howd'y," he said. "Got th' waggin where you want it?"

"Howd'y, friend," replied Buffalo, looking out from under bushy brows. "I reckon so. 'Most any place'll do. Ain't nothin' 'round'll scratch th' polish off it," he grinned.

Johnny laughed and began unhitching the tired, patient horses, and his deft fingers had it done before Buffalo had any more than started. "Fine hosses," he complimented, slapping the big gray at his side. "You must treat 'em well."

"I do," said Buffalo. "I may abuse myself, some times, but not these here fellers. They'll pull all day, an' are as gentle as kittens."

"How do you find freightin'?" asked Johnny, leading his pair into the shed.

"Pickin' up, an' pickin fast," answered Buffalo, following with the second team. "It's gettin' too much for one old man an' this waggin. An' top of that I got th' mail contract I been askin' for for years. So I got to put on another waggin an' make th' trip every week 'stead of only when th' freight piles up enough to make it worth while. Reckon I'll break my boy in on th' new waggin."

"I'll leave th' feedin' to you," said Johnny, leaning against the wall. "You know what they need."

"All right, friend; much obliged to you. I just let 'em eat all th' hay they can hold an' give 'em their measures of oats. I have to carry them with me— can't get none away from Highbank, everythin' up here bein' grass fed."

"I feed oats when I can get 'em," replied Johnny. "I allus reckon a corn-fed hoss has more bottom."

"Shore has—if they're that kind," agreed Buffalo.

"Travel th' same way all th' time?"

"Yes. I won't gain nothin' goin' t'other way 'round," answered Buffalo, busy with his pets. "You see I allus come north loaded. Th' first stop, after here, is Juniper, where I loses part of th' load. That's thirty miles from here, an' th' road's good. Then I cross over to Sherman, lose th' rest of th' load, an' come back from there light—it's fifty mile of hard travelin'. Goin' like I do I has th' good, short haul with th' heavy load; comin' back I have a light waggin on th' long, mean haul. If I went to Sherman first, things would just be turned 'round."

"What do you do when you have passengers for Sherman?"

"Don't want none!" snorted Buffalo. "Wouldn't carry 'em to Sherman, anyhow. Anybody with sense that can sit a hoss wouldn't crawl along with me in th' heat an' dust on that jouncin' seat. But sometimes I has a tenderfoot to nurse, consarn 'em. They ask so many fool questions I near go *loco*. But they pays me well for it, you bet!"

"Anythin' else I can give you a hand with?" asked Johnny, following the old man out of the shed.

"No, thankee; I'm all done. Th' only man that can give me a hand now is that scamp, George. I'm goin' in to eat, friend. Got to be up an' be on my way before th' sun comes up. I get th' cool of th' mornin' for my team, an' give 'em a longer rest when she gets hot. If you see Jim Fanning, tell him I'm buyin' hides as a side line now. I pays spot cash for 'em, same price as Ol' Saunders would pay, less th' freight. He has quit th' business an' went to live with his married da'ter, ol' fool!"

"Fanning sell hides?"

"No; I just want him to know so he can tell th' Bar H an' th' Triangle an' mebby th' Double X. I want to have a good load goin' back from here. There ain't no profit in goin' all th' way back with an empty waggin. Well, good night, friend! I'm much obliged to you."

"That's all right," smiled Johnny. "I'll tell him.

Good night; an' good luckl" he added as an afterthought, and then drifted around to the saloon, where he found several men at the bar.

Dave performed the introductions, and added: "Nelson, here, says he ain't goin' back punchin' cows as long as his money lasts. He's a travelin' eddicator; in th' innercent game of draw—or was it studhoss, Nelson?"

"Draw is closer to my heart," laughed Johnny. "My friend, Tex, told me I might learn draw if I lived long enough; but I'd have to have a pack of cards buried with me an' practice in th' other world if I aimed to learn studhoss."

"It grieves me to see a young man wastin' his time in idleness," said Ben Dailey, the storekeeper. "Th' devil is allus lookin' for holts. Young men should keep workin'. Might I inquire if you feel like indulgin' in a little game of draw? You'll find us rusty, though."

"We don't play oftener than every night, an' some afternoons," said Fanning.

"I'm a little scared when a man says he's rusty," replied Johnny. "But I reckon I might as well lose tonight as later. I hope Dave is too busy to cut in— he said he don't know *nothin'* about it."

"Dave's still cuttin' his teeth," chuckled Jim Fanning; "but he uses my silver to cut 'em on. When he learns th' game I'm goin' to drift out of town while I still got a cayuse."

Two punchers came stamping in and Dave nodded to them. "Here's yore victims; here's them infants from th' Double X. Boys, say 'Howd'y' to Mr. Nelson.

Nelson, that tall, red-headed feller is Slim Hawkes; an' that bowlegged towhead is Tom Wilkes. They ain't been in here in three months, an' they've rid twenty miles to rob us."

"An' we might walk home," retorted Wilkes. "Let's lay th' dust before we starts anythin'. Nelson, yo're in bad company. This gang would rob a church. You want to get a kneehold an' hang onto th' pommel after *this* game starts. Here's how!"

As the game progressed the few newcomers who straggled in felt their interest grow. As each finished his drink, Dave would lean forward and whisper:, "There's what I call a poker game. Four highwaymen playin' 'em close. To listen to 'em you'd think they never saw a card before."

Johnny was complaining. "Gents, I know I'm ignorant—but would you advise me to draw to a pair of treys? Shall I hold up an ace, or take three cards? I'll chance it; I never hold a sider. Gimme three."

"Ain't that just my luck," sighed Ben. "An' me with three of a kind."

A little later Johnny picked up another hand and frowned at it. "Well, seein' as I allus hold up a sider, I'll have two, this time."

Hoofbeats drummed up and stopped, and a voice was heard outside. Dave looked at the calendar. "Big Tom's a day ahead—he ain't due for his spree till pay-day. Hello, Huff! What you doin' so fur from home?"

"Hello, Dave! Hello, boys!" said the newcomer. "I feel purty good tonight. Just got word that McCullough wants two thousand head from us fellers up here. He'll be along with his reg'lar trail outfit in a few weeks. Sixteen men, a four-mule chuck waggin, an' nine saddle hosses to th' man. I'm sendin' word that I can give him a thousand head, an' th' Triangle is goin' to give him five hundred; so he'll want five hundred from th' Double X, which Slim an' Tom can tell Sherwood."

"Shore," growled Slim, and his ranch mate nodded.

"Goin' up to Dodge again?" queried Dailey.

"He didn't say," answered Big Tom. "Who's doin' the scalpin'?" he asked, going over to the table, where he gradually grew more restless as he watched.

"Some of these days, when I grows up," grinned Wilkes, "I'm goin' up th' trail with a herd, like a reg'lar cow-puncher. Dodge may be top-heavy with marshals, but I'd like to see it again, with money in my pockets."

Slim grunted. "Huh!" He looked over his hand, and drawled: "Th' last time you went up you put on too many airs. Just because Cimarron let you play *segundo* once in a while when he went on ahead to size up th' water or some river we would have to cross, you got too puffed up. I'm aimin' to be th' second boss th' next trip, an' I'll hand you a few jobs that'll keep you out of mischief."

Big Tom watched the winner rake in the chips and could stand it no longer. "Say," he growled, "anybody gettin' tired, an' want to drop out?"

Dailey looked up. "I only won two dollars in two hours, an' I got some work to do. Everybody bein' willin', I'll go out an' bury my winnin's."

Big Tom took his place. "I'm shore of one thing: I can't lose th' ranch, for I don't own it."

A round or two had been played when Big Tom drew his first openers. Johnny raised it and cards were drawn. After it had gone around twice, the others dropped out. Big Tom raised and Johnny helped it along. The betting became stiffer and Big Tom laughed. "I hope you keep on boostin' her."

"You can't get me out of this pot with dynamite," replied Johnny, pushing out a raise.

Big Tom's gun was out before he left his seat. His chair crashed backward and he leaned over the table. "Meanin'?" he snarled.

Johnny, surprised, kept his hand on the chips. "What I said," he answered, evenly.

"Tom!" yelled Dave. "He don't mean nothin'! He's a stranger down here."

Big Tom's scowl faded at the words. "I reckon I was hasty, Nelson," he said.

Johnny spoke slowly, his voice metallic "You was so hasty you come near never gettin' over it. Put down th' gun."

"I'm a mite touchy at—"

"If you has anythin' to say, put—down—that— gun.

"No offense?"

"For th' third time: Put—down—that—gun."

Big Tom shook his head and appeared to be genuinely sorry. He slid the gun back and picked up his chair. "You raised?"

"I did. I advise you to call—and end it."

"She's called. Five little hearts," said Big Tom, lying down his cards.

"They're hasty, too. Queen full, count 'em. Let's liquor."

The foreman paused in indecision. "Nelson—"

"We all get touchy," interrupted Johnny, scraping in the winnings. "Will you drink with me?"

"I'll take the same," said Big Tom, and he bought the next round, nodded his good night and went out.

Johnny turned to Dave. "Will you oblige me by tellin' me what Mr. Huff got huffy about?"

Dave hesitated, but Slim Hawkes laughed and answered for him, his slow drawl enhancing the humor of his tale, and wrinkles playing about his eyes and lips told of the enjoyment the picture gave to him. "Clear River crossed our range, flowed through Little Canyon, made a big bend on th' Bar H, passed out of East Canyon, an' flowed down the middle of th' SV. Three years ago a piece of Little Canyon busted loose an' slid down, blockin' th' river, which backed up, gettin' higher an' higher, an' began to cut through its bank about three miles above. Big Tom got busy, *pronto*. He sends for a box of dynamite, sticks it around in th' *debris* an' let's her go—*all* of it. When th' earthquake stopped there was a second one in th' dust an' smoke—we all thought it was a delayed charge. It wasn't. It was a section of th' canyon wall, near a hundred feet long an' almost two hundred feet high. There was a shale fault runnin' down from th' top, back about forty feet. Everythin' in front of that was jarred loose an' slid. Th' canyon was choked so hard an' fast that it won't never get open again. Clear River kept right on a-cuttin', an' it now flows on th' other side of Pine Mountain, which means th' Bar H ain't got no water of its own, except a few muddy holes south an' west of th' ranch buildings. That's why he's touchy. But that's a long speech, an' a dry one. Let's all liquor again."

RANGE HORSES

CHARLES M. RUSSELL

"Range hosses," says Rawhide Rawlins, "don't ask nothin' of men. Since Cortez brought them, they've been takin' care of themselves. They've been a long time learnin'—from the land of drought to the country of deep snows and long winters, they ranged.

"The Injuns used to tame wolves to move their camps till the Spaniard came. These dogs bein' meat eaters, it kept the red man busy feedin' his folks and his dogs. It's a cinch that lots of the time the whole outfit went hungry. I'm guessin' that in those days that nobody knows about, the red men followed the wolf and when able, drove him from his kill, and the wolf had the best end of it. But with a hoss under him it was different. The wolf followed the red man and got part of his kill. Some Injuns call the hoss 'the big dog,' but I'm tellin' about hosses.

"All other animals cached their young when they went to water. When a colt was born, his mother never left him and in a short time, he would travel with his maw. Wolves don't have much chance. Hosses stay in bands—if a wolf or wolves show up, they won't run like other animals, they bunch; and range hosses are dangerous at both ends, strikin' and kickin'. A wolf likes somethin' easy. After he feels the hoofs of a range mare a few times, he quits—it takes his appetite.

"When winter comes, the range hoss don't hug the brush like cows and starve to death—he hunts the ridges where the snow blows off. When he gets cold, the whole band will run and warm up—if the snow's deep, he paws to the grass. This keeps him warm. Nature gives him a winter coat. Sometimes, when his belly's full, he'll hunt a wind-break. Sometimes a lion will get a colt, but not often. Range hosses like open country, and won't stay in the brush only long enough to water.

"Hosses love pure cold water. In running water, which they like best, most of them drink with their heads up stream, every hoss tryin' to get up stream above the rile. I've seen bands of hosses at a prairie spring waitin' their turn to drink where it was cold and clear. As I said before, hosses like good water, but in countries where water ain't good, they drink anythin' that's wet. In fly time they bunch and stand heads and tails, each hoss using the tail of his pardner as a fly brush. If there's a breeze they hunt high ground; if it's still, they pick bare ground where there's lots of dust. In saddle bands, like you'll see on roundups, hosses will stay in groups from two to four or five.

"Some hosses will stay friends for years; others, like men, are changeable. A band of hosses turn their hind quarters to a rain or snow storm. They will, if driven, face a storm, but it's hard to make them go sideways. Range hosses in a hilly country stand with their heads down hill. You could drive a band of hosses up the steepest kind of a hill but nobody that I ever knowed could drive a bunch straight down (that goes with cows, too)—they'd sidle it every time.

"Hosses raised on the plains don't like the mountains, and if there's any chance they pull out. A hoss loves the range where he was foaled and will drift hundreds of miles to get back. If you're traveling with strange hosses, and camp, as long as they are tired and hungry they stay, but if there's a bunch quitter watch him when he fills up—he'll drift and travel.

"Most hosses are good swimmers, but few of them like it. If you want to play safe, swimming a hoss, loosen your cinches and jerk your bridle off. Maybe you won't come out just where you wanted, but you'll come out. Many a man has drowned himself and hoss by pullin' his hoss over. If you're lost in a blizzard, give your cayuse his head—he'll take you to shelter—it's hard to lose an animal.

"In the dark, don't spur a hoss where he don't want to go. There's lots of times a hoss knows more than a man. A man that says a hoss don't know nothin' don't know much about hosses."

* * * * *

I read in the papers a while back where there's seventy thousand wild hosses on the ranges of Montana," says Rawhide Rawlins. "They say these animals are a menace to stockmen. Mebbe this is right, but I think it would bother this old state to round up that many tame ones.

"A few years ago a hoss was considered kind of handy to have around. He was needed everywhere and used all ways. Up hill or down, mud or dust, he worked. They made no good roads for him. There's not a city in mighty near the whole world he didn't help build. There's a few ice-bound countries where the hoss don't live, and in these same lands it ain't easy for humans to live.

"This last war was a machine-made hell, but I doubt if it could have been win without hosses, an' the same kind that some folks say is a menace to men now. There was thousands of branded hosses died with our fighters on the other side. The range hoss was God-made, an' like all of His makin', the best. These hosses cost the man that branded an' claimed 'em nothing. They lived on the grass an' water the Almighty gave 'em.

"Many thousand years ago, when folks was all a-foot, lizards, horned toads, an' bullfrogs measured from thirty to a hundred feet in length an' stood from forty to sixty hands. Besides these, there was tigers and laffin' hyenas that would eat an elephant for breakfast. From what I've read, in the days I'm talkin' about man wasn't much, an' he sure lived simple. A good, stout cave was his home. He fed mostly on bugs an' snails, an' a grasshopper that happened to 'light anywhere near him or his family was out of luck. Sometimes some real game gent would slip out with his stone tomahawk an' bring back a skunk or two. Then's when they pulled a regular feed, but there wasn't no set date for these feasts, an' they mostly came far apart. With a hyena that weighed seven ton a-laffin' around the door, man loved his home, an' Maw never worried about where Paw was.

"But one day one of these old home-livers was sunnin' himself an' layin' for a grasshopper, when he looks down from his ledge to the valley below where all these animals is busy eatin' one another, an' notices one species that don't take no part in this feast, but can out-run an' out-dodge all others. This cave man is pro-gressive, an' has learned to think. He sees this animal is small compared to the rest, an' ain't got no horns, tusks or claws, eatin' nothin' but grass. There's other grass-eaters, but they all wear horns that don't look good to Mister Cave Man.

"He remembers when his Maw used to pack him on her back. Bein' a lazy gent he's lookin' for somethin' easy, an' he figgers that if he could get this horn-less animal under him, he could ride once more like he did in his childhood. Right then is when man starts thinkin' of somethin' besides eatin'.

"Not far from the cave there's a trail where herds of hosses come to water, so one day Mister Man climbs into a tree that hangs over the trail, an' with a grapevine loop he snares one of these animals. But he finds out that though this beast ain't got horns or claws, he's mighty handy with all four feet, and when Paw sneaks home that evenin' he's got hoof marks all over him an' he ain't had a ride yet. Sore as he is, he goes back next day an' tries again. About the sixth day this poor hoss is so starved that Mister Man gets up to him, an' tyin' a strip of bark to his under jaw an' another around his belly, he steps across the hoss. The bronc sinks his head an' goes in the air. Mister Man stays, but he breaks all the rules in a ridin' contest of to-day. He don't pull leather, but tears all the mane out from ears to withers, an' that bark hand-hold of his is all that keeps the hoss from unloadin' him. A few days later his bronc is plumb gentle. Paw mounts, goes out an' with a stone-headed spear kills a wild cow, an' he comes back to the cave with the hide an' more meat than the folks ever seen before. The family is so pleased with this useful pet that they bring him in the cave nights, an' all get busy pullin' grass for him.

"Mister Man finds that with four legs under him instead of two, he can ride rings around them big lizards, an' there ain't any of them claw-wearin', tusk-bearin' critters can overtake him. The old gent snares more hosses, an' it ain't long till the whole family's hoss-back. When this bunch starts out, armed an' mounted, they sure bring home the bacon. Meat—I'd tell a man. This cave looks ah' smells like a packin' plant before the pure food law. It's now mankind sheds the leaf garments of old Granddad Adam an' starts wearin' new clothes.

"Paw's wearin' a head-an'-tail cowskin; the boys has a yearlin' robe apiece. Maw an' the girls wouldn't be in style at all these days. Mebbe it's modesty—it might be the chill in the weather—but they're sure covered from ears to heels in deer an' elk skins, an' from that day to just lately man never knowed whether his sweetheart was knock-kneed or bow-legged.

"Since that old bug-eater snared that first cayuse, his descendants have been climbin', an' the hoss has been with 'em. It was this animal that took 'em from a cave. For thousands of years the hoss an' his long-eared cousins furnished all transportation on land for man an' broke all the ground for their farmin'. He has helped build every railroad in the world. Even now he builds the roads for the automobile that has made him nearly useless, an' I'm here to tell these machine-lovers that it will take a million years for the gas wagon to catch up with the hoss in what he's done for man. To-day some of these auto drivers want to kill him off to make fertilizer out of his body. Mebbe I'm sentimental, but I think it's a damned hard finish for one that has been as good a friend to man as the hoss."

GOOD SAMARITAN COWBOYS

H. H. HALSELL

One of the boldest deeds I can ever think of was one performed by O. D. Halsell in the year 1885 while our cattle were ranging on the south side of the Cimarron. At this time there was a soldier camp in a large grove of timber in the bend of the Cimarron about five miles northeast of the present city of Guthrie. On a certain day O. D. was riding through the range, and at a point about three miles south of the soldier camp he found the head of a big four-year-old steer of his. The steer had just been slaughtered and loaded into a wagon. Trailing the wagon, he found it led into the soldier camp. The captain's tent was in the center of the camp. O. D. rode up to the tent and called him out. He said, "You have no right to hold cattle in Oklahoma." O. D. said, "I may not, but you have no right to eat my beef steers." The Captain then asked him what he was going to do about it. O. D. said, "I am giving you five minutes to pay me forty-five dollars, or I'll kill you." That old Captain looked at him, saw he meant it, and handed him the forty-five dollars. Steers were worth at that time about half that amount. The Captain happened to be a brave man and admired a brave one.

How old-time cowboys die. There was in our camp on the Cimarron a cowboy who went by the name of Bednego; we never knew what his real name was. This boy was taken sick with pneumonia, and we had him hauled to Pawnee Agency, where there was an agency doctor. O. D. and I took time about staying with him. The agency was fifty miles from our camp. While I was on duty with him he became so bad that the doctor said: "Your man is dying and won't live until morning. You had better find out where his people are and ask him if he wants to send any word or message to them." I dreaded the job of telling this old boy but had to do it. Our cook was also devoted to Bednego and was sitting on the end of his bed. The boy was propped up with pillows and looked to me to be dying. About all he could take was buttermilk, and he always loved that drink. I sat on the bed and began to break the news as gently as possible to him. I said, "Bednego, you know we are your friends, and we will stay with you till the last, but you are a very sick man and may not get well. We will do all we can for you; but we want to know, should you not get well, is there any word you want to send to your folks." It seemed to hurt his feelings to think we were weakening when he had no idea of giving up the fight. Then in a weak voice, between breaths, he said, "Harry, I reckon you better—better—give me another—glass of—buttermilk." I said, "Old boy, your kind don't die." We held his head up, and that old puncher sucked slowly at that glass of milk until it was all gone. By morning he was on the way to recovery, and in two weeks he was back on the Cimarron.

While on a general roundup between the Canadian and Cimarron Rivers and near the Chisholm Trail, O. D. rode up to me just after noon and said, "There are some men stealing strays out of these herds while the men are on the roundup. I figure they have already gone northwest toward New Mexico, and one of us must follow them." I wanted to shield him from danger, so I said, "I'll go." There was a camp and ranch north of the Cimarron. O. D. and I cut out what cattle we had in the roundup, and I drove them north to this ranch and spent the night, leaving my cattle in this outfit's horse pasture. Next morning I started west to catch up with that stray bunch of cattle if possible. This same night a man by name of Brady Bryan stayed at this camp. He was what was called a rustler—that is to say, he often rustled things which belonged to someone else. And his territory of operations often reached into Kansas. I wrote some poetry about him one day, and Bryan rather enjoyed the notoriety. Bryan asked me for permission to go; and while I felt sure he could be of no help to me, still it was a lonesome ride and any company was better than none. So early in the morning we rode west into a country of fine grass, a beautiful cattle country, but no ranch, no cattle, nothing but unending prairie. We were riding west, making about seven or eight miles an hour. I was on my favorite buckskin horse. This horse was good in every way, a fast runner, a fine saddle horse, and faithful. About three o'clock in the afternoon I looked ahead about two miles and saw a bunch of cattle and told Bryan it was the stolen cattle. He said, "How do you know?" I said, "All of them are lying down, and that shows they are worn out by a long drive." There was a branch with some clusters of bushes and elm trees just south of the cattle about fifty yards. We rode on the north side of the cattle to the west side, then crossed the stream and were riding down the south side about twenty steps from the branch when suddenly I saw three men sitting under the bank. I said, "Brady, there they are." Immediately Bryan hit his big brown horse in the flank with his quirt, and the last I saw of him he was passing over a divide. I knew two of these men, and they spoke to me. I also knew the safe plan was to be friendly, frank, and open with them. I got down and walked up and sat down near them. Two of them were old-time cow hands, both fine cowboys. The other they called the Kid. These "Kids" are often fools enough to kill on any and all occasions. One of them asked me what I wanted. I said: "Boys, I only want what all cowmen have a right to do, and that is to look at any passing herd. If you have no cattle belonging to our outfit or our neighbors, I'll ride on; but if you have any of those, I want them." Lincoln said: "We have none of your cattle, but you can look at the herd." These two men were not what would be classed as thieves or bad men at all, but they rustled strays just too much. Ordinarily strays that were far from home, and easy to appropriate, fell an easy prey to a fast rider. While I knew these two men well, at the same time, it would have been safer for them to have gotten rid of me, for dead men tell no tales. Then there was the fact that the man who ran away could tell the tale that the last he saw of me was with those men, for he, too, knew both of the men. I told them I would never tell that I saw them, and they trusted my word. I kept my eyes on the Kid all of the time I was with them. I then mounted Buck and rode on down the south side of the branch. I had my Winchester in my hands and rode up on another man sitting in the trail crossing of that branch. He rose up and said, "Harry, you can't go to that herd." I said, "Ben Grant (that was his name, and he was sure enough a killer), I am going to look at that herd; and you step out of the way, or I'll bore a hole through you." Now Grant was a gambler and would kill if he got the drop, but he would not face the cold steel. There is a character called Trampas, representing just such a man, in Owen Wister's book, *The Virginian,* and when I read the story of his shooting at the Virginian it reminded me of Ben Grant. Grant moved out of the way. I went to the drove of cattle and cut out five head of ZV and Diamond Tail cattle, and started east. By daylight I was at camp, ate breakfast, and put these five with my other bunch, which together made about forty head. I then moved on southeast and in two or three days arrived at our camp on the south bank of the Cimarron, pretty well worn out, having had little to eat on the way and being alone.

During the winter of 1885 and 1886 we built a winter camp on the north bank of the Cimarron. The camp was located in the timber. There were two hills with a twenty-foot space between. We cut out a dugout in each, facing each other, and covered over the space between; and the north end of this hall was roofed in, so we had two large rooms with a hall between. We lined the dugouts inside with split cedar logs, and this made a very comfortable, warm home. During a fearful cold spell I was away, and O. D. and about four or five other men were at this camp. There was a wagon loaded with feed and supplies in front of the hall. It being an awful cold night, the men had put prairie hay on the floor, spread some blankets over that, and were having a good time playing cards. This they kept up till about midnight, then went to bed. About 2 AM O. D. was awakened by flames of fire in the hay and bedding. He immediately aroused all the men, and they tried to put the fire out. Failing in that, Halsell instructed the men to get out all the things they could. He told one man to carry out a five-gallon can of coal oil. This man, in his excitement, carried it just outside the door and set it down. If the men had listened to O. D., they could have saved the bedding; but owing to the fact that they had just been aroused out of deep sleep and the fearful, numbing cold, there was much confusion and nothing was accomplished. Presently belts of cartridges began firing, three whole boxes included. This drove all the men to the horse sheds. O. D. and another men tried to pull the wagon out of reach of the flames, but the wheels were frozen, and about this time the can of coal oil exploded, and that ruined it all. The horses were in the lot under a hay shed. There the cold, shivering men gathered and saddled their horses. Halsell sent some of them to the B. & M. camp, ten miles down the river, some he sent to a ranch forty miles southwest, and he and another man went to a camp about thirty miles south on the Canadian. I was with Tom Love at Welston the night of the fire, and next day we two rode up to. the river to the camp where O. D. Halsell and four other men were playing poker. That day he won between two and three hundred dollars. He was the only successful poker player outside of regular gamblers or professionals I ever saw, but he always played fair. And all men who knew him understood what it would cost to try to cheat him.

Gambling as a profession is almost as bad as stealing, for regular gamblers who follow that as a trade will cheat and rob; but in our cow camps we used all sorts of games as pastimes, and almost all cowboys played fair. Most men who are not regular gamblers and who play poker are deluded into thinking they can win; however, there is a real art to successful poker playing. First, you must have an affidavit face which no man can read. Second, you must have the nerve to plank down plenty of the long green at the right time. Third, you must have the ability to read the other man's face. And fourth, you must have common sense enough to quit at the right time. Now all these qualifications are rarely ever possessed by one person, so my advice is to cut it all out. There is just one way to earn money, and that it is by honest labor ; that is, it pays well to earn it that way, and no short cut to fortune is ever permanently satisfactory. I guess the Creator knew what he was talking about when he gave one of his first commandments, "In the sweat of your face ye shall earn your bread."

On one occasion our outfit was riding out to Hunnewell, returning down the trail due south, when opposite the shipping pens we heard guns firing; and looking east, we saw a drunk cowboy running out of town, yelling and having a good time by himself. He did not know that there were some officers behind a group of houses shooting at him. But O. D. Halsell saw it, and it made him good and mad to see those officers shooting at that cowboy just because he was happy. Although we had just finished a long, hard trip on the trail, O. D. said he was going back. George Ricker said, "I am going with you." I was perfectly sober and realized the danger and did not want to go, but went; and we three went fast. The officers saw us coming and deputized some additional men. As we ran up we jumped from our horses with drawn pistols. With our bridle reins in our left hands we stepped onto the sidewalk, facing six officers, and Ben Grant, who had turned renegade—that is, he was what confederates once called "turned coat." He had started into gambling and standing in with the cut-throats of Hunnewell. Now he came running up the sidewalk in his shirtsleeves, buckling on his belt and six-shooter, and calling out, "Oscar, I am deputized to help arrest you." If I should live another hundred years, I never would forget the fire that seemed to flash from O. D.'s face as he hurled at old Ben Grant these burning words, "Yes, and you son—, if they are all like you, it will take a cow pen full to do that." That paralyzed Grant so that he could not even buckle his belt.

I think I was the only one of the three of us who was at all scared, but I was the only sober man there and also the youngest. One of the officers denied shooting at the man when O. D. accused them of a cowardly attack on a drunk cowboy. When the officer said he didn't shoot, George Ricker called him a liar. I tried to quiet him, but old George was feeling proud as he stood by O. D., who was looked upon by all men who knew him as not only the bravest of the brave and a devoted friend to all cowboys, and especially to those who were in need, but he was also a very fine-looking man whose very presence commanded respect. He was cursing these men and was in a furious mood. The Chief Marshal said, "Oscar, you will be killed." O. D. said, "Yes, I know it; but I'll kill you the first one." Now as I look back and recall these wild scenes, I can hardly believe such a period of wild, lawless life ever existed on the Kansas border, but it did.

The chief officer was no coward, but he knew his men had done wrong in shooting at that defenseless cowboy; and, as there was no law to right and wrong, O. D. took the law into his own hands to defend the weak against the strong. Turn back to the days of chivalry and read where such gallant knights as Ivanhoe, Chevalier Baird, and Sir Philip Sidney, at the altar, took vows to make battle for the weak against the strong, to right wrongs, and the bold acts of these cowboys in the rough days will not appear so bad.

We had one advantage—we had our guns in our hands and our seven opponents did not. We were within eight feet of them and could, of course, and would have killed three before any one of them could have been ready. And it is a fact, proved on many occasions, that if you get the leaders, you have the fight won. This Chief Marshal was thinking fast, and so he said, "Oscar, let's all take a drink together, call it square, and you all leave town, and that will be the last of it." O. D. said, "All right; I'll set 'em up." All of them filed in but Ben Grant. I saw him hanging back, and I hung back. As he came to the door he said, "You go in." I replied, "No, you are going in." He tucked his head and went in. I stood near the door, watched him, and drank lemonade. Now it was considered dishonorable to pledge friendship in a drink and then violate that pledge, and very few men would fuss with a man he had touched glasses with. But there are exceptions, and Ben Grant was one. We filed out and went on our way down the Chisholm Trail.

Returning to Texas from a trail drive in the year 1885 or 1886, there were about six of us riding horseback with a pack horse. When we arrived in the

Arbuckle Mountains, we stopped at a beautiful running branch, and all of us got down under some small elm trees and dipped up the cool water to drink. After a rest of about fifteen minutes, I said, "Mount, forward, march!" All the men mounted but one young fellow. I looked and saw him standing by his horse with his head leaning against the saddle and his hand with a finger through his tin cup, gripping the horn. I jumped down and felt his pulse, and he seemed to be dead. I pulled his hand loose from the saddle horn and laid him down on his back with his head against a tree, at the same time asking God for a doctor. When I turned around there stood by me a man holding the bridle reins of his horse with a medicine bag in one hand. I said, "Are you a doctor?" He said, "Yes." I then told him to do something for the man. He gave him some kind of medicine and said we ought to get a wagon and haul him on to Texas. He also said if the boy did not regain consciousness by morning, he would die. To get a wagon was a serious problem, but somehow I believed I could find one. Starting east, I rode rapidly for approximately eight miles and came on to a man and woman sitting in a two-horse wagon by the roadside. I told him I wanted him to go with me and haul a sick man to Texas. He said, "All right." Some would say this all just accidentally happened. I do not think so. Two years after this incident I was in Bonham, Tex., and as I sat down at a table in a restaurant to have dinner, this same doctor walked in, and I knew him and had him take dinner with me. I said to him, "I want to be near you, for I feel toward you in a way that I do not toward any other man."

When I returned to the men with the wagon, we put the sick man in on a feather bed. I got in the back end and placed his head on a pillow in my lap, and we moved out at sunset. The men rode in front, two and two, together. Thus we went south all night and just at daybreak we stopped. The men built a fire. The boy roused up and said, "Help me out." We carried him out and the medicine operated and the boy became conscious. We placed him back in the wagon and moved on to Texas. When we reached there we put him in a sanitarium. That young man had been sick for several days and had never complained or let us know he was ill. There are many men of that disposition. Of late years I enjoy complaining and grunting in order to relieve the strain on my system. If this story is ever published, it is likely some readers will not believe that doctor was standing there when I called for him. All the same it is true, just as I tell it, just as true as the story of the big Tonkaway Indian falling in my bed at midnight one July night in 1880, about one hundred miles east of the Pecos, as I was on my way from Mexico to Decatur.

BUCK PETERS MAKES FRIENDS

CLARENCE E. MULFORD

AND

JOHN WOOD CLAY

The town of Twin River straggled with indifferent impartiality along the banks of the Black Jack and Little Jill branches where they ran together to form the Jones' Luck River, two or three houses lying farther north along the main stream. The trail from Wayback, the nearest railway point, hugged the east bank of Jones' Luck, shaded throughout its course by the trees which lined the river, as they did all the streams in this part of the country: cottonwoods mostly, with an occasional ash or elm. Looking to the east, the rolling ground sloped upward toward a chain of hills; to the west, beyond the river, the country lay level to the horizon. On both sides of the trail the underbrush grew thick; spring made of it a perfect paradise of blossoms.

Boomerang, pet hobo of Twin River and the only one who ever dared to come back, left Little Nell's with his characteristic hurried shuffle and approached the wooden bridge where the Wayback trail crossed the Jill, and continued south to Big Moose. Boomerang was errand boy just now, useful man about the hotel or one of the saloons when necessity drove, at other times just plain bum. He was suspected of having been a soldier. A sharp "'tention" would startle him into a second's upright stiffness which after a furtive look around would relax into his customary shambling lack of backbone. He had one other amusing peculiarity: let a gun be discharged in his vicinity and there was trouble right away, trouble the gunner was not looking for; Boomerang would fly into such a fury of fighting rage, it was a town wonder that some indignant citizen had not sent him long ago where he never could come back.

Coming to the bridge he looked casually and from habit along the trail and espied a horseman riding his way. He studied him reflectively a few seconds and then spat vigorously at something moving on one of the bridge planks, much as the practised gun-man snaps without appearing to aim. "Stranger," he affirmed; "Cow-punch," he added; "Old man," he shrewdly surmised, and shook his head; "Dunno 'im" and he glanced at the stain on the plank to see what he had bagged. Among his other pleasing human habits "Boom "used tobacco—as a masticant—there was the evidence of the fact. But he had missed and after a wistful look for something to inspire him to a more successful effort, he shuffled on.

The horseman came at a steady gait, his horse, a likely-looking bay with black spots, getting over the ground considerably faster than the cow-ponies common to the locality; approaching the bridge he was slowed to a walk while his rider took in the town with comprehensive glance. A tall man, lean and grizzled, with the far-seeing, almost vacant eye of the plainsman, there was nothing, to any one but such a student of humanity as "Boom," to indicate his calling, much less his position in it. The felt hat, soft shirt and rough, heavy suit, the trousers pushed into the tops of his boots, were such as a man in the town might wear and many did wear. He forded the stream near the bridge at a walk. Pop Snow, better known as Dirty, cleverly balancing himself within an inch of safety in front of tile "I-Call" saloon, greeted him affably: "Come a long way, stranger?" asked Dirty.

"From Wayback," announced the other and paused in interested suspense. Dirty had become seized with some internal convulsion, which momentarily threatened disaster to his balance. His feet swung back and forth in. spasmodic jerks, the while his sinful old carcass shook like a man with the Chagres fever.

Finally a strangled wheeze burst from his throat and explained the crinkle about his eyes: he was laughing.

"Wayback ain't fur," he declared, licking his lips in anticipation of the kernel of his joke about to come. "You can a'most see it frum here through the bottom uv—"

"How d' you know it ain't?" the horseman abruptly interrupted.

Dirty was hurt. This was not according to Hoyle. Two more words and no self-respecting "gent" could refuse to look toward Wayback through a glass—and certainly not alone. The weather was already too cold to sit fishing for such fish as this; and here was one who had swallowed the bait, rejecting the hook.

"Why, stranger, I been there," explained Dirty, in aggrieved remonstrance.

"How long since you been there? Not since two-at-once, was you? Didn't it used to be at Drigg's Worry? Did n't it?"

Snow lost his balance. He nodded in open-mouthed silence.

"Course it was—at Drigg's Worry—and now it's way back," and with a grim chuckle the stranger pressed in his knees and loped on down the trail to the Sweet-Echo Hotel.

Dirty stared after him. "Who in hell's that?" he asked himself in profane astonishment. "It's never Black Jack—too old; an' it ain't Lucky Jones—too young. He sure said 'two-at-once.' Two-at-once: I ain't heard that in more 'n twenty years." His air-dried throat compelled inward attention and he got up from his box and turned and looked at it. "Used to be at Drigg's Worry, didn't it?" he mimicked. "Did n't it? An' now it's way back." He kicked the box viciously against the tavern wall. "D—n yer! This yer blasted town's gettin' too smart," and he proceeded to make the only change of base he ever undertook during the day, by stamping across the bridge to the "Why-Not."

The door of the I-Call opened and a man appeared. He glanced around carelessly until he noticed the box, which he viewed with an appearance of lively interest, coming outside and walking around it at a respectful distance. "Huh!" he grunted. Having satisfied himself of its condition he drawlingly announced it for the benefit of those inside. "Dirty's busted his chair," he informed, and turned to look curiously after Pop Snow, who was at that moment slamming the door of the Why-Not behind him.

Through the open door three other men came out. They all looked at the box. One of them stopped and turned it over with his thumb. "Kicked it," he said, and they all looked across at the Why-Not, considering. A roar from behind them smote upon their ears like a mine blast: "Shut that door! "With one accord they turned and trooped back again.

The rider meanwhile was talking to his horse as he covered the short distance to the Sweet-Echo Hotel. "Wonderful climate, Allday. If twenty years don't wear you down no more 'n old Snow you'll shore be a grand horse t' own," and he playfully banged him alongside the neck with his stirrup. Allday limited his resentment to a flattening of the ears and the rider shook his head sorrowfully. "Yo 're one good li'l hoss but yore patience'd discourage a saint." He swung off the trail to ride around the building in search of a shelter of some kind, catching sight of Boomerang just disappearing through the door of the bar-room. "Things has been a-movin' 'round Twin River since Frenchy an' me went after Slippery an' his gang: bridges, reg'lar hotels, an' tramps. An' oblige *me* by squintin' at th' stable. If Cowan'd wake up an' find that at th' back door, he'd fall dead."

He dismounted and led his horse through the stable door, stopping in contemplation of the interior. He was plainly surprised. "One, two, three, four," he counted, "twenty stalls—twenty tie-'em-by-th'-head stalls—no, there's a rope behind 'em. Well, I'm d—d! He ain't meanin' to build again in fifty years; no, not never!"

Allday went willingly enough into one of the stalls—they were nothing new to him—and fell to eating with no loss of time. Buck watched him for a few moments and then, throwing saddle and bridle onto his shoulder, he walked back the way he had come and into the hotel bar. No one noticed him as he entered, all, even the bartender, being deeply intent on watching a game of cards. Buck grunted, dropped his belongings in a corner, and paused to examine the group. A grand collie dog, lying near the stove in the middle of the room, got up, came and sniffed at him, and went back and lay down again.

The game was going on at a table close to the bar, over which the bartender leaned, standing on some elevation to enable him to draw closer. Only two men were playing. The one facing Buck was a big man, in the forties, his brown hair and beard thickly sprinkled with gray; brown eyes, red-rimmed from dissipation, set wide apart from a big, bold nose, stared down at the cards squeezed in a big hand. The other man was of slight build, with black hair, and the motions of his hands, which Buck had caught as he entered, were those of a gambler: accurate, assured, easy with a smooth swiftness that baffled the eye. He was dressed like a cow-punch; he looked like a cow-punch—all but the hands; these, browned as they were, and dirty, exhibited a suppleness that had never been injured by hard work. Buck walked up to the bar and a soft oath escaped him as he caught sight of the thin, brown face, the straight nose, the out-standing ears, the keen black eyes -— Buck's glance leaped around the circle of on-lookers in the effort to discover how many of the gambler's friends were with him. He was satisfied that the man was playing a lone hand. There was a tenseness in the air which Buck knew well, but from across the hall came a most incongruous sound. "Piano, by G—-d!" breathed Buck in amazement. The intentness on the game of those in the room explained why he had seen no one about the place and he was at a loss to account, for the indifference of the musician.

At the big man's left, standing in the corner between the bar and the wall, was a woman. Her blonde hair and blue eyes set off a face with some pretensions to beauty, and in point of size she was a fitting mate for the big man at whom she stared with lowering gaze. Close to her stood the hobo, and Buck rightly concluded he was a privileged character. Surrounding the table were several men quite evidently punchers, two or three who might be miners, and an unmistakable travelling salesman of that race whose business acumen brings them to the top though they start at the bottom. Buck had gauged them all in that one glance. Afterward he watched the gambler's hands and a puzzled expression gradually appeared on his face; he frowned and moved uneasily. Was the man playing fair or were his eyes getting old? Suddenly the frown disappeared and he breathed a sigh of relief: the motion itself had been invisible but Buck had caught the well-remembered preliminary flourish; thereafter he studied the faces of the others; the game had lost interest, even the low voices of the players fell on deaf ears. His interest quickened as the big man stood up.

"I'm done," he declared. "That lets me out, Dave. You've got th' pile. After to-night I '11 have to pound leather for forty a month and my keep." He turned to the woman, while an air of relief appeared among the others at his game acceptance of the loss. "Go on home, Nell. I won't be up yet a while."

"You won't be up at all," was the level-voiced reply.

"Eh?" he exclaimed, in surprised questioning.

She pushed past him and walked to the door. "You won't be up at all," she repeated, facing him. "You've lost your pile and sent mine after it in a game you don't play any better than a four-year-old. I warned you not to play. Now you take the consequences." The door slammed after her. "Boom" silently opened the door into the hall and vanished.

The big man looked around, dazed. No one met his eye. Dave was sliding the cards noiselessly through his fingers and the rest appeared fascinated by the motion. The big man turned to the bartender. "Slick, gimme a bottle," he demanded. Slick complied without a word and he bore it in his hand to the table behind the door, where he sat drinking alone, staring out morosely at the gathering darkness.

Buck dropped into the vacated chair and laid his roll on the table. "The time to set in at a two-hand game of draw," he remarked with easy good nature, "is when th' other feller is feelin' all flushed up with win-nin'. If you like to add my pile to that load you got a'ready, I'm on." He beamed pleasantly on the surrounding faces and a cynical smile played for a moment on the thin lips of the man facing him. "Sure," he agreed, and pushed the cards across the table.

"Bar-keep, set 'em up," said Buck, flicking a bill behind him. Slick became busy at once and Buck, in a matter-of-fact manner, placed bis gun on the table at his left hand and picked up the pack. "Yes," he went on with vacuous cheerfulness, "the best man with a full deck I ever saw told me that. We crossed trails down in Cheyenne. They was shore some terrors in that li'l town, but he was th' one original." He shook his head in reminiscent wonder, and raised his glass. "Here's to a growin' pile, Bud," and nodding to the others, who responded with indistinct murmurs, the drink was drained in the customary gulp. "One more, bar-keep, before we start her," he demanded. "I never drink when I'm a-playin'." Here he leaned forward and raised his voice. "Friend, you over there by th' winder, yo 're not drinkin'." The big man slowly turned his head and looked at Buck with blood-shot eyes, then at the extra glass on his table. "Here's better luck ner mine, friend—not wishin' you no harm, Dave," and he added the drink to the generous quantity he had already consumed. Buck waved his hand in acknowledgment, then he smiled again on his opponent.

"Same game you was playin', Bud?" he asked, genially.

"Suits me," was the laconic reply.

Buck raised the second drink. "Here's to Tex Ewalt, th' man who showed me th' error of my ways." The tail of his eye was on Dave.

The name of Tex must have shocked him like a bucket of ice water but he did not betray it by so much as the flicker of an eyelid. Ewalt and he had been friends in the Panhandle and both had escaped the fate of Trendley and his crowd more by luck than merit. Buck knew Dave's history in Texas, related by Ewalt himself, who had illustrated the tell-tale flourish with which Dave introduced a crooked play; but he did not know that Dave Owens was Black Jack, returned after years of wandering, to the place of his nativity.

The boy and girl history of David Jones (Black Jack) and his sister, Veia (called Jill) was well known to some of the old timers who went to Montana in the first gold rush and stayed there. It was difficult to get them to tell it and one was sorry to have heard it, if successful. Buck shuffled the cards slowly and then with a careful exaggeration of the flourish, dealt the hand in a swift shower of dropping units. A sigh of appreciation escaped the observant group and this time Buck got results: at sight of the exaggerated flourish an involuntary contraction of the muscles hardened the deceptively boyish form and face of the younger man and the black eyes stared a challenging question at the smiling gray ones opposite before dropping to the cards he had unconsciously gathered up.

Luck smiled on Buck from the start. He meant that it should. Always a good player, his acquaintance with Tex, who had taught him all he knew of crooked plays, had made him an apt pupil in the school in which his slippery opponent was a master. With everything coming his way Buck was quite comfortable. Sooner or later the other would force the fighting. Time enough to sit up and take notice when the flourishing danger signal appeared.

It came at last. Dave leaned forward and spoke. "Cheyenne, how'd jack-pots strike yer? I got ter hit th' trail before six an' it's pretty nigh time to feed."

"Shore!" assented Buck, heartily. The pot grew in a manner scandalous to watch. "Double the ante," softly suggested Dave. "Shore," agreed Buck, with genial alacrity. "Double her ag'in."

"Double she is," was Buck's agreeable response.

Pass after pass and Slick stretched out over the bar and craned his neck. At last, with a graceful flourish a good hand fell to Buck, a suspiciously good hand, while Dave's thin lips were twisted into a onesided smile. Buck looked at him reproachfully. "Bud, you should oughter knowed better'n that. I got six cards."

The smile faded from Dave's face and he stared at the cards like a man who sees ghosts. The stare rose slowly to Buck's face, but no one could possibly suspect such grieved reproach to be mere duplicity. It was too ridiculous—only Dave knew quite well that he had *not* dealt six cards. "Funny," he said. "Funny how a man'll make mistakes."

"I forgive you this once, but don't do it no more," , and Buck shuffled the cards, executed a particularly outrageous flourish, and dealt.

"Ha! Ha!" barked Bow-Wow Baker. "D—n if they ain't both makin' th' same sign. Must belong to th' same lodge."

Chesty Sutton dug him in the ribs with an elbow. "Shut up!" he hissed, never taking his eyes from the game.

Dave passed and Buck opened. Dave drew three cards to two high ones. Buck stood pat. Dave scanned his hand; whatever suspicion he might have had, vanished: he had never seen the man who could deal him a straight in that fashion. He backed his hand steadily until Buck's assurance and his own depleted cash made him pause, and he called. Buck solemnly laid down four aces. Four!—and Dave would have taken his oath the diamond ace had been on the bottom of the deck before the deal—and Buck had not drawn cards.

"They're good," said Dave shortly, dropping his hand into the discard. "If you're goin' to stay around here, Cheyenne, I'll get revenge to-morrer." He started to rise.

"Nope, I guess not, Bud. I never play yore kind of a game with th' same man twice."

Dave froze in his position. "Meanin'?" he asked, coldly.

"I don't like th' way you deal," was the frank answer.

"D—n you!" cursed Dave. His hand flew to his guii—and stopped. Over the edge of the table a forty-five was threatening with steady mouth.

"Don't do it, Bud," warned Buck.

Dave's hand slowly moved forward. "A two-gun man, eh?" he sneered.

"Shore. Never bet on th' gun on th' table, Bud. You got a lot to learn. Hit her up or you'll be late—an' down where I came from it's unhealthy to look through a winder without first makin' a noise."

"Yore argument is good. But I reckon it'd be a good bet as how you'll learn somethin' in Twin River you ain't never learned nowhere else." Dave sauntered carelessly to the front door.

"You ain't never too old to learn," agreed Buck, sententiously. The front door closed quietly after Dave and half a minute later his pony's hoofs were heard pounding along the trail that led toward Big Moose:

"Cheyenne, put her there! I like yore style!" Chesty Sutton, late puncher for the Circle X, shoved his hand under Buck's nose with unmistakable friendliness. "*I* like th' way *you* play, all right."

"Me, too," chimed in Bow-Wow. "Dave Owens has got th' lickin' of his life. An' between you an' I, Cheyenne, I ain't never seed Dave get licked afore—not reg'lar."

The chorus of congratulations that followed was so sincere that Buck's heart warmed toward the company. Chesty secured attention by pointing his finger at Buck and wagging it impressively. "But you hear me, Cheyenne," he warned. "Dave ain't no quitter. He's got it agin' you an' he's h—l on th' shoot. I ain't never heerd of his killin' nobody but he's right handy spoilin' yore aim. Ain't he, Bow-Wow?"

"Look a-here. How often have I told you? You sez so. He *is*. Don't alius leave it to me." Bow-Wow's tone was indignant as he rubbed his right arm reflectively.

"Gentlemen, I'm not sayin' a word against anybody, not one word," and Slick glanced from man to man, shaking his head to emphasize his perfect belief in the high standard of morality prevalent in Twin River. "But I begs leave to remark that I like Cheyenne's game—which it is th' first time in my brief but eventful career that I seen five dealt cards turn into six. You all seen it. It sure happened. Mr. Cheyenne, you have my joyous admiration. Let's celebrate. An' in th' meantime, might I inquire, without offence, if Cheyenne has a habit of complainin' of too many cards ?" They haol lined up before the bar and all glasses were filled before Buck answered. Slick stood directly before him and every face, showing nothing beyond polite interest, was turned his way. But Buck well knew that on his reply depended his position in the community and the gravity of the occasion was in his voice when he spoke.

"Gentlemen, Mr. Slick has called. There's two ways of playin'. When I plays with any gentleman here, I plays one way. Dave Owens played th' other way. I played his game."

He glanced at the silent figure by the window, set down his glass, and started to cross the room. Chesty Sutton put out his hand and stopped him. "I would n't worry him none, Cheyenne. Ned Monroe's th' best boss I ever worked for but hard luck has been pilin' up on him higher 'n th' Rockies since he lost his ranch. Better let him fight it out alone, friend."

Lost his ranch—Ned Monroe—Buck's intention was doubly strengthened. "Leave it to me," was his confident assurance, and he strode across the room and around the table in front of the window. The sombre eyes of the big man were forced to take notice of him.

"Friend, it's on th' house. Mr. Slick is a right pleasant man, an' he's waitin'." A rapid glance at the bottle told him that Monroe, in his complete oblivion, had forgotten it. Ned eyed him with a puzzled frown while the words slowly illumined his clouded mind. At length he turned, slowly, sensed the situation, and rose heavily to his feet. "Sure," was the simple reply. At the bar significant looks were exchanged. "I'm beginnin' to *like* Cheyenne," declared Slick, thoughtfully, rubbing the palm of his left hand against the bar; "which his persuadin' language is fascinatin' to see."

"It sure is," Chesty Sutton endorsed promptly, while the others about him nodded their heads in silent assent.

"Well, gentlemen," said Slick, "here's to th' continued good health of Mr. Cheyenne." Down the line ran the salutation and Buck laughed as he replaced his empty glass.

"I shore hope you-all ain't tryin' to scare me none," he insinuated; "because I'm aimin' to stop up here an'—who in h—l's poundin' that pie-anner?" he broke off, turning to glare in the direction of the melancholy sound.

"Ha! Ha!" barked in his ear, and Buck wheeled as if he had been kicked. "That's Sandy," explained Bow-Wow Baker. "He thinks he's some player. An' he is. There ain't nothin' like it between here an' Salt Lake."

"Oh, yes; there is," contradicted Buck. "You an' him's a good team. I bet if you was in th' same room you'd set up on yore hind laigs an' howl." Bow-Wow drew back, abashed.

"Set 'em up, Mr. Slick," chuckled the salesman.

"Don't notice him, Cheyenne," advised Chesty in a disgusted aside. "He don't mean nothin' by it. It's just a habit. It's got so I'm alius expectin' him to raise his foot an' scratch for fleas," and he withered the crestfallen Bow-Wow with a look of scorn.

"You was sayin' as how you was aimin' to stop here," suggested Ned Monroe, his interest awakened at thought of a rising star so often following the fall of his own.

"Yes," acknowledged Buck. "If I find —" Crash! Ding-dong! Ding-dong! The noise of the bell was deafening. Buck set down his glass with extreme care and looked at Slick with an air of helpless wonder, but Bow-Bow was ready with the explanation. "Grub-pile!" he shouted, making for the side door, grasping hold of Chesty's hand as he went out and dragging that exasperated puncher after him by strength of muscle and purpose. "Come on, Cheyenne! No angel-in-th'-pot,' but a good, square meal, all right."

Chesty Sutton cast behind him at Buck a glance of miserable apology, seized the door-frame in passing, and delivered to Bow-Wow a well-placed and energetic kick. Relieved of the drag of Chesty's protesting weight and with the added impetus of the impact of Chesty's foot, Bow-Wow shot across the wide hall, struggling frantically to regain his equilibrium, and passed through the door of the dining-room like a quarter-horse with the blind staggers. The bell-ringing ended in a crash of broken crockery, succeeded by a fearful uproar of struggling and profanity.

The collie bounded to his feet, his hair bristling along his spine, and rushed at the door with a low growl. Ned caught him by the collar and held him. "Down, Bruce, down!" he commanded, and the dog subsided into menacing growls.

Chesty, at the door, snorted in derision. "D—n fool!" he informed those behind him. "He's tryin' to climb th' table. Hey, Ned; let th' other dog loose," he suggested, hopefully.

By the time the highly entertained group had gathered about the dining-room door, the oaths and imprecations had resolved themselves into a steady railing. Bow-Wow sat sprawled in a chair, gazing in awed silence along the path of wreckage wrought by the flying bell; opposite him, waving a pair of pugnacious fists in close proximity to Bow-Wow's face, stood Sandy McQueen, proprietor of the Sweet-Echo. It appeared that he was angry and the spectators waited with absorbed expectancy on what would happen next.

"Ye gilravagin' deevil!" he shouted, "canna ye see an inch afore yer ain nase? Gin ye hae nae better manners na a gyte bull, gang oot to grass like thae ither cattle. Lord preserv's," he prayed, following the strained intensity of Bow-Wow's gaze, "look at the cheeny! A'm ruined!" He started to gather up the broken crockery when the roar of laughter, no longer to be restrained, assailed his outraged ears. He looked sourly at his guests. "Ou, ay, ye maun lauch, but wha's to pay for the cheeny? Ou, ay! A ken weel eneuch!"

The hilarious company pushed into the dining-room and began to help him in his task, casting many jocose reproaches on the overburdened Bow-Wow. Slick returned to the bar-room to clean off the bar before eating, and Buck went after him. "Hey, what have I struck?" he asked, with much curiosity. "He sounds worse 'n a circus."

"He's mad," explained Slick. "Nobody on God's green earth can understand him when he's mad. Which a circus is music alongside o' him. When he's ca'm, he talks purty good American."

"You shore relieves my mind. What is he—Roosian?"

"Claims to be Scotch. But I dunno—a Scotchman's a sort of Englishman, ain't he?"

"That was alius my opinion," agreed Buck.

"Well—I dunno," and Slick shook his head doubtfully as he hung the towel onto a handy hook and stooped to come under the bar. "Sounds funny to me, all right. 'Tain't English; not by a h—l of a sight."

"Sounds funny to me," echoed Buck. "I'm *shore* it ain't English. But, say, Slick; gimme a room. I'm stoppin' here an' I'd like to drop my things where I can find 'em."

"Right," said Slick, and he led the way into the hall and toward a bedroom at the rear. Chesty Sutton stood in the doorway of the dining-room. "Better git in on th' jump, Cheyenne," he advised, anxiously. "Bow-Wow's that savage, he's boltin' his grub in chunks an' there ain't goin' to be a whole lot left for stragglers."

"Muzzle him," replied Buck, over his saddle-weighted shoulder, while Slick only grinned, "If I goes hungry, I eats Bow-Wow. Dog ain't so bad." Chesty chuckled and returned to the sulky Bow-Wow with the warning.

Despite Chesty's fears, there was plenty to eat and to spare. Little talking was done, as every one was hungry, with the possible exception of Ned, and even he would have passed for a hungry man. Sandy McQueen and the cook offici-ated and the race was so nearly a dead heat that the first to finish was hardly across the hall before the last pushed his chair back from the table.

An immediate adjournment to the bar-room was the customary with-drawal, and Buck, doing as the others, found Ned in his former seat beside a table. Buck joined him and showed such an evident desire for privacy that the others forbore to intrude.

"Ned," said Buck, leaning towards him across the table, "it ain't none of my business, an' it ain't as I'm just curious, but was that straight, what you said about bein' broke?"

"That's straight," Ned assured him, gloomily.

"An' lookin' for a job?" asked Buck, quietly.

"You bet," was the emphatic reply.

"Chesty said as how he used to work for you. Was you foreman?"

"I was foreman an' boss of the NM ranch till them blood-suckers back East druv me off 'n it—d—n 'em."

"Boss, was you? Then I reckon you wouldn't refuse a job as foreman, would you?"

Ned's interest became practical. "Where's yore ranch?" he asked, with some show of eagerness.

"Why, I was aimin' to stop 'round here some'rs."

"H—l! There ain't a foot o' ground within eighty mile o' where yo 're sittin' as ain't grazed a heap over, less 'n it's some nester hangin' on by his fingers an' toes—an' blamed few o' them, neither. Leastaways, none but th' NM an' Schatz's range, which they says belongs to th' old Double Y, both of 'em."

"What's keepin' them free ?"

"'Bout a regiment o' deputies, I reckon." He smiled grimly. "It's costin' 'em somethin' to keep th' range free o' cattle. Mebby you could lease it. That McAllister feller ain't never goin' to get a man to run it for long. Some o' th' boys is feelin' mighty sore an' Schatz is a tough nut. It's goin' to be a mighty big job, when he starts, an' that's certain."

"I'd like to see it. We'll go t'morrow."

Buck's careless defiance of the situation pleased Ned. With the first evidence of good humor he had shown he hit Buck a resounding slap on the back. "That's you," was his admiring comment.

The door opened to admit the short, broad figure of a man who, after a glance around the room, made his bow-legged way to their table. His tone betrayed some anxiety as he asked: "Ned, haf you seen mein Fritz?"

"Nope," answered Ned, "I have n't, Dutch. Hey, boys!" he called," Anybody seen Pickles?"

A chorus of denials arose and Chesty sauntered over to get details. "W'y, you durned ol' Dutch Onion, you ain't gone an' lost him again, have you?"

"Ach! Dot leetle *Kobold!* Alvays ven I looks, like a flea he iss someveres else."

"How'd you lose him?" demanded Chesty.

Dutch stole a look askance at Ned and turned on Chesty a reproachful face. He laid a glove on the edge of the table. "Dot's Fritz. I turn 'round, like dot," suiting action to word, in a complete turn, his right hand reaching out, taking up the glove and whirling it behind his back as he faced the table again. He looked at the empty spot with vast surprise, in delicious pantomime.

The glove, meanwhile, had fallen against the nose of Bruce, who sniffed at it and then picked it up and carried it to Slick behind the bar, returning to his resting place with the air of a duty accomplished.

Dutch continued to stare at the table for several seconds. Then he glanced around and called: "Fritz! Fritz! *Komm' zu mir*—und Fritz iss gone," he finished, turning to those at the table an expression of comical bewilderment. He took a couple of steps in the direction where he supposed the glove to be. Bruce was just lying down. Dutch looked more carefully, stooping to see along the floor. A light broke in on him. He straightened up and excitedly declared: "Yoost like dot! Yoost like der glove iss Fritz: I know ver he iss bud I can't see him."

"Dutch, come here." Ned's voice was stern and Dutch approached with hanging countenance. "Where was you when you c turn 'round like dot'?" asked Ned.

"Only a minute, Ned; yoost a minute! "

"Where?"

"In Ike's I vas; yoost a minute."

"Ain't I told you to keep out o' there ?"

Dutch moved his feet, licked his lips, and cleared his throat; words seemed to fail him.

While he hesitated the door opened again, something more than six inches, and Boomerang squeezed through. He shuffled up to Dutch and touched him on the shoulder. "Hey, Dutch, I been chasin' you all over. Pickles went home wit' Little Nell, see? An' she sent me ter tell you."

"Vat I mit dot —" he broke off and turned to Ned. "I begs your pardon, but Fritz, he iss leetle—he learn quick. Right avay I go." He was at the door when Slick hailed him.

"Hey, Dutchy, this yourn?" The other caught the tossed glove, and nodded.

"Yah, first der glove, soon iss Fritz," and the door closed behind him.

"Good as a circus," laughingly declared Buck. "About pay now—how would eighty a month hit you, for a starter?"

"Fine," declared Ned.

"Then here she is, first month," and Buck handed it over. "Will that be enough to square up what you owe?" he added.

"W'y, I don't owe nothin'," declared Ned.

"Well—now—I was just a-thinkin' 'bout th' lady as seemed right vexed when you dropped yore roll to Dave." He looked casually at Slick, behind the bar, while he was saying it.

"Little Nell? I don't owe her nothin', neither. It was my pile,— all of it."

Buck heaved a sigh of relief. "I'm right glad to hear it. Then you'll be all ready to hit th' trail with me in th' mornin'?" he asked.

"Shore; but s'pos'n you can't get th' ranch?" suggested Ned.

"I'll get it. An' when I get it I'll run it, too, less'n they load me with lead too heavy to sit a horse—then you'll run it." His smile was infectious.

"Cheyenne, I like yore style. Put 'er there," and he shoved a huge, hairy fist at Buck. "'Nother thing," he went on, "Chesty an' Bow-Wow was a-goin' over to th' Bitter Root. I'll tell 'em to hang 'round for a spell. Them's two good boys. So's Dutchy—when he ain't a-runnin' after Pickles."

"All right; you talk to 'em. See you in th' mornin'," and with a general good-night, Buck went to his room.

Chesty and Bow-Wow joined Ned to have a "night cap" and say good-bye, intending to start early next morning. "No, boys, I've had enough," said Ned. "I've took a job with Cheyenne, an' you boys better hang 'round. Find Dutch in th' mornin' an' tell him. An' I'm a-goin' to turn in, too. I'm cussed sleepy." The other two sat staring across the table at one another. The news seemed too good to be true.

"Ha! Ha!" barked Bow-Wow, "I never did like them d—n Bitters, not nohow."

Chesty nodded his head. "Me, too," he agreed. "Son, there's a big time due in these parts: I feel it in my bones."

Seized with a common impulse they sprang to their feet and began a war-dance around the stove, chanting some Indian gibberish that was a series of grunts, snarls, and yells. Their profane demands for information meeting with no response, the others one by one joined them, until a howling, bobbing ring of men circled the stove, and, growling and barking at their heels, the dog danced with them. Slick looked on with an indulgent grin and the row did not cease until Sandy stuck his head in at the hall door. "Deil tak' ye I" he shouted. "Canna ye let a body sleep?"

A minute later the room had settled down into its customary decorum and Bruce, with a wary look about, now and then, was preparing to resume his rudely interrupted doze.

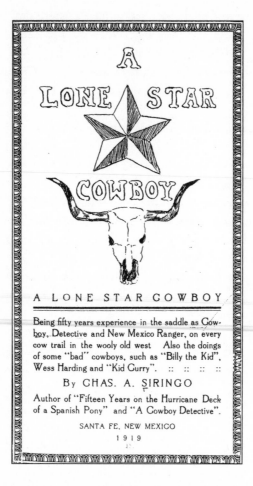

A LONE STAR COWBOY

Being fifty years experience in the saddle as Cowboy, Detective and New Mexico Ranger, on every cow trail in the wooly old west   Also the doings of some "bad" cowboys, such as "Billy the Kid", Wess Harding and "Kid Curry".   ::   ::   ::   ::

By CHAS. A. SIRINGO

Author of "Fifteen Years on the Hurricane Deck of a Spanish Pony" and "A Cowboy Detective".

SANTA FE, NEW MEXICO

1919

ON A TARE IN WICHITA, KANSAS

CHARLES SIRINGO

On the fourth day of July, after being on the trail just three months, we landed on the "Ninnasquaw" river, thirty miles west of Wichita, Kansas.

Nearly all the boys, the boss included, struck out for Wichita right away to take the train for Houston, Texas, the nearest railroad point to their respective homes. Mr. Grimes paid their railroad fares according to custom in those days. I concluded I would remain until fall.

Mr. Grimes had come around by rail, consequently he was on hand to receive us. He already had several thousand steers—besides our herd—on hand; some that he drove up the year before and others he bought around there. He had them divided up into several different herds—about eight hundred to the herd—and scattered out into different places, that is each camp off by itself, from five to ten miles from any other. With each herd or bunch would be a cook and "chuck" wagon, four riders, a "boss" included—and five horses to the rider. During the day two men would "herd" or watch the cattle until noon and the other two until time to "bed" them, which would be about dark. By "bedding" we mean take them to camp, to a certain high piece of ground suitable for a "bed ground" where they would all lie down until morning, unless disturbed by a storm or otherwise. The nights would be divided up into four equal parts—one man "on" at a time, unless storming, tormented with mosquitos or something of the kind, when every one except the cook would have to be "out" singing to them.

The herd I came up the trail with was split into three bunches and I was put with one of them under a man by the name of Phillups, but shortly afterwards changed and put with a Mr. Taylor.

I spent all my extra time when not on duty, visiting a couple of New York damsels, who lived with their parents five miles east of our camp. They were the only young ladies in the neighborhood, the country being very thinly settled then, therefore the boys thought I was very "cheeky"—getting on courting terms with them so quick. One of them finally "put a head on me"—or in grammatical words, gave me a black eye—which chopped my visits short off; she didn't understand the Texas way of proposing for one's hand in marriage, was what caused the fracas. She was cleaning roasting-ears for dinner when I asked her how she would like to jump into double harness and trot through life with me? The air was full of flying roasting-ears for a few seconds—one of them striking me over the left eye—and shortly afterwards a young Cow Puncher rode into camp with one eye in a sling. You can imagine the boys giving it to me about monkeying with civilized girls, etc.

After that I became very lonesome; had nothing to think of but my little Texas girl—the only one on earth I loved. While sitting "on herd" in the hot sun, or lounging around camp in the shade of the wagon-there being no trees in that country to supply us with shade—my mind would be on nothing but her. I finally concluded to write to her and find out just how I stood. As often as I had been with her I had never let her know my thoughts. She being only fourteen years of age, I thought there was plenty time. I wrote a long letter explaining everything and then waited patiently for an answer. I felt sure she would give me encouragement, if nothing more.

A month passed by and still no answer. Can it be possible that she don't think enough of me to answer my letter? thought I. "No," I would finally decide, "she is too much of an angel to be guilty of such."

At last the supply wagon arrived from Wichita and among the mail was a letter for me. I was on herd that forenoon and when the other boys came out to relieve Collier and I, they told me about there being a letter in camp for me, written by a female, judging from the fine hand-writing on the envelope.

I was happy until I opened the letter and read a few lines. It then dropped from my fingers and I turned deathly pale. Mr. Collier wanted to know if some of my relations wasn't dead? Suffice it to say that the object of my heart was married to my old playmate Billy Williams. The letter went on to state that she had given her love to another and that she never thought I loved her only as a friend, etc. She furthermore went on advising me to grin and bear it, as there were just as good fish in the sea as ever was caught etc.

I wanted some one to kill me, so concluded to go to the Black hills—as everyone was flocking there then. Mr. Collier, the same man I traded the crippled horse to—agreed to go with me. So we both struck out for Wichita to settle up with daddy Grimes. Mr. Collier had a good horse of his own and so did I; mine was a California pony that I had given fifty-five dollars for quite awhile before. My intention was to take him home and make a race horse of him; he was only three years old and according to my views a "lightning striker."

After settling up, we, like other "locoed" Cow Punchers proceeded to take in the town, and the result was, after two or three days carousing around, we left there "busted" with the exception of a few dollars.

As we didn't have money enough to take us to the Black hills, we concluded to pull for the Medicine river, one hundred miles west.

We arrived in Kiowa, a little one-horse town on the Medicine, about dark one cold and disagreeable evening.

We put up at the Davis House, which was kept by a man named Davis—by the way one of the whitest men that ever wore shoes. Collier made arrangements that night with Mr. Davis to board us on "tick" until we could get work. But I wouldn't agree to that.

The next morning after paying my night's lodging I had just one dollar left and I gave that to Mr. Collier as I bade him adieu. I then headed southwest across the hills, not having any destination in view; I wanted to go somewhere but didn't care where. To tell the truth I was still somewhat rattled over my recent bad luck.

That night I lay out in the brush by myself and next morning changed my course to southeast, down a creek called Driftwood. About noon I accidentally landed in Gus Johnson's Cow camp at the forks of Driftwood and "Little Mule" creeks.

I remained there all night and next morning when I was fixing to pull out—God only knows where, the boss, Bill Hudson, asked me if I wouldn't stay and work in his place until he went to Hutchison, Kansas and back? I agreed to do so finally if he would furnish "Whisky-peat," my pony, all the corn he could eat—over and above my wages, which were to be twenty-five dollars a month. The outfit consisted of only about twenty-five hundred Texas steers, a chuck wagon, cook and five riders besides the boss.

A few days after Mr. Hudson left we experienced a terrible severe snow storm. We had to stay with the drifting herd night and day, therefore it went rough with us—myself especially, being from a warm climate and only clad in common garments, while the other boys were fixed for winter.

When Mr. Hudson came back from Hutchison he pulled up stakes and drifted south down into the Indian territory—our camp was then on the territory and Kansas line—in search of good winter quarters.

We located on the "Eagle Chief" river, a place where cattle had never been held before. Cattlemen in that section of country considered it better policy to hug the Kansas line on account of indians.

About the time we became settled in our new quarters, my month was up and Mr. Hudson paid me twenty-five dollars, telling me to make that my home all winter if I wished.

My "pile" now amounted to forty-five dollars, having won twenty dollars from one of the boys, Ike Berry, on a horse race. They had a race horse in camp called "Gray-dog," who had never been beaten, so they said, but I and Whisky-peat done him up, to the extent of twenty dollars, in fine shape.

I made up my mind that I would build me a "dugout" somewhere close to the Johnson camp and put in the winter hunting and trapping. Therefore as Hudson was going to Kiowa, with the wagon, after a load of provisions, etc., I went along to lay me in a supply also.

On arriving at Kiowa I found that my old "pard" Mr. Collier had struck a job with a cattleman whose ranch was close to town. But before spring he left for good "Hold Hengland" where a large pile of money was awaiting him; one of his rich relations had died and willed him everything he had. We suppose he is now putting on lots of "agony," if not dead, and telling his green countrymen of his hairbreadth escapes on the wild Texas plains.

We often wonder if he forgets to tell of his experience with "old gray," the pony I traded to him for the boat.

After sending mother twenty dollars by registered mail and laying in a supply of corn, provisions, ammunition, etc., I pulled back to Eagle Chief, to make war with wild animals—especially those that their hides would bring me in some money, such as gray wolves, coyotes, wild oats, buffaloes and bears. I left Kiowa with just three dollars in money.

The next morning after arriving in camp I took my stuff and moved down the river about a mile to where I had already selected a spot for my winter quarters.

I worked like a turk all day long building me a house out of dry poles—covered with grass. In the north end I built a "sod" chimney and in the south end, left an opening for a door. When finished it lacked about two feet of being high enough for me to stand up straight.

It was almost dark and snowing terribly when I got it finished and a fire burning in the low, Jim Crow fire-place. I then fed Whiskey-peat some corn and stepped out a few yards after an armful of good solid wood for morning. On getting about half an armful of wood gathered I heard something crackling and looking over my shoulder discovered my mansion in flames. I got there in time to save nearly everything in the shape of bedding, etc. Some of the grub, being next to the fireplace, was lost. I slept at Johnson's camp that night.

The next morning I went about two miles down the river and located another camp. This time I built a dug-out right on the bank of the stream, in a thick bunch of timber.

I made the dug-out in a curious shape; started in at the edge of the steep bank and dug a place six feet long, three deep and three wide, leaving the end next to the creek open for a door. I then commenced at the further end and dug another place same size in an opposite direction, which formed an "L." I then dug still another place, same size, straight out from the river which made the whole concern almost in the shape of a "Z." In the end furthest from the stream I made a fire-place by digging the earth away—in the shape of a regular fire-place. And then to make a chimney I dug a round hole, with the aid of a butcher knife, straight up as far as I could reach; then commencing at the top and connecting the two holes. The next thing was to make it "draw," and I did that by cutting and piling sods of dirt around the hole, until about two feet above the level.

I then proceeded to build a roof over my 3 x 18 mansion. To do that I cut green poles four feet long and laid them across the top, two or three inches apart. Then a layer of grass and finally, to finish it off a foot of solid earth. She was then ready for business. My idea in making it so crooked was, to keep the indians, should any happen along at night, from seeing my fire. After getting established in my new quarters I put out quite a number of wolf baits and next morning in going to look at them found several dead wolves besides scores of skunks, etc. But they were frozen too stiff to skin, therefore I left them until a warmer day.

The next morning on crawling out to feed my horse I discovered it snowing terribly, accompanied with a piercing cold norther. I crawled back into my hole after making Whisky-peat as comfortable as possible and remained there until late in the evening, when suddenly disturbed by a horny visitor.

It was three or four o'clock in the evening, while humped up before a blazing fire, thinking of days gone by, that all at once, before I had time to think, a large red steer came tumbling down head first, just missing me by a few inches. In traveling ahead of the storm the whole Johnson herd had passed right over me, but luckily only one broke through.

Talk about your ticklish places! That was truly one of them; a steer jammed in between me and daylight, and a hot fire roasting me by inches.

I tried to get up through the roof—it being only a foot above my head—but failed. Finally the old steer made a terrible struggle, just about the time I was fixing to turn my wicked soul over to the Lord, and I got a glimpse of daylight under his flanks. I made a dive for it and by tight squeezing I saved my life.

After getting out and shaking myself I made a vow that I would leave that God-forsaken country in less than twenty-four hours; and I did so.

HOPALONG'S ROUND UP

CLARENCE E. MULFORD

The texan sky seemed a huge mirror upon which were reflected the white fleecy clouds sailing northward; the warm spring air was full of that magnetism which calls forth from their earthy beds the gramma grass and the flowers; the scant vegetation had taken on new dress and traces of green now showed against the more sombre-colored stems; while in the distance, rippling in glistening patches where, disturbed by the wind, the river sparkled like a tinsel ribbon flung carelessly on the grays and greens of the plain. Birds winged their joyous way and filled the air with song; and far overhead a battalion of tardy geese flew, arrow-like, towards the cool lakes of the north, their faint honking pathetic and continuous. Skulking in the coulees or speeding across the skyline of some distant rise occasionally could be seen a coyote or gray wolf. The cattle, less gregarious than they had been in the colder months, made tentative sorties from the lessening herd, and began to stray off in search of the tender green grass which pushed up recklessly from the closely cropped, withered tufts. Rattlesnakes slid out and uncoiled their sinuous lengths in the warm sunlight, and copperheads raised their burnished armor from their winter retreats. All nature had felt the magic touch of the warm winds, and life in its multitudinous forms was discernible on all sides. The gaunt tragedy of a hard winter for that southern range had added its chilling share to the horrors of the past and now the cattle took heart and lost their weakness in the sunlight, hungry but contented.

The winter had indeed been hard, one to be remembered for years to come, and many cattle had died because of it; many skeletons, stripped clean by coyotes and wolves, dotted the arroyos and coulees. The cold weather had broken suddenly, and several days of rain, followed by sleet, had drenched the cattle thoroughly. Then from out of the north came one of those unusual rages of nature, locally known as a "Norther," freezing pitilessly; and the cattle, weakened by cold and starvation, had dumbly succumbed to this last blow. Their backs were covered with an icy shroud, and the deadly cold gripped their vitals with a power not to be resisted. A glittering sheet formed over the grasses as far as eye could see, and the cattle, unlike the horses, not knowing enough to stamp through it, nosed in vain at the sustenance beneath, until weakness compelled them to lie down in the driving snow, and once down, they never arose. The storm had raged for the greater part of a week, and then suddenly one morning the sun shown down on a velvety plain, blinding in its whiteness; and when spring had sent the snow mantle roaring through the arroyos and water courses in a turmoil of yellow water and driftwood, and when the range riders rode forth to read the losses on the plain, the remaining cattle were staggering weakly in search of food. Skeletons in the coulees told the story of the hopeless fight, how the unfortunate cattle had drifted before the wind to what shelter they could find and how, huddled together for warmth, they had died one by one. The valley along Conroy Creek had provided a rough shelter with its scattered groves and these had stopped the cattle drift, so much dreaded by cowmen.

It had grieved Buck Peters and his men to the heart to see so many cattle swept away in one storm, but they had done all that courage and brains could do to save them. So now, when the plain was green again and the warm air made riding a joy, they were to hold the calf roundup. When Buck left his blanket after the first night spent in the roundup camp and rode off to the horse herd, he smiled from suppressed elation, and was glad that he was alive.

Peaceful as the scene appeared there was trouble brewing, and it was in expectation of this that Buck had begun the roundup earlier than usual. The unreasoning stubbornness of one man, and the cunning machinations of a natural rogue, threatened to bring about, from what should have been only a misunderstanding, as pretty a range war as the Southwest had seen. Those immediately involved were only a few when compared to the number which might eventually be brought into the strife, but if this had been pointed out to Jim Meeker he would have replied that he "didn't give a d—n."

Jim Meeker was a Montana man who thought to carry out on the H& range, of which he was foreman, the same system of things which had served where he had come from. This meant trouble right away, for the Bar-20, already short in range, would not stand idly by and see him encroach upon their land for grass and water, more especially when he broke a solemn compact as to range rights which had been made by the former owners of the H2 with the Bar-20. It meant not only the forcible use of Bar-20 range, but also a great hardship upon the herds for which Buck Peters was responsible.

Meeker's obstinacy was covertly prodded by Antonio for his own personal gains, but this the Bar-20 foreman did not know; if he had known it there would have been much trouble averted, and one more Mexican sent to the spirit world.

Buck Peters was probably the only man of all of them who realized just what such a war would mean, to what an extent rustling would flourish while the cowmen fought. His best efforts had been used to avert trouble, so far successfully; but that he would continue to do so was doubtful. He had an outfit which, while meaning to obey him in all things and to turn from any overt act of war, was not of the kind to stand much forcing or personal abuse; their nervous systems were constructed on the hair-trigger plan, and their very loyalty might set the range ablaze with war. However, on this most perfect of mornings Meeker's persistent aggression did not bother him, he was free from worry for the time.

Just north of Big Coulee, in which was a goodly sized water hole, a group of blanket-swathed figures lay about a fire near the chuck wagon, while the sleepy cook prepared breakfast for his own outfit, and for the eight men which the foreman of the C80 and the Double Arrow had insisted upon Buck taking. The sun had not yet risen, but the morning glow showed gray over the plain, and it would not be long before the increasing daylight broke suddenly. The cook fires crackled and blazed steadily, the iron pots hissing under their dancing and noisy lids, while the coffee pots bubbled and sent up an aromatic steam, and the odor of freshly baked biscuits swept forth as the cook uncovered a pan. A pile of tin plates was stacked on the tail-board of the wagon while a large sheet-iron pail contained tin cups. The figures, feet to the fire, looked like huge, grotesque cocoons, for the men had rolled themselves in their blankets, their heads resting on their saddles, and in many cases folded sombreros next to the leather made softer pillows.

Back of the chuck wagon the eastern sky grew rapidly brighter, and suddenly daylight in all its power dissipated the grayish light of the moment before. As the rim of the golden sun arose above the low sand hills to the east the foreman rode into camp. Some distance behind him Harry Jones and two other C80 men drove up the horse herd and enclosed it in a flimsy corral quickly extemporized from lariats; flimsy it was, but it sufficed for cow-ponies that had learned the lesson of the rope.

"All ready, Buck," called Harry before his words were literally true.

With assumed ferocity but real vociferation Buck uttered a shout and watched the effect. The cocoons became animated, stirred and rapidly unrolled, with the exception of one, and the sleepers leaped to their feet and folded the blankets. The exception stirred, subsided, stirred again and then was quiet. Buck and Red stepped forward while the others looked on grinning to see the fun, grasped the free end of the blanket and suddenly straightened up, their hands going high above their heads. Johnny Nelson, squawking, rolled over and over and, with a yell of surprise, sat bolt upright and felt for his gun.

"Huh!" he snorted. "Reckon yo're smart, don't you!"

"Purty near a shore 'nuf pin-wheel, Kid," laughed Red.

"Don't you care, Johnny; you can finish it tonight," consoled Frenchy McAllister, now one of Buck's outfit.

"Breakfast, Kid, breakfast!" sang out Hopalong as he finished drying his face.

The breakfast was speedily out of the way, and pipes were started for a short smoke as the punchers walked over to the horse herd to make their selections. By exercising patience, profanity, and perseverance they roped their horses and began to saddle up. Ed Porter, of the C80, and Skinny Thompson, Bar-20, cast their ropes with a sweeping, preliminary whirl over their heads, but the others used only a quick flit and twist of the wrist. A few mildly exciting struggles for the mastery took place between riders and mounts, for some cow-ponies are not always ready to accept their proper place in the scheme of things.

"Slab-sided jumpin' jack!" yelled Rich Finn, a Double Arrow puncher, as he fought his horse. ." Alius' raisin' th' devil afore I'm all awake! "

"Lemme hold her head, Rich," jeered Billy Williams.

"Her laigs, Billy, not her head," corrected Lanky Smith, the Bar-20 rope expert, whose own horse had just become sensible.

"Don't hurt him, bronc; we need him," cautioned Red.

"Come on, fellers; gettin' late," called Buck.

Away they went, tearing across the plain, Buck in the lead. After some time had passed the foreman raised his arm and Pete Wilson stopped and filled his pipe anew, the west-end man of the cordon. Again Buck's arm went up and Skinny Thompson dropped out, and so on until the last man had been placed and the line completed. At a signal from Buck the whole line rode forward, gradually converging on a central point and driving the scattered cattle before it.

Hopalong, on the east end of the line, sharing with Billy the posts of honor, was now kept busy dashing here and there, wheeling, stopping, and manoeuvring as certain strong-minded cattle, preferring the freedom of the range they had just quitted, tried to break through the cordon. All but branded steers and cows without calves had their labors in vain, although the escape of these often set examples for ambitious cows with calves. Here was where reckless and expert riding saved the day, for the cow-ponies, trained in the art of punching cows, entered into the game with zest and executed quick turns which more than once threatened a catastrophe to themselves and riders. Range cattle can run away from their domesticated kin, covering the ground with an awkward gait that is deceiving; but the ponies can run faster and turn as quickly.

Hopalong, determined to turn back one stubborn mother cow, pushed her too hard, and she wheeled to attack him. Again the nimble pony had reason to move quickly and Hopalong swore as he felt the horns touch his leg.

"On th' prod, hey! Well, stay on it!" he shouted, well knowing that she would. "Pig-headed old fool—*all right*, Johnny; I'm comin'!" and he raced away to turn a handful of cows which were proving too much for his friend. "*Ki-yi-yeow-eow-eow-eow-eow!*" he yelled, imitating the coyote howl.

The cook had moved his wagon as soon as breakfast was over and journeyed southeast with the cavvieyh; and as the cordon neared its objective the punchers could see his camp about half a mile from the level pasture where the herd would be held for the cutting-out and branding. Cookie regarded himself as the most important unit of the roundup and acted accordingly, and he was not far wrong.

"Hey, Hoppy!" called Johnny through the dust of the herd, "there's cookie. I was 'most scared he'd get lost."

"Can't you think of anythin' else but grub ?" asked Billy Jordan from the rear.

"Can you tell me anything better to think of?"

There were from three to four thousand cattle in the herd when it neared the stopping point, and dust arose in low-hanging clouds above it. Its pattern of differing shades of brown, with yellow and black and white relieving it, constantly shifted like a kaleidoscope as the cattle changed positions; and the rattle of horns on horns and the muffled bellowing could be heard for many rods.

Gradually the cordon surrounded the herd and, when the destination was reached, the punchers rode before the front ranks of cattle and stopped them. There was a sudden tremor, a compactness in the herd, and the cattle in the rear crowded forward against those before; another tremor, and the herd was quiet. Cow-punchers took their places around it, and kept the cattle from breaking out and back to the range, while every second man, told off by the foreman, raced at top speed towards the camp, there to eat a hasty dinner and get a fresh horse from his *remuda*, as his string of from five to seven horses was called. Then he galloped back to the herd and relieved his nearest neighbor. When all had reassembled at the herd the work of cutting-out began.

Lanky Smith, Panhandle Lukins, and two more Bar men rode some distance east of the herd, there to take care of the cow-and-calf cut as it grew by the cutting-out. Hopalong, Red, Johnny, and three others were assigned to the task of getting the mother cows and their calves out of the main herd and into the new one, while the other punchers held the herd and took care of the stray herd when they should be needed. Each of the cutters-out rode after some calf, and the victim, led by its mother, worked its way after her into the very heart of the mass; and in getting the pair out again care must be taken not to unduly excite the other cattle. Wiry, happy, and conceited cow-ponies unerringly and patiently followed mother and calf into the press, nipping the pursued when too slow and gradually forcing them to the outer edge of the herd; and when the mother tried to lead its offspring back into the herd to repeat the performance, she was in almost every case cleverly blocked and driven out on the plain where the other punchers took charge of her and added her to the cow-and-calf cut.

Johnny jammed his sombrero on his head with reckless strength and swore luridly as he wheeled to go back into the herd.

"What's th' matter, Kid ?" laughingly asked Skinny as he turned his charges over to another man.

"None of yore d—d business!" blazed Johnny. Under his breath he made a resolve. "If I get you two out here again I'll keep you here if I have to shoot you!"

"Are they slippery, Johnny?" jibed Red, whose guess was correct. Johnny refused to heed such asinine remarks and stood on his dignity.

As the cow-and-calf herd grew in size and the main herd dwindled, more punchers were shifted to hold it; and it was not long before the main herd was comprised entirely of cattle without calves, when it was driven off to freedom after being examined for other brands. As soon as the second herd became of any size it was not necessary to drive the cows and calves to it when they were driven out of the first herd, as they made straight for it. The main herd, driven away, broke up as it would, while the guarded cows stood idly beside their resting offspring awaiting further indignities.

The drive had covered so much ground and taken so much time that approaching darkness warned Buck not to attempt the branding until the morrow, and he divided his force into three shifts. Two of these hastened to the camp, gulped down their supper, and rolling into their blankets, were soon sound asleep. The horse herd was driven off to where the grazing was better, and night soon fell over the plain.

The cook's fires gleamed through the darkness and piles of biscuits were heaped on the tail-board of the wagon, while pots of beef and coffee simmered over the fires, handy for the guards as they rode in during the night to awaken brother punchers, who would take their places while they slept. Soon the cocoons were quiet in the grotesque shadows caused by the fires and a deep silence reigned over the camp. Occasionally some puncher would awaken long enough to look at the sky to see if the weather had changed, and satisfied, return to sleep.

Over the plain sleepy cowboys rode slowly around the herd, glad to be relieved by some other member of the outfit, who always sang as he approached the cattle to reassure them and save a possible stampede. For cattle, if suddenly disturbed at night by anything, even the waving of a slicker in the hands of some careless rider, or a wind-blown paper, will rise in a body—all up at once, frightened and nervous. The sky was clear and the stars bright and when the moon rose it flooded the plain with a silvery light and made fairy patterns in the shadows.

Snatches of song floated down the gentle wind as the riders slowly circled the herd, for the human voice, no matter how discordant, was quieting. A low and plaintive "Don't let this par-ting grieve y-o-u" passed from hearing around the resting cows, soon to be followed by "When-n in thy dream-ing, nights like t-h-e-s-e shall come a-gain —" as another watcher made the circuit. The serene cows, trusting in the prowess and vigilance of these low-voiced centaurs to protect them from danger, dozed and chewed their cuds in peace and quiet, while the natural noises of the night relieved the silence in unobtruding harmony.

Far out on the plain a solitary rider watched the herd from cover and swore because it was guarded so closely. He glanced aloft to see if there was any hope of a storm and finding that there was not, muttered savagely and rode away. It was Antonio, wishing that he could start a stampede and so undo the work of the day and inflict heavy losses on the Bar-20. He did not dare to start a grass fire for at the first flicker of a light he would be charged by one or more of the night riders and if caught, death would be his reward.

While the third shift rode and sang the eastern sky became a dome of light reflected from below and the sunrise, majestic in all its fiery splendor, heralded the birth of another perfect day.

Through the early morning hours the branding continued, and the bleating of the cattle told of the hot stamping irons indelibly burning the sign of the Bar-20 on the tender hides of calves. Mother cows fought and plunged and called in reply to the terrified bawling of their offspring, and sympathetically licked the burns when the frightened calves had been allowed to join them. Cowboys were deftly roping calves by their hind legs and dragging them to the fires of the branding men. Two men would hold a calf, one doubling the foreleg back on itself at the knee and the other, planting one booted foot against the calf's under hind leg close to its body, pulled back on the other leg while his companion, who held the foreleg, rested on the animal's head. The third man, drawing the hot iron from the fire, raised and held it suspended for a second over the calf's flank, and then there was an odor and a puff of smoke; and the calf was branded with a mark which neither water nor age would wipe out.

Pete Wilson came riding up dragging a calf at the end of his rope, and turned the captive over to Billy Williams and his two helpers, none of them paying any attention to the cow which followed a short distance behind him. Lanky seized the unfortunate calf and leaned over to secure the belly hold, when someone shouted a warning and he dropped the struggling animal and leaped back and to one side as the mother charged past. Wheeling to return the attack, the cow suddenly flopped over and struck the earth with a thud as Buck's rope went home. He dragged her away and then releasing her, chased her back into the herd.

"*Hi!* Get that little devil!" shouted Billy to Hopalong, pointing to the fleeing calf.

"Why didn't you watch for her, you half-breed!" demanded the indignant Lanky of Pete. "Do you think this is a ten-pin alley!"

Hopalong came riding up with the calf, which swiftly became recorded property.

"Bar-20; tally one," sang out the monotonous voice of the tally-man. "Why didn't you grab her when she went by, Lanky ?" he asked, putting a new point on his pencil.

"Hope th' next one heads yore way!" retorted Lanky, grinning.

"Won't. I ain't abusin' th' kids."

"Bar-20; tally one," droned a voice at the next fire.

All was noise, laughter, dust, and a seeming confusion, but every man knew his work thoroughly and was doing it in a methodical way, and the confusion was confined to the victims and their mothers.

When the herd had been branded and allowed to return to the plain, the outfit moved on into a new territory and the work was repeated until the whole range, with the exception of the valley, had been covered. When the valley was worked it required more time in comparison with the amount of ground covered than had been heretofore spent on any part of the range; for the cattle were far more numerous, and it was no unusual thing to have a herd of great size before the roundup place had been reached. This heavy increase in the numbers of the cattle to be herded made a corresponding increase in the time and labor required for the cutting-out and branding. Five days were required in working the eastern and central parts of the valley and it took three more days to clean up around the White Horse Hills, where the ground was rougher and the riding harder. And at every cutting-out there was a large stray-herd made up of H2 and Three Triangle cattle. The H2 had been formerly the Three Triangle. Buck had been earnest in his instructions to his men regarding the strays, for now was the opportunity to rid his range of Meeker's cattle in a way natural and without especial significance; once over the line it would be a comparatively easy matter to keep them there.

For taking care of this extra herd and also because Buck courted scrutiny during the branding, the foreman accepted the services of three H2 men. This addition to his forces made the work move somewhat more rapidly and when, at the end of each day's ycutting-out, the stray herd was complete, it was driven south across the boundary line by Meeker's men. When the last stray-herd started south Buck rode over to the punchers and told them to tell their foreman to let him know when he could assist in the southern roundup and thus return the favor.

As the Bar-20 outfit and the C80 and Double Arrow men rode north towards the ranch house they were met by Lucas, foreman of the C80, who joined them near Medicine Bend.

"Well, got it all over, hey?" he cried as he rode up.

"Yep; bigger job than I thought, too. It gets bigger every year an' that blizzard didn't make much difference in th' work, neither," Buck replied. "I'll help you out when you get ready to drive."

"No you won't; you can help me an' Bartlett more by keeping all yore men watchin' that line," quickly responded Lucas. "We'll work together, me an' Bartlett, an' we'll have all th' men we want. You just show that man Meeker that range grabbin' ain't healthy down here—that's all we want. Did he send you any help in th' valley ?"

"Yes, three men," Buck replied. "But we'll break even on that when he works along th' boundary."

"Have any trouble with 'em ?"

"Not a bit."

"I sent Wood Wright down to Eagle th' other day, an' he says th' town is shore there'll be a big range war," remarked Lucas. "He said there's lots of excitement down there an' they act like they wish th' trouble would hurry up an' happen. We've got to watch that town, all right."

"If there's a war th' rustlers'll flock here from all over," interposed Rich Finn.

"Huh!" snorted Hopalong. "They'll flock out again if we get a chance to look for 'em. An' that town'U shore get into trouble if it don't live plumb easy. You know what happened th' last time rustlin' got to be th' style, don't you ?"

"Well," replied Lucas, "I've fixed it with Cowan to get news to me an' Bartlett if anything sudden comes up. If you need us just let him know an' we'll be with you in two shakes."

"That's good, but I don't reckon I'll need any help, leastwise not for a long time," Buck responded. "But I tell you what you might do, when you can; make up a vigilance committee from yore outfits an' ride range for rustlers. We can take care of all that comes on us, but we won't have.no time to bother about th' rest of th' range! An' if you do that it'll shut 'em out of our north range."

"We'll do it," Lucas promised. "Bartlett is going to watch th' trails north to see if he can catch anybody runnin' cattle to th' railroad construction camps. Every suspicious lookin' stranger is going to be held up an* asked questions; an' if we find any runnin' irons, you know what that means."

"I reckon we can handle th' situation, all right, no matter how hard it gets," laughed the Bar-20 foreman.

"Well, I'll be leavin' you now," Lucas remarked as they reached the Bar-20 bunk house. "We begin to round up next week, an' there's lots to be done before then. Say, can I use yore chuck wagon? Mine is shore done for."

"Why, of course," replied Buck heartily. "Take it now, if you want, or any time you send for it."

"Much obliged; come on, fellers," Lucas cried to his men. "We're goin' home."

ON THE TRAIL

ZANE GREY

Shefford was awakened next morning by a sound he had never heard before—the plunging of hobbled horses on soft turf. It was clear daylight, with a ruddy color in the sky and a tinge of red along the cañon rim. He saw Withers, Lake, and the Indian driving the mustangs toward camp.

The burros appeared lazy, yet willing. But the mustangs and the mule Withers called Red and the gray mare Dynamite were determined not to be driven into camp. It was astonishing how much action they had, how much ground they could cover with their forefeet hobbled together. They were exceedingly skilful; they lifted both forefeet at once, and then plunged. And they all went in different directions. Nas Ta Bega darted in here and there to head off escape.

Shefford pulled on his boots and went out to help. He got too close to the gray mare and, warned by a yell from Withers, he jumped back just in time to avoid her vicious heels. Then Shefford turned his attention to Nack-yal and chased him all over the flat in a futile effort to catch him. Nas Ta Bega came to Shefford's assistance and put a rope over Nack-yal's head.

"Don't ever get behind one of these mustangs," said Withers, warningly, as Shefford came up. "You might be killed. . . . Eat your bite now. We'll soon be out of here."

Shefford had been late in awakening. The others had breakfasted. He found eating somewhat difficult in the excitement that ensued. Nas Ta Bega held ropes which were round the necks of Red and Dynamite. The mule showed his cunning and always appeared to present his heels to Withers, who tried to approach him with a pack-saddle. The patience of the trader was a revelation to Shefford. And at length Red was cornered by the three men, the pack-saddle was strapped on, and then the packs. Red promptly bucked the packs off, and the work had to be done over again. Then Red dropped his long ears and seemed ready to be tractable.

When Shefford turned his attention to Dynamite he decided that this was his first sight of a wild horse. The gray mare had fiery eyes that rolled and showed the white. She jumped straight up, screamed, pawed, bit, and then plunged down to shoot her hind hoofs into the air as high as her head had been. She was amazingly agile and she seemed mad to kill something. She dragged the Indian about, and when Joe Lake got a rope on her hind foot she dragged them both. They lashed her with the ends of the lassoes, which action only made her kick harder. She plunged into camp, drove Shefford flying for his life, knocked down two of the burros, and played havoc with the unstrapped packs. Withers ran to the assistance of Lake, and the two of them hauled back with all their strength and weight. They were both powerful and heavy men. Dynamite circled round and finally, after kicking the camp-fire to bits, fell down on her haunches in the hot embers. "Let—her—set—there!" panted Withers. And Joe Lake shouted, "Burn up, you durn coyote!" Both men appeared delighted that she had brought upon herself just punishment. Dynamite sat in the remains of the fire long enough to get burnt, and then she got up and meekly allowed Withers to throw a tarpaulin and a roll of blankets over her and tie them fast.

Lake and Withers were sweating freely when this job was finished.

"Say, is that a usual morning's task with the pack-animals?" asked Shefford.

"They're all pretty decent to-day, except Dynamite," replied Withers. "She's got to be worked out."

Shefford felt both amusement and consternation. The sun was just rising over the ramparts of the cañon, and he had already seen more difficult and dangerous work accomplished than half a dozen men of his type could do in a whole day. He liked the outlook of his new duty as Withers's assistant, but he felt helplessly inefficient. Still, all he needed was experience. He passed over what he anticipated would be pain and peril—the cost was of no moment.

Soon the pack-train was on the move, with the Indian leading. This morning Nack-yal began his strange swinging off to the left, precisely as he had done the day before. It got to be annoying to Shefford, and he lost patience with the mustang and jerked him sharply round. This, however, had no great effect upon Nack-yal.

As the train headed straight up the cañon Joe Lake dropped back to ride beside Shefford. The Mormon had been amiable and friendly.

"Flock of deer up that draw," he said, pointing up a narrow side cañon.

Shefford gazed to see a half-dozen small, brown, long-eared objects, very like burros, watching the pack-train pass.

"Are they deer?" he asked, delightedly.

"Sure are," replied Joe, sincerely. "Get down and shoot one. There's a rifle in your saddle-sheath."

Shefford had already discovered that he had been armed this morning, a matter which had caused him reflection. These animals certainly looked like deer; he had seen a few deer, though not in their native wild haunts; and he experienced the thrill of the hunter. Dismounting, he drew the rifle out of the sheath and started toward the little cañon.

"Hyar! Where you going with that gun?" yelled Withers. "That's a bunch of burros. . . . Joe's up to his old tricks. Shefford, look out for Joe!"

Rather sheepishly Shefford returned to his mustang and sheathed the rifle, and then took a long look at the animals up the draw. They resembled deer, but upon second glance they surely were burros.

"Durn me! Now if I didn't think they sure were deer!" exclaimed Joe. He appeared absolutely sincere and innocent. Shefford hardly knew how to take this likable Mormon, but vowed he would be on his guard in the future.

Nas Ta Bega soon led the pack-train toward the left wall of the cañon, and evidently intended to scale it. Shefford could not see any trail, and the wall appeared steep and insurmountable. But upon nearing the cliff he saw a narrow broken trail leading zigzag up over smooth rock, weathered slope, and through cracks.

"Spread out, and careful now!" yelled Withers.

The need of both advices soon became manifest to Shefford. The burros started stones rolling, making danger for those below. Shefford dismounted and led Nack-yal and turned aside many a rolling rock. The Indian and the burros, with the red mule leading, climbed steadily. But the mustangs had trouble. Joe's spirited bay had to be coaxed to face the ascent; Nack-yal balked at every difficult step; and Dynamite slipped on a flat slant of rock and slid down forty feet. Withers and Lake with ropes hauled the mare out of the dangerous position. Shefford, who brought up the rear, saw all the action, and it was exciting, but his pleasure in the climb was spoiled by sight of blood and hair on the stones. The ascent was crooked, steep, and long, and when Shefford reached the top of the wall he was glad to rest. It made him gasp to look down and see what he had surmounted. The cañon floor, green and level, lay a thousand feet below; and the wild burros which had followed on the trail looked like rabbits.

Shefford mounted presently, and rode out upon a wide, smooth trail leading into a cedar forest. There were bunches of gray sage in the open places. The air was cool and crisp, laden with a sweet fragrance. He saw Lake and Withers bobbing along, now on one side of the trail, now on the other, and they kept to a steady trot. Occasionally the Indian and his bright-red saddle-blanket showed in an opening of the cedars.

It was level country, and there was nothing for Shefford to see except cedar and sage, an outcropping of red rock in places, and the winding trail. Mockingbirds made melody everywhere. Shefford seemed full of a strange pleasure, and the hours flew by. Nack-yal still wanted to be everlastingly turning off the trail, and, moreover, now he wanted to go faster. He was eager, restless, dissatisfied.

At noon the pack-train descended into a deep draw, well covered with cedar and sage. There was plenty of grass and shade, but no water. Shefford was surprised to see that every pack was removed; however, the roll of blankets was left on Dynamite.

The men made a fire and began to cook a noonday meal. Shefford, tired and warm, sat in a shady spot and watched. He had become all eyes. He had almost forgotten Fay Larkin; he had forgotten his trouble; and the present seemed sweet and full. Presently his ears were filled by a pattering roar and, looking up the draw, he saw two streams of sheep and goats coming down. Soon an Indian shepherd appeared, riding a fine mustang. A cream-colored colt bounded along behind, and presently a shaggy dog came in sight. The Indian dismounted at the camp, and his flock spread by in two white and black streams. The dog went with them. Withers and Joe shook hands with the Indian, whom Joe called "Navvy," and Shefford lost no time in doing likewise. Then Nas Ta Bega came in, and he and the Navajo talked. When the meal was ready all of them sat down round the canvas. The shepherd did not tie his horse.

Presently Shefford noticed that Nack-yal had returned to camp and was acting strangely. Evidently he was attracted by the Indian's mustang or the cream-colored colt. At any rate, Nack-yal hung around, tossed his head, whinnied in a low, nervous manner, and looked strangely eager and wild. Shefford was at first amused, then curious. Nack-yal approached too close to the mother of the colt, and she gave him a sounding kick in the ribs. Nack-yal uttered a plaintive snort and backed away, to stand, crestfallen, with all his eagerness and fire vanished.

Nas Ta Bega pointed to the mustang and said something in his own tongue. Then Withers addressed the visiting Indian, and they exchanged some words, whereupon the trader turned to Shefford.

"I bought Nack-yal from this Indian three years ago. This mare is Nack-yal's mother. He was born over here to the south. That's why he always swung left off the trail. He wanted to go home. Just now he recognized his mother and she whaled away and gave him a whack for his pains. She's got a colt now and probably didn't recognize Nack-yal. But he's broken-hearted."

The trader laughed, and Joe said, "You can't tell what these durn mustangs will do." Shefford felt sorry for Nack-yal, and when it came time to saddle him again found him easier to handle than ever before. Nack-yal stood with head down, broken-spirited.

Shefford was the first to ride up out of the draw, and once upon the top of the ridge he halted to gaze, wide-eyed and entranced. A rolling, endless plain sloped down beneath him, and led him on to a distant round-topped mountain. To the right a red cañon opened its jagged jaws, and away to the north rose a whorled and strange sea of curved ridges, crags, and domes.

Nas Ta Bega rode up then, leading the pack-train.

"Bi Nai, that is Na-tsis-an," he said, pointing to the mountain. "Navajo Mountain. And there in the north are the cañons."

Shefford followed the Indian down the trail and soon lost sight of that wide green-and-red wilderness. Nas Ta Bega turned at an intersecting trail, rode down into the cañon, and climbed out on the other side. Shefford got a glimpse now and then of the black dome of the mountain, but for the most part the distant points of the country were hidden. They crossed many trails, and went up and down the sides of many shallow cañons. Troops of wild mustangs whistled at them, stood on ridge-tops to watch, and then dashed away with manes and tails flying.

Withers rode forward presently and halted the pack-train. He had some conversation with Nas Ta Bega, whereupon the Indian turned his horse and trotted back, to disappear in the cedars.

"I'm some worried," explained Withers. "Joe thinks he saw a bunch of horsemen trailing us. My eyes are bad and I can't see far. The Indian will find out. I took a roundabout way to reach the village because I'm always dodging Shadd." This communication lent an added zest to the journey. Shefford could hardly believe the truth that his eyes and his ears brought to his consciousness. He turned in behind Withers and rode down the rough trail, helping the mustang all in his power. It occurred to him that Nack-yal had been entirely different since that meeting with his mother in the draw. He turned no more off the trail; he answered readily to the rein; he did not look afar from every ridge. Shefford conceived a liking for the mustang.

Withers turned sidewise in his saddle and let his mustang pick the way.

"Another time we'll go up round the base of the mountain, where you can look down on the grandest scene in the world," said he. "Two hundred miles of wind-worn rock, all smooth and bare, without a single straight line—cañons, caves, bridges—the most wonderful country in the world! Even the Indians haven't explored it. It's haunted, for them, and they have strange gods. The Navajos will hunt on this side of the mountain, but not on the other. That north side is consecrated ground. My wife has long been trying to get the Navajos to tell her the secret of Nonnezoshe. Nonnezoshe means Rainbow Bridge. The Indians worship it, but as far as she can find out only a few have ever seen it. I imagine it 'd be worth some trouble."

"Maybe that's the bridge Venters talked about—the one overarching the entrance to Surprise Valley," said Shefford.

"It might be," replied the trader. "You've got a good chance of finding out. Nas Ta Bega is the man. You stick to that Indian. . . . Well, we start down here into this cañon, and we go down *some*, I reckon. In half an hour you'll see sago-lilies and Indian paint-brush and vermilion cactus."

About the middle of the afternoon the pack-train and its drivers arrived at the hidden Mormon village. Nas Ta Bega had not returned from his scout back along the trail.

Shefford's sensibilities had all been overstrained, but he had left in him enthusiasm and appreciation that made the situation of this village a fairyland. It was a valley, a cañon floor, so long that he could not see the end, and perhaps a quarter of a mile wide. The air was hot, still, and sweetly odorous of unfamiliar flowers. Piñon and cedar trees surrounded the little log and stone houses, and along the walls of the cañon stood sharp-pointed, dark-green spruce-trees. These walls were singular of shape and color. They were not imposing in height, but they waved like the long, undulating swell of a sea. Every foot of surface was perfectly smooth, and the long curved lines of darker tinge that streaked the red followed the rounded line of the slope at the top. Far above, yet overhanging, were great yellow crags and peaks, and between these, still higher, showed the pine-fringed slope of Navajo Mountain with snow in the sheltered places, and glistening streams, like silver threads, running down.

All this Shefford noticed as he entered the valley from round a corner of wall. Upon nearer view he saw and heard a host of children, who, looking up to see the intruders, scattered like frightened quail. Long gray grass covered the ground, and here and there wide, smooth paths had been worn. A swift and murmuring brook ran through the middle of the valley, and its banks were bordered with flowers.

Withers led the way to one side near the wall, where a clump of cedar-trees and a dark, swift spring boiling out of the rocks and banks of amber moss with purple blossoms made a beautiful camp site. Here the mustangs were unsaddled and turned loose without hobbles. It was certainly unlikely that they would leave such a spot. Some of the burros were unpacked, and the others Withers drove off into the village.

"Sure's pretty nice," said Joe, wiping his sweaty face. "I'll never want to leave. It suits me to lie on this moss. . . . Take a drink of that spring."

Shefford complied with alacrity and found the water cool and sweet, and he seemed to feel it all through him. Then he returned to the mossy bank. He did not reply to Joe. In fact, all his faculties were absorbed in watching and feeling, and he lay there long after Joe went off to the village. The murmur of water, the hum of bees, the songs of strange birds, the sweet, warm air, the dreamy summer somnolence of the valley—all these added drowsiness to Shefford's weary lassitude, and he fell asleep. When he awoke Nas Ta Bega was sitting near him and Joe was busy near a camp-fire.

"Hello, Nas Ta Bega!" said Shefford. "Was there any one trailing us?"

The Navajo nodded.

Joe raised his head and with forceful brevity said, "Shadd."

"Shadd!" echoed Shefford, remembering the dark, sinister face of his visitor that night in the Sagi. "Joe, is it serious—his trailing us?"

"Well, I don't know how durn serious it is, but I'm scared to death," replied Lake. "He and his gang will hold us up somewhere on the way home."

Shefford regarded Joe with both concern and doubt. Joe's words were at variance with his looks.

"Say, pard, can you shoot a rifle?" queried Joe.

"Yes. I'm a fair shot at targets."

The Mormon nodded his head as if pleased. "That's good. These outlaws are all poor shots with a rifle. So'm I. But I can handle a six-shooter. I reckon we'll make Shadd sweat if he pushes us."

Withers returned, driving the burros, all of which had been unpacked down to the saddles. Two gray-bearded men accompanied him. One of them appeared to be very old and venerable, and walked with a stick. The other had a sad-lined face and kind, mild blue eyes. Shefford observed that Lake seemed unusually respectful. Withers introduced these Mormons merely as Smith and Henninger. They were very cordial and pleasant in their greetings to Shefford. Presently another, somewhat younger, man joined the group, a stalwart, jovial fellow with ruddy face. There was certainly no mistaking his kindly welcome as he shook Shefford's hand. His name was Beal. The three stood round the camp-fire for a while, evidently glad of the presence of fellow-men and to hear news from the outside. Finally they went away, taking Joe with them. Withers took up the task of getting supper where Joe had been made to leave it.

"Shefford, listen," he said, presently, as he knelt before the fire. "I told them right out that you'd been a Gentile clergyman—that you'd gone back on your religion. It impressed them and you've been well received. I'll tell the same thing over at Stonebridge. You'll get in right. Of course I don't expect they'll make a Mormon of you. But they'll try to. Meanwhile you can be square and friendly all the time you're trying to find your Fay Larkin. To-morrow you'll meet some of the women. They're good souls, but, like any women, crazy for news. Think what it is to be shut up in here between these walls!"

"Withers, I'm intensely interested," replied Shefford, "and excited, too. Shall we stay here long?"

"I'll stay a couple of days, then go to Stonebridge with Joe. He'll come back here, and when you both feel like leaving, and if Nas Ta Bega thinks it safe, you'll take a trail over to some Indian hogans and pack me out a load of skins and blankets. . . . My boy, you've all the time there is, and I wish you luck. This isn't a bad place to loaf. I always get sentimental over here. Maybe it's the women. Some of them are pretty, and one of them—Shefford, they call her the

Sago Lily. Her first name is Mary, I'm told. Don't know her last name. She's lovely. And I'll bet you forget Fay Larkin in a flash. Only—be careful. You drop in here with rather peculiar credentials, so to speak—as my helper and as a man with no religion! You'll not only be fully trusted, but you'll be welcome to these lonely women. So be careful. Remember it's my secret belief they are sealed wives and are visited occasionally at night by their husbands. I don't *know* this, but I believe it. And you're not supposed to dream of that."

"How many men in the village?" asked Shefford.

"Three. You met them."

"Have they wives?" asked Shefford, curiously.

"Wives! Well, I guess. But only one each that I know of. Joe Lake is the only unmarried Mormon I've met."

"And no men—strangers, cowboys, outlaws—ever come to this village?"

"Except to Indians, it seems to be a secret so far," replied the trader, earnestly. "But it can't be kept secret. I've said that time after time over in Stonebridge. With Mormons it's 'sufficient unto the day is the evil thereof.'"

"What 'll happen when outsiders do learn and ride in here?"

"There'll be trouble—maybe bloodshed. Mormon women are absolutely good, but they're human, and want and need a little life. And, strange to say, Mormon men are pig-headedly jealous. . . . Why, if some of the cowboys I knew in Durango would ride over here there'd simply be hell. But that's a long way, and probably this village will be deserted before news of it ever reaches Colorado. There's more danger of Shadd and his gang coming in. Shadd's half Piute. He must know of this place. And he's got some white outlaws in his gang. . . . Come on. Grub's ready, and I'm too hungry to talk."

Later, when shadows began to gather in the valley and the lofty peaks above were gold in the sunset glow, Withers left camp to look after the straying mustangs, and Shefford strolled to and fro under the cedars. The lights and shades in the Sagi that first night had moved him to enthusiastic watchfulness, but here they were so weird and beautiful that he was enraptured. He actually saw great shafts of gold and shadows of purple streaming from the peaks down into the valley. It was day on the heights and twilight in the valley. The swiftly changing colors were like rainbows.

While he strolled up and down several women came to the spring and filled their buckets. They wore shawls or hoods and their garments were somber, but, nevertheless, they appeared to have youth and comeliness. They saw him, looked at him curiously, and then, without speaking, went back on the well-trodden path. Presently down the path appeared a woman—a girl in lighter garb. It was almost white. She was shapely and walked with free, graceful step, reminding him of the Indian girl, Glen Naspa. This one wore a hood shaped like a huge sunbonnet and it concealed her face. She carried a bucket. When she reached the spring and went down the few stone steps Shefford saw that she did not have on shoes. As she braced herself to lift the bucket her bare foot clung to the mossy stone. It was a strong, sinewy, beautiful foot, instinct with youth. He was curious enough, he thought, but the awakening artist in him made him more so. She dragged at the full bucket and had difficulty in lifting it out of the hole. Shefford strode forward and took the bucket-handle from her.

"Won't you let me help you?" he said, lifting the bucket. "Indeed—it's very heavy."

"Oh—thank you," she said, without raising her head. Her voice seemed singularly young and sweet. He had not heard a voice like it. She moved down the path and he walked beside her. He felt embarrassed, yet more curious than ever; he wanted to say something, to turn and look at her, but he kept on for a dozen paces without making up his mind.

Finally he said: "Do you really carry this heavy bucket? Why, it makes my arm ache."

"Twice every day—morning and evening," she replied. "I'm very strong."

Then he stole a look out of the corner of his eye, and, seeing that her face was hidden from him by the hood, he turned to observe her at better advantage. A long braid of hair hung down her back. In the twilight it gleamed dull gold. She came up to his shoulder. The sleeve nearest him was rolled up to her elbow, revealing a fine round arm. Her hand, like her foot, was brown, strong, and well shaped. It was a hand that had been developed by labor. She was full-bosomed, yet slender, and she walked with a free stride that made Shefford admire and wonder.

They passed several of the little stone and log houses, and women greeted them as they went by, and children peered shyly from the doors. He kept trying to think of something to say, and, failing in that, determined to have one good look under the hood before he left her.

"You walk lame," she said, solicitously. "Let me carry the bucket now—please. My house is near."

"Am I lame? . . . Guess so, a little," he replied. "It was a hard ride for me. But I'll carry the bucket just the same."

They went on under some piñon-trees, down a path to a little house identical with the others, except that it had a stone porch. Shefford smelled fragrant wood-smoke and saw a column curling from the low, flat, stone chimney. Then he set the bucket down on the porch.

"Thank you, Mr. Shefford," she said.

"You know my name?" he asked.

"Yes. Mr. Withers spoke to my nearest neighbor and she told me."

"Oh, I see. And you—"

He did not go on and she did not reply. When she stepped upon the porch and turned he was able to see under the hood. The face there was in shadow, and for that very reason he answered to ungovernable impulse and took a step closer to her. Dark, grave, sad eyes looked down at him, and he felt as if he could never draw his own glance away. He seemed not to see the rest of her face, and yet felt that it was lovely. Then a downward movement of the hood hid from him the strange eyes and the shadowy loveliness.

"I—I beg your pardon," he said, quickly, drawing back. "I'm rude. . . . Withers told me about a girl he called—he said looked like a sago-lily. That's no excuse to stare under your hood. But I—I was curious. I wondered if—"

He hesitated, realizing how foolish his talk was. She stood a moment, probably watching him, but he could not be sure, for her face was hidden.

"They call me that," she said. "But my name is Mary."

"Mary—what ?" he asked.

"Just Mary," she said, simply. "Good night."

He did not say good night and could not have told why. She took up the bucket and went into the dark house. Shefford hurried away into the gathering darkness.

SOME LIARS OF THE OLD WEST

CHARLES M. RUSSELL

Speakin' of liars, the Old West could put in its claim for more of 'em than any other land under the sun. The mountains and plains seemed to stimulate man's imagination. A man in the States might have been a liar in a small way, but when he comes west he soon takes lessons from the prairies, where ranges a hundred miles away seem within touchin' distance, streams run uphill and Nature appears to lie some herself.

These men weren't vicious liars. It was love of romance, lack of reading matter, and the wish to be entertainin' that makes 'em stretch facts and invent yarns. Jack McGowan, a well-known old-timer now livin' in Great Falls, tells of a man known as Lyin' Jack, who was famous from Mexico to the Arctic.

McGowan says one of Jack's favorite tales is of an elk he once killed that measured 15-feet spread between the antlers. He used to tell that he kept these horns in the loft of his cabin.

"One time I hadn't seen Jack for years," said McGowan, "when he shows up in Benton. The crowd's all glad to see Jack, an' after a round or two of drinks, asks him to tell them a yarn.

"'No, boys,' says Jack, 'I'm through. For years I've been tellin' these lies—told 'em so often I got to believin' 'em myself. That story of mine about the elk with the 15-foot horns is what cured me. I told about that elk so often that I knowed the place I killed it. One night I lit a candle and crawled up in the loft to view the horns—an' I'm damned if they was there.'"

Once up in Yogo, Bill Cameron pointed out Old Man Babcock an' another old-timer, Patrick, sayin', "there's three of the biggest liars in the world."

"Who's the third?" inquired a bystander.

"Patrick's one, an' old Bab's the other two," says Cameron.

This Babcock one night is telling about getting jumped by 50 hostile Sioux, a war party, that's giving him a close run. The bullets an' arrows are tearin' the dirt all around, when he hits the mouth of a deep canyon. He thinks he's safe, but after ridin' up it a way, discovers it's a box gulch, with walls straight up from 600 to 1,000 feet. His only get-away's where he come in, an' the Indians are already whippin' their ponies into it.

Right here old Bab rares back in his chair, closes his eyes, an' starts fondlin' his whiskers. This seems to be the end of the story, when one of the listeners asks:

"What happened then?"

Old Bab, with his eyes still closed, takin' a fresh chew, whispered: "They killed me, b' God!"

The upper Missouri River steamboats, they used to say, would run on a light dew, an' certainly they used to get by where there was mighty little water. X. Beidler an' his friend, Major Reed, are traveling by boat to Fort Benton. One night they drink more than they should. X. is awakened in the morning by the cries of Reed. On entering his stateroom, X. finds Reed begging for water, as he's dying of thirst.

X. steps to the bedside, and takin' his friend's hand, says: "I'm sorry, Major, I can't do anything for you. That damned pilot got drunk, too, last night, and we're eight miles up a dry coulee!"

"Some say rattlers ain't pizen," said Buckskin Williams, an old freighter, "but I know different. I'm pullin' out of Milk River one day with 14, when I notice my line hoss swing out an' every hoss on the near side crowds the. chain. My near wheel hoss, that I'm ridin', rares up an' straddles the tongue. It's then I see what the trouble is—a big rattler has struck, misses my hoss an' hits the tongue. The tongue starts to swell up. I have to chop it off to save the wagon, an' I'm damn quick doin' it, too!"

"Cap" Nelse, a well-known old-timer around Benton in the early days, tells of coming south from Edmonton with a string of half-breed carts. They were traveling through big herds of buffalo. It was spring and there were many calves. They had no trouble with the full-grown buffalo, Cap said, but were forced to stop often to take the calves from between the spokes of the cart-wheels!

A traveling man in White Sulphur Springs makes a bet of drinks for the town with Coates, a saloon keeper, that Coates can't find a man that will hold up his hand and take his oath that he has seen 100,000 buffalo at one sight. When the bet's decided, it's agreed to ring the triangle at the hotel, which will call the town to their drinks.

Many old-timers said they had seen that many buffalo, but refused to swear to it, and it looked like Coates would lose his bet until Milt Crowthers showed up. Then a smile of confidence spread over Coates' face as he introduces Crowthers to the drummer.

"Mr. Crowthers," said the traveling man," how many antelope have you seen at one time?"

Crowthers straightens up and looks wise, like he's turning back over the pages of the past. "Two hundred thousand," says he.

"How many elk?" asks the traveling man.

"Somethin' over a million," replies Crowthers.

"Mr. Crowthers, how many buffalo will you hold up your hand and swear you have seen at one sight?"

Crowthers holds up his hand. "As near as I can figure," says he, "about three million billion."

This is where Coates starts for the triangle, but the traveling man halts him, saying, "Where were you when you saw these buffalo, Mr. Crowthers?"

"I was a boy travelin' with a wagon train," replies Crowthers. "We was south of the Platte when we was forced to corral our wagons to keep our stock from bein' stampeded by buffalo. For five days an' nights 50 men kep' their guns hot killin' buffalo to keep 'em off the wagons. The sixth day the herd spread, givin' us time to yoke up an' cross the Platte, an' it's a damn good thing we did."

"Why?" asks the traveling man.

"Well," says Crowthers, "we no more than hit the high country north of the Platte, than lookin' back, here comes the main herd!"

PECOS BILL

MODY C. BOATRIGHT

THE GENESIS OF PECOS BILL

"I suppose," said Lanky, as he sat by the camp-fire with Red and Hank and Joe, now his fast friends, "that the cowboy's life is about the most interesting one there is. I'd like it. Live outdoors, plenty of fresh air to breathe, interesting work—that's the life"

"I ain't kickin'," said Joe. "You see I'm still at it, though I've cussed it as much as anybody in my time, and swore off and quit, too, more than once. But somehow when spring comes, and the grass gits green, and I know the calves is comin', somethin' jest naturally gits under my hide, and I come back to the smell of burnt hair and the creak of saddle-leather."

"Yeah," said Red, "it's jist like a dream I had once. I dreamt I died and went up to a place where there was big pearly gates, and I walked up and knocked on the door, and it come wide open. I went in, and there stood Saint Peter.

"Come in; welcome to our city' he says. 'I've been lookin' for you. Go over to the commissary and git you a harp and a pair of wings'

" 'All right,' says I, feelin' mighty lucky to git in.

"As I walked along on the gold sidewalk, I sees a lot of fellers roped and hobbled and hog-tied.

" 'What's the matter?' says I; 'Saint Peter, you're not tryin' to buffalo me, are you?'

" 'Naw,' he says, 'what makes you think so? Your record ain't nothin' extra good, but you didn't git cut back, did you? Here you are. You're in. Ain't that enough?'

" 'Ain't this hell?' I says.

" 'Naw,' says Peter, 'this ain't hell a-tall.'

" 'Are you shore this ain't hell?' I asks.

" 'Naw,' he says, 'this ain't hell. What makes you think it is?'

" 'Why,' I says, 'what you got all them fellers roped and tied down for?'

"Oh,' he says, 'them fellers over there? You see them's cowboys from the Southwest, and I have to keep 'em tied to keep 'em from goin' back. I think maybe they'll git range broke after while so I can turn 'em loose, but it seems like it's takin' a long time."

"However," said Joe, "the cow business ain't what it used to be, what with barbed wire, windmills, automobiles and trucks, and the like. They don't want cowhands anymore; what they want is blacksmiths, mechanics, and the like. Still, I reckon it's a good thing, for they couldn't git cowhands if they did want 'em.

"Now, here's Red and Hank. Good boys, both of 'em. And I've leaned 'em a lot about cattle; and they take money at the rodeos, but they ain't like the old cowhands. I don't know jest what it is, but they ain't the same.

"And they ain't but mighty few real cowmen any more. Now, take the big mogul of this outfit. Good feller, always pays wages every month— which is more than some of the old-timers could do. But he ain't no cowman. Sets up all day at a big desk in town—has a secretary, stenographer, and the like. Why, if Pecos Bill had a-done a thing like that, he would of been so ashamed of his self, he would of jest naturally laid down and died."

"Who is this Pecos Bill I've heard you mention?" asked Lanky.

"Who is he? Why, ain't you ever heard of Pecos Bill?"

"Not till I came here."

"Well, well, I reckon you've heard of Sam Houston, and Sam Bass and General Lee and George Washington and Pat Garrett, ain't you?"

"Oh, yes, I've heard a little about them but not anything about Pecos Bill."

"That jest shows that the fellers that make our books don't know what to put in 'em. The idear of leavin' out Pecos Bill."

"But who was Pecos Bill?"

"Who was he? Why he was jest about the most celebrated man in the whole dang cow country."

"What was his real name?"

"So far as I know the only real name he ever had was Pecos Bill. Don't suppose anybody knows what his daddy's name was. You see, in his day it wasn't good manners to ask a feller his name, and besides it wasn't good judgment either. And it ain't been so long. Many a greenhorn bein' ignorant of that little point of good manners has looked down the muzzle of a six-shooter and then died.

"Pecos Bill's daddy didn't say what they called him back in the States, and nobody asked him. They jest called him the Ole Man, for he was old—about seventy some odd when he came to Texas."

"When did he come to Texas?" asked Lanky.

"I couldn't say about that exactly," said Joe. "It must of been right about the time Sam Houston discovered Texas. Anyhow, the Ole Man loaded up all his twelve kids and his Ole Woman and his rifle, and all his other stuff in an oxwagon and lit out hell-bent for Texas as soon as he found out there was sech a place. They say other people that come later didn't have no trouble fmdin' the way. They jest went by the Indian skeletons that the Ole Man left along his road.

"Well, they finally got to the Sabine River. The Ole Man stops his oxen, old Spot and Buck, he calls 'em, and rounds up all his younguns and has 'em set down and listen while he makes 'em a speech. 'Younguns,' he says, 'that land you see on the other side of the river is Texas, wild and woolly and full of fleas. And if you ain't that way only more so, you ain't no brats of mine.'"

"I'd always heard that Pecos Bill was born in Texas," interrupted Red.

"Jest wait," said Joe. "Jest wait; have I said he wasn't? Them was the other kids.

"As I was about to say, they crossed the river and camped for the night. That was in Texas, savvy. And that night Pecos Bill was born. The next mornin' the Ole Woman put him on a bear's skin and left him to play with his self while she made the corn-pone for breakfast. And right then's when they come dang near losin' Pecos Bill."

"Bears or Indians?" asked Lanky.

"Neither one," said Joe. "Bears and Indians didn't mean nothin' to that old man. He would have et 'em for breakfast. Once later when the Ole Man and the older brats was gone, the Comanches did try to git Bill, but the Ole Woman lit into 'em with the broom-handle and killed forty-nine right on the spot. She never knowed how many she crippled and let git away. No, it wasn't the Indians. It was miskeeters."

"Malaria?" said Lanky.

"You guessed wrong again," said Joe. "This is what happened. The Ole Woman was cookin' corn-pone, and all of a sudden it got dark, and there was the dangest singin' and hummin' you ever heard. Then they see it was a swarm of big black miskeeters; and they was so thick around Bill that you jest couldn't see him.

"The Ole Man felt his way to the wagon and got out his gun. He thought he'd shoot it off in the air and scere them miskeeters away. He pointed the muzzle of the gun toward the sky and pulled the trigger. What he seen then was a little beam of light come through. It was just like bein' in a dark room and lookin' out through a piece of windmill pipe. That was jest for a minute, for right away the hole shet up, and them miskeeters swarmed around Pecos, and the Ole Man seen they was goin' to pack him off if he didn't do somethin' right away.

"Then he happened to recollect that he'd brought his hog-renderin' kettle along; so he fought his way back to the wagon and rolled it out and turned it over the kid. He was scered the lad would git lonesome under there by his self, so he jest slipped the choppin' axe under the edge of the kettle for the chap to play with.

"Well, them danged miskeeters jest buzzed and buzzed around the kettle, tryin' to find a way to git in. D'rec'ly they all backed off, and the Old Man and the Ole Woman thought they'd give up and was goin' way. Then all at once one of them miskeeters comes at that kettle like a bat out of hell. He hit the kettle and rammed his bill clean through it; and he stuck there. Then another one come at the kettle jest like the first one had; and he stuck, too. Then they kept comin', and every one stuck. The Ole Man and. the Ole woman and the older brats stood there watchin' them miskeeters ram that kettle. After each one of them varmints (they was too \ big to be called insects) hit the kettle, there would be a little ring—*dingl* Like that. Purty soon the old folks got on to what was happenin'. Every time a miskeeter would ram his bill through the kettle, Pecos would brad it with the choppin' axe. Well, after while them miskeeters jest naturally lifted that kettle right up and flew off with it. The others thought they had Pecos Bill and follered the kettle off. Of course the Ole Man hated to lose his utensil. He said he didn't know how the Old Woman was going to render up the lard and bear's grease now; but it was worth a hundred kettles to know he had such a smart brat. And from that time the Ole Man would always talk about Bill as a chap of Great Possibilities. He 'lowed that if the brat jest had the proper raisin', he'd make a great man some day. He said he was goin' to try to do his part by him; so he begun givin' him a diet of jerked game with whiskey and onions for breakfast. He lapped it up so well that in three days the Ole Woman weaned him."

"Did the Ole Man settle there on the Sabine?" asked Lanky.

"Naw," said Joe. "He squatted on a little sandy hill on the Trinity somewheres east of where Dallas is now. It was jest an accident that he stopped where he did."

"How was that?" asked Lanky.

"Well," said Joe, "you see, it was like this. They was travelin' west in their customary and habitual manner, which was with the Ole Man and the six oldest kids walkin' alongside Spot and Buck, and the Ole Woman and the seven youngest kids in the wagon. Jest as they was comin' to the foot of a sandy hill, a big rain come up. It rained so hard that the Ole Man couldn't see the wagon, but he stuck close to them trusty oxen of his, and they went right up the hill. When he got to the top, he seen that it had about quit rainin'; and he looked back and seen the wagon still at the bottom of the hill, and there was the brats that had been walkin' with him under it."

"Did the harness break?" asked Lanky.

"Naw, it wasn't that," said Joe. "You see, he was usin' a rawhide lariat for a log-chain, and it had got wet. I reckon you know what rawhide does when it gits wet, don't you, Lanky? It stretches. There ain't no rubber that will stretch like wet rawhide. Well, that's what happened to that lariat. It stretched so that the Ole Man drove his oxen a mile up the hill without movin' the wagon an inch. Not an inch had he moved her, by gar."

"Well, the sun was shinin' now, and it got brighter and brighter, and while the Ole Man was wonderin' what in the dickens to do next, Ole Spot jest dropped down dead from sunstroke. That sort of got next to the Ole Man, for he said that brute had been a real friend to him, and besides he was worth his weight in gold. Still, he lowed he'd might as well skin him. So he got out his old Bowie knife and started to work.

"Well, sir, while he was skinnin' Spot, a norther came up, and damn me, if Ole Buck didn't keel over, froze to death.

"So the Ole Man decided he'd jest as well stop there where he was. So he told the Ole Woman to bring up the brats. He threw the ox yoke over a stump; and the Ole Woman brought up some chuck and some beddin' from the wagon. Then they et supper and tucked the kids into bed. The Ole Man tried to blow out the lantern, but she wouldn't blow. He raised up the globe, and there was the flame froze still as an icicle. He jest broke it off and buried it in the sand and turned in and went to sleep.

"The next mornin' when he woke up, it was clear and the sun was warm. Well, the Ole Woman cooked a bite, and while they was eatin' here come the wagon right up the hill. You see the rawhide was dryin' out. That's the way it does."

"That's what it does, all right," said Red. "Once I knowed a clodhopper that made his self a rawhide hat. It worked fine till one day he got caught out in the rain. Then the sun come out, and that hat drawed up so he couldn't git it off. And it was drawin' up and mashin' his head somthin' terrible. Lucky for him, it wasn't very far to a tank, and he got off and stood on his head in the water a few minutes and it come right off."

"Well," said Joe, "that's what the rawhide log-chain done. It dried out, and that wagon come right up the hill; and when it got up to where the Ole Man and the Ole Woman was, the Ole Man got his chippin' axe and begun cuttin' down trees to make him a cabin. And that's where he settled."

"Did Pecos Bill grow up there in East Texas?" asked Lanky.

"He left when he was a mere lad," said Joe. "But he lived there a little while. The Ole Man got along fine till his corn give out, because there was plenty of game. But he jest couldn't do without his corn-pone and his corn whiskey. So he cleared a little patch and put it in corn."

"And worked it without his steers?" asked Lanky.

"Why not?" said Joe. "He made him a light Georgie-stock out of wood, and the Ole Woman and one of the bigger kids could pull it fine. He made some harness out of the hide of Old Spot, and he'd hitch 'em and plough all day.

"They used to all go out in the field and leave Pecos Bill in the cabin by his self. One day when Bill was about three years old, the Ole Man was ploughin', and jest as he turned the Ole Woman and the kid he had hitched up with her around to start a new row, the Ole Woman begun yellin' and tryin' to get out of the harness.

"'What's eatin' on you, Ole Woman?' says the Ole Man. 'I never seen you do like this before. Must have a tick in your ear.'

"The Ole Woman yelled that she see a panther go in the cabin where Bill was.

"The Ole Man told her not to git exicted.'It's a half hour by sun till dinner time yet,' he says,'and that dang panther needn't expect no help from me nohow. The fool critter ought to of had more sense than to go in there. He'll jest have to make out the best way he can.'

"So they ploughed on till dinner time, and when they come back to the cabin, there was Pecos Bill a-chewin' on a piece of raw panther flank.

"They lived there another year or two before the Ole Man taken a notion to leave."

"I reckon you know how he come to git the idear in his head, don't you, Joe?" said Red.

"I'll bite," said Joe. "Go ahead."

"Why, this ain't no sell," said Red. "I've heard Windy Williams tell it a hundred times.

"One time the Ole Man had the Ole Woman and one of the big kids hitched up to the plough in his customary and habitual manner, jist as Joe has been tellin' about, and all at once here comes piece of paper blowin' across the field. The Ole Woman shied a little bit off to one side; then the kid got to prancin', and then they tore loose and went lickity-split, rearm' and tearin' across that corn patch, draggin' the Ole Man with 'em. The Ole Man stumped his toe on a root, and then they got loose from him and tore up the Georgie-stock. After while they quieted down, and the Ole Man got up and fetched 'em in. Then he went out and picked up the piece of paper where it was hung on a stump. He seen it was an old newspaper. That set him to wonderin'.

"The next mornin' he got his rifle and begun lookin' around. About five miles from his place he found some wagon tracks, and he follered the tracks till he come to a new cabin about fifty miles up the creek. Then he come home and told the Ole Woman and the kids to git ready to leave. He calkilated the country was gittin' too thickly settled for him."

"How did he get away without a team?" asked Lanky.

"Oh, that was easy," said Red. "He sent Pecos Bill out to ketch a couple of mustangs, and in about an hour the lad run 'em down. The Ole Man fixed up the harness he'd been usin' to plough with, and loaded in his stuff and his wife and kids, and pulled out.

"They kept goin' west till finally they come to the Pecos River, which the Ole Man said he'd ford or bust. He got across all right, but as he was drivin' up the bank on the west side, the end-gate come out of the wagon, and Pecos Bill fell out. The Ole Man and the Ole Woman never missed him till they got about thirty miles further on; then they said it wasn't worth while turnin' back. They said they guessed the chap could take kere of his self, and if he couldn't he wasn't worth turnin' back for nohow. So that's how Pecos Bill come to be called Pecos Bill."

"What became of him?" asked Lanky. "What happened to him then?"

"What happened to him then?" said Red. "That would take a long time to tell."

"We'll tell you about that some other time, Lanky," said Joe.

ADVENTURES OF PECOS BILL

"How old was Pecos Bill when he was lost on the Pecos River?" Lanky asked Joe on the next night when supper was finished and the four were sitting around the fire smoking.

"I guess he must of been about four year old," said Joe. "Some says he was jest a year old, but that can't be right. The Ole Man made two or three crops down on the Trinity before the country got so thickly settled that he had to leave."

"What became of the family?" asked Lanky.

"That would be hard to answer," said Joe; "hard to answer. I don't suppose there's a soul that knows for certain. There's been tales about 'em bein' et up by wild beasts, but that ain't likely; and there's been tales about 'em bein' killed by the Indians, but that ain't likely neither. Why, them Red-Skins would run like scered jack-rabbits when they seen the Ole Man comin', or the Ole Woman either. Then there's tales about 'em dyin' for water in the desert, which may be so; but more than likely they settled somewhere and lived a happy and peaceful life."

"The chances are," said Red, "that they settled in the Lost Canyon, and their offspring may be livin' there yet for all anybody knows."

"Where is the Lost Canyon?" asked Lanky.

"That's jist what nobody don't know," said Red; "but it's out in the Big Bend Country somewheres, and it opens into the Rio Grande. It gits wide, and there's springs in it, and buffalo a-grazin' on the grass, and it's a fine country."

"How do you know about it?" asked Lanky. "Have you ever been there?"

"Naw," said Red,"but people has. But you never can find it when you're lookin' for itfThem that finds it, finds it accidentally, and then they can't go back. That's jist the place that would of suited Pecos Bill's Ole Man, and the chances are that's where he stopped. Some day I'm goin' to happen on that canyon myself, and if I do, I'll jist stake me out a ranch; that is unless it's inhabited by Pecos Bill's race. If it is, I reckon I'll let 'em have it."

"And what became of Pecos Bill?" asked Lanky.

"Why," said Joe, "he jest growed up with the country.There wasn't nothin' else he could do. He got to runnin' with a bunch of coyotes and took up with 'em. He learned their language and took up all their bad habits. He could set on the ground and howl with the best of'em, and run down a jack-rabbit jest as quick, too. He used to run ahead of the pack, and pull down a forty-eight point buck and bite a hole in his neck before the rest of the coyotes got there. But he always divided with the pack, and that's probably the reason they throwed off on him like they did."

"Did he ever teach anybody else the coyote language?" asked Lanky.

"Jest one old prospector that befriended him once. That was all. You see the old man couldn't find no gold and he went to trappin', and he used the language that Bill had taught him to call up the coyotes and git 'em in his traps. Bill said it was a dirty trick, and he wouldn't teach nobody else how to speak coyote. Bill would of killed the old prospector if it hadn't of been that the old man done him a favor once."

"What did he do?" asked Lanky.

"Why, it was him that found Bill and brought him back to civilization and liquor, which Bill had jest about forgot the taste of."

"How old was BiE at that time?" asked Lanky.

"Oh, I guess he was about ten years old," said Joe. "One day this old prospector comes along and he hears the most terrible racket anybody ever heard of—rocks a-rollin' down the canyon, brush a-poppin', and the awfullest howlin' and squallin' you could imagine; and he looks up the canyon and sees what he first thinks is a cloud comin' up, but purty soon he discovers it's fur a-flyin'.

"Well, he decides to walk up the canyon a piece and investigate, and purty soon he comes on Pecos Bill, who has a big grizzly bear under each arm just mortally squeezin' the stuffin' out of 'em. And while the old prospector stands there a-watchin', Bill tears off a hind leg and begins eatin' on it.

" 'A game scrap, son,' says the old prospector, 'and who be ye?'

" 'Me?' says Bill. 'I'm a varmit.'

' " 'Naw, ye ain't a varmit,' says the old prospector; 'you're a human.'

" 'Naw,' says Bill, 'I ain't no human; I'm a varmit.'

" 'How come?' says the prospector.

" 'Don't I go naked?' says Bill.

" 'Shore ye do,' says the old prospector. 'Shore ye're naked. So is the Indians and them critters is part human, anyway. That don't spell nothin'.'

" 'Don't I have fleas?' says Bill.

" 'Shore ye do,' says the old prospector, 'but all Texians has fleas.'

" 'Don't I howl?' says Bill.

" 'Yeah, ye howl all right,' says the old prospector, 'but nearly all Texians is howlin' most of the time. That don't spell nothin' neither.'

" 'Well, jest the same I'm a coyote,' says Bill.

" 'Naw, ye ain't a coyote,' says the old prospector. 'A coyote's got a tail, ain't he?'

" 'Yeah,' says Bill, 'a coyote's got a tail.'

" 'But you ain't got no tail,' says the old prospector. 'Jest feel and see if you have.'

"Bill felt and shore nuff, he didn't have no tail.

" 'Well, I'll be danged,' he says. 'I never did notice that before. I guess I ain't a coyote, after all. Show me them humans, and if I like their looks, maybe I'll throw in with 'em.'

"Well, he showed Bill the way to an outfit, and it wasn't long till he was the most famous and noted man in the whole cow country."

"It was him," said Hank, "that invented ropin'. He had a rope that reached from the Rio Grande to the Big Bow, and he shore did swing a mean loop. He used to amuse his self by throwin' a little *Julian*[1] up in the sky and fetchin' down the buzzards and eagles that flew over. He roped everything he ever seen: bears and wolves and panthers, elk and buffalo. The first time he seen a train, he thought it was some kind of varmit, and damn me if he didn't slip a loop over it and dang near wreck the thing.

---

1   A type of loop. Pronounced *hoolidn*.

"One time his ropin' shore did come in handy, for he saved the life of a very dear friend."

"How was that?" asked Lanky.

"Well, Bill had a hoss that he thought the world of, and he had a good reason to, too, for he had raised him from a colt, feedin' him on a special diet of nitroglycerin and barbed wire, which made him very tough and also very ornery when anybody tried to handle him but Bill. The hoss thought the world of Bill, but when anybody else come around, it was all off. He had more ways of pitchin' than Carter had oats. Lots of men tried to ride him, but only one man besides Bill ever mounted that hoss and lived. That's the reason Bill named him Widow-Maker."

"Who was that man?" asked Lanky.

"That was Bill's friend that I was goin' to tell you about Bill savin' his life," said Hank. "You see this feller gits his heart set on ridin' Widow-Maker. Bill tried to talk him out of it, but he wouldn't listen. He said he could ride anything that had hair. It had been his ambition from youth, he said, to find a critter that could make him pull leather. So Bill, seein' the pore feller's heart was about to break, finally told him to go ahead.

"He gits on Widow-Maker, and that hoss begins to go through his gaits, doin' the end-to-end, the sunfish, and the back-throw; and about that time the rider goes up in the sky. Bill watches him through a spyglass and sees him land on Pike's Peak. No doubt he would of starved to death up there, but Bill roped him by the neck and drug him down, thus savin' his life."

"Yeah," said Red, "Widow-Maker was jist the sort of hoss that suited Bill exactly, For one thing, it saved him a lot of shootin', because he didn't have no trouble keepin' other people off his mount; and as for Bill, he could ride anything that had hair and some things that didn't have. Once, jist for fun, he throwed a surcingle on a streak of lightin' and rode it over Pike's Peak.

"Another time he bet a Stetson hat he could ride a cyclone. He went up on the Kansas line and simply eared that tornado down and got on it. Down he come across Oklahoma and the Panhandle a-settin' on that tornado, a-curlin' his mustache and a-spurrin' it in the withers. Seein' it couldn't throw him, it jist naturally rained out from under him, and that's the way Bill got the only spill he ever had.

"Yeah," continued Red, "I reckon Bill was mighty hard to throw. A smart lad he was, and a playful sort of feller, too. In his spare time he used to amuse his self puttin' thorns on things—bushes and cactuses and the like, and he even stuck horns on the toads so they'd match up with the rest of the country."

"I see he's been at work in this country," said Lanky. "Did he live all his life in Texas?"

"Naw, he didn't," said Joe. "Bill was a good deal like his old man. When he had killed all the Indians and bad men, and the country got all peaceful and quiet, he jest couldn't stand it any longer, and he saddled up his hoss and started west. Out on the New Mexico line he met an old trapper, and they got to talkin', and Bill told him why he was leavin', and said if the old man knowed where there was a tough outfit, he'd be much obliged if he would tell him how to git to it.

" 'Ride up the draw about two hundred miles,' says the old traper, 'and you'll find a bunch of buys so tough that they bite nails in two jest for the fun of it.'

"So Bill rides on in a hurry, gittin' somewhat reckless on account of wantin' to git to that outfit and git a look at the bad *hombres* that the old man has told him about. The first thing Bill knowed, his hoss stumps his toe on a mountain and breaks his fool neck rollin' down the side, and so Bill finds his self afoot.

"He takes off his saddle and goes walkin' on, packin' it, till all at once he comes to a big rattlesnake. He was twelve feet long and had fangs like the tushes of a *javelina;* and he rears up and sings at Bill and sticks out his tongue like he was lookin' for a scrap. There wasn't nothin' that Bill wouldn't fight, and he always fought fair; and jest to be shore that rattlesnake had a fair show and couldn't claim he took advantage of him, Bill let him have three bites before he begun. Then he jest naturally lit into that reptile and mortally flailed the stuffm' out of him. Bill was always quick to forgive, though, and let by-gones be by-gones, and when the snake give up, Bill took him up. and curled him around his neck, and picked up his saddle and outfit and went on his way.

"As he was goin' along through a canyon, all at once a big mountain lion jumped off of a cliff and spraddled out all over Bill. Bill never got excited. He jest took his time and laid down his saddle and his snake, and then he turned loose on that cougar. Well, sir, the hair flew so it rose up like a cloud and the jack-rabbits and road-runners thought it was sundown. It wasn't long till that cougar had jest all he could stand, and be begun to lick Bill's hand and cry like a kitten.

"Well, Bill jest ears him down and slips his .bridle on his head, throws on the saddle and cinches her tight, and mounts the beast. Well, that cat jest tears out across the mountains and canyons with Bill on his back a-spurrin' him in the shoulders and quirtin' him down the flank with the rattlesnake.

"And that's the way Bill rode into the camp of the outfit the old trapper had told him about. When he gits there, he reaches out and cheeks down the cougar and sets him on his haunches and gits down and looks at his saddle.

"There was them tough *hombres* a-settin' around the fire playin' *monte*. There was a pot of coffee and a bucket of beans a-boilin' on the fire, and as Bill hadn't had nothing to eat for several days, he was hungry; so he stuck his hand down in the bucket and grabbed a handful of beans and crammed 'em into his mouth. Then he gabbed the coffee pot and washed 'em down, and wiped his mouth on a prickly-pear. Then he turned to the men and said, 'Who in the hell is boss around here, anyway?'

"'I was,' says a big stout feller about seven feet tall, 'but you are now, stranger.'

"And that was the beginning of Bill's outfit."

"But it was only the beginnin's," said Red; "for it wasn't long after that that he staked out New Mexico and fenced Arizona for a calf-pasture. He built a big ranch-house and had a big yard around it. It was so far from the yard gate to the front door, that he used to keep a string of saddle hosses at stations along the way, for the convenience of visitors. Bill always was a hospitable sort of chap, and when company come, lie always tried to persuade them to stay as long as he could git 'em to. Deputy sheriffs and brand inspectors he never would let leave a-tall.

"One time his outfit was so big that he would have his cooks jist dam up a draw to mix the biscuit dough in. They would dump in the flour and the salt and the bakin'-powder and mix it up with teams and fresnoes. You can still see places where the dough was left in the bottom of the draw -when they moved on. Alkali lakes they call 'em. That's the bakin'-powder that stayed in the ground.

"One time when there was a big drought and water got scerce on Bill's range, he lit in and dug the Rio Grande and ditched water from the Gulf of Mexico. Old man Windy Williams was water boy on the job, and he said Bill shore drove his men hard for a few days till they got through, and it kept him busy carryin' water."

"I guess it took about all of Bill's time to manage a ranch like that," said Lanky.

"Not all, not all," said Joe. "That was his main vocation and callin', but he found time for a good many other things. He was always goin' in for somethin' else when the cattle business got slack.

"When the S. P. come through, he got a contract furnishin' 'em wood. Bill went down into Mexico and rounded up a bunch of greasers and put 'em to cuttin' wood. He made a contract with 'em that they was to git half the wood they cut. When the time was up, they all had big stacks of cordwood, Mex'can cords, you understand, that they don't know what to do with. So Bill talked it over with 'em and finally agreed to take it off their hands without chargin' 'em a cent. Bill always was liberal.

"He done some of the gradin' on the S. P. too. This time he went out and rounded up ten thousand badgers and put 'em to diggin'. He said they was better laborers than Chinks, because he could learn 'em how to work sooner. Bill had some trouble, however, gittin' 'em to go in a straight line, and that's why the S. P. is so crooked in places.

"He also got a contract fencin' the right-of-way. The first thing that he done was to go out on the line of Texas and New Mexico and buy up all the dry holes old Bob Sanford had made out there tryin' to git water. He pulled 'em up and sawed 'em up into two-foot lengths for post-holes."

"I've heard the Paul Bunyan did that with dry oil-wells," said Lanky.

"Paul Bunyan might of for all I know," said Joe. "But if he did, he learned the trick from Pecos Bill, for this was before oil had been invented.

"However, it cost so much to freight the holes down that Bill give up the plan long before he had used up all of Bob Sanford's wells, and found a cheaper and better way of makin' post-holes."

"What was his new method?" asked Lanky.

"Why, he jest went out and rounded up a big bunch of prairie-dogs, and turned 'em loose where he wanted the fence, and of course every critter of 'em begun diggin' a hole, for it's jest a prairie-dog's nature to dig holes. As soon as a prairie-dog would git down about two feet, Bill would yank him out and stick a post in the hole. Then the fool prairie-dog would go start another one, and Bill would git it. Bill said he found the prairie-dog labor very satisfactory. The only trouble was that sometimes durin' off hours, the badgers that he had gradin' would make a raid on the prairie-dogs, and Bill would have to git up and drive 'em back to their own camp."

"Did Bill have any other occupations?" asked Lanky.

"Well," said Joe, "he used to fight Indians jest for recreation, but he never did make a business of it like some did, huntin' 'em for a dollar a scalp. In fact Bill was not bloodthirsty and cruel, and he never scalped an Indian in his life. He'd just skin 'em and tan their hides."

"That reminds me," said Hank, "of another business he used to carry on as a sort of side-line, and that was huntin' buffalo. You see, it was the hides that was valuable, and Bill thought it was too much of a waste to kill a buffalo jest for the hide; so he'd jest hold the critters and skin 'em alive and then turn 'em aloose to grow a new hide. A profitable business he built up, too, but he jest made one mistake."

"What was that?" asked Lanky.

"One spring he skinned too early, and a norther come up, and all the buffalo took cold and died. Mighty few of'em left after that." "Did Bill ever get married?" asked Lanky.

"Oh, yes," said Joe. "He married lots of women in his day, but he never had the real tender affection for any of the rest of'em that he had for his first wife, Slue-Foot Sue.

"Bill savvied courtin' the ladies all right; yet he never took much stock in petticoats till he met Slue-Foot Sue; but when he saw that gal come ridin' down the Rio Grande on a catfish, it jest got next to him, and he married her right off.

"I say right off—but she made him wait a few days till she could send to San Antonio for a suitable and proper outfit, the principal garment bein' a big steel wire bustle, like all the women wore when they dressed up in them days.

"Well, everything would have gone off fine, but on the very day of the weddin' Sue took a fool notion into her head that she jest had to ride Widow-Maker. For a long time Bill wouldn't hear to it, but finally she begun to cry, and said Bill didn't love her any more. Bill jest couldn't stand to see her cry; so he told her to go ahead but to be keerful.

"Well, she got on that hoss, and he give about two jumps, and she left the saddle. He threwed her'so high that she had to duck as she went up to keep from bumpin' her head on the moon. Then she come down, landin' right on that steel bustle, and that made her bounce up jest as high, nearly, as she had went before. Well, she jest kept on bouncin' like that for ten days and nights, and finally Bill had to shoot her to keep her from starvin' to death. It nearly broke his heart. That was the only time Bill had ever been known to shed tears, and he was so tore up that he wouldn't have nothin' to do with a woman for two weeks."

THE EXODUS OF PECOS BILL

Lanky had been sent for, and this was his last night in camp. His face was tanned; he had gained in weight; he had earned money in his own right. He felt that he was now a man.

He and his cronies sat around the fire in silence. Joe and the boys would miss the kid, and he hated to leave. This silence wouldn't do.

"What became of Pecos Bill?" asked Lanky.

"That would be hard to say," said Joe, "hard to say. Everybody knows he's gone, jest like the open range and the longhorn steer; but jest how and where he passed in his checks, I don't suppose anybody will ever find out for certain. A lot of the fellers that knowed him are dead, and a lot of'em has bad memories—a lot of the old-timers has bad memories—and some of 'em are sech damn liars that you can't go by what they say."

"You've seen Pecos Bill, haven't you, Joe?" said Lanky.

"Well, yes, that is I seen him when I was a young buck. But I never seen him die, and I never could find out jest how he was took off. I've seen some mighty hot arguments on the subject, and I've knowed one or two fellers to die with their boots on after gittin' in a quarrel in jest that way."

"I heard one account a few years ago," said Red, "that may be right. There was a feller in Amarillo named Gabriel Asbury Jackson. He'd worked his self out of a job in Kansas and had come to Texas to buck the cigarette evil. One time he cornered a bunch of us that was too drunk to make a git-away and begun talkin' to us about smokin'.

" 'Young men,' he says, 'beware of cigarettes. You think you're smart to smoke a sack of Bull Durham every day, do you? Well, look at Pecos Bill. A stalwart young man he was, tough as nails, a fine specimen. But he got to foolin' with cigarettes. What did they do for him?' he says. 'Why, nothin' at first. But did he quit? No!' he says. 'He puffed away for ninety years, but they finally got him. And they'll git you, every mother's son of you, if you don't leave 'em alone.'"

"That ain't so," said Joe. "That man was jest a liar. Cigarettes never killed Pecos Bill. He was, however, a great smoker, but he never smoked Bull Durham. He made him up a mixture of his own, the principal ingredients bein' Kentucky home-spun, sulphur, and gun-powder. Why, he would have thought he was a sissy if he'd smoked Bull Durham.

"When the matches was scerce Bill used to ride out into a thunderstorm and light his cigarette with a streak of lightnin', and that's no doubt what's back of a tale you hear every once in a while about him bein' struck and kilt. But nobody that knows how Bill throwed a surcingle over a streak of lightnin' and rode it over Pike's Peak will ever believe that story."

"I heard it was liquor that killed pore Bill," said Hank.

"Must of been boot-leg," said Red.

"Naw," said Hank. "You see, Bill bein' brought up as he was from tender youth on whiskey and onions, was still a young man when whiskey lost its kick for him. He got to puttin' nitroglycerin in his drinks. That worked all right for a while, but soon he had to go to wolf-bait; and when that got so it didn't work, he went to fish-hooks. Bill used to say, rather sorrowful-like, that that was the only way he could git an idear from his booze. But after about fifty years the fish-hooks rusted out his interior parts and brought pore Bill to an early grave."

"I don't know who told you that windy," said Joe. "It might have been your own daddy. But it ain't so. It's jest another damn lie concocted by them damn prohibition men."

"I heard another tale," said Red, "which may be right for all I know. I heard that Bill went to Fort Worth one time, and there he seen a Boston man who had jist come to Texas with a mail-order cowboy outfit on; and when Bill seen him, he jist naturally laid down and laughed his self to death."

"That may be so," said Joe, "but I doubt it. I heard one tale about the death of Pecos Bill that I believe is the real correct and true account."

"And what was that?" asked Lanky.

"Well, Bill happened to drift into Cheyenne jest as the first rodeo was bein' put on. Bein' a bit curious to know what it was all about, he went out to the grounds to look the thing over. When he seen the ropers and the riders, he begun to weep; the first tears he's shed since the death of Slue-Foot Sue. Well, finally when a country lawyer jest three years out of Mississippi got up to make a speech and referred to the men on horseback as cowboys, Bill turned white and begun to tremble. And then when the country lawyer went on to talk about 'keepin' inviolate the sacred traditions of the Old West,' Bill jest went out and crawled in a prairie-dog hole and died of solemncholy."

Lanky looked at Red and Hank. They had not missed the point, but they chose to ignore it.

Joe talked on. "After several years," he said, "when all Bill's would-be rivals was sure he was dead, they all begun to try to ruin his reputation and defame his character. They said he was a hot-headed, overbearin' sort of feller. They was too scered to use the word, even after Bill died, but what they meant was that he was a *killer.*

"Now, Pecos Bill did kill lots of men. He never kept no tally hisself, and I don't suppose nobody will ever know jest how many he took off. Of course I'm not referrin' to Mex'cans and Indians. Bill didn't count them. But Bill wasn't a bad man, and he hardly ever killed a man without just cause.

"For instance, there was big Ike that he shot for snorin', that Bill's enemies talked up so much. But them that was doin' the talkin would for-git to mention that Bill had been.standin' guard over Mexico steers every night for six weeks and was gittin' a bit sleepy.

"Then there was Ris Risbone. Ris was one of these practical jokers, and he ramrodded an outfit that fell in behind Bill's on the trail. Ris had a dozen or so jokes, and when he pulled one, he slapped his knees and laughed and laughed whether anybody else was a-Iaughin' or not. One day Ris rode up to Bill's chuck-wagon when there wasn't nobody there but the cook, and he was asleep in the shade of the wagon with his head between the wheels. Ris slipped up and gabbed the trace chains and begun rattlin' 'em and yellin' 'Whoa! Whoa!' The pore spick woke up thinkin' that the team was runnin' away, and that he was about to git his pass to Saint Peter. He jumped up and bumped his head on the wagon; then he wakes up and looks around, and there stands Ris slappin' his knees and laughin'. Jest then Bill rides up, but he never said nothin'.

"When the outfits got to Abilene, Bill was in the White Elephant with some of his men, fixin' to take a drink. Jest as Bill was about to drop his fish-hooks in his glass, Ris poked his head in at the winder and yelled, 'Fire! Fire!'— and Bill did.

"In one killin', however, Bill acted a bit hasty, as he admitted his self. One day he called Three-Fingered Ed out of the saloon, sayin' he'd like to speak with him in private. Bill led Ed out into a back alley, and there they stopped.

" 'Say, Ed,' he says, lookin' him right in the eye, 'didn't you say that Mike said I was a hot-headed, over-bearing' sort of feller?'

" 'Naw,' says Ed, 'You mistook me. He never said that.'

" 'Well, doggone,' says Bill, 'ain't that too bad. I've gone and killed an inno-cent man.'

"Well, Lanky, maybe your pa'll let you come back next fall."
The End

A Cracker Cowboy. *Painting in "21" Club Collection—Peter Kriendler, President.*

CRACKER COWBOYS
OF FLORIDA

FREDERIC REMINGTON

One can thresh the straw of history until he is well worn out, and also is running some risk of wearing others out who may have to listen, so I will waive the telling of who the first cowboy was, even if I knew; but the last one who has come under my observation lives down in Florida, and the way it happened was this: I was sitting in a "sto' do'," as the "Crackers" say, waiting for the clerk to load some "number eights," when my friend said, "Look at the cowboys!" This immediately caught my interest. With me cowboys are what gems and porcelains are to some others. Two very emaciated Texas ponies pattered down the street, bearing wild-looking individuals, whose hanging hair and drooping hats and generally bedraggled appearance would remind you at once of the Spanish-moss which hangs so quietly and helplessly to the limbs of the oaks out in the swamps. There was none of the bilious fierceness and rearing plunge which I had associated with my friends out West, but as a fox-terrier is to a yellow cur, so were these last. They had on about four dollars' worth of clothes between them, and rode McClellan saddles, with saddle-bags and guns tied on before. The only things they did which were conventional were to tie their ponies up by the head in brutal disregard, and then get drunk in about fifteen minutes. I could see that in this case, while some of the tail feathers were the same, they would easily classify as new birds.

"And so you have cowboys down here?" I said to the man who ran the meat-market.

He picked a tiny piece of raw liver out of the meshes of his long black beard, tilted his big black hat, shoved his arms into his white apron front, and said:

"Gawd! yes, stranger; I was one myself."

The plot thickened so fast that I was losing much, so I became more deliberate. "Do the boys come into town often?" I inquired further.

"Oh yes, 'mos' every little spell," replied the butcher, as he reached behind his weighing-scales and picked up a double-barrelled shot-gun, sawed off. "We-uns are expectin' of they-uns to-day." And he broke the barrels and took out the shells to examine them.

"Do they come shooting?" I interposed.

He shut the gun with a snap. "We split even, stranger."

Seeing that the butcher was a fragile piece of bric-à-brac, and that I might need him for future study, I bethought me of the banker down the street. Bankers are bound to be broad-gauged, intelligent, and conservative, so I would, go to him and get at the ancient history of this neck of woods. I introduced myself, and was invited behind the counter. The look of things reminded me of one of those great green terraces which conceal fortifications and ugly cannon. It was boards and wire screen in front, but behind it were shot-guns and six-shooters hung in the handiest way, on a sort of disappearing gun-carriage arrangement. Shortly one of the cowboys of the street scene floundered in. He was two-thirds drunk, with brutal, shifty eyes and a flabby lower lip.

"I want twenty dollars on the old man. Ken I have it?"

I rather expected that the bank would go into "action front," but the clerk said, "Certainly," and completed this rather odd financial transaction, whereat the bull-hunter stumbled out.

"Who is the old man in this case?" I ventured.

"Oh, it's his boss, old Colonel Zuigg, of Crow City. I gave some money to some of his boys some weeks ago, and when the colonel was down here I asked him if he wanted the boys to draw against him in that way, and he said, 'Yes—for a small amount; they will steal a cow or two, and pay me that way.'"

Here was something tangible.

"What happens when a man steals another man's brand in this country?"

"He mustn't get caught; that's all. They all do it, but they never bring their troubles into court. They just shoot it out there in the bresh. The last time old Colonel Zuigg brought Zorn Zuidden in here and had him indicted for stealing cattle, said Zorn: 'Now see here, old man Zuigg, what do you want for to go and git me arrested fer? I have stole thousands of cattle and put your mark and brand on 'em, and jes because I have stole a couple of hundred from you, you go and have me indicted. You jes better go and get that whole deal nol prossed;' and it was done."

The argument was perfect.

"From that I should imagine that the cow-people have no more idea of law than the 'gray apes,'" I commented.

"Yes, that's about it. Old Colonel Zuigg was a judge fer a spell, till some feller filled him with buckshot, and he had to resign; and I remember he decided a case aginst me once. I was hot about it, and the old colonel he saw I was. Says he, 'Now yer mad, ain't you?' And I allowed I was. 'Well,' says he, 'you hain't got no call to get mad. I have decided the last eight cases in yer favor, and you kain't have it go yer way all the time; it wouldn't look right;' and I had to be satisfied."

The courts in that locality were but the faint and sickly flame of a taper offered at the shrine of a justice which was traditional only, it seemed. Moral forces having ceased to operate, the large owners began to brand everything in sight, never realizing that they were sowing the wind. This action naturally demoralized the cowboys, who shortly began to brand a little on their own account—and then the deluge. The rights of property having been destroyed, the large owners put strong outfits in the field, composed of desperate men armed to the teeth, and what happens in the lonely pine woods no one knows but the desperadoes themselves, albeit some of them never come back to the little fringe of settlements. The winter visitor from the North kicks up the jack-snipe along the beach or tarponizes in the estuaries of the Gulf, and when he comes to the hotel for dinner he eats Chicago dressed beef, but out in the wilderness low-browed cow-folks shoot and stab each other for the possession of scrawny creatures not fit for a pointer-dog to mess on. One cannot but feel the force of Buckle's law of "the physical aspects of nature" in this sad country. Flat and sandy, with miles of straight pine timber, each tree an exact duplicate of its neighbor tree, and underneath the scrub palmettoes, the twisted brakes and hammocks, and the gnarled water-oaks festooned with the sad gray Spanish-moss—truly not a country for a high-spirited race or moral giants.

The land gives only a tough wiregrass, and the poor little cattle, no bigger than a donkey, wander half starved and horribly emaciated in search of it. There used to be a trade with Cuba, but now that has gone; and beyond the supplying of Key West and the small fringe of settlements they have no market. How well the cowboys serve their masters I can only guess, since the big owners do not dare go into the woods, or even to their own doors at night, and they do not keep a light burning in the houses. One, indeed, attempted to assert his rights, but some one pumped sixteen buckshot into him as he bent over a spring to drink, and he left the country. They do tell of a late encounter between two rival foremen, who rode on to each other in the woods, and drawing, fired, and both were found stretched dying under the palmettoes, one calling deliriously the name of his boss. The unknown reaches of the Everglades lie just below, and with a half-hour's start a man who knew the country would be safe from pursuit, even if it were attempted; and, as one man cheerfully confided to me, "A boat don't leave no trail, stranger."

That might makes right, and that they steal by wholesale, any cattle-hunter will admit; and why they brand at all I cannot see, since one boy tried to make it plain to me, as he shifted his body in drunken abandon and grabbed my pencil and a sheet of wrapping paper: "See yer; ye see that?" And he drew a circle O; and then another ring around it, thus: ◎. "That brand ain't no good. Well, then—" And again his knotted and dirty fingers essayed the brand IO. He laboriously drew upon it and made EO which of course destroyed the former brand.

"Then here," he continued, as he drew 13, "all ye've got ter do is this—313."
I gasped in amazement, not at his cleverness as a brand-destroyer, but at his
honest abandon. With a horrible operatic laugh, such as is painted in "The Cos-
sack's Answer," he again laboriously drew ⊕ (the circle cross), and then added
some marks which made it look like this: ⊕. And again breaking into his devil's
"ha, ha!" said, "Make the damned thing whirl."

I did not protest. He would have shot me for that. But I did wish he
was living in the northwest quarter of New Mexico, where Mr. Cooper and
Dan could throw their eyes over the trail of his pony. Of course each man has
adjusted himself to this lawless rustling, and only calculates that he can steal
as much as his opponent. It is rarely that their affairs are brought to court, but
when they are, the men come *en masse* to the room, armed with knives and rifles,
so that any decision is bound to be a compromise, or it will bring on a general
engagement.

There is also a noticeable absence of negroes among them, as they still
retain some *ante bellum* theories, and it is only very lately that they have "recon-
structed." Their general ignorance is "miraculous," and quite mystifying to an
outside man. Some whom I met did not even know where the Texas was which
furnishes them their ponies. The railroads of Florida have had their ups and
downs with them in a petty way on account of the running over of their cattle by
the trains; and then some longhaired old Cracker drops into the nearest station
with his gun and pistol, and wants the telegraph operator to settle immediately
on the basis of the Cracker's claim for damages, which is always absurdly high.
At first the railroads demurred, but the cowboys lined up in the "bresh" on some
dark night and pumped Winchesters into the train in a highly picturesque way.
The trainmen at once recognized the force of the Cracker's views on cattle-
killing, but it took some considerable "potting" at the more conservative super-
intendents before the latter could bestir themselves and invent a "cow-attorney,"
as the company adjuster is called, who now settles with the bushmen as best he
can. Certainly no worse people ever lived since the big killing up Muscleshell
way, and the romance is taken out of it by the cowardly assassination which is
the practice. They are well paid for their desperate work, and always eat fresh
beef or "razor-backs," and deer which they kill in the woods. The heat, the poor
grass, their brutality, and the pest of the flies kill their ponies, and, as a rule, they
lack dash and are indifferent riders, but they are picturesque in their unkempt,
almost unearthly wildness. A strange effect is added by their use of large, fierce
cur-dogs, one of which accompanies each cattle-hunter, and is taught to pursue

cattle, and to even take them by the nose, which is another instance of their brutality. Still, as they only have a couple of horses apiece, it saves them much extra running. These men do not use the rope, unless to noose a pony in a corral, but work their cattle in strong log corrals, which are made at about a day's march apart all through the woods. Indeed, ropes are hardly necessary, since the cattle are so small and thin that two men can successfully "wrestle" a three-year-old. A man goes into the corral, grabs a cow by one horn, and throwing his other arm over her back, waits until some other man takes her hind leg, whereat ensues some very entertaining Græco-Roman style.

Cowboys Wrestling a Bull. *Authors' photoengraving.*

When the cow is successful, she finds her audience of Cracker cowboys sitting on the fence awaiting another opening, and gasping for breath. The best bull will not go over three hundred pounds, while I have seen a yearling at a hundred and fifty—if you, O knights of the riata, can imagine it! Still, it is desperate work. Some of the men are so reckless and active that they do not hesitate to encounter a wild bull in the open. The cattle are as wild as deer, they race off at scent; and when "rounded up" many will not drive, whereupon these are promptly shot. It frequently happens that when the herd is being driven quietly along a bull will turn on the drivers, charging at once. Then there is a scamper and great shooting. The bulls often become so maddened in these forays that they drop and die in their tracks, for which strange fact no one can account, but as a rule they are too scrawny and mean to make their handling difficult.

So this is the Cracker cowboy, whose chief interest would be found in the tales of some bushwhacking enterprise, which I very much fear would be a one-sided story, and not worth the telling. At best they must be revolting, having no note of the savage encounters which used to characterize the easy days in West Texas and New Mexico, when every man tossed his life away to the crackle of his own revolver. The moon shows pale through the leafy canopy on their evening fires, and the mists, the miasma, and the mosquitoes settle over their dreary camp talk. In place of the wild stampede, there is only the bellowing in the pens, and instead of the plains shaking under the dusty air as the bedizened vaqueros plough their fiery broncos through the milling herds, the cattle-hunter wends his lonely way through the ooze and rank grass, while the dreary pine trunks line up and shut the view.